THE BEST AMERICAN NOIR OF THE CENTURY

THE BEST AMERICAN NOIR OF THE CENTURY

EDITED BY

JAMES ELLROY and
OTTO PENZLER

WITH AN INTRODUCTION BY

JAMES ELLROY

HOUGHTON MIFFLIN HARCOURT
BOSTON • NEW YORK

www.hmhco.com

Library of Congress Cataloging-in-Publication Data

The best American noir of the century / edited by James Ellroy and Otto Penzler; with an introduction by James Ellroy.

p. cm. — (The best American series)

ISBN 978-0-547-57744-9 (pbk.)

1. Noir fiction, American. 2. Detective and mystery stories, American. 3. American fiction — 20th century. I. Ellroy, James, date. II. Penzler, Otto.

PS648.N64B47 2010

813'.087208 — dc22 2010017204

Printed in the United States of America

DOC 10 9 8 7

4500737822

"Missing the Morning Bus" by Lorenzo Carcaterra. First published in *Dead Man's Hand,* 2007. Copyright © 2007 by the author. Reprinted by permission of the author.

"All Through the House" by Christopher Coake. First published in *Gettysburg Review,* 2003. Copyright © 2003 by Christopher Coake; published in *We're in Trouble* by Christopher Coake, Harcourt, 2005. Reprinted by permission of Houghton Mifflin Harcourt.

"What She Offered" by Thomas H. Cook. First published in *Dangerous Women,* 2005. Copyright © 2005 by Thomas H. Cook. Reprinted by permission of the author.

"Hot Springs" by James Crumley. First published in *Murder for Love,* 1996. Copyright © 1996 by James Crumley. Reprinted by permission of the Estate of James Crumley.

"The Weekender" by Jeffery Deaver. First published in *Alfred Hitchcock's Mystery Magazine,* December 1996. Copyright © 1996 by Jeffery W. Deaver. Reprinted by permission of the author.

"A Ticket Out" by Brendan DuBois. First published in *Ellery Queen's Mystery Magazine,* January 1987. Copyright © 1987 by Brendan DuBois. Reprinted by permission of the author.

"Mefisto in Onyx" by Harlan Ellison. From *The Essential Ellison: A 50-Year Retrospective,* 2005. Copyright © 1993 by the Kilimanjaro Corporation. Reprinted by arrangement with, and permission of, the Author and the Author's agent, Richard Curtis Associates, Inc., New York. All rights reserved. Harlan Ellison is a registered trademark of the Kilimanjaro Corporation.

"Since I Don't Have You" by James Ellroy. First published in *A Matter of Crime,* vol. 4. Copyright © 1988 by James Ellroy. Reprinted by permission of Sobel Weber Associates.

"You'll Always Remember Me" by Steve Fisher. First published in *Black Mask Magazine,* March 1938. Copyright © 1938 by the author. Reprinted by permission of Keith Alan Deutsch.

"Poachers" by Tom Franklin. From *Poachers.* Copyright © 1999 by Tom Franklin. Reprinted by permission of HarperCollins Publishers.

"The Paperhanger" by William Gay. First published in *Harper's Magazine,* February 2000. Copyright © 2000 by William Gay. Reprinted by permission of the author.

"Out There in the Darkness" by Ed Gorman. First published in *Out There in the Darkness,* 1995. Copyright © 1995 by Ed Gorman. Reprinted by permission of the author.

"Iris" by Stephen Greenleaf. First published in *The Eyes Have It,* 1984. Copyright © 1984 by Stephen Greenleaf. Reprinted by permission of the author.

"Crack" by James W. Hall. First published in *Murder and Obsession,* 1999. Copyright © 1999 by James W. Hall. Reprinted by permission of the author.

"Slowly, Slowly in the Wind" by Patricia Highsmith. First published in *Slowly, Slowly in the Wind.* Copyright © 1972, 1973, 1974, 1976, 1977, and 1979 by Patricia Highsmith. Copyright © by Diogenes Verlag AG Zurich. Reprinted by permission of W. W. Norton & Company, Inc.

"The Homecoming" by Dorothy B. Hughes. First published in *Murder Cavalcade,* 1946. Copyright © 1946 by Dorothy B. Hughes, *Murder Cavalcade,* New York: Duell, Sloan & Pearce. Permission granted by Blanche C. Gregory, Inc.

"The Last Spin" by Evan Hunter. First published in *Manhunt,* September 1956. Copyright © 1956 by Evan Hunter. Reprinted by permission of Gelfman Schneider Literary Agents, Inc.

"Gun Crazy" by MacKinlay Kantor. First published in the *Saturday Evening Post,* February 13, 1940. Copyright © 1940 by MacKinlay Kantor. Reprinted by permission of Layne Schroder, Lydia Kantor and Melissa Poplazarova and by agreement with the estate's agent, Donald Maass Literary Agency, 121 West 27th Street, Suite 801, NY, NY 10001.

"Nothing to Worry About" by Day Keene. First published in *Detective Tales Magazine,* August 1945. Copyright © 1945 by Popular Publications, Inc. Copyright renewed © 1973 and assigned to Argosy Communications, Inc. All rights reserved. Reprinted with permission by arrangement with Argosy Communications, Inc.

"Her Lord and Master" by Andrew Klavan. First published in *Dangerous Women,* 2005. Copyright © 2005 by Andrew Klavan. Reprinted by permission of the author.

"Running Out of Dog" by Dennis Lehane. First published in *Murder and Obsession,* 1999. Copyright © 1999 by Dennis Lehane. Reprinted with permission of Ann Rittenberg Literary Agency, Inc.

CONTENTS

FOREWORD

The French word *noir* (which means "black") was first connected to the word *film* by a French critic in 1946, and has subsequently become a prodigiously overused term to describe a certain type of film or literary work. Curiously, *noir* is not unlike *pornography,* in the sense that it is virtually impossible to define, but everyone thinks they know it when they see it. Like many other certainties, it is often wildly inaccurate.

This volume is devoted to short noir fiction of the past century, but it is impossible to divorce the literary genre entirely from its film counterpart. Certainly, *noir* most commonly evokes the great crime films of the 1940s and 1950s that were shot in black-and-white with cinematography that was heavily influenced by early-twentieth-century German expressionism: sharp angles (venetian blinds, windows, railroad tracks) and strong contrasts between light and dark. Most of us have a collective impression of film noir as having certain essentials: a femme fatale, some tough criminals, an equally tough cop or private eye, an urban environment, and night . . . endless night. There are bars, nightclubs, menacing alleys, seedy hotel rooms.

While it may be comforting to recognize these elements as the very definition of *film noir,* it is as simplistic a view as that which limits the mystery genre to detective fiction, failing to accept the numerous other elements of that rich literature, such as the crime novel and suspense stories.

Certainly the golden age of film noir occurred in those decades, the '40s and '50s, but there were superb examples in the 1930s, such as *M* (1931), in which Peter Lorre had his first starring role, and *Freaks* (1932), Tod Browning's unforgettable biopic in which the principal actors were actual carnival "human curiosities." And no one is likely to dispute that the noir motion picture continued into the 1960s and beyond, as evidenced by such classics as *The Manchurian Candidate* (1962), *Taxi Driver* (1976), *Body Heat* (1981), and *L.A. Confidential* (1997).

Much of film noir lacks some or all of the usual clichéd visual set pieces of the genre, of course, but the absolutist elements by which the films are known are less evident in the literature, which relies more on plot, tone, and theme than on the chiaroscuro effects choreographed by directors and cinematographers.

Allowing for the differences of the two mediums, I also believe that most film and literary critics are entirely wrong about their definitions of *noir,* a genre which famously—but erroneously—has its roots in the American hard-boiled private eye novel. In fact, the two subcategories of the mystery genre, private detective stories and noir fiction, are diametrically opposed, with mutually exclusive philosophical premises.

Noir works, whether films, novels, or short stories, are existential, pessimistic tales about people, including (or especially) protagonists, who are seriously flawed and morally questionable. The tone is generally bleak and nihilistic, with characters whose greed, lust, jealousy, and alienation lead them into a downward spiral as their plans and schemes inevitably go awry. Whether their motivation is as overt as a bank robbery, or as subtle as the willingness to compromise integrity for personal gain, the central figures in noir stories are doomed to hopelessness. They may be motivated by the pursuit of seemingly easy money or by love—or, more commonly, physical desire—almost certainly for the wrong member of the opposite sex. The machinations of their relentless lust will cause them to lie, steal, cheat, and even kill as they become more and more entangled in a web from which they cannot possibly extricate themselves. And, while engaged in this hopeless quest, they will be double-crossed, betrayed, and, ultimately, ruined. The likelihood of a happy ending in a noir story is remote, even if the protagonist's own view of a satisfactory resolution is the criterion for defining *happy.* No, it will end badly, because the characters are inherently corrupt and that is the fate that inevitably awaits them.

The private detective story is a different matter entirely. Raymond Chandler famously likened the private eye to a knight, a man who could walk mean streets but not himself be mean, and this is true of the overwhelming majority of those heroic figures. They may well be brought into an exceedingly dark situation, and encounter characters who are deceptive, violent, paranoid, and lacking a moral center, but the American private detective retains his sense of honor in the face of all the adversity and duplicity with which he must do battle. Sam Spade avenged the murder of a partner because he knew he "was supposed to do something about it." Mike Hammer found it easy to kill a woman to whom he had become attached because he learned she had murdered his friend. Lew Archer, Spenser, Elvis Cole, and other iconic private eyes, as well as policemen who, like Harry Bosch and Dave Robicheaux, often act as if they are unconstrained by their official positions, may bend (or break) the law, but their own sense of morality will be used in the pursuit of justice. Although not every one of their cases may have a happy conclusion, the hero nonetheless will emerge with a clean ethical slate.

Film noir blurs the distinction between hard-boiled private eye narratives and true noir stories by employing similar design and camerawork techniques for both genres, though the discerning viewer will easily recognize the opposing life-views of a moral, even heroic, often romantic detective, and the lost characters in noir who are caught in the inescapable prisons of their own construction, forever trapped by their isolation from their own souls, as well as from society and the moral restrictions that permit it to be regarded as civilized.

This massive collection seldom allows exceptions to these fundamental principles of noir stories. They are dark and often oppressive, failing to allow redemption for most of the people who inhabit their sad, violent, amoral world. Carefully wrought plans crumble, lovers deceive, normality morphs into decadence, and decency is scarce and unrewarded. Nonetheless, the writers who toil in this oppressive landscape have created stories of such relentless fascination that they rank among the giants of the literary world. Some, like Cornell Woolrich, David Goodis, and Jim Thompson, wrote prolifically but produced little that did not fall into the noir category, accurately reflecting their own troubled, tragic lives. Others, like Elmore Leonard, Evan Hunter, and Lawrence Block, have written across a more varied range of crime fiction, from dark to light, from morose to hilarious. Just not in this volume. If you find light and hilarity in these pages, I strongly recommend a visit to a mental health professional.

Otto Penzler
May 2009

INTRODUCTION

We created it, but they love it more in France than they do here. Noir is the most scrutinized offshoot of the hard-boiled school of fiction. It's the long drop off the short pier, and the wrong man and the wrong woman in perfect misalliance. It's the nightmare of flawed souls with big dreams and the precise *how* and *why* of the all-time sure thing that goes bad. Noir is opportunity as fatality, social justice as sanctified shuck, and sexual love as a one-way ticket to hell. Noir indicts the other subgenres of the hard-boiled school as sissified, and canonizes the inherent human urge toward self-destruction.

Noir sparked before the Big War and burned like a four-coil hot plate up to 1960. Cheap novels and cheap films about cheap people ran concurrent with American boosterism and yahooism and made a subversive point just by being. They described a fully existing fringe America and fed viewers and readers the demography of a Secret Pervert Republic. It was just garish enough to be laughed off as unreal and just pathetic enough to be recognizably human. The concurrence said: *Something is wrong here.* The subtext was: *Malign fate has a great and unpredictable power and none of us is safe.*

The thrill of noir is the rush of moral forfeit and the abandonment to titillation. The social importance of noir is its grounding in the big themes of race, class, gender, and systemic corruption. The overarching joy and lasting appeal of noir is that it makes doom fun.

The inhabitants of the Secret Pervert Republic are a gas. Their intransigence and psychopathy are delightful. They relentlessly pursue the score, big and small. They only succeed at a horrific cost that renders it all futile. They are wildly delusional and possessed of verbal flair. Their overall job description is "grandiose lowlife." They speak their own language. Safecrackers are "box men" who employ explosive "soup." Grifters perfect the long con, the short con, and the dime hustle. Race-wire scams utilize teams of scouts who place last-minute bets and relay information to bookmaking networks. A twisted professionalism defines all strata of the Secret Pervert Republic. This society grants women a unique power to seduce and destroy. A six-week chronology from first kiss to gas chamber is common in noir.

The subgenre officially died in 1960. New writer generations have resurrected it and redefined it as a sub-subgenre, tailored to meet their dramatic needs. *Doom is fun.* Great sex preceded the gas-chamber bounce. Older Secret Pervert Republicans blew their wads on mink coats for evil women. Present-day SPRs go broke on crack cocaine. Lethal injection has replaced the green room. Noir will never die — it's too dementedly funny not to flourish in the heads of hip writers who wish they could time-trip to 1948 and live postwar malaise and psychoses. The young and feckless will inhabit the Secret Pervert Republic, reinvent it, wring it dry, and reinvent it all over again.

The short stories in this volume are a groove. Exercise your skeevy curiosity and read every one. You'll be repulsed and titillated. You'll endure moral forfeit. Doom is fun. You're a perv for reading this introduction. Read the whole book and you'll die on a gurney with a spike in your arm.

James Ellroy
July 2009

THE BEST AMERICAN NOIR OF THE CENTURY

1923

TOD ROBBINS

SPURS

Clarence Aaron "Tod" Robbins (1888–1949) graduated from Washington and Lee University in Virginia and soon became an expatriate, moving to the French Riviera. When World War II erupted and the Nazis occupied France, he refused to leave and was put into a concentration camp for the duration of the war.

He wrote mostly horror and dark fantasy fiction for the pulps, publishing two collections of these stories, *Silent, White, and Beautiful and Other Stories* (1920) and *Who Wants a Green Bottle? and Other Uneasy Tales* (1926). Among his novels, the most successful was *The Unholy Three* (1917), twice adapted for films of the same title: a silent directed by Tod Browning in 1925 and a sound version in 1930 directed by Jack Conway, both of which starred Lon Chaney. Robbins's earlier novel, *Mysterious Martin* (1912), was about a man who creates art that can be deadly; he later rewrote the enigmatic story and published it as *The Master of Murder* (1933). He also wrote *In the Shadow* (1929) and *Close Their Eyes Tenderly* (1947), published only in Monaco in a tiny edition, an anti-Communist novel in which murder is treated as comedy and farce.

"Spurs" was the basis for the classic noir film *Freaks,* which was released by MGM in 1932. It was directed by Robbins's friend Tod Browning, who enjoyed enormous success with *Dracula,* starring Bela Lugosi, which was released the previous year. *Freaks* used real-life carnival performers for most roles, horrifying audiences so much that it was banned in England and the studio cut the ninety-minute film to sixty-four minutes. Public outrage led to the swift end of Tod Browning's career as a director. It featured the midget Harry Earles, who had also appeared in *The Unholy Three.*

This very dark film retained little of the equally dark story on which it was based. It remains the story of carnival people and a midget, Jacques Courbé (Hans in the film), who falls in love with the bareback rider Jeanne Marie (Cleopatra in the film), a beautiful tall blonde.

"Spurs" was first published in the famous pulp magazine *Munsey's* (February 1923) and first collected in book form in *Who Wants a Green Bottle? and Other Uneasy Tales* (London: Philip Allan, 1926).

■ ■ ■

I

JACQUES COURBÉ WAS a romanticist. He measured only twenty-eight inches from the soles of his diminutive feet to the crown of his head; but there were times, as he rode into the arena on his gallant charger, St. Eustache, when he felt himself a doughty knight of old about to do battle for his lady.

What matter that St. Eustache was not a gallant charger except in his master's imagination—not even a pony, indeed, but a large dog of a nondescript breed, with the long snout and upstanding aura of a wolf? What matter that M. Courbé's entrance was invariably greeted with shouts of derisive laughter and bombardments of banana skins and orange peel? What matter that he had no lady, and that his daring deeds were severely curtailed to a mimicry of the bareback riders who preceded him? What mattered all these things to the tiny man who lived in dreams, and who resolutely closed his shoe-button eyes to the drab realities of life?

The dwarf had no friends among the other freaks in Copo's Circus. They considered him ill-tempered and egotistical, and he loathed them for their acceptance of things as they were. Imagination was the armor that protected him from the curious glances of a cruel, gaping world, from the stinging lash of ridicule, from the bombardments of banana skins and orange peel. Without it, he must have shriveled up and died. But those others? Ah, they had no armor except their own thick hides! The door that opened on the kingdom of imagination was closed and locked to them; and although they did not wish to open this door, although they did not miss what lay beyond it, they resented and mistrusted anyone who possessed the key.

Now it came about, after many humiliating performances in the arena, made palatable only by dreams, that love entered the circus tent and beckoned commandingly to M. Jacques Courbé. In an instant the dwarf was engulfed in a sea of wild, tumultuous passion.

Mlle. Jeanne Marie was a daring bareback rider. It made M. Jacques Courbé's tiny heart stand still to see her that first night of her appearance in the arena, performing brilliantly on the broad back of her aged mare, Sappho. A tall, blond woman of the amazon type, she had round eyes of baby blue which held no spark of her avaricious peasant's soul, carmine lips and cheeks, large white teeth which flashed continually in a smile, and hands which, when doubled up, were nearly the size of the dwarf's head.

Her partner in the act was Simon Lafleur, the Romeo of the circus tent—a swarthy, herculean young man with bold black eyes and hair that glistened with grease, like the back of Solon, the trained seal.

From the first performance, M. Jacques Courbé loved Mlle. Jeanne Marie. All his tiny body was shaken with longing for her. Her buxom charms, so generously revealed in tights and spangles, made him flush and cast down his eyes. The familiarities allowed to Simon Lafleur, the bodily acrobatic contacts of the two performers, made the dwarf's blood boil. Mounted on St. Eustache, awaiting his turn at the entrance, he would grind his teeth in impotent rage to see Simon circling round and round the ring, standing proudly on the back of Sappho and holding Mlle. Jeanne Marie in an ecstatic embrace, while she kicked one shapely, bespangled leg skyward.

"Ah, the dog!" M. Jacques Courbé would mutter. "Some day I shall teach this hulking stable boy his place! *Ma foi,* I will clip his ears for him!"

St. Eustache did not share his master's admiration for Mlle. Jeanne Marie. From the first, he evinced his hearty detestation of her by low growls and a ferocious display of long, sharp fangs. It was little consolation for the dwarf to know that St. Eustache showed still more marked signs of rage when Simon Lafleur approached him. It pained M. Jacques Courbé to think that his gallant charger, his sole companion, his bedfellow, should not also love and admire the splendid giantess who each night risked life and limb before the awed populace. Often, when they were alone together, he would chide St. Eustache on his churlishness.

"Ah, you devil of a dog!" the dwarf would cry. "Why must you always growl and show your ugly teeth when the lovely Jeanne Marie condescends to notice you? Have you no feelings under your tough hide? Cur, she is an angel, and you snarl at her! Do you not remember how I found you, starving puppy in a Paris gutter? And now you must threaten the hand of my princess! So this is your gratitude, great hairy pig!"

M. Jacques Courbé had one living relative—not a dwarf, like himself, but a fine figure of a man, a prosperous farmer living just outside the town of Roubaix. The elder Courbé had never married; and so one day, when he was found dead from heart failure, his tiny nephew—for whom, it must be confessed, the farmer had always felt an instinctive aversion—fell heir to a comfortable property. When the tidings were brought to him, the dwarf threw both arms about the shaggy neck of St. Eustache and cried out:

"Ah, now we can retire, marry and settle down, old friend! I am worth many times my weight in gold!"

That evening as Mlle. Jeanne Marie was changing her gaudy costume after the performance, a light tap sounded on the door.

"Enter!" she called, believing it to be Simon Lafleur, who had promised to take her that evening to the Sign of the Wild Boar for a glass of wine to wash the sawdust out of her throat. "Enter, *mon chéri!*"

The door swung slowly open; and in stepped M. Jacques Courbé, very proud and upright, in the silks and laces of a courtier, with a tiny gold-hilted sword swinging at his hip. Up he came, his shoe-button eyes all aglitter to see the more than partially revealed charms of his robust lady. Up he came to within a yard of where she sat; and down on one knee he went and pressed his lips to her red-slippered foot.

"Oh, most beautiful and daring lady," he cried, in a voice as shrill as a pin scratching on a windowpane, "will you not take mercy on the unfortunate Jacques Courbé? He is hungry for your smiles, he is starving for your lips! All night long he tosses on his couch and dreams of Jeanne Marie!"

"What play-acting is this, my brave little fellow?" she asked, bending down with the smile of an ogress. "Has Simon Lafleur sent you to tease me?"

"May the black plague have Simon!" the dwarf cried, his eyes seeming to flash blue sparks. "I am not play-acting. It is only too true that I love you, mademoiselle; that I wish to make you my lady. And now that I have a fortune, not that—" He broke off suddenly, and his face resembled a withered apple. "What is this, mademoiselle?" he said, in the low, droning tone of a hornet about to sting. "Do you laugh at my love? I warn you, mademoiselle—do not laugh at Jacques Courbé!"

Mlle. Jeanne Marie's large, florid face had turned purple from suppressed merriment. Her lips twitched at the corners. It was all she could do not to burst out into a roar of laughter.

Why, this ridiculous little manikin was serious in his lovemaking! This pocket-sized edition of a courtier was proposing marriage to her! He, this splinter of a fellow, wished to make her his wife! Why, she could carry him about on her shoulder like a trained marmoset!

What a joke this was—what a colossal, corset-creaking joke! Wait till she told Simon Lafleur! She could fairly see him throw back his sleek head, open his mouth to its widest dimensions, and shake with silent laughter. But she must not laugh—not now. First she must listen to everything the dwarf had to say; draw all the sweetness of this bonbon of humor before she crushed it under the heel of ridicule.

"I am not laughing," she managed to say. "You have taken me by surprise. I never thought, I never even guessed—"

"That is well, mademoiselle," the dwarf broke in. "I do not tolerate laughter. In the arena I am paid to make laughter; but these others pay to laugh at me. I always make people pay to laugh at me!"

"But do I understand you aright, M. Courbé? Are you proposing an honorable marriage?"

The dwarf rested his hand on his heart and bowed. "Yes, mademoiselle, an honorable marriage, and the wherewithal to keep the wolf from the door. A week ago my uncle died and left me a large estate. We shall have a servant to wait on our wants, a horse and carriage, food and wine of the best, and leisure to amuse ourselves. And you? Why, you will be a fine lady! I will clothe that beautiful big body of yours with silks and laces! You will be as happy, mademoiselle, as a cherry tree in June!"

The dark blood slowly receded from Mlle. Jeanne Marie's full cheeks, her lips no longer twitched at the corners, her eyes had narrowed slightly. She had been a bareback rider for years, and she was weary of it. The life of the circus tent had lost its tinsel. She loved the dashing Simon Lafleur; but she knew well enough that this Romeo in tights would never espouse a dowerless girl.

The dwarf's words had woven themselves into a rich mental tapestry. She saw herself a proud lady, ruling over a country estate, and later welcoming Simon Lafleur with all the luxuries that were so near his heart. Simon would be overjoyed to marry into a country estate. These pygmies were a puny lot. They died young! She would do nothing to hasten the end of Jacques Courbé. No, she would be kindness itself to the poor little fellow; but, on the other hand, she would not lose her beauty mourning for him.

"Nothing that you wish shall be withheld from you as long as you love me, mademoiselle," the dwarf continued. "Your answer?"

Mlle. Jeanne Marie bent forward, and with a single movement of her powerful arms, raised M. Jacques Courbé and placed him on her knee. For an ecstatic instant she held him thus, as if he were a large French doll, with his tiny sword cocked coquettishly out behind. Then she planted on his cheek a huge kiss that covered his entire face from chin to brow.

"I am yours!" she murmured, pressing him to her ample bosom. "From the first I loved you, M. Jacques Courbé!"

II

The wedding of Mlle. Jeanne Marie was celebrated in the town of Roubaix, where Copo's Circus had taken up its temporary quarters. Following the ceremony, a feast was served in one of the tents, which was attended by a whole galaxy of celebrities.

The bridegroom, his dark little face flushed with happiness and wine, sat at the head of the board. His chin was just above the tablecloth, so that his head looked like a large orange that had rolled off the fruit dish. Immediately beneath his dangling feet, St. Eustache, who had more than once evinced by deep growls his disapproval of the proceedings, now worried a bone with quick, sly glances from time to time at the plump legs of his new mistress. Papa Copo was on the dwarf's right, his large round face as red and benevolent as a harvest moon. Next to him sat Griffo, the giraffe boy, who was covered with spots and whose neck was so long that he looked down on all the rest, including M. Hercule Hippo the giant. The rest of the company included Mlle. Lupa, who had sharp white teeth of an incredible length and who growled when she tried to talk; the tiresome M. Jegongle, who insisted on juggling fruit, plates, and knives, although the whole company was heartily sick of his tricks; Mme. Samson, with her trained boa constrictors coiled about her neck and peeping out timidly, one above each ear; Simon Lafleur, and a score of others.

The bareback rider had laughed silently and almost continually ever since Jeanne Marie had told him of her engagement. Now he sat next to her in his crimson tights. His black hair was brushed back from his forehead and so glistened with grease that it reflected the lights overhead, like a burnished helmet. From time to time, he tossed off a brimming goblet of burgundy, nudged the bride in the ribs with his elbow, and threw back his sleek head in another silent outburst of laughter.

"And you are sure you will not forget me, Simon?" she whispered. "It may be some time before I can get the little ape's money."

"Forget you, Jeanne?" he muttered. "By all the dancing devils in champagne, never! I will wait as patiently as Job till you have fed that mouse some poisoned cheese. But what will you do with him in the meantime, Jeanne? You must allow him some liberties. I grind my teeth to think of you in his arms!"

The bride smiled, and regarded her diminutive husband with an appraising glance. What an atom of a man! And yet life might linger in his bones for a long time to come. M. Jacques Courbé had allowed himself only one glass of wine, and yet he was far gone in intoxication. His tiny face was suffused with blood, and he stared at Simon Lafleur belligerently. Did he suspect the truth?

"Your husband is flushed with wine!" the bareback rider whispered.

"*Ma foi,* madame, later he may knock you about! Possibly he is a dangerous fellow in his cups. Should he maltreat you, Jeanne, do not forget that you have a protector in Simon Lafleur."

"You clown!" Jeanne Marie rolled her large eyes roguishly and laid her hand for an instant on the bareback rider's knee. "Simon, I could crack his skull between my finger and thumb, like a hickory nut!" She paused to illustrate her example, and then added reflectively: "And, perhaps, I shall do that very thing, if he attempts any familiarities. Ugh! The little ape turns my stomach!"

By now the wedding guests were beginning to show the effects of their potations. This was especially marked in the case of M. Jacques Courbé's associates in the sideshow.

Griffo, the giraffe boy, had closed his large brown eyes and was swaying his small head languidly above the assembly, while a slightly supercilious expression drew his lips down at the corners. M. Hercule Hippo, swollen out by his libations to even more colossal proportions, was repeating over and over: "I tell you I am not like other men. When I walk, the earth trembles!" Mlle. Lupa, her hairy upper lip lifted above her long white teeth, was gnawing at a bone, growling unintelligible phrases to herself and shooting savage, suspicious glances at her companions. M. Jejongle's hands had grown unsteady, and as he insisted on juggling the knives and plates of each new course, broken bits of crockery littered the floor. Mme. Samson, uncoiling her necklace of baby boa constrictors, was feeding them lumps of sugar soaked in rum. M. Jacques Courbé had finished his second glass of wine, and was surveying the whispering Simon Lafleur through narrowed eyes.

There can be no genial companionship among great egotists who have drunk too much. Each one of these human oddities thought that he or she was responsible for the crowds that daily gathered at Copo's Circus; so now, heated with the good Burgundy, they were not slow in asserting themselves. Their separate egos rattled angrily together, like so many pebbles in a bag. Here was gunpowder which needed only a spark.

"I am a big—a very big man!" M. Hercule Hippo said sleepily. "Women love me. The pretty little creatures leave their pygmy husbands, so that they may come and stare at Hercule Hippo of Copo's Circus. Ha, and when they return home, they laugh at other men always! 'You may kiss me again when you grow up,' they tell their sweethearts."

"Fat bullock, here is one woman who has no love for you!" cried Mlle. Lupa, glaring sidewise at the giant over her bone. "That great carcass of yours is only so much food gone to waste. You have cheated the butcher, my friend. Fool, women do not come to see you! As well might they stare at the cattle being led through the street. Ah, no, they come from far and near to see one of their own sex who is not a cat!"

"Quite right," cried Papa Copo in a conciliatory tone, smiling and rubbing his hands together. "Not a cat, mademoiselle, but a wolf. Ah, you have a sense of humor! How droll!"

"I have a sense of humor," Mlle. Lupa agreed, returning to her bone, "and also sharp teeth. Let the erring hand not stray too near!"

"You, M. Hippo and Mlle. Lupa, are both wrong," said a voice which seemed to come from the roof. "Surely it is none other than me whom the people come to stare at!"

All raised their eyes to the supercilious face of Griffo, the giraffe boy, which swayed slowly from side to side on its long, pipe-stem neck. It was he who had spoken, although his eyes were still closed.

"Of all the colossal impudence!" cried the matronly Mme. Samson. "As if my little dears had nothing to say on the subject!" She picked up the two baby boa constrictors, which lay in drunken slumber on her lap, and shook them like whips at the wedding guests. "Papa Copo knows only too well that it is on account of these little charmers, Mark Antony and Cleopatra, that the sideshow is so well-attended!"

The circus owner, thus directly appealed to, frowned in perplexity. He felt himself in a quandary. These freaks of his were difficult to handle. Why had he been fool enough to come to M. Jacques Courbé's wedding feast? Whatever he said would be used against him.

As Papa Copo hesitated, his round, red face wreathed in ingratiating smiles, the long deferred spark suddenly alighted in the powder. It all came about on account of the carelessness of M. Jejongle, who had become engrossed in the conversation and wished to put in a word for himself. Absent-mindedly juggling two heavy plates and a spoon, he said in a petulant tone:

"You all appear to forget me!"

Scarcely were the words out of his mouth, when one of the heavy plates descended with a crash on the thick skull of M. Hippo; and M. Jejongle was instantly remembered. Indeed he was more than remembered; for the giant, already irritated to the boiling point by Mlle. Lupa's insults, at the new affront struck out savagely past her and knocked the juggler head-over-heels under the table.

Mlle. Lupa, always quick-tempered and especially so when her attention was focused on a juicy chicken bone, evidently considered her dinner companion's conduct far from decorous, and promptly inserted her sharp teeth in the offending hand that had administered the blow. M. Hippo, squealing from rage and pain like a wounded elephant, bounded to his feet, overturning the table.

Pandemonium followed. Every freak's hands, teeth, feet, were turned against the others. Above the shouts, screams, growls, and hisses of the combat, Papa Copo's voice could be heard bellowing for peace.

"Ah, my children, my children! This is no way to behave! Calm yourselves, I pray you! Mlle. Lupa, remember that you are a lady as well as a wolf!"

There is no doubt that M. Jacques Courbé would have suffered most in this undignified fracas, had it not been for St. Eustache, who had stationed himself over his tiny master and who now drove off all would-be assailants. As it was, Griffo, the unfortunate giraffe boy, was the most defenseless and therefore became the victim. His small, round head swayed back and forth to blows like a punching bag. He was bitten by Mlle. Lupa, buffeted by M. Hippo, kicked by M. Jejongle, clawed by Mme. Samson, and nearly strangled by both of the baby boa constrictors which had wound themselves about his neck like hangmen's nooses. Undoubtedly he would have fallen a victim to circumstances, had it not been for Simon Lafleur, the bride, and half a dozen of her acrobatic friends, whom Papa Copo had implored to restore peace. Roaring with laughter, they sprang forward and tore the combatants apart.

M. Jacques Courbé was found sitting grimly under a fold of tablecloth. He held a broken bottle of wine in one hand. The dwarf was very drunk, and in a towering rage. As Simon Lafleur approached with one of his silent laughs, M. Jacques Courbé hurled the bottle at his head.

"Ah, the little wasp!" the bareback rider cried, picking up the dwarf by his waistband. "Here is your fine husband, Jeanne! Take him away before he does me some mischief. *Parbleu,* he is a bloodthirsty fellow in his cups!"

The bride approached, her blond face crimson from wine and laughter. Now that she was safely married to a country estate, she took no more pains to conceal her true feelings.

"Oh, la, la!" she cried, seizing the struggling dwarf and holding him forcibly on her shoulder. "What a temper the little ape has! Well, we shall spank it out of him before long!"

"Let me down!" M. Jacques Courbé screamed in a paroxysm of fury. "You will regret this, madame! Let me down, I say!"

But the stalwart bride shook her head. "No, no, my little one!" she laughed. "You cannot escape your wife so easily! What, you would fly from my arms before the honeymoon!"

"Let me down!" he cried again. "Can't you see that they are laughing at me!"

"And why should they not laugh, my little ape? Let them laugh, if they will; but I will not put you down. No, I will carry you thus, perched on my shoulder, to the farm. It will set a precedent which brides of the future may find a certain difficulty in following!"

"But the farm is quite a distance from here, my Jeanne," said Simon Lafleur. "You are strong as an ox, and he is only a marmoset; still I will wager a bottle of Burgundy that you set him down by the roadside."

"Done, Simon!" the bride cried, with a flash of her strong white teeth. "You shall lose your wager, for I swear that I could carry my little ape from one end of France to the other!"

M. Jacques Courbé no longer struggled. He now sat bolt upright on his bride's broad shoulder. From the flaming peaks of blind passion, he had fallen into an abyss of cold fury. His love was dead, but some quite alien emotion was rearing an evil head from its ashes.

"Come!" cried the bride suddenly. "I am off. Do you and the others, Simon, follow to see me win my wager."

They all trooped out of the tent. A full moon rode the heavens and showed the road, lying as white and straight through the meadows as the parting in Simon Lafleur's black, oily hair. The bride, still holding the diminutive bridegroom on her shoulder, burst out into song as she strode forward. The wedding guests followed. Some walked none too steadily. Griffo, the giraffe boy, staggered pitifully on his long, thin legs. Papa Copo alone remained behind.

"What a strange world!" he muttered, standing in the tent door and following them with his round blue eyes. "Ah, these children of mine are difficult at times—very difficult!"

III

A year had rolled by since the marriage of Mlle. Jeanne Marie and M. Jacques Courbé. Copo's Circus had once more taken up its quarters in the town of Roubaix. For more than a week the country people for miles around had flocked to the sideshow to get a peep at Griffo, the giraffe boy; M. Hercule Hippo, the giant; Mlle. Lupa, the wolf lady; Mme. Samson, with her baby boa constrictors; and M. Jejongle, the famous juggler. Each was still firmly convinced that he or she alone was responsible for the popularity of the circus.

Simon Lafleur sat in his lodgings at the Sign of the Wild Boar. He wore nothing but red tights. His powerful torso, stripped to the waist, glistened with oil. He was kneading his biceps tenderly with some strong-smelling fluid.

Suddenly there came the sound of heavy, laborious footsteps on the stairs. Simon Lafleur looked up. His rather gloomy expression lifted, giving place to the brilliant smile that had won for him the hearts of so many lady acrobats.

"Ah, this is Marcelle!" he told himself. "Or perhaps it is Rose, the English girl; or, yet again, little Francesca, although she walks more lightly. Well, no matter — whoever it is, I will welcome her!"

By now, the lagging, heavy footfalls were in the hall; and, a moment later, they came to a halt outside the door. There was a timid knock.

Simon Lafleur's brilliant smile broadened. "Perhaps some new admirer that needs encouragement," he told himself. But aloud he said, "Enter, mademoiselle!"

The door swung slowly open and revealed the visitor. She was a tall, gaunt woman dressed like a peasant. The wind had blown her hair into her eyes. Now she raised a large, toil-worn hand, brushed it back across her forehead and looked long and attentively at the bareback rider.

"Do you not remember me?" she said at length.

Two lines of perplexity appeared above Simon Lafleur's Roman nose; he slowly shook his head. He, who had known so many women in his time, was now at a loss. Was it a fair question to ask a man who was no longer a boy and who had lived? Women change so in a brief time! Now this bag of bones might at one time have appeared desirable to him.

Parbleu! Fate was a conjurer! She waved her wand; and beautiful women were transformed into hogs, jewels into pebbles, silks and laces into hempen cords. The brave fellow who danced tonight at the prince's ball, might tomorrow dance more lightly on the gallows tree. The thing was to live and die with a full belly. To digest all that one could — that was life!

"You do not remember me?" she said again.

Simon Lafleur once more shook his sleek, black head. "I have a poor memory for faces, madame," he said politely. "It is my misfortune, when there are such beautiful faces."

"Ah, but you should have remembered, Simon!" the woman cried, a sob rising in her throat. "We were very close together, you and I. Do you not remember Jeanne Marie?"

"Jeanne Marie!" the bareback rider cried. "Jeanne Marie, who married a marmoset and a country estate? Don't tell me, madame, that you — "

He broke off and stared at her, open-mouthed. His sharp black eyes wandered from the wisps of wet, straggling hair down her gaunt person till they rested at last on her thick cowhide boots encrusted with layer on layer of mud from the countryside.

"It is impossible!" he said at last.

"It is indeed Jeanne Marie," the woman answered, "or what is left of her. Ah, Simon, what a life he has led me! I have been merely a beast of burden! There are no ignominies which he has not made me suffer!"

"To whom do you refer?" Simon Lafleur demanded. "Surely you cannot mean that pocket-edition husband of yours—that dwarf, Jacques Courbé?"

"Ah, but I do, Simon! Alas, he has broken me!"

"He—that toothpick of a man?" the bareback rider cried with one of his silent laughs. "Why, it is impossible! As you once said yourself, Jeanne, you could crack his skull between finger and thumb like a hickory nut!"

"So I thought once. Ah, but I did not know him then, Simon! Because he was small, I thought I could do with him as I liked. It seemed to me that I was marrying a manikin. 'I will play Punch and Judy with this little fellow,' I said to myself. Simon, you may imagine my surprise when he began playing Punch and Judy with me!"

"But I do not understand, Jeanne. Surely at any time you could have slapped him into obedience!"

"Perhaps," she assented wearily, "had it not been for St. Eustache. From the first that wolf-dog of his hated me. If I so much as answered his master back, he would show his teeth. Once, at the beginning, when I raised my hand to cuff Jacques Courbé, he sprang at my throat and would have torn me limb from limb had the dwarf not called him off. I was a strong woman, but even then I was no match for a wolf!"

"There was poison, was there not?" Simon Lafleur suggested.

"Ah, yes, I, too, thought of poison; but it was of no avail. St. Eustache would eat nothing that I gave him; and the dwarf forced me to taste first of all food that was placed before him and his dog. Unless I myself wished to die, there was no way of poisoning either of them."

"My poor girl!" the bareback rider said pityingly. "I begin to understand; but sit down and tell me everything. This is a revelation to me, after seeing you stalking homeward so triumphantly with your bridegroom on your shoulder. You must begin at the beginning."

"It was just because I carried him thus on my shoulder that I have had to suffer so cruelly," she said, seating herself on the only other chair the room afforded. "He has never forgiven me the insult which he says I put upon him. Do you remember how I boasted that I could carry him from one end of France to the other?"

"I remember. Well, Jeanne?"

"Well, Simon, the little demon has figured out the exact distance in leagues. Each morning, rain or shine, we sally out of the house — he on my back, and the wolf-dog at my heels — and I tramp along the dusty roads till my knees tremble beneath me from fatigue. If I so much as slacken my pace, if I falter, he goads me with cruel little golden spurs; while, at the same time, St. Eustache nips my ankles. When we return home, he strikes so many leagues off a score which he says is the number of leagues from one end of France to the other. Not half that distance has been covered, and I am no longer a strong woman, Simon. Look at these shoes!"

She held up one of her feet for his inspection. The sole of the cowhide boot had been worn through; Simon Lafleur caught a glimpse of bruised flesh caked with the mire of the highway.

"This is the third pair that I have had," she continued hoarsely. "Now he tells me that the price of shoe leather is too high, that I shall have to finish my pilgrimage barefooted."

"But why do you put up with all this, Jeanne?" Simon Lafleur asked angrily. "You, who have a carriage and a servant, should not walk at all!"

"At first there was a carriage and a servant," she said, wiping the tears from her eyes with the back of her hand, "but they did not last a week. He sent the servant about his business and sold the carriage at a nearby fair. Now there is no one but me to wait on him and his dog."

"But the neighbors?" Simon Lafleur persisted. "Surely you could appeal to them?"

"We have no neighbors; the farm is quite isolated. I would have run away many months ago, if I could have escaped unnoticed; but they keep a continual watch on me. Once I tried, but I hadn't traveled more than a league before the wolf-dog was snapping at my ankles. He drove me back to the farm, and the following day I was compelled to carry the little fiend until I fell from sheer exhaustion."

"But tonight you got away?"

"Yes," she said with a quick, frightened glance at the door. "Tonight I slipped out while they were both sleeping, and came here to you. I knew that you would protect me, Simon, because of what we have been to each other. Get Papa Copo to take me back in the circus, and I will work my fingers to the bone! Save me, Simon!"

Jeanne Marie could no longer suppress her sobs. They rose in her throat, choking her, making her incapable of further speech.

"Calm yourself, Jeanne," Simon Lafleur told her soothingly. "I will do what I can for you. I shall discuss the matter with Papa Copo tomorrow. Of course, you are no longer the woman that you were a year ago. You have aged since then, but perhaps our good Papa Copo could find you something to do."

He broke off and eyed her intently. She had sat up in the chair; her face, even under its coat of grime, had turned a sickly white.

"What troubles you, Jeanne?" he asked a trifle breathlessly.

"Hush!" she said, with a finger to her lips. "Listen!"

Simon Lafleur could hear nothing but the tapping of the rain on the roof and the sighing of the wind through the trees. An unusual silence seemed to pervade the Sign of the Wild Boar.

"Now don't you hear it?" she cried with an inarticulate gasp. "Simon, it is in the house — it is on the stairs!"

At last the bareback rider's less-sensitive ears caught the sound his companion had heard a full minute before. It was a steady pit-pat, pit-pat, on the stairs, hard to dissociate from the drip of the rain from the eaves; but each instant it came nearer, grew more distinct.

"Oh, save me, Simon; save me!" Jeanne Marie cried, throwing herself at his feet and clasping him about his knees. "Save me! It is St. Eustache!"

"Nonsense, woman!" the bareback rider said angrily, but nevertheless he rose. "There are other dogs in the world. On the second landing, there is a blind fellow who owns a dog. Perhaps that is what you hear."

"No, no — it is St. Eustache's step! My God, if you had lived with him a year, you would know it, too! Close the door and lock it!"

"That I will not," Simon Lafleur said contemptuously. "Do you think I am frightened so easily? If it is the wolf-dog, so much the worse for him. He will not be the first cur I have choked to death with these two hands!"

Pit-pat, pit-pat — it was on the second landing. Pit-pat, pit-pat — now it was in the corridor, and coming fast. Pit-pat — all at once it stopped.

There was a moment's breathless silence, and then into the room trotted St. Eustache. M. Jacques sat astride the dog's broad back, as he had so often done in the circus ring. He held a tiny drawn sword; his shoe-button eyes seemed to reflect its steely glitter.

The dwarf brought the dog to a halt in the middle of the room, and took in, at a single glance, the prostrate figure of Jeanne Marie. St. Eustache, too, seemed to take silent note of it. The stiff hair on his back rose up, he showed his long white fangs hungrily, and his eyes glowed like two live coals.

"So I find you thus, madame!" M. Jacques Courbé said at last. "It is fortunate that I have a charger here who can scent out my enemies as well as hunt them down in the open. Without him, I might have had some difficulty in discovering you. Well, the little game is up. I find you with your lover!"

"Simon Lafleur is not my lover!" she sobbed. "I have not seen him once since I married you until tonight! I swear it!"

"Once is enough," the dwarf said grimly. "The imprudent stable boy must be chastised!"

"Oh, spare him!" Jeanne Marie implored. "Do not harm him, I beg of you! It is not his fault that I came! I—"

But at this point Simon Lafleur drowned her out in a roar of laughter.

"Ha, ha!" he roared, putting his hands on his hips. "You would chastise me, eh? *Nom d'un chien!* Don't try your circus tricks on me! Why, hop-o'-my-thumb, you who ride on a dog's back like a flea, out of this room before I squash you. Begone, melt, fade away!" He paused, expanded his barrel-like chest, puffed out his cheeks, and blew a great breath at the dwarf. "Blow away, insect," he bellowed, "lest I put my heel on you!"

M. Jacques Courbé was unmoved by this torrent of abuse. He sat very upright on St. Eustache's back, his tiny sword resting on his tiny shoulder.

"Are you done?" he said at last, when the bareback rider had run dry of invectives. "Very well, monsieur! Prepare to receive cavalry!" He paused for an instant, then added in a high, clear voice: "Get him, St. Eustache!"

The dog crouched, and at almost the same moment, sprang at Simon Lafleur. The bareback rider had no time to avoid him and his tiny rider. Almost instantaneously the three of them had come to death grips. It was a gory business.

Simon Lafleur, strong man as he was, was bowled over by the dog's unexpected leap. St. Eustache's clashing jaws closed on his right arm and crushed it to the bone. A moment later the dwarf, still clinging to his dog's back, thrust the point of his tiny sword into the body of the prostrate bareback rider.

Simon Lafleur struggled valiantly, but to no purpose. Now he felt the fetid breath of the dog fanning his neck, and the wasp-like sting of the dwarf's blade, which this time found a mortal spot. A convulsive tremor shook him and he rolled over on his back. The circus Romeo was dead.

M. Jacques Courbé cleansed his sword on a kerchief of lace, dismounted, and approached Jeanne Marie. She was still crouching on the floor, her eyes closed, her head held tightly between both hands. The dwarf touched her imperiously on the broad shoulder which had so often carried him.

"Madame," he said, "we now can return home. You must be more careful hereafter. *Ma foi,* it is an ungentlemanly business cutting the throats of stable boys!"

She rose to her feet, like a large trained animal at the word of command.

"Do you wish to be carried?" she said between livid lips.

"Ah, that is true, madame," he murmured. "I was forgetting our little wager. Ah, yes! Well, you are to be congratulated, madame—you have covered nearly half the distance."

"Nearly half the distance," she repeated in a lifeless voice.

"Yes, madame," M. Jacques Courbé continued. "I fancy that you will be quite a docile wife by the time you have done." He paused, and then added reflectively: "It is truly remarkable how speedily one can ride the devil out of a woman—with spurs!"

Papa Copo had been spending a convivial evening at the Sign of the Wild Boar. As he stepped out into the street, he saw three familiar figures preceding him—a tall woman, a tiny man, and a large dog with upstanding ears. The woman carried the man on her shoulder; the dog trotted at her heels.

The circus owner came to a halt and stared after them. His round eyes were full of childish astonishment.

"Can it be?" he murmured. "Yes, it is! Three old friends! And so Jeanne carries him! Ah, but she should not poke fun at M. Jacques Courbé! He is so sensitive; but, alas, they are the kind that are always henpecked!"

1928

JAMES M. CAIN

PASTORALE

JAMES M(ALLAHAN) CAIN (1892–1977) was born in Annapolis, and grew up in Maryland, returning to the state permanently (after seventeen years as a screenwriter in California) in 1947. He received his BA from Washington College at the age of eighteen, then taught mathematics and English for four years before receiving his MA. He became a journalist, also submitting articles and stories to magazines while still in his twenties. His first full-length novel, *The Postman Always Rings Twice* (1934), became a huge bestseller and was filmed by MGM (with a script by Raymond Chandler) in 1946, starring Lana Turner and John Garfield, and again in 1981, with Jessica Lange and Jack Nicholson. Cain did not write detective stories, but is lumped with other hard-boiled writers for his tough, gritty crime novels of sex and violence, most of which follow a familiar plot of a man falling for a woman and engaging in a criminal plot for her, only to have her betray him. In addition to *Postman,* the formula also worked in *Double Indemnity* (1943), filmed by Billy Wilder in 1944 with Barbara Stanwyck, Fred MacMurray, and Edward G. Robinson. The other classic film noir made from his work, *Mildred Pierce* (1941), was as bleak as his other books and films, but this time it is the titular character who is betrayed by a woman — her daughter.

"Pastorale" is Cain's first published story and established the template for what was to become his more serious work. The familiar story of a man and woman in an illicit affair planning to murder her husband is told in the humorous style of Ring Lardner's "Haircut," but nonetheless leads to inevitable darkness. It was first published in the March 1928 issue of *American Mercury* and first collected in book form in Cain's *The Baby in the Icebox* (1981).

■ ■ ■

1

WELL, IT LOOKS like Burbie is going to get hung. And if he does; what he can lay it on is, he always figured he was so damn smart.

You see, Burbie, he left town when he was about sixteen year old. He run away with one of them traveling shows, "East Lynne" I think it was, and he stayed away about ten years. And when he come back he thought he knowed a lot. Burbie, he's got them watery blue eyes what kind of stick out from his face, and how he killed the time was to sit around and listen to the boys talk down at the poolroom or over at the barber shop or a couple other places where he hung out, and then wink at you like they was all making a fool of theirself or something and nobody didn't know it but him.

But when you come right down to what Burbie had in his head, why, it wasn't much. 'Course, he generally always had a job, painting around or maybe helping out on a new house, like of that, but what he used to do was to play baseball with the high school team. And they had a big fight over it, 'cause Burbie was so old nobody wouldn't believe he went to the school, and them other teams was all the time putting up a squawk. So then he couldn't play no more. And another thing he liked to do was sing at the entertainments. I reckon he liked that most of all, 'cause he claimed that a whole lot of the time he was away he was on the stage, and I reckon maybe he was at that, 'cause he was pretty good, 'specially when he dressed hisself up like a old-time Rube and come out and spoke a piece what he knowed.

Well, when he come back to town he seen Lida and it was a natural. 'Cause Lida, she was just about the same kind of a thing for a woman as Burbie was for a man. She used to work in the store, selling dry goods to the men, and kind of making hats on the side. 'Cepting only she didn't stay on the dry goods side no more'n she had to. She was generally over where the boys was drinking Coca-Cola, and all the time carrying on about did they like it with ammonia or lemon, and could she have a swallow outen their glass. And what she had her mind on was the clothes she had on, and was she dated up for Sunday night. Them clothes was pretty snappy, and she made them herself. And I heard some of them say she wasn't hard to date up, and after you done kept your date why maybe you wasn't going to be disappointed. And why Lida married the old man I don't know, lessen she got tired working at the store and tooken a look at the big farm where he lived at, about two mile from town.

By the time Burbie got back she'd been married about a year and she was about due. So her and him commence meeting each other, out in the orchard back of the old man's house. The old man would go to bed right after supper and then she'd sneak out and meet Burbie. And nobody wasn't supposed to know nothing about it. Only everybody did, 'cause Burbie, after he'd get back to town about eleven o'clock at night, he'd kind of slide into the poolroom and set down easy like. And then somebody'd say, "Yay, Burbie, where you been?" And Burbie, he'd kind of look around, and then he'd pick out somebody and wink at him, and that was how Burbie give it some good advertising.

So the way Burbie tells it, and he tells it plenty since he done got religion down to the jailhouse, it wasn't long before him and Lida thought it would be a good idea to kill the old man. They figured he didn't have long to live nohow, so he might as well go now as wait a couple of years. And another thing, the old man had kind of got hep that something was going on, and they figured if he throwed Lida out it wouldn't be no easy job to get his money even if he died regular. And another thing, by that time the Klux was kind of talking around, so Burbie figured it would be better if him and Lida was to get married, else maybe he'd have to leave town again.

So that was how come he got Hutch in it. You see, he was afeared to kill the old man hisself and he wanted some help. And then he figured it would be pretty good if Lida wasn't nowheres around and it would look like robbery. If it would've been me, I would've left Hutch out of it. 'Cause Hutch, he was mean. He'd been away for a while too, but him going away, that wasn't the same as Burbie going away. Hutch was sent. He was sent for ripping a mail sack while he was driving the mail wagon up from the station, and before he come back he done two years down to Atlanta.

But what I mean, he wasn't only crooked, he was mean. He had a ugly look to him, like when he'd order hisself a couple of fried eggs over to the restaurant, and then set and eat them with his head humped down low and his arm curled around his plate like he thought somebody was going to steal it off him, and handle his knife with his thumb down near the tip, kind of like a nigger does a razor. Nobody didn't have much to say to Hutch, and I reckon that's why he ain't heard nothing about Burbie and Lida, and et it all up what Burbie told him about the old man having a pot of money hid in the fireplace in the back room.

So one night early in March, Burbie and Hutch went out and done the job. Burbie he'd already got Lida out of the way. She'd let on she had to go to the city to buy some things, and she went away on No. 6, so everybody knowed she was gone. Hutch, he seen her go, and come running to Burbie saying now was a good time, which was just what Burbie wanted. 'Cause her and Burbie had already put the money in the pot, so Hutch wouldn't think it was no put-up job. Well, anyway, they put $23 in the pot, all changed into pennies and nickels and dimes so it would look like a big pile, and that was all the money Burbie had. It was kind of like you might say the savings of a lifetime.

And then Burbie and Hutch got in the horse and wagon what Hutch had, 'cause Hutch was in the hauling business again, and they went out to the old man's place. Only they went around the back way, and tied the horse back of the house so nobody couldn't see it from the road, and knocked on the back door and made out like they was just coming through the place on their way back to town and had stopped by to get warmed up, 'cause it was cold as hell. So the old man let them in and give them a drink of some hard cider what he had, and they got canned up a little more. They was already pretty canned, 'cause they both of them had a pint of corn on their hip for to give them some nerve.

And then Hutch he got back of the old man and crowned him with a wrench what he had hid in his coat.

2

Well, next off Hutch gets sore as hell at Burbie 'cause there ain't no more'n $23 in the pot. He didn't do nothing. He just set there, first looking at the money, what he had piled up on a table, and then looking at Burbie.

And then Burbie commences soft-soaping him. He says hope my die he thought there was a thousand dollars anyway in the pot, on account the old man being like he was. And he says hope my die it sure was a big surprise to him how little there was there. And he says hope my die it sure does make him feel bad, on account he's the one had the idea first. And he says hope my die it's all his fault and he's going to let Hutch keep all the money, damn if he ain't. He ain't going to take none of it for hisself at all, on account of how bad he feels. And Hutch, he don't say nothing at all, only look at Burbie and look at the money.

And right in the middle of while Burbie was talking, they heard a whole lot of hollering out in front of the house and somebody blowing a automobile horn. And Hutch jumps up and scoops the money and the wrench off the table in his pockets, and hides the pot back in the fireplace. And then he grabs the old man and him and Burbie carries him out the back door, hists him in the wagon, and drives off. And how they was to drive off without them people seeing them was because they come in the back way and that was the way they went. And them people in the automobile, they was a bunch of old folks from the Methodist church what knowed Lida was away and didn't think so much of Lida nohow and come out to say hello. And when they come in and didn't see nothing, they figured the old man had went in to town and so they went back.

Well, Hutch and Burbie was in a hell of a fix all right. 'Cause there they was, driving along somewheres with the old man in the wagon and they didn't have no more idea than a baldheaded coot where they was going or what they was going to do with him. So Burbie, he commence to whimper. But Hutch kept a-setting there, driving the horse, and he don't say nothing.

So pretty soon they come to a place where they was building a piece of county road, and it was all tore up and a whole lot of toolboxes laying out on the side. So Hutch gets out and twists the lock off one of them with the wrench, and takes out a pick and a shovel and throws them in the wagon. And then he got in again and drove on for a while till he come to the Whooping Nannie woods, what some of them says has got a ghost in it on dark nights, and it's about three miles from the old man's farm. And Hutch turns in there and pretty soon he come to a kind of a clear place and he stopped. And then, first thing he's said to Burbie, he says,

"Dig that grave!"

So Burbie dug the grave. He dug for two hours, until he got so damn tired he couldn't hardly stand up. But he ain't hardly made no hole at all. 'Cause the ground is froze and even with the pick he couldn't hardly make a dent in it scarcely. But anyhow Hutch stopped him and they throwed the old man in and covered him up. But after they got him covered up his head was sticking out. So Hutch beat the head down good as he could and piled the dirt up around it and they got in and drove off.

After they'd went a little ways, Hutch commence to cuss Burbie. Then he said Burbie'd been lying to him. But Burbie, he swears he ain't been lying. And then Hutch says he *was* lying and with that he hit Burbie. And after he knocked Burbie down in the bottom of the wagon he kicked him and then pretty soon Burbie up and told him about Lida. And when Burbie got done telling him about Lida, Hutch turned the horse around. Burbie asked then what they was going back for and Hutch says they're going back for to git a present for Lida. So they come back for to git a present for Lida. So they come back to the grave and Hutch made Burbie cut off the old man's head with the shovel. It made Burbie sick, but Hutch made him stick at it, and after a while Burbie had it off. So Hutch throwed it in the wagon and they get in and start back to town once more.

Well, they wasn't no more'n out of the woods before Hutch takes hisself a slug of corn and commence to holler. He kind of raved to hisself, all about how he was going to make Burbie put the head in a box and tie it up with a string and take it out to Lida for a present, so she'd get a nice surprise when she opened it. Soon as Lida comes back he says Burbie has got to do it, and then he's going to kill Burbie. "I'll kill you!" he says. "I'll kill you, damn you! I'll kill you!" And he says it kind of singsongy, over and over again.

And then he takes hisself another slug of corn and stands up and whoops. Then he beat on the horse with the whip and the horse commence to run. What I mean, he commence to gallop. And then Hutch hit him some more. And then he commence to screech as loud as he could. "Ride him, cowboy!" he hollers. "Going East! Here come old broadcuff down the road! Whe-e-e-e-e!" And sure enough, here they come down the road, the horse a-running hell to split, and Hutch a-hollering, and Burbie a-shivering, and the head a-rolling around in the bottom of the wagon, and bouncing up in the air when they hit a bump, and Burbie damn near dying every time it hit his feet.

3

After a while the horse got tired so it wouldn't run no more, and they had to let him walk and Hutch set down and commence to grunt. So Burbie, he tries to figure out what the hell he's going to do with the head. And pretty soon he remembers a creek what they got to cross, what they ain't crossed on the way out 'cause they come the back way. So he figures he'll throw the head overboard when Hutch ain't looking. So he done it. They come to the creek, and on the way down to the bridge there's a little hill, and when the wagon tilted going down the hill the head rolled up between Burbie's feet, and he held it there, and when they got in the middle of the bridge he reached down and heaved it overboard.

Next off, Hutch give a yell and drop down in the bottom of the wagon. 'Cause what it sounded like was a pistol shot. You see, Burbie done forgot that it was a cold night and the creek done froze over. Not much, just a thin skim about a inch thick, but enough that when that head hit it, it cracked pretty loud in different directions. And that was what scared Hutch. So when he got up and seen the head setting out there on the ice in the moonlight, and got it straight what Burbie done, he let on he was going to kill Burbie right there. And he reached for the pick. And Burbie jumped out and run, and he didn't never stop till he got home at the place where he lived at, and locked the door, and climbed in bed and pulled the covers over his head.

Well, the next morning a fellow come running into town and says there's hell to pay down at the bridge. So we all went down there and first thing we seen was that head laying out there on the ice, kind of rolled over on one ear. And next thing we seen was Hutch's horse and wagon tied to the bridge rail, and the horse damn near froze to death. And the next thing we seen was the hole in the ice where Hutch fell through. And the next thing we seen down on the bottom next to one of the bridge pilings, was Hutch.

So the first thing we went to work and done was to get the head. And believe me a head laying out on thin ice is a pretty damn hard thing to get, and what we had to do was to lasso it. And the next thing we done was to get Hutch. And after we fished him out he had the wrench and the $23 in his pockets and the pint of corn on his hip and he was stiff as a board. And near as I can figure out, what happened to him was that after Burbie run away he climbed down on the bridge piling and tried to reach the head and fell in.

But we didn't know nothing about it then, and after we done got the head and the old man was gone and a couple of boys that afternoon found the body and not the head on it, and the pot was found, and them old people from the Methodist church done told their story and one thing and another, we figured out that Hutch done it, 'specially on account he must have been drunk and he done time in the pen and all like of that, and nobody ain't thought nothing about Burbie at all. They had the funeral and Lida cried like hell and everybody tried to figure out what Hutch wanted with the head and things went along thataway for three weeks.

Then one night down to the poolroom they was having it some more about the head, and one says one thing and one says another, and Benny Heath, what's a kind of a constable around town, he started a long bum argument about how Hutch must of figured if they couldn't find the head to the body they couldn't prove no murder. So right in the middle of it Burbie kind of looked around like he always done and then he winked. And Benny Heath, he kept on a-talking, and after he got done Burbie kind of leaned over and commence to talk to him. And in a couple of minutes you couldn't of heard a man catch his breath in that place, accounten they was all listening at Burbie.

I already told you Burbie was pretty good when it comes to giving a spiel at a entertainment. Well, this here was a kind of spiel too. Burbie act like he had it all learned by heart. His voice trimmled and ever couple of minutes he'd kind of cry and wipe his eyes and make out like he can't say no more, and then he'd go on.

And the big idea was what a whole lot of hell he done raised in his life. Burbie said it was drink and women what done ruined him. He told about all the women what he knowed, and all the saloons he's been in, and some of it was a lie 'cause if all the saloons was as swell as he said they was they'd of throwed him out. And then he told about how sorry he was about the life he done led, and how hope my die he come home to his old hometown just to get out the devilment and settle down. And he told about Lida, and how she wouldn't let him cut it out. And then he told how she done led him on till he got the idea to kill the old man. And then he told about how him and Hutch done it, and all about the money and the head and all the rest of it.

And what it sounded like was a piece what he knowed called "The Face on the Floor," what was about a bum what drawed a picture on the barroom floor of the woman what done ruined him. Only the funny part was that Burbie wasn't ashamed of hisself like he made out he was. You could see he was proud of hisself. He was proud of all them women and all the liquor he'd drunk and he was proud about Lida and he was proud about the old man and the head and being slick enough not to fall in the creek with Hutch. And after he got done he give a yelp and flopped down on the floor and I reckon maybe he thought he was going to die on the spot like the bum what drawed the face on the barroom floor, only he didn't. He kind of lain there a couple of minutes till Benny got him up and put him in the car and tooken him off to jail.

So that's where he's at now, and he's went to work and got religion down there, and all the people what comes to see him, why he sings hymns to them and then he speaks them his piece. And I hear tell he knows it pretty good by now and has got the crying down pat. And Lida, they got her down there too, only she won't say nothing 'cepting she done it same as Hutch and Burbie. So Burbie, he's going to get hung, sure as hell. And if he hadn't felt so smart, he would've been a free man yet.

Only I reckon he done been holding it all so long he just had to spill it.

1938

STEVE FISHER

YOU'LL ALWAYS REMEMBER ME

STEVE (STEPHEN GOULD) FISHER (1912–1980) was born in Marine City, Illinois, and joined the Marines at the age of sixteen, moving to California when he was discharged in 1932. His first short story had been published when he was thirteen, so he soon moved to New York to write for pulps, producing hundreds of stories, mostly mysteries but also stories about war, sex, and romance, graduating to the better-paying "slicks" such as *Esquire* and the *Saturday Evening Post.* When Hollywood money looked more enticing, he went to Los Angeles and became an equally prolific writer for motion pictures, with fifty-three screenplays to his credit, including *Johnny Angel* (1945, with Frank Gruber), Raymond Chandler's *The Lady in the Lake* (1946), *Song of the Thin Man* (1947), and Cornell Woolrich's *I Wouldn't Be in Your Shoes* (1948). Fisher was an even more prolific writer for television, producing more than 200 scripts for such long-running series as *McMillan and Wife, Barnaby Jones, Starsky and Hutch, Cannon,* and *77 Sunset Strip,* among many others.

What had been a moderately successful career changed in 1941 when he wrote *I Wake Up Screaming,* which was adapted in the same year into what is generally regarded as the first film noir. With the action moving from the novel's Hollywood setting of palm trees and sunshine to the dark alleys and nightclubs of New York City, it starred Victor Mature, Betty Grable, and Carole Landis. It was remade twelve years later as *Vicki,* this time set entirely in California, and starred Jeanne Crain, Elliott Reid, Jean Peters, and Richard Boone.

"You'll Always Remember Me" was first published in the March 1938 issue of *Black Mask.*

■ ■ ■

I COULD TELL it was Pushton blowing the bugle and I got out of bed tearing half of the bedclothes with me. I ran to the door and yelled, "Drown it! Drown it! Drown it!" and then I slammed the door and went along the row of beds and pulled the covers off the rest of the guys and said:

"Come on, get up. Get up! Don't you hear Pushton out there blowing his stinky lungs out?"

I hate bugles anyway, but the way this guy Pushton all but murders reveille kills me. I hadn't slept very well, thinking of the news I was going to hear this morning, one way or the other, and then to be jarred out of what sleep I could get by Pushton climaxed everything.

I went back to my bed and grabbed my shoes and puttees and slammed them on the floor in front of me, then I began unbuttoning my pajamas. I knew it wouldn't do any good to ask the guys in this wing. They wouldn't know anything. When they did see a paper all they read was the funnies. That's the trouble with Clark's. I know it's one of the best military academies in the West and that it costs my old man plenty of dough to keep me here, but they sure have some dopey ideas on how to handle kids. Like dividing the dormitories according to ages. Anybody with any sense knows that it should be according to grades because just take for instance this wing. I swear there isn't a fourteen-year-old punk in it that I could talk to without wanting to push in his face. And I have to live with the little pukes.

So I kept my mouth shut and got dressed, then I beat it out into the company street before the battalion got lined up for the flag raising. That's a silly thing, isn't it? Making us stand around with empty stomachs, shivering goose pimples while they pull up the flag and Pushton blows the bugle again. But at that I guess I'd have been in a worse place than Clark's Military Academy if my pop hadn't had a lot of influence and plenty of dollars. I'd be in a big school where they knock you around and don't ask you whether you like it or not. I know. I was there a month. So I guess the best thing for me to do was to let the academy have their Simple Simon flag-waving fun and not kick about it.

I was running around among the older guys now, collaring each one and asking the same question: "Were you on home-going yesterday? Did you see a paper last night? What about Tommy Smith?" That was what I wanted to know. What about Tommy Smith.

"He didn't get it," a senior told me.

"You mean the governor turned him down?"

"Yeah. He hangs Friday."

That hit me like a sledge on the back of my head and I felt words rushing to the tip of my tongue and then sliding back down my throat. I felt weak, like my stomach was all tied up in a knot. I'd thought sure Tommy Smith would have had his sentence changed to life. I didn't think they really had enough evidence to swing him. Not that I cared, particularly, only he had lived across the street and when they took him in for putting a knife through his old man's back—that was what they charged him with—it had left his two sisters minus both father and brother and feeling pretty badly.

Where I come in is that I got a crush on Marie, the youngest sister. She's fifteen. A year older than me. But as I explained, I'm not any little dumb dope still in grammar school. I'm what you'd call bright.

So that was it; they were going to swing Tommy after all, and Marie would be bawling on my shoulder for six months. Maybe I'd drop the little dame. I certainly wasn't going to go over and take that for the rest of my life.

I got lined up in the twelve-year-old company, at the right end because I was line sergeant. We did squads right and started marching toward the flagpole. I felt like hell. We swung to a company front and halted.

Pushton started in on the bugle. I watched him with my eyes burning. Gee, I hate buglers, and Pushton is easy to hate anyway. He's fat and wears horn-rimmed glasses. He's got a body like a bowling ball and a head like a pimple. His face looks like yesterday's oatmeal. And does he think being bugler is an important job! The little runt struts around like he was Gabriel, and he walks with his buttocks sticking out one way and his chest the other.

I watched him now, but I was thinking more about Tommy Smith. Earlier that night of the murder I had been there seeing Marie and I had heard part of Tommy's argument with his old man. Some silly thing. A girl Tommy wanted to marry and the old man couldn't see it that way. I will say he deserved killing, the old grouch. He used to chase me with his cane. Marie says he used to get up at night and wander around stomping that cane as he walked.

Tommy's defense was that the old boy lifted the cane to bean him. At least that was the defense the lawyer wanted to present. He wanted to present that, with Tommy pleading guilty, and hope for an acquittal. But Tommy stuck to straight denials on everything. Said he hadn't killed his father. The way everything shaped up the state proved he was a drunken liar and the jury saw it that way.

Tommy was a nice enough sort. He played football at his university, was a big guy with blond hair and a ruddy face, and blue eyes. He had a nice smile, white and clean like he scrubbed his teeth a lot. I guess his old man had been right about that girl, though, because when all this trouble started she dropped right out of the picture, went to New York or somewhere with her folks.

I was thinking about this when we began marching again; and I was still thinking about it when we came in for breakfast about forty minutes later, after having had our arms thrown out of joint in some more silly stuff called setting-up exercises. What they won't think of! As though we didn't get enough exercise running around all day!

Then we all trooped in to eat.

I sat at the breakfast table cracking my egg and watching the guy across from me hog six of them. I wanted to laugh. People think big private schools are the ritz and that their sons, when they go there, mix with the cream of young America. Bushwa! There are a few kids whose last names you might see across the front of a department store like Harker Bros., and there are some movie stars' sons, but most of us are a tough, outcast bunch that couldn't get along in public school and weren't wanted at home. Tutors wouldn't handle most of us for love or money. So they put us here.

Clark's will handle any kid and you can leave the love out of it so long as you lay the money on the line. Then the brat is taken care of so far as his parents are concerned, and he has the prestige of a fancy Clark uniform.

There wasn't another school in the state that would have taken me, public or private, after looking at my record. But when old man Clark had dough-ray-me clutched in his right fist he was blind to records like that. Well, that's the kind of a bunch we were.

Well, as I say, I was watching this glutton stuff eggs down his gullet which he thought was a smart thing to do even though he got a bellyache afterward, when the guy on my right said:

"I see Tommy Smith is going to hang."

"Yeah," I said, "that's rotten, ain't it?"

"Rotten?" he replied. "It's wonderful. It's what that rat has coming to him."

"Listen," said I, "one more crack like that and I'll smack your stinking little face in."

"You and how many others?" he said.

"Just me," I said, "and if you want to come outside I'll do it right now."

The kid who was table captain yelled: "Hey, you two pipe down. What's the argument anyway?"

"They're going to hang Tommy Smith," I said, "and I think it's a dirty rotten shame. He's as innocent as a babe in the woods."

"Ha-ha," said the table captain, "you're just bothered about Marie Smith."

"Skirt crazy! Skirt crazy!" mumbled the guy stuffing down the eggs.

I threw my water in his face, then I got up, facing the table captain and the guy on my right. "Listen," I said, "Tommy Smith is innocent. I was there an hour before the murder happened, wasn't I? What do you loudmouthed half-wits think you know about it? All you morons know is what you read in the papers. Tommy didn't do it. I should know, shouldn't I? I was right there in the house before it happened. I've been around there plenty since. I've talked to the detectives."

I sat down, plenty mad. I sat down because I had seen a faculty officer coming into the dining room. We all kept still until he walked on through. Then the table captain sneered and said:

"Tommy Smith is a dirty stinker. He's the one that killed his father all right. He stuck a knife right through his back!"

"A lie! A lie!" I screamed.

"How do you know it's a lie?"

"Well, I — I know, that's all," I said.

"Yeah, you know! Listen to him! You know! That's hot. I think I'll laugh!"

"Damn it," I said. "I *do* know!"

"How? How? Tell us that!"

"Well, maybe *I* did it. What do you think about that?"

"You!" shouted the table captain. "A little fourteen-year-old wart like you killing anybody! Ha!"

"Aw, go to hell," I said, "that's what you can do. Go straight to hell!"

"A little wart like you killing anybody," the table captain kept saying, and he was holding his sides and laughing.

All that Monday I felt pretty bad thinking about Tommy, what a really swell guy he had been, always laughing, always having a pat on the back for you. I knew he must be in a cell up in San Quentin now, waiting, counting the hours, maybe hearing them build his scaffold.

I imagine a guy doesn't feel so hot waiting for a thing like that, pacing in a cell, smoking up cigarettes, wondering what it's like when you're dead. I've read some about it. I read about Two Gun Crowley, I think it was, who went to the chair with his head thrown back and his chest out like he was proud of it. But there must have been something underneath, and Crowley, at least, knew that *he* had it coming to him. The real thing must be different than what you read in the papers. It must be pretty awful.

But in spite of all this I had sense enough to stay away from Marie all day. I could easily have gone to her house, which was across the street from the campus, but I knew that she and her sister, Ruth, and that Duff

Ryan, the young detective who had made the arrest—because, as he said, he thought it was his duty—had counted on the commutation of sentence. They figured they'd have plenty of time to clear up some angles of the case which had been plenty shaky even in court. No, sir. Sweet Marie would be in no mood for my consolation, and besides I was sick of saying the same things over and over and watching her burst into tears every time I mentioned Tommy's name.

I sat in the study hall Monday evening thinking about the whole thing. Outside the window I could see the stars crystal clear; and though it was warm in the classroom I could feel the cold of the air in the smoky blue of the night, so that I shivered. When they marched us into the dormitory at eight-thirty, Simmons, the mess captain, started razzing me about Tommy being innocent again, and I said:

"Listen, putrid, you wanta get hurt?"

"No," he said, then he added: "Sore head."

"You'll have one sore face," I said, "if you don't shut that big yap of yours."

There was no more said, and when I went to bed and the lights went off I lay there squirming while that fat-cheeked Pushton staggered through taps with his bugle. I was glad that Myers had bugle duty tomorrow and I wouldn't have to listen to Pushton.

But long after taps I still couldn't sleep for thinking of Tommy. What a damn thing that was—robbing me of my sleep! But I tell you, I did some real fretting, and honestly, if it hadn't been for the fact that God and I parted company so long ago, I might have even been sap enough to pray for him. But I didn't. I finally went to sleep. It must have been ten o'clock.

I didn't show around Marie's Tuesday afternoon either, figuring it was best to keep away. But after chow, that is, supper, an orderly came beating it out to the study hall for me and told me I was wanted on the telephone. I chased up to the main building and got right on the wire. It was Duff Ryan, that young detective I told you about.

"You've left me with quite a load, young man," he said.

"Explain," I said. "I've no time for nonsense." I guess I must have been nervous to say a thing like that to the law, but there was something about Duff Ryan's cool gray eyes that upset me and I imagined I could see those eyes right through the telephone.

"I mean about Ruth," he said softly, "she feels pretty badly. Now I can take care of her all right, but little Marie is crying her eyes out and I can't do anything with her."

"So what?" I said.

"She's your girl, isn't she, Martin?" he asked.

"Listen," I said, "in this school guys get called by their last name. Martin sounds sissy. My name is Thorpe."

"I'm sorry I bothered you, Martin," Duff said in that same soft voice. "If you don't want to cooperate —"

"Oh, I'll cooperate," I said. "I'll get right over. That is, provided I can get permission."

"I've already arranged that," Duff told me. "You just come on across the street and don't bother mentioning anything about it to anyone."

"OK," I said, and hung up. I sat there for a minute. This sounded fishy to me. Of course, Duff *might* be on the level, but I doubted it. You can never tell what a guy working for the law is going to do.

I trotted out to the campus and on across to the Smith house. Their mother had died a long while ago, so with the father murdered, and Tommy in the death house, there were only the two girls left.

Duff answered the door himself. I looked up at the big bruiser and then I sucked in my breath. I wouldn't have known him! His face was almost gray. Under his eyes were the biggest black rings I had ever seen. I don't mean the kind you get fighting. I mean the other kind, the serious kind you get from worry. He had short clipped hair that was sort of reddish, and shoulders that squared off his figure, tapering it down to a nice V.

Of course, he was plenty old, around twenty-six, but at this his being a detective surprised you because ordinarily he looked so much like a college kid. He always spoke in a modulated voice and never got excited over anything. And he had a way of looking at you that I hated. A quiet sort of way that asked and answered all of its own questions.

Personally, as a detective, I thought he was a big flop. The kind of detectives that I prefer seeing are those giant fighters that blaze their way through a gangster barricade. Duff Ryan was none of this. I suppose he was tough but he never showed it. Worst of all, I'd never even seen his gun!

"Glad you came over, Martin," he said.

"The name is Thorpe," I said.

He didn't answer, just stepped aside so I could come in. I didn't see Ruth, but I spotted Marie right away. She was sitting on the divan with her legs pulled up under her and her face hidden. She had a handkerchief pressed in her hand. She was a slim kid, but well developed for fifteen, so well developed in fact that for a while I had been razzed about this at school.

Like Tommy, she had blond hair, only hers was fluffy and came partway to her shoulders. She turned now and her face was all red from crying, but I still thought she was pretty. I'm a sucker that way. I've been a sucker for women ever since I was nine.

She had wide-spaced green eyes, and soft, rosy skin, and a generous mouth. Her only trouble, if any, was that she was a prude. Wouldn't speak to anybody on the Clark campus except me. Maybe you think I didn't like that! I'd met her at Sunday school, or rather coming out, since I had been hiding around waiting for it to let out, and I walked home with her four Sundays straight before she would speak to me. That is, I walked along beside her holding a one-way conversation. Finally I skipped a Sunday, then the next one she asked me where I had been, and that started the ball rolling.

"Thorpe," she said — that was another thing, *she* always called me by my last name because that was the one I had given her to start with — "Thorpe, I'm so glad you're here. Come over here and sit down beside me."

I went over and sat down and she straightened up, like she was ashamed that she had been crying, and put on a pretty good imitation of a smile. "How's everything been?" she said.

"Oh, pretty good," I said. "The freshmen are bellyaching about Latin this week, and just like algebra, I'm already so far ahead of them it's a crying shame."

"You're so smart, Thorpe," she told me.

"Too bad about Tommy," I said. "There's always the chance for a reprieve though."

"No," she said, and her eyes began to get dim again, "no, there isn't. This — this decision that went through Sunday night — that's the — Unless, of course, something comes up that we — the lawyer can —" and she began crying.

I put my arm around her, which was a thing she hadn't let me do much, and I said, "Come on, kid. Straighten up. Tommy wouldn't want you to cry."

About five minutes later she did straighten up. Duff Ryan was sitting over in the corner looking out the window, but it was just like we were alone.

"I'll play the piano," she said.

"Do you know anything hot yet?"

"Hot?" she said.

"Something popular, Marie," I explained. Blood was coming up into my face.

"Why, no," she replied. "I thought I would—"

"Play hymns!" I half screamed. "No! I don't want to hear any of those damned hymns!"

"Why, Thorpe!"

"I can't help it," I said. "I've told you about that enough times. Those kinds of songs just drone along in the same pitch and never get anywhere. If you can't play something decent stay away from the piano."

My fists were tight now and my fingers were going in and out. She knew better than to bring up that subject. It was the only thing we had ever argued about. Playing hymns. I wanted to go nuts every time I heard "Lead Kindly Light" or one of those other goofy things. I'd get so mad I couldn't see straight. Just an obsession with me, I guess.

"All right," she said, "but I wish you wouldn't swear in this house."

I said, "All right, I won't swear in this house."

"Or anywhere else," she said.

I was feeling good now. "OK, honey, if you say so."

She seemed pleased, and at least the argument had gotten her to quit thinking about Tommy for a minute. But it was then that her sister came downstairs.

Ruth was built on a smaller scale than Marie so that even though she was nineteen she wasn't any taller. She had darker hair too, and an oval face, very white now, making her brown eyes seem brighter. Brighter though more hollow. I will say she was beautiful.

She wore only a rich blue lounging robe, which was figure-fitting though it came down past her heels and was clasped in a high collar around her pale throat.

"I think it's time for you to come to bed, Marie," she said. "Hello, Thorpe."

"Hello," I said.

Marie got up wordlessly and pressed my hand, and smiled again, that faint imitation, and went off. Ruth stood there in the doorway from the dining room and as though it was a signal—which I suspect it was—Duff Ryan got up.

"I guess it's time for us to go, Martin," he said.

"You don't say," I said.

He looked at me fishily. "Yeah. I do say. We've got a job to do. Do you know what it is, Martin? We've got to kill a kitten. A poor little kitten."

I started to answer but didn't. The way he was saying that, and looking at me, put a chill up my back that made me suddenly ice cold. I began to tremble all over. He opened the door and motioned for me to go out.

That cat thing was a gag of some kind, I thought, and I was wide awake for any funny stuff from detectives, but Duff Ryan actually had a little kitten hidden in a box under the front steps of the house. He picked it up now and petted it.

"Got hit by a car," he said. "It's in terrible pain and there isn't a chance for recovery. I gave it a shot of stuff that eased the pain for a while but it must be coming back. We'll have to kill the cat."

I wanted to ask him why he hadn't killed it in the first place, whenever he had picked it up from under the car, but I kept my mouth shut and we walked along, back across the street to the Clark campus. There were no lights at all here and we walked in darkness, our feet scuffing on the dirt of the football gridiron.

"About that night of the murder, Martin," Duff said. "You won't mind a few more questions, will you? We want to do something to save Tommy. I made the arrest but I've been convinced since that he's innocent. I want desperately to save him before it's too late. It's apparent that we missed on something because — well, the way things are."

I said, "Are you sure of Tommy's innocence, or are you stuck on Ruth?"

"Sure of his innocence," he said in that soft voice. "You want to help, don't you, Martin? You don't want to see Tommy die?"

"Quit talking to me like a kid," I said. "Sure I want to help."

"All right. What were you doing over there that night?"

"I've answered that a dozen times. Once in court. I was seeing Marie."

"Mr. Smith — that is, her father — chased you out of the house though, didn't he?"

"He asked me to leave," I said.

"No, he didn't, Martin. He ordered you out and told you not to come back again."

I stopped and whirled toward him. "Who told you that?"

"Marie," he said. "She was the only one who heard him. She didn't want to say it before because she was afraid Ruth would keep her from seeing you. That little kid has a crush on you and she didn't think that had any bearing on the case."

"Well, it hasn't, has it?"

"Maybe not," snapped Duff Ryan, "but he did chase you out, didn't he? He threatened to use his cane on you?"

"I won't answer," I said.

"You don't have to," he told me. "But I wish you'd told the truth about it in the first place."

"Why?" We started walking again. "You don't think *I* killed him, do you?" I shot a quick glance in his direction and held my breath.

"No," he said, "nothing like that, only—"

"Only what?"

"Well, Martin, haven't you been kicked out of about every school in the state?"

"I wouldn't go so far as to say *every* school."

Duff said, "Quite a few though, eh?"

"Enough," I said.

"That's what I thought." He went on quietly, "I went over and had a look at your record, Martin. I wish I had thought of doing that sooner."

"Listen—"

"Oh, don't get excited," he said, "this may give us new leads, that's all. We've nothing against you. But when you were going to school at Hadden, you took the goat, which was a class mascot, upstairs with you one night and then pushed him down the stairs so that he broke all his legs. You did that, didn't you?"

"The goat slipped," I said.

"Maybe," whispered Duff. He lit a cigarette, holding on to the crippled cat with one hand. "But you stood at the top of the stairs and watched the goat suffer until somebody came along."

"I was so scared I couldn't move."

"Another time," Duff continued, "at another school, you pushed a kid into an oil hole that he couldn't get out of and you were ducking him—maybe trying to kill him—when someone came along and stopped you."

"He was a sissy. I was just having some fun!"

"At another school you were expelled for roping a newly born calf and pulling it up on top of a barn where you stabbed it and watched it bleed to death."

"I didn't stab it! It got caught on a piece of tin from the drain while I was pulling it up. You haven't told any of this to Marie, have you?"

"No," Duff said.

"All those things are just natural things," I said. "Any kid is liable to do them. You're just nuts because you can't pin the guilt on anybody but the guy who is going to die Friday and you're trying to make me look bad!"

"Maybe," Duff answered quietly, and we came into the chapel now and stopped. He dropped his cigarette, stepped on it, then patted the cat. Moonlight shone jaggedly through the rotting pillars. I could see the cat's eyes shining. "Maybe," Duff breathed again, "but didn't you land in a reform school once?"

"Twice," I said.

"And once in an institution where you were observed by a staff of doctors? It was a state institution, I think. Sort of a rest home."

"I was there a month," I said. "Some crab sent me there, or had me sent. But my dad got me out."

"Yes," Duff replied, "the crab had you sent there because you poisoned two of his Great Dane dogs. Your dad had to bribe somebody to get you out, and right now he pays double tuition for you here at Clark's."

I knew all this but it wasn't anything sweet to hear coming from a detective. "What of it?" I said. "You had plenty of chance to find that out."

"But we weren't allowed to see your records before," Duff answered. "As a matter of fact I paid an orderly to steal them for me, and then return them."

"Why, you dirty crook!"

I could see the funny twist of his smile there in the moonlight. His face looked pale and somehow far away. He looked at the cat and petted it some more. I was still shaking. Scared, I guess.

He said, "Too bad we have to kill you, kitten, but it's better than that pain."

Then, all at once I thought he had gone mad. He swung the cat around and began batting its head against the pillar in the chapel. I could see the whole thing clearly in the moonlight, his arm swinging back and forth, the cat's head being battered off, the bright crimson blood spurting all over.

He kept on doing it and my temples began to pound. My heart went like wildfire. I wanted to reach over and help him. I wanted to take that little cat and squeeze the living guts out of it. I wanted to help him smash its brains all over the chapel. I felt dizzy. Everything was going around. I felt myself reaching for the cat.

But I'm smart. I'm no dummy. I'm at the head of my class. I'm in high school. I knew what he was doing. He was testing me. *He wanted me to help him.* The son of a —— wasn't going to trick *me* like that. Not Martin Thorpe. I put my arms behind me and grabbed my wrists and with all my might I held my arms there and looked the other way.

I heard the cat drop with a thud to the cement, then I looked up, gasping to catch my breath. Duff Ryan looked at me with cool gray eyes, then he walked off. I stood there, still trying to get my breath and watching his shadow blend with the shadows of the dark study hall. I was having one hell of a time getting my breath.

But I slept good all night. I was mad and I didn't care about Tommy anymore. Let him hang. I slept good but I woke up ten minutes before reveille remembering that it was Pushton's turn at the bugle again. He and Myers traded off duty every other day.

I felt pretty cocky and got up putting on only my slippers and went down to the eleven-year-old wing. Pushton was sitting on the edge of the bed working his arms back and forth and yawning. The fat little punk looked like an old man. He took himself that seriously. You would have thought maybe he was a general.

"What you want, Thorpe?" he said.

"I want your bugle. I'm going to break the damn thing."

"You leave my bugle alone," he said. "My folks aren't as rich as yours and I had to save all my spending money to buy it." This was true. They furnished bugles at school but they were awful and Pushton took his music so seriously that he had saved up and bought his own instrument.

"I know it," I said, "so the school won't be on my neck if I break it." I looked around. "Where is it?"

"I won't tell you!"

I looked under the bed, under his pillow, then I grabbed him by the nose. "Come on, Heinie. Where is it?"

"Leave me alone!" he wailed. "Keep your hands off me." He was talking so loud now that half the wing was waking up.

"All right, punk," I said. "Go ahead and blow that thing, and I hope you blow your tonsils out."

I went back to my bed and held my ears. Pushton blew the bugle all right, I never did find out where he had the thing hidden.

I dressed thinking, well, only two more days and Tommy gets it. I'd be glad when it was over. Maybe all this tension would ease up then and Marie wouldn't cry so much because once he was dead there wouldn't be anything she could do about it. Time would go by and eventually she would forget him. One person more or less isn't so important in the world anyway, no matter how good a guy he is.

Everything went swell Wednesday right through breakfast and until after we were marching out of the chapel and into the schoolroom. Then I ran into Pushton, who was trotting around with his bugle tucked under his arm. I stopped and looked him up and down.

His little black eyes didn't flicker. He just said, "Next time you bother me, Thorpe, I'm going to report you."

"Go ahead, punk," I said, "and see what happens to you."

I went on into school then, burning up at his guts, talking to *me* that way.

I was still burned up and sore at the guy when a lucky break came, for me, that is, not Pushton. It was during the afternoon right after we had been dismissed from the classroom for the two-hour recreation period.

I went into the main building, which was prohibited in the daytime so that I had to sneak in, to get a book I wanted to read. It was under my pillow. I slipped up the stairs, crept into my wing, got the book, and started out. It was then that I heard a pounding noise.

I looked around, then saw it was coming from the eleven-year-old wing.

I walked in and there it was! You wouldn't have believed anything so beautiful could have been if you hadn't seen it with your own eyes. At least that was the way I felt about it. For who was it but Pushton.

The bugler on duty has the run of the main building and it was natural enough that he was here, but I hadn't thought about it. There was a new radio set, a small portable, beside his bed. I saw that the wires and earphone—which you have to use in the dormitory—were connected with the adjoining bed as well and guessed that it belonged to another cadet. But Pushton was hooking it up. He was leaning halfway out the window trying, pounding with a hammer, to make some kind of a connection on the aerial wire.

Nothing could have been better. The window was six stories from the ground, with cement down below. No one knew I was in the building. I felt blood surge into my temples. My face got red, hot red, and I could feel fever throbbing in my throat. I moved forward slowly, on cat feet, my hands straight at my sides. I didn't want him to hear me. But I was getting that dizzy feeling now. My fingers were itching.

Then suddenly I lunged over, I shoved against him. He looked back once, and that was what I wanted. He looked back for an instant, his fat face green with the most unholy fear I have ever seen. Then I gave him another shove and he was gone. Before he could call out, before he could say a word, he was gone, falling through the air!

I risked jumping up on the bed so I could see him hit, and I did see him hit. Then I got down and straightened the bed and beat it out.

I ran down the stairs as fast as I could. I didn't see anybody. More important, no one saw me. But when I was on the second floor I ran down the hall to the end and lifted the window. I jumped out here, landing squarely on my feet.

I waited for a minute, then I circled the building from an opposite direction. My heart was pounding inside me. It was difficult for me to breathe. I managed to get back to the play field through an indirect route.

Funny thing, Pushton wasn't seen right away. No one but myself had seen him fall. I was on the play field at least ten minutes, plenty long enough to establish myself as being there, before the cry went up. The kids went wild. We ran in packs to the scene.

I stood there with the rest of them looking at what was left of Pushton. He wouldn't blow any more bugles. His flesh was like a sack of water that had fallen and burst full of holes. The blood was splattered out in jagged streaks all around him.

We stood around about five minutes, the rest of the kids and I, nobody saying anything. Then a faculty officer chased us away, and that was the last I saw of Pushton.

Supper was served as usual but there wasn't much talk. What there was of it seemed to establish the fact that Pushton had been a thick-witted sort and had undoubtedly leaned out too far trying to fix the aerial wire and had fallen.

I thought that that could have easily been the case, all right, and since I had hated the little punk I had no conscience about it. It didn't bother me nearly so much as the fact that Tommy Smith was going to die. I had liked Tommy. And I was nuts about his sister, wasn't I?

That night study hall was converted into a little inquest meeting. We were all herded into one big room and Major Clark talked to us as though we were a bunch of Boy Scouts. After ascertaining that no one knew any more about Pushton's death than what they had seen on the cement, he assured us that the whole thing had been unavoidable and even went so far as to suggest that we might spare our parents the worry of telling them of so unfortunate an incident. All the bloated donkey was worrying about was losing a few tuitions.

Toward the end of the session Duff Ryan came in and nodded at me, and then sat down. He looked around at the kids, watched Major Clark a while, and then glanced back at me. He kept doing that until we were dismissed. He made me nervous.

Friday morning I woke up and listened for reveille but it didn't come. I lay there, feeling comfortable in the bedclothes and half lazy, but feeling every minute that reveille would blast me out of my place. Then I suddenly realized why the bugle hadn't blown. I heard the splash of rain across the window and knew that we wouldn't have to raise the flag or take our exercises this morning. On rainy days we got to sleep an extra half-hour.

I felt pretty good about this and put my hands behind my head there on the pillow and began thinking. They were pleasant, what you might call mellow, thoughts. A little thing like an extra half-hour in bed will do that.

Things were working out fine and after tonight I wouldn't have anything to worry about. For Duff Ryan to prove Tommy was innocent *after* the hanging would only make him out a damn fool. I was glad it was raining. It would make it easier for me to lay low, to stay away from Marie until the final word came . . .

That was what I thought in the morning, lying there in bed. But no. Seven-thirty that night Duff came over to the school in a slicker. He came into the study hall and got me. His eyes were wild. His face was strained.

"Ruth and I are going to see the lawyer again," he said. "You've got to stay with Marie."

"Nuts," I said.

He jerked me out of the seat, then he took his hands off me as though he were ashamed. "Come on," he said. "This is no time for smart talk."

So I went.

Ruth had on a slicker too and was waiting there on the front porch. I could see her pretty face. It was pinched, sort of terrible. Her eyes were wild too. She patted my hand, half crying, and said, "You be good to Marie, honey. She likes you, and you're the only one in the world now that can console her."

"What time does Tommy go?" I asked.

"Ten-thirty," said Duff.

I nodded. "OK." I stood there as they crossed the sidewalk and got into Duff Ryan's car and drove away. Then I went in to see Marie. The kid looked scared, white as a ghost.

"Oh, Thorpe," she said, "they're going to kill him tonight!"

"Well, I guess there's nothing we can do," I said.

She put her arms around me and cried on my shoulder. I could feel her against me, and believe me, she was nice. She had figure, all right. I put my arms around her waist and then I kissed her neck and her ears. She looked at me, tears on her cheeks, and shook her head. "Don't."

She said that because I had never kissed her before, but now I saw her lips and I kissed her. She didn't do anything about it, but kept crying.

Finally I said, "Well, let's make fudge. Let's play a game. Let's play the radio. Let's do *something*. This thing's beginning to get me."

We went to the kitchen and made fudge for a while.

But I was restless. The rain had increased. There was thunder and lightning in the sky now. Again I had that strange feeling of being cold, although the room was warm. I looked at the clock and it said ten minutes after eight. Only ten minutes after eight! And Tommy wasn't going to hang until ten-thirty!

"You'll always stay with me, won't you, Thorpe?" said Marie.

"Sure," I told her, but right then I felt like I wanted to push her face in. I had never felt that way before. I couldn't understand what was the matter with me. Everything that had been me was gone. My wit and good humor.

I kept watching the clock, watching every minute that ticked by, and thinking of Tommy up there in San Quentin in the death cell pacing back and forth. I guess maybe he was watching the minutes too. I wondered if it was raining up there and if rain made any difference in a hanging.

We wandered back into the living room and sat down at opposite ends of the divan. Marie looking at nothing, her eyes glassy, and me watching and hating the rain, and hearing the clock.

Then suddenly Marie got up and went to the piano. She didn't ask me if she could or anything about it. She just went to the piano and sat down. I stared after her, even opened my mouth to speak. But I didn't say anything. After all, it was *her* brother who was going to die, wasn't it? I guess for one night at least she could do anything she wanted to do.

But then she began playing. First, right off, "Lead Kindly Light," and then "Onward Christian Soldiers," and then "Little Church in the Wildwood." I sat there wringing my hands with that agony beating in my ears. Then I leapt to my feet and began to shout at her.

"Stop that! Stop it! Do you want to drive me crazy?"

But her face was frozen now. It was as though she was in a trance. I ran to her and shook her shoulder, but she pulled away from me and played on.

I backed away from her and my face felt as though it was contorted. I backed away and stared at her, her slim, arched back. I began biting my fingernails, and then my fingers. That music was killing me. Those hymns . . . those silly, inane hymns. Why didn't she stop it? The piano and the rain were seeping into my bloodstream.

I walked up and down the room. I walked up and down the room faster and faster. I stopped and picked up a flower vase and dropped it, yelling: *"Stop it! For the love of heaven, stop!"*

But she kept right on. Again I began staring at her, at her back, and her throat, and the profile of her face. I felt blood surging in me. I felt those hammers in my temples . . .

I tried to fight it off this time. I tried to go toward her to pull her away from that damn piano but I didn't have the strength to move in her direction. I stood there feeling the breath go out of me, feeling my skin tingle. And I didn't want to be like that. I looked at my hands, and one minute they were tight fists and the next my fingers were working in and out like mad.

I looked toward the kitchen, and then I moved quietly into it. She was still slamming at the piano when I opened the drawer and pulled out the knife I had used to kill her father.

At least it was a knife like it. I put it behind me and tiptoed back into the room. She wasn't aware that I had moved. I crept up on her, waited.

Her hands were flying over the piano keys. Once more I shouted, and my voice was getting hoarse: "Stop it!"

But of course she didn't. She didn't and I swore. I swore at her. She didn't hear this either. But I'd show the little slut a thing or two.

I was breathing hard, looking around the room to make sure no one was here. Then I lifted the knife and plunged down with it.

I swear I never knew where Duff Ryan came from. It must have been from behind the divan. A simple place like that and I hadn't seen him, merely because I had been convinced that he went away in the car. But he'd been in the room all the time waiting for me to do what I almost did.

It had been a trick, of course, and this time I'd been sap enough to fall into his trap. He had heard me denounce hymns, he knew I'd be nervous tonight, highly excitable, so he had set the stage and remained hidden, and Marie had done the rest.

He had told Marie then, after all.

Duff Ryan grabbed my wrist just at the right moment, as he had planned on doing, and of course being fourteen I didn't have much chance against him. He wrested away the knife, then he grabbed me and shouted:

"Why did you murder Marie's father?"

"Because the old boy hated me! Because he thought Marie was too young to know boys! Because he kicked me out and hit me with his cane!" I said all this, trying to jerk away from him, but I couldn't so I went on:

"That's why I did it. Because I had a lot of fun doing it! So what? What are you going to do about it? I'm a kid, you can't hang *me!* There's a law against hanging kids. I murdered Pushton too. I shoved him out the window! How do you like that? All you can do is put me in reform school!"

As my voice faded, and it faded because I had begun to choke, I heard Ruth at the telephone. She had come back in too. She was calling long distance. San Quentin.

Marie was sitting on the divan, her face in her hands. You would have thought she was sorry for me. When I got my breath I went on:

"I came back afterward, while Tommy was in the other room. I got in the kitchen door. The old man was standing there and I just picked up the knife and let him have it. I ran before I could see much. But Pushton. Let me tell you about Pushton—"

Duff Ryan shoved me back against the piano. "Shut up," he said. "You didn't kill Pushton. You're just bragging now. But you did kill the old man and that's what we wanted to know!"

Bragging? I was enraged. But Duff Ryan clipped me and I went out cold.

So I'm in reform school now and—will you believe it?—I can't convince anyone that I murdered Pushton. Is it that grownups are so unbelieving because I'm pretty young? Are they so stupid that they still look upon fourteen-year-old boys as little innocents who have no minds of their own? That is the bitterness of youth. And I am sure that I won't change or see things any differently. I told the dopes that too, but everyone assures me I will.

But the only thing I'm really worried about is that no one will believe about Pushton, not even the kids here at the reform school, and that hurts. It does something to my pride.

I'm not in the least worried about anything else. Things here aren't so bad, nor so different from Clark's. Doctors come and see me now and then but they don't think anything is wrong with my mind.

They think I knifed old man Smith because I was in a blind rage when I did it, and looking at it that way, it would only be second-degree murder even if I were older. I'm not considered serious. There are lots worse cases here than mine. Legally, a kid isn't responsible for what he does, so I'll be out when I'm twenty-one. Maybe before, because my old man's got money . . .

You'll always remember me, won't you? Because I'll be out when I'm older and you might be the one I'll be seeing.

1940

MACKINLAY KANTOR

GUN CRAZY

MacKinlay Kantor (1904–1977) was born in Webster City, Iowa, becoming a journalist at seventeen, and soon after began selling hard-boiled mystery stories to various pulp magazines. He wrote numerous crime stories, as well as several novels in the genre, such as *Diversey* (1928), about Chicago gangsters, and *Signal Thirty-Two* (1950), an excellent police procedural, given verisimilitude by virtue of Kantor's receiving permission from the acting police commissioner of New York to accompany the police on their activities to gather background information. His most famous crime novel is *Midnight Lace* (1948), the suspenseful tale of a young woman terrorized by an anonymous telephone caller; it was filmed twelve years later, starring Doris Day and Rex Harrison.

Kantor is far better known for his mainstream novels, such as the sentimental dog story *The Voice of Bugle Ann* (1936), filmed the same year; the long narrative poem *Glory for Me* (1945), filmed as *The Best Years of Our Lives* (1946), which won the Academy Award for Best Picture; and the outstanding Civil War novel *Andersonville* (1955), about the notorious Confederate prisoner of war camp, for which he won the Pulitzer Prize.

"Gun Crazy" was first published in the February 13, 1940, issue of the *Saturday Evening Post.* It has seldom been reprinted, even though it served as the basis for the famous noir cult film of the same title, for which Kantor wrote the screenplay. Released in 1949, it was directed by Joseph H. Lewis. The film, an excellent though more violent expansion of the short story, features a clean-cut gun nut, Bart (Nelly in the story), played by John Dall, who meets a good-looking sharpshooter, Laurie Starr (Antoinette McReady in the story), played by Peggy Cummins, and their subsequent spree of bank robberies and shootings.

■ ■ ■

I first met Nelson Tare when he was around five or six years old, and I was around the same. I had watched his family moving into the creek house on a cold, snowless morning in early winter.

Two lumber wagons went by, with iron beds and old kitchen chairs and mattresses tied all over them. They rumbled down the hill past Mr. Boston's barn and stopped in front of the creek house. I could see men and girls working, carrying the stuff inside.

In midafternoon I was outdoors again, and I coasted to the corner in my little wagon to see whether the moving-in activities were still going on.

Then Nelson Tare appeared. He had climbed the hill by himself; probably he was looking for guns, although I couldn't know that at the time. He was a gaunt little child with bright blue beads for eyes, and a sharp-pointed nose.

He said, "Hello, kid. Want to pway?"

Nelson was only about a month younger than I, it turned out, but he still talked a lot of baby talk. I think kids are apt to do that more when their parents don't talk to them much.

I told him that I did want to play, and asked him what he wanted to do.

He asked, "Have you got any guns?" What he actually said was, "Dot any duns?" and for a while I didn't know what he was talking about. Then, when I understood, I coasted back to the house in my wagon, with Nelson walking beside me. We went into the living room.

I had three guns: a popgun with the pop gone, and a glass pistol that used to have candy inside — but now the candy was all eaten up — and a cap gun and holster.

The cap gun was the best. It was nickel-plated, and the holster was made of black patent leather. It was the shape and possibly half the size of an ordinary .32-caliber revolver.

Nelson Tare's eyes pushed out a little when he saw it. He made a grab, and belted it on before I had time to protest and tell him that I wanted to play with the cap gun and he could play with the glass pistol or the broken pop rifle. He went swaggering around with the gun on, and it kind of scared me the way he did it — all of a sudden he'd snatch the revolver out of its holster and aim it at me.

I took the glass pistol and tried to imitate him. But the glass pistol couldn't click, and at least the hammer of the cap gun would come down with a resounding click. Nelson, or Nelly, as I came to know him, fairly shot the daylights out of me. I began to protest, and he kept on advancing and kind of wrangling and threatening me, until he had me backed up in a corner.

He hadn't taken off his little red coat with its yellow horn buttons, and he was perspiring inside it. I still recollect how he smelled when he got close enough to wool me around; I had never smelled a smell like that before. I remember his face, too, when he came close — the tiny, expressionless turquoise eyes, the receding chin and baby mouth still marked with the tag ends of his dinner; and in between them, that inhuman nose whittled out to a point.

I tried to push him away as he kept battling me and shooting me, and I guess I began to cry.

Nelson said that it wasn't a real gun.

"It might go off!"

He said that it couldn't go off; that it wasn't "weal."

"'Course it isn't real!" I cried. "I guess there isn't any boy in the world got a real gun!"

Well, he said that he had one, and when I was still disbelieving he said that he would go home and fetch it. His coat had come unbuttoned in our scufflings, and I remember how he looked as I watched through the window and saw him flapping down the last length of concrete sidewalk past the big maple tree.

My mother came from upstairs while I waited at the window. She said that she had heard voices. "Did you have company?" she asked.

"It was a new boy."

"What new boy?"

"He moved into the creek house down there."

My mother said doubtfully, "Oh, yes. I heard there was a ditcher's family moving in down there."

Well, I wanted to know what a ditcher was, and while Mother was explaining to me about drainage ditches out on the prairie and how the tile was laid in them, here came Nelly hustling up the road as fast as he could leg it. He had something big and heavy that he had to carry in both hands. When he got into the yard we could see that he did have a revolver, and it looked like a real one.

Mother exclaimed, and went to open the door for him. He ducked inside, bareheaded and cold, with his dirty, thin, straw-colored hair sticking every which way, and the old red coat still dangling loose.

"I dot my dun," he said.

It was a large revolver — probably about a .44. It had a yellow handle, but the metal parts were a mass of rust. The cylinder and hammer were rusted tight and couldn't be moved.

"Why, little boy," Mother exclaimed in horror, "where on earth did you get this?"

He said that he got it at home.

Mother lured it out of his hands, but only after she had praised it extravagantly. She got him to put the revolver on the library table, and then she took us both out to the kitchen, where we had milk and molasses cookies.

My father came home from his newspaper office before Nelly had gone. We showed Father the gun, and he lighted the lamp on the library table and examined the revolver thoroughly.

"My goodness, Ethel," he said to my mother, "it's got cartridges in it!"

"Cartridges?"

"Yes, it sure has. They're here in the cylinder, all rusted in tight. Good thing the rest of it is just as rusty."

He put on his coat again and said that he'd take Nelson home. It was growing dark and was almost suppertime, and he was afraid the boy might be lost there in the new surroundings of Elm City. Nelson wanted his gun, but my father said no and put it in his own overcoat pocket. I was allowed to go along with them.

When we got to the creek house, Father rapped on the door and Nelly's mother opened it. She was a scrawny, pale-faced woman, very round-shouldered, in a calico dress. Nelly's father wasn't there; he had gone to take one of the teams back. There were several girls — Nelly's sisters — strung out all the way from little kids to a big, bony creature as tall as her mother.

Father brought out the gun and said that it wasn't wise to let little kids go carrying things like that around.

"You little devil!" said Nelly's mother to Nelly, and she laughed when she said it. "What on earth were you doing with that?"

The girls crowded close and looked. "Why, it's Jay's gun!" said the eldest one.

Father wanted to know who Jay was. They laughed a lot while they were telling him, although they were remarkably close-lipped about it at the same time. All that Father could get out of them was the fact that they used to live in Oklahoma, and Jay was somebody who used to stay at their house. He had left that gun there once, and they still kept it — as a kind of memorial for Jay, it would seem.

"I swear Nelly must have taken it out of the bureau drawer," said Mrs. Tare, still smiling. "You little devil, you got to behave yourself, you got to!" And she gave him a kind of spat with her hand, but not as if she were mad. They all seemed to think it was cute, for him to sneak off with that gun.

Father said goodbye and we went home. It was dark now, and all the way up the hill and past Mr. Boston's farmyard, I kept wondering about this new little boy and the rusty revolver. I kept breathing hard, trying to breathe that strange oily smell out of my nose. It was the odor of their house and of themselves — the same odor I had noticed when Nelly tussled with me.

My father said quite calmly that he supposed Jay was an Oklahoma outlaw. Unintentionally, he thus gave Nelson Tare a fantastic importance in my eyes. I did not dream then that Jay, instead of old Barton Tare with his sloppy mustache, might have been Nelly's own father. Perhaps it is a dream, even as I write the words now. But I think not.

When Nelly grew older, he possessed a great many physical virtues. He was remarkably agile in the use of his hands and arms. He had no fear of height; he would climb any windmill within reach and he could stump any boy in that end of town when it came to Stump-the-Leader. But Nelly Tare liked guns better than he did games.

At the air-rifle stage of our development, Nelly could shoot rings around any of us. He and I used to go up in our barn and lie on the moldy, abandoned hay of the old mow. There were rats that sometimes came into the chicken run next door, to eat the chickens' food. I never did shoot a rat with my BB gun, and for some reason Nelly never did either. That was funny, because he was such a good shot. We used to amuse ourselves, while waiting for rats, by trying to peck away at the chickens' water pan. It was a good healthy distance, and I'd usually miss. But the side of the pan which faced our way had the enamel all spotted off by Nelly's accurate fire.

He owned an air-pump gun of his own, but not for long. He traded it to somebody for an old .22, and after that there was little peace in the neighborhood. He was always shooting at tin cans or bottles on the roadside dump. He was always hitting too.

In the winter of 1914, Nelly and I went hunting with Clyde Boston. Clyde was a huge, ruddy-faced young man at least ten years older than Nelly and I. He lived with his parents across from our corner.

One day there was deep snow, and Nelly and I were out exploring. He had his .22, and every now and then he'd bang away at a knot on a fence post. At last we wandered into Boston's barnyard, and found Clyde in the barn, filling his pockets with shotgun shells.

He had a shotgun too — a fine repeater, gleaming blue steel — and Nelly wanted to know what Clyde was doing. "Going hunting?"

"Come on, Clyde," I said, "let us go! Nelly's got his gun."

Clyde took the little rifle and examined it critically. "This won't do for hunting around here," he said. "I'm going out after rabbits, and you got to have a shotgun for that. Rifle bullets are apt to carry too far and hit somebody, or maybe hit a pig or something. Anyway, you couldn't hit a cottontail on the run with that."

"Hell I couldn't," said Nelly.

I said, "Clyde, you let us go with you and we'll beat up the game. We'll scare the rabbits out of the weeds, because you haven't got any dog. Then you can shoot them when they run out. Maybe you'll let us have one shot each, huh, Clyde — maybe?"

Clyde said that he would see, and he made Nelly leave his rifle at the barn. We went quartering off through the truck garden on the hillside.

The snow had fallen freshly, but already there was a mass of rabbit tracks everywhere. You could see where the cottontails had run into the thickest, weediest coverts to feed upon dry seeds.

Clyde walked in the middle, with his face apple-colored with the cold and his breath blowing out. Nelly and I spread wide, to scare up the game. We used sticks and snowballs to alarm the thickets, and we worked hard at it. The big twelve-gauge gun began to bang every once in a while. Clyde had three cottontails hanging furry from his belt before we got to the bend in the creek opposite the Catholic cemetery. Then finally he passed the gun over to me and told me I could have the next chance.

It came pretty soon. We saw a cottontail in his set — a gray little mound among the vervain stalks. I lifted the muzzle, but Clyde said that it wasn't fair to shoot rabbits in the set, and made Nelly throw a snowball. The cottontail romped out of there in a hurry, and I whaled away with the shotgun and managed to wound the rabbit and slow him down. I fired again and missed, and Clyde caught up with the rabbit after a few strides. He put the poor peeping thing out of its misery by rapping it on the head.

I tied the rabbit to the belt of my mackinaw, and Clyde passed the shotgun over to Nelly.

Nelly's face was pale.

"Watch your step," said Clyde. "Remember to keep the safety on until you see something to shoot."

"Sure," said Nelly Tare.

We crossed the creek without starting any more rabbits, and came down the opposite side of the stream. Then a long-legged jack jumped up out of a deep furrow where there had been some fall plowing, and ran like a mule ahead of us.

"Look at those black ears!" Clyde sang out. "It's a jack! Get him, Nelly — get him!"

Well, Nelson had the gun at his shoulder; at first I thought he had neglected to touch the safety — I thought he couldn't pull the trigger because the safety was on. He kept swinging the muzzle of the gun, following the jackrabbit in its erratic course, until the rabbit slowed up a little.

The jack bobbed around behind a tree stump, and then came out on the other side. It squatted down on top of the snow and sat looking at us. It hopped a few feet farther and then sat up again to watch.

"For gosh sakes," said Clyde Boston, "what's the matter with you, kid? There he is, looking at you."

Nelson Tare just stood like a snow man, or rather like a snow boy. He kept the rabbit covered; his dirty blue finger didn't move. The trigger waited, the shell in the barrel waited, and so did we.

Nelly's face was deathly white under the dirt that streaked it. The eyes were blank little marbles, as always; even his nose seemed pointed like the sights of a gun. And yet he did not shoot.

Clyde said, half under his breath, "I guess that's what they call buck fever. You got the buck, Nelly." He hurried over to take the shotgun.

Blood from the last-killed rabbit made little dots on the snow around my feet, though the animal was freezing fast.

"Can't you see him, Nelly?"

Nelson said, "Yes. I —"

Clyde lost all patience. "Oh, for gosh sake!" he exclaimed, and grabbed the gun. But our combined motions startled the jackrabbit, and he vanished into the creek gorge beyond.

Something had happened there in the snow; none of us knew exactly what had happened. But whatever it was, it took the edge off our sport. We tramped along a cattle path next to the stream, with Clyde carrying the shotgun. We boys didn't scare up any more game. Nelly kept looking at the rabbits, which bounced and rubbed their frozen red against Clyde Boston's overalls.

Clyde teased him, all the way back to the Boston barnyard. He'd say, "Nelly, I thought you were supposed to be the Daniel Boone of the neighborhood. Gosh, Nelly, I thought you could shoot. I thought you were just gun crazy!"

We walked through the fresh warm mire behind the Boston barn.

Clyde said that he didn't need three rabbits; that his mother could use only two, and would Nelly want the other one?

"No," said Nelson. We went into the barn, and Nelly picked up his .22 rifle.

"Look out while you're on the way home," said Clyde, red-faced and jovial as ever. "Look out you don't meet a bear. Maybe he wouldn't set around and wait like that jackrabbit did."

Nelson Tare sucked in his breath. "You said I couldn't shoot, didn't you, Mister Clyde?"

"You had your chance. Look at Dave there. He's got a rabbit to take home that he shot himself, even though he didn't kill it first crack."

"I can shoot," said Nelly. He worked a cartridge into the breech of his rifle. "Dave," he said to me, "you throw up a snowball."

"Can't anybody hit a snowball with a twenty-two," said big Clyde Boston.

Nelly said, "Throw a snowball, Dave."

I stepped down from the sill of the barn door and made a ball about the size of a Duchess apple. I threw it high toward the telephone wires across the road. Nelly Tare pinked it apart with his .22 before the ball ever got to the wires. Then he went down the road to the creek house, with Clyde Boston and me looking after him. Clyde was scratching his head, but I just looked.

Nelly began to get into trouble when he was around fourteen. His first trouble that anyone knew about happened in the cloakroom of the eighth grade at school. Miss Cora Petersen was a great believer in corporal punishment, and when Nelly was guilty of some infraction of rules, Miss Petersen prepared to thrash him with a little piece of white rubber hose. Teachers used to be allowed to do that.

But if the pupil did not permit it to be done to him, but instead drew a loaded revolver from inside his shirt and threatened to kill his teacher, that was a different story. It was a story in which the superintendent of schools and the local chief of police and hard-faced old Mr. Tare were all mixed together in the climax.

There was some talk about the reform school, too, but the reform school did not materialize until a year later.

That was after Meisner's Hardware and Harness Store had been robbed. The thief or thieves had a peculiar taste in robbery; the cash drawer was untouched, but five revolvers and a lot of ammunition were taken away. A mile and a quarter away, to be exact. They were hidden beneath planks and straw in Mr. Barton Tare's wagon shed, and Chief of Police Kelcy found them after the simplest kind of detective work.

This time the story had to be put in the paper, no matter how much my father regretted it. This time it was the reform school for sure.

We boys in the south end of town sat solemnly on our new concrete curbstone and talked of Nelly Tare in hushed voices. The judge had believed, sternly and simply, that Nelly was better off at Eldora than at home. He gave him two years. Nelly didn't serve all of that time. He got several months off for good behavior, which must have come as a surprise to many people in Elm City.

He emerged from the Eldora reformatory in the spring of 1918. His parents were out of the picture by this time. His mother was dead; his father had moved to South Dakota with the two youngest girls, and the other girls had married or drifted away.

Nelly may have been under age, but when he expressed a preference for the cavalry, and when he flourished a good report sheet from the reformatory superintendent, no one cared to say him nay. Once he came home on furlough from a camp in New Mexico. I remember how he looked, standing in front of Frank Wanda's Recreation Pool Hall, with the flashing badge of a pistol expert pinned upon his left breast, and all the little kids grouped around to admire the polish on his half-leather putts.

He never got a chance to use any guns against the Germans. He wasn't sent to France, and came back to Elm City in the spring of 1919. It was reasonable for him to come there. Elm City was the only real hometown he had, and one of his sisters was married to Ira Flagler, a garage mechanic who lived out on West Water Street. Nelly went to live with the Flaglers.

He began working at Frank Wanda's pool hall. I have spoken about his skill with his hands; he employed that skill to good advantage in the pool hall. He had developed into a remarkable player during his year in the Army. He also ran the cigar counter and soft drinks for Frank Wanda, who was getting old and couldn't stand on his feet very long at a time.

It used to be that in every pool hall there was somebody who played for the house, if people came along and really wanted to bet anything. Nelly would play on his own, too, taking money away from farm boys or from some out-of-towner who thought he was good. He was soon making real money, but he didn't spend it in the usual channels. He spent it on guns.

All sorts. Sometimes he'd have an especially good revolver down there in the billiard parlor with him, and he'd show it to me when I dropped in for cigarettes. He had a kind of private place out along the Burlington tracks where he used to practice shooting on Sundays. And in 1923 a carnival came to town.

Miss Antoinette McReady, the Outstanding Six-Gun Artiste of Two Nations, was supposed to come from Canada. Maybe she did. They built up a phony Royal Canadian Mounted Police atmosphere for her act. A fellow in a shabby red coat and yellow-striped breeches sold tickets out in front. An extra girl in the same kind of comic uniform assisted the artiste with her fancy shooting. They had a steel backstop at the rear of the enclosure to stop the bullets. I went to the carnival on the first night, and dropped in to see the shooting act.

The girl was pretty good. Her lady assistant put on a kind of crown with white chalks sticking up in it, and Miss McReady shot the chalks out of the crown quite accurately, missing only one or two shots and not killing the lady assistant at all. She did mirror shooting and upside-down-leaning-backward shooting; she balanced on a chair and shot. She was a very pretty redhead, though necessarily painted.

Then the Royal Canadian Mounted manager made a speech. He said that frequently during her extensive travels, Miss McReady had been challenged by local pistol-artists, but that she was so confident of her ability that she had a standing offer of one hundred dollars to anybody who could outshoot her.

The only condition was that the challenging local artist should agree to award Miss McReady an honorarium of twenty dollars, provided she outshot him.

Nelly Tare climbed up on the platform; he showed the color of his money and the bet was on.

Miss Antoinette McReady shot first, shooting at the tiny target gong with great deliberation; she rang the gong five out of six times. Nelly took her gun, aimed, and snapped it a few times before ejecting the empty shells, to acquaint himself with the trigger pull. Then he loaded up, with the whole audience standing to watch him. He fired his six rounds, rapid fire, and everyone yipped when he rang the gong with every shot.

Miss Antoinette McReady smiled and bowed as if she had done the shooting instead of Nelly; she went over to congratulate him. They got ready for the next competition. The girl assistant started to put on the crown thing with its chalks sticking out of the sockets. Nelly talked to her a minute in a low voice; he took the crown and put it on his own head.

He stood against the backstop. His face was very red, but he stood there stiff at Army attention, with his hands against his sides.

"Go ahead, sister," he told Miss McReady.

Well, they made him sign a waiver first, in case of accident. You could have heard an ant sneeze in that place when Miss McReady stood up to do her shooting. She fired six times and broke four of the chalks. The people in the audience proceeded to wake up babies two blocks away, and Miss Antoinette McReady went over to Nelly with those little dancing, running steps that circus and vaudeville folks use. She made him come down to the front and take applause with her. Then she said she'd wear the crown for Nelly, and this time there was no waiver signed.

Nelly broke all six chalks in six steady shots, and Miss Antoinette McReady kissed him, and Frank Wanda had to get a new fellow for the pool hall when Nelly left town with the show after the last performance on Saturday night.

It was six months later when I heard my father exclaim, while he was taking press dispatches over the out-of-town wire. He often did that when some news came through which particularly interested or excited him. I left my desk and went to look over his shoulder, while his fat old fingers pushed out the story on the typewriter.

HAMPTON, COLORADO, April 2.—Two desperate trick-shot artists gave Hampton residents an unscheduled exhibition today. When the smoke had cleared away the Hampton County Savings Bank discovered it had paid more than $7,000 to watch the show.

Shortly after the bank opened this morning, a young man and a young woman, identified by witnesses as "Cowboy" Nelson Tare and Miss Antoinette McReady, walked into the bank and commanded tellers and customers to lie down on the floor. They scooped up $7,150 in small bills, and were backing toward an exit, when Vice-President O. E. Simms tried to reach for a telephone.

The trick-shot bandits promptly shot the telephone off the desk. They pulverized chandeliers, interior glass, and window lights in a rapid fusillade which covered their retreat to their car.

Within a few minutes a posse was in hot pursuit, but lost the trail near Elwin, ten miles south of this place. A stolen car, identified as the one used by the bandits, was found abandoned this noon near Hastings City. State and county officers immediately spread a dragnet on surrounding highways.

Nelson Tare and his female companion were easily recognized as stunt shooters with a traveling carnival which became stranded in Elwin a week ago. A full description of the hard-shooting pair has been broadcast to officials of five nearby states.

All the time I was reading it, I kept thinking of Nelly Tare, half-pint size in a dirty red coat, asking me, "Dot any duns?"

They were captured in Oklahoma that summer, after another robbery. Antoinette McReady, whose real name turned out to be Ruth Riley, was sent to a women's penal institution; Nelly Tare went to McAlester Prison. He managed his escape during the winter two years later, and started off on a long series of holdups which carried him south into Texas, over to Arkansas, and north into Missouri.

Those were the days of frequent and daring bank robberies throughout that region. There were a lot of other bad boys around, and Nelly was only one of the herd. Still, he began to appear in the news dispatches with increasing regularity, and when some enterprising reporter called him Nice Nelly, the name stuck and spread. It was a good news name, like Baby Face or Pretty Boy.

They recaptured him in Sedalia; the story of his escape from the Jefferson City Penitentiary in 1933 was front-page stuff all over the nation. It was always the same — he was always just as hard to catch up with. He was always just as able to puncture the tires of pursuing cars, to blast the headlights that tried to pick him out through the midnight dust.

Federal men didn't enter the picture until the next January, when Nelly kidnapped a bank cashier in Hiawatha, Kansas, and carried him nearly to Lincoln, Nebraska. That little state line made all the difference in the world. The so-called Lindbergh Law had come into existence, and Nice Nelly Tare became a public enemy on an elaborate scale.

It is not astonishing that some people of Elm City basked in this reflected notoriety.

Reporters from big-city papers, photographers from national magazines, came poking around all the time. They interviewed Nelly's sister, poor Mrs. Ira Flagler, until she was black in the face — until she was afraid to let her children play in the yard.

They took pictures of Frank Wanda's pool hall, and they would have taken pictures of Frank if he hadn't been dead. They managed to shake Miss Cora Petersen, late of Elm City's eighth grade, from asthmatic retirement. Her homely double-chinned face appeared in a fine-screen cut, in ugly halftones — a million different impressions of it. READ

TEACHER'S STORY OF HOW NICE NELLY, BABY BANDIT, DREW HIS FIRST BEAD ON HER. OTHER PICTURES ON PAGE SEVEN.

Clyde Boston and I used to talk about it, over in Clyde's office in the courthouse. Clyde Boston had been sheriff for two terms; he was just as apple-cheeked and good-natured as ever, though most of his hair was gone. He would shake his head when we talked about Nelly Tare, which we did often.

"You know," he'd say, "a lot of people probably doubt those stories about Nelly's fancy shooting—people who haven't seen him shoot. But I still remember that time he had you throw a snowball for him to break with a rifle. He certainly is gun crazy."

It was during the late summer of 1934—the bad drought year—when Nelly held up a bank at Northfield, Minnesota, and was promptly dubbed the Modern Jesse James.

Officers picked up Nelly's trail in Sioux Falls, and that was a relief to us in Elm City, because people had always feared that Nelly might be struck with a desire to revisit his boyhood haunts and stage a little shooting right there in the lobby of the Farmers' National Bank. Nelly's trail was lost again, and for two weeks he slid out of the news.

Then came the big story. Federal men very nearly recaptured him in Council Bluffs, though he got away from them even there. Then silence again.

About two o'clock of the following Thursday afternoon, I went up to the courthouse on printing business. I had stopped in at Sheriff Clyde Boston's office and was chewing the rag with Clyde, when his telephone rang.

Clyde picked up the phone. He said, "Yes . . . Yes, Barney . . . He did? . . . Yes . . . Glad you called me." He hung up the receiver and sat drumming his fingers against a desk blotter.

"Funny thing," he said. "That was young Barney Meisner, down at the hardware store."

"What did he have to say?"

"He said that one of the Flagler kids was in there a while ago and bought two boxes of forty-five shells. Funny, isn't it?"

We looked at each other. "Maybe Ira Flagler's decided to emulate his wife's folks," I said, "and take up trick shooting on the side."

Clyde Boston squeezed out a smile. "Guess I'll ride up to their house and ask about it."

So I went along with him, and when we got to the green-and-white

Flagler house on West Water Street, we saw a coupe parked in the drive. Clyde breathed rapidly for a moment; I saw his hands tighten on the steering wheel, until he could read the license number of the car. Clyde relaxed. It was a Vera Cruz County number; it was one of our own local cars; I remembered that I had seen Ira Flagler driving that car sometimes.

Clyde parked across the street, although down a little way. He got out on the driver's side and I got out on the other side. When I walked around the rear of the car and looked up at the Flagler house, Nelly Tare was standing on the porch with a revolver in his hand.

I guess neither Clyde nor I could have said anything if we had been paid. Clyde didn't have his own gun on; sheriffs didn't habitually carry guns in our county anymore. There was Nelly on the porch, covering us and looking just about the same as ever, except that his shoulders had sagged and his chin seemed to have receded a good deal more.

He said, "Lay down on the ground. That's right—both of you. Lay down. That's right—keep your hands up."

When we were on the ground, or rather on the asphalt pavement which formed the last block of Water Street, Nelly fired four shots. He put them all into the hood and engine of the car, and then we heard his feet running on the ground. I didn't look for a minute, but Clyde had more nerve than I, and got up on his haunches immediately.

By that time Nelly was in the Flagler coupe. He drove it right across their vegetable garden, across Lou Miller's yard, and out onto the pavement of Prospect Street. Prospect Street connected with a wide gravel road that went south toward the Rivermouth country and the town of Liberty beyond. Nelly put his foot on the gas; dust went high.

Those four bullets had made hash out of the motor. The starter was dead when Clyde got his foot on it; gas and water were leaking out underneath. Mrs. Ira Flagler stumbled out upon the porch with one of her children; they were both crying hysterically.

She said, "Oh, thank God he didn't shoot you, Mr. Boston!"

Later she told her story. Nelly had showed up there via boxcar early that morning, but Ira was working on a hurry-up job at the garage and didn't know about it. Nelly had made his sister and the children stay in the house all day. Finally he persuaded the youngest boy that it would be great fun and a joke on everybody if he would go downtown and buy him two boxes of .45 shells.

But all this revelation came later, for Clyde Boston was well occupied at the telephone. He called the courthouse and sent a carload of vigilantes after Nelly on Primary No. 37. He called the telephone office and had them notify authorities in Liberty, Prairie Flower, Mannville, and Fort Hood. Then he called the state capital and talked to federal authorities himself. Government men started arriving by auto and airplane within two hours.

About suppertime Nelly showed up at a farmhouse owned by Larry Larsen, fourteen miles southwest of Elm City. He had been circling around all afternoon, trying to break through the cordon. They had heavy trucks across all the roads; late-summer cornfields don't make for good auto travel, even when there has been a drought.

He took Larsen's sedan and made the farmer fill it with gas out of his tractor tank. Nelly had cut the telephone wires; he forced the farmer's family to tie one another up, and then he tied the last one himself. Nelly saw to it that the tying was well done; it was after eight o'clock before one of the kids got loose and they shouted forth their story over a neighbor's telephone.

Things were wild enough down at the *Chronicle* office that evening. But I had a reliable staff, and at eight-thirty I thought it was safe to take a run up to the courthouse.

"I kind of expected you'd be up, Dave," said Clyde Boston.

I told him that I thought he'd be out on the road somewhere.

"Been out for the last four hours." He took his feet down off the desk, and then put them up again. "If I can get loose from all these state and national efficiency experts, how'd you like to take a little drive with me in your car? Mine's kind of out of order."

Well, I told him that I'd be glad to drive him anywhere he said, but I didn't want to come back with bullet holes in the cowling. So he got loose from the efficiency experts, and he made me strike out south of town and then east, on Primary No. 6.

Clyde didn't talk. Usually it was his way to talk a lot, in a blissful, middle-aged, baldheaded fashion. We passed two gangs of guards and identified ourselves each time, and finally Clyde had me stop at a farm where some cousins of his lived. He borrowed a log chain — a good big one with heavy links. This rusty mass Clyde dumped down into my clean back seat, and then he directed me to drive south again.

The katydids exclaimed in every grove.

"You know," said Clyde, "I used to do a lot of rabbit hunting and prairie-chicken hunting down this way, when I was younger. And you used to do a lot of hiking around down here with the boys. Fact is, only boys who were raised in these parts would know this country completely. Isn't that a fact? Outside officers wouldn't know it."

Well, I agreed that they wouldn't, and then Clyde began to talk about

Nelly Tare. He said that Nelly's one chance to get out of those several hundred square miles that he was surrounded in was to ride out on a railroad train. He wouldn't be likely to try it on foot, not unless he was crazy, and Clyde Boston didn't think he was crazy. Except gun crazy, as always.

"Now, the railroads all cross up here in this end of the county, up north of the river. Don't they?"

"That's right."

"So to get from where Nelly was at suppertime to where he'd like to be, he'd have to go diagonally from southwest to northeast. Now, the river timber runs diagonally from southwest to northeast—"

I began to see a little light. "You're talking about the old Rivermouth road." And Clyde said that he was.

He said that he had picnicked there with his family in recent years. The ancient timber road was still passable by car, if a driver proceeded slowly and cautiously enough. It meant fording several creeks; it couldn't be managed when the creeks were up.

"It comes out on the prairie just below the old Bemis farm," said Clyde. "You go down between pastures on a branch-off lane, and then you're right in the woods. That's where I think maybe he'll come out."

When he got to the Bemis place we turned off on the side lane and drove to the edge of the timber. The forest road emerged—a wandering sluice with yellow leaves carpeting it. We left my car parked at the roadside, and Clyde dragged the log chain down the timber road until he found a good place.

Cottonwoods and thin saplings made a wall along either side, where the road twisted out of the gully. A driver couldn't tell that the road was blocked until he had climbed the last curve in low gear.

Clyde wrapped the log chain around two cottonwoods. It sagged, stiff and heavy, across the path.

I said, "He'll kill you, Clyde. Don't expect me to help you try to grab him and get killed at the same time."

"There won't be any killing." Clyde settled himself in the darkness. "I'm going to take Nelly Tare back to Elm City. Alive."

Old logs and gullies are thick in the Rivermouth country; hazel brush fairly blocks the forgotten road in a hundred places. It was long before Nelly's headlights came sneaking through the trees. The katydids spoke a welcome; the dull parking lights went in and out, twisting, exploring, poking through the brush; they came on, with the motor growling in low.

Nelly made quite a spurt and went into second for a moment as the car swung up out of the gorge; sleek leaves flew from under his rear wheels; little rocks pattered back into the shrubbery.

Then Nelly saw the log chain. He jammed his brakes and the car slewed around until it was broadside. Nelly turned off the motor and lights in half a second; the car door swung; he was out on the log-chain side, and he had a gun in his hand.

"Don't shoot, Nelly," said Clyde Boston, stepping in front of the trees and turning on his flashlight.

I didn't want to be killed, so I stood behind a tree and watched them. The flashlight thrust out a long, strong beam; Clyde stood fifteen feet away from the car's radiator, but the shaft of his lamp was like whitewash on Nelly Tare.

"It's Clyde," the sheriff said. "Clyde Boston. You remember me? I was up at your sister's place today."

Nelly cried, "Turn off that light!"

"No," Clyde said. "And I'm warning you not to shoot the light out, because I'm holding it right in front of my stomach. My stomach's a big target. You wouldn't want to shoot my stomach, would you, Nelly?"

Nelson Tare's hair was too long, and he needed a shave. He looked like some wild thing that had been dug out of the woods. "Clyde! I'm telling you for the last time! Turn it off!"

Clyde's voice was a smooth rumble. "Remember one time when we went hunting rabbits?" He edged forward a little. "You and Dave and me. Remember? A big jack sat down, waiting for you to kill him. And you couldn't pull the trigger. You couldn't kill him."

Nelly had his face screwed into a wad, and his teeth showed between his lips.

"Never shot anything or anybody, did you, Nelly?" There was a snapping sound, and I jumped. It was only a stick breaking under Clyde's foot as he moved nearer to the car. "You never shot a soul. Not a jackrabbit or anything. You couldn't."

He was only ten feet away from Nelly and Nelly's gun.

"You just pretended you could. But the guards in Oklahoma and Missouri didn't know you the way I do. They hadn't ever gone hunting with you, had they?"

He took another step forward. Another. Nelly was something out of a waxworks in a sideshow, watching him come. Then a vague suffusion of light began to show around them; a carload of deputies had spotted my car at the head of the lane; their headlamps came hurtling toward us.

"You shot telephones off of desks," Clyde purred to Nelly, "and tires off of cars. You've been around and you've done a lot of shooting. But you never shot things that the blood ran out of . . . Now, you drop your gun, Nelly. Drop it on the ground. Gosh, I was crazy this afternoon. I shouldn't have laid down when you told me to. I should have just stood there."

Maybe he was right and maybe he was wrong, I don't know. The car stopped and I heard men yell, "Look out, Sheriff!" They were ready with their machine guns, trying to hustle themselves into some position where they could spatter the daylights out of Nelly Tare without shooting Clyde Boston too. Clyde didn't give them a chance to do it. He dove forward; he flung his arms around Nelly and crushed him to the ground.

Nelly cried, and I don't like to think about it; sometimes I wake up in the night and think I hear him crying. My memory goes back to our haymow days and to the rats in the chicken pen — the rats that Nelly couldn't shoot — and I remember the bloody cottontails dangling from Clyde's belt.

Nelly cried, but not solely because he was captured and would never be free again. He wept because the world realized something he had tried to keep hidden, even from himself. When he was taken back into prison, he wore an expression of tragic perplexity. It must have been hideous for him to know that he, who had loved guns his whole life long, should at last be betrayed by them.

1945

DAY KEENE

NOTHING TO WORRY ABOUT

DAY KEENE, the pseudonym of Gunard Hjertstedt (1904–1969), was born on the south side of Chicago. As a young man he became active as an actor and playwright in repertory theater with such friends as Melvyn Douglas and Barton MacLane. When they decided to go to Hollywood, Keene instead opted to become a full-time writer, mainly for radio soap operas. He was the head writer for the wildly successful *Little Orphan Annie,* which premiered on NBC's Blue Network on April 6, 1931, and ran for nearly thirteen years, as well as the mystery series *Kitty Keene, Incorporated,* about a beautiful female private eye with a showgirl past; it began on the NBC Red Network on September 13, 1937, and ran for four years. Keene then abandoned radio to write mostly crime and mystery stories for the pulps, then for the newly popular world of paperback originals, for which his dark, violent, and relentlessly fast-paced stories were perfectly suited, producing nearly fifty mysteries between 1949 and 1965. Among his best and most successful novels were his first, *Framed in Guilt* (1949), the recently reissued classic noir *Home Is the Sailor* (1952), *Joy House* (1954, filmed by MGM in 1964 and also released as *The Love Cage,* with Alain Delon, Jane Fonda, and Lola Albright), and *Chautauqua* (1960), written with Dwight Vincent, the pseudonym of mystery writer Dwight Babcock; it was filmed by MGM in 1969 and also released as *The Trouble with Girls,* starring Elvis Presley and Marlyn Mason.

"Nothing to Worry About" was first published in the August 1945 issue of *Detective Tales.*

▪ ▪ ▪

IF THERE WERE any letters of fire on Assistant State's Attorney John Sorrel's broad and distinguished brow, they were invisible to his fellow passengers in the lighted cabin of the Washington–Chicago plane, as it circled the Cicero Airport at fifteen minutes to midnight. The stewardess, appraising his broad shoulders, graying temples, and hearty laughter, considered the woman to whom he was returning very fortunate indeed. His seat mate had found him intelligent and sympathetic.

At no time during the flight, or during the hours preceding it, had there been anything in Sorrel's voice or demeanor to which anyone could point and say, "I knew it at the time. He was nervous. He couldn't concentrate. His conversation was forced. He talked and acted like a man about to kill his wife."

It was no sudden decision on Sorrel's part. He had considered killing Frances, often; only a firm respect for the law that he himself represented had deterred him. He had, in the name of the state, asked for, and been given, the lives of too many men to be careless with his own. Intolerable as his marital situation had become, it was preferable to facing a jury whom he had lost the right to challenge.

The NO SMOKING and PLEASE FASTEN YOUR SEAT BELT panels over the door of the pilot's compartment blinked on. The lights of the field rushed up to meet the plane.

This is it, Sorrel thought. *In twenty minutes, thirty at the most, Frances will be dead. Poor soul.*

His seat mate wound up the telling of the involved argument and verbal slug-fest in which he had just engaged with the Office of Price Administration. Sorrel gave him one-half of his mind, sympathizing hugely, assuring him he had been right, that it couldn't last forever, and agreeing that it seemed that private business was headed for a boom.

The other half of his mind considered the thing that he had to do. It would not be pleasant. In his search for a solution to his problem, he had inspected, weighed, and judged the none-too-many means by which murder could be done. The alleged clever methods — accidental death, suicide, death by misadventure — he had rejected almost immediately. They left too many loopholes for failure; few of them ever succeeded. There was a reason. No matter how brilliant a killer might be, he was seldom, if ever, a match for the combined technical, executive, and judicial branches of the law.

Crime detection, trial, and judgment had become akin to an exact science.

The art of killing, the three Ms, means, method, motive, had changed little in the known history of man. To take a life, one still had to shoot, knife, drown, strike, strangle, or poison the party of the unwanted part. And, as with most basic refinements to the art of living, the first known method of murder used — that of striking the party to be removed with whatever object came first to hand — was still the most difficult of detection, providing of course that the party who did the striking could maintain a reasonable plea of being elsewhere at the time.

* * *

It was, after mature consideration, that method that Sorrel had chosen. He had even chosen his weapon, one of the heavy cut-glass candlesticks that stood on Frances's dressing table.

"Murphy. J. P. Murphy is the name," his seat mate identified himself. He shook Sorrel's hand vigorously. "It's been a pleasure to meet you, Prosecutor. And if you decide to enter the senatorial race, as I've seen hinted at in the papers, you can count on my vote as certain."

Sorrel's hearty laugh filled the plane. "Thanks. I'll remember that, Murphy."

His only luggage was his briefcase. The stewardess insisted on getting it down from the rack for him. He tucked a forbidden bill in the breast pocket of her uniform. "Nice trip." He smiled. "And thanks."

"Thank *you,* Mr. Sorrel!" She beamed. One met such few really nice men. Most tipping hands brushed or hovered, seeking a partial return on their investment.

Sorrel stood in the open door of the plane a moment, sniffing the night air. The fine weather was still holding. It was neither too hot nor too cold.

He descended the steps and lifted a hand in greeting to the pilot as he passed the nose of the plane. He did so habitually on his not-infrequent trips. There must be no departure from the norm, no errors of omission or commission, no nervously spilled milk in which the bacteria of suspicion might breed.

He, John Sorrel, assistant state's attorney, was returning from Washington with nothing on his mind but the successful conclusion of the business that had taken him there. He wasn't nervous. He felt fine. He assured himself that he did.

In the doorway of the terminal, Murphy touched his arm. "I'm taking a cab to the Loop. If you'd like to share it, Sorrel . . ."

"Thanks, no," Sorrel said. "My car should be waiting." He managed to edge his words with the proper amount of innuendo without being vulgar. "You see, I—well, I'm not going directly home."

The other man winked. "I—see."

They parted after shaking hands again. He was, Sorrel realized, running the risk of being slightly too clever. But the more people who knew, or who thought they knew, that he had gone directly from the plane to Evelyn's apartment, the stronger would be his alibi.

He had never kept their affair a secret. He doubted that any prosecutor, judge, or jury—if it should come to that—would question so embarrassing an alibi as a husband's being forced to admit that, while his wife had been killed, he had been with another woman, railing against the deceased because she had refused to divorce him.

Despite the lateness of the hour, the terminal was crowded. He saw three or four men whom he knew and nodded cordially to as he passed through the terminal.

Jackson was waiting behind the wheel of a department car. Sorrel tossed his case into the back seat and slid in beside him. "So you got my wire."

"And why not?" Jackson asked. "You wanna go home, the office, or . . ." He left the question open.

Sorrel sighed. "Home, I suppose. But let's drop by the Eldorado first."

"I figured that," Jackson said.

Sorrel rode, the night wind cool on his cheeks, eager to be done with what he had to do, wishing that Frances had been reasonable. If she had been, if she had been willing to divorce him, none of this would have to be.

In front of the building he told Jackson, "I won't be long, I think."

Jackson fished in his vest pocket for a toothpick, found one. "Take your time."

He meant it. He liked Sorrel. He liked Evelyn, too. For all of her good looks, she was a lady. Frances Sorrel wasn't, what with her calling a spade a dirty shovel and her drinking and her fighting—she was no wife for a man who soon might be a senator. Although, at that, he reflected, he had heard someone say that she had worked like a dog for the money that had put Sorrel through law school, and she had always sworn she hadn't started to drink and chase until he had gone lace curtain Irish on her.

Under the marquee of the building, the colored doorman grinned whitely at Sorrel. "Glad to see you back, Mr. Smith. Been missin' you for a week now."

Sorrel creased a five-dollar bill and slipped it into his hand. "I've been in Washington saving the nation."

The doorman chuckled, hugely amused. "He say he been in Washington savin' the nation," he confided to Jackson.

Jackson continued to pick at his teeth. "Yair."

Inside the lobby, Sorrel paused briefly, suddenly short of breath. This was murder. He, John Sorrel, an assistant state's attorney who would have been state's attorney had it not been for his wife, and who was being considered by the party as a senatorial candidate, was proposing to steal into his own home by stealth and remove the sole obstacle who stood in the path of his political success.

That angle would not enter the case, however. It would not be considered a motive. None of the powers-that-were had ever mentioned Frances. But, he knew, there was the feminine vote to consider. And what with things as they were, the party couldn't afford to take a chance. Frances's scenes were too well known. She drank; she cursed; she was unfaithful. Not that he had ever been so fortunate as to obtain proof that would stand in a court of law.

He closed his eyes and saw his wife as he had seen her, fat, slovenly dressed, her face puffed with drink, during the last public scene that she had made. That had been in the lobby of the Chalmer's House, before a delighted ring of onlookers.

"Sure I'm drunk. An' I'm a tramp," she had taunted while he had tried vainly to hush her. "An' don't you tell me to shut up. Wash a hell. I'm human. The trouble with you is that you've got too big for your bed. You're one of them whitened sepelcurs like Father Ryan wash always talking about." She had turned to the crowd, her voice suddenly gin-throaty, maudlin tears spilling down her cheeks. "I'm not good enough for him anymore. Me, who put him through school, who loved him when he didn't have a dime." She had attempted to embrace him. "Cansha understand? I still love you, Johnny." The tears had dried as abruptly as they had come. "An' I'll shee you in hell before I'll let some painted young tart make a bigger fool of you than you are. Now go ahead an' hit me. I dare you to, you blankety blankety blank."

Sorrel opened his eyes, his moment of weakness gone. There was only the one thing to do. But at least in one respect she was wrong. He was very human. He wanted to feel Evelyn's arms soft and cool around his neck, hear her assure him again that someday everything would be all right, if only they were patient.

His jaw muscles tightening, he opened the door of the self-service elevator and punched the twelfth-floor button. He was finished with being patient. He had been patient for ten years. It was not his fault, it was her own fault, that Frances had not grown with him. One thing he knew, he could no longer stand the sight or sound or touch of her.

Tonight must end it.

In front of Evelyn's door he slipped his key from his pocket, paused at the realization that if he saw her now he would make her a party to his crime. More, she would attempt to dissuade him. It was best that she know nothing about it, until the affair was over.

Light streamed out from under her door. Her radio was playing softly. He could hear the sound of movement, a drawer being opened and closed. It was enough to know that she was home, that she had received his wire and was waiting. Good girl. Evelyn was a brick. Whatever happened, he could count on her.

He descended to the second floor, left the elevator and walked down the service stairs and out of the side door. The coupe was parked where he had left it. His one fear had been that he might find it stripped.

The motor started easily. He glanced at his watch in the dash light. Five of the thirty minutes that he had allotted himself were gone. Driving at forty miles an hour, the three miles he had to travel would take him two minutes each way. It was fifteen minutes of one. Allow even six more minutes for mishaps and he still had plenty of time to do what he had to do and be back in Evelyn's apartment within a half hour from the time that he had left Jackson. At one-fifteen he would phone down to the doorman and ask him to have Jackson bring up his briefcase and the bottle of rye it contained.

He had no fear that Frances would not be at home. His telegram had stated that his plane was arriving at midnight. Clinging to the tattered remnants of their marriage, she always made it a practice to be home and more or less sober whenever he returned.

"You'll never catch me that way," she had told him once. "I'm a good wife to you, Johnny, see? And I'm willing to be a better one if you would only let me. Why can't we start all over?"

There were a dozen answers to that one, the best of which was Evelyn. The two women had never met. Frances knew that she existed, that was all. That was enough.

As he slowed for the intersection at Sixty-third Street, Sorrel smiled wryly at a suggestion that Evelyn, intrigued by the fact that they had never met, had made.

"We know she's not true to you, Johnny," she had pointed out. "She has no right to point a finger. She doesn't know me. So why can't I strike up a drinking acquaintance with her, or take a job as her maid, or something, and get some concrete proof that would stand up in a divorce court?"

Sorrel had refused to hear of it. Frances was shrewd. A scene between the two was unthinkable. Frances fought as they fought in back of the yards, where both of them had been born — for keeps. Then, too, a sense of guilt had assailed him. His own hands were not clean. He, and he alone, was responsible for Frances's infidelities. She was merely reaching out for the love that he denied her. He had told Evelyn at the time that whatever was done, he would do. He was keeping his word now.

There were few cars on Sixty-third Street. There were none on the darker residential street onto which he turned. He drove for another quarter mile and parked a half a block and across the street from his home.

There were lights in both the kitchen and in Frances's bedroom. The shades of the bedroom were drawn, but, as he watched, a vague figure crossed the room, too far back of the shade to seem more than a passing shadow.

His eyes felt suddenly hot and strained. His throat contracted. His mouth was dry. His hands felt cold and clammy on the wheel. He sat a moment longer, wondering at himself, revolted by the thing he had come to do. This was murder. This was what other men had done for reasons no better than his own, and he, in his smug superiority, safe in the law's ivory tower, had thundered against them and denounced them as cool-blooded conniving scoundrels.

He stepped from the car with an effort and crossed the street. He had come a long way in his climb up — he intended to go still further. With Frances dead and Evelyn beside him, there was no goal to which he might not aspire.

He stopped under a spreading elm tree in the yard and cursed his shaking hands. There was no reason to be afraid. The law would never touch him. He had planned too well. There would be no insurance angle. Frances had none. His only gain would be peace of mind and that wasn't considered a motive for murder. A few of the boys in his own office might suspect him but no one would be able to prove a thing.

Frances's failings were well known. She had come home drunk. She had left the door unlocked. A night prowler had entered and killed her. No one would be more surprised and shocked than he when he returned with Jackson an hour from now and found her — dead.

He slipped his key in the front door. The inner bolt was shot and it refused to open. He considered ringing the bell and killing her in the hall. He decided to stay, as far as possible, with his original plan. There was no convenient weapon in the hall. A single scream would shatter the stillness of the sleeping street. What he had to do must be done in silence.

The back door leading into the kitchen was open but the screen door was locked. He slipped on a pair of gloves and fumbled in one corner of the porch where he had remembered seeing a rusty ice pick. His luck was holding. The pick was there. He probed it through the screen and lifted the hood from its eyes.

The door open, he waited, listening, hearing nothing. There was a half-emptied bottle of milk, a clouded glass, and the remains of a peanut butter sandwich on the kitchen table.

Frances, he decided, was playing the sober and repentant wife this time.

Believe me, John. I love you. I'll stop drinking. I'll do anything you say. You're all that matters to me. Why can't we start all over?

He had heard it so many times that he could play the record by heart. He noted that the kitchen shade was up. Anyone entering the kitchen would be visible from the darkened windows of the house next door. Sweat beading on his forehead, he slipped in a hand before him and snapped the switch, thankful that he had noticed the shade in time. It was the little things of murder that sent men to the chair.

The darkness magnified his strain. His mouth grew even drier. He heard, or thought he heard, the pounding of his heart. He had to force himself to cross the kitchen, feeling his way along the wall to the rear stairs.

Now he could hear sounds in the bedroom. She seemed to be opening and closing drawers, probably in search of one of the bottles she was always hiding from herself.

He crossed the dark hall toward the closed bedroom door and his weight caused a board to creak. The light in the bedroom went out and the door opened. They stood only feet apart in the black hallway, aware of each other but unable to see.

The blood, Sorrel thought suddenly. *It will splatter. I'll be covered with blood. Damn it! Why didn't I think of that!*

Then he realized he still was clutching the rusted ice pick in his hand. It was as good a weapon as any, better than most. Murder Incorporated had used them as the chief tool of their trade. An ice pick had been used in the case of the State versus Manny Capper. The sweat on his brow turned cold. Manny had gone to the chair.

Galvanized by his own terror, crying out hoarsely, Sorrel sprang forward. His groping hand felt teeth in time to clamp his palm over the welling scream. It died stillborn as he plunged the pick in his hand repeatedly into the yielding flesh. The body he held ceased squirming and sagged limply. He allowed it to fall to the floor, relieved to be rid of it.

The ice pick fell from his nerveless hand. He tried to fumble a match from his pocket and could not. His hands were shaking too badly. Afraid of the dark, afraid of the woman whom he had killed, he squatted beside the body and felt for a pulse with the back of his wrist, where flesh gaped between glove and coat cuff. There was no pulse. It was over, done with, *finis*. He was free.

He crept back down the stairs and out through the kitchen to the porch. Then he remembered the pick. It would have no fingerprints on it. He considered returning for it and his stomach rebelled.

So there were no fingerprints on the death weapon. So what? Most house prowlers with the sense of gnats wore gloves. It was nothing for him to worry over.

He walked silently, unseen, back to his car and examined his gloves in the dash light. One was slightly splattered with blood but there seemed to be none on the cuffs of his suit. All that remained to be done was to rid himself of the gloves.

It was over, done. He was free. There was nothing to stop him now, nothing to stop the boys from running him for whatever office they pleased. Frances had made her last scene. He was young, under forty. His new life was just beginning.

As he drove, the horror of the thing that he had been forced to do left him. He wanted to sing, to yell, to shout to the stars that he was free. He contented himself with a grin.

It had been a relatively simple matter, after all. He wadded the gloves into a ball and tossed them out the car window. They could not be traced to him. There was nothing to tie him to the murder but the fact that he and Frances were married. Back at the Eldorado, he parked the coupe in the same space it had occupied before and glanced at his watch before switching off the lights. It was eleven minutes past one. He was four minutes ahead of schedule.

He expended them by walking to the corner and peering around it cautiously. The doorman and Jackson were deep in some discussion. Satisfied that he had not been missed, he entered the side door.

Telling Evelyn would take some doing. She would be horrified at first, but she was quick-witted enough to realize that no other course had been open to him. It didn't matter now. All that mattered was that the thing was done.

His throat and mouth were normal again. In the bright light of the cage he could see no bloodstains on his suit. He had been fortunate. He was whistling softly, almost cheerfully, as he inserted his key in the door.

The radio was still playing softly. A bottle of his best scotch beside her, Frances was sitting in one of Evelyn's easy chairs. "I knew you'd come here first," she said. "What's a matter? Was your plane late?"

He stared at her open-mouthed, screams he was unable to utter tearing at his throat.

"You poor damn fool," his wife continued. "Why didn't you let me meet her? Why didn't you make me realize what a swell kid she really was? Why didn't you tell me that the boys wanted to run you for senator? You should have known me better, John. You're my man. You always will be. No tramp was goin' to take you from me. But a sweet kid like that is another matter." She fluffed at her frowsy hair. "I feel kind of honored like."

Sorrel managed to gasp one word, "Evelyn . . ."

Frances nipped at the scotch. "Oh, you didn't know. Well, she showed at the house this morning and gave me a song and dance about being a maid out of work, her with fingernails that long." She laughed, shortly. "So I hired her and I pumped her. She's probably goin' through all my things right now, spyin' on me." Frances picked an oblong scrap of yellow paper from the table. "She never even got a chance to see her telegram because I copped her key from her purse and come over here shortly after I got the telegram that you sent me. Mine was all right. But after I read this one I kinda wondered." She read it aloud: "'Sweetheart. Be in your apartment at twelve tonight. Don't leave it for any reason. And don't let anyone in but me. This is important, more important than you realize.'"

His voice sounding strange to himself, Sorrel asked, "You — knew?"

Frances Sorrel smiled thinly. "I know you," she admitted. "But don't worry. Think nothing of it. As long as your plane was late, you've got nothing to worry about."

1946

DOROTHY B. HUGHES

THE HOMECOMING

Dorothy B(elle) Hughes (1904–1993). Born in Kansas City, Missouri, Hughes received her journalism degree from the University of Missouri and did postgraduate work at the University of New Mexico and Columbia University. She worked as a journalist in Missouri, New York, and New Mexico before becoming a mystery writer.

This underappreciated author is historically important as being the first female to fall squarely in the hard-boiled school. She wrote eleven novels in the 1940s, beginning with *The So Blue Marble* (1940) and including *The Cross-Eyed Bear* (1940), *The Bamboo Blonde* (1941), *The Fallen Sparrow* (1942), *Ride the Pink Horse* (1946), and *In a Lonely Place* (1947), the latter three all made into successful films noir. *The Fallen Sparrow* was filmed by RKO in 1943 and starred John Garfield and Maureen O'Hara; *Ride the Pink Horse* (Universal, 1947) starred Robert Montgomery and Thomas Gomez; *In a Lonely Place* (Columbia, 1950) was a vehicle for Humphrey Bogart, Gloria Grahame, and Martha Stewart, and was directed by Nicholas Ray. This classic film noir portrays an alcoholic screenwriter who is prone to violent outbursts and is accused of murdering a hatcheck girl. He is given an alibi by his attractive blond neighbor, who soon becomes fearful that he really did commit the crime, and that she might be next. In the book, the writer is, in fact, a psychopathic killer, but the director found it too dark and softened the plot.

At the height of her powers and success, Hughes largely quit writing due to domestic responsibilities. She reviewed mysteries for many years, winning an Edgar Award from the Mystery Writers of America for her critical acumen in 1951; in 1978 the organization named her a Grand Master for lifetime achievement.

"The Homecoming" was first published in *Murder Cavalcade,* the first Mystery Writers of America anthology (New York: Duell, Sloan and Pearce, 1946).

▪ ▪ ▪

It was a dark night, a small-wind night, the night on which evil things could happen, might happen. He didn't feel uneasy walking the two dark blocks from the streetcar to her house. The reason he kept peering over his shoulder was because he heard things behind him, things like the rustle of an ancient bombazine skirt, like footsteps trying to walk without sound, things like crawling and scuttling and pawing. The things you'd hear in a too-old forest place, not on the concrete pavement of a city street. He had to look behind him to know that the sounds were the ordinary sounds of a city street in the autumn. Browned leaves shriveled and fallen, blown in small whirlpools by the small wind. Warped elm boughs scraping together in lonely nakedness. The sounds you'd expect on a night in autumn when the grotesquerie of shadows was commonplace. Elm fingers beckoning, leaves drifting to earth, shadows on an empty street. The little moans of the wind quivering his own flung shadow, and his own steps solid in the night, moving to her house.

He'd be there. The hero. Korea Jim. He'd be there a long time, since supper. She'd have asked him to supper because this was her folks' night out. Her folks always went out Thursday nights, ladies' night at the club. Cards and bingo and dancing and eats and they wouldn't get home till after one o'clock at least.

She'd say it cute, "Come over for supper Thursday. I'm a terrible cook. All I can fix is pancakes." And you'd know there was nothing you'd rather eat Thursday night than her pancakes. Better than thick steak, better than chicken and dumplings, better than turkey and all the fixings would be pancakes on Thursday night. She'd say it coaxing, "If you don't come I'll be here all by myself. The family always goes out on Thursday night." And even if there weren't going to be pancakes with sorghum or real maple syrup, your choice, your chest would swell until it was tight enough to bust, wanting to protect her from a lonely night at home with the folks out.

She was such a little thing. Not tall enough to reach the second shelf in the kitchen without standing on tiptoes. Not even in her pencil-point heels was she high enough to reach his chin. She was little and soft as fur and her hair was like yellow silk. She was always fooling you with her hair. You'd get used to the memory of her looking like a kid sister with her hair down her back, maybe curled a little, and the next time she'd have it pinned on top of her head like she was playing grownup. Or she'd have it curled up short or once or twice in two stiff pigtails with ribbon bows like a real kid. Wondering about her hair he forgot for a moment the dark and the wind and the things crawling in his mind and heart; he quickened his steps to cover the blocks to her house.

Then he remembered. It wasn't he who had been invited to pancakes for supper; it was the boy with the medals, the hero, Korea Jim. By now she and Jim would be sitting on the couch, sitting close together so they'd both avoid the place where the couch sagged. Her brother, the one in the Navy, had busted it when he was a kid.

She and Jim would be sitting there close and only the one lamp on. Too much light hurt her eyes. Her eyes were big as cartwheels, blue sometimes, a smoky blue, and sometimes sort of purple-gray. You didn't know what color her eyes were until you looked into them. It was like her hair only she did it to her hair and her eyes did themselves. Her nose didn't change, it was little and cute like she was. Just turned up the least bit, enough to make her cuter when she put her eyelashes up at you and said, "Aw, Benny!" Her mouth changed colors, red like a Jonathan sometimes, sometimes like holly, sometimes like mulberries. Her father didn't like that purple color. He'd say, "Take it off, Nan. You look like a stuck pig." Red like blood. But the colors didn't change her mouth really, red like fire, red like soft warm wool. Her mouth . . .

He picked up his steps and shadows flickered as he moved. This time he didn't look over his shoulder. Nothing was back there. And beyond, a block beyond her house, he could see the blur of green light, the precinct police station house. It was somehow reassuring. There couldn't be anything behind you with the police station ahead of you. Besides he had the gun.

It was heavy in his overcoat pocket. On the streetcar riding out to her neighborhood he'd felt everyone's eyes looking through the pocket and wondering why a nice young fellow was carrying a gun. He could have told them he was going to Nan's house though she wasn't expecting him. Though she'd told him for the twelfth night in a row, "I'm so sorry, Benny, but I'm busy tonight." Except the one night he hadn't phoned, the night he'd walked the streets in the chill autumn rain until his shoes were soggy and his mind a tight red knot.

He could have told them he was going to surprise Nan and especially surprise Hero Jim, Korea Jim. He'd find out how much of a hero Jim was. He'd see what big bold Jim would do up against a real gun. She'd see, too.

They'd be sitting on the couch so close, and the lamp over on the far table the only light. Not much light from that lamp. Her mother had made the lampshade. She'd bought a regular paper shade at the ten-cent store for thirty-nine cents, then she'd pasted on it colored pictures of kids and dogs and handsome sailors and soldiers and Marines. All put together sort of like a patchwork quilt in diamond shapes. After that she'd shellacked over the pictures and it made a swell shade. Only it didn't give much light.

When he'd ring the doorbell they'd sort of jump apart, she and Jim, wondering who it was. Wondering if her folks had left the club early, before the spread. Wondering who it could be. She'd say, "I wonder who it could possibly be this time of night." The way she'd said it the night the wire came that her brother was married in San Diego. Jim would say, "Probably your folks," just the way Benny had said it the night of the telegram. And she'd say, wrinkling her forehead the way she did when she was disturbed by something, "It couldn't be. Pop would never leave before the cheese. Unless someone's sick—"

Then Jim would go to the door. She wouldn't come because she'd be wondering who it was. Besides she was nervous at night, even walking down the street with a man she was nervous, looking over her shoulder, skipping along faster. As if she felt something was after her, something that someday would catch up to her. It might have been from her that he got the nervousness of walking down this street at night. No reason why he should be nervous. It wasn't late, hardly eleven yet. He'd only sat through half the show. He'd seen it before.

Jim would come to the door. He ought to let Jim have it right then and there. The dirty, cheating, lying—. Sitting around saying, "I don't want to talk about it, Nan." Waiting to be coaxed. And she'd coaxed him, turning the sweet smell of her body to big Jim, handsome Jim, the hero of Korea. She got him started, bringing up things about the raid that had been printed in the newspapers along with the picture of Jim. He didn't want to talk about it but once she got him started, you couldn't turn him off. He went on and on, not even seeming to see her big blue smoky eyes, not even seeming to hear her little soft furry hurt cries. On and on, practically crawling around the floor, and then he'd stopped and the sweat had broken out all over his red face. "I'm sorry, Nan," he'd said so quietly you could hardly hear him.

She didn't say anything. She just was looking at Jim. He, Benny, had put a hot number on the phonograph, a new Les Brown, and he'd said, "Come on, Nan. Let's start the joint jumping." He'd had enough of Jim's showing off. He'd said it again louder but she didn't answer him. She sat there looking at Jim, and Jim looking at the floor. Les Brown played on and on not knowing nobody was listening to him. Benny knew that night what was going to happen. Her and Jim. And him out of it.

It had always been like that for Jim. He got everything. In High he was the one elected captain of the basketball team. He was the junior class president. He was the one the girls were always looking their eyes out at in the halls. He was the one the fellows wanted to double-date with. He'd always got everything. Nan and him sitting together in assembly. Everything. When other guys had pimples, Jim didn't. When other guys had to sleep in stocking tops and grease their hair to keep it out of their eyes, Jim's yellow hair was crisp enough to stay where it belonged. When other guys' pants needed pressing and they forgot their dirty fingernails, Jim didn't. Korea Jim. The hero. Even in the war he'd come out the big stuff.

War was supposed to make all men the same. Not one guy with more stripes a hero and another guy already back in civvies. It wasn't Benny's fault he hadn't been sent over. The Army didn't say, "Would you like to go to Korea and be a hero?" They said you were doing your part just as much being a soldier in your own hometown in the recruiting office. Benny had been pretty lucky being in his own hometown for the war, being in clean work, in safe work. He'd thought he'd been lucky until Jim came back with all those pretty ribbons and his picture in the paper. It wasn't Benny's fault. He didn't ask the Army not to send him over; if he'd been sent he could have been a hero too. He could have led the raiders through frontline fire and liberated those poor starved guys. High school kids like yourself only they were men now, old men. It made Benny shiver to see them in the newsreels. It made him know he was lucky to have been in the recruiting office, addressing envelopes and filing papers.

Even if Jim had come back a big-shot hero. Jim who'd always had everything and now had this. And Nan, too. He wasn't going to get away with it this time. He wasn't going to have Nan. Nan was Benny's girl. She'd been his girl for almost two years. Jim hadn't meant anything to her those years. Just one of the gang in Korea. She didn't talk about him any more than she did about any of the other kids, wondering what they were doing on certain nights while she and Benny were out jumping and jiving at the USO.

Jim wasn't going to come back and bust up Benny and Nan. He wasn't going to be let do it. He could get him plenty of other girls; there were always plenty of girls for a good-looking guy like Jim. All he had to do was whistle. Just because he'd been Nan's fellow in high school before the war started didn't mean he could walk back in and take over. Not after leaving her for four years. Jim had left her. He hadn't even waited for the draft. He'd quit high school and signed up right away.

It wasn't Benny's fault he'd had to wait to be drafted. Jim's folks had given him permission to sign up. Benny's mom had just cried and cried and wouldn't talk about it. So he'd had to wait for the draft. Besides he wasn't as strong as Jim. He always had colds in the winter just like Mom said. Besides none of that made any difference. He'd been a soldier just like Jim. It wasn't his fault he hadn't got to be a hero. None of that mattered at all. There was only one thing counting. Nan. His girl. Benny's girl. Jim was going to find that out. Tonight.

He was there at the white cement steps, the familiar steps, gray in the night. He didn't walk on by like he had the night he walked in the soggy rain, his stomach curdled and his thoughts tied in wet red knots. Tonight he climbed the steps without breaking the firmness of his stride. Without trying to be quiet. He wasn't afraid of Jim. He had as much right here as Jim had. He continued up the short cement walk to the gray stoop, climbed the gray steps and was on the porch.

The drapes were drawn across the front parlor windows. Only the little light was on inside. He knew from the dim red glow against the drapes, almost purple-red. He pushed the bell once, hard and firm and not afraid. Like he had a right. Like he'd been pushing it for the two years since he ran into Nan at a USO party.

It happened the way he knew it was going to happen. A wait. Waiting while she and Jim jumped apart and she smoothed her hair while she was wondering who it could possibly be. The wait and then the footsteps of a man coming to the door. Of Jim. Benny's hand gripped tight on the gun in his pocket. Holding tight that way kept his stomach from jumping around. He had to keep tight so he wouldn't let Jim have it the way he ought to when Jim opened the door. The dirty, double-crossing, lying . . .

The door opened sudden. Before he was quite ready for it to open. Jim was standing there, tall and lanky in the dim hallway, peering out to see who was standing outside. Not expecting Benny. Not expecting him at all. Because his face came over with a real surprised look when he figured out who it was. Jim said, "For gos' sake! It's Benny." He said it more to her, back there in the parlor, than to himself.

Benny didn't say anything. He stepped in and Jim had to stand aside and let him pass. She was just starting over to the archway from the couch when Benny walked into the parlor. He didn't say anything to her either; he simply stood with his hands in his overcoat pockets looking at her. He didn't even take off his hat. He couldn't, not without letting her see how his hands were shaking. Keeping his hand gripped on the gun kept it steady, and the other hand a tight fist in his pocket. There wasn't any reason for them to be shaking; he wasn't afraid of anything. It wasn't because he was afraid his voice would shake that he didn't speak; it wasn't that at all. It was that he didn't have anything to say to them. Keeping his mouth shut was easy. Nan started talking the minute he came in.

She was mad. Her eyes were like sparklers and her words came out of her mouth like little spits of lead. He'd seen her mad before but just a little bit, kind of cute. This was different. If he hadn't been bigger than she, she'd have used her fists on him. If he hadn't had a gun . . . She didn't know about the gun. But he could hardly hear what she was saying from looking at her. Because she was so pretty she was like a lump in his heart, so little and soft and her cheeks bright and her mouth . . . His hand was so tight on the gun that his fingers ached like his heart. He set his teeth together tight as his knuckles so that his head hurt too, so that all the hurts could fuse and he could keep from thinking about the bad one, the inside one. So he wouldn't cry. He wanted to cry, to bawl like a kid. But he wouldn't, not with Jim standing there like he owned the parlor, like he was the head of the house waiting to see what this peddler wanted.

She was saying, "What are you doing here, Benny? You knew very well I was busy tonight. I told you that. What's the idea of coming here when I told you I was busy? And at this time of night?" He had a feeling she'd been saying it over and over again.

She was funny sputtering out words that way and not having any idea why he was here or what he was going to do. He wanted to laugh at her, to laugh and laugh until he doubled up from laughing. As if he'd eaten green apples. But he didn't. He just stood there listening to her until Jim said, "Shush, Nan." Said it sharp, like he was giving orders to a soldier.

Benny turned his eyes over to Jim then. The way Jim had said it you'd have thought he was nervous. You'd have thought he knew why Benny had come and that he didn't want to have it happen, to be shown up in front of Nan.

Jim said, "Why don't you take off your things and join us, Benny? We're just sitting around waiting for Nan's folks to get home from the club."

As if he didn't know what they were doing. As if he hadn't known all evening every minute what they were doing. From when Jim got there at seven and she tied an apron around his waist and let him help drip the batter on the griddle. Right through every minute of it. Sitting down together in the breakfast nook and her saying, "Isn't this fun? Like—"

and breaking off and looking embarrassed. That's the way she was, nice, sort of shy, not like most girls who'd say anything and never be embarrassed.

Jim said, "Come on, Benny, take off your hat and coat. We'll have some jive. I brought Nan some new records tonight. There's a swell new Tatum — have you heard it?"

Shaming him because he never brought any records to Nan. He'd have brought them if he'd thought of it. He'd just never thought of it. Nan always had the new records.

Jim didn't stop talking. He kept on like Benny was a little kid, coaxing him. "— let me have your coat. How about having a Coke with us?"

Hero Jim. Asking Benny to have a Coke like he was still a high school kid instead of a man. Hero Jim, the plaster saint, acting like he'd never had a slug of gin. Trying to make her think he was a Galahad and Benny a no-good bum.

"— I was just telling Nan we hadn't seen you for a long time. Wondered what happened to you. Why you didn't come around."

Yeah. Sure. Rubbing salt in the wounds. That's what he learned in Korea. Scrub salt in the bleeding. Acting like it was his house. Acting like he and Nan were married. Trying to show Benny up for the outsider. Talking and talking, so sure of himself, so big and brave and handsome and sure of himself.

Nan stopped Jim. Stopped him by breaking in with a hard icy crust of anger around her soft red mouth.

"What do you want, Benny?" she asked. Hard and cold and cruel. "If you have anything to say, say it and get out. If you haven't, get out!" Her voice was like a whip.

Jim cried, "Nan!" He shook his head. "You shouldn't have said that, Nan." He was talking to her soft now, like she was the child. "It wasn't right to say that. Benny's come to see you —"

"I told him I wouldn't see him tonight." She didn't bend to Jim. She was too mad. "He knew I was busy tonight." She turned her eyes again on Benny. They weren't like Nan's eyes, they were black like hate. "I'll tell him now to his face what I told you." The words came from her frozen mouth, each one like a whip. "I don't ever want to see you again. Now get out."

"Nan," Jim cried again. His voice wasn't steady. It was shaky. "Oh, Nan!" He twisted some kind of a smile at Benny. "Come on, Benny, sit down and let's talk everything over. Nan didn't mean it. We're all friends. We've been friends for years. Sit down and have a Coke —"

Benny brought his hand out of his pocket then. He had a smile on his face too, he could feel it there. It hurt his mouth. He had a little trouble getting his hand out of his pocket. Getting it out and holding on to that thing at the same time. But it came out and the gun was still in his hand.

Jim saw it. Jim saw it and he had sweat on his upper lip and above his eyebrows. He was yellow. Just like Benny had known he'd be. Yellow. Korea Jim, Hero Jim, was scared to death.

Jim's voice didn't sound scared. It was quiet and calm and easy. "Where did you get that, Benny? Let me see it, will you?"

Benny didn't say anything. He just held the gun and Jim put his hand down to his side again, slowly, creakingly.

The sweat was trickling down Jim's nose. He laughed but it wasn't a good laugh. "What do you want with a gun, Benny? You might hurt somebody if you aren't careful with it. Let me see it, will you? Come on, let me have it."

He'd had enough. Hero Jim, standing there like a gook, like he'd never seen a gun before and didn't know what to do about it. Now was Benny's time to laugh, but the gun made too much noise. Nobody could have heard him laughing with all that noise. Even if Nan hadn't started screaming. Standing there, her eyes crazy and her face like an old woman's, just screaming and screaming and screaming. He only turned the gun on her to make her keep quiet. He didn't mean that she should fall down and spread on the floor like Jim. She shouldn't have dropped like Jim. She had on her good blue dress. They looked silly, the two of them, like big sawdust dolls, crumpled there on the rug. Scared to death. Scared to get up. Scared even to look at him. That's the way a hero acted when a real guy came around. Like a girl. Like a soft, silly girl. Lying down on his face, not moving a muscle, lying on his face like a dog.

They looked like shadows, the two of them, big shadows on the rug. When the gun clicked instead of blasting, Benny stopped laughing. The room was so quiet he could hear the beat of his heart. He didn't like it so quiet. Not at all.

He said, "Get up." He'd had enough of their wallowing, of their being scared.

"Get up."

He said, "You look crazy lying there. Get up." Suddenly he shrilled it.

"Get up."

Louder. "Get up! Get up! Get up!"

Scared to death . . . scared to death . . .

The gun made such a little noise dropping to the rug. Because his fingers couldn't hold it. Because his fingers were soft as her hair. They couldn't get up. They couldn't ever get up.

Not ever.

He hadn't meant to do it. He didn't do it on purpose. He wouldn't hurt Nan. He wouldn't hurt Nan for anything in the world, he loved her.

She was his girl.

He wouldn't hurt Nan. He wouldn't kill — he wouldn't kill anyone.

He hadn't! They were doing this to get even with him. He began shouting again, "Get up! Get up!"

But his voice didn't sound like his own voice. It was shaky like his mouth and his hands and the wet back of his neck.

"Get up!"

He heard his mouth say it and he started over to take hold of Jim and make him stop acting like he was dead.

He started.

He took one step and that was all. Because he knew. He knew whatever he said or did couldn't make them move. They were dead, really dead.

When his mind actually spoke the word, he ran. Bolting out of the house, stumbling off the stoop down the steps to the curb. He didn't get there too soon.

He retched.

When he was through being sick, he sat down on the curb. He was too weak to stand. He was like the leaves blowing down the street in the little moans of wind.

He was like the shadows wavering against the houses across the street.

There were lights in most of the houses. You'd think the neighbors would have heard all the noise. Would have come running out to see what was going on. They probably thought it was the radio.

They should have come. If they had come, they'd have stopped him. He didn't want to kill anyone. He didn't want even to kill Jim. Just to scare him off. Just give him a scare.

She couldn't be dead. She couldn't be, she couldn't be, she couldn't be. He sobbed the words into the wind and the dark and the dead brown leaves.

He sat there a long, long time. When he stood up his face was wet. He rubbed his eyes, trying to dry them so he could see where he was going.

But the rain came into them again, spilling down his cheeks, filling up, overflowing, refilling, over and over again.

He ought to go back and close the blurred door. The house would get cold with it standing wide open, letting the cold dark wind sweep through.

He couldn't go back there. Not even for his gun.

He started down the street, not knowing where he was going, not seeing anything but the wet dark world.

He no longer feared the sound and shadow behind him.

There was no terror as bad as the hurt in his head and his heart.

As he moved on without direction he saw through the mist the pinprick of green in the night. He knew then where he was going, where he must go. The tears ran down his cheeks into his mouth. They tasted like blood.

1952

HOWARD BROWNE

MAN IN THE DARK

Howard Browne (1908–1999) was born in Omaha, Nebraska, and from 1929 worked for more than a dozen years in various jobs, many of them in department stores, before becoming a full-time writer and editor. Beginning in 1942, he worked for nearly fifteen years as the editor of several Ziff-Davis science-fiction magazines (a genre he actively disliked, preferring mysteries), including *Amazing Stories* and *Fantastic Adventures.* During this time, he wrote numerous stories for pulp magazines, as well as several novels under the pseudonym John Evans, most successfully the somewhat controversial series about Chicago private detective Paul Pine. The Pine novels were probably closer in style to Raymond Chandler than any other writer (with the exception of the early Lew Archer novels by Ross Macdonald) of his time. *Halo in Blood* (1946) was the first; *Halo for Satan* (1948) is about a manuscript purportedly written by Jesus Christ; *Halo in Brass* (1949) deals with the then-unmentionable subject of lesbianism; and *The Taste of Ashes* (1957) was published under his own name and is among the earliest works of fiction to deal with child molestation.

Browne went to Hollywood in 1956 and wrote more than 100 episodes of numerous television series, including *Playhouse 90, Maverick, Ben Casey, The Virginian,* and *Columbo.* He also wrote numerous screenplays, notably *Portrait of a Mobster* (1961) with Vic Morrow playing Dutch Schultz, *The St. Valentine's Day Massacre* (1967) with George Segal and Jason Robards, and *Capone* (1975), with Ben Gazzara.

In 1952, while Browne was editor of *Fantastic,* he called his friend Roy Huggins (creator of such famous television series as *Maverick, 77 Sunset Strip,* and *The Fugitive*) and asked him if he could write a detective story with fantasy elements in it. Huggins agreed, but when the time came to turn to it, he was too busy writing a screenplay to do the story. Since Browne already had the cover of the fall issue of the magazine ready to go, with Huggins's name on it, he wrote "Man in the Dark" himself, under the "pseudonym" of Roy Huggins.

▪ ▪ ▪

I

SHE CALLED ME at four-ten. "Hi, Poopsie."

I scowled at her picture in the leather frame on my desk. "For Christ's sake, Donna, will you lay off that 'Poopsie' stuff? It's bad enough in the bedroom, but this is over the phone and in broad daylight."

She laughed. "It kind of slipped out. You know I'd never say it where anyone else could hear. Would I, Poopsie?"

"What's all that noise?"

"The man's here fixing the vacuum. Hey, we eating home tonight, or out? Or are you in another deadline dilemma?"

"No dilemma. Might as well —"

"Can't hear you, Clay."

I could hardly hear *her.* I raised my voice. "Tell the guy to turn that goddamn thing off. I started to say we might as well eat out and then take in that picture at the Paramount. Okay?"

"All right. What time'll you get home?"

"Hour — hour'n a half."

The vacuum cleaner buzz died out just as she said, "Bye now," and the two words sounded loud and unnatural. I put back the receiver and took off my hat and sat down behind the desk. We were doing a radio adaptation of *Echo of a Scream* that coming Saturday and I was just back from a very unsatisfactory rehearsal. When things don't go right, it's the producer who gets it in the neck, and mine was still sensitive from the previous week. I kept a small office in a building at Las Palmas and Yucca, instead of using the room allotted me at NBS. Some producers do that, since you can accomplish a lot more without a secretary breathing down your neck and the actors dropping in for gin rummy or a recital of their love life.

The telephone rang. A man's voice, deep and solemn, said, "Is this Hillside 7–8691?"

"That's right," I said.

"Like to speak to Mr. Clay Kane."

"I'm Clay Kane. Who's this?"

"The name's Lindstrom, Mr. Kane. Sergeant Lindstrom, out of the sheriff's office, Hollywood substation."

"What's on your mind, Sergeant?"

"We got a car here, Mr. Kane," the deep slow voice went on. "Dark blue '51 Chevrolet, two-door, license 2W78–40. Registered to Mrs. Donna Kane, 7722 Fountain Avenue, Los Angeles."

I could feel my forehead wrinkling into a scowl. "That's my wife's car. What do you mean: you 'got' it?"

"Well, now, I'm afraid I got some bad news for you, Mr. Kane." The voice went from solemn to grave. "Seems your wife's car went off the road up near the Stone Canyon Reservoir. I don't know if you know it or not, but there's some pretty bad hills up —"

"I know the section," I said. "Who was in the car?"

". . . Just your wife, Mr. Kane."

My reaction was a mixture of annoyance and mild anger. "Not *my* wife, Sergeant. I spoke to her on the phone not five minutes ago. She's at home. Either somebody stole the car or, more likely, she loaned it to one of her friends. How bad is it?"

There was a pause at the other end. When the voice spoke again, the solemnity was still there, but now a vague thread of suspicion was running through it.

"The car burned, Mr. Kane. The driver was still in it."

"That's terrible," I said. "When did it happen?"

"We don't know exactly. That's pretty deserted country. Another car went by after it happened, spotted the wreck, and called us. We figure it happened around two-thirty."

"Not my wife," I said again. "You want to call her, she can tell you who borrowed the car. Unless, like I say, somebody swiped it. You mean you found no identification at all?"

". . . Hold on a minute, Mr. Kane."

There followed the indistinct mumble you get when a hand is held over the receiver at the other end of the wire. I waited, doodling on a scratch pad, wondering vaguely if my car insurance would cover this kind of situation. Donna had never loaned the car before, at least not to my knowledge.

The sergeant came back. "Hate to trouble you, Mr. Kane, but I expect you better get out here. You got transportation, or would you want one of our men to pick you up?"

This would just about kill our plans for the evening. I tried reasoning with him. "Look here, Officer, I don't want to sound cold-blooded about this, but what can I do out there? If the car was stolen, there's nothing I can tell you. If Mrs. Kane let somebody use it, she can tell you who it was over the phone. Far as the car's concerned, my insurance company'll take care of that."

The deep slow voice turned a little hard. "Afraid it's not that simple. We're going to have to insist on this, Mr. Kane. Take Stone Canyon until you come to Fontenelle Way, half a mile or so south of Mulholland

Drive. The accident happened about halfway between those two points. I'll have one of the boys keep an eye out for you. Shouldn't take you more'n an hour at the most."

I gave it another try. "You must've found *some* identification, Sergeant. Something that —"

He cut in sharply. "Yeah, we found something. Your wife's handbag. Maybe she loaned it along with the car."

A dry click meant I was alone on the wire. I hung up slowly and sat there staring at the wall calendar. That handbag bothered me. If Donna had loaned the Chevy to someone, she wouldn't have gone off and left the bag. And if she'd left it on the seat while visiting or shopping, she would have discovered the theft of the car and told me long before this.

There was one sure way of bypassing all this guesswork. I picked up the receiver again and dialed the apartment.

After the twelfth ring I broke the connection. Southern California in August is as warm as anybody would want, but I was beginning to get chilly along the backbone. She could be at the corner grocery or at the Feldmans' across the hall, but I would have liked it a lot better if she had been in the apartment and answered my call.

It seemed I had a trip ahead of me. Stone Canyon Road came in between Beverly Glen Boulevard and Sepulveda, north of Sunset. That was out past Beverly Hills, and the whole district was made up of hills and canyons, with widely scattered homes clinging to the slopes. A car could go off almost any one of the twisting roads through there and not be noticed for a lot longer than two hours. It was the right place for privacy, if privacy was what you were looking for.

The thing to do, I decided, was to stop at the apartment first. It was on the way, so I wouldn't lose much time, and I could take Donna along with me. Getting an explanation direct from her ought to satisfy the cops, and we could still get in a couple of drinks and a fast dinner, and make that premiere.

I covered the typewriter, put on my hat, locked up, and went down to the parking lot. It was a little past four-twenty.

II

It was a five-minute trip to the apartment building where Donna and I had been living since our marriage seven months before. I waited while a fat woman in red slacks and a purple and burnt-orange blouse pulled a yellow Buick away from the curb, banging a fender or two in the process, then parked and got out onto the walk.

It had started to cool off a little, the way it does in this part of the country along toward late afternoon. A slow breeze rustled the dusty fronds of palm trees lining the parkways along Fountain Avenue. A thin pattern of traffic moved past, and the few pedestrians in sight had the look of belonging there.

I crossed to the building entrance and went in. The small foyer was deserted and the mailbox for 2C, our apartment, was empty. I unlocked the inner door and climbed the carpeted stairs to the second floor and walked slowly down the dimly lighted corridor.

Strains of a radio newscast filtered through the closed door of the apartment across from 2C. Ruth Feldman was home. She might have word, if I needed it. I hoped I wouldn't need it. There was the faint scent of jasmine on the air.

I unlocked the door to my apartment and went in and said, loudly: "Hey, Donna. It's your ever-lovin'."

All that came back was silence. Quite a lot of it. I closed the door and leaned against it and heard my heart thumping away. The white metal venetian blinds at the living room windows overlooking the street were lowered but not turned, and there was a pattern of sunlight on the maroon carpeting. Our tank-type vacuum cleaner was on the floor in front of the fireplace, its hose tracing a lazy S along the rug like a gray python, the cord plugged into a wall socket.

The silence was beginning to rub against my nerves. I went into the bedroom. The blind was closed and I switched on one of the red-shaded lamps on Donna's dressing table. Nobody there. The double bed was made up, with her blue silk robe across the foot and her slippers with the powder blue pompons under the trailing edge of the pale yellow spread.

My face in the vanity's triple mirrors had that strained look. I turned off the light and walked out of there and on into the bathroom, then the kitchen and breakfast nook. I knew all the time Donna wouldn't be in any of them; I had known it from the moment that first wave of silence answered me.

But I looked anyway . . .

She might have left a note for me, I thought. I returned to the bedroom and looked on the nightstand next to the telephone. No note. Just the day's mail: two bills, unopened; a business envelope from my agent, unopened, and a letter from Donna's mother out in Omaha, opened and thrust carelessly back into the envelope.

The mail's being there added up to one thing at least: Donna had been in the apartment after three o'clock that afternoon. What with all this economy wave at the post offices around the country, we were getting one delivery a day and that not before the middle of the afternoon. The phone call, the vacuum sweeper, the mail on the nightstand: they were enough to prove that my wife was around somewhere. Out for a lipstick, more than likely, or a carton of Fatimas, or to get a bet down on a horse.

I left the apartment and crossed the hall and rang the bell to 2D. The news clicked off in the middle of the day's baseball scores and after a moment the door opened and Ruth Feldman was standing there.

"Oh. Clay." She was a black-haired little thing, with not enough color from being indoors too much, and a pair of brown eyes that, in a prettier face, would have made her something to moon over on long winter evenings. "I *thought* it was too early for Ralph; he won't be home for two hours yet."

"I'm looking for Donna," I said. "You seen her?"

She leaned negligently against the door edge and moved her lashes at me. The blouse she was wearing was cut much too low. "No-o-o. Not since this morning anyway. She came in about eleven for coffee and a cigarette. Stayed maybe half an hour, I guess it was."

"Did she say anything about her plans for the day? You know: whether she was going to see anybody special, something like that?"

She lifted a shoulder. "Hunh-uh. She did say something about her agent wanting her to have lunch with this producer — what's his name? — who does the *Snow Soap* television show. They're casting for a new musical and she thinks that's why this lunch. But I suppose you know about that. You like to come in for a drink?"

I told her no and thanked her and she pouted her lips at me. I could come in early any afternoon and drink her liquor and give her a roll in the hay, no questions asked, no obligations and no recriminations. Not just because it was me, either. It was there for anyone who was friendly, no stranger, and had clean fingernails. You find at least one like her in any apartment house, where the husband falls asleep on the couch every night over a newspaper or the television set.

I asked her to keep an eye out for Donna and tell her I had to run out to Stone Canyon on some urgent and unexpected business and that I'd call in the first chance I got. She gave me a big smile and an up-from-under stare and closed the door very gently.

I lit a cigarette and went back to the apartment to leave a note for Donna next to the telephone. Then I took a last look around and walked down one flight to the street, got into the car, and headed for Stone Canyon.

III

It was a quarter past five by the time I got out there. There was an especially nasty curve in the road just to the north of Yestone, and off on the left shoulder where the bend was sharpest, three department cars were drawn up in a bunch. A uniformed man was taking a smoke behind the wheel of the lead car; he looked up sharply as I made a U-turn and stopped behind the last car.

By the time I had cut off the motor and opened the door, he was standing there scowling at me. "Where d'ya think you're goin', Mac?"

"Sergeant Lindstrom telephoned me," I said, getting out onto the sparse sun-baked growth they call grass in California.

He ran the ball of a thumb lightly along one cheek and eyed me stonily from under the stiff brim of his campaign hat. "Your name Kane?"

"That's it."

He took the thumb off his face and used it to point. "Down there. They're waitin' for you. Better take a deep breath, Mac. You won't like what they show you."

I didn't say anything. I went past him and on around the department car. The ground fell away in what almost amounted to a forty-five-degree slope, and a hundred yards down the slope was level ground. Down there a knot of men were standing near the scorched ruins of what had been an automobile. It could have been Donna's Chevy or it could have been any other light job. From its condition and across the distance I couldn't tell.

It took some time and a good deal of care for me to work my way to the valley floor without breaking my neck. There were patches of scarred earth spaced out in a reasonably straight line all the way down the incline where the car had hit and bounced and hit again, over and over. Splinters of broken glass lay scattered about, and about halfway along was a twisted bumper and a section of grillwork. There was a good deal of brush around and it came in handy for hanging on while I found footholds. It was a tough place to get down, but the car at the bottom hadn't had any trouble making it.

A tall, slender, quiet-faced man in gray slacks and a matching sports shirt buttoned at the neck but without a tie was waiting for me. He nodded briefly and looked at me out of light blue eyes under thick dark brows.

"Are you Clay Kane?" It was a soft, pleasant voice, not a cop's voice at all.

I nodded, looking past him at the pile of twisted metal. The four men near it were looking my way, their faces empty of expression.

The quiet-faced man said, "I'm Chief Deputy Martell, out of Hollywood. They tell me it's your wife's car, but that your wife wasn't using it. Has she told you yet who was?"

"Not yet; no. She was out when I called the apartment, although I'd spoken to her only a few minutes before."

"Any idea where she might be?"

I shrugged. "Several, but I didn't have a chance to do any checking. The sergeant said you were in a hurry."

"I see . . . I think I'll ask you to take a quick glance at the body we took out of the car. It probably won't do much good, but you never know. I'd better warn you: it won't be pleasant."

"That's all right," I said. "I spent some time in the Pacific during the war. We opened up pillboxes with flamethrowers."

"That should help." He turned and moved off, skirting the wreckage, and I followed. A small khaki tarpaulin was spread out on the ground, bulged in the center where it covered an oblong object. Not a very big object. I began to catch the acrid-sweetish odor of burned meat, mixed with the faint biting scent of gasoline.

Martell bent and took hold of a corner of the tarpaulin. He said flatly, "Do the best you can, Mr. Kane," and flipped back the heavy canvas.

It looked like nothing human. Except for the contours of legs and arms, it could have been a side of beef hauled out of a burning barn. Where the face had been was a smear of splintered and charred bone that bore no resemblance to a face. No hair, no clothing except for the remains of a woman's shoe still clinging to the left foot; only blackened, flame-gnawed flesh and bones. And over it all the stench of a charnel house.

I backed away abruptly and clamped down on my teeth, fighting back a wave of nausea. Martell allowed the canvas to fall back into place. "Sorry, Mr. Kane. We can't overlook any chances."

"It's all right," I mumbled.

"You couldn't identify . . . her?"

I shuddered. "Christ, no! Nobody could!"

"Let's have a look at the car."

I circled the wreck twice. It had stopped right-side up, the tires flat, the hood ripped to shreds, the engine shoved halfway into the front seat. The steering wheel was snapped off and the dashboard appeared to have been worked over with a sledgehammer. Flames had eaten away the upholstery and blackened the entire interior.

It was Donna's car; no doubt about that. The license plates showed the right number and a couple of rust spots on the right rear fender were as I remembered them. I said as much to Chief Deputy Martell and he nodded briefly and went over to say something I couldn't hear to the four men.

He came back to me after a minute or two. "I've a few questions. Nothing more for you down here. Let's go back upstairs."

He was holding something in one hand. It was a woman's bag: blue suede, small, with a gold clasp shaped like a question mark. I recognized it and my mouth felt a little dry.

It was a job getting up the steep slope. The red loam was dry and crumbled under my feet. The sun was still high enough to be hot on my back and my hands were sticky with ooze from the sagebrush.

Martell was waiting for me when I reached the road. I sat down on the front bumper of one of the department cars and shook the loose dirt out of my shoes, wiped most of the sage ooze off my palms, and brushed the knees of my trousers. The man in the green khaki uniform was still behind the wheel of the lead car but he wasn't smoking now.

I followed the sheriff into the front seat of a black-and-white Mercury with a buggy-whip aerial at the rear bumper and a radio phone on the dash. He lit up a small yellow cigar in violation of a fire-hazard signboard across the road from us. He dropped the match into the dashboard ashtray and leaned back in the seat and bounced the suede bag lightly on one of his broad palms.

IV

He said, "One of the boys found this in a clump of sage halfway down the slope. You ever see it before?"

"My wife has one like it."

He cocked an eye at me. "Not like it, Mr. Kane. This is hers. Personal effects, identification cards, all that. No doubt at all."

". . . OK."

"And that's your wife's car?"

"Yeah."

"But you say it's not your wife who was in it?"

"No question about it," I said firmly.

"When did you see her last?"

"Around nine-thirty this morning."

"But you talked to her later, I understand."

"That's right."

"What time?"

"A few minutes past four this afternoon."

He puffed out some blue smoke. "Sure it was your wife?"

"If I wouldn't know, who would?"

His strong face was thoughtful, his blue eyes distant. "Mrs. Kane's a singer, I understand."

"That's right," I told him. "Uses her maiden name: Donna Collins."

He smiled suddenly, showing good teeth. "Oh, sure. The missus and I heard her on the *Dancing in Velvet* program last week. She's good — and a mighty lovely young woman, Mr. Kane."

I muttered something polite. He put some cigar ash into the tray and leaned back again and said, "They must pay her pretty good, being a radio star."

"Not a star," I explained patiently. "Just a singer. It pays well, of course — but nothing like the top names pull down. However, Donna's well fixed in her own right; her father died a while back and left her what amounts to quite a bit of money . . . Look, Sheriff, what's the point of keeping me here? I don't know who the dead woman is, but since she was using my wife's car, the one to talk to is Mrs. Kane. She's bound to be home by this time; why not ride into town with me and ask her?"

He was still holding the handbag. He put it down on the seat between us and looked off toward the blue haze that marked the foothills south of Burbank. "Your wife's not home, Mr. Kane," he said very quietly.

A vague feeling of alarm stirred within me. "How do you know that?" I demanded.

He gestured at the two-way radio. "The office is calling your apartment at ten-minute intervals. As soon as Mrs. Kane answers her phone, I'm to get word. I haven't got it yet."

I said harshly, "What am I supposed to do — sit here until they call you?"

He sighed a little and turned sideways on the seat far enough to cross his legs. The light blue of his eyes was frosted over now, and his jaw was a grim line.

"I'm going to have to talk to you like a Dutch uncle, Mr. Kane. As you saw, we've got a dead woman down there as the result of what, to all intents and purposes, was an unfortunate accident. Everything points to the victim's being your wife except for two things, one of them your insistence that you spoke to her on the phone nearly two hours *after* the accident. That leaves us wondering — and with any one of several answers. One is that you're lying; that you didn't speak to her at all. If that's the right answer, we can't figure out the reason behind it. Two: your wife loaned a friend the car. Three: somebody lifted it from where it was parked. Four: you drove up here with her, knocked her in the head, and let the car roll over the edge."

"Of all the goddamn — !"

He held up a hand, cutting me off. "Let's take 'em one at a time. I can't see any reason, even if you murdered her, why you'd say your wife telephoned you afterwards. So until and unless something turns up to show us why you'd lie about it, I'll have to believe she did make that call. As for her loaning the car, that could very well have happened, only it doesn't explain why she's missing now. This business of the car's being stolen doesn't hold up, because the key was still in the ignition and in this case."

He took a folded handkerchief from the side pocket of his coat and opened it. A badly scorched leather case came to light, containing the ignition and trunk keys. The rest of the hooks were empty. I sat there staring at it, feeling my insides slowly and painfully contracting.

"Recognize it?" Martell asked softly.

I nodded numbly. "It's Donna's."

He picked up the handbag with his free hand and thrust it at me. "Take a look through it."

Still numb, I released the clasp and pawed through the contents. A small green-leather wallet containing seventy or eighty dollars and the usual identification cards, one of them with my office, address, and phone number. Lipstick, compact, mirror, comb, two initialed handkerchiefs, a few hairpins. The French enamel cigarette case and matching lighter I'd given her on her twenty-fifth birthday three months ago. Less than a dollar in change.

That was all. Nothing else. I shoved the stuff back in the bag and closed the clasp with stiff fingers and sat there looking dully at Martell.

He was refolding the handkerchief around the key case. He returned it to his pocket carefully, took the cigar out of his mouth and inspected the glowing tip.

"Your wife wear any jewelry, Mr. Kane?" he asked casually.

I nodded. "A wristwatch. Her wedding and engagement rings."

"We didn't find them. No jewelry at all."

"You wouldn't," I said. "Whoever that is down there, she's not Donna Kane."

He sat there and looked out through the windshield and appeared to be thinking. He wore no hat and there was a strong sprinkling of gray in his hair and a bald spot about the size of a silver dollar at the crown. There was a network of fine wrinkles at the corners of his eyes, as there so often is in men who spend a great deal of time in the sun. He looked calm and confident and competent and not at all heroic.

Presently he said, "That phone call. No doubt at all that it was your wife?"

"None."

"Recognized her voice, eh?"

I frowned. "Not so much that. It was more what she said. You know, certain expressions nobody else'd use. Pet name — you know."

His lips quirked and I felt my cheeks burn. He said, "Near as you can remember, tell me about that call. If she sounded nervous or upset — the works."

I put it all together for him, forgetting nothing. Then I went on about stopping off at the apartment, what I'd found there and what Ruth Feldman had said. Martell didn't interrupt, only sat there drawing on his cigar and soaking it all in.

After I was finished, he didn't move or say anything for what seemed a long time. Then he leaned forward and ground out the stub of the cigar and put a hand in the coat pocket next to me and brought out one of those flapped bags women use for formal dress, about the size of a business envelope and with an appliquéd design worked into it. Wordlessly he turned back the flap and let a square gold compact and matching lipstick holder slide out into the other hand.

"Ever see these before, Kane?"

I took them from him. His expression was impossible to read. There was nothing unusual about the lipstick tube, but the compact had a circle of brilliants in one corner and the initials H.W. in the circle.

I handed them back. "New to me, Sheriff."

He was watching me closely. "Think a minute. This can be important. Either you or your wife know a woman with the initials H.W.?"

". . . Not that I . . . Helen? Helen! Sure; Helen Wainhope! Dave Wainhope's wife." I frowned. "I don't get it, Sheriff."

He said slowly, "We found this bag a few feet from the wreck. Any idea how it might have gotten there?"

"Not that I can think of."

"How well do you know these Wainhopes?"

"About as well as you get to know anybody. Dave is business manager for some pretty prominent radio people. A producer, couple of directors, seven or eight actors that I know of."

"You mean he's an agent?"

"Not that. These are people who make big money but can't seem to hang on to it. Dave collects their checks, puts 'em on an allowance, pays their bills, and invests the rest. Any number of men in that line around town."

"How long have you known them?"

"Dave and Helen? Two, three years. Shortly after I got out here. As a matter of fact, he introduced me to Donna. She's one of his clients."

"The four of you go out together?"

"Now and then; sure."

"In your wife's car?"

". . . I see what you're getting at. You figure Helen might have left her bag there. Not a chance, Sheriff. We always used Dave's Cadillac. Helen has a Pontiac convertible."

"When did you see them last?"

"Well, I don't know about Donna, but I had lunch with Dave . . . let's see . . . day before yesterday. He has an office in the Taft Building."

"Where do they live?"

"Over on one of those little roads off Beverly Glen. Not far from here, come to think about it."

With slow care he pushed the compact and lipstick back in the folder and dropped it into the pocket it had come out of. "Taft Building, hunh?" he murmured. "Think he's there now?"

I looked at my strapwatch. Four minutes till six. "I doubt it, Sheriff. He should be home by this time."

"You know the exact address?"

"Well, it's on Angola, overlooking the southern tip of the Reservoir. A good-sized redwood ranch house on the hill there. It's the only house within a couple miles. You can't miss it."

He leaned past me and swung open the door. "Go on home, Kane. Soon as your wife shows up, call the station and leave word for me. I may call you later."

"What about her car?"

He smiled without humor. "Nobody's going to swipe it. Notify your insurance agent in the morning. But I still want to talk to Mrs. Kane."

I slid out and walked back to my car. As I started the motor, the black-and-white Mercury made a tight turn on screaming tires and headed north. I pulled back onto the road and tipped a hand at the deputy. He glared at me over the cigarette he was lighting.

I drove much too fast all the way back to Hollywood.

V

She wasn't there.

I snapped the switch that lit the end-table lamps flanking the couch and walked over to the window and stood there for a few minutes, staring down into Fountain Avenue. At seven o'clock it was still light outside. A small girl on roller skates scooted by, her sun-bleached hair flying. A tall, thin number in a pale blue sports coat and dark glasses got leisurely out of a green convertible with a wolf tail tied to the radiator emblem and sauntered into the apartment building across the street.

A formless fear was beginning to rise within me. I knew now that it had been born at four-thirty when I stopped off on my way to Stone Canyon and found the apartment empty. Seeing the charred body an hour later had strengthened that fear, even though I knew the dead woman couldn't be Donna. Now that I had come home and found the place deserted, the fear was crawling into my throat, closing it to the point where breathing seemed a conscious effort.

Where was Donna?

I lit a cigarette and began to pace the floor. Let's use a little logic on this, Kane. You used to be a top detective-story writer; let's see you go to work on this the way one of your private eyes would operate.

All right, we've got a missing woman to find. To complicate matters, the missing woman's car was found earlier in the day with a dead woman at the wheel. Impossible to identify her, but we know it's not the one we're after because *that* one called her husband *after* the accident.

Now, since your wife's obviously alive, Mr. Kane, she's missing for one of two reasons: either she can't come home or she doesn't want to. "Can't" would mean she's being held against her will; we've nothing to indicate *that.* That leaves the possibility of her not wanting to come home. What reason would a woman have for staying away from her husband? The more likely one would be that she was either sore at him for something or had left him for another man.

I said a short ugly word and threw my cigarette savagely into the fireplace. Donna would never pull a stunt like that! Hell, we'd only been married a few months and still as much in love as the day the knot was tied.

Yeah? How do you know? A lot of guys kid themselves into thinking the same thing, then wake up one morning and find the milkman has taken over. Or they find some hot love letters tied in blue ribbon and shoved under the mattress.

I stopped short. It was an idea. Not love letters, of course; but there might be something among her personal files that could furnish a lead. It was about as faint a possibility as they come, but at least it would give me something to do.

The big bottom drawer of her desk in the bedroom was locked. I remembered that she carried the key in the same case with those to the apartment and the car, so I used the fireplace poker to force the lock. Donna would raise hell about that when she got home, but I wasn't going to worry about that now.

There was a big manila folder inside, crammed with letters, tax returns, receipted bills, bankbooks, and miscellaneous papers; I dumped them out and began to paw through the collection. A lot of the stuff had come from Dave Wainhope's office, and there were at least a dozen letters signed by him explaining why he was sending her such-and-such.

The phone rang suddenly. I damned near knocked the chair over getting to it. It was Chief Deputy Martell.

"Mrs. Kane show up?"

"Not yet. No."

He must have caught the disappointment in my voice. It was there to catch. He said, "That's funny . . . Anyway, the body we found in that car wasn't her."

"I told you that. Who was it?"

"This Helen Wainhope. We brought the remains into the Georgia Street Hospital and her husband made the ID about fifteen minutes ago."

I shivered, remembering. "How could he?"

"There was enough left of one of her shoes. That and the compact did the trick."

"He tell you why she was driving my wife's car?"

Martell hesitated. "Not exactly. He said the two women had a date in town for today. He didn't know what time, but Mrs. Wainhope's car was on the fritz, so the theory is that your wife drove out there and picked her up."

"News to me," I said.

He hesitated again. ". . . Any bad blood between your wife and . . . and Mrs. Wainhope?"

"That's a hell of a question!"

"You want to answer it?" he said quietly.

"You bet I do! They got along fine!"

"If you say so." His voice was mild. "I just don't like this coincidence of Mrs. Kane's being missing at the same time her car goes off a cliff with a friend in it."

"I don't care about that. I want my wife back."

He sighed. "OK. Give me a description and I'll get out an all-points on her."

I described Donna to him at length and he took it all down and said he'd be in touch with me later. I put back the receiver and went into the living room to make myself a drink. I hadn't eaten a thing since one o'clock that afternoon, but I was too tightened up with worry to be at all hungry.

Time crawled by. I finished my drink while standing at the window, put together a second, and took it back into the bedroom and started through the papers from Donna's desk. At eight-fifteen the phone rang.

"Clay? This is Dave—Dave Wainhope." His voice was flat and not very steady.

I said, "Hello, Dave. Sorry to hear about Helen." It sounded pretty lame, but it was the best I could do at the time.

"You know about it then?"

"Certainly I know about it. It was Donna's car, remember?"

"Of course, Clay." He sounded very tired. "I guess I'm not thinking too clearly. I called you about something else."

"Yeah?"

"Look, Clay, it's none of my business, I suppose. But what's wrong between you and Donna?"

I felt my jaw sag a little. "Who said anything was wrong?"

"All I know is, she was acting awfully strange. She wanted all the ready cash I had on hand, no explanation, no—"

My fingers were biting into the receiver. "Wait a minute!" I shouted. "Dave, listen to me! You *saw* Donna?"

"That's what I'm trying to tell you. She—"

"When?"

". . . Why, not ten minutes ago. She—"

"Where? Where was she? Where did you see her?"

"Right here. At my office." He was beginning to get excited himself. "I stopped by on my way from the Georgia—"

I cut him off. "Christ, Dave, I've been going nuts! I've been looking for her since four-thirty this afternoon. What'd she say? What kind of trouble is she in?"

"I don't know. She wouldn't tell me anything—just wanted money quick. No checks. I thought maybe you and she had had a fight or something. I had around nine hundred in the safe; I gave it all to her and she beat—"

I shook the receiver savagely. "But she must have said *something!* She wouldn't just leave without . . . you know . . ."

"She said she sent you a letter earlier in the day."

I dropped down on the desk chair. My hands were shaking and my mouth was dry. "A letter," I said dully. "A letter. Not in person, not even a phone call. Just a letter."

By this time Dave was making comforting sounds. "I'm sure it's nothing serious, Clay. You know how women are. The letter'll probably tell you where she is and you can talk her out of it."

I thanked him and hung up and sat there and stared at my thumb. For some reason I felt even more depressed than before. I couldn't understand why Donna wouldn't have turned to me if she was in trouble. That was always a big thing with us: all difficulties had to be shared . . .

I went into the kitchen and made myself a couple of cold salami sandwiches and washed them down with another highball. At nine-twenty I telephoned the Hollywood substation to let Martell know what Dave Wainhope had told me. Whoever answered said the chief deputy was out and to call back in an hour. I tried to leave a message on what it was about, but was told again to call back and got myself hung up on.

About ten minutes later the buzzer from downstairs sounded. I pushed the button and was standing in the hall door when a young fellow in a postman's gray uniform showed up with a special-delivery letter. I signed for it and closed the door and leaned there and ripped open the envelope.

A single sheet of dime-store paper containing a few neatly typed lines and signed in ink in Donna's usual scrawl.

> Clay darling:
>
> I'm terribly sorry, but something that happened a long time ago has come back to plague me and I have to get away for a few days. Please don't try to find me, I'll be all right as long as you trust me.
>
> You know I love you so much that I won't remain away a day longer than I have to. Please don't worry, darling, I'll explain everything the moment I get back.
>
> All my love,
> *Donna*

And that was that. Nothing that I could get my teeth into; no leads, nothing to cut away even a small part of my burden of concern. I walked into the bedroom with no spring in my step and dropped the letter on the desk and reached for the phone. But there was no point to that. Martell wouldn't be back at the station yet.

Maybe I had missed something. Maybe the envelope was a clue? A clue to what? I looked at it. Carefully. The postmark was Hollywood. That meant it had gone through the branch at Wilcox and Selma. At five-twelve that afternoon. At five-twelve I was just about pulling up behind those department cars out on Stone Canyon Road. She would have had to mail it at the post office instead of a drop box for me to get it four hours later.

No return address, front or back, as was to be expected. Just a cheap envelope, the kind you pick up at Woolworth's or Kress's. My name and the address neatly typed. The *e* key was twisted very slightly to the right and the *t* was tilted just far enough to be noticeable if you looked at it long enough.

I let the envelope drift out of my fingers and stood there staring down at Donna's letter. My eyes wandered to the other papers next to it . . .

I said, "Jesus Christ!" You could spend the next ten years in church and never say it more devoutly than I did at that moment. My eyes were locked to one of the letters David Wainhope had written to Donna—and in its typewritten lines two individual characters stood out like bright and shining beacons: a tilted *t* and a twisted *e!*

VI

It took some time—I don't know how much—before I was able to do any straight-line thinking. The fact that those two letters had come out of the same typewriter opened up so many possible paths to the truth behind Donna's disappearance that—well, I was like the mule standing between two stacks of hay.

Finally I simply turned away and walked into the living room and poured a good half-inch of bonded bourbon into a glass and drank it down like water after an aspirin. I damned near strangled on the stuff; and by the time I stopped gasping for air and wiping the tears out of my eyes, I was ready to do some thinking.

Back at the desk again, I sat down and picked up the two sheets of paper. A careful comparison removed the last lingering doubt that they had come out of the same machine. Other points began to fall into place:

the fact that the typing in Donna's letter had been done by a professional. You can always tell by the even impression of the letters, instead of the dark-light-erasure-strike-over touch you find in an amateur job. And I knew that Donna had never used a typewriter in her life!

All right, what did it mean? On the surface, simply that somebody had typed the letter for Donna, and at Dave Wainhope's office. It had to be his office, for he would hardly write business letters at home—and besides I was pretty sure Dave was strictly a pen-and-pencil man himself.

Now what? Well, since it was typed in Dave's office, but not by Dave or Donna, it would indicate Dave's secretary had done the work. Does that hold up? It's got to hold up, friend; no one else works in that office but Dave and his secretary.

Let's kind of dig into that a little. Let's say that Donna dropped in on Dave earlier in the afternoon, upset about something. Let's say that Dave is out, so Donna dictates a note to me and the secretary types it out. Very simple . . . But is it?

No.

And here's why. Here are the holes: first, the note is on dime-store paper, sent in a dime-store envelope. Dave wouldn't have that kind of stationery in his office—not a big-front guy like Dave. OK, stretch it all the way out; say that Donna had brought her own paper and had the girl use it. You still can't tell me Dave's secretary wouldn't have told her boss about it when he got back to the office. And if she told *him*, he would certainly have told *me* during our phone conversation.

But none of those points compares with the biggest flaw of them all: why would Donna have *anyone* type the letter for her when a handwritten note would do just as well—especially on a very private and personal matter like telling your husband you're in trouble?

I got up and walked down the room and lit a cigarette and looked out the window without seeing anything. A small voice in the back of my mind said, "If all this brain work of yours is right, you know what it adds up to, don't you, pal?"

I knew. Sure, I knew. It meant that Donna Kane was a threat to somebody. It meant that she was being held somewhere; that she had been forced to sign a note to keep me from reporting her disappearance to the cops until whoever was responsible could make a getaway.

It sounded like a bad movie, and I tried hard to make myself believe that's all it was. But the more I dug into it, the more I went over the results of my reasoning, the more evident it became that there was no other explanation.

You do only one thing in a case like that. I picked up the phone and called Martell again. He was still out. I took a stab at telling the desk sergeant, or whoever it was at the other end, what was going on. But it sounded so complex and confused, even to me, that he finally stopped me. "Look, neighbor, call back in about fifteen, twenty minutes. Martell's the man you want to talk to." He hung up before I could give him an argument.

His advice was good and I intended to take it. Amateur detectives usually end up with both feet stuck in their esophagus. This was a police job. My part in it was to let them know what I'd found out, then get out of their way.

That secretary would know. She was in this up to the hilt. I had seen her a few times: a dark-haired girl, quite pretty, a little on the small side but built right. Big blue eyes; I remembered that. Quiet. A little shy, if I remembered right. What was her name? Nora. Nora something. Campbell? Kenton? No. Kemper? That was it: Nora Kemper.

I found her listed in the Central District phone book. In the 300 block on North Hobart, a few doors below Beverly Boulevard. I knew the section. Mostly apartment houses along there. Nothing fancy, but a long way from being a slum. The right neighborhood for private secretaries. As I remembered, she had been married but was now divorced.

I looked at my watch. Less than five minutes since I'd called the sheriff's office. I thought of Donna tied and gagged and stuck away in, say, the trunk of some car. It was more than I could take.

I was on my way out the door when I thought of something else. I went back into the bedroom and dug under a pile of sports shirts in the bottom dresser drawer and took out the gun I'd picked up in San Francisco the year before. It was a Smith & Wesson .38, the model they called the Terrier. I made sure it was loaded, shoved it under the waistband of my slacks in the approved pulp-magazine style, and left the apartment.

VII

It was a quiet street, bordered with tall palms, not much in the way of streetlights. Both curbs were lined with cars, and I had to park half a block down and across the way from the number I wanted.

I got out and walked slowly back through the darkness. I was a little jittery, but that was to be expected. Radio music drifted from a bungalow court and a woman laughed thinly. A couple passed me, arm in arm, the man in an army officer's uniform. I didn't see anyone else around.

The number I was after belonged to a good-sized apartment building, three floors and three separate entrances. Five stone steps, flanked by a wrought-iron balustrade, up to the front door. A couple of squat Italian cypresses in front of the landing.

There was no one in the foyer. In the light from a yellow bulb in a ceiling fixture I could make out the names above the bell buttons. Nora Kemper's apartment was 205. Automatically I reached for the button, then hesitated. There was no inner door to block off the stairs. Why not go right on up and knock on her door? No warning, no chance for her to think up answers before I asked the questions.

I walked up the carpeted steps to the second floor and on down the hall. It was very quiet. Soft light from overhead fixtures glinted on pale green walls and dark green doors. At the far end of the hall, a large window looked out on the night sky.

Number 205 was well down the corridor. No light showed under the edge of the door. I pushed a thumb against a small pearl button set flush in the jamb and heard a single flatted bell note.

Nothing happened. No answering steps, no questioning voice. A telephone rang twice in one of the other apartments and a car horn sounded from the street below.

I tried the bell again, with the same result. Now what? Force the door? No sense to that, and besides, illegal entry was against the law. I wouldn't know how to go about it anyway.

She would have to come home eventually. Thing to do was stake out somewhere and wait for her to show up. If she didn't arrive within the next half hour, say, then I would hunt up a phone and call Martell.

I went back to the stairs and was on the point of descending to the first floor when I heard the street door close and light steps against the tile flooring down there. It could be Nora Kemper. Moving silently, I took the steps to the third floor and stood close to the wall where the light failed to reach.

A woman came quickly up the steps to the second floor. From where I stood I couldn't see her face clearly, but her build and the color of her hair were right. She was wearing a light coat and carrying a white drawstring bag, and she was in a hurry. She turned in the right direction, and the moment she was out of sight I raced back to the second floor.

It was Nora Kemper, all right. She was standing in front of the door to 205 and digging into her bag for the key. I had a picture of her getting inside and closing the door and refusing to let me in.

I said, "Hold it a minute, Miss Kemper."

She jerked her head up and around, startled. I moved toward her slowly. When the light reached my face, she gasped and made a frantic jab into the bag, yanked out her keys, and tried hurriedly to get one of them into the lock.

I couldn't afford to have that door between us. I brought the gun out and said sharply, "Stay right there. I want to talk to you."

The hand holding the keys dropped limply to her side. She began to back away, retreating toward the dead end of the corridor. Her face gleamed whitely, set in a frozen mask of fear.

She stopped only when she could go no farther. Her back pressed hard against the wall next to the window, her eyes rolled, showing the whites.

Her voice came out in a ragged whisper. "Wha-what do you want?"

I said, "You know me, Miss Kemper. You know who I am. What are you afraid of?"

Her eyes wavered, dropped to the .38 in my hand. "The gun. I—"

"Hunh-uh," I said. "You were scared stiff before I brought it out. Recognizing me is what scared you. Why?"

Her lips shook. Against the pallor of her skin they looked almost black. "I don't know what . . . Don't stand . . . Please. Let me go."

She tried to squeeze past me. I reached out and grabbed her by one arm. She gasped and jerked away—and her open handbag fell to the floor, spilling the contents.

She started after them, but I was there ahead of her. I had seen something—something that shook me like a solid right to the jaw.

Three of them, close together on the carpet. I scooped them up and straightened and jerked Nora Kemper around to face me. I shoved my open hand in front of her eyes, letting her see what was in it.

"Keys!" I said hoarsely. "Take a good look, lady! They came out of your purse. The keys to my apartment, my mailbox. *My wife's keys!*"

A small breeze would have knocked her down. I took a long look at her stricken expression, then I put a hand on her shoulder and pushed her ahead of me down the hall. I didn't have to tell her what I wanted: she unlocked the door and we went in.

When the lights were on, she sank down on the couch. I stood over her, still holding the gun. My face must have told her what was going on behind it, for she began to shake uncontrollably.

I said, "I'm a man in the dark, Miss Kemper. I'm scared, and when I get scared I get mad. If you don't want a mouth full of busted teeth, tell me one thing: *where is my wife?*"

She had sense enough to believe me. She gasped and drew back. "He didn't tell me," she wailed. "I only did what he told me to do, Mr. Kane."

"What *who* told you?"

"David. Mr. Wainhope."

I breathed in and out. "You wrote that letter?"

". . . Yes."

"Did you see my wife sign it?"

She wet her lips. "She wasn't there. David signed it. There are samples of her signature at the office. He copied from one of them."

I hadn't thought of that. "What's behind all this?"

"I—I don't know." She couldn't take her eyes off the gun. "Really I don't, Mr. Kane."

"You know a hell of a lot more than I do," I growled. "Start at the beginning and give it to me. All of it."

She pushed a wick of black hair off her forehead. Some of the color was beginning to seep back into her cheeks, but her eyes were still clouded with fear.

"When I got back to the office from lunch this afternoon," she said, "David was out. He called me a little after three and told me to meet him at the corner of Fountain and Courtney. I was to take the Hollywood streetcar instead of a cab and wait for him there."

"Did he say why?"

"No. He sounded nervous, upset. I was there within fifteen minutes, but he didn't show up until almost a quarter to four."

"Go on," I said when she hesitated.

"Well, we went into an apartment building on Fountain. Dave took out some keys and used one of them to take mail out of a box with your name on it. Then he unlocked the inner door and we went up to your apartment. He had the key to it, too. He gave me the keys and we went into the bedroom. He told me to call you and what to say. Before that, though, he hunted up the vacuum cleaner and started it going. Then I talked to you on the phone."

I stared at her. "You did fine. The cleaner kept me from realizing it wasn't Donna's voice, and I suppose at one time or another Helen must've found out Donna called me 'Poopsie' and told Dave about it. Big laugh! What happened after that?"

Her hands were clenched in her lap, whitening the knuckles. Her small breasts rose and fell under quick shallow breathing. Fear had taken most of the beauty out of her face.

"Dave opened one of the letters he had brought upstairs," she said tonelessly, "and left it next to the phone. We went back downstairs and drove back to the office. On the way Dave stopped off and bought some cheap stationery. I used some of it to write that letter. He told me to mail it at the post office right away, then he walked out. I haven't seen him since."

"Secretaries like you," I said sourly, "must take some finding. Whatever the boss says goes. You don't find 'em like that around the broadcasting studios."

Her head swung up sharply. "I happen to love Dave . . . and he loves me. We're going to be married — now that he's free."

My face ached from keeping my expression unchanged. "How nice for both of you. Only he's got a wife, remember?"

She looked at me soberly. "Didn't you know about that?"

"About what?"

"Helen Wainhope. She was killed in an automobile accident this afternoon."

"When did you hear that?"

"David told me when he called in around three o'clock."

I let my eyes drift to the gun in my hand. There was no point in flashing it around any longer. I slid it into one of my coat pockets and fished a cigarette out and used a green and gold table lighter to get it going. I said, "And all this hocus-pocus about signing my wife's name to a phony letter, calling me on the phone and pretending to be her — all this on the same day Dave Wainhope's wife dies — and you don't even work up a healthy curiosity? I find that hard to believe, Miss Kemper. You must have known he was into something way over his head."

"I love David," she said simply.

I blew out some smoke. "Love isn't good for a girl like you. Leave it alone. It makes you stupid. Good night, Miss Kemper."

She didn't move. A tear began to trace a jagged curve along her left cheek. I left her sitting there and went over to the door and out, closing it softly behind me.

VIII

At eleven o'clock at night there's not much traffic on Sunset, especially when you get out past the bright two-mile stretch of the Strip with its Technicolor neons, its plush nightclubs crowded with columnists and casting-couch starlets and vacationing Iowans, its modernistic stucco buildings with agents' names in stylized lettering across the fronts. I drove by them and dropped on down into Beverly Hills, where most of the homes were dark at this hour, through Brentwood, where a lot of stars hide out in big estates behind hedges and burglar alarms, and finally all that was behind me and I turned off Sunset onto Beverly Glen

Boulevard and followed the climbing curves up into the foothills to the north.

The pattern was beginning to form. Dave Wainhope had known his wife was dead long before Sheriff Martell drove out to break the news to him. I saw that as meaning one thing: he must have had a hand in that "accident" on Stone Canyon Road. He could have driven out there with Helen, then let the car roll over the lip of the canyon with her in it. The motive was an old, old one: in love with another woman and his wife in the way.

That left only Donna's disappearance to account for. In a loose way I had that figured out too. She might have arrived at Dave's home at the wrong time. I saw her walking in and seeing too much and getting herself bound and gagged and tucked away somewhere while Dave finished the job. Why he had used Donna's car to stage the accident was something I couldn't fit in for sure, although Sheriff Martell had mentioned that Helen's car hadn't been working.

It added up — and in the way it added up was the proof that Donna was still alive. Even with the certainty that Dave Wainhope had coldbloodedly sent his wife plunging to a horrible death, I was equally sure he had not harmed Donna. Otherwise the obvious move would have been to place her in the car with Helen and drop them both over the edge. A nice clean job, no witnesses, no complications. Two friends on their way into town, a second of carelessness in negotiating a dangerous curve — and the funeral will be held Tuesday!

The more I thought of it, the more trouble I was having in fitting Dave Wainhope into the role of murderer at all. He was on the short side, thick in the waistline, balding, and with the round guileless face you find on some infants. As far as I knew he had never done anything more violent in his life than refuse to tip a waiter.

None of that proved anything, of course. If murders were committed only by people who looked the part, there would be a lot more pinochle played in homicide bureaus.

I turned off Beverly Glen at one of the narrow unpaved roads well up into the hills and began to zigzag across the countryside. The dank smell of the distant sea drifted in through the open windows, bringing with it the too-sweet odor of sage blossoms. The only sounds were the quiet purr of the motor and the rattle of loose stones against the underside of the fenders.

Then suddenly I was out in the open, with Stone Canyon Reservoir below me behind a border of scrub oak and manzanita and the sheen of moonlight on water. On my left, higher up, bulked a dark sharp-angled building of wood and stone and glass among flowering shrubs and bushes and more of the scrub oak. I followed a graveled driveway around a sweeping half-circle and pulled up alongside the porch.

I cut off the motor and sat there. Water gurgled in the radiator. With the headlights off, the night closed in on me. A bird said something in its sleep and there was a brief rustling among the bushes.

The house stood big and silent. Not a light showed. I put my hand into my pocket next to the gun and got out onto the gravel. It crunched under my shoes on my way to the porch. I went up eight steps and across the flagstones and turned the big brass doorknob.

Locked. I hadn't expected it not to be. I shrugged and put a finger against the bell and heard a strident buzz inside that seemed to rock the building.

No lights came on. I waited a minute or two, then tried again, holding the button down for what seemed a long time. All it did was use up some of the battery.

Now what? I tried to imagine David Wainhope crouched among the portières with his hands full of guns, but it wouldn't come off. The more obvious answer would be the right one: he simply wasn't home.

I wondered if he would be coming home at all. By now he might be halfway to Mexico, with a bundle of his clients' cash in the back seat and no intention of setting foot in the States ever again. He would have to get away before somebody found Donna Kane and turned her loose to tell what had actually happened. I had a sharp picture of her trussed up and shoved under one of the beds. It was all I needed.

I walked over to one of the porch windows and tried it. It was fastened on the inside. I took out my gun and tapped the butt hard against the glass. It shattered with a sound like the breaking up of an ice jam. I reached through and turned the catch and slid the frame up far enough for me to step over the sill.

Nobody else around. I moved through the blackness until I found an arched doorway and a light switch on the wall next to that.

I was in a living room which ran the full length of the house. Modern furniture scattered tastefully about. Sponge-rubber easy chairs in pastel shades. An enormous wood-burning fireplace. Framed Greenwich Village smears grouped on one wall. A shiny black baby grand with a tasseled gold scarf across it and a picture in a leather frame of Helen Wainhope. Everything looked neat and orderly and recently dusted.

I walked on down the room and through another archway into a dining room. Beyond it was a hall into the back of the house, with three bedrooms, one of them huge, the others ordinary in size with a connecting bath. I went through all of them. The closets had nothing in them but clothing. There was nothing under the beds, not even a little honest dirt. Everything had a place and everything was in its place.

The kitchen was white and large, with all the latest gadgets. Off it was a service porch, with a refrigerator, a deep freeze big enough to hold a body (but without one in it), and a washing machine. The house was heated with gas, with a central unit under the house. No basement.

Donna was still missing.

I left the lights on and went outside and around the corner of the house to the three-car garage. The foldback doors were closed and locked, but a side entrance wasn't. One car inside: a gray Pontiac convertible I recognized as Helen's. Nobody in it and the trunk was locked. I gave the lid a halfhearted rap and said, "Donna? Are you in there?"

No answer. No wild drumming of heels, no thrashing about. No sound at all except the blood rushing through my veins, and I probably imagined that.

Right then I knew I was licked. He had hidden her somewhere else or he had taken her with him. That last made no sense at all, but then he probably wasn't thinking sensibly.

Nothing left but to call the sheriff and let him know how much I'd learned and how little I'd found. I should have done that long before this. I went back to the house to hunt up the telephone. I remembered seeing it on a nightstand in one of the bedrooms, and I walked slowly back along the hall to learn which one.

Halfway down I spotted a narrow door I had missed the first time. I opened it and a light went on automatically. A utility closet, fairly deep, shelves loaded with luggage and blankets, a couple of electric heaters stored away for use on the long winter nights. And that was all.

I was on the point of leaving when I noticed that a sizable portion of the flooring was actually a removable trapdoor. I bent down and tugged it loose and slid it to one side, revealing a cement-lined recess about five feet deep and a good eight feet square. Stone steps, four of them, very steep, went down into it. In there was the central gas furnace and a network of flat pipes extending in all directions. The only illumination came from the small naked bulb over my head, and at first I could see nothing beyond the unit itself.

My eyes began to get used to the dimness. Something else was down there on the cement next to the furnace. Something dark and shapeless . . . A pale oval seemed to swell and float up toward me.

"Donna!" I croaked. "My good God, it's Donna!"

I half fell down the stone steps and lifted the lifeless body into my arms. Getting back up those steps and along the hall to the nearest bedroom is something I would never remember.

And then she was on the bed and I was staring down at her. My heart seemed to leap once and shudder to a full stop, and a wordless cry tore at my throat.

The girl on the bed was Helen Wainhope!

IX

I once heard it said that a man's life is made up of many small deaths, the least of them being the final one. I stood there looking at the dead woman, remembering the charred ruins of another body beside a twisted heap of blackened metal, and in that moment a part of me stumbled and fell and whimpered and died.

The telephone was there, waiting. I looked at it for a long time. Then I took a slow uneven breath and shook my head to clear it and picked up the receiver.

"Put it down, Clay."

I turned slowly. He was standing in the doorway, holding a gun down low, his round face drawn and haggard.

I said, "You killed her, you son of a bitch."

He wet his lips nervously. "Put it down, Clay. I can't let you call the police."

It didn't matter. Not really. Nothing mattered anymore except that he was standing where I could reach him. I let the receiver drop back into place. "Like something left in the oven too long," I said. "That's how I have to remember her."

I started toward him. Not fast. I was in no hurry. The longer it lasted, the more I would like it.

He brought the gun up sharply. "Don't make me shoot you. Stay right there. Please, Clay."

I stopped. It took more than I had to walk into the muzzle of a gun. You have to be crazy, I guess, and I wasn't that crazy.

He began to talk, his tongue racing, the words spilling out. "I didn't kill Donna, Clay. It was an accident. You've got to believe that, Clay! I liked her; I always liked Donna. You know that."

I could feel my lips twisting into a crooked line. "Sure. You always liked Donna. You always liked me, too. Put down the gun, Dave."

He wasn't listening. A muscle twitched high up on his left cheek. "You've got to understand how it happened, Clay. It was quick like a nightmare. I want you to know about it, to understand that I didn't intend . . ."

There was a gun in my pocket. I thought of it and I nodded. "I'm listening, Dave."

His eyes flicked to the body on the bed, then back to me. They were tired eyes, a little wild, the whites bloodshot. "Not in here," he said. He moved to one side. "Go into the living room. Ahead of me. Don't do anything . . . foolish."

I went past him and on along the hall. He was close behind me, but not close enough. In the silence I could hear him breathing.

I sat down on a sponge-rubber chair without arms. I said, "I'd like a cigarette, Dave. You know, to steady my nerves. I'm very nervous right now. You know how it is. I'll just put my hand in my pocket and take one out. Will that be all right with you?"

He said, "Go ahead," not caring, not even really listening.

Very slowly I let my hand slide into the side pocket of my coat. His gun went on pointing at me. The muzzle looked as big as the Second Street tunnel. My fingers brushed against the grip of the .38. A knuckle touched the trigger guard and the chill feel was like an electric shock. His gun went on staring at me.

My hand came out again. Empty. I breathed a shallow breath and took a cigarette and my matches from behind my display handkerchief. My forehead was wet. Whatever heroes had, I didn't have it. I struck a match and lit the cigarette and blew out a long plume of smoke. My hand wasn't shaking as much as I had expected.

"Tell me about it," I said.

He perched on the edge of the couch across from me, a little round man in a painful blue suit, white shirt, gray tie, and brown pointed shoes. He had never been one to go in for casual dress like everyone else in Southern California. Lamplight glistened along his scalp below the receding hairline and the muscle in his cheek twanged spasmodically.

"You knew Helen," he said in a kind of faraway voice. "She was a wonderful woman. We were married twelve years, Clay. I must have been crazy. But I'm not making much sense, am I?" He tried to smile but it broke on him.

I blew out some more smoke and said nothing. He looked at the gun as though he had never seen it before, but he kept on pointing it at me.

"About eight months ago," he continued, "I made some bad investments with my own money. I tried to get it back by other investments, this time with Donna's money. It was very foolish of me. I lost that, too."

He shook his head with slow regret. "It was quite a large sum, Clay. But I wasn't greatly worried. Things would break right before long and I could put it back. And then Helen found out about it . . .

"She loved me, Clay. But she wouldn't stand for my dipping into Donna's money. She said unless I made good the shortage immediately she would tell Donna. If anything like that got out it would ruin me. I promised I would do it within two or three weeks."

He stopped there and the room was silent. A breeze came in at the open window and rustled the drapes.

"Then," David Wainhope said, "something else happened, something that ruined everything. This isn't easy for me to say, but . . . well, I was having an . . . affair with my secretary. Miss Kemper. A lovely girl. You met her."

"Yes," I said. "I met her."

"I thought we were being very—well, careful. But Helen is—was a smart woman, Clay. She suspected something and she hired a private detective. I had no idea, of course . . .

"Today, Helen called me at the office. I was alone; Miss Kemper was at lunch. Helen seemed very upset; she told me to get home immediately if I knew what was good for me. That's the way she put it: 'if you know what's good for you'!"

I said, "Uh-*hunh!*" and went on looking at the gun.

"Naturally, I went home at once. When I got here, Donna was just getting out of her car in front. Helen's convertible was also in the driveway, so I put my car in the garage and came into the living room. I was terribly upset, feeling that Helen was going to tell Donna about the money.

"They were standing over there, in front of the fireplace. Helen was furious; I had never seen her quite so furious before. She told me she was going to tell Donna everything. I pleaded with her not to. Donna, of course, didn't know what was going on.

"Helen told her about the shortage, Clay. Right there in front of me. Donna took it better than I'd hoped. She said she would have to get someone else to look after her affairs but that she didn't intend to press charges against me. That was when Helen really lost her temper.

"She said she was going to sue me for divorce and name Miss Kemper; that she had hired a private detective and he had given her a report that same morning. She started to tell me all the things the detective had told her. Right in front of Donna. I shouted for her to stop but she went right on. I couldn't stand it, Clay. I picked up the poker and I hit her. Just once, on the head. I didn't know what I was doing. It—it was like a reflex. She died on the floor at my feet."

I said, "What am I supposed to do—feel sorry for you?"

He looked at me woodenly. I might as well have spoken to the wall. "Donna was terribly frightened. I think she screamed, then she turned and ran out of the house. I heard her car start before I realized she would tell them I killed Helen.

"I ran out, shouting for her to wait, to listen to me. But she was already turning into the road. My car was in the garage, so I jumped into Helen's and went after her. I wasn't going to do anything to her, Clay; I just wanted her to understand that I hadn't meant to kill Helen, that it only happened that way.

"By the time we reached that curve on Stone Canyon I was close behind her. She was driving too fast and the car skidded on the turn and went over. I could hear it. All the way down I heard it. I'll never get that sound out of my mind."

I shivered and closed my eyes. There was no emotion in me anymore—only a numbness that would never really go away.

His unsteady voice went on and on. "She must have died instantly. The whole front of her face . . . My mind began to work fast. If I could make the police think it was my wife who had died in the accident, then I could hide Helen's body and nobody would know. That way Donna would be the one missing and they'd ask you questions, not me.

"The wreckage was saturated with gasoline. I—I threw a match into it. The fire couldn't hurt her, Clay. She was already dead. I swear it. Then I went up to the car and looked through it for something of Helen's I could leave near the scene.

"I came back here," he went on tonelessly, "and hid Helen's body. And all the time thoughts kept spinning through my head. Nobody must doubt that it was Helen in that car. If I could just convince you that Donna was not only alive *after* the accident, but that she had gone away . . .

"It came to me almost at once. I don't know from where. Maybe when staying alive depends on quick thinking, another part of your mind takes over. Miss Kemper would have to help me—"

I waved a hand, stopping him. "I know all about that. She told me. And for Christ's sake stop calling her Miss Kemper! You've been sleeping with her—remember?"

He was staring at me. "She told you? Why? I was sure—"

"You made a mistake," I said. "That note you signed Donna's name to was typed on the office machine. When I found that out I called on your Miss Kemper. She told me enough to get me started on the right track."

The gun was very steady in his hand now. Hollows deepened under his cheeks. "You—you told the police?"

"Certainly."

He shook his head. "No. You didn't tell them. They would be here now if you had." He stood up slowly, with a kind of quiet agony. "I'm sorry, Clay."

My throat began to tighten. "The hell with being sorry. I know. I'm the only one left. The only one who can put you in that gas chamber out at San Quentin. Now you make it number three."

His face seemed strangely at peace. "I've told you what happened. I wanted you to hear it from me, exactly the way it happened. I wanted you to know I couldn't deliberately kill anyone."

He turned the gun around and reached out and laid it in my hand. He said, "I suppose you had better call the police now."

I looked stupidly down at the gun and then back at him. He had forgotten me. He settled back on the couch and put his hands gently down on his knees and stared past me at the night sky beyond the windows.

I wanted to feel sorry for him. But I couldn't. It was too soon. Maybe some day I would be able to.

After a while I got up and went into the bedroom and put through the call.

1953

MICKEY SPILLANE

THE LADY SAYS DIE!

MICKEY (born FRANCIS MORRISON) SPILLANE (1918–2006) was born in Brooklyn, New York, and raised in a tough neighborhood in Elizabeth, New Jersey. He sold his first stories to the top American magazines at the age of seventeen, then switched to pulp magazines and comic books; he was one of the creators of superheroes Captain Marvel and Captain America. He took time out for World War II, in which he flew combat missions and trained pilots for the Air Force, then he returned to continue his writing career while also becoming a trampoline performer for Ringling Bros. and Barnum & Bailey circus and working with the Federal Bureau of Investigation to break up a narcotics ring.

Spillane created his most famous character, Mike Hammer, for a comic book, but when the publisher failed he converted the story and hero into a novel, *I, the Jury* (1947), which became a national phenomenon, selling many millions of copies, as did his next six books. At one time, his first seven books all ranked among the top-ten best-selling novels in U.S. history. While most critics savaged them, partly because of their relatively (for the time) graphic depictions of violence and references to sex, partly because of his avowed right-wing patriotism, readers loved him, and the objectivist philosopher Ayn Rand wrote of him admiringly, comparing reading his books to listening to a military band in a public park. Most of his early novels were made into motion pictures, including *I, the Jury* (1953), with Biff Elliot as Hammer; the noir classic *Kiss Me Deadly* (1955), with Ralph Meeker as Hammer; and *The Girl Hunters* (1963), in which Spillane himself played the detective. The Mystery Writers of America named him a Grand Master for lifetime achievement in 1995.

Although Spillane was a better novelist than short story writer, his name on a magazine cover was certain to increase circulation; he was eagerly pursued for new works and was often accommodating. "The Lady Says Die!" originally appeared in the October 1953 issue of *Manhunt,* the ultimate hard-boiled digest magazine of its time.

▪ ▪ ▪

THE STOCKY MAN handed his coat and hat to the attendant and went through the foyer to the main lounge of the club. He stood in the doorway for a scant second, but in that time his eyes had seen all that was to be seen; the chess game beside the windows, the foursome at cards, and the lone man at the rear of the room sipping a drink.

He crossed between the tables, nodding briefly to the card players, and went directly to the back of the room. The other man looked up from his drink with a smile. "Afternoon, Inspector. Sit down. Drink?"

"Hello, Dunc. Same as you're drinking."

Almost languidly, the fellow made a motion with his hand. The waiter nodded and left. The inspector settled himself in his chair with a sigh. He was a big man, heavy without being given to fat. Only his high shoes proclaimed him for what he was. When he looked at Chester Duncan he grimaced inwardly, envying him his poise and manner, yet not willing to trade him for anything.

Here, he thought smugly, *is a man who should have everything, yet has nothing. True, he has money and position, but the finest of all things, a family life, was denied him.* And with a brood of five in all stages of growth at home, the inspector felt that he had achieved his purpose in life.

The drink came and the inspector took his, sipping it gratefully. When he put it down he said, "I came to thank you for that, er . . . tip. You know, that was the first time I've ever played the market."

"Glad to do it," Duncan said. His hands played with the glass, rolling it around in his palms. His eyebrows shot up suddenly, as though he was amused at something. "I suppose you heard all the ugly rumors."

A flush reddened the inspector's face. "In an offhand way, yes. Some of them were downright ugly." He sipped his drink again and tapped a cigarette on the side table. "You know," he said, "if Walter Harrison's death hadn't been so definitely a suicide, you might be standing an investigation right now."

Duncan smiled slowly. "Come now, Inspector. The market didn't budge until after his death, you know."

"True enough. But rumor has it that you engineered it in some manner." He paused long enough to study Duncan's face. "Tell me, did you?"

"Why should I incriminate myself?"

"It's over and done with. Harrison leaped to his death from the window of a hotel room. The door was locked, and there was no possible way anyone could have gotten in that room to give him a push. No, we're quite satisfied that it was suicide, and everybody that ever came in contact with Harrison agrees that he did the world a favor when he died. However, there's still some speculation about you having a hand in things."

"Tell me, Inspector, do you really think I had the courage or the brains to oppose a man like Harrison, and force him to kill himself?"

The inspector frowned, then nodded. "As a matter of fact, yes. You *did* profit by his death."

"So did *you*." Duncan laughed.

"Ummmm."

"Though it's nothing to be ashamed about," Duncan added. "When Harrison died, the financial world naturally expected that the stocks he financed were no good and tried to unload. It so happened that I was one of the few who knew they were as good as gold and bought while I could. And, of course, I passed the word on to my friends. Somebody had might as well profit by the death of a . . . a rat."

Through the haze of the smoke, Inspector Early saw his face tighten around the mouth. He scowled again, leaning forward in his chair. "Duncan, we've been friends quite a while. I'm just cop enough to be curious and I'm thinking that our late Walter Harrison was cursing you just before he died."

Duncan twirled his glass around. "I've no doubt of it," he said. His eyes met the inspector's. "Would you really like to hear about it?"

"Not if it means your confessing to murder. If that has to happen, I'd much rather you spoke directly to the DA."

"Oh, it's nothing like that at all. No, not a bit, Inspector. No matter how hard they tried, they couldn't do a thing that would impair either my honor or reputation. You see, Walter Harrison went to his death through his own greediness."

The inspector settled back in his chair. The waiter came with drinks to replace the empties and the two men toasted each other silently.

"Some of this you probably know already, Inspector," Duncan said . . .

Nevertheless, I'll start at the beginning and tell you everything that happened. Walter Harrison and I met in law school. We were both young and not too studious. We had one thing in common and only one. Both of us were the products of wealthy parents who tried their best to spoil their children. Since we were the only ones who could afford certain—er—pleasures, we naturally gravitated to each other, though when I think back, even at that time, there was little true friendship involved.

It so happened that I had a flair for my studies, whereas Walter didn't give a damn. At examination time, I had to carry him. It seemed like a big joke at the time, but actually I was doing all the work while he was having his fling around town. Nor was I the only one he imposed upon in such a way. Many students, impressed with having his friendship, gladly took over his papers. Walter could charm the devil himself if he had to.

And quite often he had to. Many's the time he's talked his way out of spending a weekend in jail for some minor offense — and I've even seen him twist the dean around his little finger, so to speak. Oh, but I remained his loyal friend. I shared everything I had with him, including my women, and even thought it amusing when I went out on a date and met him, only to have him take my girl home.

In the last year of school the crash came. It meant little to me, because my father had seen it coming and got out with his fortune increased. Walter's father tried to stick it out and went under. He was one of the ones who killed himself that day.

Walter was quite stricken, of course. He was in a blue funk and got stinking drunk. We had quite a talk, and he was for quitting school at once, but I talked him into accepting the money from me and graduating. Come to think of it, he never did pay me back that money. However, it really doesn't matter.

After we left school I went into business with my father and took over the firm when he died. It was that same month that Walter showed up. He stopped in for a visit and wound up with a position, though at no time did he deceive me as to the real intent of his visit. He got what he came after and in a way it was a good thing for me. Walter was a shrewd businessman.

His rise in the financial world was slightly less than meteoric. He was much too astute to remain in anyone's employ for long, and with the Street talking about Harrison, the boy wonder of Wall Street, in every other breath, it was inevitable that he open up his own office. In a sense, we became competitors after that, but always friends.

Pardon me, Inspector, let's say that I was his friend, he never was mine. His ruthlessness was appalling at times, but even then he managed to charm his victims into accepting their lot with a smile. I for one know that he managed the market to make himself a cool million on a deal that left me gasping. More than once he almost cut the bottom out of my business, yet he was always in with a grin and a big hello the next day as if it had been only a tennis match he had won.

If you've followed his rise then you're familiar with the social side of his life. Walter cut quite a swath for himself. Twice, he was almost killed by irate husbands, and if he had been, no jury on earth would have convicted his murderer. There was the time a young girl killed herself rather than let her parents know that she had been having an affair with Walter and had been trapped. He was very generous about it. He offered her money to travel, her choice of doctors, and anything she wanted . . . except his name for her child. No, he wasn't ready to give his name away then. That came a few weeks later.

I was engaged to be married at the time. Adrianne was a girl I had loved from the moment I saw her, and there aren't words enough to tell how happy I was when she said she'd marry me. We spent most of our waking hours poring over plans for the future. We even selected a site for our house out on the Island and began construction. We were timing the wedding to coincide with the completion of the house, and if ever I was a man living in a dream world, it was then. My happiness was complete, as was Adrianne's, or so I thought. Fortune seemed to favor me with more than one smile at the time. For some reason my own career took a sudden spurt and whatever I touched turned to gold, and in no time the Street had taken to following me rather than Walter Harrison. Without realizing it, I turned several deals that had him on his knees, though I doubt if many ever realized it. Walter would never give up the amazing front he affected.

At this point Duncan paused to study his glass, his eyes narrowing. Inspector Early remained motionless, waiting for him to go on . . .

Walter came to see me, Duncan said. It was a day I shall never forget. I had a dinner engagement with Adrianne and invited him along. Now I know that what he did was done out of sheer spite, nothing else. At first I believed that it was my fault, or hers, never giving Walter a thought . . .

Forgive me if I pass over the details lightly, Inspector. They aren't very pleasant to recall. I had to sit there and watch Adrianne captivated by this charming rat to the point where I was merely a decoration in the chair opposite her. I had to see him join us day after day, night after night, then hear the rumors that they were seeing each other without me, then discover for myself that she was in love with him.

Yes, it was quite an experience. I had the idea of killing them both, then killing myself. When I saw that that could never solve the problem, I gave it up.

Adrianne came to me one night. She sat and told me how much she hated to hurt me, but she had fallen in love with Walter Harrison and wanted to marry him. What else was there to do? Naturally, I acted the part of a good loser and called off the engagement. They didn't wait long. A week later they were married and I was the laughingstock of the Street.

Perhaps time might have cured everything if things hadn't turned out the way they did. It wasn't very long afterwards that I learned of a break in their marriage. Word came that Adrianne had changed, and I knew for a fact that Walter was far from being true to her.

You see, now I realized the truth. Walter never loved her. He never loved anybody but himself. He married Adrianne because he wanted to hurt me more than anything else in the world. He hated me because I had something he lacked . . . happiness. It was something he searched after desperately himself and always found just out of reach.

In December of that year Adrianne took sick. She wasted away for a month and died. In the final moments, she called for me, asking me to forgive her; this much I learned from a servant of hers. Walter, by the way, was enjoying himself at a party when she died. He came home for the funeral and took off immediately for a sojourn in Florida with some attractive showgirl.

God, how I hated that man! I used to dream of killing him! Do you know, if ever my mind drifted from the work I was doing, I always pictured myself standing over his corpse with a knife in my hand, laughing my head off.

Every so often I would get word of Walter's various escapades, and they seemed to follow a definite pattern. I made it my business to learn more about him, and before long I realized that Walter was almost frenzied in his search to find a woman he could really love. Since he was a fabulously wealthy man, he was always suspicious of a woman wanting him more than his wealth, and this very suspicion always was the thing that drove a woman away from him.

It may seem strange to you, but regardless of my attitude, I saw him quite regularly. And equally strange, he never realized that I hated him so. He realized, of course, that he was far from popular in any quarter, but he never suspected me of anything else save a stupid idea of friendship. But having learned my lesson the hard way, he never got the chance to impose upon me again, though he never really had need to.

It was a curious thing, the solution I saw to my problem. It had been there all the time, I was aware of it being there, yet using the circumstances never occurred to me until the day I was sitting on my veranda reading a memo from my office manager. The note stated that Walter had pulled another coup in the market and had the Street rocking on its heels. It was one of those times when any variation in Wall Street reflected the economy of the country, and what he did was undermine the entire economic structure of the United States. It was with the greatest effort that we got back to normal without toppling, but in doing so a lot of places had to close up. Walter Harrison, however, had doubled the wealth he could never hope to spend anyway.

As I said, I was sitting there reading the note when I saw her behind the window in the house across the way. The sun was streaming in, reflecting the gold in her hair, making a picture of beauty so exquisite as to be unbelievable. A servant came and brought her a tray, and as she sat down to lunch I lost sight of her behind the hedges and the thought came to me of how simple it would all be.

I met Walter for lunch the next day. He was quite exuberant over his latest adventure, treating it like a joke.

I said, "Say, you've never been out to my place on the Island, have you?"

He laughed, and I noticed a little guilt in his eyes. "To tell you the truth," he said, "I would have dropped in if you hadn't built the place for Adrianne. After all . . ."

"Don't be ridiculous, Walter. What's done is done. Look, until things get back to normal, how about staying with me a few days. You need a rest after your little deal."

"Fine, Duncan, fine! Anytime you say."

"All right, I'll pick you up tonight."

We had quite a ride out, stopping at a few places for drinks and hashing over the old days at school. At any other time I might have laughed, but all those reminiscences had taken on an unpleasant air. When we reached the house I had a few friends in to meet the fabulous Walter Harrison, left him accepting their plaudits, and went to bed.

We had breakfast on the veranda. Walter ate with relish, breathing deeply of the sea air with animal-like pleasure. At exactly nine o'clock the sunlight flashed off the windows of the house behind mine as the servant threw them open to the morning breeze.

Then she was there. I waved and she waved back. Walter's head turned to look, and I heard his breath catch in his throat. She was lovely, her hair a golden cascade that tumbled around her shoulders. Her blouse was a radiant white that enhanced the swell of her breasts, a gleaming contrast to the smooth tanned flesh of her shoulders.

Walter looked like a man in a dream. "Lord, she's lovely!" he said. "Who is she, Dunc?"

I sipped my coffee. "A neighbor," I said lightly.

"Do you . . . do you think I could get to meet her?"

"Perhaps. She's quite young and just a little bit shy and it would be better to have her see me with you a few times before introductions are in order."

He sounded hoarse. His face had taken on an avid, hungry look. "Anything you say, but I have to meet her." He turned around with a grin. "By golly, I'll stay here until I do, too!"

We laughed over that and went back to our cigarettes, but every so often I caught him glancing back toward the hedge with that desperate expression creasing his face.

Being familiar with her schedule, I knew that we wouldn't see her again that day, but Walter knew nothing of this. He tried to keep away from the subject, yet it persisted in coming back. Finally he said, "Incidentally, just who is she?"

"Her name is Evelyn Vaughn. Comes from quite a well-to-do family."

"She here alone?"

"No, besides the servants she has a nurse and a doctor in attendance. She hasn't been quite well."

"Hell, she looks the picture of health."

"Oh, she is now," I agreed. I walked over and turned on the television and we watched the fights. For the sixth time a call came in for Walter, but his reply was the same. He wasn't going back to New York. I felt the anticipation in his voice, knowing why he was staying, and had to concentrate on the screen to keep from smiling.

Evelyn was there the next day and the next. Walter had taken to waving when I did, and when she waved back his face seemed to light up until it looked almost boyish. The sun had tanned him nicely and he pranced around like a colt, especially when she could see him. He pestered me with questions and received evasive answers. Somehow he got the idea that his importance warranted a visit from the house across the way. When I told him that to Evelyn neither wealth nor position meant a thing, he looked at me sharply to see if I was telling the truth. To have become what he was he had to be a good reader of faces, and he knew that it *was* the truth, beyond the shadow of a doubt.

So I sat there day after day watching Walter Harrison fall helplessly in love with a woman he hadn't met yet. He fell in love with the way she waved, until each movement of her hand seemed to be for him alone. He fell in love with the luxuriant beauty of her body, letting his eyes follow her as she walked to the water from the house, aching to be close to her. She would turn sometimes and see us watching, and wave.

At night he would stand by the window, not hearing what I said because he was watching her windows, hoping for just one glimpse of her, and often I would hear him repeating her name slowly, letting it roll off his tongue like a precious thing.

It couldn't go on that way. I knew it and he knew it. She had just come up from the beach and the water glistened on her skin. She laughed at something the woman said who was with her and shook her head back so that her hair flowed down her back.

Walter shouted and waved and she laughed again, waving back. The wind brought her voice to him and Walter stood there, his breath hot in my face. "Look here, Duncan, I'm going over and meet her. I can't stand this waiting. Good Lord, what does a guy have to go through to meet a woman?"

"You've never had any trouble before, have you?"

"Never like this!" he said. "Usually they're dropping at my feet. I haven't changed, have I? There's nothing repulsive about me, is there?"

I wanted to tell the truth, but I laughed instead. "You're the same as ever. It wouldn't surprise me if she was dying to meet you, too. I can tell you this . . . she's never been outside as much as since you've been here."

His eyes lit up boyishly. "Really, Dunc. Do you think so?"

"I think so. I can assure you of this, too. If she does seem to like you, it's certainly for yourself alone."

As crudely as the barb was placed, it went home. Walter never so much as glanced at me. He was lost in thought for a long time, then: "I'm going over there now, Duncan. I'm crazy about that girl. By God, I'll marry her if it's the last thing I do."

"Don't spoil it, Walter. Tomorrow, I promise you. I'll go over with you."

His eagerness was pathetic. I don't think he slept a wink that night. Long before breakfast, he was waiting for me on the veranda; we ate in silence, each minute an eternity for him. He turned repeatedly to look over the hedge, and I caught a flash of worry when she didn't appear.

Tight little lines had appeared at the corners of his eyes, and he said, "Where is she, Dunc? She should be there by now, shouldn't she?"

"I don't know," I said. "It does seem strange. Just a moment." I rang the bell on the table and my housekeeper came to the door. "Have you seen the Vaughns, Martha?" I asked her.

She nodded sagely. "Oh, yes, sir. They left very early this morning to go back to the city."

Walter turned to me. "Hell!"

"Well, she'll be back," I assured him.

"Damn it, Dunc, that isn't the point!" He stood up and threw his napkin on the seat. "Can't you realize that I'm in love with the girl? I can't wait for her to get back!"

His face flushed with frustration. There was no anger, only the crazy hunger for the woman. I held back my smile. It happened. It happened the way I planned for it to happen. Walter Harrison had fallen so deeply in love, so truly in love, that he couldn't control himself. I might have felt sorry for him at that moment if I hadn't asked him, "Walter, as I told you, I know very little about her. Supposing she is already married."

He answered my question with a nasty grimace. "Then she'll get a divorce if I have to break the guy in pieces. I'll break anything that stands in my way, Duncan. I'm going to have her if it's the last thing I do!"

He stalked off to his room. Later I heard the car roar down the road. I let myself laugh then.

I went back to New York and was there a week when my contacts told me of Walter's fruitless search. He used every means at his disposal, but he couldn't locate the girl. I gave him seven days, exactly seven days. You see, that seventh day was the anniversary of the date I introduced him to Adrianne. I'll never forget it. Wherever Walter is now, neither will he.

When I called him, I was amazed at the change in his voice. He sounded weak and lost. We exchanged the usual formalities; then I said, "Walter, have you found Evelyn yet?"

He took a long time to answer. "No, she's disappeared completely."

"Oh, I wouldn't say that," I said.

He didn't get it at first. It was almost too much to hope for. "You . . . mean you know where she is?"

"Exactly."

"Where? Please, Dunc . . . where is she?" In a split second he became a vital being again. He was bursting with life and energy, demanding that I tell him.

I laughed and told him to let me get a word in and I would. The silence was ominous then. "She's not very far from here, Walter, in a small hotel right off Fifth Avenue." I gave him the address and had hardly finished when I heard his phone slam against the desk. He was in such a hurry he hadn't bothered to hang up . . .

Duncan stopped and drained his glass, then stared at it remorsefully. The inspector coughed lightly to attract his attention, his curiosity prompting him to speak. "He found her?" he asked eagerly.

"Oh yes, he found her. He burst right in over all protests, expecting to sweep her off her feet."

This time the inspector fidgeted nervously. "Well, go on."

Duncan motioned for the waiter and lifted a fresh glass in a toast. The inspector did the same. Duncan smiled gently. "When she saw him, she laughed and waved. Walter Harrison died an hour later . . . from a window in the same hotel."

It was too much for the inspector. He leaned forward in his chair, his forehead knotted in a frown. "But what happened? Who was she? Damn it, Duncan . . ."

Duncan took a deep breath, then gulped the drink down.

"Evelyn Vaughn was a hopeless imbecile," he said.

"She had the beauty of a goddess and the mentality of a two-year-old. They kept her well tended and dressed so she wouldn't be an object of curiosity. But the only habit she ever learned was to wave bye-bye . . ."

1953

DAVID GOODIS

PROFESSIONAL MAN

DAVID GOODIS (1917–1967) was born in Philadelphia and received a BS in journalism from Temple University, briefly working for an advertising agency after graduation. He quickly became a prolific freelance fiction writer, his first novel, *Retreat from Oblivion,* being published in 1939. After numerous short stories sold to various pulp magazines, under both his own name and several pseudonyms, he had tremendous success with his second novel, *Dark Passage* (1946), which was serialized in the *Saturday Evening Post* and was bought for the movies. Delmer Daves directed and wrote the screenplay, and Humphrey Bogart starred as Vincent Parry, the wrongfully imprisoned convict who escapes from prison in order to find the real killer of his wife; Lauren Bacall also starred. Other films made from his work include *Down There* (1956), filmed by François Truffaut as *Shoot the Piano Player* (1960); *Street of No Return* (1954), a 1989 film directed by Samuel Fuller; *The Burglar* (1953), adapted for a 1957 film with a screenplay by Goodis; and many others, mainly in France. Although his early novels and some short stories are powerful and memorable, his later work is so hopelessly dark that he has failed to maintain his place among the top rank of noir or hard-boiled writers. The people in his books are losers and know it. This sense of utter despair seems to appeal to the French, where Goodis is ranked among the greatest American crime writers. Goodis himself was a recluse, and his appraisal of his own work suggests a familiarity with depression. "My first novel was published when I was twenty-two," he wrote in a letter shortly before he died. "It was nothing and the same applies to most of the sixteen others published since then."

"Professional Man" was televised as an episode of the Showtime series *Fallen Angels,* on October 15, 1995. The script was by Howard A. Rodman, Steven Soderbergh was the director, and it starred Peter Coyote as the Boss and Brendan Fraser as Johnny Lamb. It was first published in the October 1953 issue of *Manhunt.*

■ ■ ■

AT FIVE PAST FIVE the elevator operated by Freddy Lamb came to a stop on the street floor. Freddy smiled courteously to the departing passengers. As he said good night to the office-weary faces of secretaries and bookkeepers and executives, his voice was soothing and cool-sweet, almost like a caress for the women and a pat on the shoulder for the men. People were very fond of Freddy. He was always so pleasant, so polite and quietly cheerful. Of the five elevator-men in the Chambers Trust Building, Freddy Lamb was the favorite.

His appearance blended with his voice and manner. He was neat and clean and his hair was nicely trimmed. He had light brown hair parted on the side and brushed flat across his head. His eyes were the same color, focused level when he addressed you, but never too intent, never probing. He looked at you as though he liked and trusted you, no matter who you were. When you looked at him you felt mildly stimulated. He seemed much younger than his thirty-three years. There were no lines on his face, no sign of worry or sluggishness or dissipation. The trait that made him an ideal elevator man was the fact that he never asked questions and never talked about himself.

At twenty past five, Freddy got the go-home sign from the starter, changed places with the night man, and walked down the corridor to the locker room. Taking off the uniform and putting on his street clothes, he yawned a few times. And while he was sitting on the bench and tying his shoelaces, he closed his eyes for a long moment, as though trying to catch a quick nap. His fingers fell away from the shoelaces and his shoulders drooped and he was in that position when the starter came in.

"Tired?" the starter asked.

"Just a little." Freddy looked up.

"Long day," the starter said. He was always saying that. As though each day was longer than any other.

Freddy finished with the shoelaces. He stood up and said, "You got the dollar-fifty?"

"What dollar-fifty?"

"The loan," Freddy said. He smiled offhandedly. "From last week. You ran short and needed dinner money. Remember?"

The starter's face was blank for a moment. Then he snapped his fingers and nodded emphatically. "You're absolutely right," he declared. "I'm glad you reminded me."

He handed Freddy a dollar bill and two quarters. Freddy thanked him and said good night and walked out. The starter stood there, lighting a cigarette and nodding to himself and thinking, *Nice guy, he waited a week before he asked me, and then he asked me so nice, he's really a nice guy.*

At precisely eight-ten, Freddy Lamb climbed out of the bathtub on the third floor of the uptown rooming house in which he lived. In his room, he opened a dresser drawer, took out silk underwear, silk socks, and a silk handkerchief. When he was fully dressed, he wore a pale gray roll-collar shirt that had cost fourteen dollars, a gray silk gabardine suit costing ninety-seven fifty, and dark gray suede shoes that had set him back twenty-three ninety-five. He broke open a fresh pack of cigarettes and slipped them into a wafer-thin sterling silver case, and then he changed wristwatches. The one he had been wearing was of mediocre quality and had a steel case. The one he wore now was fourteen-karat white gold. But both kept perfect time. He was very particular about the watches he bought. He wouldn't wear a watch that didn't keep absolutely perfect time.

The white-gold watch showed eight-twenty when Freddy walked out of the rooming house. He walked down Sixteenth to Ontario, then over to Broad and caught a cab. He gave the driver an address downtown. The cab's headlights merged with the flooded glare of southbound traffic. Freddy leaned back and lit a cigarette.

"Nice weather," the driver commented.

"Yes, it certainly is," Freddy said.

"I like it this time of year," the driver said, "it ain't too hot and it ain't too cold. It's just right." He glanced at the rearview mirror and saw that his passenger was putting on a pair of dark glasses. He said, "You in show business?"

"No," Freddy said.

"What's the glasses for?"

Freddy didn't say anything.

"What's the glasses for?" the driver asked.

"The headlights hurt my eyes," Freddy said. He said it somewhat slowly, his tone indicating that he was rather tired and didn't feel like talking.

The driver shrugged and remained quiet for the rest of the ride. He brought the cab to a stop at the corner of Eleventh and Locust. The fare was a dollar twenty. Freddy gave him two dollars and told him to keep the change. As the cab drove away, Freddy walked west on Locust to Twelfth, walked south on Twelfth, then turned west again, moving through a narrow alley. There were no lights in the alley except for a rectangle of green neon far down toward the other end. The rectangle was a glowing frame for the neon wording, BILLY'S HUT. It was also a beckoning finger for that special type of citizen who was never happy unless he was being ripped off in a clip joint. They'd soon be flocking through the front entrance on Locust Street. But Freddy Lamb, moving toward the back entrance, had it checked in his mind that the place was empty now. The dial of his wristwatch showed eight fifty-seven, and he knew it was too early for customers. He also knew that Billy Donofrio was sound asleep on a sofa in the backroom used as a private office. He knew it because he'd been watching Donofrio for more than two weeks and he was well acquainted with Donofrio's nightly habits.

When Freddy was fifteen yards away from Billy's Hut, he reached into his inner jacket pocket and took out a pair of white cotton gloves. When he was five yards away, he came to a stop and stood motionless, listening. There was the sound of a record player from some upstairs flat on the other side of the alley. From another upstairs flat there was the noise of lesbian voices saying, "You did," and "I didn't," and "You did, you did—"

He listened for other sounds and there were none. He let the tip of his tongue come out just a little to moisten the center of his lower lip. Then he took a few forward steps that brought him to a section of brick wall where the bricks were loose. He counted up from the bottom, the light from the green neon showing him the fourth brick, the fifth, the sixth, and the seventh. The eighth brick was the one he wanted. He got a grip on its edges jutting away from the wall, pulled at it very slowly and carefully. Then he held it in one hand and his other hand reached into the empty space and made contact with the bone handle of a switchblade. It was a six-inch blade and he'd planted it there two nights ago.

He put the brick back in place and walked to the back door of Billy's Hut. Bending to the side to see through the window, he caught sight of Billy Donofrio on the sofa. Billy was flat on his back, one short leg dangling over the side of the sofa, one arm also dangling, with fat fingers holding the stub of an unlit cigar. Billy was very short and very fat, and in his sleep he breathed as though it were a great effort. Billy was almost completely bald and what hair he had was more white than black. Billy was fifty-three years old and would never get to be fifty-four.

Freddy Lamb used a skeleton key to open the back door. He did it without a sound. And then, without a sound, he moved toward the sofa, his eyes focused on the crease of flesh between Billy's third chin and

Billy's shirt collar. His arm went up and came down and the blade went into the crease, went in deep to cut the jugular vein, moved left, moved right, to widen the cut so that it was almost from ear to ear. Billy opened his eyes and tried to open his mouth but that was as far as he could take it. He tried to breathe and he couldn't breathe. He heard the voice of Freddy Lamb saying very softly, almost gently, "Good night, Billy." Then he heard Freddy's footsteps moving toward the door, and the door opening, and the footsteps walking out.

Billy didn't hear the door as it closed. By that time he was far away from hearing anything.

On Freddy's wrist, the hands of the white-gold watch pointed to nine twenty-six. He stood on the sidewalk near the entrance of a nightclub called Yellow Cat. The place was located in a low-rent area of South Philadelphia, and the neighboring structures were mostly tenements and garages and vacant lots heaped with rubbish. The club's exterior complied with the general trend; it was dingy and there was no paint on the wooden walls. But inside it was a different proposition. It was glittering and lavish, the drinks were expensive, and the floorshow featured a first-rate orchestra and singers and dancers. It also featured a unique type of striptease entertainment, a quintet of young females who took off their clothes while they sat at your table. For a reasonable bonus they'd let you keep the brassiere or garter or whatnot for a souvenir.

The white-gold watch showed nine twenty-eight. Freddy decided to wait another two minutes. His appointment with the owner of Yellow Cat had been arranged for nine-thirty. He knew that Herman Charn was waiting anxiously for his arrival, but his personal theory of punctuality stipulated split-second precision, and since they'd made it for nine-thirty he'd see Herman at nine-thirty, not a moment earlier or later.

A taxi pulled up and a blonde stepped out. She paid the driver and walked toward Freddy and he said, "Hello, Pearl."

Pearl smiled at him. "Kiss me hello."

"Not here," he said.

"Later?"

He nodded. He looked her up and down. She was five-five and weighed 110 and nature had given her a body that caused men's eyes to bulge. Freddy's eyes didn't bulge, although he told himself she was something to see. He always enjoyed looking at her. He wondered if he still enjoyed the nights with her. He'd been sharing the nights with her for the past several months and it had reached the point where he wasn't seeing any other women and maybe he was missing out on something. For just a moment he gazed past Pearl, telling himself that she needed him more than he needed her, and knowing it wouldn't be easy to get off the hook.

Well, there wasn't any hurry. He hadn't seen anything else around that interested him. But he wished Pearl would let up on the clinging routine. Maybe he'd really go for her if she wasn't so hungry for him all the time.

Pearl stepped closer to him. The hunger showed in her eyes. She said, "Know what I did today? I took a walk in the park."

"You did?"

"Yeah," she said. "I went to Fairmount Park and took a long walk. All by myself."

"That's nice," he said. He wondered what she was getting at.

She said, "Let's do it together sometimes. Let's go for a walk in the park. It's something we ain't never done. All we do is drink and listen to jazz and find all sorts of ways to knock ourselves out."

He gave her a closer look. This was a former call girl who'd done a stretch for prostitution, a longer stretch for selling cocaine, and had finally decided she'd done enough time and she might as well go legitimate. She'd learned the art of stripping off her clothes before an audience, and now at twenty-six she was earning a hundred-and-a-half a week. It was clean money, as far as the law was concerned, but maybe in her mind it wasn't clean enough. Maybe she was getting funny ideas, like this walk-in-the-park routine. Maybe she'd soon be thinking in terms of a cottage for two and a little lawn in the front and shopping for a baby carriage.

He wondered what she'd look like, wearing an apron and standing at a sink and washing dishes.

For some reason the thought disturbed him. He couldn't understand why it should disturb him. He heard her saying, "Can we do it, Freddy? Let's do it on Sunday. We'll go to Fairmount Park."

"We'll talk about it," he cut in quickly. He glanced at his wristwatch. "See you after the show."

He hurried through the club entrance, went past the hatcheck counter, past the tables and across the dance floor and toward a door marked PRIVATE. There was a button adjoining the door and he pressed the button: one short, two longs, another short, and then there was a buzzing sound. He opened the door and walked into the office. It was a large room and the color motif was yellow and gray. The walls and ceiling were gray and the thick carpet was pale yellow. The furniture was bright yellow. There was a short skinny man standing near the desk and his face was gray. Seated at the desk was a large man whose face was a mixture of yellow and gray.

Freddy closed the door behind him. He walked toward the desk. He nodded to the short, skinny man and then he looked at the large man and said, "Hello, Herman."

Herman glanced at a clock on the desk. He said, "You're right on time."

"He's always on time," said the short, skinny man.

Herman looked at Freddy Lamb and said, "You do it?"

Before Freddy could answer, the short, skinny man said, "Sure he did it."

"Shut up, Ziggy," Herman said. He had a soft, sort of gooey voice, as though he spoke with a lot of marshmallow in his mouth. He wore a suit of very soft fabric, thin and fleecy, and his thick hands were pressed softly on the desktop. On the little finger of his left hand he wore a large star emerald that radiated a soft green light. Everything about him was soft, except for his eyes. His eyes were iron.

"You do it?" he repeated softly.

Freddy nodded.

"Any trouble?" Herman asked.

"He never has trouble," Ziggy said.

Herman looked at Ziggy. "I told you to shut up." Then, very softly, "Come here, Ziggy."

Ziggy hesitated. He had a ferret face that always looked sort of worried and now it looked very worried.

"Come here," Herman purred.

Ziggy approached the large man. Ziggy was blinking and swallowing hard. Herman reached out and slowly took hold of Ziggy's hand. Herman's thick fingers closed tightly on Ziggy's bony fingers and gave a yank. Ziggy moaned.

"When I tell you to shut up," Herman said, "you'll shut up." He smiled softly and paternally at Ziggy. "Right?"

"Right," Ziggy said. Then he moaned again. His fingers were free now and he looked down at them as an animal gazes sadly at its own crushed paws. He said, "They're all busted."

"They're not all busted," Herman said. "They're damaged just enough to let you know your place. That's one thing you must never forget. Every man who works for me has to know his place." He was still smiling at Ziggy. "Right?"

"Right," Ziggy moaned.

Then Herman looked at Freddy Lamb and said, "Right?"

Freddy didn't say anything. He was looking at Ziggy's fingers. Then his gaze climbed to Ziggy's face. The lips quivered, as though Ziggy was trying to hold back sobs. Freddy remembered the time when nothing could hurt Ziggy, when Ziggy and he were their own bosses and did their engineering on the waterfront. There were a lot of people on the waterfront who were willing to pay good money to have other people placed on stretchers or in caskets. In those days the rates had been fifteen dollars for a broken jaw, thirty for a fractured pelvis, and a hundred for the complete job. Ziggy handled the blackjack work and the bullet work and Freddy took care of such special functions as switchblade slicing, lye in the eyes, and various powders and pills slipped into a glass of beer or wine or a cup of coffee. There were orders for all sorts of jobs in those days.

Fifteen months ago, he was thinking. And times had sure changed. The independent operator was swallowed up by the big combines. It was especially true in this line of business, which followed the theory that competition, no matter how small, was not good for the overall picture. So the moment had come when he and Ziggy had been approached with an offer, and they knew they had to accept, there wasn't any choice, if they didn't accept they'd be erased. They didn't need to be told about that. They just knew. As much as they hated to do it, they had to do it. The proposition was handed to them on a Wednesday afternoon and that same night they went to work for Herman Charn.

He heard Herman saying, "I'm talking to you, Freddy."

"I hear you," he said.

"You sure?" Herman asked softly. "You sure you hear me?"

Freddy looked at Herman. He said quietly, "I'm on your payroll. I do what you tell me to do. I've done every job exactly the way you wanted it done. Can I do any more than that?"

"Yes," Herman said. His tone was matter-of-fact. He glanced at Ziggy and said, "From here on it's a private discussion. Me and Freddy. Take a walk."

Ziggy's mouth opened just a little. He didn't seem to understand the command. He'd always been included in all the business conferences, and now the look in his eyes was a mixture of puzzlement and injury.

Herman smiled at Ziggy. He pointed to the door. Ziggy bit hard on his lip and moved toward the door and opened it and walked out of the room.

For some moments it was quiet in the room and Freddy had a feeling it was too quiet. He sensed that Herman Charn was aiming something at him, something that had nothing to do with the ordinary run of business.

There was the creaking sound of leather as Herman leaned back in the desk chair. He folded his big soft fingers across his big soft belly and said, "Sit down, Freddy. Sit down and make yourself comfortable."

Freddy pulled a chair toward the desk. He sat down. He looked at the face of Herman and for just a moment the face became a wall that moved toward him. He winced; his insides quivered. It was a strange sensation, he'd never had it before and he couldn't understand it. But then the moment was gone and he sat there relaxed, his features expressionless, as he waited for Herman to speak.

Herman said, "Want a drink?"

Freddy shook his head.

"Smoke?" Herman lifted the lid of an enamel cigarette box.

"I got my own," Freddy murmured. He reached into his pocket and took out the flat silver case.

"Smoke one of mine," Herman said. He paused to signify it wasn't a suggestion, it was an order. And then, as though Freddy were a guest, rather than an employee, "These smokes are special-made. Come from Egypt. Cost a dime apiece."

Freddy took one. Herman flicked a table-lighter, applied the flame to Freddy's cigarette, lit one for himself, took a slow, soft drag, and let the smoke come out of his nose. Herman waited until all of the smoke was out and then said, "You didn't like what I did to Ziggy."

It was a flat statement that didn't ask for an answer. Freddy sipped at the cigarette, not looking at Herman.

"You didn't like it," Herman persisted softly. "You never like it when I let Ziggy know who's boss."

Freddy shrugged. "That's between you and Ziggy."

"No," Herman said. And he spoke very slowly, with a pause between each word. "It isn't that way at all. I don't do it for Ziggy's benefit. He already knows who's top man around here."

Freddy didn't say anything. But he almost winced. And again his insides quivered.

Herman leaned forward. "Do you know who the top man is?"

"You," Freddy said.

Herman smiled. "Thanks, Freddy. Thanks for saying it." Then the smile vanished and Herman's eyes were hammerheads. "But I'm not sure you mean it."

Freddy took another sip from the Egyptian cigarette. It was strongly flavored tobacco but somehow he wasn't getting any taste from it.

Herman kept leaning forward. "I gotta be sure, Freddy," he said. "You been working for me more than a year. And just like you said, you do all the jobs exactly the way I want them done. You plan them perfect, it's always clean and neat from start to finish. I don't mind saying you're one of the best. I don't think I've ever seen a cooler head. You're as cool as they come, an icicle on wheels."

"That's plenty cool," Freddy murmured.

"It sure is," Herman said. He let the pause drift in again. Then, his lips scarcely moving, "Maybe it's too cool."

Freddy looked at the hammerhead eyes. He wondered what showed in his own eyes. He wondered what thoughts were burning under the cool surface of his own brain.

He heard Herman saying, "I've done a lot of thinking about you. A lot more than you'd ever imagine. You're a puzzler, and one thing I always like to do is play stud poker with a puzzler."

Freddy smiled dimly. "Want to play stud poker?"

"We're playing it now. Without cards." Herman gazed down at the desktop. His right hand was on the desktop and he flicked his wrist as though he was turning over the hole card. His voice was very soft as he said, "I want you to break it up with Pearl."

Freddy heard himself saying, "All right, Herman."

It was as though Freddy hadn't spoken. Herman said, "I'm waiting, Freddy."

"Waiting for what?" He told the dim smile to stay on his lips. It stayed there. He murmured, "You tell me to give her up and I say all right. What more do you want me to say."

"I want you to ask me why. Don't you want to know why?"

Freddy didn't reply. He still wore the dim smile and he was gazing past Herman's head.

"Come on, Freddy. I'm waiting to see your hole card."

Freddy remained quiet.

"All right," Herman said. "I'll keep on showing you mine. I go for Pearl. I went for her the first time I laid eyes on her. That same night I took her home with me and she stayed over. She did what I wanted her to do but it didn't mean a thing to her, it was just like turning a trick. I thought it wouldn't bother me, once I have them in bed I can put them out of my mind. But this thing with Pearl, it's different. I've had her on my mind and it gets worse all the time and now it's gotten to the point where I have to do something about it. First thing I gotta do is clear the road."

"It's cleared," Freddy said. "I'll tell her tonight I'm not seeing her anymore."

"Just like that?" And Herman snapped his fingers.

"Yes," Freddy said. His fingers made the same sound. "Just like that."

Herman leaned back in the soft leather chair. He looked at the face of Freddy Lamb as though he was trying to solve a cryptogram. Finally he shook his head slowly, and then he gave a heavy sigh and he said, "All right, Freddy. That's all for now."

Freddy stood up. He started toward the door. Halfway across the room he stopped and turned and said, "You promised me a bonus for the Donofrio job."

"This is Monday," Herman said. "I hand out the pay on Friday."

"You said I'd be paid right off."

"Did I?" Herman smiled softly.

"Yes," Freddy said. "You said the deal on Donofrio was something special and the customer was paying fifteen hundred. You told me there was five hundred in it for me and I'd get the bonus the same night I did the job."

Herman opened a desk drawer and took out a thick roll of bills.

"Can I have it in tens and twenties?" Freddy asked.

Herman lifted his eyebrows. "Why the small change?"

"I'm an elevator man," Freddy said. "The bank would wonder what I was doing with fifties."

"You're right," Herman said. He counted off the five hundred in tens and twenties, and handed the money to Freddy. He leaned back in the chair and watched Freddy folding the bills and pocketing them and walking out of the room. When the door was closed Herman said aloud to himself, "Don't try to figure him out, he's all ice and no soul, strictly a professional."

The white-gold watch showed eleven thirty-five. Freddy sat at a table watching the floorshow and drinking from a tall glass of gin and ginger ale. The Yellow Cat was crowded now and Freddy wore the dark glasses and his table was in a darkly shadowed section of the room. He sat there with Ziggy and some other men who worked for Herman. There was Dino, who did his jobs at long range and always used a rifle. There was Shikey, six foot six and weighing three hundred pounds, an expert at bone cracking, gouging, and the removing of teeth. There was Riley, another bone-cracker and strangling specialist.

A tall, pretty boy stood in front of the orchestra, clutching the mike as though it was the only support he had in the world. He sang with an ache in his voice, begging someone to "—please understand." The audience liked it and he sang it again. Then two colored lap-dancers came out and worked themselves into a sweat and were gasping for breath as they finished the act. The MC walked on and motioned the orchestra to quiet down and grinned at ringside faces as he said, "Ready for dessert?"

"Yeah," a man shouted from ringside. "Let's have the dessert."

"All right," the MC said. He cupped his hands to his mouth and called offstage, "Bring it out, we're all starved for that sweetmeat."

The orchestra went into medium tempo, the lights changing from glaring yellow to a soft violet. And then they came out, seven girls wearing horn-rimmed glasses and ultraconservative costumes. They walked primly, and all together they resembled the stiff-necked females in a cartoon lampooning the WCTU. It got a big laugh from the audience, and there was some appreciative applause. The young ladies formed a line and slowly waved black parasols as they sang, "—Father, oh father, come home with me now." But then it became, "—Daddy, oh daddy, come home with me now." And as they emphasized the daddy angle, they broke up the line and discarded the parasols and took off their ankle-length dark blue coats. Then, their fingers loosening the buttons of dark blue dresses, they moved separately toward the ringside tables. The patrons in the back stood up to get a better look and in the balcony the lenses of seven lamps were focused on seven young women getting undressed.

Dino, who had a footwear fetish, said loudly, "I'll pay forty for a high-heeled shoe."

One of the girls took off her shoe and flung it toward Freddy's table. Shikey caught it and handed it to Dino. A waiter came over and Dino handed him four tens and he took the money to the girl. Riley looked puzzledly at Dino and said, "Whatcha gonna do with a high-heeled shoe?" And Shikey said, "He boils 'em and eats 'em." But Ziggy had another theory. "He bangs the heel against his head," Ziggy said. "That's the way he gets his kicks." Dino sat there gazing lovingly at the shoe in his hand while his other hand caressed the kidskin surface. Then gradually his eyes closed and he murmured, "This is nice, this is so nice."

Riley was watching Dino and saying, "I don't get it."

Ziggy shrugged philosophically. "Some things," he said, "just can't be understood."

"You're so right." It was Freddy talking. He didn't know his lips were making sounds. He was looking across the tables at Pearl. She sat with some ringsiders and already she'd taken off considerable clothing; she was half-naked. On her face there was a detached look and her hands moved mechanically as she unbuttoned the buttons and unzipped the zippers. There were three men sitting with her and their eyes feasted on her, they had their mouths open in a sort of mingled fascination and worship. At nearby tables the other strippers were performing but they weren't getting undivided attention. Most of the men were watching Pearl. One of them offered a hundred dollars for her stocking. She took off the stocking and let it dangle from her fingers. In a semiwhisper she asked if there were any higher bids. Freddy told himself that she wasn't happy doing what she was doing. Again he could hear her plaintive voice as she asked him to take her for a walk in the park. Suddenly, he knew that he'd like that very much. He wanted to see the sun shining on her hair, instead of the nightclub lights. He heard himself saying aloud, "Five hundred."

He didn't shout it, but at the ringside tables they all heard it, and for a moment there was stunned silence. At his own table the silence was very thick. He could feel the pressure of it, and the moment seemed to have substance, something on the order of iron wheels going around and around, making no sound and getting nowhere.

Some things just can't be understood, he thought. He was taking the tens and twenties from his jacket pocket. The five hundred seemed to prove the truth of Ziggy's vague philosophy. Freddy got up from his chair and moved toward an empty table behind some potted ferns adjacent to the orchestra stand. He sat down and placed green money on a yellow tablecloth. He wasn't looking at Pearl as she approached the table. From ringside an awed voice was saying, "For one silk stocking she gets half a grand—"

She seated herself at the table. He shoved the money toward her. He said, "There's your cash. Let's have the stocking."

"This a gag?" she asked quietly. Her eyes were somewhat sullen. There was some laughter from the table where Ziggy and some of the others were seated; they now had the notion it was some sort of joke.

Freddy said, "Take off the stocking."

She looked at the pile of tens and twenties. She said, "Whatcha want the stocking for?"

"Souvenir," he said.

It was the tone of his voice that did it. Her face paled. She started to shake her head very slowly, as though she couldn't believe him.

"Yes," he said, with just the trace of a sigh. "It's all over, Pearl. It's the end of the line."

She went on shaking her head. She couldn't talk.

He said, "I'll hang the stocking in my bedroom."

She was biting her lip. "It's a long time till Christmas."

"For some people it's never Christmas."

"Freddy—" She leaned toward him. "What's it all about? Why're you doing this?"

He shrugged. He didn't say anything.

Her eyes were getting wet. "You won't even give me a reason?"

All he gave her was a cool smile. Then his head was turned and he saw the faces at Ziggy's table and then he focused on the face of the large man who stood behind the table. He saw the iron in the eyes of Herman Charn. He told himself he was doing what Herman had told him to do. And just then he felt the quiver in his insides. It was mostly in the spine, as though his spine was gradually turning to jelly.

He spoke to himself without a sound. He said, *No, it isn't that, it can't be that.*

Pearl was saying, "All right, Freddy, if that's the way it is."

He nodded very slowly.

Pearl bent over and took the stocking off her leg. She placed the stocking on the table. She picked up the five hundred, counted it off to make sure it was all there.

Then she stood up and said, "No charge, mister. I'd rather keep the memories."

She put the tens and twenties on the tablecloth and walked away. Freddy glanced off to the side and saw a soft smile on the face of Herman Charn.

The floorshow had ended and Freddy was still sitting there at the table. There was a bottle of bourbon in front of him. It had been there for less than twenty minutes and already it was half empty. There was also a pitcher of ice water and the pitcher was full. He didn't need a chaser because he couldn't taste the whiskey. He was drinking the whiskey from the water glass.

A voice said, "Freddy—"

And then a hand tugged at his arm. He looked up and saw Ziggy sitting beside him.

He smiled at Ziggy. He motioned toward the bottle and shot glass and said, "Have a drink."

Ziggy shrugged. "I might as well while I got the chance. At the rate you're going, that bottle'll soon be empty."

"It's very good bourbon," Freddy said.

"Yeah?" Ziggy was pouring a glass for himself. He swished the liquor into his mouth. Then, looking closely at Freddy, "You don't care whether it's good or not. You'd be gulping it if it was shoe polish."

Freddy was staring at the tablecloth. "Let's go somewhere and drink some shoe polish."

Ziggy tugged again at Freddy's arm. He said, "Come out of it."

"Come out of what?"

"The clouds," Ziggy said. "You're in the clouds."

"It's nice in the clouds," Freddy said. "I'm up here having a dandy time. I'm floating."

"Floating? You're drowning." Ziggy pulled urgently at his arm, to get his hand away from a water glass filled with whiskey. "You're not a drinker, Freddy. What do you want to do, drink yourself into a hospital?"

Freddy grinned. He aimed the grin at nothing in particular. For some moments he sat there motionless. Then he reached into his jacket pocket and took out the silk stocking. He showed it to Ziggy and said, "Look what I got."

"Yeah," Ziggy said. "I seen her give it to you. What's the score on that routine?"

"No score," Freddy said. He went on grinning. "It's a funny way to end a game. Nothing on the scoreboard. Nothing at all."

Ziggy frowned. "You trying to tell me something?"

Freddy looked at the whiskey in the water glass. He said, "I packed her in."

"No," Ziggy said. His tone was incredulous. "Not Pearl. Not that pigeon. That ain't no ordinary merchandise. You wouldn't walk out on Pearl unless you had a very special reason."

"It was special, all right."

"Tell me about it, Freddy." There was something plaintive in Ziggy's voice, a certain feeling for Freddy that he couldn't put into words. The closest he could get to it was: "After all, I'm on your side, ain't I?"

"No," Freddy said. The grin was slowly fading. "You're on Herman's side." He gazed past Ziggy's head. "We're all on Herman's side."

"Herman? What's he got to do with it?"

"Everything," Freddy said. "Herman's the boss, remember?" He looked at the swollen fingers of Ziggy's right hand. "If Herman wants something done, it's got to be done. He gave me orders to break with Pearl. He's the employer and I'm the hired man, so I did what I had to do. I carried out his orders."

Ziggy was quiet for some moments. Then, very quietly, "Well, it figures he wants her for himself. But it don't seem right. It just ain't fair."

"Don't make me laugh," Freddy said. "Who the hell are we to say what's fair?"

"We're human, aren't we?"

"No," Freddy said. He gazed past Ziggy's head. "I don't know what we are. But I know one thing, we're not human. We can't afford to be human, not in this line of business."

Ziggy didn't get it. It was just a little too deep for him. All he could say was "You getting funny ideas?"

"I'm not reaching for them, they're just coming to me."

"Take another drink," Ziggy said.

"I'd rather have the laughs." Freddy showed the grin again. "It's really comical, you know? Especially this thing with Pearl. I was thinking of calling it quits anyway. You know how it is with me, Ziggy. I never like to be tied down to one skirt. But tonight Pearl said something that spun me around. We were talking outside the club and she brought it in out of left field. She asked me to take her for a walk in the park."

Ziggy blinked a few times. "What?"

"A walk in the park," Freddy said.

"What for?" Ziggy wanted to know. "She gettin' square all of a sudden? She wanna go around picking flowers?"

"I don't know," Freddy said. "All she said was 'It's very nice in Fairmount Park.' She asked me to take her there and we'd be together in the park, just taking a walk."

Ziggy pointed to the glass. "You better take that drink."

Freddy reached for the glass. But someone else's hand was there first. He saw the thick soft fingers, the soft green glow of the star emerald. As the glass of whiskey was shoved out of his reach, he looked up and saw the soft smile on the face of Herman Charn.

"Too much liquor is bad for the kidneys," Herman said. He bent down lower to peer at Freddy's eyes. "You look knocked out, Freddy. There's a soft couch in the office. Go in there and lie down for a while."

Freddy got up from the chair. He was somewhat unsteady on his feet. Herman took his arm and helped him make it down the aisle, past the tables to the door of the office. He could feel the pressure of Herman's hand on his arm. It was very soft pressure but somehow it felt like a clamp of iron biting into his flesh.

Herman opened the office door and guided him toward the couch. He fell onto the couch, sent an idiotic grin toward the ceiling, then closed his eyes and went to sleep.

* * *

He slept until four-forty in the morning. The sound that woke him up was a scream.

At first it was all blurred, there was too much whiskey-fog in his brain, he had no idea where he was or what was happening. He pushed his knuckles against his eyes. Then, sitting up, he focused on the faces in the room. He saw Shikey and Riley and they had girls sitting in their laps. They were on the other couch at the opposite side of the room. He saw Dino standing near the couch with his arm around the waist of a slim brunette. Then he glanced toward the door and he saw Ziggy. That made seven faces for him to look at. He told himself to keep looking at them. If he concentrated on that, maybe he wouldn't hear the screaming.

But he heard it. The scream was an animal sound and yet he recognized the voice. It came from near the desk, and he turned his head very slowly, telling himself he didn't want to look but knowing he had to look.

He saw Pearl kneeling on the floor. Herman stood behind her. With one hand he was twisting her arm up high between her shoulder blades. His other hand was on her head and he was pulling her hair so that her face was drawn back, her throat stretched.

Herman spoke very softly. "You make me very unhappy, Pearl. I don't like to be unhappy."

Then Herman gave her arm another upward twist and pulled tighter on her hair and she screamed again.

The girl in Shikey's lap gave Pearl a scornful look and said, "You're a damn fool."

"In spades." It came from the stripper who nestled against Riley. "All he wants her to do is kiss him like she means it."

Freddy told himself to get up and walk out of the room. He lifted himself from the couch and took a few steps toward the door and heard Herman saying, "Not yet, Freddy. I'll tell you when to go."

He went back to the couch and sat down.

Herman said, "Be sensible, Pearl. Why can't you be sensible?"

Pearl opened her mouth to scream again. But no sound came out. There was too much pain and it was choking her.

The brunette who stood with Dino was saying, "It's a waste of time, Herman, she can't give you what she hasn't got. She just don't have it for you, Herman."

"She'll have it for him," Dino said. "Before he's finished, he'll have her crawling on her belly."

Herman looked at Dino. “No,” he said. “She won’t do that. I wouldn’t let her do that.” He cast a downward glance at Pearl. His lips shaped a soft smile. There was something tender in the smile and in his voice. “Pearl, tell me something, why don’t you want me?”

He gave her a chance to reply, his fingers slackening the grip on her wrist and her hair. She groaned a few times and then she said, “You got my body, Herman. You can have my body anytime you want it.”

“That isn’t enough,” Herman said. “I want you all the way, a hundred percent. It’s got to be like that, Pearl. You’re in me so deep it just can’t take any other route. It’s got to be you and me from here on in, you gotta need me just as much as I need you.”

“But Herman —” She gave a dry sob. “I can’t lie to you. I just don’t feel that way.”

“You’re gonna feel that way,” Herman said.

“No.” Pearl sobbed again. “No. No.”

“Why not?” He was pulling her hair again, twisting her arm. But it seemed he was suffering more than Pearl. The pain racked his pleading voice. “Why can’t you feel something for me?”

Her reply was made without sound. She managed to turn her head just a little, toward the couch. And everyone in the room saw her looking at Freddy.

Herman’s face became very pale. His features tightened and twisted and it seemed he was about to burst into tears. He stared up at the ceiling.

Herman shivered. His body shook spasmodically, as though he stood on a vibrating platform. Then all at once the tormented look faded from his eyes, the iron came into his eyes, and the soft smile came onto his lips. He released Pearl, turned away from her, went to the desk, and opened the cigarette box. It was very quiet in the room while Herman stood there lighting the cigarette. He took a slow, easy drag and then he said quietly, “All right, Pearl, you can go home now.”

She started to get up from the floor. The brunette came over and helped her up.

“I’ll call a cab for you,” Herman said. He reached for the telephone and put in the call. As he lowered the phone, he was looking at Pearl and saying, “You want to go home alone?”

Pearl didn’t say anything. Her head was lowered and she was leaning against the shoulder of the brunette.

Herman said, “You want Freddy to take you home?”

Pearl raised her head just a little and looked at the face of Freddy Lamb.

Herman laughed softly. "All right," he said. "Freddy'll take you home."

Freddy winced. He sat there staring at the carpet.

Herman told the brunette to fix a drink for Pearl. He said, "Take her to the bar and give her anything she wants." He motioned to the other girls and they got up from the laps of Shikey and Riley. Then all the girls walked out of the room. Herman was quiet for some moments, taking slow drags at the cigarette and looking at the door. Then gradually his head turned and he looked at Freddy. He said, "You're slated, Freddy."

Freddy went on staring at the carpet.

"You're gonna bump her," Herman said.

Freddy closed his eyes.

"Take her somewhere and bump her and bury her," Herman said.

Shikey and Riley looked at each other. Dino had his mouth open and he was staring at Herman. Standing next to the door, Ziggy had his eyes glued to Freddy's face.

"She goes," Herman said. And then, speaking aloud to himself, "She goes because she gives me grief." He hit his hand against his chest. "She hits me here, where I live. Hits me too hard. Hurts me. I don't appreciate getting hurt. Especially here." Again his hand thumped his chest. He said, "You'll do it, Freddy. You'll see to it that I get rid of the hurt."

"Let me do it," Ziggy said. Herman shook his head. He pointed a finger at Freddy. His finger jabbed empty air, and he said, "Freddy does it. Freddy."

Ziggy opened his mouth, tried to close it, couldn't close it, and blurted, "Why take it out on him?"

"That's a stupid question," Herman said mildly. "I'm not taking it out on anybody. I'm giving the job to Freddy because I know he's dependable. I can always depend on Freddy."

Ziggy made a final, frantic try. "Please, Herman," he said. "Please don't make him do it."

Herman didn't bother to reply. All he did was give Ziggy a slow appraising look up and down. It was like a soundless warning to Ziggy, letting him know he was walking on thin ice and the ice would crack if he opened his mouth again.

Then Herman turned to Freddy and said, "Where's your blade?"

"Stashed," Freddy said. He was still staring at the carpet.

Herman opened a desk drawer. He took out a black-handled switchblade. "Use this," he said, coming toward the couch. He handed the knife to Freddy. "Give it a try," he said.

Freddy pressed the button. The blade flicked out. It glimmered blue-white. He pushed the blade into the handle and tried the button again. He went on trying the button and watching the flash of the blade. It was quiet in the room as the blade went in and out, in and out. Then from the street there was the sound of a horn. Herman said, "That's the taxi." Freddy nodded and got up from the sofa and walked out of the room. As he moved toward the girls who stood at the cocktail bar, he could feel the weight of the knife in the inner pocket of his jacket. He was looking at Pearl and saying, "Come on, let's go," and as he said it, the blade seemed to come out of the knife and slice into his own flesh.

The taxi was cruising north on Sixteenth Street. On Freddy's wrist the white-gold watch said five-twenty. He was watching the parade of unlit windows along the dark street. Pearl was saying something but he didn't hear her. She spoke just a bit louder and he turned and looked at her. He smiled and murmured, "Sorry, I wasn't listening."

"Can't you sit closer?"

He moved closer to her. A mixture of moonlight and streetlamp glow came pouring into the back seat of the taxi and illuminated her face. He saw something in her eyes that caused him to blink several times.

She noticed the way he was blinking and said, "What's the matter?"

He didn't answer. He tried to stop blinking and he couldn't stop.

"Hangover?" Pearl asked.

"No," he said. "I feel all right now, I feel fine."

For some moments she didn't say anything. She was rubbing her sore arm. She tried to stretch it, winced and gasped with pain, and said, "Oh Jesus, it hurts. It really hurts. Maybe it's broken."

"Let me feel it," he said. He put his hand on her arm. He ran his fingers down from above her elbow to her wrist. "It isn't broken," he murmured. "Just a little swollen, that's all. Sprained some ligaments."

She smiled at him. "The hurt goes away when you touch it."

He tried not to look at her, but something fastened his eyes to her face. He kept his hand on her arm. He heard himself saying, "I feel sorry for Herman. If he could see you now, I mean if you'd look at him like you're looking at me —"

"Freddy," she said. "Freddy." Then she leaned toward him. She rested her head on his shoulder.

Then somehow everything was quiet and still and he didn't hear the noise of the taxi's engine, he didn't feel the bumps as the wheels hit the ruts in the cobblestone surface of Sixteenth Street. But suddenly there was a deep rut and the taxi gave a lurch. He looked up and heard the driver cursing the city engineers. "Goddamn it," the driver said. "They got a deal with the tire companies."

Freddy stared past the driver's head, his eyes aimed through the windshield to see the wide intersection where Sixteenth Street met the Parkway. The Parkway was a six-laned drive slanting to the left of the downtown area, going away from the concrete of Philadelphia skyscrapers and pointing toward the green of Fairmount Park.

"Turn left," Freddy said.

They were approaching the intersection, and the driver gave a backward glance. "Left?" the driver asked. "That takes us outta the way. You gave me an address on Seventeenth near Lehigh. We gotta hit it from Sixteenth—"

"I know," Freddy said quietly. "But turn left anyway."

The driver shrugged. "You're the captain." He beat the yellow of a traffic light and the taxi made a left turn onto the Parkway.

Pearl said, "What's this, Freddy? Where're we going?"

"In the park." He wasn't looking at her. "We're gonna do what you said we should do. We're gonna take a walk in the park."

"For real?" Her eyes were lit up. She shook her head as though she could scarcely believe what he'd just said.

"We'll take a nice walk," he murmured. "Just the two of us. The way you wanted it."

"Oh," she breathed. "Oh, Freddy—"

The driver shrugged again. The taxi went past the big monuments and fountains of Logan Circle, past the Rodin Museum and the Art Museum and onto River Drive. For a mile or so they stayed on the highway, bordering the moonlit water of the river and then, without being told, the driver made a turn off the highway, made a series of turns that took them deep into the park. They came to a section where there were no lights, no movement, no sound except the autumn wind drifting through the trees and bushes and tall grass and flowers.

"Stop here," Freddy said.

The taxi came to a stop. They got out and he paid the driver. The driver gave him a queer look and said, "You sure picked a lonely spot."

Freddy looked at the cabman. He didn't say anything.

The driver said, "You're at least three miles off the highway. It's gonna be a problem getting a ride home."

"Is it your problem?" Freddy asked gently.

"Well, no—"

"Then don't worry about it," Freddy said. He smiled amiably. The driver threw a glance at the blonde, smiled, and told himself that the man might have the right idea, after all. With an item like that, any man would want complete privacy. He thought of the bony, bucktoothed woman who waited for him at home, crinkled his face in a distasteful grimace, put the car in gear, and drove away.

"Ain't it nice?" Pearl said. "Ain't it wonderful?"

They were walking through a glade where the moonlight showed the autumn colors of fallen leaves. The night air was fragrant with the blended aromas of wildflowers. He had his arm around her shoulder and was leading her toward a narrow lane sloping downward through the trees.

She laughed lightly, happily. "It's like as if you know the place. As if you've been here before."

"No," he said. "I've never been here before."

There was the tinkling sound of a nearby brook. A bird chirped in the bushes. Another bird sang a tender reply.

"Listen," Pearl murmured. "Listen to them."

He listened to the singing of the birds. Now he was guiding Pearl down along the slope and seeing the way it leveled at the bottom and then went up again on all sides. It was a tiny valley down there with the brook running along the edge. He told himself it would happen when they reached the bottom.

He heard Pearl saying, "Wouldn't it be nice if we could stay here?"

He looked at her. "Stay here?"

"Yes," she said. "If we could live here for the rest of our lives. Just be here, away from everything—"

"We'd get lonesome."

"No we wouldn't," she said. "We'd always have company. I'd have you and you'd have me."

They were nearing the bottom of the slope. It was sort of steep now and they had to move slowly. All at once she stumbled and pitched forward and he caught her before she could fall on her face. He steadied her, smiled at her, and said, "OK?"

She nodded. She stood very close to him and gazed into his eyes and said, "You wouldn't let me fall, would you?"

The smile faded. He stared past her. "Not if I could help it."

"I know," she said. "You don't have to tell me."

He went on staring past her. "Tell you what?"

"The situation." She spoke softly, almost in a whisper. "I got it figured, Freddy. It's so easy to figure."

He wanted to close his eyes; he didn't know why he wanted to close his eyes.

He heard her saying, "I know why you packed me in tonight. Orders from Herman."

"That's right." He said it automatically, as though the mention of the name was the shifting of a gear.

"And another thing," she said. "I know why you brought me here." There was a pause, and then, very softly, "Herman."

He nodded.

She started to cry. It was quiet weeping and contained no fear, no hysteria. It was the weeping of farewell. She was crying because she was sad. Then, very slowly, she took the few remaining steps going down to the bottom of the slope. He stood there and watched her face as she turned to look up at him.

He walked down to where she stood, smiling at her and trying to pretend his hand was not on the switchblade in his pocket. He tried to make himself believe he wasn't going to do it, but he knew that wasn't true. He'd been slated for this job. The combine had him listed as a top-rated operator, one of the best in the business. He'd expended a lot of effort to attain that reputation, to be known as the grade-A expert who'd never muffed an assignment.

He begged himself to stop. He couldn't stop. The knife was open in his hand and his arm flashed out and sideways with the blade sliding in neatly and precisely, cutting the flesh of her throat. She went down very slowly, tried to cough, made a few gurgling sounds, and then rolled over on her back and died looking up at him.

For a long time he stared at her face. There was no expression on her features now. At first he didn't feel anything, and then he realized she was dead, and he had killed her.

He tried to tell himself there was nothing else he could have done, but even though that was true it didn't do any good. He took his glance away from her face and looked down at the white-gold watch to check the hour and the minute, automatically. But somehow the dial was blurred, as though the hands were spinning like tiny propellers. He had the weird feeling that the watch was showing time traveling backward, so that he found himself checking it in terms of years and decades. He went all the way back to the day when he was eleven years old and they took him to reform school.

In reform school he was taught a lot of things. The thing he learned best was the way to use a knife. The knife became his profession. But somewhere along the line he caught onto the idea of holding a daytime job to cover his nighttime activities. He worked in stockrooms and he did some window cleaning and drove a truck for a fruit dealer. And finally he became an elevator operator and that was the job he liked best. He'd never realized why he liked it so much but he realized now. He knew that the elevator was nothing more than a moving cell, and that the only place for him was a cell. The passengers were just a lot of friendly visitors walking in and out, saying "Good morning, Freddy," and "Good night, Freddy," and they were such nice people. Just the thought of them brought a tender smile to his lips.

Then he realized he was smiling down at her. He sensed a faint glow coming from somewhere, lighting her face. For an instant he had no idea what it was. Then he realized it came from the sky. It was the first signal of approaching sunrise.

The white-gold watch showed five fifty-three. Freddy Lamb told himself to get moving. For some reason he couldn't move. He was looking down at the dead girl. His hand was still clenched about the switchblade, and as he tried to relax it he almost dropped the knife. He looked down at it.

The combine was a cell, too, he told himself. The combine was an elevator from which he could never escape. It was going steadily downward and there were no stops until the end. There was no way to get out.

Herman had made him kill the girl. Herman would make him do other things. And there was no getting away from that. If he killed Herman there would be someone else.

The elevator was carrying Freddy steadily downward. Already, he had left Pearl somewhere far above him. He realized it all at once, and an unreasonable terror filled him.

Freddy looked at the white-gold watch again. A minute had passed and he knew suddenly that he was slated to do a job on someone in exactly three minutes now. The minutes passed and he stood there alone.

At precisely five fifty-seven he said goodbye to his profession and plunged the blade into his heart.

1955

CHARLES BEAUMONT

THE HUNGER

Charles Beaumont (1929–1967) was born Charles Leroy Nutt in Chicago; ridiculed because of his last name, he dropped out of high school and joined the Army. He found solace in science fiction and fantasy and began writing them himself, selling his first story, "The Devil, You Say?" at the age of twenty-one to *Astounding Stories;* it was later adapted as an episode of *The Twilight Zone,* as was his second story, "The Beautiful People," and six others. He also wrote more than twenty episodes for the series. His short career (essentially ending at the age of thirty-four when he was diagnosed with a "mysterious brain disease") was a prolific one, with scores of short stories, teleplays (in addition to *The Twilight Zone,* he wrote for *Four Star Playhouse; Alfred Hitchcock Presents; Naked City; Route 66; Richard Diamond, Private Detective; Have Gun — Will Travel,* and many other programs), and fourteen screenplays, most of which were low-budget fantasy and horror films, including *Queen of Outer Space* (1958), *Premature Burial* (1962), *The Wonderful World of the Brothers Grimm* (1962), *7 Faces of Dr. Lao* (1964), *The Masque of the Red Death* (1964), and *The Intruder* (1962), which was based on his 1959 novel of the same name. He also coauthored a novel, *Run from the Hunter,* with John E. Tomerlin under the pseudonym Keith Grantland in 1957. *Playboy* published "Black Country" in its issue of September 1954 — its first piece of fiction. Beaumont was given a posthumous Bram Stoker Award in 1988 by the Horror Writers Association for his *Collected Stories.*

"The Hunger" was first published in the April 1955 issue of *Playboy;* it was collected in the author's *The Hunger and Other Stories* (1957).

▪ ▪ ▪

Now, with the sun almost gone, the sky looked wounded — as if a gigantic razor had been drawn across it, slicing deep. It bled richly. And the wind, which came down from High Mountain, cool as rain, sounded a little like children crying: a soft, unhappy kind of sound, rising and falling.

Afraid, somehow, it seemed to Julia. Terribly afraid.

She quickened her step. I'm an idiot, she thought, looking away from the sky. A complete idiot. That's why I'm frightened now; and if anything happens—which it won't, and can't—then I'll have no one to blame but myself.

She shifted the bag of groceries to her other arm and turned, slightly. There was no one in sight, except old Mr. Hannaford, pulling in his newspaper stands, preparing to close up the drugstore, and Jake Spiker, barely moving across to the Blue Haven for a glass of beer: no one else. The rippling red-brick streets were silent.

But even if she got nearly all the way home, she could scream and someone would hear her. Who would be fool enough to try anything right out in the open? Not even a lunatic. Besides, it wasn't dark yet, not technically, anyway.

Still, as she passed the vacant lots, all shoulder-high in wild grass, Julia could not help thinking, He might be hiding there, right now. It was possible. Hiding there, all crouched up, waiting. And he'd only have to grab her, and—she wouldn't scream. She knew that suddenly, and the thought terrified her. Sometimes you *can't* scream . . .

If only she'd not bothered to get that spool of yellow thread over at Younger's, it would be bright daylight now, bright clear daylight. And—

Nonsense! This was the middle of the town. She was surrounded by houses full of people. People all around. Everywhere.

(He was a hunger; a need; a force. Dark emptiness filled him. He moved, when he moved, like a leaf caught in some dark and secret river, rushing. But mostly he slept now, an animal, always ready to wake and leap and be gone . . .)

The shadows came to life, dancing where Julia walked. Now the sky was ugly and festered, and the wind had become stronger, colder. She clicked along the sidewalk, looking straight ahead, wondering, Why, why am I so infernally stupid? What's the matter with me?

Then she was home, and it was all over. The trip had taken not more than half an hour. And here was Maud, running. Julia felt her sister's arms fly around her, hugging. "God, my God."

And Louise's voice: "We were just about to call Mick to go after you."

Julia pulled free and went into the kitchen and put down the bag of groceries.

"Where in the world have you been?" Maud demanded.

"I had to get something at Younger's." Julia took off her coat. "They had to go look for it, and—I didn't keep track of the time."

Maud shook her head. "Well, I don't know," she said wearily. "You're just lucky you're alive, that's all."

"Now—"

"You listen! He's out there somewhere. Don't you understand that? It's a fact. They haven't even come close to catching him yet."

"They will," Julia said, not knowing why: she wasn't entirely convinced of it.

"Of course they will. Meantime, how many more is he going to murder? Can you answer me that?"

"I'm going to put my coat away." Julia brushed past her sister. Then she turned and said, "I'm sorry you were worried. It won't happen again." She went to the closet, feeling strangely upset. They would talk about it tonight. All night. Analyzing, hinting, questioning. They would talk of nothing else, as from the very first. And they would not be able to conceal their delight.

"Wasn't it awful about poor Eva Schillings?"

No, Julia had thought: from her sisters' point of view it was not awful at all. It was wonderful. It was priceless.

It was news.

Julia's sisters . . . Sometimes she thought of them as mice. Giant gray mice, in high white collars: groaning a little, panting a little, working about the house. Endlessly, untiringly: they would squint at pictures, knock them crooked, then straighten them again; they swept invisible dust from clean carpets and took the invisible dust outside in shining pans and dumped it carefully into spotless apple-baskets; they stood by beds whose sheets shone gleaming white and tight, and clucked in soft disgust, and replaced the sheets with others. All day, every day, from six in the morning until most definite dusk. Never questioning, never doubting that the work had to be done.

They ran like arteries through the old house, keeping it alive. For it had become now a part of them, and they part of it—like the hand-crank mahogany Victrola in the hall, or the lion-pelted sofa, or the Boutelle piano (ten years silent, its keys yellowed and decayed and ferocious, like the teeth of an aged mule).

Nights, they spoke of sin. Also of other times and better days: Maud and Louise—sitting there in the bellying heat of the obsolete but steadfast stove, hooking rugs, crocheting doilies, sewing linen, chatting, chatting.

Occasionally Julia listened, because she was there and there was nothing else to do; but mostly she didn't. It had become a simple thing to rock and nod and think of nothing at all, while *they* traded dreams of dead husbands, constantly relishing their mutual widowhood—relishing it!—pitching these fragile ghosts into moral combat. "Ernie, God rest him, was an honorable man." (So were they all, Julia would think, all honorable men; but we are here to praise Caesar, not to bury him . . .) "Jack would be alive today if it hadn't been for that trunk lid slamming down on his head: that's what started it all." Poor Ernie! Poor Jack!

(He walked along the railroad tracks, blending with the night. He could have been young or old: an age-hiding beard dirtied his face and throat. He wore a blue sweater, ripped in a dozen places. On the front of the sweater was sewn a large felt letter: E. Also sewn there was a small design showing a football and calipers. His gray trousers were dark with stain where he had fouled them. He walked along the tracks, seeing and not seeing the pulse of light far ahead; thinking and not thinking. Perhaps I'll find it there. Perhaps they won't catch me. Perhaps I won't be hungry anymore . . .)

"You forgot the margarine," Louise said, holding the large sack upside down.

"Did I? I'm sorry." Julia took her place at the table. The food immediately began to make her ill: the sight of it, the smell of it. Great bowls of beans, crisp-skinned chunks of turkey, mashed potatoes. She put some on her plate, and watched her sisters. They ate earnestly; and now, for no reason, this, too, was upsetting.

She looked away. What was it? What was wrong?

"Mick says that fellow didn't die," Maud announced. "Julia —"

"What fellow?"

"At the asylum, that got choked. He's going to be all right."

"That's good."

Louise broke a square of toast. She addressed Maud: "What else did he say, when you talked to him? Are they making any progress?"

"Some. I understand there's a bunch of police coming down from Seattle. If they don't get him in a few days, they'll bring in some bloodhounds from out of state. Of course, you can imagine how much Mick likes *that!*"

"Well, it's his own fault. If he was any kind of a sheriff, he'd've caught that fellow a long time before this. I mean, after all, Burlington just isn't that big." Louise dismembered a turkey leg, ripped little shreds of the meat off, put them into her mouth.

Maud shook her head. "I don't know. Mick claims it isn't like catching an ordinary criminal. With this one, you never can guess what he's going to do, or where he'll be. Nobody has figured out how he stays alive, for instance."

"Probably," Louise said, "he eats bugs and things."

Julia folded her napkin quickly and pressed it onto the table.

Maud said, "No. Most likely he finds stray dogs and cats."

They finished the meal in silence. Not, Julia knew, because there was any lull in thought: merely so the rest could be savored in the living room, next to the fire. A proper place for everything.

They moved out of the kitchen. Louise insisted on doing the dishes, while Maud settled at the radio and tried to find a local news broadcast. Finally she snapped the radio off angrily. "You'd think they'd at least keep us informed! Isn't that the least they could do?"

Louise materialized in her favorite chair. The kitchen was dark. The stove warmed noisily, its metal sides undulating.

And it was time.

"Where do you suppose he is right now?" Maud asked.

Louise shrugged. "Out there somewhere. If they'd got him, Mick would've called us. He's out there somewhere."

"Yes. Laughing at all of us, too, I'll wager. Trying to figure out who'll be next."

Julia sat in the rocker and tried not to listen. Outside, there was a wind. A cold wind, biting; the kind that slips right through window putty, that you can feel on the glass. Was there ever such a cold wind? she wondered.

Then Louise's words started to echo. "He's out there somewhere . . ."

Julia looked away from the window and attempted to take an interest in the lacework in her lap.

Louise was talking. Her fingers flashed long silver needles. ". . . spoke to Mrs. Schillings today."

"I don't want to hear about it." Maud's eyes flashed like the needles.

"God love her heart, she's about crazy. Could barely talk."

"God, God."

"I tried to comfort her, of course, but it didn't do any good."

Julia was glad she had been spared that conversation. It sent a shudder across her, even to think about it. Mrs. Schillings was Eva's mother, and Eva — only seventeen . . . The thoughts she vowed not to think came back. She remembered Mick's description of the body, and his words: ". . . she'd got through with work over at the telephone office around about nine. Carl Jasperson offered to see her home, but he says she said not to bother, it was only a few blocks. Our boy must have been hiding around the other side of the cannery. Just as Eva passed, he jumped. Raped her and then strangled her. I figure he's a pretty man-sized bugger. Thumbs like to went clean through the throat . . ."

In two weeks, three women had died. First, Charlotte Adams, the librarian. She had been taking her usual shortcut across the school playground, about 9:15 P.M. They found her by the slide, her clothes ripped from her body, her throat raw and bruised.

Julia tried very hard not to think of it, but when her mind would clear, there were her sisters' voices, droning, pulling her back, deeper.

She remembered how the town had reacted. It was the first murder Burlington had had in fifteen years. It was the very first mystery. Who was the sex-crazed killer? Who could have done this terrible thing to Charlotte Adams? One of her gentleman friends, perhaps. Or a hobo, from one of the nearby jungles, or . . .

Mick Daniels and his tiny force of deputies had swung into action immediately. Everyone in town took up the topic, chewed it, talked it, chewed it, until it lost its shape completely. The air became electrically charged. And a grim gaiety swept Burlington, reminding Julia of a circus where everyone is forbidden to smile.

Days passed uneventfully. Vagrants were pulled in and released. People were questioned. A few were booked, temporarily.

Then, when the hum of it had begun to die, it happened again. Mrs. Dovie Samuelson, member of the local PTA, mother of two, moderately attractive and moderately young, was found in her garden, sprawled across a rhododendron bush, dead. She was naked, and it was established that she had been attacked. Of the killer, once again, there was no trace.

Then the State Hospital for the Criminally Insane released the information that one of its inmates — a Robert Oakes — had escaped. Mick, and many others, had known this all along. Oakes had originally been placed in the asylum on a charge of raping and murdering his cousin, a girl named Patsy Blair.

After he had broken into his former home and stolen some old school clothes, he had disappeared, totally.

Now he was loose.

Burlington, population 3,000, went into a state of ecstasy: delicious fear gripped the town. The men foraged out at night with torches and weapons; the women squeaked and looked under their beds and . . . chatted.

But still no progress was made. The maniac eluded hundreds of searchers. They knew he was near, perhaps at times only a few feet away, hidden; but always they returned home, defeated.

They looked in the forests and in the fields and along the riverbanks.

They covered High Mountain — a miniature hill at the south end of town — like ants, poking at every clump of brush, investigating every abandoned tunnel and water tank. They broke into deserted houses, searched barns, silos, haystacks, treetops. They looked everywhere, everywhere. And found nothing.

When they decided for sure that their killer had gone far away, that he couldn't conceivably be within fifty miles of Burlington, a third crime was committed. Young Eva Schillings's body had been found less than a hundred yards from her home.

And that was three days ago . . .

". . . they get him," Louise was saying, "they ought to kill him by little pieces for what he's done."

Maud nodded. "Yes; but they won't."

"Of course they —"

"No! You wait. They'll shake his hand and lead him back to the bughouse and wait on him hand and foot — till he gets a notion to bust out again."

"Well, I'm of a mind the people will have something to say about that."

"Anyway," Maud continued, never lifting her eyes from her knitting, "what makes you so sure they *will* catch him? Supposing he just drops out of sight for six months, and —"

"You stop that! They'll get him. Even if he is a maniac, he's still human."

"I really doubt that. I doubt that a human could have done these awful things." Maud sniffed. Suddenly, like small rivers, tears began to course down her snowbound cheeks, cutting and melting the hard white-packed powder, revealing flesh underneath even paler. Her hair was shot with gray, and her dress was the color of rocks and moths; yet she did not succeed in looking either old or frail. There was nothing whatever frail about Maud.

"He's a man," she said. Her lips seemed to curl at the word. Louise nodded, and they were quiet.

(His ragged tennis shoes padded softly on the gravel bed. Now his heart was trying to tear loose from his chest. The men, the men . . . They had almost stepped on him, they were that close. But he had been silent. They had gone past him, and away. He could see their flares back in the distance. And far ahead, the pulsing light. Also a square building: the depot, yes. He must be careful. He must walk in the shadows. He must be very still.

The fury burned him, and he fought it.

Soon.

It would be all right, soon . . .)

". . . Think about it, this here maniac is only doing what every man would *like* to do but can't."

"Maud!"

"I mean it. It's a man's natural instinct — it's all they ever think about." Maud smiled. She looked up. "Julia, you're feeling sick. Don't tell me you're not."

"I'm all right," Julia said, tightening her grip on the chair-arms slightly. She thought, They've been married! They talk this way about men, as they always have, and yet soft words have been spoken to them, and strong arms placed around their shoulders . . .

Maud made tiny circles with her fingers. "Well, I can't force you to take care of yourself. Except, when you land in the hospital again, I suppose you know who'll be doing the worrying and staying up nights — as per usual."

"I'll . . . go on to bed in a minute." But why was she hesitating? Didn't she want to be alone?

Why didn't she want to be alone?

Louise was testing the door. She rattled the knob vigorously and returned to her chair.

"What would he want, anyway," Maud said, "with two old biddies like us?"

"We're not so old," Louise said, saying, actually: "That's true; we're old."

But it wasn't true, not at all. Looking at them, studying them, it suddenly occurred to Julia that her sisters were ashamed of their essential attractiveness. Beneath the '20s hairdos, the ill-used cosmetics, the ancient dresses (which did not quite succeed in concealing their still-voluptuous physiques), Maud and Louise were youthfully full and pretty. They were. Not even the birch-twig toothbrushes and traditional snuff could hide it.

Yet, Julia thought, they envy me.

They envy my plainness.

"What kind of man would do such heinous things?" Louise said, pronouncing the word carefully: *heen-ious.*

And Julia, without calling or forming the thought, discovered an answer grown in her mind: an impression, a feeling.

What kind of a man?

A lonely man.

It came upon her like a chill. She rose from the pillowed chair, lightly. "I think," she said, "I'll go on to my room."

"Are your windows good and locked?"

"Yes."

"You'd better make sure. All he'd have to do is climb up the drainpipe." Maud's expression was peculiar. Was she really saying, "This is only to comfort you, dear. Of the three of us, it's unlikely he'd pick on you."

"I'll make sure." Julia walked to the hallway. "Good night."

"Try to get some sleep." Louise smiled. "And don't think about him, hear? We're perfectly safe. He couldn't possibly get in, even if he tried. Besides," she said, "I'll be awake."

(He stopped and leaned against a pole and looked up at the deaf and swollen sky. It was a movement of dark shapes, a hurrying, a running.

He closed his eyes.

"The moon is the shepherd,
The clouds are his sheep . . ."

He tried to hold the words, tried very hard, but they scattered and were gone.

"No."

He pushed away from the pole, turned, and walked back to the gravel bed.

The hunger grew: with every step it grew. He thought that it had died, that he had killed it at last and now he could rest, but it had not died. It sat inside him, inside his mind, gnawing, calling, howling to be released. Stronger than before. Stronger than ever before.

"The moon is the shepherd . . ."

A cold wind raced across the surrounding fields of wild grass, turning the land into a heavy dark green ocean. It sighed up through the branches of cherry trees and rattled the thick leaves. Sometimes a cherry would break loose, tumble in the gale, fall, and split, filling the night with its fragrance. The air was iron and loam and growth.

He walked and tried to pull these things into his lungs, the silence and coolness of them.

But someone was screaming, deep inside him. Someone was talking.

"What are you going to do — "

He balled his fingers into fists.

"Get away from me! Get away!"

"Don't — "

The scream faded.

The girl's face remained. Her lips and her smooth white skin and her eyes, her eyes . . .

He shook the vision away.

The hunger continued to grow. It wrapped his body in sheets of living fire. It got inside his mind and bubbled in hot acids, filling and filling him.

He stumbled, fell, plunged his hands deep into the gravel, withdrew fists full of the grit and sharp stones, and squeezed them until blood trailed down his wrists.

He groaned softly.

Ahead, the light glowed and pulsed and whispered, Here, Here, Here, Here, Here.

He dropped the stones and opened his mouth to the wind and walked on . . .)

Julia closed the door and slipped the lock noiselessly. She could no longer hear the drone of voices: it was quiet, still, but for the sighing breeze.

What kind of a man . . .

She did not move, waiting for her heart to stop throbbing. But it would not stop.

She went to the bed and sat down. Her eyes traveled to the window, held there.

"He's out there somewhere . . ."

Julia felt her hands move along her dress. It was an old dress, once purple, now gray with faded gray flowers. The cloth was tissue-thin. Her fingers touched it and moved upward to her throat. They undid the top button.

For some reason, her body trembled. The chill had turned to heat, tiny needles of heat, puncturing her all over.

She threw the dress over a chair and removed the underclothing. Then she walked to the bureau and took from the top drawer a flannel nightdress, and turned.

What she saw in the tall mirror caused her to stop and make a small sound.

Julia Landon stared back at her from the polished glass.

Julia Landon, thirty-eight, neither young nor old, attractive nor unattractive, a woman so plain she was almost invisible. All angles and sharpnesses, and flesh that would once have been called milky but was now only white, pale white. A little too tall. A little too thin. And faded.

Only the eyes had softness. Only the eyes burned with life and youth and—

Julia moved away from the mirror. She snapped off the light. She touched the window shade, pulled it slightly, guided it soundlessly upward.

Then she unfastened the window latch.

Night came into the room and filled it. Outside, giant clouds roved across the moon, obscuring it, revealing it, obscuring it again.

It was cold. Soon there would be rain.

Julia looked out beyond the yard, in the direction of the depot, dark and silent now, and the tracks and the jungles beyond the tracks where lost people lived.

"I wonder if he can see me."

She thought of the man who had brought terror and excitement to the town. She thought of him openly, for the first time, trying to imagine his features.

He was probably miles away.

Or perhaps he was nearby. Behind the tree, there, or under the hedge . . .

"I'm afraid of you, Robert Oakes," she whispered to the night. "You're insane, and a killer. You would frighten the wits out of me."

The fresh smell swept into Julia's mind. She wished she were surrounded by it, in it, just for a little while.

Just for a few minutes.

A walk. A short walk in the evening.

She felt the urge strengthening.

"You're dirty, young man. And heartless—ask Mick, if you don't believe me. You want love so badly you must kill for it—but nevertheless, you're heartless. Understand? And you're not terribly bright, either, they say. Have you read Shakespeare's sonnets? Herrick? How about Shelley, then? There, you see! I'd detest you on sight. Just look at your fingernails!"

She said these things silently, but as she said them she moved toward her clothes.

She paused, went to the closet.

The green dress. It was warmer.

A warm dress and a short walk—that will clear my head. Then I'll come back and sleep.

It's perfectly safe.

She started for the door, stopped, returned to the window. Maud and Louise would still be up, talking.

She slid one leg over the sill; then the other leg.

Softly she dropped to the frosted lawn.

The gate did not creak.

She walked into the darkness.

Better! So much better. Good clean air that you can breathe!

The town was a silence. A few lights gleamed in distant houses, up ahead; behind, there was only blackness. And the wind.

In the heavy green frock, which was still too light to keep out the cold — though she felt no cold; only the needled heat — she walked away from the house and toward the depot.

It was a small structure, unchanged by passing years, like the Landon home and most of the homes in Burlington. There were tracks on either side of it.

Now it was deserted. Perhaps Mr. Gaffey was inside, making insect sounds on the wireless. Perhaps he was not.

Julia stepped over the first track and stood, wondering what had happened and why she was here. Vaguely she understood something. Something about the yellow thread that had made her late and forced her to return home through the gathering dusk. And this dress — had she chosen it because it was warmer than the others . . . or because it was prettier?

Beyond this point there was wilderness, for miles. Marshes and fields overgrown with weeds and thick foliage. The hobo jungles: some tents, dead campfires, empty tins of canned heat.

She stepped over the second rail and began to follow the gravel bed. Heat consumed her. She could not keep her hands still.

In a dim way, she realized — with a tiny part of her — why she had come out tonight.

She was looking for someone.

The words formed in her mind, unwilled: "Robert Oakes, listen, listen to me. You're not the only one who is lonely. But you can't steal what we're lonely for, you can't take it by force. Don't you know that? Haven't you learned that yet?"

I'll talk to him, she thought, and he'll go along with me and give himself up . . .

No.

That isn't why you're out tonight. You don't care whether he gives himself up or not. You . . . only want him to know that you understand. Isn't that it?

You couldn't have any other reason.

It isn't possible that you're seeking out a lunatic for any other reason.

Certainly you don't want him to touch you.

Assuredly you don't want him to put his arms around you and kiss you, because no man has ever done that — assuredly, assuredly.

It isn't you he wants. It isn't love. He wouldn't be taking Julia Landon . . .

"But what if he doesn't!" The words spilled out in a small choked cry. "What if he sees me and runs away! Or I don't find him. Others have been looking. What makes me think I'll — "

Now the air swelled with sounds of life: frogs and birds and locusts, moving; and the wind, running across the trees and reeds and foliage at immense speed, whining, sighing.

Everywhere there was this loudness, and a dark like none Julia had ever known. The moon was gone entirely. Shadowless, the surrounding fields were great pools of liquid black, stretching infinitely, without horizon.

Fear came up in her chest, clutching.

She tried to scream.

She stood paralyzed, moveless, a pale terror drying into her throat and into her heart.

Then, from far away, indistinctly, there came a sound. A sound like footsteps on gravel.

Julia listened, and tried to pierce the darkness. The sounds grew louder. And louder. Someone was on the tracks. Coming closer.

She waited. Years passed, slowly. Her breath turned into a ball of expanding ice in her lungs.

Now she could see, just a bit.

It was a man. A black man-form. Perhaps — the thought increased her fear — a hobo. It mustn't be one of the hoboes.

No. It was a young man. Mick! Mick, come to tell her, "Well, we got the bastard!" and to ask, narrowly, "What the devil you doing out here, Julie?" Was it?

She saw the sweater. The ball of ice in her lungs began to melt a little. A sweater. And shoes that seemed almost white.

Not a hobo. Not Mick. Not anyone she knew.

She waited an instant longer. Then, at once, she knew without question who the young man was.

And she knew that he had seen her.

The fear went away. She moved to the center of the tracks.

"I've been looking for you," she said soundlessly. "Every night I've thought of you. I have." She walked toward the man. "Don't be afraid, Mr. Oakes. Please don't be afraid. I'm not."

The young man stopped. He seemed to freeze, like an animal prepared for flight.

He did not move for several seconds.

Then he began to walk toward Julia, lightly, hesitantly, rubbing his hands along his trousers.

When Julia was close enough to see his eyes, she relaxed, and smiled.

Perhaps, she thought, feeling the first drops of rain upon her face, perhaps if I don't scream he'll let me live.

That would be nice.

1956

GIL BREWER

THE GESTURE

GIL(BERT) BREWER (1922–1983) was born in Canandaigua, New York. While he was serving in the Army during World War II, his family moved to Florida; he joined them after his discharge. He decided to become a writer like his father when he was nine years old, dropping out of school to work at various blue-collar jobs while practicing his craft. Although his bibliography shows numerous sales to pulps such as *Zeppelin Stories* in 1929 and to various detective magazines between 1931 and 1934, they are obviously inaccurate. His first book, *13 French Street,* was published in 1951—the first of his twenty-three novels to be issued in that decade—the same year in which he sold what is probably his first published short story, "With This Gun," to *Detective Tales.* He published nearly one hundred stories in all, mostly under his own name, but also under the pseudonyms Eric Fitzgerald and Bailey Morgan. He also ghost-wrote novels for Ellery Queen, Hal Ellson, Al Conroy, and five novels for an Israeli soldier named Harry Arvay.

Early in his career, Brewer came to the attention of Joseph T. Shaw, who became his agent. The famous editor of *Black Mask* saw in Brewer a special talent and thought he could rival the biggest names, but Shaw died of a heart attack in 1952, soon after their association began. Thereafter Brewer cranked out paperback originals at a prodigious rate, often completing a book in a week or less. They are generally dark stories, compared by the editor Anthony Boucher to the work of James M. Cain and Jim Thompson, mostly about ordinary men led down the road to ruin by unscrupulous women. His best-selling book, *The Red Scarf* (1958), one of two hardcover books he published, sold more than a million copies. After the 1950s, however, his output diminished, both quantitatively and qualitatively, largely due to alcoholism and serious injuries sustained in a car crash—a good career that, with better advice and a little more luck, could have been a great one.

"The Gesture" was originally published in the March 1956 issue of *The Saint Mystery Magazine.*

▪ ▪ ▪

NOLAN PLACED BOTH hands on the railing of the veranda, and unconsciously squeezed the wood until the muscles in his arms corded and ached. He looked down, across the immaculately trimmed green lawn, past the palms and the Australian pines, to the beach, gleaming whitely under the late-morning sun.

The Gulf was crisply green today, and calm, broken only by the happy frolicking of the man and woman — laughing, swimming. His wife, Helen, and Latimer, the photographer from the magazine in New York, down to do a picture story of the island.

Nolan turned his gaze away, lifted his hands, and stared at his palms. His hands were trembling and his thin cotton shirt was soaked with perspiration.

He couldn't stand it. He left the veranda and walked swiftly into the sprawling living room of his home. He paced back and forth for a moment, his feet whispering on the grass rug. Then he stood quietly in the center of the room, trying to think. For two weeks it had been going on. At first he'd thought he would last. Now he knew it no longer mattered, about lasting.

He would have to do something. He strode rapidly across the room into his study, opened the top drawer of his desk, and looked down at the .45 automatic. He slammed the drawer shut, whirled, and went back into the living room.

Why had he ever allowed the man entrance to the island?

Oh, he knew why, well enough. Because Helen had wanted it. And now he couldn't order Latimer away. It would be as good as telling Helen the reason. She knew how much he loved her; why did she act this way? Why did she torture him? She *must* realize, after all these years, that he couldn't stand another man even looking at her beauty.

Why did she think they lived here — severed from all mainland life?

He stiffened, making an effort to wipe away the frown on his face. He reached for his handkerchief and swabbed at the perspiration on his arms and forehead. They were coming, laughing and talking, up across the lawn.

Quickly, he selected a magazine from the rack and settled into a wicker chair with his back to the front entrance. He flipped the periodical open and was engrossed in a month-old mystery story when they stomped loudly across the veranda.

Every step was a kind of unbearable thunder to Nolan. He was reaching such a pitch of helpless irritability that he nearly screamed.

"Darling!" Helen called. "Where are you — oh, there!"

She stepped toward him, her bare feet softly thumping the grass rug. He half-glanced up at her. She was coffee-brown, her eyes excited and happier than he'd seen them in a long time. She wore one of the violent-hued red, yellow, and green cloth swimming suits that she'd designed for herself.

He abruptly realized how meager the suit was and his neck burned. He had contrived to have her make the suit with the least expenditure of material. It was his pleasure to look at her.

But not now — not with Latimer here!

"What *have* you been doing?" she asked.

He started to reply, looking across at Latimer standing at the entranceway, but she rippled on. "You really should have come swimming with us, dear. It was wonderful this morning." She reached out and tousled his hair. "You haven't been near the water in days."

Nolan cleared his throat. "Well," he said. "Well, Mr. Latimer. About caught up? About ready with your story?"

He wanted to shout: *When are you leaving!* He could not. He sat there, staring at Latimer. The sunny days here on the island had done the man good. He was bronzed and healthy and young and abrim with a vitality that had not been present when he'd first come over from the mainland.

"A few more days, I guess," Latimer said. "I wish you'd call me Jack. And I sure wish you two would pose for a few pictures. It's nice enough, the way you've been about letting me photograph the island, your home, but —" Latimer left the protest unspoken, smiling halfheartedly.

Nolan glanced at his wife. She reached down and touched his arm, her fingers trembling. "After lunch Jack and I are going to take a walk, clear around the island," she said. "You know, we haven't done that in a terribly long while. Why don't you come along?"

"Sorry," Nolan said quickly. "I've some things I've got to attend to."

"Sure wish you'd come," Latimer said.

Nolan said nothing.

"Well," Latimer said. "I've got to write a letter. Guess I'll do it while you're fixing lunch, Helen."

"Right," Helen said. "I'd better get busy." She turned and hurried off toward the kitchen, humming softly.

"By the way," Latimer said to Nolan. "Anything you'd like done in town? I'll be taking the boat across this evening, so I can mail some stuff off."

"Thank you," Nolan said. "There's nothing."

"Well," Latimer said. He sighed and started across the room toward the hallway leading to his bedroom. It had been a storage room, but Nolan had fixed it up with a bed and a table for Latimer's typewriter when Helen insisted the photographer stay on the island. Latimer paused by the hallway. "Sure you won't come with us this afternoon?"

Nolan didn't bother to answer. He couldn't answer. If he had tried, he knew he might have shouted, even cursed — maybe actually gone at the man with his bare hands.

He would not use his bare hands. He wouldn't soil them. He would use the gun. He listened as Latimer left the room, and sat there breathing stiffly, his fingers clenched into the magazine's crumpled pages.

Yes, that's what he would do. Latimer's saying he was going to remain on the island longer still clinched it. Nolan knew why Latimer had said that. He wasn't fooling anybody. Taking advantage of hospitality for his own sneaking reasons. Didn't Helen see what kind of a man Latimer was? Was she blind? Or did she want it this way?

The very thought of such a thing sent Nolan out of the chair, stalking back and forth across the room. He could hear Latimer's typewriter ticking away from the far side of the house.

Their paradise. Their home. Their love. Torn and twisted and broken by this insensitive person. He heard Helen call them to lunch then, and moving toward the table in the dining room, he felt slightly relieved. He knew that while they were gone this afternoon, he would get everything ready.

With Latimer's unconscious aid, Nolan knew exactly how he was going to do it. He sat at the table, picking at his food, listening to them talk and laugh. He tried vainly to concentrate away from the sounds of their voices.

"This salad's terrific," Latimer said. "Helen, you're wonderful! You two've got it made out here!"

Helen lowered her gaze to her plate. Nolan stared directly at Latimer and Latimer reddened and looked away. Nolan grinned inside. He had caught the man. But the victory was empty. The long afternoon, thinking about her out there with Latimer, would be painful.

They finished lunch in silence. Almost before Nolan realized it, the house was again empty. He could hear them laughing still, their voices growing faint as they moved down along the beach.

Helen had even insisted on taking several bottles of cold beer wrapped in insulated bags to keep cool, and carried in the old musette.

Nolan could not stand still. He paced back and forth across the extent of the house, thinking about tonight. If he didn't do it tonight, it might be too late. He did not want Helen too attached to Latimer, and he felt sure it had gone very far already.

He knew Latimer intended to stay on and stay on — until he could take Helen away with him. But tonight would end it. He would go along with Latimer to the mainland. Only, Latimer would never reach the mainland. The boat would swamp.

Nolan knew how to swamp a boat. He knew Latimer wasn't much of a swimmer, and anyhow, a man couldn't swim with a .45 slug in his heart. But Nolan could swim well. He would kill Latimer, take him out into the Gulf, weight him, and sink him. Then he'd bring the boat in and swamp it and swim ashore. He would report it, and rent a boat and come home. He knew they were in for a bit of heavy weather tonight. It would be just perfect.

And Helen and he would be happy again. The way they had always been.

He looked back, thinking over the good times. The time before they'd come to the island, when he'd been hard-working at the glass-cutting business he'd inherited from his father. Then more and more he'd become conscious of Helen's beauty and the effect she had on men. And loving her as wildly as he did, he could no longer bear the endless suspense; the knowledge that sooner or later she would leave him. So he sold the business, retired. His little lie. So far as she knew, he simply wanted island life — quiet, unhurried, alone with her. It was true. But not a complete truth.

All this time they had been happy. Until now. Somebody'd got wind of the beauty of the island and Latimer had shown up to do his story. Under conditions imposed by Nolan — no pictures of either himself or Helen. He had allowed one fuzzy negative of them standing against a blossoming hibiscus near the house, at twilight — that was all.

Wandering through the house, trying not to think of what they were doing now, he found himself in Latimer's room. The unmade bed, the photographic equipment, the typewriter set up on the table.

Beside the machine was a typewritten letter.

Nolan turned away. But something drew him over to the table. Pure curiosity in this man Latimer. He stood there, staring down at the obviously unfinished letter. An addressed envelope lay beside it. There was a half-completed sentence on the sheet in the typewriter, numbered Page 2.

The letter was addressed to the editor of the magazine where Latimer worked.

Nolan began reading, at first leisurely, then feverishly.

Dear Bart:

Really have this thing wrapped up, but I'm staying on a while longer, just to settle a few things in my own mind and maybe I'll come up with a bunch of pix and a yarn that'll knock your head off . . . sure beautiful scenery on the island . . . house is a regular bamboo and cypress mansion . . . unhealthy, Bart, really sick . . . he watches her like a hawk. He's ripped with jealousy and it would be laughable, except that they're both so very old. He must be in his eighties, but she's a bit harder to read. I did a lousy thing. I confronted her with it. You would have, too. She's so obviously just enduring everything for his sake. Humoring him. My God, think of it! All these years he's kept her out here, away from everybody, imprisoned. It's pure hell. She as much as admitted it. I'm staying on, just to see if I can't work it somehow. Get her back to civilization, if only for a vacation, Bart. She deserves it. You should hear her ask how things are out there—it would break your damned heart . . .

There was more, and Nolan read all of it through twice. For a moment longer he stood there, seeing everything clearly for the first time in nearly a half century.

Then he walked through the house to his study, opened the desk drawer, took out the .45 automatic. He sat down in his chair by the desk, put the muzzle of the gun into his mouth, and pulled the trigger.

1956

EVAN HUNTER

THE LAST SPIN

EVAN HUNTER (1926–2005) was born Salvatore A. Lombino, legally changing his name in 1952. He was admitted to New York's Cooper Union after winning a scholarship to the Art Students League, then served in the Navy during World War II; he graduated from Hunter College after his return from the Pacific theater. He had begun writing stories while based on a destroyer, then wrote numerous short stories and several novels in the years after the war. After several unsuccessful adult and children's books, he published *The Blackboard Jungle* in 1954, which was an instant success, filmed the following year and starring Glenn Ford, Anne Francis, and Sidney Poitier. In 1956 he created the Ed McBain byline, which became more famous than his own, as he wrote the iconic Eighty-seventh Precinct series, in which the members of an entire squad room, rather than a single police officer, serve as the hero. Fifty-four novels succeeded *Cop Hater,* the first book in the series. Under the McBain name, he also produced thirteen novels about Matthew Hope, a Florida lawyer, and several standalone mysteries. Hunter also wrote under the pseudonyms Richard Marston, Hunt Collins, Ezra Hannon, Curt Cannon, and John Abbott, producing more than one hundred books. Other films made from his works include *Strangers When We Meet* (1960), *High and Low* (1962), *Last Summer* (1969), *Fuzz* (1972), *Blood Relatives* (1977), and *The Chisholms* (1979). He also wrote the screenplay for Alfred Hitchcock's *The Birds* (1963).

The Blackboard Jungle was the first significant book to deal with juvenile delinquents and gang violence in New York, and many of Hunter's early short stories, collected in *Learning to Kill* (2006), deal with these subjects, often in a sympathetic manner.

"The Last Spin" was first published in the September 1956 issue of *Manhunt;* it was collected in Hunter's *The Jungle Kids* the same year.

■ ■ ■

THE BOY SITTING opposite him was his enemy.

The boy sitting opposite him was called Tigo, and he wore a green silk jacket with an orange stripe on each sleeve. The jacket told Danny that Tigo was his enemy. The jacket shrieked, "Enemy, enemy!"

"This is a good piece," Tigo said, indicating the gun on the table. "This runs you close to forty-five bucks, you try to buy it in a store. That's a lot of money."

The gun on the table was a Smith & Wesson .38 Police Special.

It rested exactly in the center of the table, its sawed-off, two-inch barrel abruptly terminating the otherwise lethal grace of the weapon. There was a checked walnut stock on the gun, and the gun was finished in a flat blue. Alongside the gun were three .38 Special cartridges.

Danny looked at the gun disinterestedly. He was nervous and apprehensive, but he kept tight control of his face. He could not show Tigo what he was feeling. Tigo was the enemy, and so he presented a mask to the enemy, cocking one eyebrow and saying, "I seen pieces before. There's nothing special about this one."

"Except what we got to do with it," Tigo said. Tigo was studying him with large brown eyes. The eyes were moist-looking. He was not a bad-looking kid, Tigo, with thick black hair and maybe a nose that was too long, but his mouth and chin were good. You could usually tell a cat by his mouth and his chin. Tigo would not turkey out of this particular rumble. Of that, Danny was sure.

"Why don't we start?" Danny asked. He wet his lips and looked across at Tigo.

"You understand," Tigo said, "I got no bad blood for you."

"I understand."

"This is what the club said. This is how the club said we should settle it. Without a big street diddlebop, you dig? But I want you to know I don't know you from a hole in the wall—except you wear a blue and gold jacket."

"And you wear a green and orange one," Danny said, "and that's enough for me."

"Sure, but what I was trying to say . . ."

"We going to sit and talk all night, or we going to get this thing rolling?" Danny asked.

"What I'm trying to say," Tigo went on, "is that I just happened to be picked for this, you know? Like to settle this thing that's between the two clubs. I mean, you got to admit your boys shouldn't have come in our territory last night."

"I got to admit nothing," Danny said flatly.

"Well, anyway, they shot at the candy store. That wasn't right. There's supposed to be a truce on."

"OK, OK," Danny said.

"So like . . . like this is the way we agreed to settle it. I mean, one of us and . . . and one of you. Fair and square. Without any street boppin', and without any law trouble."

"Let's get on with it," Danny said.

"I'm trying to say, I never even seen you on the street before this. So this ain't nothin' personal with me. Whichever way it turns out, like . . ."

"I never seen you neither," Danny said.

Tigo stared at him for a long time. "That's cause you're new around here. Where you from originally?"

"My people come down from the Bronx."

"You got a big family?"

"A sister and two brothers, that's all."

"Yeah, I only got a sister." Tigo shrugged. "Well." He sighed. "So." He sighed again. "Let's make it, huh?"

"I'm waitin'," Danny said.

Tigo picked up the gun, and then he took one of the cartridges from the tabletop. He broke open the gun, slid the cartridge into the cylinder, and then snapped the gun shut and twirled the cylinder. "Round and round she goes," he said, "and where she stops, nobody knows. There's six chambers in the cylinder and only one cartridge. That makes the odds five to one that the cartridge'll be in firing position when the cylinder stops whirling. You dig?"

"I dig."

"I'll go first," Tigo said.

Danny looked at him suspiciously. "Why?"

"You want to go first?"

"I don't know."

"I'm giving you a break." Tigo grinned. "I may blow my head off first time out."

"Why you giving me a break?" Danny asked.

Tigo shrugged. "What the hell's the difference?" He gave the cylinder a fast twirl.

"The Russians invented this, huh?" Danny asked.

"Yeah."

"I always said they was crazy bastards."

"Yeah, I always . . ." Tigo stopped talking. The cylinder was stopped now. He took a deep breath, put the barrel of the .38 to his temple, and then squeezed the trigger.

The firing pin clicked on an empty chamber.

"Well, that was easy, wasn't it?" he asked. He shoved the gun across the table. "Your turn, Danny."

Danny reached for the gun. It was cold in the basement room, but he was sweating now. He pulled the gun toward him, then left it on the table while he dried his palms on his trousers. He picked up the gun then and stared at it.

"It's a nifty piece," Tigo said. "I like a good piece."

"Yeah, I do too," Danny said. "You can tell a good piece just by the way it feels in your hand."

Tigo looked surprised. "I mentioned that to one of the guys yesterday, and he thought I was nuts."

"Lots of guys don't know about pieces," Danny said, shrugging.

"I was thinking," Tigo said, "when I get old enough, I'll join the Army, you know? I'd like to work around pieces."

"I thought of that, too. I'd join now only my old lady won't give me permission. She's got to sign if I join now."

"Yeah, they're all the same," Tigo said, smiling. "Your old lady born here or the old country?"

"The old country," Danny said.

"Yeah, well, you know they got these old-fashioned ideas."

"I better spin," Danny said.

"Yeah," Tigo agreed.

Danny slapped the cylinder with his left hand. The cylinder whirled, whirled, and then stopped. Slowly, Danny put the gun to his head. He wanted to close his eyes, but he didn't dare. Tigo, the enemy, was watching him. He returned Tigo's stare, and then he squeezed the trigger.

His heart skipped a beat, and then over the roar of his blood he heard the empty click. Hastily, he put the gun down on the table.

"Makes you sweat, don't it?" Tigo said.

Danny nodded, saying nothing. He watched Tigo. Tigo was looking at the gun.

"Me now, huh?" Tigo said. He took a deep breath, then picked up the .38. He twirled the cylinder, waited for it to stop, and then put the gun to his head.

"Bang!" Tigo said, and then he squeezed the trigger. Again the firing pin clicked on an empty chamber. Tigo let out his breath and put the gun down.

"I thought I was dead that time," he said.

"I could hear the harps," Danny said.

"This is a good way to lose weight, you know that?" Tigo laughed nervously, and then his laugh became honest when he saw Danny was laughing with him. "Ain't it the truth? You could lose ten pounds this way."

"My old lady's like a house," Danny said, laughing. "She ought to try this kind of diet." He laughed at his own humor, pleased when Tigo joined him.

"That's the trouble," Tigo said. "You see a nice deb in the street, you think it's crazy, you know? Then they get to be our people's age, and they turn to fat." He shook his head.

"You got a chick?" Danny asked.

"Yeah, I got one."

"What's her name?"

"Aw, you don't know her."

"Maybe I do," Danny said.

"Her name is Juana." Tigo watched him. "She's about five-two, got these brown eyes . . ."

"I think I know her," Danny said. He nodded. "Yeah, I think I know her."

"She's nice, ain't she?" Tigo asked. He leaned forward, as if Danny's answer was of great importance to him.

"Yeah, she's nice," Danny said.

"The guys rib me about her. You know, all they're after . . . well, you know . . . they don't understand something like Juana."

"I got a chick, too," Danny said.

"Yeah. Hey, maybe sometime we could . . ." Tigo cut himself short. He looked down at the gun, and his sudden enthusiasm seemed to ebb completely. "It's your turn," he said.

"Here goes nothing," Danny said. He twirled the cylinder, sucked in his breath, and then fired.

The empty click was loud in the stillness of the room.

"Man!" Danny said.

"We're pretty lucky, you know?" Tigo said.

"So far."

"We better lower the odds. The boys won't like it if we . . ." He stopped himself again, and then reached for one of the cartridges on the table. He broke open the gun again, and slipped the second cartridge into the cylinder. "Now we got two cartridges in here," he said. "Two cartridges, six chambers. That's four to two. Divide it, and you get two to one." He paused. "You game?"

"That's . . . that's what we're here for, ain't it?"

"Sure."

"OK then."

"Gone," Tigo said, nodding his head. "You got courage, Danny."

"You're the one needs the courage," Danny said gently. "It's your spin."

Tigo lifted the gun. Idly, he began spinning the cylinder.

"You live on the next block, don't you?" Danny asked.

"Yeah." Tigo kept slapping the cylinder. It spun with a gently whirring sound.

"That's how come we never crossed paths, I guess. Also, I'm new on the scene."

"Yeah, well you know, you get hooked up with one club, that's the way it is."

"You like the guys on your club?" Danny asked, wondering why he was asking such a stupid question, listening to the whirring of the cylinder at the same time.

"They're OK." Tigo shrugged. "None of them really send me, but that's the club on my block, so what're you gonna do, huh?" His hand left the cylinder. It stopped spinning. He put the gun to his head.

"Wait!" Danny said.

Tigo looked puzzled. "What's the matter?"

"Nothing. I just wanted to say . . . I mean . . ." Danny frowned. "I don't dig too many of the guys on my club, either."

Tigo nodded. For a moment, their eyes locked. Then Tigo shrugged, and fired.

The empty click filled the basement room.

"Phew," Tigo said.

"Man, you can say that again."

Tigo slid the gun across the table.

Danny hesitated an instant. He did not want to pick up the gun. He felt sure that this time the firing pin would strike the percussion cap of one of the cartridges. He was sure that this time he would shoot himself.

"Sometimes I think I'm turkey," he said to Tigo, surprised that his thoughts had found voice.

"I feel that way sometimes, too," Tigo said.

"I never told that to nobody," Danny said. "The guys on my club would laugh at me, I ever told them that."

"Some things you got to keep to yourself. There ain't nobody you can trust in this world."

"There should be somebody you can trust," Danny said. "Hell, you can't tell nothing to your people. They don't understand."

Tigo laughed. "That's an old story. But that's the way things are. What're you gonna do?"

"Yeah. Still, sometimes I think I'm turkey."

"Sure, sure," Tigo said. "It ain't only that, though. Like sometimes . . . well, don't you wonder what you're doing stomping some guy in the street? Like . . . you know what I mean? Like . . . who's the guy to you? What you got to beat him up for? 'Cause he messed with somebody else's girl?" Tigo shook his head. "It gets complicated sometimes."

"Yeah, but . . ." Danny frowned again. "You got to stick with the club. Don't you?"

"Sure, sure . . . hell yes." Again their eyes locked.

"Well, here goes," Danny said. He lifted the gun. "It's just . . ." He shook his head, and then twirled the cylinder. The cylinder spun, and then stopped. He studied the gun, wondering if one of the cartridges would roar from the barrel when he squeezed the trigger.

Then he fired.

Click.

"I didn't think you was going through with it," Tigo said.

"I didn't neither."

"You got heart, Danny," Tigo said. He looked at the gun. He picked it up and broke it open.

"What you doing?" Danny asked.

"Another cartridge," Tigo said. "Six chambers, three cartridges. That makes it even money. You game?"

"You?"

"The boys said . . ." Tigo stopped talking. "Yeah, I'm game," he added, his voice curiously low.

"It's your turn, you know."

"I know."

Danny watched as Tigo picked up the gun.

"You ever been rowboating on the lake?"

Tigo looked across the table at Danny, his eyes wide. "Once," he said. "I went with Juana."

"Is it . . . is it any kicks?"

"Yeah. Yeah, it's grand kicks. You mean you never been?"

"No," Danny said.

"Hey, you got to try it, man," Tigo said excitedly. "You'll like it. Hey, you try it."

"Yeah, I was thinking maybe this Sunday I'd . . ." He did not complete the sentence.

"My spin," Tigo said wearily. He twirled the cylinder. "Here goes a good man," he said, and he put the revolver to his head and squeezed the trigger.

Click.

Danny smiled nervously. "No rest for the weary," he said. "But Jesus you've got heart. I don't know if I can go through with it."

"Sure, you can," Tigo assured him. "Listen, what's there to be afraid of?" He slid the gun across the table.

"We keep this up all night?" Danny asked.

"They said . . . you know . . ."

"Well, it ain't so bad. I mean, hell, we didn't have this operation, we wouldn'ta got a chance to talk, huh?" He grinned feebly.

"Yeah," Tigo said, his face splitting in a wide grin. "It ain't been so bad, huh?"

"No, it's been . . . well, you know, these guys on the club, who can talk to them?"

He picked up the gun.

"We could . . ." Tigo started.

"What?"

"We could say . . . well . . . like we kept shootin' an' nothing happened, so . . ." Tigo shrugged. "What the hell! We can't do this all night, can we?"

"I don't know."

"Let's make this the last spin. Listen, they don't like it, they can take a flying leap, you know?"

"I don't think they'll like it. We're supposed to settle this for the clubs."

"Screw the clubs!" Tigo said. "Can't we pick our own . . ." The word was hard coming. When it came, his eyes did not leave Danny's face. ". . . friends?"

"Sure we can," Danny said vehemently. "Sure we can! Why not?"

"The last spin," Tigo said. "Come on, the last spin."

"Gone," Danny said. "Hey, you know, I'm *glad* they got this idea. You know that? I'm actually glad!" He twirled the cylinder. "Look, you want to go on the lake this Sunday? I mean with your girl and mine? We could get two boats. Or even one if you want."

"Yeah, one boat," Tigo said. "Hey, your girl'll like Juana, I mean it. She's a swell chick."

The cylinder stopped. Danny put the gun to his head quickly.

"Here's to Sunday," he said. He grinned at Tigo, and Tigo grinned back, and then Danny fired.

The explosion rocked the small basement room, ripping away half of Danny's head, shattering his face. A small cry escaped Tigo's throat, and a look of incredulous shock knifed his eyes.

Then he put his head on the table and began weeping.

1960

JIM THOMPSON

FOREVER AFTER

JIM (JAMES MEYERS) THOMPSON (1906–1977) was born in Anadarko, Oklahoma Territory, and worked numerous hard, physical jobs, including as an oil-well and pipeline laborer (his father was a wildcatter), while trying to write. He received commissions from the Works Projects Administration Writers' Project during the Depression, producing guidebooks of Oklahoma, among other works, and worked as a journalist, mainly covering crime stories.

His first novel, *Now and on Earth* (1942), is a tale of sex, sin, violence, and revenge. The book most readers regard as his masterpiece, *The Killer Inside Me* (1952), was the first of sixteen paperback originals he produced during the 1950s, his only prolific era. His other critically successful novels during the '50s include *Savage Night* (1953), *A Swell-Looking Babe* (1954), and *The Getaway* (1959). After *The Grifters* (1963) and *Pop. 1280* (1964), the quality of his work, already extremely erratic, declined rapidly. When he died in 1977, not a single book of his was in print in the United States until Quill included *The Killer Inside Me* in a series of classic hard-boiled novels in 1983; the following year, Black Lizard reprinted most of his other titles. While his bleak novels of psychopaths, losers, alcoholics, and unreliable narrators never achieved sales beyond a vocal cult following in his own country, he enjoyed substantial commercial and critical success in France, where he has often been regarded as America's greatest hard-boiled writer. Several films were made from his work, with varying aesthetic success, including *The Killer Inside Me,* a dud filmed in 1976 with Stacy Keach as Sheriff Lou Ford; *The Getaway,* filmed twice (both with endings absurdly changed from very noir to happy), first in 1972 with Steve McQueen and Ali MacGraw, then in 1994 with Alec Baldwin and Kim Basinger; and the superb *The Grifters* (1990), for which Donald E. Westlake's screenplay received one of the film's four Academy Award nominations. Directed by Stephen Frears, it starred John Cusack, Anjelica Huston, Annette Bening, and Pat Hingle. Thompson also wrote several screenplays, including the caper film *The Killing* (1956) and the antiwar film *Paths of Glory* (1957), both directed by Stanley Kubrick, but was cheated out of a screenwriting credit both times.

"Forever After" was published in the May 1960 issue of *Shock* magazine.

▪ ▪ ▪

IT WAS A FEW minutes before five o'clock when Ardis Clinton unlocked the rear door of her apartment and admitted her lover. He was a cow-eyed young man with a wild mass of curly black hair. He worked as a dishwasher at Joe's Diner, which was directly across the alley.

They embraced passionately. Her body pressed against the meat cleaver concealed inside his shirt, and Ardis shivered with delicious anticipation. Very soon now, it would all be over. That stupid ox, her husband, would be dead. He and his stupid cracks — all the dullness and boredom — would be gone forever. And with the twenty thousand insurance money, ten thousand dollars double-indemnity . . .

"We're going to be so happy, Tony," she whispered. "You'll have your own place, a real swank little restaurant with what they call one of those intimate bars. And you'll just manage it, just kind of saunter around in a dress suit, and —"

"And we'll live happily ever after," Tony said. "Just me and you, baby, walking down life's highway together."

Ardis let out a gasp. She shoved him away from her, glaring up into his handsome empty face. "Don't!" she snapped. "Don't say things like that! I've told you and told you not to do it, and if I have to tell you again, I'll —!"

"But what'd I say?" he protested. "I didn't say nothin'."

"Well . . ." She got control of herself, forcing a smile. "Never mind, darling. You haven't had any opportunities and we've never really had a chance to know each other, so — so never mind. Things will be different after we're married." She patted his cheek, kissed him again. "You got away from the diner all right? No one saw you leave?"

"Huh-uh. I already took the stuff up to the steam-table for Joe, and the waitress was up front too, y'know, filling the sugar bowls and the salt and pepper shakers like she always does just before dinner. And —"

"Good. Now, suppose someone comes back to the kitchen and finds out you're not there. What's your story going to be?"

"Well . . . I was out in the alley dumping some garbage. I mean —" He corrected himself hastily, "maybe I was. Or maybe I was down in the basement, getting some supplies. Or maybe I was in the john — the lavatory, I mean — or —"

"Fine," Ardis said approvingly. "You don't say where you were, so they can't prove you weren't there. You just don't remember where you were, understand, darling? You might have been any number of places."

Tony nodded. Looking over her shoulder into the bedroom, he frowned worriedly. "Why'd you do that now, honey? I know this has got to look like a robbery. But tearin' up the room now, before he gets here—"

"There won't be time afterwards. Don't worry, Tony. I'll keep the door closed."

"But he might open it and look in. And if he sees all them dresser drawers dumped around, and—"

"He won't. He won't look into the bedroom. I know exactly what he'll do, exactly what he'll say, the same things that he's always done and said ever since we've been married. All the stupid, maddening, dull, tiresome—!" She broke off abruptly, conscious that her voice was rising. "Well, forget it," she said, forcing another smile. "He won't give us any trouble."

"Whatever you say." Tony nodded docilely. "If you say so, that's the way it is, Ardis."

"But there'll be trouble—from the cops. I know I've already warned you about it, darling. But it'll be pretty bad, worse than anything you've ever gone through. They won't have any proof, but they're bound to be suspicious, and if you ever start talking, admitting anything—"

"I won't. They won't get anything out of me."

"You're sure? They'll try to trick you. They'll probably tell you that I've confessed. They may even slap you around. So if you're not absolutely sure . . ."

"They won't get anything out of me," he repeated stolidly. "I won't talk."

And studying him, Ardis knew that he wouldn't.

She led the way down the hall to the bathroom. He parted the shower curtains and stepped into the tub. Drawing a pair of gloves from his pocket, he pulled them onto his hands. Awkwardly, he fumbled the meat cleaver from beneath his shirt.

"Ardis. Uh—look, honey."

"Yes?"

"Do I have to hit you? Couldn't I just maybe give you a little shove, or—"

"No, darling," she said gently. "You have to hit me. This is supposed to be a robbery. If you killed my husband without doing anything to me, well, you know how it would look."

"But I never hit no woman—any woman—before. I might hit you too hard, and—"

"Tony!"

"Well, all right," he said sullenly. "I don't like it, but all right."

Ardis murmured soothing endearments. Then, brushing his lips quickly with her own, she returned to the living room. It was a quarter after five, exactly five minutes—but *exactly*—until her husband, Bill, would come home. Closing the bedroom door, she lay down on the lounge. Her negligee fell open, and she left it that way, grinning meanly as she studied the curving length of her thighs.

Give the dope a treat for a change, she thought. *Let him get one last good look before he gets his.*

Her expression changed. Wearily, resentfully, she pulled the material of the negligee over her legs. Because, of course, Bill would never notice. She could wear a ring in her nose, paint a bull's-eye around her navel, and he'd never notice.

If he had ever noticed, just once paid her a pretty compliment . . .

If he had ever done anything different, ever said or done anything different at all—even the teensiest little bit . . .

But he hadn't. Maybe he couldn't. So what else could she do but what she was doing? She could get a divorce, sure, but that was all she'd get. No money; nothing with which to build a new life. Nothing to make up for those fifteen years of slowly being driven mad.

It's his own fault, she thought bitterly. *I can't take any more. If I had to put up with him for just one more night, even one more hour . . . !*

She heard heavy footsteps in the hallway. Then a key turned in the door latch, and Bill came in. He was a master machinist, a solidly built man of about forty-five. The old-fashioned gold-rimmed glasses on his pudgy nose gave him a look of owlish solemnity.

"Well," he said, setting down his lunch bucket. "Another day, another dollar."

Ardis grimaced. He plodded across to the lounge, stooped, and gave her a halfhearted peck on the cheek.

"Long time no see," he said. "What we havin' for supper?"

Ardis gritted her teeth. It shouldn't matter now; in a few minutes it would all be over. Yet somehow it *did* matter. He was as maddening to her as he had ever been.

"Bill . . ." She managed a seductive smile, slowly drawing the negligee apart. "How do I look, Bill?"

"OK," he yawned. "Got a little hole in your drawers, though. What'd you say we was havin' for supper?"

"Slop," she said. "Garbage. Trash salad with dirt dressing."

"Sounds good. We got any hot water?"

Ardis sucked in her breath. She let it out again in a kind of infuriated moan. "Of course we've got hot water! Don't we always have? Well, don't we? Why do you have to ask every night?"

"So what's to get excited about?" He shrugged. "Well, guess I'll go splash the chassis."

He plodded off down the hall. Ardis heard the bathroom door open and close. She got up, stood waiting by the telephone. The door banged open again, and Tony came racing up the hall.

He had washed off the cleaver. While he hastily tucked it back inside his shirt, Ardis dialed the operator. "Help," she cried weakly. "Help . . . police . . . murder!"

She let the receiver drop to the floor, spoke to Tony in a whisper. "He's dead? You're sure of it?"

"Yeah, yeah, sure I'm sure. What do you think?"

"All right. Now, there's just one more thing . . ."

"I can't, Ardis. I don't want to. I—"

"Hit me," she commanded, and thrust out her chin. "Tony, I said to hit me!"

He hit her. A thousand stars blazed through her brain and disappeared. And she crumpled silently to the floor.

. . . When she regained consciousness, she was lying on the lounge. A heavyset man, a detective obviously, was seated at her side, and a white-jacketed young man with a stethoscope draped around his neck hovered nearby.

She had never felt better in her life. Even the lower part of her face, where Tony had smashed her, was surprisingly free of pain. Still, because it was what she should do, she moaned softly; spoke in a weak, hazy voice.

"Where am I?" she said. "What happened?"

"Lieutenant Powers," the detective said. "Suppose you tell me what happened, Mrs. Clinton."

"I . . . I don't remember. I mean, well, my husband had just come home, and gone back to the bathroom. And there was a knock on the door, and I supposed it was the paperboy or someone like that. So—"

"You opened the door and he rushed in and slugged you, right? Then what happened?"

"Well, then he rushed into the bedroom and started searching it. Yanking out the dresser drawers and—"

"What was he searching for, Mrs. Clinton? You don't have any considerable amount of money around, do you? Or any jewelry aside from what you're wearing? And it wasn't your husband's payday, was it?"

"Well, no. But—"

"Yes?"

"I don't know. Maybe he was crazy. All I know is what he did."

"I see. He must have made quite a racket, seems to me. How come your husband didn't hear it?"

"He couldn't have. He had the shower running, and—"

She caught herself, fear constricting her throat. Lieutenant Powers grinned grimly.

"Missed a bet, huh, Mrs. Clinton?"

"I—I don't know what you're—"

"Come off of it! The bathtub's dry as an oven. The shower was never turned on, and you know why it wasn't. Because there was a guy standing inside of it."

"B-but—but I don't know anything. I was unconscious, and—"

"Then, how do you know what happened? How do you know this guy went into the bedroom and started tearing it apart? And how did you make that telephone call?"

"Well, I . . . I wasn't completely unconscious. I sort of knew what was going on without really—"

"Now, you listen to me," he said harshly. "You made that fake call of yours—yes, I said *fake*—to the operator at twenty-three minutes after five. There happened to be a prowl car right here in the neighborhood, so two minutes later, at five twenty-five, there were cops here in your apartment. You were unconscious then, more than an hour ago. You've been unconscious until just now."

Ardis's brain whirled. Then it cleared suddenly, and a great calm came over her.

"I don't see quite what you're hinting at, Lieutenant. If you're saying that I was confused, mixed up—that I must have dreamed or imagined some of the things I told you—I'll admit it."

"You know what I'm saying! I'm saying that no guy could have got in and out of this place, and done what this one did, in any two minutes!"

"Then the telephone operator must have been mistaken about the time," Ardis said brightly. "I don't know how else to explain it."

Powers grunted. He said he could give her a better explanation—and he gave it to her. The right one. Ardis listened to it placidly, murmuring polite objections.

"That's ridiculous, Lieutenant. Regardless of any gossip you may have heard, I don't know this, uh, Tony person. And I most certainly did not plot with him or anyone else to kill my husband. Why—"

"He says you did. We got a signed confession from him."

"Have you?" But of course they didn't have. They might have found out about Tony, but he would never have talked. "That hardly proves anything, does it?"

"Now, you listen to me, Mrs. Clinton! Maybe you think that—"

"How is my husband, anyway? I do hope he wasn't seriously hurt."

"How is he?" the lieutenant snarled. "How would he be after gettin' worked over with—" He broke off, his eyes flickering. "As a matter of fact," he said heavily, "he's going to be all right. He was pretty badly injured, but he was able to give us a statement and—"

"I'm so glad. But why are you questioning me, then?" It was another trick. Bill had to be dead. "If he gave you a statement, then you must know that everything happened just like I said."

She waited, looked at him quizzically. Powers scowled, his stern face wrinkling with exasperation.

"All right," he said at last. "All right, Mrs. Clinton. Your husband is dead. We don't have any statement from him, and we don't have any confession from Tony."

"Yes?"

"But we know that you're guilty, and you know that you are. And you'd better get it off your conscience while you still can."

"While I still can?"

"Doc"—Powers jerked his head at the doctor. At the man, that is, who appeared to be a doctor. "Lay it on the line, Doc. Tell her that her boyfriend hit her a little too hard."

The man came forward hesitantly. He said, "I'm sorry, Mrs. Clinton. You have a—uh—you've sustained a very serious injury."

"Have I?" Ardis smiled. "I feel fine."

"I don't think," the doctor said judiciously, "that that's quite true. What you mean is that you don't feel anything at all. You couldn't. You see, with an injury such as yours—"

"Get out," Ardis said. "Both of you get out."

"Please, Mrs. Clinton. Believe me, this isn't a trick. I haven't wanted to alarm you, but—"

"And you haven't," she said. "You haven't scared me even a little bit, mister. Now, clear out!"

She closed her eyes, kept them closed firmly. When, at last, she reopened them, Powers and the doctor—if he really had been a doctor—were gone. And the room was in darkness.

She lay smiling to herself, congratulating herself. In the corridor outside, she heard heavy footsteps approaching; and she tensed for a moment. Then, remembering, she relaxed again.

Not Bill, of course. She was through with that jerk forever. He'd driven her half out of her mind, got her to the point where she couldn't have taken another minute of him if her life depended on it. But now . . .

The footsteps stopped in front of her door. A key turned in the lock, the door opened and closed.

There was a clatter of a lunch pail being set down; then a familiar voice — maddeningly familiar words:

"Well. Another day, another dollar."

Ardis's mouth tightened; it twisted slowly in a malicious grin. So they hadn't given up yet! They were pulling this one last trick. Well, let them; she'd play along with the gag.

The man plodded across the room, stooped, and gave her a half-hearted peck on the cheek. "Long time no see," he said. "What we havin' for supper?"

"Bill . . ." Ardis said. "How do I look, Bill?"

"OK. Got your lipstick smeared, though. What'd you say we was having for supper?"

"Stewed owls! Now, look, mister. I don't know who you —"

"Sounds good. We got any hot water?"

"Of course, we've got hot water! Don't we always have? Why do you always have to ask if — if —"

She couldn't go through with it. Even as a gag — even someone who merely sounded and acted like he did — it was too much to bear.

"Y-you get out of here!" she quavered. "I don't have to stand for this! I *c-can't* stand it! I did it for fifteen years, and —"

"So what's to get excited about?" he said. "Well, guess I'll go splash the chassis."

"Stop it! *STOP IT!*" Her screams filled the room . . . silent screams ripping through silence. "He's — you're dead! I know you are! You're dead, and I don't have to put up with you for another minute. And — and — !"

"Wouldn't take no bets on that if I was you," he said mildly. "Not with a broken neck like yours."

He trudged off toward the bathroom, wherever the bathroom is in Eternity.

1968

CORNELL WOOLRICH

FOR THE REST OF HER LIFE

CORNELL (GEORGE HOPLEY) WOOLRICH (1903–1968) was born in New York City but divided his early years between Latin America and Mexico, with his father, and New York, with his Manhattan socialite mother. While still an undergraduate at Columbia University, he wrote his first novel, a romance, *Cover Charge* (1926). Another romantic novel, *Children of the Ritz* (1927), quickly followed, and it won a $10,000 prize jointly offered by *College Humor* magazine and First National Pictures, which filmed it in 1929. Four more romantic novels, favorably compared to F. Scott Fitzgerald, followed. Woolrich had also begun to write short stories, and his first mystery was published in 1934. Most of his subsequent work (more than two hundred stories and sixteen novels) was in that genre. A reclusive alcoholic, he rarely left his hotel room for the last three decades of his life.

Arguably the greatest suspense writer of the twentieth century, Woolrich, under his own name and the pseudonyms William Irish and George Hopley, was able to construct plots that stretched credulity, especially in their dependence on coincidence, yet relentlessly gripped readers. He is noted for producing stories of the everyday gone wrong, as terrible things happen to ordinary people. More than twenty of his novels and stories were filmed, including *The Leopard Man* (1943), based on *Black Alibi* (1942), directed by Jacques Tourneur; *Phantom Lady* (1944), directed by Robert Siodmak; *Rear Window* (1954), based on "It Had to Be Murder" and directed by Alfred Hitchcock; and *The Bride Wore Black* (1967), directed by François Truffaut. More true of the literary works than the motion pictures (since Hollywood preferred happy endings), Woolrich was able to heighten suspense by being totally unpredictable, with readers never knowing if the suspense would be relieved or if it would be worse when the tale was ended.

"For the Rest of Her Life," the last Woolrich story published during his lifetime, first appeared in the May 1968 issue of *Ellery Queen's Mystery Magazine*, and was first collected in his *Angels of Darkness* (1978). It was made into a two-hour television movie in West Germany in 1974, directed and adapted for the screen by Rainer Werner Fassbinder.

■ ■ ■

THEIR EYES MET in Rome. On a street in Rome — the Via Piemonte. He was coming down it, coming along toward her, when she first saw him. She didn't know it but he was also coming into her life, into her destiny — bringing what was meant to be.

Every life is a mystery. And every story of every life is a mystery. But it is not what *happens* that is the mystery. It is whether it *has* to happen no matter what, whether it is ordered and ordained, fixed and fated, or whether it can be missed, avoided, circumvented, passed by; *that* is the mystery.

If she had not come along the Via Piemonte that day, would it still have happened? If she had come along the Via Piemonte that day, but ten minutes later than she did, would it *still* have happened? Therein lies the real mystery. And no one ever knows, and no one ever will.

As their eyes met, they held. For just a heartbeat.

He wasn't cheap. He wasn't sidewalk riffraff. His clothes were good clothes, and his air was a good air.

He was a personable-looking man. First your eye said: he's not young anymore, he's not a boy anymore. Then your eye said: but he's not old. There was something of youth hovering over and about him, and yet refusing to land in any one particular place. As though it were about to take off and leave him. Yet not quite that, either. More as though it had never fully been there in the first place. In short, the impression it was, was agelessness. Not young, not old, not callow, not mature — but ageless. Thirty-six looking fifty-six, or fifty-six looking thirty-six, but which it was you could not say.

Their eyes met — and held. For just a heartbeat.

Then they passed one another by, on the Via Piemonte, but without any turn of their heads to prolong the look.

I wonder who that was, she thought.

What he thought couldn't be known — at least, not by her.

Three nights later they met again, at a party the friend she was staying with took her to.

He came over to her, and she said, "I've seen you before. I passed you on Monday on the Via Piemonte. At about four in the afternoon."

"I remember you, too," he said. "I noticed you that day, going by."

I wonder why we remember each other like that, she mused; I've passed dozens, hundreds of other people since, and he must have too. I don't remember any of *them.*

"I'm Mark Ramsey," he said.

"I'm Linda Harris."

An attachment grew up. What is an attachment? It is the most difficult of all the human interrelationships to explain, because it is the vaguest, the most impalpable. It has all the good points of love, and none of its drawbacks. No jealousy, no quarrels, no greed to possess, no fear of losing possession, no hatred (which is very much a part of love), no surge of passion, and no hangover afterward. It never reaches the heights, and it never reaches the depths.

As a rule it comes on subtly. As theirs did. As a rule the two involved are not even aware of it at first. As they were not. As a rule it only becomes noticeable when it is interrupted in some way, or broken off by circumstances. As theirs was. In other words, its presence only becomes known in its absence. It is only missed after it stops. While it is still going on, little thought is given to it, because little thought needs to be.

It is pleasant to meet, it is pleasant to be together. To put your shopping packages down on a little wire-backed chair at a little table at a sidewalk café, and sit down and have a vermouth with someone who has been waiting there for you. And will be waiting there again tomorrow afternoon. Same time, same table, same sidewalk café. Or to watch Italian youth going through the gyrations of the latest dance craze in some inexpensive indigenous night-place — while you, who come from the country where the dance originated, only get up to do a sedate fox trot. It is even pleasant to part, because this simply means preparing the way for the next meeting.

One long continuous being-together, even in a love affair, might make the thing wilt. In an attachment it would surely kill the thing off altogether. But to meet, to part, then to meet again in a few days, keeps the thing going, encourages it to flower.

And yet it requires a certain amount of vanity, as love does: a desire to please, to look one's best, to elicit compliments. It inspires a certain amount of flirtation, for the two are of opposite sex. A wink of understanding over the rim of a raised glass, a low-voiced confidential aside about something and the smile of intimacy that answers it, a small impromptu gift — a necktie on the one part because of an accidental spill on the one he was wearing, or of a small bunch of flowers on the other part because of the color of the dress she has on.

So it goes.

And suddenly they part, and suddenly there's a void, and suddenly they discover they have had an attachment.

Rome passed into the past, and became New York.

Now, if they had never come together again, or only after a long time and in different circumstances, then the attachment would have faded and died. But if they suddenly do come together again — while the sharp sting of missing one another is still smarting — then the attachment will revive full force, full strength. But never again as merely an attachment. It has to go on from there, it has to build, to pick up speed. And sometimes it is so glad to be brought back again that it makes the mistake of thinking it is love.

She was thinking of him at the moment the phone rang. And that helped, too, by its immediacy, by its telephonic answer to her wistful wish of remembrance. Memory is a mirage that fools the heart . . .

"You'll never guess what I'm holding in my hand, right while I'm talking to you . . .

"I picked it up only a moment ago, and just as I was standing and looking at it, the phone rang. Isn't that the strangest thing! . . .

"Do you remember the day we stopped in and you bought it . . .

"I have a little one-room apartment on East Seventieth Street. I'm by myself now, Dorothy stayed on in Rome . . ."

A couple of months later, they were married . . .

They call this love, she said to herself. I know what it is now. I never thought I would know, but I do now.

But she failed to add: If you can step back and identify it, is it really there? Shouldn't you be unable to know what the whole thing's about? Just blindly clutch and hold and fear that it will get away. But unable to stop, to think, to give it any name.

Just two more people sharing a common human experience. Infinite in its complexity, tricky at times, but almost always successfully surmounted in one of two ways: either blandly content with the results as they are, or else vaguely discontent but chained by habit. Most women don't marry a man, they marry a habit. Even when a habit is good, it can become monotonous; most do. When it is bad in just the average degree it usually becomes no more than a nuisance and an irritant; and most do.

But when it is darkly, starkly evil in the deepest sense of the word, then it can truly become a hell on earth.

Theirs seemed to fall midway between the first two, for just a little while. Then it started veering over slowly toward the last. Very slowly, at the start, but very steadily . . .

They spent their honeymoon at a New Hampshire lakeshore resort. This lake had an Indian name which, though certainly barbaric in sound to the average English-speaker, in her special case presented such an impassable block both in speech and in mental pre-speech imagery (for some obscure reason, Freudian perhaps, or else simply an instinctive retreat from something with distressful connotations) that she gave up trying to say it and it became simply "the lake." Then as time drew it backward, not into forgetfulness but into distance, it became "that lake."

Here the first of the things that happened, happened. The first of the things important enough to notice and to remember afterward, among a great many trifling but kindred ones that were not. Some so slight they were not more than gloating, zestful glints of eye or curt hurtful gestures. (Once he accidentally poured a spurt of scalding tea on the back of a waitress's wrist, by not waiting long enough for the waitress to withdraw her hand in setting the cup down, and by turning his head momentarily the other way. The waitress yelped, and he apologized, but he showed his teeth as he did so, and you don't show your teeth in remorse.)

One morning when she woke up, he had already dressed and gone out of the room. They had a beautifully situated front-view of rooms which overlooked the lake itself (the bridal suite, as a matter of fact), and when she went to the window she saw him out there on the white-painted little pier which jutted out into the water on knock-kneed piles. He'd put on a turtleneck sweater instead of a coat and shirt, and that, over his spare figure, with the shoreward breeze alternately lifting and then flattening his hair, made him look younger than when he was close by. A ripple of the old attraction, of the old attachment, coursed through her and then was quickly gone. Just like the breeze out there. The little sidewalk-café chairs of Rome with the braided-wire backs and the piles of parcels on them, where were they now? Gone forever; they couldn't enchant anymore.

The lake water was dark blue, pebbly-surfaced by the insistent breeze that kept sweeping it like the strokes of invisible broom-straws, and mottled with gold flecks that were like floating freckles in the nine o'clock September sunshine.

There was a little boy in bathing trunks, tanned as a caramel, sitting on the side of the pier, dangling his legs above the water. She'd noticed him about in recent days. And there was his dog, a noisy, friendly, ungainly little mite, a Scotch terrier that was under everyone's feet all the time.

The boy was throwing a stick in, and the dog was splashing after it, retrieving it, and paddling back. Over and over, with that tirelessness and simplicity of interest peculiar to all small boys and their dogs. Off to one side a man was bringing up one of the motorboats that were for rent, for Mark to take out.

She could hear him in it for a while after that, making a long slashing ellipse around the lake, the din of its vibration alternately soaring and lulling as it passed from the far side to the near and then back to the far side again.

Then it cut off suddenly, and when she went back to look it was rocking there sheepishly engineless. The boy was weeping and the dog lay huddled dead on the lake rim, strangled by the boiling backwash of the boat that had dragged it — how many times? — around and around in its sweep of the lake. The dog's collar had become snagged some way in a line with a grappling hook attached, left carelessly loose over the side of the boat. (Or aimed and pitched over as the boat went slashing by?) The line trailed limp now, and the lifeless dog had been detached from it.

"If you'd only looked back," the boy's mother said ruefully to Mark. "He was a good swimmer, but I guess the strain was too much and his little heart gave out."

"He did look! He did! He did! I saw him!" the boy screamed, agonized, peering accusingly from in back of her skirt.

"The spray was in the way," Mark refuted instantly. But she wondered why he said it so quickly. Shouldn't he have taken a moment's time to think about it first, and then say, "The spray must have been — " or "I guess maybe the spray — " But he said it as quickly as though he'd been ready to say it even before the need had arisen.

Everyone for some reason acted furtively ashamed, as if something unclean had happened. Everyone but the boy, of course. There were no adult nuances to his pain.

The boy would eventually forget his dog.

But would she? Would she?

They left the lake — the farewells to Mark were a bit on the cool side, she noticed — and moved into a large rambling country house in the Berkshire region of Massachusetts, not far from Pittsfield, which he told her had been in his family for almost seventy-five years. They had a car, an Alfa Romeo, which he had brought over from Italy, and, at least in all its outward aspects, they had a not too unpleasant life together. He was an art importer, and financially a highly successful one; he used to commute back and forth to Boston, where he had a gallery with a small-size apartment above it. As a rule he would stay over in the city, and then drive out Friday night and spend the weekend in the country with her.

(She always slept so well on Mondays, Tuesdays, and Wednesdays. Thursdays she always lay awake half the night reminding herself that the following night was Friday. She never stopped to analyze this; if she had, what would it have told her? What *could* it have, if she didn't realize it already?)

As far as the house was concerned, let it be said at once that it was not a depressing house in itself. People can take their moods from a house, but by the same token a house can take its mood from the people who live in it. If it became what it became, it was due to him — or rather, her reaction to him.

The interior of the house had crystallized into a very seldom evoked period, the pre–World War I era of rococo and gimcrack elegance. Either its last occupant before them (an unmarried older sister of his) had had a penchant for this out of some girlhood memory of a war-blighted romance and had deliberately tried to re-create it, or what was more likely, all renovations had stopped around that time and it had just stayed that way by default.

Linda discovered things she had heard about but never seen before. Claw legs on the bathtub, nacre in-and-out pushbuttons for the lights, a hanging stained-glass dome lamp over the dining-room table, a gramophone with a crank handle — she wondered if they'd first rolled back the rug and then danced the hesitation or the one-step to it. The whole house, inside and out, cried out to have women in the straight-up-and-down endlessly long tunics of 1913, with side-puffs of hair over their ears, in patent-leather shoes with beige suede tops up to the middle of the calf, suddenly step out of some of the rooms; and in front of the door, instead of his slender-bodied, bullet-fast Italian compact, perhaps a four-cornered Chalmers or Pierce-Arrow or Hupmobile shaking all over to the beat of its motor.

Sometimes she felt like an interloper, catching herself in some full-length mirror as she passed it, in her over-the-kneetop skirt and short free down-blown hair. Sometimes she felt as if she were under a magic spell, waiting to be disenchanted. But it wasn't a good kind of spell, and it didn't come wholly from the house or its furnishings . . .

One day at the home of some people Mark knew who lived in the area, where he had taken her on a New Year's Day drop-in visit, she met a young man named Garrett Hill. He was branch head for a company in Pittsfield.

It was as simple as that — they met. As simple as only beautiful things can be simple, as only life-changing things, turning-point things, can be simple.

Then she met him a second time, by accident. Then a third, by coincidence. A fourth, by chance . . . Or directed by unseen forces?

Then she started to see him on a regular basis, without meaning anything, certainly without meaning any harm. The first night he brought her home they chatted on the way in his car; and then at the door, as he held out his hand, she quickly put hers out of sight behind her back.

"Why are you afraid to shake my hand?"

"I thought you'd hurt me."

"How can anyone hurt you by just shaking your hand?"

When he tried to kiss her, she turned and fled into the house, as frightened as though he'd brandished a whip at her.

When he tried it again, on a later night, again she recoiled sharply—as if she were flinching from some sort of punishment.

He looked at her, and his eyes widened, both in sudden understanding and in disbelief. "You're *afraid physically,*" he said, almost whispering. "I thought it was some wifely scruple the other night. But you're physically afraid of being kissed! As if there were pain attached to it."

Before she could stop herself or think twice she blurted out, "Well, there is, isn't there?"

He said, his voice deadly serious, "*What* kind of kissing have you been used to?"

She hung her head. And almost the whole story had been told.

His face was white as a sheet. He didn't say another word. But one man understands another well; all are born with that particular insight.

The next week she went into the town to do some small shopping—shopping she could have done as easily over the phone. Did she hope to run across him during the course of it? Is that why she attended to it in person? And after it was taken care of she stepped into a restaurant to sit down over a cup of coffee while waiting for her bus. He came into the place almost immediately afterward; he must have been sitting in his car outside watching for her.

He didn't ask to sit down; he simply leaned over with his knuckles resting on the table, across the way from her, and with a quick back glance toward the door by which he had just entered, took a book out from under his jacket and put it down in front of her, its title visible.

"I sent down to New York to get this for you," he said. "I'm trying to help you in the only way I know how."

She glanced down at it. The title was: *The Marquis de Sade: The Complete Writings.*

"Who was he?" she asked, looking up. She pronounced it with the long *a,* as if it were an English name. "Sayd."

"Sod," he instructed. "He was a Frenchman. Just read the book" was all he would say. "Just read the book."

He turned to leave her, and then he came back for a moment and added, "Don't let anyone else see—" Then he changed it to "Don't let *him* see you with it. Put a piece of brown wrapping paper around it so the title won't be conspicuous. As soon as you've finished, bring it back; don't leave it lying around the house."

After he'd gone she kept staring at it. Just kept staring.

They met again three days later at the same little coffee shop off the main business street. It had become their regular meeting place by now. No fixed arrangement to it; he would go in and find her there, or she would go in and find him there.

"Was he the first one?" she asked when she returned the book.

"No, of course not. This is as old as man—this getting pleasure by giving pain. There are some of them born in every generation. Fortunately not too many. He simply was the first one to write it up and so when the world became more specialized and needed a separate tag for everything, they used his name. It became a word—*sadism,* meaning sexual pleasure got by causing pain, the sheer pleasure of being cruel."

She started shaking all over as if the place were drafty. "It is that." She had to whisper it, she was so heartsick with the discovery. "Oh, God, yes, it is that."

"You had to know the truth. That was the first thing. You had to know, you had to be told. It isn't just a vagary or a whim on his part. It isn't just a—well, a clumsiness or roughness in making love. This is a frightful thing, a deviation, an affliction, and—a terrible danger to you. You had to understand the truth first."

"Sometimes he takes his electric shaver—" She stared with frozen eyes at nowhere out before her. "He doesn't use the shaver itself, just the cord—connects it and—"

She backed her hand into her mouth, sealing it up.

Garrett did something she'd never seen a man do before. He lowered his head, all the way over. Not just onto his chest, but all the way down until his chin was resting on the tabletop. And his eyes, looking up at her, were smoldering red with anger. But literally red, the whites all suffused. Then something wet came along and quenched the burning in them.

"Now you know what you're up against," he said, straightening finally. "Now what do you want to do?"

"I don't know." She started to sob very gently, in pantomime, without a sound. He got up and stood beside her and held her head pressed against him. "I only know one thing," she said. "I want to see the stars at night again, and not just the blackness and the shadows. I want to wake up in the morning as if it was my right, and not have to say a prayer of thanks that I lived through the night. I want to be able to tell myself there won't be another night like the last one."

The fear Mark had put into her had seeped and oozed into all parts of her; she not only feared fear, she even feared rescue from fear.

"I don't want to make a move that's too sudden," she said in a smothered voice.

"I'll be standing by, when you want to and when you do."

And on that note they left each other. For one more time.

On Friday he was sitting there waiting for her at their regular table, smoking a cigarette. And another lay out in the ashtray, finished. And another. And another.

She came up behind him and touched him briefly but warmly on the shoulder, as if she were afraid to trust herself to speak.

He turned and greeted her animatedly. "Don't tell me you've been in there that *long!* I thought you hadn't come in yet. I've been sitting out here twenty minutes, watching the door for you."

Then when she sat down opposite him and he got a good look at her face, he quickly sobered.

"I couldn't help it. I broke down in there. I couldn't come out any sooner. I didn't want everyone in the place to see me, the way I was."

She was still shaking irrepressibly from the aftermath of long-continued sobs.

"Here, have one of these," he offered soothingly. "May make you feel better — " He held out his cigarettes toward her.

"No!" she protested sharply, when she looked down and saw what it was. She recoiled so violently that her whole chair bounced a little across the floor. He saw the back of her hand go to the upper part of her breast in an unconscious gesture of protection, of warding off.

His face turned white when he understood the implication. White with anger, with revulsion. "So that's it," he breathed softly. "My God, oh, my God."

They sat on for a long while after that, both looking down without saying anything. What was there to say? Two little cups of black coffee had arrived by now — just as an excuse for them to stay there.

Finally he raised his head, looked at her, and put words to what he'd been thinking. "You can't go back anymore, not even once. You're out of the house and away from it now, so you've got to stay out. You can't go near it again, not even one more time. One more night may be one night too many. He'll kill you one of these nights — he will even if he doesn't mean to. What to him is just a thrill, an excitement, will take away your life. Think about that — you've *got* to think about that."

"I have already," she admitted. "Often."

"You don't want to go to the police?"

"I'm ashamed." She covered her eyes reluctantly with her hand for a moment. "I know I'm not the one who should be, he's the one. But I am nevertheless. I couldn't bear to tell it to an outsider, to put it on record, to file a complaint — it's so intimate. Like taking off all your clothes in public. I can hardly bring myself even to have you know about it. And I haven't told you everything — not everything."

He gave her a shake of the head, as though he knew.

"If I try to hide out in Pittsfield, he'll find me sooner or later — it's not that big a place — and come after me and force me to come back, and either way there'll be a scandal. And I don't want that. I couldn't stand that. The newspapers . . ."

All at once, before they quite knew how it had come about, or even realized that it had come about, they were deep in the final plans, the final strategy and staging that they had been drawing slowly nearer and nearer to all these months. Nearer to with every meeting, with every look and with every word. The plans for her liberation and her salvation.

He took her hands across the table.

"No, listen. This is the way, this is how. New York. It has to be New York; he won't be able to get you back; it's too big; he won't even be able to find you. The company's holding a business conference there on Tuesday, with each of the regional offices sending a representative the way they always do. I was slated to go, long before this came up. I was going to call you on Monday before I left. But what I'm going to do now is to leave ahead of time, tonight, and take you with me."

He raised one of her hands and patted it encouragingly.

"You wait for me here in the restaurant. I have to go back to the office, wind up a few things, then I'll come back and pick you up — shouldn't take me more than half an hour."

She looked around her uneasily. "I don't want to sit here alone. They're already giving me knowing looks each time they pass, the waitresses, as if they sense something's wrong."

"Let them, the hell with them," he said shortly, with the defiance of a man in the opening stages of love.

"Can't you call your office from here? Do it over the phone?"

"No, there are some papers that have to be signed — they're waiting for me on my desk."

"Then you run me back to the house and while you're doing what you have to at the office I'll pick up a few things; then you can stop by for me and we'll start out from there."

"Isn't that cutting it a little close?" he said doubtfully. "I don't want you to go back there." He pivoted his wristwatch closer to him. "What time does he usually come home on Fridays?"

"Never before ten at night."

He said the first critical thing he'd ever said to her. "Just like a girl. All for the sake of a hairbrush and a cuddly negligee you're willing to stick your head back into that house."

"It's more than just a hairbrush," she pointed out. "I have some money there. It's not his, it's mine. Even if this friend from my days in Rome — the one I've spoken to you about — even if she takes me in with her at the start, I'll need some money to tide me over until I can get a job and find a place of my own. And there are other things, like my birth certificate, that I may need later on; he'll never give them up willingly once I leave."

"All right," he gave in. "We'll do it your way."

Then just before they got up from the table that had witnessed such a change in both their lives, they gave each other a last look. A last, and yet a first one. And they understood each other.

She didn't wait for him to say it, to ask it. There is no decorum in desperation, no coyness in a crisis. She knew it had been asked unsaid, anyway. "I want to rediscover the meaning of gentle love. I want to lie in your bed, in your arms. I want to be your wife."

He took hold of her left hand, raised the third finger, stripped off the wedding band and in its place firmly guided downward a massive fraternity ring that had been on his own hand until that very moment. Heavy, ungainly, much too large for her — and yet everything that love should be.

She put it to her lips and kissed it.

They were married now.

The emptied ring rolled off the table and fell on the floor, and as they moved away his foot stepped on it, not on purpose, and distorted it into something warped, misshapen, no longer round, no longer true. Like what it had stood for.

He drove her back out to the house and dropped her off at the door, and they parted almost in silence, so complete was their understanding by now, just three muted words between them: "About thirty minutes."

It was dark now, and broodingly sluggish. Like something supine waiting to spring, with just the tip of its tail twitching. Leaves stood still on the trees. An evil green star glinted in the black sky like a hostile eye, like an evil spying eye.

His car had hummed off; she'd finished and brought down a small packed bag to the ground floor when the phone rang. It would be Garry, naturally, telling her he'd finished at the office and was about to leave.

"Hello — " she began, urgently and vitally and confidentially, the way you share a secret with just one person and this was the one.

Mark's voice was at the other end.

"You sound more chipper than you usually do when I call up to tell you I'm on the way home."

Her expectancy stopped. And everything else with it. She didn't know what to say. "Do I?" And then, "Oh, I see."

"Did you have a good day? You must have had a *very* good day."

She knew what he meant, she knew what he was implying.

"I — I — oh, I did nothing, really. I haven't been out of the house all day."

"That's strange," she heard him say. "I called you earlier — about an hour ago?" It was a question, a pitfall of a question. "You didn't come to the phone."

"I didn't hear it ring," she said hastily, too hastily. "I might have been out front for a few minutes. I remember I went out there to broom the gravel in the drivew — "

Too late she realized he hadn't called at all. But now he knew that she hadn't been in the house all day, that she'd been out somewhere during part of it.

"I'll be a little late." And then something that sounded like "That's what you want to hear, isn't it?"

"What?" she said quickly. "What?"

"I said I'll be a little late."

"What was it you said after that?"

"What was it you said after that?" he quoted studiedly, giving her back her own words.

She knew he wasn't going to repeat it, but by that very token she knew she'd heard it right the first time.

He *knows,* she told herself with a shudder of premonition as she got off the phone and finally away from him. (His voice could hold fast to you and enthrall you, too; his very voice could torture you, as well as his wicked, cruel fingers.) He knows there's someone; he may not know who yet, but he knows there is someone.

A remark from one of the nightmare nights came back to her: "There's somebody else who wouldn't do this, isn't there? There's somebody else who wouldn't make you cry."

She should have told Garry about it long before this. Because now she had to get away from Mark at all cost, even more than she had had to ever before. Now there would be a terrible vindictiveness, a violent jealousy sparking the horrors, where before there had sometimes been just an irrational impulse, sometimes dying as quickly as it was born. Turned aside by a tear or a prayer or a run around a chair.

And then another thing occurred to her, and it frightened her even more immediately, here and now. What assurance was there that he was where he'd said he was, still in the city waiting to start out for here? He might have been much closer, ready to jump out at her unexpectedly, hoping to throw her off-guard and catch her away from the house with someone, or (as if she could have possibly been that sort of person) with that someone right here in the very house with her. He'd lied about calling the first time; why wouldn't he lie about where he was?

And now that she thought of it, there was a filling station with a public telephone less than five minutes' drive from here, on the main thruway that came up from Boston. An eddy of fear swirled around her, like dust rising off the floor in some barren, drafty place. She had to do one of two things immediately—there was no time to do both. Either call Garry at his office and warn him to hurry, that their time limit had shrunk. Or try to trace Mark's call and find out just how much margin of safety was still left to them.

She chose the latter course, which was the mistaken one to choose.

Long before she'd been able to identify the filling station exactly for the information operator to get its number, the whole thing had become academic. There was a slither and shuffle on the gravel outside and a car, someone's car, had come to a stop in front of the house.

Her first impulse, carried out immediately without thinking why, was to snap off all the room lights. Probably so she could see out without being seen from out there.

She sprang over to the window, and then stood there rigidly motionless, leaning a little to peer intently out. The car had stopped at an unlucky angle of perspective—unlucky for her. They had a trellis with tendrils of wisteria twining all over it like bunches of dangling grapes. It blanked out the midsection of the car, its body shape, completely. The beams of the acetylene-bright headlights shone out past one side, but they told her nothing; they could have come from any car. The little glimmer of color on the driveway, at the other side, told her no more.

She heard the door crack open and clump closed. Someone's feet, obviously a man's, chopped up the wooden steps to the entrance veranda, and she saw a figure cross it, but it was too dark to make out who he was.

She had turned now to face the other way, and without knowing it her hand was holding the place where her heart was. This was Mark's house, he had the front-door key. Garry would have to ring. She waited to hear the doorbell clarinet out and tell her she was safe, she would be loved, she would live.

Instead there was a double click, back then forth, the knob twined around, and the door opened. A spurt of cool air told her it had opened.

Frightened back into childhood fears, she turned and scurried, like some little girl with pigtails flying out behind her, scurried back along the shadowed hall, around behind the stairs, and into a closet that lay back there, remote as any place in the house could be. She pushed herself as far to the back as she could, and crouched down, pulling hanging things in front of her to screen and to protect her, to make her invisible. Sweaters and mackintoshes and old forgotten coveralls. And she hid her head down between her knees — the way children do when a goblin or an ogre is after them, thinking that if they can't see it, that fact alone will make the terror go away.

The steps went up the stairs, on over her, up past her head. She could feel the shake if not hear the sound. Then she heard her name called out, but the voice was blurred by the many partitions and separations between — as if she were listening to it from underwater. Then the step came down again, and the man stood there at the foot of the stairs, uncertain. She tried to teach herself how to forget to breathe, but she learned badly.

There was a little *tick!* of a sound, and he'd given himself more light. Then each step started to sound clearer than the one before, as the distance to her thinned away. Her heart began to stutter and turn over, and say: here he comes, here he comes. Light cracked into the closet around three sides of the door, and two arms reached in and started to make swimming motions among the hanging things, trying to find her.

Then they found her, one at each shoulder, and lifted her and drew her outside to him. (With surprising gentleness.) And pressed her to his breast. And her tears made a new pattern of little wet polka dots all over what had been Garry's solid-colored necktie until now.

All she could say was "Hurry, hurry, get me out of here!"

"You must have left the door open in your hurry when you came back here. I tried it, found it unlocked, and just walked right in. When I looked back here, I saw that the sleeve of that old smock had got caught in the closet door and was sticking out. Almost like an arm, beckoning me on to show me where you were hiding. It was uncanny. Your guardian angel must love you very much, Linda."

But will he always? she wondered. Will he always?

He took her to the front door, detoured for a moment to pick up the bag, then led her outside and closed the door behind them for good and all.

"Just a minute," she said, and stopped, one foot on the ground, one still on the wooden front steps.

She opened her handbag and took out her key — the key to what had been her home and her marriage. She flung it back at the door, and it hit and fell, with a cheap shabby little *clop!* — like something of not much value.

Once they were in the car they just drove; they didn't say anything more for a long time.

All the old things had been said. All the new things to be said were still to come.

In her mind's eye she could see the saw-toothed towers of New York climbing slowly up above the horizon before her at the end of the long road. Shimmering there, iridescent, opalescent, rainbows of chrome and glass and hope. Like Jerusalem, like Mecca, or some other holy spot. Beckoning, offering heaven. And of all the things New York has meant to various people at various times — fame, success, fulfillment — it probably never meant as much before as it meant to her tonight: a place of refuge, a sanctuary, a place to be safe in.

"How long does the trip take?" she asked him wistful-eyed.

"I usually make it in less than four hours. Tonight I'll make it in less than three."

I'll never stray out of New York again, she promised herself. Once I'm safely there, I'll never go out in the country again. I never want to see a tree again, except way down below me in Central Park from a window high up.

"Oh, get me there, Garry, get me there."

"I'll get you there," Garry promised, like any new bridegroom, and bent to kiss the hand she had placed over his on the wheel.

Two car headlights from the opposite direction hissed by them — like parallel tracer bullets going so fast they seemed to swirl around rather than undulate with the road's flaws.

She purposely waited a moment, then said in a curiously surreptitious voice, as though it shouldn't be mentioned too loudly, "Did you see that?"

All he answered, noncommittally, was "Mmm."

"That was the Italian compact."

"You couldn't tell what it was," he said, trying to distract her from her fear. "Went by too fast."

"I know it too well. I recognized it."

Again she waited a moment, as though afraid to make the movement she was about to. Then she turned and looked back, staring hard and steadily into the funneling darkness behind them.

Two back lights had flattened out into a bar, an ingot. Suddenly this flashed to the other side of the road, then reversed. Then, like a ghastly scimitar chopping down all the tree trunks in sight, the headlights reappeared, rounded out into two spheres, gleaming, small — but coming back after them.

"I told you. It's turned and doubled back."

He was still trying to keep her from panic. "May have nothing to do with us. May not be the same car we saw go by just now."

"It is. Why would he make a complete about-turn like that in the middle of nowhere? There's no intersection or side road back there — we haven't passed one for miles."

She looked again.

"They keep coming. And they already look bigger than when they started back. I think they're gaining on us."

He said, with an unconcern that he didn't feel, "Then we'll have to put a stop to that."

They burst into greater velocity, with a surge like a forward billow of air.

She looked, and she looked again. Finally, to keep from turning so constantly, she got up on the seat on the point of one knee and faced backward, her hair pouring forward all around her, jumping with an electricity that was really speed.

"Stay down," he warned. "You're liable to get thrown that way. We're up to sixty-five now." He gave her a quick tug for additional emphasis, and she subsided into the seat once more.

"How is it now?" he checked presently. The rearview mirror couldn't reflect that far back.

"They haven't grown smaller, but they haven't grown larger."

"We've stabilized, then," he translated. "Dead heat."

Then after another while and another look, "Wait a minute!" she said suddenly on a note of breath-holding hope. Then, "No," she mourned quickly afterward. "For a minute I thought—but they're back again. It was only a dip in the road.

"They hang on like leeches, can't seem to shake them off," she complained in a fretful voice, as though talking to herself. "Why don't they go away? Why *don't* they?"

Another look, and he could sense the sudden stiffening of her body.

"They're getting bigger. I know I'm not mistaken."

He could see that, too. They were finally peering into the rearview mirror for the first time. They'd go offside, then they'd come back in again. In his irritation he took one hand off the wheel long enough to give the mirror a backhand slap that moved it out of focus altogether.

"Suppose I stop, get out, and face him when he comes up, and we have it out here and now. What can he do? I'm younger, I can outslug him."

Her refusal to consent was an outright scream of protest. All her fears and all her aversion were in it.

"All right," he said. "Then we'll run him into the ground if we have to."

She covered her face with both hands—not at the speed they were making, but at the futility of it.

"They sure build good cars in Torino, damn them to hell!" he swore in angry frustration.

She uncovered and looked. The headlights were closer than before. She began to lose control of herself.

"Oh, this is like every nightmare I ever had when I was a little girl! When something was chasing me, and I couldn't get away from it. Only now there'll be no waking up in the nick of time."

"Stop that," he shouted at her. "Stop it. It only makes it worse, it doesn't help."

"I think I can feel his breath blowing down the back of my neck."

He looked at her briefly, but she could tell by the look on his face he hadn't been able to make out what she'd said.

Streaks of wet that were not tears were coursing down his face in uneven lengths. "My necktie," he called out to her suddenly, and raised his chin to show her what he meant. She reached over, careful not to place herself in front of him, and pulled the knot down until it was loose. Then she freed the buttonhole from the top button of his shirt.

A long curve in the road cut them off for a while, from those eyes, those unrelenting eyes behind them. Then the curve ended, and the eyes came back again. It was worse somehow, after they'd been gone like that, than when they remained steadily in sight the whole time.

"He holds on and holds on and *holds on*—like a mad dog with his teeth locked into you."

"He's a mad dog all right." All pretense of composure had long since left him. He was lividly angry at not being able to win the race, to shake the pursuer off. She was mortally frightened. The long-sustained tension of the speed duel, which seemed to have been going on for hours, compounded her fears, raised them at last to the pitch of hysteria.

Their car swerved erratically, the two outer wheels jogged briefly over marginal stones and roots that felt as if they were as big as boulders and logs. He flung his chest forward across the wheel as if it were something alive that he was desperately trying to hold down; then the car recovered, came back to the road, straightened out safely again with a catarrhal shudder of its rear axle.

"Don't," he warned her tautly in the short-lived lull before they picked up hissing momentum again. "Don't grab me like that again. It went right through the shoulder of my jacket. I can't manage the car, can't hold it, if you do that. I'll get you away. Don't worry, I'll get you away from him."

She threw her head back in despair, looking straight up overhead. "We seem to be standing still. The road has petrified. The trees aren't moving backwards anymore. The stars don't either. Neither do the rocks along the side. Oh, faster, Garry, faster!"

"You're hallucinating. Your senses are being tricked by fear."

"Faster, Garry, faster!"

"Eighty-five, eighty-six. We're on two wheels most of the time—two are off the ground. I can't even breathe, my breath's being pulled out of me."

She started to beat her two clenched fists against her forehead in a tattoo of hypnotic inability to escape. "I don't care, Garry! Faster, faster! If I've got to die, let it be with you, not with him!"

"I'll get you away from him. If it kills me."

That was the last thing he said.

If it kills me.

And as though it had overheard, and snatched at the collateral offered it, that unpropitious sickly greenish star up there — surely Mark's star, not theirs — at that very moment a huge tremendous thing came into view around a turn in the road. A skyscraper of a long-haul van, its multiple tiers beaded with red warning lights. But what good were they that high up, except to warn off planes?

It couldn't maneuver. It would have required a turntable. And they had no time or room.

There was a soft crunchy sound, like someone shearing the top off a soft-boiled egg with a knife. At just one quick slice. Then a brief straight-into-the face blizzard effect, but with tiny particles of glass instead of frozen flakes. Just a one-gust blizzard — and then over with. Then an immense whirl of light started to spin, like a huge Ferris wheel all lit up and going around and around, with parabolas of light streaking off in every direction and dimming. Like shooting stars, or the tails of comets.

Then the whole thing died down and went out, like a blazing amusement park sinking to earth. Or the spouts of illuminated fountains settling back into their basins . . .

She could tell the side of her face was resting against the ground, because blades of grass were brushing against it with a feathery tickling feeling. And some inquisitive little insect kept flitting about just inside the rim of her ear. She tried to raise her hand to brush it away, but then forgot where it was and what it was.

But then forgot . . .

When they picked her up at last, more out of this world than in it, all her senses gone except for reflex-actions, her lips were still quivering with the unspoken sounds of "Faster, Garry, faster! Take me away — "

Then the long nights, that were also days, in the hospital. And the long blanks, that were also nights. Needles, and angled glass rods to suck water through. Needles, and curious enamel wedges slid under your middle. Needles, and — needles and needles and needles. Like swarms of persistent mosquitoes with unbreakable drills. The way a pincushion feels, if it could feel. Or the target of a porcupine. Or a case of not just momentary but permanently endured static electricity after you scuff across a woolen rug and then put your finger on a light switch. Even food was a needle — a jab into a vein . . .

Then at last her head cleared, her eyes cleared, her mind and voice came back from where they'd been. Each day she became a little stronger, and each day became a little longer. Until they were back for good, good as ever before. Life came back into her lungs and heart. She could feel it there, the swift current of it. Moving again, eager again. Sun again, sky again, rain and pain and love and hope again. Life again — the beautiful thing called life.

Each day they propped her up in a chair for a little while. Close beside the bed, for each day for a little while longer.

Then at last she asked, after many starts that she could never finish, "Why doesn't Garry come to me? Doesn't he know I've been hurt?"

"Garry can't come to you," the nurse answered. And then, in the way that you whip off a bandage that has adhered to a wound fast, in order to make the pain that much shorter than it would be if you lingeringly edged it off a little at a time, then the nurse quickly told her, "Garry won't come to you anymore."

The black tears, *so* many of them, such a rain of them, blotted out the light and brought on the darkness . . .

Then the light was back again, and no more tears. Just — Garry won't come to you anymore.

Now the silent words were: Not so fast, Garry, not so fast; you've left me behind and I've lost my way.

Then in a little while she asked the nurse, "Why don't you ever let me get up from this chair? I'm better now, I eat well, the strength has come back to my arms, my hands, my fingers, my whole body feels strong. Shouldn't I be allowed to move around and exercise a little? To stand up and take a few steps?"

"The doctor will tell you about that," the nurse said evasively.

The doctor came in later and he told her about it. Bluntly, in the modern way, without subterfuges and without false hopes. The kind, the sensible, the straight-from-the-shoulder modern way.

"Now listen to me. The world is a beautiful world, and life is a beautiful life. In this beautiful world everything is comparative; luck is comparative. You could have come out of it stone-blind from the shattered glass, with both your eyes gone. You could have come out of it minus an arm, crushed and having to be taken off. You could have come out of it with your face hideously scarred, wearing a repulsive mask for the rest of your life that would make people sicken and turn away. You could have come out of it dead, as — as someone else did. Who is to say you are lucky, who is to say you are not? You have come out of it beautiful of face. You have come out of it keen and sensitive of mind, a mind with all the precision and delicate adjustment of the works inside a fine Swiss watch. A mind that not only *thinks,* but *feels.* You have come out of it with a strong brave youthful heart that will carry you through for half a century yet, come what may."

"But— "

She looked at him with eyes that didn't fear.

"You will never again take a single step for all the rest of your life. You are hopelessly, irreparably paralyzed from the waist down. Surgery, everything, has been tried. Accept this . . . Now you know—and so now be brave."

"I am. I will be," she said trustfully. "I'll learn a craft of some kind, that will occupy my days and earn me a living. Perhaps you can find a nursing home for me at the start until I get adjusted, and then maybe later I can find a little place all to myself and manage there on my own. There are such places, with ramps instead of stairs— "

He smiled deprecatingly at her oversight.

"All that won't be necessary. You're forgetting. There is someone who will look after you. Look after you well. You'll be in good capable hands. Your husband is coming to take you home with him today."

Her scream was like the death cry of a wounded animal. So strident, so unbelievable, that in the stillness of its aftermath could be heard the slithering and rustling of people looking out the other ward-room doors along the corridor, nurses and ambulatory patients, asking one another what that terrified cry had been and where it had come from.

"Two cc's of M, and hurry," the doctor instructed the nurse tautly. "It's just the reaction from what she's been through. This sometimes happens—going-home happiness becomes hysteria."

The wet kiss of alcohol on her arm. Then the needle again—the needle meant to be kind.

One of them patted her on the head and said, "You'll be all right now."

A tear came to the corner of her eyes, and just lay there, unable to retreat, unable to fall . . .

Myopically she watched them dress her and put her in her chair. Her mind remained awake, but everything was downgraded in intensity—the will to struggle had become reluctance, fear had become unease. She still knew there was cause to scream, but the distance had become too great, the message had too far to travel.

Through lazy, contracting pupils she looked over and saw Mark standing in the doorway, talking to the doctor, shaking the nurse's hand and leaving something behind in it for which she smiled her thanks.

Then he went around in back of her wheelchair, with a phantom breath for a kiss to the top of her head, and started to sidle it toward the door that was being held open for the two of them. He tipped the front of the chair ever so slightly, careful to avoid the least jar or impact or roughness, as if determined that she reach her destination with him in impeccable condition, unmarked and unmarred.

And as she craned her neck and looked up overhead, and then around and into his face, backward, the unspoken message was so plain, in his shining eyes and in the grim grin he showed his teeth in, that though he didn't say it aloud, there was no need to; it reached from his mind into hers without sound or the need of sound just as surely as though he had said it aloud.

Now I've got you.

Now he had her — for the rest of her life.

1972

DAVID MORRELL

THE DRIPPING

DAVID MORRELL (1934–) was born in Kitchener, Ontario, and was still a teenager when he decided to become a writer, inspired by the *Route 66* television series created by Stirling Silliphant, and encouraged by Hemingway scholar Philip Young at Penn State University, where Morrell eventually received his BA and MA. In 1970 he took a job as an English professor at the University of Iowa, and produced his initial novel, *First Blood,* two years later.

This book, since described as the father of the modern adventure novel, introduced the world to Rambo, who went on to become one of the most famous fictional characters in the world, largely through film adaptations starring Sylvester Stallone. John Rambo (the famous name came from a variety of apple) is a Vietnam War vet, a troubled, violent former Green Beret warrior trained in survival, hand-to-hand combat, and other special martial skills. The film series began with *First Blood* (1982), and has continued with *Rambo: First Blood Part II* (1985), *Rambo III* (1988), *Rambo* (2008), and *Rambo V* (scheduled for release in 2011).

Morrell has enjoyed numerous other bestsellers among his twenty-eight novels, including *The Brotherhood of the Rose* (1984), which became a popular TV miniseries starring Robert Mitchum in 1989. In addition to his ambitious international thrillers, he has written highly popular horror fiction, notably *Creepers* (2005), which won a Bram Stoker Award from the Horror Writers Association. He is also the cofounder of the organization International Thriller Writers.

"The Dripping" is the author's first published story. It was originally published in the August 1972 issue of *Ellery Queen's Mystery Magazine.*

■ ■ ■

THAT AUTUMN WE live in a house in the country, my mother's house, the house I was raised in. I have been to the village, struck more by how nothing in it has changed, yet everything has, because I am older now, seeing it differently. It is as though I am both here now and back then, at once with the mind of a boy and a man. It is so strange a doubling, so intense, so unsettling, that I am moved to work again, to try to paint it.

So I study the hardware store, the grain barrels in front, the twin square pillars holding up the drooping balcony onto which seared wax-faced men and women from the old people's hotel above come to sit and rock and watch. They look like the same aging people I saw as a boy, the wood of the pillars and balcony looks as splintered.

Forgetful of time while I work, I do not begin the long walk home until late, at dusk. The day has been warm, but now in my shirt I am cold, and a half mile along I am caught in a sudden shower and forced to leave the gravel road for the shelter of a tree, its leaves already brown and yellow. The rain becomes a storm, streaking at me sideways, drenching me; I cinch the neck of my canvas bag to protect my painting and equipment, and decide to run, socks spongy in my shoes, when at last I reach the lane down to the house and barn.

The house and barn. They and my mother, they alone have changed, as if as one, warping, weathering, joints twisted and strained, their gray so unlike the white I recall as a boy. The place is weakening her. She is in tune with it, matches its decay. That is why we have come here to live. To revive. Once I thought to convince her to move away. But of her sixty-five years she has spent forty here, and she insists she will spend the rest, what is left to her.

The rain falls stronger as I hurry past the side of the house, the light on in the kitchen, suppertime and I am late. The house is connected with the barn the way the small base of an *L* is connected to its stem. The entrance I always use is directly at the joining, and when I enter out of breath, clothes clinging to me cold and wet, the door to the barn to my left, the door to the kitchen straight ahead, I hear the dripping in the basement down the stairs to my right.

"Meg. Sorry I'm late," I call to my wife, setting down the water-beaded canvas sack, opening the kitchen door. There is no one. No settings on the table. Nothing on the stove. Only the yellow light from the 60-watt bulb in the ceiling. The kind my mother prefers to the white of 100. It reminds her of candlelight, she says.

"Meg," I call again, and still no one answers. Asleep, I think. Dusk coming on, the dark clouds of the storm have lulled them, and they have lain down for a nap, expecting to wake before I return.

Still the dripping. Although the house is very old, the barn long disused, roofs crumbling, I have not thought it all so ill-maintained, the storm so strong that water can be seeping past the cellar windows, trickling, pattering on the old stone floor. I switch on the light to the basement, descend the wood stairs to the right, worn and squeaking, reach where the stairs turn to the left the rest of the way down to the floor, and see not water dripping. Milk. Milk everywhere. On the rafters, on the walls, dripping on the film of milk on the stones, gathering speckled with dirt in the channels between them. From side to side and everywhere.

Sarah, my child, has done this, I think. She has been fascinated by the big wood dollhouse that my father made for me when I was quite young, its blue paint chipped and peeling now. She has pulled it from the far corner to the middle of the basement. There are games and toy soldiers and blocks that have been taken from the wicker storage chest and played with on the floor, all covered with milk, the dollhouse, the chest, the scattered toys, milk dripping on them from the rafters, milk trickling on them.

Why has she done this, I think. Where can she have gotten so much milk? What was in her mind to do this thing?

"Sarah," I call. "Meg." Angry now, I mount the stairs into the quiet kitchen. "Sarah," I shout. She will clean the mess and stay indoors the remainder of the week.

I cross the kitchen, turn through the sitting room past the padded flower-patterned chairs and sofa that have faded since I knew them as a boy, past several of my paintings that my mother has hung up on the wall, bright-colored old ones of pastures and woods from when I was in grade school, brown-shaded new ones of the town, tinted as if old photographs. Two stairs at a time up to the bedrooms, wet shoes on the soft worn carpet on the stairs, hand streaking on the smooth polished maple banister.

At the top I swing down the hall. The door to Sarah's room is open, it is dark in there. I switch on the light. She is not on the bed, nor has been; the satin spread is unrumpled, the rain pelting in through the open window, the wind fresh and cool. I have the feeling then and go uneasy into our bedroom; it is dark as well, empty too. My stomach has become hollow. Where are they? All in Mother's room?

No. As I stand at the open door to Mother's room I see from the yellow light I have turned on in the hall that only she is in there, her small torso stretched across the bed.

"Mother," I say, intending to add, "Where are Meg and Sarah?" But I stop before I do. One of my mother's shoes is off, the other askew on her foot. There is mud on the shoes. There is blood on her cotton dress. It is torn, her brittle hair disrupted, blood on her face, her bruised lips are swollen.

For several moments I am silent with shock. "My God, Mother," I finally manage to say, and as if the words are a spring releasing me to action I touch her to wake her. But I see that her eyes are open, staring ceilingward, unseeing though alive, and each breath is a sudden full gasp, then slow exhalation.

"Mother, what has happened? Who did this to you? Meg? Sarah?"

But she does not look at me, only constant toward the ceiling.

"For God's sake, Mother, answer me! Look at me! What has happened?"

Nothing. Eyes sightless. Between gasps she is like a statue.

What I think is hysterical. Disjointed, contradictory. I must find Meg and Sarah. They must be somewhere, beaten like my mother. Or worse. Find them. Where? But I cannot leave my mother. When she comes to consciousness, she too will be hysterical, frightened, in great pain. How did she end up on the bed?

In her room there is no sign of the struggle she must have put up against her attacker. It must have happened somewhere else. She crawled from there to here. Then I see the blood on the floor, the swath of blood down the hall from the stairs. Who did this? Where is he? Who would beat a gray, wrinkled, arthritic old woman? Why in God's name would he do it? I shudder. The pain of the arthritis as she struggled with him.

Perhaps he is still in the house, waiting for me.

To the hollow sickness in my stomach now comes fear, hot, pulsing, and I am frantic before I realize what I am doing — grabbing the spare cane my mother always keeps by her bed, flicking on the light in her room, throwing open the closet door and striking in with the cane. Viciously, sounds coming from my throat, the cane flailing among the faded dresses.

No one. Under the bed. No one. Behind the door. No one.

I search all the upstairs rooms that way, terrified, constantly checking behind me, clutching the cane and whacking into closets, under beds, behind doors, with a force that would certainly crack a skull. No one.

"Meg! Sarah!"

No answer, not even an echo in this sound-absorbing house.

There is no attic, just an overhead entry to a crawlspace under the eaves, and that opening has long been sealed. No sign of tampering. No one has gone up.

I rush down the stairs, seeing the trail of blood my mother has left on the carpet, imagining her pain as she crawled, and search the rooms downstairs with the same desperate thoroughness. In the front closet. Behind the sofa and chairs. Behind the drapes.

No one.

I lock the front door, lest he be outside in the storm waiting to come in behind me. I remember to draw every blind, close every drape, lest he be out there peering at me. The rain pelts insistently against the windowpanes.

I cry out again and again for Meg and Sarah. The police. My mother. A doctor. I grab for the phone on the wall by the front stairs, fearful to listen to it, afraid he has cut the line outside. But it is droning. Droning. I ring for the police, working the handle at the side around and around and around.

They are coming, they say. A doctor with them. Stay where I am, they say. But I cannot. Meg and Sarah, I must find them. I know they are not in the basement where the milk is dripping—all the basement is open to view. Except for my childhood things, we have cleared out all the boxes and barrels and the shelves of jars the Saturday before.

But under the stairs. I have forgotten about under the stairs and now I race down and stand dreading in the milk; but there are only cobwebs there, already re-formed from Saturday when we cleared them. I look up at the side door I first came through, and as if I am seeing through a telescope I focus largely on the handle. It seems to fidget. I have a panicked vision of the intruder bursting through, and I charge up to lock the door, and the door to the barn.

And then I think: if Meg and Sarah are not in the house they are likely in the barn. But I cannot bring myself to unlock the barn door and go through. *He* must be there as well. Not in the rain outside but in the shelter of the barn, and there are no lights to turn on there.

And why the milk? Did he do it and where did he get it? And why? Or did Sarah do it before? No, the milk is too freshly dripping. It has been put there too recently. By him. But why? And who is he? A tramp? An escapee from some prison? Or asylum? No, the nearest institution is far away, hundreds of miles. From the town then. Or a nearby farm.

I know my questions are for delay, to keep me from entering the barn. But I must. I take the flashlight from the kitchen drawer and unlock the door to the barn, force myself to go in quickly, cane ready, flashing my light. The stalls are still there, listing; and some of the equipment, churners, separators, dull and rusted, webbed and dirty. The must of decaying wood and crumbled hay, the fresh wet smell of the rain gusting through cracks in the walls. Once this was a dairy, as the other farms around still are.

Flicking my light toward the corners, edging toward the stalls, boards creaking, echoing, I try to control my fright, try to remember as a boy how the cows waited in the stalls for my father to milk them, how the barn was once board-tight and solid, warm to be in, how there was no connecting door from the barn to the house because my father did not want my mother to smell the animals in her kitchen.

I run my light down the walls, sweep it in arcs through the darkness before me as I draw nearer to the stalls, and in spite of myself I recall that other autumn when the snow came early, four feet deep by morning and still storming thickly, how my father went out to the barn to milk and never returned for lunch, nor supper. There was no phone then, no way to get help, and my mother and I waited all night, unable to make our way through the storm, listening to the slowly dying wind; and the next morning was clear and bright and blinding as we shoveled out to find the cows in agony in their stalls from not having been milked and my father dead, frozen rock-solid in the snow in the middle of the next field where he must have wandered when he lost his bearings in the storm.

There was a fox, risen earlier than us, nosing at him under the snow, and my father had to be sealed in his coffin before he could lie in state. Days after, the snow was melted, gone, the barnyard a sea of mud, and it was autumn again and my mother had the connecting door put in. My father should have tied a rope from the house to his waist to guide him back in case he lost his way. Certainly he knew enough. But then he was like that, always in a rush. When I was ten.

Thus I think as I light the shadows near the stalls, terrified of what I may find in any one of them, Meg and Sarah, or him, thinking of how my mother and I searched for my father and how I now search for my wife and child, trying to think of how it was once warm in here and pleasant, chatting with my father, helping him to milk, the sweet smell of new hay and grain, the different sweet smell of fresh droppings, something I always liked and neither my father nor my mother could understand. I know that if I do not think of these good times I will surely go mad in awful anticipation of what I may find. Pray God they have not died!

What can he have done to them? To assault a five-year-old girl? Split her. The hemorrhaging alone can have killed her.

And then, even in the barn, I hear my mother cry out for me. The relief I feel to leave and go to her unnerves me. I do want to find Meg and Sarah, to try to save them. Yet I am relieved to go. I think my mother will tell me what has happened, tell me where to find them. That is how I justify my leaving as I wave the light in circles around me, guarding my back, retreating through the door and locking it.

Upstairs she sits stiffly on her bed. I want to make her answer my questions, to shake her, to force her to help, but I know it will only frighten her more, maybe push her mind down to where I can never reach.

"Mother," I say to her softly, touching her gently. "What has happened?" My impatience can barely be contained. "Who did this? Where are Meg and Sarah?"

She smiles at me, reassured by the safety of my presence. Still she cannot answer.

"Mother. Please," I say. "I know how bad it must have been. But you must try to help. I must know where they are so I can help them."

She says, "Dolls."

It chills me. "What dolls, Mother? Did a man come here with dolls? What did he want? You mean he looked like a doll? Wearing a mask like one?"

Too many questions. All she can do is blink.

"Please, Mother. You must try your best to tell me. Where are Meg and Sarah?"

"Dolls," she says.

As I first had the foreboding of disaster at the sight of Sarah's unrumpled satin bedspread, now I am beginning to understand, rejecting it, fighting it.

"Yes, Mother, the dolls," I say, refusing to admit what I know. "Please, Mother. Where are Meg and Sarah?"

"You are a grown boy now. You must stop playing as a child. Your father. Without him you will have to be the man in the house. You must be brave."

"No, Mother." I can feel it swelling in my chest.

"There will be a great deal of work now, more than any child should know. But we have no choice. You must accept that God has chosen to take him from us, that you are all the man I have left to help me."

"No, Mother."

"Now you are a man and you must put away the things of a child."

Eyes streaming, I am barely able to straighten, leaning wearily against the doorjamb, tears rippling from my face down to my shirt, wetting it cold where it had just begun to dry. I wipe my eyes and see her reaching for me, smiling, and I recoil down the hall, stumbling down the stairs, down, through the sitting room, the kitchen, down, down to the milk, splashing through it to the dollhouse, and in there, crammed and doubled, Sarah. And in the wicker chest, Meg. The toys not on the floor for Sarah to play with, but taken out so Meg could be put in. And both of them, their stomachs slashed, stuffed with sawdust, their eyes rolled up like dolls' eyes.

The police are knocking at the side door, pounding, calling out who they are, but I am powerless to let them in. They crash through the door, their rubber raincoats dripping as they stare down at me.

"The milk," I say.

They do not understand. Even as I wait, standing in the milk, listening to the rain pelting on the windows while they come over to see what is in the dollhouse and in the wicker chest, while they go upstairs to my mother and then return so I can tell them again, "The milk." But they still do not understand.

"She killed them of course," one man says. "But I don't see why the milk."

Only when they speak to the neighbors down the road and learn how she came to them, needing the cans of milk, insisting she carry them herself to the car, the agony she was in as she carried them, only when they find the empty cans and the knife in a stall in the barn, can I say, "The milk. The blood. There was so much blood, you know. She needed to deny it, so she washed it away with milk, purified it, started the dairy again. You see, there was so much blood."

That autumn we live in a house in the country, my mother's house, the house I was raised in. I have been to the village, struck even more by how nothing in it has changed, yet everything has, because I am older now, seeing it differently. It is as though I am both here now and back then, at once with the mind of a boy and a man . . .

1979

PATRICIA HIGHSMITH

SLOWLY, SLOWLY IN THE WIND

PATRICIA HIGHSMITH (originally Mary Patricia Plangman) (1921–1995) was born in Fort Worth, Texas, and moved to New York as a child, later graduating from Barnard College. Her mother divorced her father five months before she was born, and had tried to abort her by drinking turpentine, so it is not surprising that they did not have a close relationship. Highsmith moved permanently to Europe in 1963, where she enjoyed greater success, both critical and commercial, than in America.

Her first short story, "The Heroine," was published in *Harper's Bazaar* shortly after her graduation and was selected as one of the twenty-two best stories of 1945. Her first novel, *Strangers on a Train* (1950), written while still in her twenties, was moderately successful but became a sensation when it was acquired for the movies by Alfred Hitchcock, who directed the classic film noir and released it in 1951; it starred Robert Walker and Farley Granger. More than twenty films are based on her thirty books (twenty-two novels and eight short story collections), many made in France. Apart from the first novel, she has been most avidly read for her series about the amoral, sexually ambiguous murderer and thief Tom Ripley, beginning with *The Talented Mr. Ripley* (1955) and continuing with *Ripley Under Ground* (1970), *Ripley's Game* (1974), *The Boy Who Followed Ripley* (1980), and *Ripley Under Water* (1991). Ironically, her career and book sales received a huge boost after she died, when *The Talented Mr. Ripley* was filmed in 1999 by Anthony Minghella, starring Matt Damon, Gwyneth Paltrow, Jude Law, and Cate Blanchett. It was followed by *Ripley's Game* (2002), starring John Malkovich.

"Slowly, Slowly in the Wind" was Highsmith's personal favorite of all her stories, according to an introduction she wrote for *Chillers* (1990), a collection of her stories that had been adapted for a television series. She acknowledges that the title was inspired by an aide to then-president Richard M. Nixon, who said that he'd like to see a certain enemy twisting slowly, slowly in the wind. It was first published in her collection *Slowly, Slowly in the Wind* (1976).

■ ■ ■

EDWARD "SKIP" SKIPPERTON spent most of his life feeling angry. It was his nature. When he was a boy he had a bad temper; now, as a man, he was impatient with people who were slow or stupid. He often met such people in his work, which was to give advice on managing companies. He was good at his job: he could see when people were doing something the wrong way, and he told them in a loud, clear voice how to do it better. The company directors always followed his advice.

Now Skipperton was fifty-two. His wife had left him two years ago, because she couldn't live with his bad temper. She had met a quiet university teacher in Boston, ended her marriage with Skip, and married the teacher. Skip wanted very much to keep their daughter, Maggie, who was then fifteen. With the help of clever lawyers he succeeded.

A few months after he separated from his wife, Skip had a heart attack. He was better again in six months, but his doctor gave him some strong advice.

"Stop smoking and drinking now, or you're a dead man, Skip! And I think you should leave the world of business, too—you've got enough money. Why don't you buy a small farm and live quietly in the country?"

So Skip looked around, and bought a small farm in Maine with a comfortable farmhouse. A little river, the Coldstream, ran along the bottom of the garden, and the house was called Coldstream Heights. He found a local man, Andy Humbert, to live on the farm and work for him.

Maggie was moved from her private school in New York to one in Switzerland; she would come home for the holidays. Skip did stop smoking and drinking: when he decided to do something, he always did it immediately. There was work for him on the farm. He helped Andy to plant corn in the field behind the house; he bought two sheep to keep the grass short, and a pig, which soon gave birth to twelve more.

There was only one thing that annoyed him: his neighbor. Peter Frosby owned the land next to his, including the banks of the Coldstream and the right to catch fish in it. Skip wanted to be able to fish a little. He also wanted to feel that the part of the river which he could see from the house belonged to him. But when he offered to buy the fishing rights, he was told that Frosby refused to sell. Skip did not give up easily. The next week he telephoned Frosby, inviting him to his house for a drink. Frosby arrived in a new Cadillac, driven by a young man. He introduced the young man as his son, also called Peter. Frosby was a rather small, thin man with cold gray eyes.

"The Frosbys don't sell their land," he said. "We've had the same land for nearly three hundred years, and the river's always been ours. I can't understand why you want it."

"I'd just like to do a little fishing in the summer," said Skip. "And I think you'll agree that the price I offer isn't bad — twenty thousand dollars for about two hundred meters of fishing rights. You won't get such a good offer again in your lifetime."

"I'm not interested in *my* lifetime," Frosby said with a little smile. "I've got a son here."

The son was a good-looking boy with dark hair and strong shoulders, taller than his father. He sat there with his arms across his chest, and appeared to share his father's negative attitude. Still, he smiled as they were leaving and said, "You've made this house look very nice, Mr. Skipperton." Skip was pleased. He had tried hard to choose the most suitable furniture for the sitting room.

"I see you like old-fashioned things," said Frosby. "That scarecrow in your field — we haven't seen one of those around here for many years."

"I'm trying to grow corn out there," Skip said. "I think you need a scarecrow in a cornfield."

Young Peter was looking at a photograph of Maggie, which stood on the hall table. "Pretty girl," he said.

Skip said nothing. The meeting had failed. Skip wasn't used to failing. He looked into Frosby's cold gray eyes and said: "I've one more idea. I could rent the land by the river for the rest of my life, and then it goes to you — or your son. I'll give you five thousand dollars a year."

"I don't think so, Mr. Skipperton. Thank you for the drink, and — goodbye."

"Stupid man," said Skip to Andy as the Cadillac moved off. But he smiled. Life was a game, after all. You won sometimes, you lost sometimes.

It was early May. The corn which they had planted was beginning to come up through the earth. Skip and Andy had made a scarecrow from sticks joined together — one stick for the body and head, another for the arms, and two more for the legs. They had dressed it in an old coat and trousers that Andy had found, and had put an old hat of Skip's on its head.

The weeks passed and the corn grew high. Skip tried to think of ways to annoy Frosby, to force him to rent part of the stream to him.

But he forgot about Frosby when Maggie came home for the summer holidays. Skip met her at the airport in New York, and they drove up to

Maine. Skip thought she looked taller; she was certainly more beautiful!

"I've got a surprise for you at home," Skip said.

"Oh — a horse, perhaps?"

Skip had forgotten she was learning to ride. "No, not a horse." The surprise was a red Toyota. He had remembered, at least, that Maggie's school had taught her to drive. She was very excited, and threw her arms round Skip's neck. "You're so sweet! And you're looking *very* well!"

Skip and Maggie went for a drive in the new car the next morning. In the afternoon Maggie asked her father if she could go fishing in the stream. He had to tell her that she couldn't, and he explained the reason.

"Well, never mind, there are a lot of other things to do." Maggie enjoyed going for walks, reading, and doing little jobs in the house.

Skip was surprised one evening when Maggie arrived home in her Toyota carrying three fish. He was afraid she had been fishing in the stream, against his instructions.

"Where did you get those?"

"I met the boy who lives there. We were both buying petrol, and he introduced himself — he said he'd seen my photograph in your house. Then we had coffee together —"

"The Frosby boy?"

"Yes. He's very nice. Perhaps it's only the father who's not nice. Well, Pete said, 'Come and fish with me this afternoon,' so I did."

"I don't — please, Maggie, I don't want you to mix with the Frosbys."

Maggie was surprised, but said nothing.

The next day, Maggie said she wanted to go to the village to buy some shoes. She was away for nearly three hours. With a great effort, Skip didn't question her.

Then on Saturday morning, Maggie said there was a dance in the nearest town, and she was going.

"I can guess who you're going with," Skip said angrily.

"I'm going alone, I promise you. Girls don't need a boy to take them to dances now."

Skip realized that he couldn't order her not to go to a dance. But he knew the Frosby boy would be there. And he knew what was going to happen. His daughter was falling in love with Pete Frosby.

Maggie got home very late that night, after Skip had gone to bed. At breakfast, she looked fresh and happy.

"I expect the Frosby boy was at the dance?" said Skip.

"I don't know what you've got against him, Father."

"I don't want you to fall in love with an uneducated country boy. I sent you to a good school."

"Pete had three years at Harvard University." Maggie stood up. "I'm almost eighteen, Father. I don't want to be told who I can and can't see."

Skip shouted at her: "They're not our kind of people!"

Maggie left the room.

During the next week Skip was in a terrible state. In his business life he had always been able to force people to do what he wanted—but he couldn't think of a way to do that with his daughter.

The following Saturday evening, Maggie said she was going to a party. It was at the house of a boy called Wilmers, who she had met at the dance. By Sunday morning, Maggie hadn't come home. Skip telephoned the Wilmerses' house.

A boy's voice said that Maggie had left the party early.

"Was she alone?"

"No, she was with Pete Frosby. She left her car here."

Skip felt the blood rush to his face. His hand was shaking as he picked up the telephone to call the Frosby house. Old Frosby answered. He said Maggie was not there. And his son was out at the moment.

"What do you mean? He was there and he went out?"

"Mr. Skipperton, my son has his own ways, his own room, his own key—his own life. I'm not going to—"

Skip put the telephone down.

Maggie was not home by Sunday evening or Monday morning. Skip didn't want to inform the police. On Tuesday there was a letter from Maggie, written from Boston. It said that she and Pete had run away to be married.

> . . . You may think this is sudden, but we do love each other, and we know what we're doing. I didn't really want to go back to school. Please don't try to find me—you'll hear from me next week. I was sorry to leave my nice new car.
>
> Love always,
>
> MAGGIE

For two days Skip didn't go out of the house, and he ate almost nothing. He felt three-quarters dead. Andy was very worried about him. When he needed to go to the village to buy some food, he asked Skip to go with him.

While Andy did the shopping, Skip sat in the car, looking at nothing. But then a figure coming down the street caught his eye. Old Frosby!

He hoped Frosby wouldn't see him in the car, but Frosby did. He didn't pause, but he smiled his unpleasant little smile. Skip realized how much he hated Frosby. His blood boiled with anger, and he felt much better: he was himself again. Frosby must be punished! He began to make a plan.

That evening, Skip suggested to Andy that he should go away for the weekend and enjoy himself. "You've earned a holiday!" he said, and gave him three hundred dollars.

Andy left on Saturday evening, in the car. Skip then telephoned old Frosby, and said it was time they became friends. Frosby was surprised, but he agreed to come on Sunday morning at about eleven for a talk. He arrived in the Cadillac, alone.

Skip acted quickly. He had his heavy gun ready, and as soon as Frosby was inside the door he hit him on the head several times with the end of the gun until Frosby was dead. He then took off his clothes and tied an old cloth around the body. He burned Frosby's clothes in the fireplace, and hid his watch and rings in a drawer.

Then Skip put one arm around Frosby's body, and pulled him out of the house and up the field to the scarecrow. The corn had already been cut. He pulled down the old scarecrow and took the clothes off the sticks. He dressed Frosby in the old coat and trousers, tied a small cloth round his face, and pushed the hat onto his head.

When he stood the scarecrow up again it looked almost the same as before. As Skip went back to the house, he turned around many times to admire his work.

He had solved the problem of what to do with the body.

Next he buried Frosby's watch and rings under a big plant in the garden. It was now half past twelve, and he had to do something with the Cadillac. He drove it to some woods a few kilometers away and left it there, after cleaning off all his fingerprints. He hadn't seen anybody.

Soon after he got home a woman telephoned from Frosby's house (his housekeeper, Skip guessed) to ask if Frosby was with him. He told her that Frosby had left his house at about twelve, and he hadn't said where he was going. He said the same thing to the policeman who came to see him in the evening, and to Maggie when she telephoned from Boston. He found it easy to lie about Frosby.

Andy arrived back the next morning, Monday. He had already heard the story in the village, and also knew that the police had found Frosby's car not far away in the woods. He didn't ask any questions.

In the next week Skip spent a lot of time watching the scarecrow from his upstairs bedroom window. He thought with pleasure of old Frosby's body there, drying — slowly, slowly in the wind.

After ten days the policeman came back, with a detective. They looked over Skip's house and land, and they looked at his two guns. They didn't find anything.

That evening, Maggie came to see him; she and Pete were at the Frosby house. It was hard for Skip to believe she was married.

"Pete's very worried and upset," she said. "Was Mr. Frosby unhappy when he visited you?"

Skip laughed. "No, very cheerful! And pleased with the marriage. Are you going to live at the Frosby house?"

"Yes. I'll take some things back with me."

She seemed cold and sad, which made Skip unhappy.

"I know what's in that scarecrow," said Andy one day.

"Do you? What are you going to do about it?" Skip asked.

"Nothing. Nothing," Andy answered with a smile.

"Perhaps you would like some money, Andy? A little present—for keeping quiet?"

"No sir," Andy said quietly. "I'm not that kind of man."

Skip didn't understand. He was used to men who liked money, more and more of it. Andy was different. He was a good man.

The leaves were falling from the trees and winter was coming. The children in the area were getting ready to celebrate the evening of October 31, when people wore special clothes and had special things to eat, and lit great fires outside and danced around them singing songs. No one came to Skip's house that evening. There was a party at the Frosbys' house—he could hear the music in the distance. He thought of his daughter dancing, having a good time. Skip was lonely, for the first time in his life. Lonely. He very much wanted a drink, but he decided to keep his promise to himself.

At that moment he saw a spot of light moving outside the window. He looked out. There was a line of figures crossing his field, carrying lights. Anger and fear rushed through him. They were on his land! They had no right! And they were children, he realized. The figures were small.

He ran downstairs and out into the field. "What do you think you're doing?" he shouted. "Get off my property!"

The children didn't hear him. They were singing a song. "We're going to burn the scarecrow . . ."

"Get off my land!" Skip fell and hurt his knee. Now the children had heard him, he was sure, but they weren't stopping. They were going to reach the scarecrow before him. He heard a cry. They had got there.

There were more cries, of terror mixed with pleasure.

Perhaps their hands had touched the body.

Skip made his way back to his house. It was worse than the police. Every child was going to tell his parents what he had found. Skip knew he had reached the end. He had seen a lot of men in business reach the end. He had known men who had jumped out of windows.

Skip went straight to his gun. He put the end in his mouth and fired. When the children came running back across the field to the road, Skip was dead.

Andy heard the shot from his room over the garage. He had also seen the children crossing the field, and heard Skip shouting. He understood what had happened.

He began walking toward the house. He would have to call the police. Andy decided to say that he didn't know anything about the body in the scarecrow's clothes. He had been away that weekend, after all.

1984

STEPHEN GREENLEAF

IRIS

STEPHEN GREENLEAF (1942–) was born in Washington, D.C. He received a BA from Carleton College in 1964, and a law degree from the University of California, Berkeley, three years later. While serving in the Army (1967–1969), he was admitted to the California bar. He practiced and taught law, but didn't like the profession very much, and studied creative writing at the University of Iowa (where he also taught, from 1995 to 2000).

His first novel — sold "over the transom," without his having publishing experience, connections, or an agent — was *Grave Error* (1979), which introduced his series hero, the lawyer turned private detective John Marshall Tanner. "Marsh" is an exceptionally moral figure, a middle-aged loner who is drawn into cases because he discerns an injustice being done and wants to correct it. The series, set in San Francisco, is noted for Greenleaf's reasonable, understated way of tackling complex social issues through his protagonist. Among the controversial subjects with which Tanner becomes involved are radical politics, the misuse of technology, legal insanity, and surrogate motherhood. Greenleaf's nonseries books, written with the same literary grace as the Tanner series, are *The Ditto List* (1985) and *Impact* (1989). Greenleaf was nominated for the Independent Mystery Booksellers Association's Dilys Award, for *Book Case* (1991); for two Shamus Awards by the Private Eye Writers of America, for *Flesh Wounds* (1996) and *Ellipsis* (2000); and for an Edgar Allan Poe Award from the Mystery Writers of America, for *Strawberry Sundae* (1999). He won the Falcon Award for the best private eye novel published in Japan, for *Book Case.*

Although private eye stories seldom fall into the noir category, the following John Marshall Tanner tale is a rare and stunning exception. "Iris," the author's only short mystery story, was first published in the anthology *The Eyes Have It* (New York: Mysterious Press, 1984).

▪ ▪ ▪

THE BUICK TRUDGED toward the summit, each step slower than the last, the automatic gearing slipping ever lower as the air thinned and the grade steepened and the trucks were rendered snails. At the top the road leveled, and the Buick spent a brief sigh of relief before coasting thankfully down the other side, atop the stiff gray strap that was Interstate 5. As it passed from Oregon to California the car seemed cheered. Its driver shared the mood, though only momentarily.

He blinked his eyes and shrugged his shoulders and twisted his head. He straightened his leg and shook it. He turned up the volume of the radio, causing a song to be sung more loudly than it merited. But the acid fog lay still behind his eyes, eating at them. As he approached a roadside rest area he decided to give both the Buick and himself a break.

During the previous week he had chased a wild goose in the shape of a rumor all the way to Seattle, with tantalizing stops in Eugene and Portland along the way. Eight hours earlier, when he had finally recognized the goose for what it was, he had headed home, hoping to make it in one day but realizing as he slowed for the rest area that he couldn't reach San Francisco that evening without risking more than was sensible in the way of vehicular manslaughter.

He took the exit, dropped swiftly to the bank of the Klamath River, and pulled into a parking slot in the Randolph Collier safety rest area. After making use of the facilities, he pulled out his map and considered where to spend the night. Redding looked like the logical place, out of the mountains, at the head of the soporific valley that separated him from home. He was reviewing what he knew about Redding when a voice, aggressively gay and musical, greeted him from somewhere near the car. He glanced to his side, sat up straight, and rolled down the window. "Hi," the thin voice said again.

"Hi."

She was blond, her long straight tresses misbehaving in the wind that tumbled through the river canyon. Her narrow face was white and seamless, as though it lacked flesh, was only skull. Her eyes were blue and tardy. She wore a loose green blouse gathered at the neck and wrists and a long skirt of faded calico, fringed in white ruffles. Her boots were leather and well worn, their tops disappearing under her skirt the way the tops of the mountains at her back disappeared into a disk of cloud.

He pegged her for a hitchhiker, one who perpetually roams the roads and provokes either pity or disapproval in those who pass her by. He glanced around to see if she was fronting for a partner, but the only thing he saw besides the picnic and toilet facilities and travelers like himself was a large bundle resting atop a picnic table at the far end of the parking lot. Her worldly possessions, he guessed; her only aids to life. He looked at her again and considered whether he wanted to share some driving time and possibly a motel room with a girl who looked a little spacy and a little sexy and a lot heedless of the world that delivered him his living.

"My name's Iris," she said, wrapping her arms across her chest, shifting her weight from foot to foot, shivering in the autumn chill.

"Mine's Marsh."

"You look tired." Her concern seemed genuine, his common symptoms for some reason alarming to her.

"I am," he admitted.

"Been on the road long?"

"From Seattle."

"How far is that about?" The question came immediately, as though she habitually erased her ignorance.

"Four hundred miles. Maybe a little more."

She nodded as though the numbers made him wise. "I've been to Seattle."

"Good."

"I've been lots of places."

"Good."

She unwrapped her arms and placed them on the door and leaned toward him. Her musk was unadulterated. Her blouse dropped open to reveal breasts sharpened to twin points by the mountain air. "Where you headed, Marsh?"

"South."

"L.A.?"

He shook his head. "San Francisco."

"Good. Perfect."

He expected it right then, the flirting pitch for a lift, but her request was slightly different. "Could you take something down there for me?"

He frowned and thought of the package on the picnic table. Drugs? "What?" he asked.

"I'll show you in a sec. Do you think you could, though?"

He shook his head. "I don't think so. I mean, I'm kind of on a tight schedule, and . . ."

She wasn't listening. "It goes to . . ." She pulled a scrap of paper from the pocket of her skirt and uncrumpled it. "It goes to 95 Albosa Drive, in Hurley City. That's near Frisco, isn't it? Marvin said it was."

He nodded. "But I don't . . ."

She put up a hand. "Hold still. I'll be right back."

She skipped twice, her long skirt hopping high above her boots to show a shaft of gypsum thigh, then trotted to the picnic table and picked up the bundle. Halfway back to the car she proffered it like a prize soufflé.

"Is this what you want me to take?" he asked as she approached.

She nodded, then looked down at the package and frowned. "I don't like this one," she said, her voice dropping to a dismissive rasp.

"Why not?"

"Because it isn't happy. It's from the B Box, so it can't help it, I guess, but all the same it should go back, I don't care *what* Marvin says."

"What is it? A puppy?"

She thrust the package through the window. He grasped it reflexively, to keep it from dropping to his lap. As he secured his grip the girl ran off. "Hey! Wait a minute," he called after her. "I can't take this thing. You'll have to . . ."

He thought the package moved. He slid one hand beneath it and with the other peeled back the cotton strips that swaddled it. A baby—not canine but human—glared at him and screamed. He looked frantically for the girl and saw her climbing into a gray Volkswagen bug that was soon scooting out of the rest area and climbing toward the freeway.

He swore, then rocked the baby awkwardly for an instant, trying to quiet the screams it formed with every muscle. When that didn't work, he placed the child on the seat beside him, started the car, and backed out. As he started forward he had to stop to avoid another car, and then to reach out wildly to keep the child from rolling off the seat.

He moved the gear to park and gathered the seat belt on the passenger side and tried to wrap it around the baby in a way that would be more safe than throttling. The result was not reassuring. He unhooked the belt and put the baby on the floor beneath his legs, put the car in gear, and set out after the little gray VW that had disappeared with the child's presumptive mother. He caught it only after several frantic miles, when he reached the final slope that descended to the grassy plain that separated the Siskiyou range from the lordly aspect of Mount Shasta.

The VW buzzed toward the mammoth mountain like a mad mouse assaulting an elephant. He considered overtaking the car, forcing Iris to stop, returning the baby, then getting the hell away from her as fast as the Buick would take him. But something in his memory of her look and words made him keep his distance, made him keep Iris in sight while he waited for her to make a turn toward home.

The highway flattened, then crossed the high meadow that nurtured sheep and cattle and horses below the lumps of the southern Cascades and the Trinity Alps. Traffic was light, the sun low above the western peaks, the air a steady splash of autumn. He checked his gas gauge. If Iris didn't turn off in the next fifty miles he would either have to force her to stop or let her go. The piercing baby sounds that rose from beneath his knees made the latter choice impossible.

They reached Yreka, and he closed to within a hundred yards of the bug, but Iris ignored his plea that the little city be her goal. Thirty minutes later, after he had decided she was nowhere near her destination, Iris abruptly left the interstate, at the first exit to a village that was handmaiden to the mountain, a town reputed to house an odd collection of spiritual seekers and religious zealots.

The mountain itself, volcanic, abrupt, spectacular, had been held by the Indians to be holy, and the area surrounding it was replete with hot springs and mud baths and other prehistoric marvels. Modern mystics had accepted the mantle of the mountain, and the crazy girl and her silly bug fit with what he knew about the place and those who gathered there. What didn't fit was the baby she had foisted on him.

He slowed and glanced at his charge once again and failed to receive anything resembling contentment in return. Fat little arms escaped the blanket and pulled the air like taffy. Spittle dribbled down its chin. A translucent bubble appeared at a tiny nostril, then broke silently and vanished.

The bug darted through the north end of town, left, then right, then left again, quickly, as though it sensed pursuit. He lagged behind, hoping Iris was confident she had ditched him. He looked at the baby again, marveling that it could cry so loud, could for so long expend the major portion of its strength in unrequited pleas. When he looked at the road again the bug had disappeared.

He swore and slowed and looked at driveways, then began to plan what to do if he had lost her. Houses dwindled, the street became dirt, then flanked the log decks and lumber stacks and wigwam burners of a sawmill. A road sign declared it unlawful to sleigh, toboggan, or ski on a county road. He had gasped the first breaths of panic when he saw the VW nestled next to a ramshackle cabin on the back edge of town, empty, as though it had been there always.

A pair of firs sheltered the cabin and the car, made the dwindling day seem night. The driveway was mud, the yard bordered by a falling wormwood fence. He drove to the next block and stopped his car, the cabin now invisible.

He knew he couldn't keep the baby much longer. He had no idea what to do, for it or with it, had no idea what it wanted, no idea what awaited it in Hurley City, had only a sense that the girl, Iris, was goofy, perhaps pathologically so, and that he should not abet her plan.

Impossibly, the child cried louder. He had some snacks in the car — crackers, cookies, some cheese — but he was afraid the baby was too young for solids. He considered buying milk, and a bottle, and playing parent. The baby cried again, gasped and sputtered, then repeated its protest.

He reached down and picked it up. The little red face inflated, contorted, mimicked a steam machine that continuously whistled. The puffy cheeks, the tiny blue eyes, the round pug nose, all were engorged in scarlet fury. He cradled the baby in his arms as best he could and rocked it. The crying dimmed momentarily, then began again.

His mind ran the gauntlet of childhood scares — diphtheria, smallpox, measles, mumps, croup, even a pressing need to burp. God knew what ailed it. He patted its forehead and felt the sticky heat of fever.

Shifting position, he felt something hard within the blanket, felt for it, finally drew it out. A nippled baby bottle, half-filled, body-warm. He shook it and presented the nipple to the baby, who sucked it as its due. Giddy at his feat, he unwrapped his package further, enough to tell him he was holding a little girl and that she seemed whole and healthy except for her rage and fever. When she was feeding steadily he put her back on the floor and got out of the car.

The stream of smoke it emitted into the evening dusk made the cabin seem dangled from a string. Beneath the firs the ground was moist, a spongy mat of rotting twigs and needles. The air was cold and damp and smelled of burning wood. He walked slowly up the drive, courting silence, alert for the menace implied by the hand-lettered sign, nailed to the nearest tree, that ordered him to KEEP OUT.

The cabin was dark but for the variable light at a single window. The porch was piled high with firewood, both logs and kindling. A maul and wedge leaned against a stack of fruitwood piled next to the door. He walked to the far side of the cabin and looked beyond it for signs of Marvin.

A tool shed and a broken-down school bus filled the rear yard. Between the two a tethered nanny goat grazed beneath a line of drying clothes, silent but for her neck bell, the swollen udder oscillating easily beneath her, the teats extended like accusing fingers. Beyond the yard a thicket of berry bushes served as fence, and beyond the bushes a stand of pines blocked further vision. He felt alien, isolated, exposed, threatened, as Marvin doubtlessly hoped all strangers would.

He thought about the baby, wondered if it was all right, wondered if babies could drink so much they got sick or even choked. A twinge of fear sent him trotting back to the car. The baby was fine, the bottle empty on the floor beside it, its noises not wails but only muffled whimpers. He returned to the cabin and went onto the porch and knocked at the door and waited.

Iris wore the same blouse and skirt and boots, the same eyes too shallow to hold her soul. She didn't recognize him; her face pinched only with uncertainty.

He stepped toward her and she backed away and asked him what he wanted. The room behind her was a warren of vague shapes, the only source of light far in the back by a curtain that spanned the room.

"I want to give you your baby back," he said.

She looked at him more closely, then opened her mouth in silent exclamation, then slowly smiled. "How'd you know where I lived?"

"I followed you."

"Why? Did something happen to it already?"

"No, but I don't want to take it with me."

She seemed truly puzzled. "Why not? It's on your way, isn't it? Almost?"

He ignored the question. "I want to know some more about the baby."

"Like what?"

"Like whose is it? Yours?"

Iris frowned and nibbled her lower lip. "Sort of."

"What do you mean, 'sort of'? Did you give birth to it?"

"Not exactly." Iris combed her hair with her fingers, then shook it off her face with an irritated twitch. "What are you asking all these questions for?"

"Because you asked me to do you a favor and I think I have the right to know what I'm getting into. That's only fair, isn't it?"

She paused. Her pout was dubious. "I guess."

"So where did you get the baby?" he asked again.

"Marvin got it."

"From whom?"

"Those people in Hurley City. So I don't know why you won't take it back, seeing as how it's theirs and all."

"But why . . ."

His question was obliterated by a high glissando, brief and piercing. He looked at Iris, then at the shadowy interior of the cabin.

There was no sign of life, no sign of anything but the leavings of neglect and a spartan bent. A fat gray cat hopped off a shelf and sauntered toward the back of the cabin and disappeared behind the blanket that was draped on the rope that spanned the rear of the room. The cry echoed once again. "What's that?" he asked her.

Iris giggled. "What does it sound like?"

"Another baby?"

Iris nodded.

"Can I see it?"

"Why?"

"Because I like babies."

"If you like them, why won't you take the one I gave you down to Hurley City?"

"Maybe I'm changing my mind. Can I see this one?"

"I'm not supposed to let anyone in here."

"It'll be OK. Really. Marvin isn't here, is he?"

She shook her head. "But he'll be back any time. He just went to town."

He summoned reasonableness and geniality. "Just let me see your baby for a second, Iris. Please? Then I'll go. And take the other baby with me. I promise."

She pursed her lips, then nodded and stepped back. "I got more than one," she suddenly bragged. "Let me show you." She turned and walked quickly toward the rear of the cabin and disappeared behind the blanket.

When he followed he found himself in a space that was half kitchen and half nursery. Opposite the electric stove and Frigidaire, along the wall between the wood stove and the rear door, was a row of wooden boxes, seven of them, old orange crates, dividers removed, painted different colors and labeled A to G. Faint names of orchards and renderings of fruits rose through the paint on the stub ends of the crates. Inside boxes C through G were babies, buried deep in nests of rags and scraps of blanket. One of them was crying. The others slept soundly, warm and toasty, healthy and happy from all the evidence he had.

"My God," he said.

"Aren't they beautiful? They're just the best little things in the whole world. Yes they are. Just the best little babies in the whole wide world. And Iris loves them all a bunch. Yes, she does. Doesn't she?"

Beaming, Iris cooed to the babies for another moment, then her face darkened. "The one I gave you, she wasn't happy here. That's because she was a B Box baby. My B babies are always sad, I don't know why. I treat them all the same, but the B babies are just contrary. That's why the one I gave you should go back. Where is it, anyway?"

"In the car."

"By itself?"

He nodded.

"You shouldn't leave her there like that," Iris chided. "She's pouty enough already."

"What about these others?" he asked, looking at the boxes. "Do they stay here forever?"

Her whole aspect solidified. "They stay till Marvin needs them. Till he does, I give them everything they want. Everything they need. No one could be nicer to my babies than me. *No* one."

The fire in the stove lit her eyes like ice in sunlight. She gazed raptly at the boxes, one by one, and received something he sensed was sexual in return. Her breaths were rapid and shallow, her fists clenched at her sides. "Where'd you get these babies?" he asked softly.

"Marvin gets them." She was only half-listening.

"Where?"

"All over. We had one from Nevada one time, and two from Idaho I think. Most are from California, though. And Oregon. I think that C Box baby's from Spokane. That's Oregon, isn't it?"

He didn't correct her. "Have there been more besides these?"

"Some."

"How many?"

"Oh, maybe ten. No, more than that. I've had three of all the babies except G babies."

"And Marvin got them all for you?"

She nodded and went to the stove and turned on a burner. "You want some tea? It's herbal. Peppermint."

He shook his head. "What happened to the other babies? The ones that aren't here anymore?"

"Marvin took them." Iris sipped her tea.

"Where?"

"To someone that wanted to love them." The declaration was as close as she would come to gospel.

The air in the cabin seemed suddenly befouled, not breathable. "Is that what this is all about, Iris? Giving babies to people that want them?"

"That want them and will *love* them. See, Marvin gets these babies from people that *don't* want them, and gives them to people that *do.* It's his business."

"Does he get paid for it?"

She shrugged absently. "A little, I think."

"Do you go with Marvin when he picks them up?"

"Sometimes. When it's far."

"And where does he take them? To Idaho and Nevada, or just around here?"

She shrugged again. "He doesn't tell me where they go. He says he doesn't want me to try and get them back." She smiled peacefully. "He knows how I am about my babies."

"How long have you and Marvin been doing this?"

"I been with Marvin about three years."

"And you've been trading in babies all that time?"

"Just about."

She poured some more tea into a ceramic cup and sipped it. She gave no sign of guile or guilt, no sign that what he suspected could possibly be true.

"Do you have any children of your own, Iris?"

Her hand shook enough to spill her tea. "I *almost* had one once."

"What do you mean?"

She made a face. "I got pregnant, but nobody wanted me to keep it so I didn't."

"Did you put it up for adoption?"

She shook her head.

"Abortion?"

Iris nodded, apparently in pain, and mumbled something. He asked her what she'd said. "I did it myself," she repeated. "That's what I can't live with. I scraped it out of there myself. I passed out. I . . ."

She fell silent. He looked back at the row of boxes that held her penance. When she saw him look she began to sing a song. "Aren't they just perfect?" she said when she was through. "Aren't they all just perfect?"

"How do you know where the baby you gave me belongs?" he asked quietly.

"Marvin's got a book that keeps track. I sneaked a look at it one time when he was stoned."

"Where's he keep it?"

"In the van. At least that's where I found it." Iris put her hands on his chest and pushed. "You better go before Marvin gets back. You'll take the baby, won't you? It just don't belong here with the others. It fusses all the time and I can't love it like I should."

He looked at Iris's face, at the firelight washing across it, making it alive. "Where are you from, Iris?"

"Me? Minnesota."

"Did you come to California with Marvin?"

She shook her head. "I come with another guy. I was tricking for him when I got knocked up. After the abortion I told him I wouldn't trick no more so he ditched me. Then I did a lot of drugs for a while, till I met Marvin at a commune down by Mendocino."

"What's Marvin's last name?"

"Hessel. Now you got to go. Really. Marvin's liable to do something crazy if he finds you here." She walked toward him and he retreated.

"OK, Iris. Just one thing. Could you give me something for the baby to eat? She's real hungry."

Iris frowned. "She only likes goat's milk, is the problem, and I haven't milked today." She walked to the Frigidaire and returned with a bottle. "This is all I got. Now, git."

He nodded, took the bottle from her, then retreated to his car.

He opened the door on the stinging smell of ammonia. The baby greeted him with screams. He picked it up, rocked it, talked to it, hummed a tune, finally gave it the second bottle, which was the only thing it wanted.

As it sucked its sustenance he started the car and let the engine warm, and a minute later flipped the heater switch. When it seemed prudent, he unwrapped the child and unpinned her soggy diaper and patted her dumplinged bottom dry with a tissue from the glove compartment. After covering her with her blanket he got out of the car, pulled his suitcase from the trunk, and took out his last clean T-shirt, then returned to the car and fashioned a bulky diaper out of the cotton shirt and affixed it to the child, pricking his finger in the process, spotting both the garment and the baby with his blood. Then he sat for a time, considering his obligations to the children that had suddenly littered his life.

He should go to the police, but Marvin might return before they responded and might learn of Iris's deed and harm the children or flee with them. He could call the police and wait in place for them to come, but he doubted his ability to convey his precise suspicions over the phone. As he searched for other options, headlights ricocheted off his mirror and into his eyes, then veered off. When his vision was reestablished he reached into the glove compartment for his revolver. Shoving it into his pocket, he got out of the car and walked back to the driveway and disobeyed the sign again.

A new shape had joined the scene, rectangular and dark. Marvin's van, creaking as it cooled. He waited, listened, and when he sensed no other presence he approached it. A converted bread truck, painted navy blue, with sliding doors into the driver's cabin and hinged doors at the back. The right fender was dented, the rear bumper wired in place. A knobby-tired motorcycle was strapped to a rack on the top. The door on the driver's side was open, so he climbed in.

The high seat was rotted through, its stuffing erupting like white weeds through the dirty vinyl. The floorboards were littered with food wrappers and beer cans and cigarette butts. He activated his pencil flash and pawed through the refuse, pausing at the only pristine object in the van — a business card, white with black engraving, taped to a corner of the dash: "J. Arnold Rasker, Attorney at Law. Practice in all Courts. Initial Consultation Free. Phone day or night."

He looked through the cab for another minute, found nothing resembling Marvin's notebook and nothing else of interest. After listening for Marvin's return and hearing nothing he went through the narrow doorway behind the driver's seat into the cargo area in the rear, the yellow ball that dangled from his flash bouncing playfully before him.

The entire area had been carpeted, ceiling included, in a matted pink plush that was stained in unlikely places and coming unglued in others. A roundish window had been cut into one wall by hand, then covered with plastic sheeting kept in place with tape. Two upholstered chairs were bolted to the floor on one side of the van, and an Army cot stretched out along the other. Two orange crates similar to those in the cabin, though empty, lay between the chairs. Above the cot a picture of John Lennon was tacked to the carpeted wall with a rusty nail. A small propane bottle was strapped into one corner, an Igloo cooler in another. Next to the Lennon poster a lever-action rifle rested in two leather slings. The smells were of gasoline and marijuana and unwashed flesh. Again he found no notebook.

He switched off his light and backed out of the van and walked to the cabin, pausing on the porch. Music pulsed from the interior, heavy metal, obliterating all noises including his own. He walked to the window and peered inside.

Iris, carrying and feeding a baby, paced the room, eyes closed, mumbling, seemingly deranged. Alone momentarily, she was soon joined by a wide and woolly man, wearing cowboy boots and Levi's, a plaid shirt, full beard, hair to his shoulders. A light film of grease coated flesh and clothes alike, as though he had just been dipped. Marvin strode through the room without speaking, his black eyes angry, his shoulders tipping to the frenetic music as he sucked the final puffs of a joint held in an oddly dainty clip.

Both Marvin and Iris were lost in their tasks. When their paths crossed they backed away as though they feared each other. He watched them for five long minutes. When they disappeared behind the curtain in the back he hurried to the door and went inside the cabin.

The music paused, then began again, the new piece indistinguishable from the old. The heavy fog of dope washed into his lungs and lightened his head and braked his brain. Murmurs from behind the curtain erupted into a swift male curse. A pan clattered on the stove; wood scraped against wood. He drew his gun and moved to the edge of the room and sidled toward the curtain and peered around its edge.

Marvin sat in a chair at a small table, gripping a bottle of beer. Iris was at the stove, her back to Marvin, opening a can of soup. Marvin guzzled half the bottle, banged it on the table, and swore again. "How could you be so fucking stupid?"

"Don't, Marvin. Please?"

"Just tell me who you gave it to. That's all I want to know. It was your buddy Gretel, wasn't it? Had to be, she's the only one around here as loony as you."

"It wasn't anyone you know. Really. It was just a guy."

"What guy?"

"Just *a guy.* I went out to a rest area way up by Oregon, and I talked to him and he said he was going to Frisco so I gave it to him and told him where to take it. You *know* it didn't belong here, Marvin. You know how puny it was."

Marvin stood up, knocking his chair to the floor. "You stupid bitch." His hand raised high, Marvin advanced on Iris with beer dribbling from his chin. "I'll break your jaw, woman. I swear I will."

"Don't hit me, Marvin. Please don't hit me again."

"Who was it? I want a name."

"I don't *know,* I told you. Just some guy going to Frisco. His name was Mark, I think."

"And he took the kid?"

Iris nodded. "He was real nice."

"You bring him here? Huh? Did you bring the son of a bitch to the cabin? Did you tell him about the others?"

"No, Marvin. No. I swear. You know I'd never do that."

"Lying bitch."

Marvin grabbed Iris by the hair and dragged her away from the stove and slapped her across the face. She screamed and cowered. Marvin raised his hand to strike again.

Sucking a breath, he raised his gun and stepped from behind the curtain. "Hold it," he told Marvin. "Don't move."

Marvin froze, twisted his head, took in the gun, and released his grip on Iris and backed away from her, his black eyes glistening. A slow smile exposed dark and crooked teeth. "Well, now," Marvin drawled. "Just who might you be besides a fucking trespasser? Don't tell me; let me guess. You're the nice man Iris gave a baby to. The one she swore she didn't bring out here. Right?"

"She didn't bring me. I followed her."

Both men glanced at Iris. Her hand was at her mouth and she was nibbling a knuckle. "I thought you went to Frisco" was all she said.

"Not yet."

"What do you want?" Her question assumed a fearsome answer.

Marvin laughed. "You stupid bitch. He wants the *rest* of them. Then he wants to throw us in jail. He wants to be a hero, Iris. And to be a hero he has to put you and me behind bars for the rest of our fucking lives." Marvin took a step forward.

"Don't be dumb." He raised the gun to Marvin's eyes.

Marvin stopped, frowned, then grinned again. "You look like you used that piece before."

"Once or twice."

"What's your gig?"

"Detective. Private."

Marvin's lips parted around his crusted teeth. "You must be kidding. Iris flags down some bastard on the freeway and he turns out to be a private cop?"

"That's about it."

Marvin shook his head. "Judas H. Priest. And here you are. A professional hero, just like I said."

He captured Marvin's eyes. "I want the book."

"What book?" Marvin burlesqued ignorance.

"The book with the list of babies and where you got them and where you took them."

Marvin looked at Iris, stuck her with his stare. "You're dead meat, you know that? You bring the bastard here and tell him all about it and expect him to just take off and not try to *stop* us? You're too fucking dumb to breathe, Iris. I got to put you out of your misery."

"I'm sorry, Marvin."

"He's going to take them *back*, Iris. Get it? He's going to take those sweet babies away from you and give them back to the assholes that don't want them. And then he's going to the cops and they're going to say you *kidnapped* those babies, Iris, and that you were bad to them and should go to jail because of what you did. Don't you see that, you brain-fried bitch? *Don't you see what he's going to do?*"

"I . . ." Iris stopped, overwhelmed by Marvin's incantation. "Are you?" she asked, finally looking away from Marvin.

"I'm going to do what's best for the babies, Iris. That's all."

"What's best for them is with me and Marvin."

"Not anymore," he told her. "Marvin's been shucking you, Iris. He steals those babies. Takes them from their parents, parents who love them. He roams up and down the coast stealing children and then he sells them, Iris. Either back to the people he took them from or to people desperate to adopt. I think he's hooked up with a lawyer named Rasker, who arranges private adoptions for big money and splits the take with Marvin. He's not interested in who loves those kids, Iris. He's only interested in how much he can sell them for."

Something had finally activated Iris's eyes. "Marvin? Is that true?"

"No, baby. The guy's blowing smoke. He's trying to take the babies away from you and then get people to believe you did something bad, just like that time with the abortion. He's trying to say you did bad things to babies again, Iris. We can't let him do that."

He spoke quickly, to erase Marvin's words. "People don't give away babies, Iris. Not to guys like Marvin. There are agencies that arrange that kind of thing, that check to make sure the new home is in the best interests of the child. Marvin just swipes them and sells them to the highest bidder, Iris. That's all he's in it for."

"I don't believe you."

"It doesn't matter. Just give me Marvin's notebook and we can check it out, contact the parents and see what they say about their kids. Ask if they wanted to be rid of them. That's fair, isn't it?"

"I don't know. I guess."

"Iris?"

"What, Marvin?"

"I want you to pick up that pan and knock this guy on the head. Hard. Go on, Iris. He won't shoot you, you know that. Hit him on the head so he can't put us in jail."

He glanced at Iris, then as quickly to Marvin and to Iris once again. "Don't do it, Iris. Marvin's trouble. I think you know that now." He looked away from Iris and gestured at her partner. "Where's the book?"

"Iris?"

Iris began to cry. "I can't, Marvin. I can't do that."

"The book," he said to Marvin again. "Where is it?"

Marvin laughed. "You'll never know, Detective."

"OK. We'll do it your way. On the floor. Hands behind your head. Legs spread. Now."

Marvin didn't move. When he spoke the words were languid. "You don't look much like a killer, Detective, and I've known a few, believe me. So I figure if you're not gonna shoot me I don't got to do what you say. I figure I'll just take that piece away from you and feed it to you inch by inch. Huh? Why don't I do just that?"

He took two quick steps to Marvin's side and sliced open Marvin's cheek with a quick swipe of the gun barrel. "Want some more?"

Marvin pawed at his cheek with a grimy hand, then examined his bloody fingers. "You bastard. OK. I'll get the book. It's under here."

Marvin bent toward the floor, twisting away from him, sliding his hands toward the darkness below the stove. He couldn't tell what Marvin was doing, so he squinted, then moved closer. When Marvin began to stand he jumped back, but Marvin wasn't attacking, Marvin was holding a baby, not a book, holding a baby by the throat.

"OK, pal," Marvin said through his grin. "Now, you want to see this kid die before your eyes, you just keep hold of that gun. You want to see it breathe some more, you drop it."

He froze, his eyes on Marvin's fingers, which inched further around the baby's neck and began to squeeze.

The baby gurgled, gasped, twitched, was silent. Its face reddened; its eyes bulged. The tendons in Marvin's hand stretched taut. Between grimy gritted teeth, Marvin wheezed in rapid streams of glee.

He dropped his gun. Marvin told Iris to pick it up. She did, and exchanged the gun for the child. Her eyes lapped Marvin's face, as though to renew its acquaintance. Abruptly, she turned and ran around the curtain and disappeared.

"Well, now." Marvin's words slid easily. "Looks like the worm has turned, Detective. What's your name, anyhow?"

"Tanner."

"Well, Tanner, your ass is mine. No more John Wayne stunts for you. You can kiss this world goodbye."

Marvin fished in the pocket of his jeans, then drew out a small spiral notebook and flashed it. "It's all in here, Tanner. Where they came from; where they went. Now watch."

Gun in one hand, notebook in the other, Marvin went to the wood stove and flipped open the heavy door. The fire made shadows dance.

"Don't."

"Watch, bastard."

Marvin tossed the notebook into the glowing coals, fished in the box beside the stove for a stick of kindling, then tossed it in after the notebook and closed the iron door. "Bye-bye babies." Marvin's laugh was quick and cruel. "Now turn around. We're going out back."

He did as he was told, walking toward the door, hearing only a silent shuffle at his back. As he passed her he glanced at Iris. She hugged the baby Marvin had threatened, crying, not looking at him. "Remember the one in my car," he said to her. She nodded silently, then turned away.

Marvin prodded him in the back and he moved to the door. Hand on the knob, he paused, hoping for a magical deliverance, but none came. Marvin prodded him again and he moved outside, onto the porch, then into the yard. "Around back," Marvin ordered. "Get in the bus."

He staggered, tripping over weeds, stumbling over rocks, until he reached the rusting bus. The moon and stars had disappeared; the night was black and still but for the whistling wind, clearly Marvin's ally. The nanny goat laughed at them, then trotted out of reach. He glanced back at Marvin. In one hand was a pistol, in the other a blanket. "Go on in. Just pry the door open."

He fit his finger between the rubber edges of the bus door and opened it. The first step was higher than he thought, and he tripped and almost fell. "Watch it. I almost blasted you right then."

He couldn't suppress a giggle. For reasons of his own, Marvin matched his laugh. "Head on back, Tanner. Pretend you're on a field trip to the zoo."

He walked down the aisle between the broken seats, smelling rot and rust and the lingering scent of skunk. "Why here?" he asked as he reached the rear.

"Because you'll keep in here just fine till I get time to dig a hole out back and open that emergency door and dump you in. Plus it's quiet. I figure with the bus and the blanket no one will hear a thing. Sit."

He sat. Marvin draped the blanket across the arm that held the gun, then extended the shrouded weapon toward his chest. He had no doubt that Marvin would shoot without a thought or fear. "Any last words, Tanner? Any parting thoughts?"

"Just that you forgot something."

"What?"

"You left the door open."

Marvin glanced quickly toward the door in the front of the bus. He dove for Marvin's legs, sweeping at the gun with his left hand as he did so, hoping to dislodge it into the folds of the blanket where it would lie useless and unattainable.

"Cocksucker."

Marvin wrested the gun from his grasp and raised it high, tossing off the blanket in the process. He twisted frantically to protect against the blow he knew was coming, but Marvin was too heavy and strong, retained the upper hand by kneeling on his chest. The revolver glinted in the darkness, a missile poised to descend.

Sound split the air, a piercing scream of agony from the cabin or somewhere near it. "What the hell?" Marvin swore, started to retreat, then almost thoughtlessly clubbed him with the gun, once, then again. After a flash of pain a broad black creature held him down for a length of time he couldn't calculate.

When he was aware again he was alone in the bus, lying in the aisle. His head felt crushed to pulp. He put a hand to his temple and felt blood. Midst throbbing pain he struggled to his feet and made his way outside and stood leaning against the bus while the night air struggled to clear his head.

He took a step, staggered, took another and gained an equilibrium, then lost it and sat down. Back on his feet, he trudged toward the porch and opened the door. Behind him, the nanny laughed again.

The cabin was dark, the only light the faint flicker from the stove behind the curtain. He walked carefully, trying to avoid the litter on the floor, the shapes in the room. Halfway to the back his foot struck something soft. As he bent to shove it out of his way it made a human sound. He knelt, saw that it was Iris, then found a lamp and turned it on.

She was crumpled, face-down, in the center of the room, arms and legs folded under her, her body curled to avoid assault. He knelt again, heard her groan once more, and saw that what he'd thought was a piece of skirt was in fact a pool of blood and what he'd thought was shadow was a broad wet trail of the selfsame substance leading toward the rear of the cabin.

He ran his hands down her body, feeling for wounds. Finding none, he rolled Iris to her side, then to her back. Blood bubbled from a point beneath her sternum. Her eyelids fluttered, open, closed, then open again. "He shot me," she said. "It hurt so bad I couldn't stop crying so he shot me."

"I know. Don't try to talk."

"Did he shoot the babies, too? I thought I heard . . ."

"I don't know."

"Would you look? Please?"

He nodded, stood up, fought a siege of vertigo, then went behind the curtain, then returned to Iris. "They're all right."

She tried to smile her thanks. "Something scared him off. I think some people were walking by outside and heard the shot and went for help. I heard them yelling."

"Where would he go, Iris?"

"Up in the woods. On his dirt bike. He knows lots of people up there. They grow dope, live off the land. The cops'll never find him." Iris moaned again. "I'm dying, aren't I?"

"I don't know. Is there a phone here?"

She shook her head. "Down at the end of the street. By the market."

"I'm going down and call an ambulance. And the cops. How long ago did Marvin leave?"

She closed her eyes. "I blacked out. Oh, God. It's real bad now, Mr. Tanner. Real bad."

"I know, Iris. You hang on. I'll be back in a second. Try to hold this in place." He took out his handkerchief and folded it into a square and placed it on her wound. "Press as hard as you can." He took her left hand and placed it on the compress, then stood up.

"Wait. I have to . . ."

He spoke above her words. "You have to get to a hospital. I'll be back in a minute and we can talk some more."

"But . . ."

"Hang on."

He ran from the cabin and down the drive, spotted the lights of the convenience market down the street and ran to the phone booth and placed his calls. The police said they'd already been notified and a car was on the way. The ambulance said it would be six minutes. As fast as he could he ran back to the cabin, hoping it would be fast enough.

Iris had moved. Her body was straightened, her right arm outstretched toward the door, the gesture of a supplicant. The sleeve of her blouse was tattered, burned to a ragged edge above her elbow. Below the sleeve her arm was red in spots, blistered in others, dappled like burned food. The hand at its end was charred and curled into a crusty fist that was dusted with gray ash. Within the fingers was an object, blackened, burned, and treasured.

He pried it from her grasp. The cover was burned away, and the edges of the pages were curled and singed, but they remained decipherable, the written scrawl preserved. The list of names and places was organized to match the gaily painted boxes in the back. Carson City. Boise. Grant's Pass. San Bernardino. Modesto. On and on, a gazetteer of crime.

"I saved it," Iris mumbled. "I saved it for my babies."

He raised her head to his lap and held it till she died. Then he went to his car and retrieved his B Box baby and placed her in her appointed crib. For the first time since he'd known her the baby made only happy sounds, an irony that was lost on the five dead children at her flank and on the just dead woman who had feared it all.

1987

BRENDAN DUBOIS

A TICKET OUT

BRENDAN DUBOIS (1959–) was born in New Hampshire and has lived there his entire life. A former newspaper reporter, he has written a variety of novels and has been a prolific short story writer, with more than one hundred published stories to his credit.

His mystery novels, set around the New Hampshire seacoast, often feature Lewis Cole, a magazine writer who was once a research analyst for the Department of Defense. The first book in the series is *Dead Sand* (1994), followed by *Black Tide* (1995), *Shattered Shell* (1999), *Killer Waves* (2002), *Buried Dreams* (2004), and *Primary Storm* (2006). He has had even greater success with international thrillers, notably *Resurrection Day* (1999), an alternative-history novel set in 1972, a decade after the Cuban missile crisis had provoked an atomic war between the Soviet Union and the United States. It received the Sidewise Award for Best Alternative History Novel at the World Science Fiction Convention. Other thrillers include *Twilight* (2007), about the aftermath of a successful terrorist attack on the U.S.; *Final Winter* (2006), a nail biter about a planned terrorist attack on the U.S.; *Betrayed* (2003), which delves into the real-life mystery of the two thousand servicemen missing in action during the Vietnam War; and *Six Days* (2001), about a plot to overthrow the U.S. government. His short stories have received numerous awards, including two Shamus Awards from the Private Eye Writers of America. "The Dark Snow" was selected for *The Best American Mystery Stories of the Century.*

"A Ticket Out" was first published in the January 1987 issue of *Ellery Queen's Mystery Magazine.*

▪ ▪ ▪

THEN THERE ARE the nights when I can't sleep, when the blankets seem wrapped around me too tight, when the room is so stuffy that I imagine the air is full of dust and age, and when my wife Carol's sighs and breathing are enough to make me tremble with tension. On these nights I slip out of bed and put on my heavy flannel bathrobe, and in bare feet I pad down the hallway—past the twins' bedroom—and go downstairs to the kitchen. I'm smart enough to know that drinking at night will eventually cause problems, but I ignore what my doctor tells me and I mix a ginger and Jameson's in a tall glass and go to the living room and look out the large bay window at the stars and the woods and the hills. Remembering what we had planned, what we had stolen, the blood that had been spilled, the tears and the anguish, I sip at my drink and think, well, it wasn't what we wanted to do. We weren't stealing for drugs or clothes or to impress the chunky, giggly girls Brad and I went to high school with. We were stealing for a ticket, for a way out. In the end, only one of us got out. That thought doesn't help me sleep at all.

It began on an August day in 1976, about a month before Brad Leary and I were going in as seniors to our high school. That summer we worked at one of the shoe mills in Boston Falls, keeping a tradition going in each of our families. Brad's father worked in one of the stitching rooms at Devon Shoe, while my dad and two older brothers worked on the other side of the Squamscott River at Parker Shoe. My dad was an assistant bookkeeper, which meant he wore a shirt and tie and earned fifty cents more an hour than the "blue-collar boys" that worked among the grinding and dirty machinery.

Brad and I worked in the packing room, piling up cardboard boxes of shoes and dodging the kicks and punches from the older men who thought we were moving too slow or too sloppily. We usually got off at three, and after buying a couple of cans of 7-Up or Coke and a bag of Humpty Dumpty potato chips we hiked away from the mills up Mast Road to the top of Cavalry Hill, which looked over the valley where Boston Falls was nestled. Well, maybe *nestled*'s too nice a word. It was more tumbled in than nestled in.

On that day, we both wore the standard uniform of the summer, dark green T-shirts, blue jeans, and sneakers. We were on an exposed part of the hill, past the town cemetery, looking down at the dirty red-brick mill buildings with the tiny windows that rose straight up from both sides of the Squamscott River. Steam and smoke fumes boiled away from tall brick stacks, and neither of us really had gotten used to the pungent, oily smell that seemed to stay right in the back of the throat. The old-timers never mind the smell. They sniff and say, "Aah," and say, "Boys, that's the smell of money." We weren't so dumb that we didn't know if Devon Shoe and Parker Shoe and the lumberyard shut down, Boston Falls would crumple away like a fall leaf in November.

But Brad never liked the smell.

"God," he said, popping open his can of soda. "It seems worse today."

"Wind's out of the south," I replied. "Can't be helped."

Our bikes were on their sides in the tall grass. There was a low buzz of insects and Brad took a long swallow from his soda, water beading up on the side of the can. It was a hot day. Brad's long hair was combed over to one side in a long swoop, and I was jealous of him because my dad made me keep my hair about two inches long, with no sideburns. But then again, Brad wore thick glasses and my vision was perfect.

"Brad," I said, "we're in trouble."

He tossed his empty soda can over his shoulder. "How are you doing?"

"With the sixty from last week, I got four hundred and twelve."

"Idiot. You should have four hundred and fifteen like me. Where's the other three?"

"I had to buy a dress shirt for Aunt Sara's funeral last week. I tore my last good one in June and Mom's been bugging me."

"Mothers." Brad hunched forward and rested his chin on his knee.

"State says we need at least a thousand for the first year."

"Yeah."

"And we can't get part-time jobs this winter, there won't be any around."

"Yeah."

"So what do we do?"

"I'm thinking. Shut up, will you?"

I let it slide, knowing what he was thinking. We were both six hundred dollars' short for the first-year tuition at the state college. My dad had made some brave noises about helping out when the time came, but six months ago my oldest brother Tom had wrapped his '68 Chevy around a telephone pole and now he was wired up to a bed in a hospital in Hanover and my parents' bank account was shrinking every month. But at least my father had offered to help. Brad's father usually came home drunk from the mill every night, sour-mad and spoiling for a fight. I'd slept over Brad's house only once, when we were both fourteen and had just become friends. It was a Friday night, and by midnight Brad's father and mother were screaming and swinging at each other with kitchen knives. Brad and I snuck out to the backyard with our blankets and pillows and we never talked about it again. But one day Brad came to school with his face lumpy and swollen from bruises, and I knew he must have told his father he wanted to go to college.

"Monroe," he said, finally speaking up.

"Go ahead."

"We're special people, aren't we?"

"Hunh?"

"I mean, compared to the rest of the kids at school, we're special, right? Who's at the top of the class? You and me, right?"

"Right."

"So we're special, we're better than they are."

"Oh, c'mon —"

"Face it, Monroe. Just sit there and face it, will you? That's all I ask right now. Just face it."

Well, he was somewhat right, but then you have to understand our regional high school, Squamscott High. Kids from Boston Falls, Machias, and Albion go there, and those other towns are no better off than ours. And in our state there's little aid for schools, so the towns have to pay the salaries and supplies. Which means a school building with crumbling plaster ceilings. Which means history books that talk about the promise of the Kennedy administration and science books that predict man will go into space one day. Which means teachers like Mr. Hensely, who stumbles into his afternoon history classes, his breath reeking of mouthwash, and Miss Tierney, the English teacher, not long out of college, who also works Saturday and Sunday mornings as a waitress at Mona's Diner on Front Street.

"All right, Brad," I said. "I guess we're special. We study hard and get good marks. We like books and we want to go places."

"But we're trapped here, Monroe," he said. "All we got here is Boston Falls, the Mohawk Cinema, Main Street — and the Wentworth Shopping Plaza ten miles away. And a lot of brick and smoke and trees and hills. Here, straight As and straight Fs will get you the same thing."

"I know. The lumberyard or Parker or Devon Shoe."

"Or maybe a store or a gas station. We're too smart for that, damn it."

"And we're too broke for college."

"That we are," he said, resting his head on his knees. "That we are."

He remained silent for a while, a trait of Brad's. We'd been friends since freshman year, when we were the only two students who were interested in joining the debate team — which lasted a week because no one else wanted to join. We shared a love of books and a desire to go to college, but no matter how many hours we spent together, there was always a dark bit of Brad I could never reach or understand. It wasn't something dramatic or apparent, just small things. Like his bedroom. Mine had the usual posters of cars and rocket ships and warplanes, but his had only one picture — a framed photograph of Joseph Stalin. I was pretty sure no one else in Brad's family recognized the picture — I got the feeling he told his father the man had been a famous scientist. When I asked Brad why Stalin of all people, he said, "The man had drive, Monroe. He grew up in a peasant society and grabbed his ticket. Look where it took him."

Brad wanted to become a lawyer and I wanted to write history books.

"Feel it," he said, his voice low, rocking back and forth. "Feel how it's strangling us?"

I felt it. If we didn't go to State, then next summer we'd be on that slippery slope where we couldn't get off, a life at the mill, a life of praying and hoping for a nickel-an-hour wage increase, of waiting for the five o'clock whistle. A life where we would find our friends and amusement at the Legion Hall, Drake's Pub, or Pete's Saloon, where we would sit comfortable on the barstools, swapping stories about who scored what winning touchdown at what state tournament, sipping our beers and feeling ourselves and our tongues getting thick with age and fear. Just getting along, getting older and slower, the old report cards with the perfect marks hidden away in some desk drawer, buried under old bills, a marriage certificate, and insurance policies.

"We gotta get out," I said.

"We do. And I know how." Brad had gotten to his feet, brushing potato-chip crumbs from his pants. "Monroe, we're going to become thieves."

The next day we were at Outland Rock, tossing pebbles into the river. We were upstream from the mills, and the waters flowed fast and clean. About another mile south, after the river passed through town, the waters were slow and slate-gray, clogged with chemical foam and wood chips and scraps of leather. Outland Rock was a large boulder that hung over the riverbank. We were too lazy to swim, so we sat and tossed pebbles into the river, watching the wide arcs of the ripples rise up and fade away.

"What are we going to steal?" I asked. "Gold? Diamonds? The bank president's Cadillac?"

Brad was on his stomach, his feet heading up to the bank, his head over the water. "Don't screw with me, Monroe. I'm serious."

I shook my head, tossing another rock in. "OK, so you're serious. Answer the question."

"Cash." He had a stick in his hand, a broken piece of pine, and he stirred it in the water like he was casting for something. "Anything else can be traced. We steal cash and we're set."

The day was warm and maybe it was the lazy August mood I was in—the comfortable, hazy feeling that the day would last forever and school and September would never come—but I decided to go along with him.

"OK, cash. But you gotta realize what we're working with."

He looked up at me, his eyes unblinking behind the thick glasses. "Go ahead, Monroe."

"Our parents still won't let us drive by ourselves, so we're stuck with our bikes. Unless you want to steal a car to get out of town—which doubles the danger. So whatever we go after has to be in Boston Falls."

"I hadn't thought of that."

"There's another thing," I said. "We can't go into the National Bank or Trussen's Jewelers in broad daylight and rob 'em. In an hour they'd be looking for two kids our age and they wouldn't have a hard time tracking us down." I lay back on the rock, the surface warm against my back, and closed my eyes, listening to some birds on the other side of the river and the swish-swish as Brad moved the stick back and forth in the water.

"Burglary," he said. I sat up, shading my face with one hand. "Burglary?"

"Yeah. We find someone who's got a lot of cash and break into their house. Do it when no one's home and they'll blame it on some drifters or something."

Somewhere a dog barked. "Do you realize we're actually talking about stealing, Brad? Not only is it a crime, but it's wrong. Are you thinking about that?"

He turned to me and his face changed—I had the strange feeling I knew what he'd look like in ten years.

"Don't get soft on me, Monroe. In another three weeks we'll be back at school. If we don't get more money this summer we're done for. 'Wrong.' Isn't it wrong that you and me have to grow up in a place like this? Isn't it wrong that we have to live alongside people who haven't read a book in years? Don't you think it's wrong that for lack of a few measly bucks we have to rot here?"

He bent over the rock and pointed. "Look." In the shallow water I saw a nesting of mussels, their shells wide open. "There you have," he continued, "the population of Boston Falls, New Hampshire. Sitting still, dumb and happy and open, letting everything go by them, ready to snap at anything that comes within reach." He pushed his stick into one of the mussels and it snapped shut against the wood. He pulled the stick out, the mussel hanging onto the stick, dripping water. "See how they grab the first thing that comes their way?"

He slammed the end of the stick onto the rock and the mussel exploded into black shards.

"We're not going to grab the first thing that comes our way, Monroe. We're going to plan and get the hell out of here. That will take cash, and if that means stealing from the fat, dumb mussels in this town, that's what we'll do."

On the ride home, Brad slowed and stopped and I pulled my rusty five-speed up next to him. A thick bank of rolling gray clouds over the hills promised a thunderstorm soon. Our T-shirts were off and tied around our waists. I was tanned from working in our garden all summer but Brad was thin and white, and his chest was a bit sunken, like he'd been punched hard there and never recovered.

"Look there," he said. I did and my stomach tightened up.

A dead woodchuck was in the middle of the road, its legs stiff. Two large black grackles hopped around the swollen brown body, their sharp beaks at work.

"So it's a burglary," I said. "Whose house?"

He shrugged his bony shoulders. "I'll find the right one. I'll go roaming."

Roaming. It was one of Brad's favorite things to do. At night, after everyone at his house was asleep, he would sneak out and roam around the dark streets and empty backyards of Boston Falls. The one time I'd gone with him, I thought he was just being a Peeping Tom or something, but it wasn't that simple. He just liked watching what people did, I think, and he moved silently from one lighted window to another. I didn't like it at all. I wasn't comfortable out on the streets or in the fields at night, and I couldn't shake off the feeling that I was trespassing.

Brad rolled his bike closer to the dead woodchuck. "Are you in, Monroe? We're running out of time."

Thunder boomed from the hills and I glanced up and saw a flash of lightning. "We better get going if we're going to beat the storm."

"I said, are you with me?"

The wind shifted, blowing the leaves on the trees in great gusts. "Brad, we gotta get moving."

"You get moving," he said, his lips tense. "You get moving wherever you're going. I'm staying here for a bit."

I pedaled away as fast as I could, pumping my legs up and down, thinking, I'll save a bit here and there, maybe deliver some papers, maybe just work an extra summer—there's got to be another way to get the money.

A week later. Suppertime at my house. My brothers Jim and Henry had eaten early and gone out, leaving me alone with my parents. My brother Tom was still in the hospital in Hanover. My parents visited him every Saturday and Sunday, bringing me along when I wasn't smart enough to leave the house early. I guess you could say I loved my brother, but the curled-over, thin figure with wires and tubes in the noisy hospital ward didn't seem to be him anymore.

We sat in the kitchen, a plastic tablecloth on the table, my mother, looking worn and tired, still wearing her apron. My dad wore his shirt and tie. His crewcut looked sweaty and he smelled of the mill. On his right shirt pocket was a plastic penholder that said PARKER DOES IT RIGHT with four pens. Supper was fried baloney, leftover mashed potatoes, and canned yellow string beans. I tried to talk about what went on at the mill that day—a pile of boxes stuffed full of leather hiking boots had fallen and almost hit me—but my parents nodded and said nothing and I finally concentrated on quietly cleaning my plate. The fried baloney left a puddle of grease that flowed into the lumpy white potatoes.

My father looked over at Mom and she hung her head, and he seemed to shrug his shoulders before he said, "Monroe?"

"Yes?"

He put his knife and fork down and folded his hands, as if we were suddenly in church.

"At work today they announced a cutback." He looked at me and then looked away, as if someone had walked past the kitchen window. "Some people are being laid off and the rest of us are having a pay cut."

"Oh." The baloney and potatoes were now very cold.

"Tom is still very sick, and until he—gets better, we still have to pay the bills. With the cutback—well, Monroe, we need the money you've saved."

I looked at my mother, but she didn't look up. "Oh," I said, feeling dumb, feeling blank.

"I know you've got your heart set on college, but this is a family emergency—that has to come first, a family has to stick together. Jim and Henry have agreed to help—"

"With what?" I said, clenching my knife and fork tight. "They don't save anything at all."

"No, but they're giving up part of their paychecks. All we ask is that you do your part."

Then Mom spoke up. "There's always next year," she said. "Not all of your friends are going to college, are they? You'll be with them next summer."

Dad gave me a weak smile. "Besides, I never went to college, and I'm doing all right. Monroe, it's just temporary, until things improve with Tom."

Until he gets better or until he dies, I thought. I didn't know what to say next, so I finished eating and went down the hallway to my bedroom and got the dark brown passbook from First Merchants of Boston Falls and brought it back and gave it to my father.

Back in my bedroom, I lay on the bed, staring up at the models of airplanes and rocket ships hanging from thin black threads attached to the ceiling. I looked at my textbooks and other books on the bookshelves I made myself. I curled up and didn't think of much at all, and after a while I fell asleep.

There was a tapping at my window and I threw the top sheet off and went over, lifting up the window screen. I stood there in my shorts, looking at Brad on the back lawn. My glow-in-the-dark clock said it was two in the morning.

"What is it?" I whispered.

"I found it," he whispered back, leaning forward so his head was almost through the open window. "I found the place."

"Whose house is it?"

"Mike Willard's."

"Mike? The ex-Marine?"

"That's right," Brad said. "I've watched him two nights in a row. He goes into his bedroom and underneath his bed he's got this little strongbox—before shutting off the light and going to bed he opens it up and goes through it. Monroe, he's got tons of money in there. Wads as big as your fist."

"You saw it?"

"Of course I did. I was in a tree in his yard. He must've been saving up all his life. You never saw so much money."

The night air was warm but goose bumps traveled up and down my arms. "How do we do it?"

"Easy. He lives out on Tanner Avenue. We can get to it by cutting through the woods. His house has hedges all around. It'll be a cinch."

I chewed on my lip. "When?" I asked.

Brad grinned at me. I could almost smell the sense of excitement. "Tomorrow. It's Saturday—your parents will be in Hanover and Mike goes to the Legion Hall every afternoon. We'll do it while he's there."

I didn't argue. "Fine," I said.

The next afternoon we were in a stand of trees facing a well-mowed backyard. Tall green hedges flanked both sides of the yard, and the two-story white house with the tall gables was quiet. Beside me, Brad was hunched over, peering around a tree trunk. We heard a door slam and saw Mike Willard walk down his drive and down the street. His posture was straight as a pine, his white hair cut in a crewcut.

"Let's give him a few minutes," Brad said. "Make sure he didn't forget anything."

I nodded. My heart was pounding so hard I wondered if Brad could hear it. I knew what we were doing was wrong, I knew it wouldn't be right to steal Mike Willard's money, but money was all I could think of. Wads as big as my fist, Brad had said.

"Go time," Brad said, and he set off across the yard. I followed. There were no toys or picnic tables or barbecue sets in Mike Willard's backyard, just a fine lawn, as if he mowed it every other day. Up on the back porch I had the strange feeling we should knock or something. I was scared Mike would come back and yell, "Boys, what the hell do you want?" or that a mailman would walk up the drive and ask if Mike was home. I almost hoped a mailman would come, but Brad picked up a rock and went to the door and it was too late. He smashed a pane of glass—the sound was so loud it seemed like every police cruiser within miles would be sent around—then he reached in and unlocked the door, motioning me to follow him inside. A small voice told me to stay outside and let him go in alone, but I followed him into the kitchen, my sneakers crunching on the glass.

The kitchen smelled clean and everything was shiny and still. There weren't even any dishes in the sink.

"God, look how clean it is," I said.

"Tell me about it. My mom should keep our house so clean."

The kitchen table was small and square, with only two chairs. There was one placemat out, a blue woven thing with stars and anchors, and I thought of Mike Willard coming home every night to this empty house, opening a can of spaghetti maybe and eating alone at his table. I looked at Brad and wanted to say, "Come on, let's not do it," because I got a bad feeling at the thought of Mike coming home and finding he'd been robbed, that someone had been in his house, but Brad looked at me hard and I followed him down the hallway.

The bedroom was small and cramped, with neatly labeled cardboard boxes piled on one side of the room and a long bureau on the other, on the other side of the bed. The labels on the boxes read CHINA 34, IWO 45, OCC, and things like that. Brad pointed at the walls, where pictures and other items were hanging. "Look, there's Mike there, I think. I wonder where it was taken. Guadalcanal, maybe?"

The faded black-and-white picture showed a group of young men standing in a jungle clearing, tired-looking, in uniforms and beards, holding rifles and automatic weapons. There was no name on the picture but I recognized a younger Mike Willard, hair short and ears sticking out, standing off to one side.

I heard a board creak. "Shh!" I said. "Did you hear that?"

"Yeah. This is an old house, Monroe."

"Well, let's get going," I said, rubbing my palms against my jeans. They were very sweaty.

"What's the rush?" Brad said, his eyes laughing at me from behind his glasses. "Old Mike's down at the Legion, telling the boys how he won the big one back in '45. Look here."

Below an American flag and a furled Japanese flag was a sheathed curved sword resting on two wooden pegs. Brad took it down and slid it out of its scabbard. He ran a thumb across the blade and took a few swings through the air. "I wonder if Mike bought it or got it off some dead Jap."

By now I was glancing out the window, wondering if anyone could see us. Brad put the sword down and climbed onto the bed. "Hold on a sec," he said.

The bed was a brown four-poster. Brad reached under the pillows and pulled out a handgun, large and oily-looking. "A .45. Can you believe it? Old Mike sleeps with a .45 under his pillow."

"Brad, stop fooling around," I said. "Let's get the box and go." But I could tell he was enjoying himself too much.

"Hold it, I just want to see if it works." He moved his hand across the top of the gun and part of it slid back and forth with a loud click-clack. "There," he said. "Just call me John Wayne. This sucker's ready to fire. I might take it with me when we leave."

He took the gun and stuck it in his waistband, then reached over and pulled a dull gray strongbox with a simple clasp lock from under the bed. My mouth felt dry and suddenly I was no longer nervous. I was thinking of all the money.

Brad rubbed his hands across the box. "Look, partner. In here's our ticket out."

Then Mike Willard was at the bedroom door, his face red, and I could smell the beer from where I was standing, almost five feet away. "You!" he roared. "What the hell are you doing in here? I'm gonna beat the crap out of you boys!"

I back-stepped quickly, tripping over the cardboard boxes and falling flat on my butt, wondering what to do next, wondering what I could say. Brad scampered across the other side of the bed, pulling out the gun and saying in a squeaky voice, "Hold it." Mike Willard swore and took two large steps, grabbing the sword and swinging it at Brad. I closed my eyes and there was a loud boom that jarred my teeth. There was a crash and an awful grunt, and another crash, then a sharp scent of smoke that seemed to cut right through me.

When I opened my eyes, Brad was sitting across from me, the gun in his lap, both of his hands pressed against his neck. He was very pale and his glasses had been knocked off—without them he looked five years younger.

"It hurts," he said. And then I saw the bright redness seep through his fingers and trickle down his bare arms.

"God," I breathed.

"I can't see," he said. "Where's Mike?"

I got up, weaving slightly, and saw Mike's feet sticking out from the other side of the bed. I crawled across the bed and peered over. Mike was on his back, his arms splayed out, his mouth open like he was still trying to yell, but his eyes were closed and there was a blossom of red spreading across his green work shirt. I stared at him for what seemed hours but his chest didn't move. When I looked up, Brad was resting his back against the bed. Both of his arms were soaked red and I gazed at him, almost fascinated by the flow of blood down his thin wrists. His face was now the color of chalk.

"Wait, I'll get a towel," I said.

"No, you idiot. If I take my hands away, I'm dead. An artery's gone. Listen. Take the box and call an ambulance."

"I think Mike's dead, Brad."

"Shut up," he said, his teeth clenched. "Just grab the box, hide it, and get help! We're juveniles—nothing's going to happen to us! Get going!" I grabbed the box and was out of the house, running through the woods, the strongbox tight against my chest. The air was fresh and smelled wonderful, and I ran all the way home.

* * *

Three days later Mike Willard was buried with full military honors and a Marine Corps honor guard at Cavalry Hill Cemetery. I learned from his front-page obituary that his wife died five years earlier and he had a daughter who lived in Jamaica Plain, Massachusetts. I also learned that Mike had been in the Marines since he was seventeen, stationed in China in the 1930s and in the Pacific in the 1940s, island-hopping, fighting the Japanese. Then after occupation duty and a year in Korea, he pulled embassy duty until he retired. His nickname had been Golden Mike, for in all his years on active duty he'd never been wounded, never been shot or scratched by shrapnel. The newspaper said he'd come home early that day to dig out a magazine clipping to show some friends at the Legion Hall. To settle a bet.

I kept the strongbox hidden in the attic. Despite the temptation and the worries and the urging, I didn't open it until that day in May after my college acceptance letter came, followed by a bill for the first year's tuition. Then I went up with a chisel and hammer and broke open the lock. The wads of money were in there, just as Brad had said, thick as my fist. They were buried under piles of fragile, yellowed letters, some newspaper and magazine clippings, and a few medals. The money was banded together by string, and in the dim light of the attic I wasn't sure of what I had. I bicycled over to Machias, to a coin shop, and the owner peered over his half-glasses and looked up at me, the money spread over his display case.

"Interesting samples," he said. He wore a dark green sweater and his hair was white. "Where did you get them?"

"From my uncle," I lied. "Can you tell me what they're worth?"

"Hmm," he said, lifting the bills up to the light. "Nineteen thirties, it looks like. What you have here is Chinese money from that time, what old soldiers and sailors called LC, or local currency. It varied from province to province, and I'd say this is some of it."

He put the bills back on the counter. "Practically worthless," he said. I thanked him and rode back to Boston Falls. That afternoon I burned some of the paper money along with my acceptance letter and tuition bill. I didn't go to college that fall and ended up never going at all.

My ginger and Jameson is gone and I continue looking out at the stars, watching the moon rise over the hill, Cavalry Hill. And even though it's miles away, I imagine I can see the white stone markers up there, marking so many graves.

In the end I stayed in Boston Falls and took a job at a bank. I worked a little and now I'm an assistant branch manager. Some years ago I married Carol, a teller I helped train, and now we're out of Boston Falls, in Machias. It's just over the line, but I get some satisfaction from getting that far.

Upstairs I still have the old strongbox with some of the money, and though I don't look at it all that often I feel like I have to have something, something I can tell myself I got from that day we broke into Mike Willard's house. I have to have something to justify what we did, and what I did. Especially what I did.

After running all that distance home, I stashed the strongbox in the attic, and as I came downstairs my parents came home. Dad patted me on the back and Mom started supper and I thought of the strongbox upstairs and the blood and the acrid smoke and Mike Willard on his back and Brad holding on to his neck like that. I knew no one had seen me. Mom offered me some lemonade and I took it and went to the living room and watched television with my dad, cheering on the Red Sox as they beat the Yankees — all the while waiting and waiting, until finally the sirens went by.

Brad was buried about a hundred feet from Mike Willard a day later. On the day of his funeral, I said I was sick and stayed home, curled up in a ball on my bed, not thinking, not doing anything, just knowing that I had the box and the money.

I put down my empty glass and open the back door, hoping the fresh air will clear my head so I can go back upstairs and try to sleep. Outside there's a slight breeze blowing in from Boston Falls, and like so many other nights I go down the porch steps and stand with my bare feet cool on the grass, the breeze on my face bringing with it the stench of the mills from Boston Falls. The smell always seems to stick in the back of my throat, and no matter how hard I try I can never get the taste of it out.

1988

JAMES ELLROY

SINCE I DON'T HAVE YOU

James Ellroy (1948–) was born Lee Earle Ellroy in Los Angeles. When he was ten years old his mother was murdered; the killer was never apprehended. There were some similarities in the case to the famous murder of Elizabeth Short, known as the Black Dahlia, and both murders obsessed Ellroy for many years. He wrote a fictionalized version of the Betty Short murder, *The Black Dahlia* (1987), which became a *New York Times* bestseller, and a memoir of his fifteen-month search for his mother's killer, *My Dark Places* (1996). As a young man, Ellroy lived a life of petty crime, alcoholism, and drug use, cleaning up his act in the late 1970s to produce his first novel, *Brown's Requiem* (1981); his second book, *Clandestine* (1982), was nominated for an Edgar Allan Poe Award for Best Paperback Original. His first hardcover book, *Blood on the Moon* (1984), began the Lloyd Hopkins trilogy. The masterly *Black Dahlia* was the first novel in what Ellroy called the L.A. Quartet, which later included *The Big Nowhere* (1988), *L.A. Confidential* (1990), and *White Jazz* (1992). Two of the books became big-budget movies. *L.A. Confidential* (1997), a critical and commercial success, was nominated for an Academy Award for Best Picture. *The Black Dahlia* (2006), on the other hand, was critically savaged, successfully warning potential audiences away.

Although he later claimed a career change from crime novels to big, ambitious political books, his Underworld trilogy, which he described as "a secret history of America in the mid-to-late twentieth century"—*American Tabloid* (1995), *The Cold Six Thousand* (2001), and *Blood's a Rover* (2009)—is heavily spiked with dark crimes and violence. Described as "the American Dostoevsky" by Joyce Carol Oates, Ellroy is arguably the most influential American crime writer of the late twentieth century; his powerful, relentlessly dark prose style of staccato sentences, infused with uniquely American slang that hammers the senses, has been emulated by any number of tough-writing young crime writers.

"Since I Don't Have You" was first published in *A Matter of Crime,* volume 4 (1988). It served as the basis for an episode of Showtime's series *Fallen Angels,* airing on September 26, 1993.

▪ ▪ ▪

DURING THE POSTWAR years I served two masters—running interference and hauling dirty laundry for the two men who defined L.A. at that time better than anyone else. To Howard Hughes I was security boss at his aircraft plant, pimp, and troubleshooter for RKO Pictures—the ex-cop who could kibosh blackmail squeezes, fix drunk drivings, and arrange abortions and dope cures. To Mickey Cohen—rackets overlord and would-be nightclub shtickster—I was a bagman to the LAPD, the former Narco detective who skimmed junk off niggertown dope rousts, allowing his Southside boys to sell it back to the hordes of schwartzes eager to fly White Powder Airlines. Big Howard: always in the news for crashing an airplane someplace inappropriate, stubbing his face on the control panel in some hicktown beanfield, then showing up at Romanoff's bandaged like the Mummy with Ava Gardner on his arm; Mickey C.: also a pussy hound par excellence, pub crawling with an entourage of psychopathic killers, press agents, gag writers, and his bulldog Mickey Cohen Jr.—a flatulent beast with a schlong so large that the Mick's stooges strapped it to a roller skate so it wouldn't drag on the ground.

Howard Hughes. Mickey Cohen. And me—Turner "Buzz" Meeks, Lizard Ridge, Oklahoma, armadillo poacher; strikebreaker goon; cop; fixer; and keeper of the secret key to his masters' psyches: they were both cowards mano a mano; airplanes and lunatic factotums their go-betweens—while I would go anywhere, anyplace—gun or billy club first, courting a front-page death to avenge my second-banana life. And the two of them courted me because I put their lack of balls in perspective: it was irrational, meshugah, bad business—a Forest Lawn crypt years before my time. But I got the last laugh there: I always knew that when faced with the grave I'd pull a smart segue to keep kicking—and I write this memoir as an old, old man—while Howard and Mickey stuff caskets, bullshit biographies their only legacy.

Howard. Mickey. Me.

Sooner or later, my work for the two of them had to produce what the yuppie lawyer kids today call "conflict of interest." Of course, it was over a woman—and, of course, being a suicidal Okie shitkicker, forty-one years old and getting tired, I decided to play both ends against the middle. A thought just hit me: that I'm writing this story because I miss Howard and Mickey, and telling it gives me a chance to be with them again. Keep that in mind—that I loved them—even though they were both world-class shitheels.

* * *

January 15, 1949.

It was cold and clear in Los Angeles, and the papers were playing up the two-year anniversary of the Black Dahlia murder case—still unsolved, still speculated on. Mickey was still mourning Hooky Rothman's death—he French-kissed a sawed-off shotgun held by an unknown perpetrator—and Howard was still pissed at me over the Bob Mitchum reefer roust: he figured that my connections with Narco Division were still so solid that I should have seen it coming. I'd been shuttling back and forth between Howard and Mickey since New Year's. The Mick's signature fruit baskets stuffed with C-notes had to be distributed to cops, judges, and City Council members he wanted to grease, and the pilot/mogul had me out bird-dogging quiff: prowling bus depots and train stations for buxom young girls who'd fall prey to RKO contracts in exchange for frequent nighttime visits. I'd been having a good run: a half-dozen Midwestern farm maidens were now ensconced in Howard's fuck pads—strategically located apartments tucked all over L.A. And I was deep in hock to a darktown bookie named Leotis Dineen, a six-foot-six jungle bunny who hated people of the Oklahoma persuasion worse than poison. I was sitting in my Quonset-hut office at Hughes Aircraft when the phone rang.

"That you, Howard?"

Howard Hughes sighed. "What happened to 'Security, may I help you'?"

"You're the only one calls this early, Boss."

"And you're alone?"

"Right. Per your instructions to call you Mr. Hughes in the presence of others. What's up?"

"Breakfast is up. Meet me at the corner of Melrose and La Brea in half an hour."

"Right, Boss."

"Two or three, Buzz? I'm hungry and having four."

Howard was on his all-chilidog diet; Pink's Dogs at Melrose and La Brea was his current in-spot. I knew for a fact that their chili was made from horse meat air-freighted up daily from Tijuana. "One kraut, no chili."

"Heathen. Pink's chili is better than Chasen's."

"I had a pony when I was a boy."

"So? I had a governess. You think I wouldn't eat—"

I said, "Half an hour," and hung up. I figured if I got there five minutes late I wouldn't have to watch the fourth-richest man in America eat.

* * *

Howard was picking strands of sauerkraut off his chin when I climbed in the back seat of his limousine. He said, "You didn't really want it, did you?"

I pressed the button that sent up the screen that shielded us from the driver. "No, coffee and doughnuts are more my style."

Howard gave me a long, slow eyeballing — a bit ill at ease because sitting down we were the same height, while standing I came up to his shoulders. "Do you need money, Buzz?"

I thought of Leotis Dineen. "Can niggers dance?"

"They certainly can. But call them colored, you never know when one might be listening."

Larry the chauffeur was Chinese; Howard's comment made me wonder if his last plane crash had dented his cabeza. I tried my standard opening line. "Getting any, Boss?"

Hughes smiled and burped; horse grease wafted through the back seat. He dug into a pile of papers beside him — blueprints, graphs, and scraps covered with airplane doodles, pulling out a snapshot of a blond girl naked from the waist up. He handed it to me and said, "Gretchen Rae Shoftel, age nineteen. Born in Prairie du Chien, Wisconsin, July 26, 1929. She was staying at the place on South Lucerne — the screening house. This is the woman, Buzz. I think I want to marry her. And she's gone — she flew the coop on the contract, me, all of it."

I examined the picture. Gretchen Rae Shoftel was prodigiously lunged — no surprise — with a blond pageboy and smarts in her eyes, like she knew Mr. Hughes's two-second screen test was strictly an audition for the sack and an occasional one-liner in some RKO turkey. "Who found her for you, Boss? It wasn't me — I'd have remembered."

Howard belched again — my hijacked sauerkraut this time. "I got the picture in the mail at the studio, along with an offer — a thousand dollars cash to a PO box in exchange for the girl's address. I did it, and met Gretchen Rae at her hotel downtown. She told me she posed for some dirty old man back in Milwaukee, that he must have pulled the routine for the thousand. Gretchen Rae and I got to be friends, and, well . . ."

"And you'll give me a bonus to find her?"

"A thousand, Buzz. Cash, off the payroll."

My debt to Leotis Dineen was eight hundred and change; I could get clean and get even on minor-league baseball — the San Diego Seals were starting their preseason games next week. "It's a deal. What else have you got on the girl?"

"She was carhopping at Scrivner's Drive-in. I know that."

"Friends, known associates, relatives here in L.A.?"

"Not to my knowledge."

I took a deep breath to let Howard know a tricky question was coming. "Boss, you think maybe this girl is working an angle on you? I mean, the picture out of nowhere, the thousand to a PO box?"

Howard Hughes harrumphed. "It had to be that piece in *Confidential*, the one that alleged my talent scouts take topless photographs and that I like my women endowed."

"*Alleged*, Boss?"

"I'm practicing coming off as irate in case I sue *Confidential* somewhere down the line. You'll get on this right away?"

"*Rápidamente.*"

"Outstanding. And don't forget Sid Weinberg's party tomorrow night. He's got a new horror picture coming out from the studio, and I need you there to keep the autograph hounds from going crazy. Eight, Sid's house."

"I'll be there."

"Find Gretchen Rae, Buzz. She's special."

Howard's one saving grace with females is that he keeps falling in love with them — albeit only after viewing Brownie snaps of their lungs. It more or less keeps him busy between crashing airplanes and designing airplanes that don't fly.

"Right, Boss."

The limousine's phone rang. Howard picked it up, listened, and murmured, "Yes. Yes, I'll tell him." Hanging up, he said, "The switchboard at the plant. Mickey Cohen wants to see you. Make it brief, you're on my time now."

"Yes, sir."

It was Howard who introduced me to Mickey, right before I got wounded in a dope shootout and took my LAPD pension. I still give him a hand with his drug dealings — unofficial liaison to Narcotics Division, point man for the Narco dicks who skim x number of grams off every ounce of junk confiscated. The LAPD has got an unofficial heroin policy: it is to be sold only to coloreds, only east of Alvarado and south of Jefferson. I don't think it should be sold anywhere, but as long as it is, I want the 5 percent. I test the shit with a chem kit I stole from the crime lab — no poor hophead is going to croak from a Mickey Cohen bindle bootjacked by Turner "Buzz" Meeks. Dubious morality: I sleep well 90 percent of the time and lay my bet action off with shine bookies, the old exploiter washing the hand that feeds him. Money was right at the top of my brain as I drove to Mickey's haberdashery on the Strip. I always need cash, and the Mick never calls unless it is in the offing.

I found the man in his back room, surrounded by sycophants and muscle: Johnny Stompanato, guinea spit curl dangling over his handsome face—he of the long-term crush on Lana Turner; Davey Goldman, Mickey's chief yes-man and the author of his nightclub shticks; and a diffident-looking little guy I recognized as Morris Hornbeck—an accountant and former trigger for Jerry Katzenbach's mob in Milwaukee. Shaking hands and pulling up a chair, I got ready to make my pitch: You pay me now; I do my job after I run a hot little errand for Howard. I opened my mouth to speak, but Mickey beat me to it. "I want you to find a woman for me."

I was about to say "What a coincidence," when Johnny Stomp handed me a snapshot. "Nice gash. Not Lana Turner quality, but USDA choice tail nonetheless."

Of course, you see it coming. The photo was a nightspot job: compliments of Preston Sturges's Players Club, Gretchen Rae Shoftel blinking against flashbulb glare, dairy-state pulchritude in a tight black dress. Mickey Cohen was draping an arm around her shoulders, aglow with love. I swallowed to keep my voice steady. "Where was the wife, Mick? Off on one of her Hadassah junkets?"

Mickey grunted. "'Israel, the New Homeland.' Ten-day tour with her mahjong club. While the cat is away, the mice will play. Va-va-va-voom. Find her, Buzzchik. A grand."

I got obstreperous, my usual reaction to being scared. "Two grand, or go take a flying fuck at a rolling doughnut."

Mickey scowled and went into a slow burn; I watched Johnny Stomp savor my bravado, Davey Goldman write down the line for his boss's shticks, and Morris Hornbeck do queasy double takes like he wasn't copacetic with the play. When the Mick's burn stretched to close to a minute, I said, "Silence implies consent. Tell me all you know about the girl, and I'll take it from there."

Mickey Cohen smiled at me—his coming-from-hunger minion. "*Goyische* shitheel. For a twosky I want satisfaction guaranteed within forty-eight hours."

I already had the money laid off on baseball, the fights, and three-horse parlays. "Forty-seven and change. Go."

Mickey eyed his boys as he spoke—probably because he was pissed at me and needed a quick intimidation fix. Davey and Johnny Stomp looked away; Morris Hornbeck just twitched, like he was trying to quash a bad case of the heebie-jeebies. "Gretchen Rae Shoftel. I met her at Scrivner's Drive-in two weeks ago. She told me she's fresh out of the Minnesota sticks, someplace like that. She—"

I interrupted. "She said 'Minnesota' specifically, Mick?"

"Right. Moosebreath, Dogturd, some boonies town—but definitely Minnesota."

Morris Hornbeck was sweating now; I had myself a hot lead. "Keep going, Mick."

"Well, we hit it off; I convince Lavonne to see Israel before them dune coons take it back; Gretchen Rae and I get together; we va-va-va-voom; it's terrific. She plays cagey with me, won't tell me where she's staying, and she keeps taking off—says she's looking for a man—some friend of her father's back in Antelope Ass or wherever the fuck she comes from. Once she's gassed on vodka Collinses and gets misty about some hide-away she says she's got. That—"

I said, "Wrap it up."

Mickey slammed his knees so hard that Mickey Cohen Jr., asleep in the doorway twenty feet away, woke up and tried to stand on all fours—until the roller skate attached to his wang pulled him back down. "I'll fucking wrap you up if you don't find her for me! That's it! I want her! Find her for me! *Do it now!*"

I got to my feet wondering how I was going to pull this one off—with the doorman gig at Sid Weinberg's party thrown smack in the middle of it. I said, "Forty-seven fifty-five and rolling," and winked at Morris Hornbeck—who just happened to hail from Milwaukee, where Howard told me Gretchen Rae Shoftel told him a dirty old man had snapped her lung shots. Hornbeck tried to wink back; it looked like his eyeball was having a grand mal seizure. Mickey said, "Find her for me. And you gonna be at Sid's tomorrow night?"

"Keeping autograph hounds at bay. You?"

"Yeah, I've got points in Sid's new picture. I want hot dope by then, Buzzchik. *Hot.*"

I said, "Scalding," and took off, almost tripping over Mickey Cohen Jr.'s appendage as I went out the door.

A potential three grand in my kick; Morris Hornbeck's hinkyness doing a slow simmer in my gourd; an instinct that Gretchen Rae Shoftel's "hideaway" was Howard Hughes's fuck pad on South Lucerne—the place where he kept the stash of specially cantilevered bras he designed to spotlight his favorite starlet's tits, cleavage gowns for his one-night inamoratas, and the stag film collection he showed to visiting defense contractors — some of them rumored to costar Mickey Cohen Jr. and a bimbo made up to resemble Howard's personal heroine: Amelia Earhart. But first there was Scrivner's Drive-in and a routine questioning of Gretchen Rae's recent coworkers. Fear adrenaline was scorching my soul as I drove there — maybe I'd played my shtick too tight to come out intact.

Scrivner's was on Sunset three blocks east of Hollywood High School, an eat-in-your-car joint featuring a rocket-ship motif — chromium scoops, dips, and portholes abounding — Jules Verne as seen by a fag set designer scraping the stars on marijuana. The carhops — all zaftig numbers — wore tight space-cadet outfits; the fry cooks wore plastic rocket helmets with clear face shields to protect them from spattering grease. Questioning a half-dozen of them was like enjoying the DTs without benefit of booze. After an hour of talk and chump-change handouts, I knew the following:

That Gretchen Rae Shoftel carhopped there for a month, was often tardy, and during midafternoon lulls tended to abandon her shift. This was tolerated because she was an atom-powered magnet that attracted men by the shitload. She could tote up tabs in her head, deftly computing sales tax — but had a marked tendency toward spilling milkshakes and French fries. When the banana-split-loving Mickey Cohen started snouting around after her, the manager gave her the go-by, no doubt leery of attracting the criminal elements who had made careers out of killing innocent bystanders while trying to kill the Mick. Aside from that I glommed one hard lead plus suppositions to hang it on: Gretchen Rae had persistently questioned the Scrivner's crew about a recent regular customer — a man with a long German surname who'd been eating at the counter, doing arithmetic tricks with meal tabs, and astounding the locals with five-minute killings of the *L.A. Times* crossword. He was an old geez with a European accent — and he stopped chowing at Scrivner's right before Gretchen Rae Shoftel hired on. Mickey told me the quail had spoken of looking for a friend of her father's; Howard had said she was from Wisconsin; German accents pointed to the dairy state in a big way. And Morris Hornbeck, Mr. Shakes just a few hours before, had been a Milwaukee mob trigger and moneyman. And — the lovely Gretchen Rae had continued carhopping after becoming the consort of two of the richest, most powerful men in Los Angeles — an eye-opener if ever there was one.

* * *

I drove to a pay phone and made some calls, straight and collect. An old LAPD pal gave me the lowdown on Morris Hornbeck—he had two California convictions for felony statch rape, both complainants thirteen-year-old girls. A guy on the Milwaukee force that I'd worked liaison with supplied Midwestern skinny: Little Mo was a glorified bookkeeper for Jerry Katzenbach's mob, run out of town by his boss in '47, when he was given excess gambling skim to invest as he saw best and opened a call house specializing in underaged poon dressed up as movie stars—greenhorn girls coiffed, cosmeticized, and gowned to resemble Rita Hayworth, Ann Sheridan, Veronica Lake, and the like. The operation was a success, but Jerry Katzenbach, Knights of Columbus family man, considered it bum PR. Adios, Morris—who obviously found an amenable home in L.A.

On Gretchen Rae Shoftel, I got bubbkis; ditto on the geezer with the arithmetic tricks similar to the carhop/vamp. The girl had no criminal record in either California or Wisconsin—but I was willing to bet she'd learned her seduction techniques at Mo Hornbeck's whorehouse.

I drove to Howard Hughes's South Lucerne Street fuck pad and let myself in with a key from my fourteen-pound Hughes Enterprises key ring. The house was furnished with leftovers from the RKO prop department, complete with appropriate female accoutrements for each of the six bedrooms. The Moroccan Room featured hammocks and settees from *Casbah Nocturne* and a rainbow array of low-cut silk lounging pajamas; the *Billy the Kid* Room—where Howard brought his Jane Russell look-alikes—was four walls of mock-saloon bars with halter-top cowgirl getups and a mattress covered by a Navajo blanket. My favorite was the Zoo Room: taxidermied cougar, bison, moose, and bobcats—shot by Ernest Hemingway—mounted with their eyes leering down on a narrow strip of sheet-covered floor. Big Ernie told me he decimated the critter population of two Montana counties in order to achieve the effect. There was a kitchen stocked with plenty of fresh milk, peanut butter, and jelly to sate teenage taste buds, a room to screen stag movies, and the master bedroom—my bet for where Howard installed Gretchen Rae Shoftel.

I took the back staircase up, walked down the hall, and pushed the door open, expecting the room's usual state: big white bed and plain white walls—the ironic accompaniment to snatched virginity. I was wrong; what I saw was some sort of testament to squarejohn American homelife.

Mixmasters, cookie sheets, toasters, and matched cutlery sets rested on the bed; the walls were festooned with Currier & Ives calendars and framed *Saturday Evening Post* covers drawn by Norman Rockwell. A menagerie of stuffed animals was admiring the artwork—pandas and tigers and Disney characters placed against the bed, heads tilted upward. There was a bentwood rocker in a corner next to the room's one window. The seat held a stack of catalogs. I leafed through them: Motorola radios, Hamilton Beach kitchen goodies, bed quilts from a mail-order place in New Hampshire. In all of them the less-expensive items were check-marked. Strange, since Howard let his master-bedroom poon have anything they wanted—top-of-the-line charge accounts, the magilla.

I checked the closet. It held the standard Hughes wardrobe—low-cut gowns and tight cashmere sweaters, plus a half-dozen Scrivner's carhop outfits, replete with built-in uplift breastplates, which Gretchen Rae Shoftel didn't need. Seeing a row of empty hangers, I checked for more catalogs and found a Bullocks Wilshire job under the bed. Flipping through it, I saw tweedy skirts and suits, flannel blazers, and prim and proper wool dresses circled; Howard's charge account number was scribbled at the top of the back page. Gretchen Rae Shoftel, math whiz, searching for another math whiz, was contemplating making herself over as Miss Upper-Middle-Class Rectitude.

I checked out the rest of the fuck pad—quick eyeball prowls of the other bedrooms, a toss of the downstairs closets. Empty Bullocks boxes were everywhere—Gretchen Rae had accomplished her transformation. Howard liked to keep his girls cash-strapped to ensure their obedience, but I was willing to guess he stretched the rules for this one. Impersonating a police officer, I called the dispatcher's office at the Yellow and Beacon cab companies. Pay dirt at Beacon: three days ago at 3:10 P.M., a cab was dispatched to 436 South Lucerne; its destination: 2281 South Mariposa.

Big pay dirt.

2281 South Mariposa was a Mickey Cohen hideout, an armed fortress where the Mick's triggers holed up during their many skirmishes with the Jack Dragna gang. It was steel-reinforced concrete; shitloads of canned goods in the bomb shelter/basement; racks of Tommys and pump shotguns behind fake walls covered by cheesecake pics. Only Mickey's boys knew about the place—making it conclusive proof that Morris Hornbeck was connected to Gretchen Rae Shoftel. I drove to Jefferson and Mariposa—quicksville.

It was a block of wood-frame houses, small, neatly tended, mostly owned by Japs sprung from the relocation camps, anxious to stick together and assert their independence in new territory. 2281 was as innocuous and sanitary as any pad on the block: Mickey had the best Jap gardener in the area. No cars were in the driveway; the cars parked curbside looked harmless enough, and the nearest local taking the sun was a guy sitting on a porch swing four houses down. I walked up to the front door, punched in a window, reached around to the latch, and let myself in.

The living room — furnished by Mickey's wife, Lavonne, with sofas and chairs from the Hadassah thrift shop — was tidy and totally silent. I was half-expecting a killer hound to pounce on me before I snapped that Lavonne had forbid the Mick to get a dog because it might whiz on the carpeting. Then I caught the smell.

Decomposition hits you in the tear ducts and gut about simultaneously. I tied my handkerchief over my mouth and nose, grabbed a lamp for a weapon, and walked toward the stink. It was in the right front bedroom, and it was a doozie.

There were two stiffs — a dead man on the floor and another on the bed. The floor man was lying face-down, with a white nightgown still pinned with a Bullocks price tag knotted around his neck. Congealed beef stew covered his face, the flesh cracked and red from scalding. A saucepan was upended a few feet away, holding the caked remains of the goo. Somebody was cooking when the altercation came down.

I laid down the lamp and gave the floor stiff a detailed eyeing. He was fortyish, blond and fat; whoever killed him had tried to burn off his fingerprints — the tips on both hands were scorched black, which meant that the killer was an amateur: the only way to eliminate prints is to do some chopping. A hot plate was tossed in a corner near the bed; I checked it out and saw seared skin stuck to the coils. The bed stiff was right there, so I took a deep breath, tightened my mask, and examined him. He was an old guy, skinny, dressed in clothes too heavy for winter L.A. There was not one mark of any kind on him; his singed-fingered hands had been folded neatly on his chest, rest in peace, like a mortician had done the job. I checked his coat and trouser pockets — goose egg — and gave him a few probes for broken bones. Double gooser. Just then a maggot crawled out of his gaping mouth, doing a spastic little lindy hop on the tip of his tongue.

I walked back into the living room, picked up the phone, and called a man who owes me a big, big favor pertaining to his wife's association with a Negro nun and a junior congressman from Whittier. The man is a crime-scene technician with the Sheriff's Department; a med school dropout adept at spot-checking cadavers and guessing causes of death. He promised to be at 2281 South Mariposa within the hour in an unmarked car — ten minutes of forensic expertise in exchange for my erasure of his debt.

I went back to the bedroom, carrying a pot of Lavonne Cohen's geraniums to help kill the stink. The floor stiff's pockets had been picked clean; the bed stiff had no bruises on his head, and there were now two maggots doing a tango across his nose. Morris Hornbeck, a pro, probably packed a silencered heater like most Mickey muscle — he looked too scrawny to be a hand-to-hand killer. I was starting to make Gretchen Rae Shoftel for the snuffs — and I was starting to like her.

Lieutenant Kirby Falwell showed up a few minutes later, tap-tap-tap on the window I broke. I let him in, and he lugged his evidence kit into the bedroom, pinching his nose. I left him there to be scientific, staying in the living room so as not to bruise his ego with my inside scoop on his wife. After half an hour he came out and greeted me:

"We're even, Meeks. The clown on the floor was hit on the head with a flat, blunt object, maybe a frying pan. It probably knocked him silly. Then somebody threw their dinner in his face and gave him second-degree burns. Then they strangled him with that negligee. I'll give you asphyxiation as cause of death. On Pops, I'd say heart attack — natural causes. I mighta said poison, but his liver isn't distended. Heart attack, fifty-fifty odds. Both dead about two days. I picked the scabs off both sets of fingers and rolled their prints. I suppose you want a forty-eight-state Teletype on them?"

I shook my head. "California and Wisconsin — but quick."

"Inside four hours. We're even, Meeks."

"Take the nightgown home to the wife, Kirby. She'll find a use for it."

"Fuck you, Meeks."

"Adios, Lieutenant."

I settled in, the lights off, figuring if Mo Hornbeck and Gretchen Rae were some kind of partners, he would be by to dump the stiffs, or she would be, or someone would drop in to say hello. I sat in a chair by the front door, the lamp in my hand ready to swing if it came to that kind of play. Danger juice was keeping me edgy; my brain fluids were roiling, trying to figure a way out of the parlay — my two benefactors hiring me to glom one woman for their exclusive use, two corpses thrown in. As hard as I brainstormed, I couldn't think up squat. With half an hour to kill before I called Kirby Falwell, I gave up and tried the Other Guy Routine.

The Other Guy Routine dates back to my days as a youth in Oklahoma, when my old man would beat the shit out of my old lady, and I'd haul a mattress out into the scrub woods so I wouldn't have to listen. I'd set my armadillo traps down, and every once in a while I'd hear a snap-squeak as some stupid 'dillo ate my bait and got his spine crunched for his trouble. When I finally fell asleep, I'd usually wake up to screeches — men hurting women — always just wind playing havoc with the scrub pines. I'd start thinking then: ways to get the old man off the old lady's back without consulting my brother Fud — in the Texas Pen for armed robbery and grievous aggravated assault. I knew I didn't have the guts to confront Pop myself, so I started thinking about other people just to get him off my mind. And that always let me develop a play: some church woman conned into dropping off a pie and religious tracts to calm the old man down; steering some local slick who thought Mom was a beauty in her direction, knowing Pop was a coward with other men and would love up the old girl for weeks and weeks just to keep her. That last play stood all of us good at the end — it was right before the old lady caught typhus. She took to bed with a fever, and the old man got in with her to keep her warm. He caught it himself — and died — sixteen days after she did. Under the circumstances, you have to believe there was nothing but love between them — right up to curtains.

So the Other Guy Routine gets you out of the hole and makes some other poor fuck feel good in the process. I worked it in niggertown as a cop: let some pathetic grasshopper slide, send him a Mickey fruit basket at Christmas, get him to snitch a horse pusher and skim 5 percent full of yuletide cheer. The only trouble with it this time is that I was locked on the horns of a jumbo dilemma: Mickey, Howard — two patrons, only one woman. And claiming failure with either man was against my religion.

I gave up thinking and called Kirby Falwell at the Sheriff's Bureau. His two-state Teletype yielded heat:

The floor stiff was Fritz Steinkamp, Chicago-Milwaukee gunsel, one conviction for attempted murder, currently on parole and believed to be a Jerry Katzenbach torpedo. Mr. Heart Attack was Voyteck Kirnipaski, three-time loser, also a known Katzenbach associate, his falls for extortion and grand larceny — specifically stock swindles. The picture getting a little less hazy, I called Howard Hughes at his flop at the Bel Air Hotel. Two rings, hang up, three rings — so he'd know it's not some gossip columnist.

"Yes?"

"Howard, you been in Milwaukee the past few years?"

"I was in Milwaukee in the spring of '47. Why?"

"Any chance you went to a whorehouse that specialized in girls made up like movie stars?"

Howard sighed. "Buzz, you know my alleged propensity in that department. Is this about Gretchen Rae?"

"Yeah. Did you?"

"Yes. I was entertaining some colleagues from the Pentagon. We had a party with several young women. My date looked just like Jean Arthur, only a bit more . . . endowed. Jean broke my heart, Buzz. You know that."

"Yeah. Did the high brass get looped and start talking shop around the girls?"

"Yes, I suppose so. What does this—"

"Howard, what did you and Gretchen Rae talk about—besides your sex fantasies?"

"Well, Gretchy seemed to be interested in business—stock mergers, the little companies I've been buying up, that sort of thing. Also politics. My Pentagon chums have told me about Korea heating up, implying lots of aircraft business. Gretchy seemed interested in that, too. A smart girl always interests herself in her lovers' endeavors, Buzz. You know that. Have you got leads on her?"

"I surely have. Boss, how have you managed to stay alive and rich so long?"

"I trust the right people, Buzz. Do you believe that?"

"I surely do."

I gave my sitting-in-the-dark stakeout another three hours, then raided the icebox for energy and took the Other Guy Routine on the road, a mitzvah for Mickey in case I had to play an angle to shoot Gretchen Rae to Howard—his very own teenage murderess. First I wrapped up Fritz Steinkamp in three windows' worth of chintz curtains and hauled him out to my car; next I mummified Voyteck Kirnipaski in a bedspread and wedged him into the trunk between Fritz and my spare tire. Then it was a routine wipe of my own possible prints, lights off, and a drive out to Topanga Canyon, to the chemical debris dump operated by the Hughes Tool Company—a reservoir bubbling with caustic agents adjacent to a day camp for underprivileged kids: a Howard tax dodge. I dumped Fritz and Voyteck into the cauldron and listened to them snap, crackle, and pop like Kellogg's Rice Krispies. Then, just after midnight, I drove to the Strip to look for Mickey and his minions.

They weren't at the Trocadero, the Mocambo, or the La Rue; they weren't at Sherry's or Dave's Blue Room. I called the DMV night information line, played cop, and got a read on Mo Hornbeck's wheels — 1946 tan Dodge Coupe, CAL-4986-J, 896¼ Moonglow Vista, South Pasadena — then took the Arroyo Seco over the hill to the address, a block of bungalow courts.

At the left side tail end of a stucco streamline job was 896¼ — rounded handrails and oblong louvers fronting tiny windows strictly for show. No lights were burning; Hornbeck's Dodge was not in the carport at the rear. Maybe Gretchen Rae was inside, armed with stuffed animals, negligee garrotes, stew pots, and frying pans — and that suddenly made me not give a fuck whether the world laid, prayed, stayed, or strayed. I kicked the door in, flipped on a wall light, and got knocked flat on my ass by a big furry mother with big, shiny, razor-white teeth.

It was a Doberman, sleek black muscle out for blood — mine. The dog snapped at my shoulder and got a snootful of Hart, Schaffner & Marx worsted; he snapped at my face and got an awkwardly thrown Meeks right jab that caused him to flinch momentarily. I dug in my pocket for my Arkansas toad stabber, popped the button, and flailed with it; I grazed the beast's paws and snout — and he still kept snapping and snarling.

Giving the fucker a stationary target was the only way. I put my left arm over my eyes and tried to stay supine; Rex the Wonder Dog went for my big, fat, juicy elbow. I hooked my shiv up at his gut, jammed it in, and yanked forward. Entrails dropped all over me; Rex vomited blood in my face and died with a snap-gurgle.

I kicked the day's third corpse off of me, stumbled to the bathroom, rummaged through the medicine cabinet, and found witch hazel. I doused my elbow bite and the blood-oozing teeth marks on my knuckles. Deep breathing, I splashed sink water on my face, looked in the mirror, and saw a middle-aged fat man, terrified and pissed to his drawers, in deep, deep shit without a depth gauge. I held the gaze, thinking it wasn't me for long seconds. Then I smashed the image with the witch hazel bottle and eyeballed the rest of the bungalow.

The larger of the two bedrooms had to be Gretchen Rae's. It was all girlish gewgaws: pandas and arcade Kewpie dolls, pinups of matinee idols and college pennants on the walls. Kitchen appliances still in their boxes were stacked on the dresser; publicity glossies of RKO pretty boys littered the bedspread.

The other bedroom reeked of VapoRub and liniment and sweat and flatulence — bare walls, the floor space almost completely taken up by a sagging Murphy bed. There was a medicine bottle on the nightstand — Dr. Revelle prescribing Demerol for Mr. Hornbeck — and checking under the pillow got me a .38 Police Special. I flipped the cylinder, extracted four of the shells, and stuck the gun in my waistband, then went back to the living room and picked up the dog, gingerly, so as not to drench myself in his gore. I noticed that it was a female; that a tag on its collar read JANET. That hit me as the funniest thing since vaudeville, and I started laughing wildly, shock coming on. I spotted an Abercrombie & Fitch dog bed in the corner, dumped Janet in it, doused the lights in the room, found a couch, and collapsed. I was heading into some sort of weird heebie-jeebie haze when wood creaking, a choked "Oh my God!" and hot yellow glare jolted me to my feet.

"Oh Janet, no!"

Mo Hornbeck beelined for the dead dog, not even noticing me. I stuck out my leg and tripped him; he hit the floor almost snout to snout with Janet. And I was right there, gun at his head, snarling like the psycho Okie killer I could have been. "Boy, you're gonna blab on you, Gretchen Rae, and them bodies on Mariposa. You're gonna spill on her and Howard Hughes, and I mean *now.*"

Hornbeck found some balls quicksville, averting his eyes from the dog, latching them onto me. "Fuck you, Meeks."

"Fuck you" was acceptable from a ranking sheriff's dick in my debt, but not from a statch raper hoodlum. I opened the .38's cylinder and showed Hornbeck the two rounds, then spun it and put the muzzle to his head. "Talk. *Now.*"

Hornbeck said, "Fuck you, Meeks"; I pulled the trigger; he gasped and looked at the dog, turning purple at the temples, red at the cheeks. Seeing myself in a cell next to Fud, the Meeks boys playing pinochle sideways through the bars, I popped off another shot, the hammer clicking on an empty chamber. Hornbeck bit at the carpet to stanch his tremors, going deep purple, then subsiding into shades of crimson, pink, death's-head white. Finally he spat dust and dog hair and gasped, "The pills by my bed and the bottle in the cupboard."

I obeyed, and the two of us sat on the porch like good buddies and killed the remains of the jug — Old Overholt Bonded. Hornbeck blasted Demerol pills along with the juice, flew to cloud nine, and told me the saddest goddamn story I'd ever heard.

Gretchen Rae Shoftel was his daughter. Mom hit the road shortly after she was born, hightailing it to parts unknown with a Schlitz Brewery driver rumored to be double-digit hung, like the human equivalent of Mickey Cohen Jr.; he raised Gretch as best he could, nursing a bad case of the hots for her, ashamed of it until he picked up scads of unrelated skinny: that his wife was servicing the entire Schlitz night shift during the time his little girl was conceived. On general principles he stayed hands-off, taking his lust out on girls from the greenhorn hooker camps up in Green Bay and Saint Paul.

Gretchy grew up strange, ashamed of her old man — a gang stooge and occasional killer. She took her old lady's maiden name and buried her head in books, loving arithmetic tricks, figures, calculations — stuff that proved she was smart. She also took up with a rough South Milwaukee crowd. One crazy Polack boyfriend beat her silly every night for a week straight when she was fifteen. Mo found out, put the kid in cement skates, and dumped him in Lake Michigan. Father and daughter were happily reunited by the revenge.

Mo moved up in Jerry Katzenbach's organization; Gretch got a bundle together tricking the hotel bars in Chicago. Mo installed Gretchen Rae as sixteen-year-old pit boss of a swank whorehouse: movie-star surrogates, the rooms bugged to pick up gangland and political skinny that might prove valuable to Jerry K. Gretch got friendly with stock swindler Voyteck Kirnipaski; she just happened to be listening through a vent one night when Howard Hughes and a cadre of Army three-stars were cavorting with Jean Arthur, Lupe Vélez, and Carole Lombard, greenhorn versions. Gretch picked up lots of juicy Wall Street gossip, and realized that this could be the start of something big. Mo contracted stomach cancer about that time and got the word: half a decade tops — enjoy life while you can. Cash skimmed off Jerry Katzenbach's books provided class-A treatment. Mo held his own against the Big C. Jerry K. got bum press for his whorehouse, kiboshed it, and banished Mo to the Coast, where Mickey Cohen welcomed him with open arms, using his juice to get Mo's two statch-rape indiscretions plea-bargained to bubbkis.

Back in Milwaukee, Gretchen Rae audited business classes at Marquette, and hauled Voyteck Kirnipaski's ashes for free when she learned he was working for Jerry K. and was dissatisfied with the pay. Then Mo had a relapse and came back to Milwaukee on a visit; Voyteck Kirnipaski skipped town with a bundle of Katzenbach's money so he could bankroll stock swindles in L.A.; Gretchen Rae, always reading the papers with an eye toward political repercussions, put her overhead dope from Howard and the high brass together with whispers on the Korea situation and decided to get more info from the man himself. Mo took some lung shots of his little girl and mailed them to Big How; he bit; Gretchy glommed leads that the on-the-lam and hotly pursued Voyteck was hanging out at Scrivner's Drive-in, and, wanting to enlist his aid in possible squeeze plays, got a job there. Mickey Cohen's crush on her put a monkey wrench into things—but she thought, somehow, that the little big man could be tapped for juice. She became his consort concurrent with Howard, father and daughter pretending to be strangers at Mickey's nightclub get-togethers. Then, at a Santa Monica motel, she located Voyteck, terrified that Katzenbach triggers were right behind him. Mo gave her the key to Mickey's Mariposa Street hideout; she ensconced Voyteck there, moving back and forth between Howard's fuck pad, pumping information subtly and pumping Kirnipaski blatantly—attempting to lure him into her web of schemes. She was making progress when Fritz Steinkamp made the scene. And damned if Gretchy didn't rise to the occasion and throttle, scald, and frying pan him to death. She attempted to soothe the terrified Voyteck afterward, but he went into cardiac arrest: the volatile combo of a murder attempt, a murder, and a murderess's tongue. Gretchen Rae panicked and took off with Voyteck's pilfered cash—and was currently trying to unload "secret insider" prospectuses on Hughes stock to a list of potential customers Kirnipaski had compiled. The girl was holed up someplace—Mo didn't know where—and tomorrow she would be calling at the homes and offices of her last wave of potential "clients."

Somewhere in the course of the story I started liking Mo almost as much as I liked Gretchen Rae. I still couldn't see any way out of the mess, but I was curious about one thing: the girly gewgaws, the appliances, all the squarejohn homey stuff Gretchy had glommed. When Mo finished his tale, I said, "What's with all the clothes and gadgets and stuffed animals?"

Morris Hornbeck, worm bait inside six months, just sighed. "Lost time, Meeks. The father-and-daughter act someplace safe, the shtick we shoulda played years ago. But that's tap city, now."

I pointed to the dead dog, its paws starting to curl with rigor mortis like it was going to be begging biscuits for eternity. "Maybe not. You sure ain't gonna have a trusty mascot, but you might get a little taste of the rest."

Morris went to his bedroom and passed out. I laid down on the homey dreambed, holding a stuffed panda, the lights off to ensure some good brainwork. Straight manipulation of Mickey and Howard fell by the wayside quick, so I shifted to the Other Guy Routine and made a snag.

Sid Weinberg.

RKO line producer.

Filthy-rich purveyor of monster cheapies, drive-in circuit turkeys that raked in the cash.

A valuable RKO mainstay—his pictures never flopped. Howard kissed his ass, worshiped his dollars-and-cents approach to moviemaking, and gave him carte blanche at the studio.

"I'd rather lose my you-know-what than lose Sid Weinberg."

Mickey Cohen was indebted to Sid Weinberg, the owner of the Blue Lagoon Saloon, where Mickey was allowed to perform his atrocious comedy routines without cops hanging around—Sid had LAPD connections.

The Mick: "I'd be without a pot to piss in without Sid. I'd have to buy my own nightclub, and that's no fun—it's like buying your own baseball team so you can play yourself."

Sid Weinberg was a widower, a man with two grown daughters who patronized him as a buffoon. He often spoke of his desire to find himself a live-in housekeeper to do light dusting and toss him a little on the side. About fifteen years ago, he was known to be in love with a dazzling blond starlet named Glenda Jensen, who hotfooted it off into the sunset one day, never to be seen again. I'd seen pictures of Glenda; she looked suspiciously like my favorite teenage killer. At eight tomorrow night Sid Weinberg was throwing a party to ballyhoo *Bride of the Surf Monster*. I was to provide security. Mickey Cohen and Howard Hughes would be guests.

I fell asleep on the thought, and dreamed that benevolent dead dogs were riding me up to heaven, my pockets full of other guys' money.

In the morning we took off after the prodigal daughter. I drove, Mo Hornbeck gave directions—where he figured Gretchen Rae would be, based on their last conversation—a panicky talk two days ago; the girl afraid of phone taps; Mo saying he would let the evidence chill, then dispose of it.

Which, of course, he didn't. According to Mo, Gretch told him Voyteck Kirnipaski had given her a list of financial-district sharks who might be interested in her Hughes Enterprises graphs: when to buy and sell shares in Toolco, Hughes Aircraft, and its myriad subsidiaries—based on her new knowledge of upcoming defense contracts and her assessment of probable stock price fluctuations. Mo stressed that was why Gretchy raped the Bullocks catalog—she wanted to look like a businesswoman, not a seductress/killer.

So we slow-lane trawled downtown, circuiting the Spring Street financial district, hoping to catch a streetside glimpse of Gretchen Rae as she made her office calls. I'd won Mo partially over with kind words and a promise to plant Janet in a ritzy West L.A. pet cemetery, but I could still tell he didn't trust me—I was too close to Mickey for too long. He gave me a steady sidelong fisheye and only acknowledged my attempts at conversation with grunts.

The morning came and went; the afternoon followed. Mo had no leads on Gretchen Rae's home calls, so we kept circling Spring Street—Third to Sixth and back again—over and over, taking piss stops at the Pig & Whistle on Fourth and Broadway every two hours. Dusk came on, and I started getting scared: my Other Guy Routine would work to perfection only if I brought Gretchy to Sid Weinberg's party right on time.

6:00.

6:30.

7:00.

7:09. I was turning the corner onto Sixth Street when Mo grabbed my arm and pointed out the window at a sharkskin-clad secretary type perusing papers by the newsstand. "There. That's my baby."

I pulled over; Mo stuck his head out the door and waved, then shouted, "No! Gretchen!"

I was setting the hand brake when I saw the girl—Gretch with her hair in a bun—notice a man on the street and start running. Mo piled out of the car and headed toward the guy; he pulled a monster handcannon, aimed, and fired twice. Mo fell dead on the sidewalk, half his face blown off; the man pursued Gretchen Rae; I pursued him.

The girl ran inside an office building, the gunman close behind. I caught up, peered in, and saw him at the top of the second-floor landing. I slammed the door and stepped back; the act coaxed two wasted shots out of the killer, glass and wood exploding all around me. Four rounds gone, two to go.

Screams on the street; two sets of footsteps scurrying upstairs; sirens in the distance. I ran to the landing and shouted, "Police!" The word drew two ricocheting bang-bangs. I hauled my fat ass up to floor 3 like a flabby dervish.

The gunman was fumbling with a pocketful of loose shells; he saw me just as he flicked his piece's cylinder open. I was within three stairs of him. Not having time to load and fire, he kicked. I grabbed his ankle and pulled him down the stairs; we fell together in a tangle of arms and legs, hitting the landing next to an open window.

We swung at each other, two octopuses, blows and gouges that never really connected. Finally he got a chokehold on my neck; I reached up through his arms and jammed my thumbs hard in his eyes. The bastard let go just long enough for me to knee his balls, squirm away, and grab him by the scalp. Blinded now, he flailed for me. I yanked him out the window head first, pushing his feet after him. He hit the pavement spread-eagled, and even from three stories up I could hear his skull crack like a giant eggshell.

I got some more breath, hauled up to the roof, and pushed the door open. Gretchen Rae Shoftel was sitting on a roll of tarpaper, smoking a cigarette, two long single tears rolling down her cheeks. She said, "Did you come to take me back to Milwaukee?"

All I could think of to say was "No."

Gretchen reached behind the tarpaper and picked up a briefcase—brand-new, Bullocks Wilshire quality. The sirens downstairs were dying out; two bodies gave lots of cops lots to do. I said, "Mickey or Howard, Miss Shoftel? You got a choice."

Gretch stubbed out her cigarette. "They both stink." She hooked a thumb over the roof in the direction of the dead gunman. "I'll take my chances with Jerry Katzenbach and his friends. Daddy went down tough. So will I."

I said, "You're not that stupid."

Gretchen Rae said, "You play the market?"

I said, "Want to meet a nice rich man who needs a friend?"

Gretchen Rae pointed to a ladder that connected the roof to the fire escape of the adjoining building. "If it's now, I'll take it."

In the cab to Beverly Hills I filled Gretchy in on the play, promising all kinds of bonuses I couldn't deliver, like the Morris Hornbeck Scholarship for impoverished Marquette University Business School students. Pulling up to Sid Weinberg's Tudor mansion, the girl had her hair down, makeup on, and was ready to do the save-my-ass tango.

At 8:03 the manse was lit up like a Christmas tree—extras in green rubber monster costumes handing out drinks on the front lawn and loudspeakers on the roof blasting the love theme from a previous Weinberg tuna, *Attack of the Atomic Gargoyles.* Mickey and Howard always arrived at parties late in order not to appear too eager, so I figured there was time to set things up.

I led Gretchen Rae inside, into an incredible scene: Hollywood's great, near-great, and non-great boogie-woogieing with scads of chorus boys and chorus girls dressed like surf monsters, atomic gargoyles, and giant rodents from Mars; bartenders sucking punch out of punchbowls with ray-gun-like siphons; tables of cold cuts dyed surf-monster green — passed up by the guests en masse in favor of good old booze — the line for which stood twenty deep. Beautiful gash was abounding, but Gretchen Rae, hair down like Sid Weinberg's old love Glenda Jensen, was getting the lion's share of the wolf stares. I stood with her by the open front door, and when Howard Hughes's limousine pulled up, I whispered, "*Now.*"

Gretchen slinked back to Sid Weinberg's glass-fronted private office in slow, slow motion; Howard, tall and handsome in a tailored tux, walked in the door, nodding to me, his loyal underling. I said, "Good evening, Mr. Hughes" out loud; under my breath, "You owe me a grand."

I pointed to Sid's office; Howard followed. We got there just as Gretchen Rae Shoftel/Glenda Jensen and Sid Weinberg went into a big open-mouthed clinch. I said, "I'll lean on Sid, boss. Kosher is kosher. He'll listen to reason. Trust me."

Inside of six seconds I saw the fourth-richest man in America go from heartsick puppy dog to hard-case robber baron and back at least a dozen times. Finally he jammed his hands in his pockets, fished out a wad of C-notes, and handed them to me. He said, "Find me another one just like her," and walked back to his limo.

I worked the door for the next few hours, chasing crashers and autograph hounds away, watching Gretchen/Glenda and Sid Weinberg work the crowd, instant velvet for the girl, youth recaptured for the sad old man. Gretchy laughed, and I could tell she did it to hold back tears; when she squeezed Sid's hand I knew she didn't know who it belonged to. I kept wishing I could be there when her tears broke for real, when she became a real little girl for a while, before going back to being a stock maven and a whore. Mickey showed up just as the movie was starting. Davey Goldman told me he was pissed: Mo Hornbeck got himself bumped off by a Kraut trigger from Milwaukee who later nosedived out a window; the Mariposa Street hideout had been burglarized, and Lavonne Cohen was back from Israel three days early and henpecking the shit out of the Mick. I barely heard the words. Gretchy and Sid were cooing at each other by the cold cuts table—and Mickey was headed straight toward them.

I couldn't hear their words, but I could read the three faces. Mickey was taken aback, but paid gracious respect to his beaming host; Gretch was twitching with the aftershocks of her old man's death. L.A.'s number one hoodlum bowed away, walked up to me, and flicked my necktie in my face. "All you get is a grand, you hump. You shoulda found her quicker."

So it worked out. Nobody made me for snuffing the Milwaukee shooter; Gretchy walked on the Steinkamp killing and her complicity in Voyteck Kirnipaski's demise—the chemical-sizzled stiffs, of course, were never discovered. Mo Hornbeck got a plot at Mount Sinai Cemetery, and Davey Goldman and I stuffed Janet into the casket with him at the mortuary—I gave the rabbi a hot tip on the trotters, and he left the room to call his bookie. I paid off Leotis Dineen and promptly went back into hock with him; Mickey took up with a stripper named Audrey Anders; Howard made a bundle off airplane parts for the Korean War and cavorted with the dozen or so Gretchen Rae Shoftel look-alikes I found him. Gretchy and Sid Weinberg fell in love, which just about broke the poor pilot-mogul's heart.

Gretchen Rae and Sid.

She did her light dusting—and must have thrown him a lot on the side. She also became Sid's personal investment banker, and made him a giant bundle, of which she took a substantial percentage cut, invested it in slum property, and watched it grow, grow, grow. Slumlord Gretch also starred in the only Sid Weinberg vehicle ever to lose money, a tear-jerker called *Glenda* about a movie producer who falls in love with a starlet who disappears off the face of the earth. The critical consensus was that Gretchen Rae Shoftel was a lousy actress, but had great lungs. Howard Hughes was rumored to have seen the movie over a hundred times.

In 1950 I got involved in a grand jury investigation that went bad in an enormous way, and I ended up taking it on the road permanently, Mr. Anonymous in a thousand small towns. Mickey Cohen did a couple of fed jolts for income tax evasion, got paroled as an old man, and settled back into L.A. as a much-appreciated local character, a reminder of the colorful old days. Howard Hughes ultimately went squirrelshit with drugs and religion, and a biography that I read said that he carried a torch for a blond whore straight off into the deep end. He'd spend hours at the Bel Air Hotel looking at her picture, playing a torchy rendition of "Since I Don't Have You" over and over. I know better: it was probably scads of different pictures, lung shots all, the music a lament for a time when love came cheap. Gretchy was special to him, though. I still believe that.

I miss Howard and Mickey, and writing this story about them has only made it worse. It's tough being a dangerous old man by yourself —you've got nothing but memories and no one with the balls to understand them.

1991

JAMES LEE BURKE

TEXAS CITY, 1947

JAMES LEE BURKE (1936–) was born in Houston but grew up on the Texas-Louisiana coast, where so much of his fiction is based. After attending the University of Louisiana at Lafayette, he received his BA and MA from the University of Missouri at Columbia. After three critically praised mainstream novels, his fourth received more than a hundred rejections over more than a decade, until the University of Louisiana Press published *The Lost Get-Back Boogie* in 1986; it was nominated for a Pulitzer Prize.

His first crime novel, *The Neon Rain* (1987), featured David Robicheaux, a Vietnam veteran and homicide detective in the New Orleans Police Department. He has been described by his creator as "Everyman from the morality plays of the Renaissance. He tries to give voice to those who have none." After stepping on too many toes in that first book, Robicheaux leaves to work on the police force in New Iberia Parish. Always present is a sidekick, Clete Purcel, also a former NOPD officer, who is now a private eye. The second novel in the series, *Heaven's Prisoners* (1988), was filmed in 1996, starring Eric Roberts, Alec Baldwin, Kelly Lynch, and Teri Hatcher. The third book, *Black Cherry Blues* (1989), won an Edgar Allan Poe Award from the Mystery Writers of America for best novel of the year. Burke won a second Edgar for *Cimarron Rose* (1997), which introduced Billy Bob Holland, a Texas Ranger turned lawyer in Missoula, Montana. MWA named Burke a Grand Master for lifetime achievement in 2009.

"Texas City, 1947," often described as Burke's finest short work of fiction, is a dark coming-of-age story that was first published in the *Southern Review* in 1991. It's first book appearance was in *New Stories from the South: The Year's Best* (1992). It was later collected in the author's *Jesus Out to Sea* (2007).

■ ■ ■

RIGHT AFTER World War II everybody in southern Louisiana thought he was going to get rich in the oil business. My father convinced himself that all his marginal jobs in the oil fields would one day give him the capital to become an independent wildcatter, perhaps even a legendary figure like Houston's Glenn McCarthy, and he would successfully hammer together a drilling operation out of wooden towers and rusted junk, punch through the top of a geological dome, and blow salt water, sand, chains, pipe casing, and oil into the next parish.

So he worked on as a roughneck on drilling rigs and as a jug-hustler with a seismograph outfit, then began contracting to build board roads in the marsh for the Texaco company. By mid-1946, he was actually leasing land in the Atchafalaya Basin and over in East Texas. But that was also the year that I developed rheumatic fever and he drove my mother off and brought Mattie home to live with us.

I remember the terrible fight they had the day she left. My mother had come home angry from her waitress job in a beer garden on that burning July afternoon, and without changing out of her pink dress with the white piping on the collar and pockets, she had begun butchering chickens on the stump in the backyard and shucking off their feathers in a big iron cauldron of scalding water. My father came home later than he should have, parked his pickup truck by the barn, and walked naked to the waist through the gate with his wadded-up shirt hanging out the back pocket of his Levi's. He was a dark Cajun, and his shoulders, chest, and back were streaked with black hair. He wore cowboy boots, a red sweat handkerchief tied around his neck, and a rakish straw hat that had an imitation snakeskin band around the crown.

Headless chickens were flopping all over the grass, and my mother's forearms were covered with wet chicken feathers. "I know you been with her. They were talking at the beer joint," she said, without looking up from where she sat with her knees apart on a wood chair in front of the steaming cauldron.

"I ain't been with nobody," he said, "except with them mosquitoes I been slapping out in that marsh."

"You said you'd leave her alone."

"You children go inside," my father said.

"That gonna make your conscience right 'cause you send them kids off, you? She gonna cut your throat one day. She been in the crazy house in Mandeville. You gonna see, Verise."

"I ain't seen her."

"You son of a bitch, I smell her on you," my mother said, and she swung a headless chicken by its feet and whipped a diagonal line of blood across my father's chest and Levi's.

"You ain't gonna act like that in front of my children, you," he said, and started toward her. Then he stopped. "Y'all get inside. You ain't got no business listening to this. This is between me and her."

My two older brothers, Weldon and Lyle, were used to our parents' quarrels, and they went inside sullenly and let the back screen slam behind them. But my little sister, Drew, whom my mother nicknamed Little Britches, stood mute and fearful and alone under the pecan tree, her cat pressed flat against her chest.

"Come on, Drew. Come see inside. We're gonna play with the Monopoly game," I said, and tried to pull her by the arm. But her body was rigid, her bare feet immobile in the dust.

Then I saw my father's large, square hand go up in the air, saw it come down hard against the side of my mother's face, heard the sound of her weeping, as I tried to step into Drew's line of vision and hold her and her cat against my body, hold the three of us tightly together outside the unrelieved sound of my mother's weeping.

Three hours later, her car went through the railing on the bridge over the Atchafalaya River. I dreamed that night that an enormous brown bubble rose from the submerged wreck, and when it burst on the surface, her drowned breath stuck against my face as wet and rank as gas released from a grave.

That fall I began to feel sick all the time, as though a gray cloud of mosquitoes were feeding at my heart. During recess at school I didn't play with the other children and instead hung about on the edges of the dusty playground or, when Brother Daniel wasn't looking, slipped around the side of the old red-brick cathedral and sat by myself on a stone bench in a bamboo-enclosed, oak-shaded garden where a statue of Mary rested in a grotto and camellia petals floated in a big goldfish pond. Sometimes Sister Roberta was there saying her rosary.

She was built like a fire hydrant. Were it not for the additional size that the swirl of her black habit and the wings of her veil gave her, she would not have been much larger than the students in her fifth-grade class. She didn't yell at us or hit our knuckles with rulers like the other nuns did, and in fact she always called us "little people" rather than children. But sometimes her round face would flare with anger below her white, starched wimple at issues which to us, in our small parochial world, seemed of little importance. She told our class once that criminals and corrupt local politicians were responsible for the slot and racehorse machines that were in every drugstore, bar, and hotel lobby in New Iberia, and another time she flung an apple core at a carload of teenagers who were baiting the Negro janitor out by the school incinerator.

She heard my feet on the dead oak leaves when I walked through the opening in the bamboo into the garden. She was seated on the stone bench, her back absolutely erect, the scarlet beads of her rosary stretched across the back of her pale hand like drops of blood. She stopped her prayer and turned her head toward me. Fine white hair grew on her upper lip.

"Do you feel sick again, Billy Bob?" she asked.

"Yes, Sister."

"Come here."

"What?"

"I said come here." Her hand reached out and held my forehead. Then she wiped the moisture off her palm with her fingers. "Have you been playing or running?"

"No, Sister."

"Has your father taken you to a doctor?"

I didn't answer.

"Look at me and answer my question," she said.

"He don't—he doesn't have money right now. He says it's because I had the flu. He boiled some honey and onions for me to eat. It made me feel better. It's true, Sister."

"I need to talk to your father."

She saw me swallow.

"Would he mind my calling him?" she asked.

"He's not home now. He works all the time."

"Will he be home tonight?"

"I'm not sure."

"Who takes care of you at night when he's not home?"

"A lady, a friend of his."

"I see. Come back to the classroom with me. It's too windy out here for you," she said.

"Sister, you don't need to call, do you? I feel OK now. My father's got a lot on his mind now. He works real hard."

"What's wrong in your house, Billy Bob?"

"Nothing. I promise, Sister." I tried to smile. I could taste bile in my throat.

"Don't lie."

"I'm not. I promise I'm not."

"Yes, I can see that clearly. Come with me."

The rest of the recess period she and I sharpened crayons in the empty room with tiny pencil sharpeners, stringing long curlicues of colored wax into the wastebasket. She was as silent and as seemingly self-absorbed as a statue. Just before the bell rang she walked down to the convent and came back with a tube of toothpaste.

"Your breath is bad. Go down to the lavatory and wash your mouth out with this," she said.

Mattie wore shorts and sleeveless blouses with sweat rings under the arms, and in the daytime she always seemed to have curlers in her hair. When she walked from room to room she carried an ashtray with her into which she constantly flicked her lipstick-stained Chesterfields. She had a hard, muscular body, and she didn't close the bathroom door all the way when she bathed, and once I saw her kneeling in the tub, scrubbing her big shoulders and chest with a large, flat brush. The area above her head was crisscrossed with improvised clotheslines from which dropped her wet underthings. Her eyes fastened on mine; I thought she was about to reprimand me for staring at her, but instead her hard-boned, shiny face continued to look back at me with a vacuous indifference that made me feel obscene.

If my father was out of town on a Friday or Saturday night, she fixed our supper (sometimes meat on Friday, the fear in our eyes not worthy of her recognition), put on her blue suit, and sat by herself in the living room, listening to the *Grand Ole Opry* or the *Louisiana Hayride,* while she drank apricot brandy from a coffee cup. She always dropped cigarette ashes on her suit and had to spot-clean the cloth with dry-cleaning fluid before she drove off for the evening in her old Ford coupe. I don't know where she went on those Friday or Saturday nights, but a boy down the road told me that Mattie used to work in Broussard's Bar on Railroad Avenue, an infamous area in New Iberia where the women sat on the galleries of the cribs, dipping their beer out of buckets and yelling at the railroad and oil-field workers in the street.

Then one morning when my father was in Morgan City, a man in a new silver Chevrolet sedan came out to see her. It was hot, and he parked his car partly on our grass to keep it in the shade. He wore sideburns, striped brown zoot slacks, two-tone shoes, suspenders, a pink shirt without a coat, and a fedora that shadowed his narrow face. While he talked to her, he put one shoe on the car bumper and wiped the dust off it with a rag. Then their voices grew louder and he said, "You like the life. Admit it, you. He ain't given you no wedding ring, has he? You don't buy the cow, no, when you can milk through the fence."

"I am currently involved with a gentleman. I do not know what you are talking about. I am not interested in anything you are talking about," she said.

He threw the rag back inside the car and opened the car door. "It's always trick, trade, or travel, darlin'," he said. "Same rules here as down on Railroad. He done made you a nigger woman for them children, Mattie."

"Are you calling me a nigra?" she said quietly.

"No, I'm calling you crazy, just like everybody say you are. No, I take that back, me. I ain't calling you nothing. I ain't got to, 'cause you gonna be back. You in the life, Mattie. You be phoning me to come out here, bring you to the crib, rub your back, put some of that warm stuff in your arm again. Ain't nobody else do that for you, huh?"

When she came back into the house, she made us take all the dishes out of the cabinets, even though they were clean, and wash them over again.

It was the following Friday that Sister Roberta called. Mattie was already dressed to go out. She didn't bother to turn down the radio when she answered the phone, and in order to compete with Red Foley's voice, she had to almost shout into the receiver.

"Mr. Sonnier is not here," she said. "Mr. Sonnier is away on business in Texas City . . . No, ma'am, I'm not the housekeeper. I'm a friend of the family who is caring for these children . . . There's nothing wrong with that boy that I can see . . . Are you calling to tell me that there's something wrong, that I'm doing something wrong? What is it that I'm doing wrong? I would like to know that. What is your name?"

I stood transfixed with terror in the hall as she bent angrily into the mouthpiece and her knuckles ridged on the receiver. A storm was blowing in from the Gulf, the air smelled of ozone, and the southern horizon was black with thunderclouds that pulsated with white veins of lightning. I heard the wind ripping through the trees in the yard and pecans rattling down on the gallery roof like grapeshot.

When Mattie hung up the phone, the skin of her face was stretched as tight as a lampshade and one liquid eye was narrowed at me like someone aiming down a rifle barrel.

The next week, when I was cutting through the neighbor's sugarcane field on the way home from school, my heart started to race for no reason, my spit tasted like pecans, and my face filmed with perspiration even though the wind was cool through the stalks of cane; then I saw the oaks and cypress trees along Bayou Teche tilt at an angle, and I dropped my books and fell forward in the dirt as though someone had wrapped a chain around my chest and snapped my breastbone.

I lay with the side of my face pressed against the dirt, my mouth gasping like a fish's, until Weldon found me and went crashing through the cane for help. A doctor came out to the house that night, examined me and gave me a shot, then talked with my father out in the hall. My father didn't understand the doctor's vocabulary, and he said, "What kind of fever that is?"

"Rheumatic, Mr. Sonnier. It attacks the heart. I could be wrong, but I think that's what your boy's got. I'll be back tomorrow."

"How much this gonna cost?"

"It's three dollars for the visit, but you can pay me when you're able."

"We never had nothing like this in our family. You sure about this?"

"No, I'm not. That's why I'll be back. Good night to you, sir."

I knew he didn't like my father, but he came to see me one afternoon a week for a month, brought me bottles of medicine, and always looked into my face with genuine concern after he listened to my heart. Then one night he and my father argued and he didn't come back.

"What good he do, huh?" my father said. "You still sick, ain't you? A doctor don't make money off well people. I think maybe you got malaria, son. There ain't nothing for that, either. It just goes away. You gonna see, you. You stay in bed, you eat cush-cush Mattie and me make for you, you drink that Hadacol vitamin tonic, you wear this dime I'm tying on you, you gonna get well and go back to school."

He hung a perforated dime on a piece of red twine around my neck. His face was lean and unshaved, his eyes as intense as a butane flame when he looked into mine. "You blame me for your mama?" he asked.

"No, sir," I lied.

"I didn't mean to hit her. But she made me look bad in front of y'all. A woman can't be doing that to a man in front of his kids."

"Make Mattie go away, Daddy."

"Don't be saying that."

"She hit Weldon with the belt. She made Drew kneel in the bathroom corner because she didn't flush the toilet."

"She's just trying to be a mother, that's all. Don't talk no more. Go to sleep. I got to drive back to Texas City tonight. You gonna be all right."

He closed my door and the inside of my room was absolutely black. Through the wall I heard him and Mattie talking, then the weight of their bodies creaking rhythmically on the bedsprings.

* * *

When Sister Roberta knew that I would not be back to school that semester, she began bringing my lessons to the house. She came three afternoons a week and had to walk two miles each way between the convent and our house. Each time I successfully completed a lesson she rewarded me with a holy card. Each holy card had a prayer on one side and a beautiful picture on the other, usually of angels and saints glowing with light or ethereal paintings of Mary with the Infant Jesus. On the day after my father had tied the dime around my neck, Sister Roberta had to walk past our neighbor's field right after he had cut his cane and burned off the stubble, and a wet wind had streaked her black habit with ashes. As soon as she came through my bedroom door her face tightened inside her wimple, and her brown eyes, which had flecks of red in them, grew round and hot. She dropped her book bag on the foot of my bed and leaned within six inches of my face as though she were looking down at a horrid presence in the bottom of a well. The hair on her upper lip looked like pieces of silver thread.

"Who put that around your neck?" she asked.

"My father says it keeps the gris-gris away."

"My suffering God," she said, and went back out the door in a swirl of cloth. Then I heard her speak to Mattie: "That's right, madam. Scissors. So I can remove that cord from his neck before he strangles to death in his sleep. Thank you kindly."

She came back into my bedroom, pulled the twine out from my throat with one finger, and snipped it in two. "Do you believe in this nonsense, Billy Bob?" she asked.

"No, Sister."

"That's good. You're a good Catholic boy, and you mustn't believe in superstition. Do you love the church?"

"I think so."

"Hmmmm. That doesn't sound entirely convincing. Do you love your father?"

"I don't know."

"I see. Do you love your sister and your brothers?"

"Yes. Most of the time I do."

"That's good. Because if you love somebody, or if you love the church, like I do, then you don't ever have to be afraid. People are only superstitious when they're afraid. That's an important lesson for little people to learn. Now, let's take a look at our math test for this week."

Over her shoulder I saw Mattie looking at us from the living room, her hair in foam rubber curlers, her face contorted as though a piece of barbed wire were twisting behind her eyes.

That winter my father started working regular hours, what he called "an indoor job," at the Monsanto Chemical Company in Texas City, and we saw him only on weekends. Mattie cooked only the evening meal and made us responsible for the care of the house and the other two meals. Weldon started to get into trouble at school. His eighth-grade teacher, a laywoman, called and said he had thumbtacked a girl's dress to the desk during class, causing her to almost tear it off her body when the bell rang, and he would either pay for the dress or be suspended. Mattie hung up the phone on her, and two days later the girl's father, a sheriff's deputy, came out to the house and made Mattie give him four dollars on the gallery.

She came back inside, slamming the door, her face burning, grabbed Weldon by the collar of his T-shirt, and walked him into the backyard, where she made him stand for two hours on an upended apple crate until he wet his pants.

Later, after she had let him come back inside and he had changed his underwear and blue jeans, he went outside into the dark by himself, without eating supper, and sat on the butcher stump, striking kitchen matches on the side of the box and throwing them at the chickens. Before we went to sleep he sat for a long time on the side of his bed, next to mine, in a square of moonlight with his hands balled into fists on his thighs. There were knots of muscle in the backs of his arms and behind his ears. Mattie had given him a burr haircut, and his head looked as hard and scalped as a baseball.

"Tomorrow's Saturday. We're going to listen to the LSU-Rice game," I said.

"Some colored kids saw me from the road and laughed."

"I don't care what they did. You're brave, Weldon. You're braver than any of us."

"I'm gonna fix her."

His voice made me afraid. The branches of the pecan trees were skeletal, like gnarled fingers against the moon.

"Don't be thinking like that," I said. "It'll just make her do worse things. She takes it out on Drew when you and Lyle aren't here."

"Go to sleep, Billy Bob," he said. His eyes were wet. "She hurts us because we let her. We ax for it. You get hurt when you don't stand up. Just like Mama did."

I heard him snuffling in the dark. Then he lay down with his face turned toward the opposite wall. His head looked carved out of gray wood in the moonlight.

I went back to school for the spring semester. Maybe because of the balmy winds off the Gulf and the heavy, fecund smell of magnolia and wisteria on the night air, I wanted to believe that a new season was beginning in my heart as well. I couldn't control what happened at home, but the school was a safe place, one where Sister Roberta ruled her little fifth-grade world like an affectionate despot.

I was always fascinated by her hands. They were like toy hands, small as a child's, as pink as an early rose, the nails not much bigger than pearls. She was wonderful at sketching and drawing with crayons and colored chalk. In minutes she could create a beautiful religious scene on the blackboard to fit the church's season, but she also drew pictures for us of Easter rabbits and talking Easter eggs. Sometimes she would draw only the outline of a figure — an archangel with enormous wings, a Roman soldier about to be dazzled by a blinding light — and she would let us take turns coloring in the solid areas. She told us the secret to great classroom art was to always keep your chalk and crayons pointy.

Then we began to hear rumors about Sister Roberta, of a kind that we had never heard about any of the nuns, who all seemed to have no lives other than the ones that were immediately visible to us. She had been heard weeping in the confessional, she had left the convent for three days without permission, two detectives from Baton Rouge had questioned her in the Mother Superior's office.

She missed a week of school and a lay teacher took her place. She returned for two weeks, then was gone again. When she came back the second time she was soft-spoken and removed, and sometimes she didn't even bother to answer simple questions that we asked her. She would gaze out the window for long periods, as though her attention were fixed on a distant object, then a noise — a creaking desk, an eraser flung from the cloakroom — would disturb her, and her eyes would return to the room, absolutely empty of thought or meaning.

I stayed after school on a Friday to help her wash the blackboards and pound erasers.

"You don't need to, Billy Bob. The janitor will take care of it," she said, staring idly out the window.

"All the kids like you, Sister," I said.

"What?" she said.

"You're the only one who plays with us at recess. You don't ever get mad at us, either. Not for real, anyway."

"It's nice of you to say that, but the other sisters are good to you, too."

"Not like you are."

"You shouldn't talk to me like that, Billy Bob." She had lost weight, and there was a solitary crease, like a line drawn by a thumbnail, in each of her cheeks.

"It's wrong for you to be sad," I said.

"You must run along home now. Don't say anything more."

I wish you were my mother, I thought I heard myself say inside my head.

"What did you say?" she asked.

"Nothing."

"Tell me what you said."

"I don't think I said anything. I really don't think I did."

My heart was beating against my rib cage, the same way it had the day I fell unconscious in the sugarcane field.

"Billy Bob, don't try to understand the world. It's not ours to understand," she said. "You must give up the things you can't change. You mustn't talk to me like this anymore. You—"

But I was already racing from the room, my soul painted with an unrelieved shame that knew no words.

The next week I found out the source of Sister Roberta's grief. A strange and seedy man by the name of Mr. Trajan, who always had an American flag pin on his lapel when you saw him inside the wire cage of the grocery and package store he operated by the Negro district, had cut an article from copies of the *Baton Rouge Morning Advocate* and the *Lafayette Daily Advertiser* and mailed it to other Catholic businessmen in town. An eighth-grader who had been held back twice, once by Sister Roberta, brought it to school one day, and after the three o'clock bell Lyle, Weldon, and I heard him reading it to a group of dumbfounded boys on the playground. The words hung in the air like our first exposure to God's name being deliberately used in vain.

Her brother had killed a child, and Sister Roberta had helped him hide in a fishing camp in West Baton Rouge Parish.

"Give me that," Weldon said, and tore the news article out of the boy's hand. He stared hard at it, then wadded it up and threw it on the ground. "Get the fuck out of here. You go around talking about this again and I'll kick your ass."

"That's right, you dumb fuck," Lyle said, putting his new baseball cap in his back pocket and setting his book satchel down by his foot.

"That's right, butt face," I added, incredulous at the boldness of my own words.

"Yeah?" the boy said, but the resolve in his voice was already breaking.

"Yeah!" Weldon said, and shoved him off balance. Then he picked up a rock and chased the boy and three of his friends toward the street. Lyle and I followed, picking up dirt clods in our hands. When the boy was almost to his father's waiting pickup truck, he turned and shot us the finger. Weldon nailed him right above the eye with the rock.

One of the brothers marched us down to Father Higgins's office and left us there to wait for Father Higgins, whose razor strop and black-Irish, crimson-faced tirades were legendary in the school. The office smelled of the cigar butts in the wastebasket and the cracked leather in the chairs. A walnut pendulum clock ticked loudly on the wall. It was overcast outside, and we sat in the gloom and silence until four o'clock.

"I ain't waiting anymore. Y'all coming?" Weldon said, and put one leg out the open window.

"You'll get expelled," I said.

"Too bad. I ain't going to wait around just to have somebody whip me," he said, and dropped out the window.

Five minutes later, Lyle followed him.

The sound of the clock was like a spoon knocking on a hollow wood box. When Father Higgins finally entered the room, he was wearing his horn-rimmed glasses and thumbing through a sheaf of papers attached to a clipboard. The hairline on the back of his neck was shaved neatly with a razor. At first he seemed distracted by my presence, then he flipped the sheets of paper to a particular page, almost as an afterthought, and studied it. He put an unlit cigar stub in his mouth, looked at me, then back at the page.

"You threw a rock at somebody?" he said.

"No, Father."

"Somebody threw a rock at you?"

"I wouldn't say that."

"Then what are you doing here?"

"I don't know," I replied.

"That's interesting. All right, since you don't know why you're here, how about going somewhere else?"

"I'll take him, Father," I heard Sister Roberta say in the doorway. She put her hand on my arm, walked me down the darkly polished corridor to the breezeway outside, then sat me down on the stone bench inside the bamboo-enclosed garden where she often said her rosary.

She sat next to me, her small white hands curved on the edges of the bench, and looked down at the goldfish pond while she talked. A crushed paper cup floated among the hyacinth leaves. "You meant well, Billy Bob, but I don't want you to defend me anymore. It's not the job of little people to defend adults."

"Sister, the newspaper said —"

"It said what?"

"You were in trouble with the police. Can they put you in jail?"

She put her hand on top of mine. Her fingernails looked like tiny pink seashells. "They're not really interested in me, Billy Bob. My brother is an alcoholic, and he killed a little boy with his car, then he ran away. But they probably won't send my brother to prison because the child was a Negro." Her hand was hot and damp on top of mine. Her voice clicked wetly in her throat. "He'll be spared, not because he's a sick man, but because it was a colored child he killed."

When I looked at her again, her long eyelashes were bright with tears. She stood up with her face turned away from me. The sun had broken through the gray seal of clouds, and the live oak tree overhead was filled with the clattering of mockingbirds and blue jays. I felt her tiny fingernails rake gently through my hair, as though she were combing a cat.

"Oh, you poor child, you have lice eggs in your hair," she said. Then she pressed my head against her breast, and I felt her tears strike hotly on the back of my neck.

Three days later, Sister saw the cigarette burn on Drew's leg in the lunchroom and reported it to the social welfare agency in town. A consumptive rail of a man in a dandruff-flecked blue suit drove out to the house and questioned Mattie on the gallery, then questioned us in front of her. Drew told him she had been burned by an ember that had popped out of a trash fire in the backyard.

He raised her chin with his knuckle. His black hair was stiff with grease. "Is that what happened?" he asked.

"Yes, sir." Drew's face was dull, her mouth down-turned at the corners. The burn was scabbed now and looked like a tightly coiled gray worm on her skin.

He smiled and took his knuckle away from her chin. "Then you shouldn't play next to the fire," he said.

"I would like to know who sent you out here," Mattie said.

"That's confidential." He coughed on the back of his hand. His shirt cuff was frayed and for some reason looked particularly pretentious and sad on his thin wrist. "And to tell you the truth, I don't really know. My supervisor didn't tell me. I guess that's how the chain of command works." He coughed again, this time loud and hard, and I could smell the nicotine that was buried in his lungs. "But everything here looks all right. Perhaps this is much ado about nothing. Not a bad day for a drive, though."

Weldon's eyes were as hard as marbles, but he didn't speak.

The man walked with Mattie to his car, and I felt like doors were slamming all around us. She put her foot on his running board and propped one arm on his car roof while she talked, so that her breasts were uplifted against her blouse and her dress made a loop between her legs.

"Let's tell him," Lyle said.

"Are you kidding? Look at him. He'd eat her shit with a spoon," Weldon said.

It was right after first period the next morning that we heard about the disaster at Texas City. Somebody shouted something about it on the playground, then suddenly the whole school was abuzz with rumors. Cars on the street pulled to the curb with their radios tuned to news stations, and we could even hear the principal's old boxwood radio blaring through the open window upstairs. A ship loaded with fertilizer had been burning in the harbor, and while people on the docks had watched firefighting boats pumping geysers of water onto the ship's decks, the fire had dripped into the hold. The explosion filled the sky with rockets of smoke and rained an umbrella of flame down on the Monsanto chemical plant. The force of the secondary explosion was so great that it blew out windows in Houston, fifty miles away. But it wasn't over yet. The fireball mushroomed laterally out into an adjacent oil field, and rows of storage tanks and wellheads went like strings of Chinese firecrackers. People said the water in the harbor boiled from the heat, the spars on steel derricks melting like licorice.

We heard nothing about the fate of my father either that afternoon or evening. Mattie got drunk that night and fell asleep in the living room chair by the radio. I felt nothing about my father's possible death, and I wondered at my own callousness. We went to school the next morning, and when we returned home in the afternoon Mattie was waiting on the gallery to tell us that a man from the Monsanto Company had telephoned and said that my father was listed as missing. Her eyes were pink with either hangover or crying, and her face was puffy and round, like a white balloon.

When we didn't respond, she said, "Your father may be dead. Do you understand what I'm saying? That was an important man from his company who called. He would not call unless he was gravely concerned. Do you children understand what is being said to you?"

Weldon brushed at the dirt with his tennis shoe, and Lyle looked into a place about six inches in front of his eyes. Drew's face was frightened, not because of the news about our father, but instead because of the strange whirring of wheels that we could almost hear from inside Mattie's head. I put my arm over her shoulders and felt her skin jump.

"He's worked like a nigra for you, maybe lost his life for you, and you have nothing to say?" Mattie asked.

"Maybe we ought to start cleaning up our rooms. You wanted us to clean up our rooms, Mattie," I said.

But it was a poor attempt to placate her.

"You stay outside. Don't even come in this house," she said.

"I have to go to the bathroom," Lyle said.

"Then you can just do it in the dirt like a darky," she said, and went inside the house and latched the screen behind her.

By the next afternoon, my father was still unaccounted for. Mattie had an argument on the phone with somebody, I think the man in zoot pants and two-tone shoes who had probably been her pimp at one time, because she told him he owed her money and she wouldn't come back and work at Broussard's Bar again until he paid her. After she hung up she breathed hard at the kitchen sink, smoking her cigarette and staring out into the yard. She snapped the cap off a bottle of Jax and drank it half empty, her throat working in one long, wet swallow, one eye cocked at me.

"Come here," she said.

"What?"

"You tracked up the kitchen. You didn't flush the toilet after you used it, either."

"I did."

"You did what?"

"I flushed the toilet."

"Then one of the others didn't flush it. Every one of you come out here. Now!"

"What is it, Mattie? We didn't do anything," I said.

"I changed my mind. Every one of you outside. All of you outside. Weldon and Lyle, you get out there right now. Where's Drew?"

"She's playing in the yard. What's wrong, Mattie?" I made no attempt to hide the fear in my voice. I could see the web of blue veins in the top of her muscular chest.

Outside, the wind was blowing through the trees in the yard, flattening the purple clumps of wisteria that grew against the barn wall.

"Each of you go to the hedge and cut the switch you want me to use on you," she said.

It was her favorite form of punishment for us. If we broke off a large switch, she hit us fewer times with it. If we came back with a thin or small switch, we would get whipped until she felt she had struck some kind of balance between size and number.

We remained motionless. Drew had been playing with her cat. She had tied a piece of twine around the cat's neck, and she held the twine in her hand like a leash. Her knees and white socks were dusty from play.

"I told you not to tie that around the kitten's neck again," Mattie said.

"It doesn't hurt anything. It's not your cat, anyway," Weldon said.

"Don't sass me," she said. "You will not sass me. None of you will sass me."

"I ain't cutting no switch," Weldon said. "You're crazy. My mama said so. You ought to be in the crazy house."

She looked hard into Weldon's eyes, then there was a moment of recognition in her colorless face, a flicker of fear, as though she had seen a growing meanness of spirit in Weldon that would soon become a challenge to her own. She wet her lips.

"We shall see who does what around here," she said. She broke off a big switch from the myrtle hedge and raked it free of flowers and leaves, except for one green sprig on the tip.

I saw the look in Drew's face, saw her drop the piece of twine from her palm as she stared up into Mattie's shadow.

Mattie jerked her by the wrist and whipped her a half-dozen times across her bare legs. Drew twisted impotently in Mattie's balled hand, her feet dancing with each blow. The switch raised welts on her skin as thick and red as centipedes.

Then suddenly Weldon ran with all his weight into Mattie's back, stiff-arming her between the shoulder blades, and sent her tripping sideways over a bucket of chicken slops. She righted herself and stared at him open-mouthed, the switch limp in her hand. Then her eyes grew hot and bright, and I could see the bone flex along her jaws.

Weldon burst out the back gate and ran down the dirt road between the sugarcane fields, the soles of his dirty tennis shoes powdering dust in the air.

She waited for him a long time, watching through the screen as the mauve-colored dusk gathered in the trees and the sun's afterglow lit the clouds on the western horizon. Then she took a bottle of apricot brandy into the bathroom and sat in the tub for almost an hour, turning the hot water tap on and off until the tank was empty. When we needed to go to the bathroom, she told us to take our problem outside. Finally she emerged in the hall, wearing only her panties and bra, her hair wrapped in a towel, the dark outline of her sex plainly visible to us.

"I'm going to dress now and go into town with a gentleman friend," she said. "Tomorrow we're going to start a new regime around here. Believe me, there will never be a reoccurrence of what happened here today. You can pass that on to young Mr. Weldon for me."

But she didn't go into town. Instead, she put on her blue suit, a flower-print blouse, her nylon stockings, and walked up and down on the gallery, her cigarette poised in the air like a movie actress.

"Why not just drive your car, Mattie?" I said quietly through the screen.

"It has no gas. Besides, a gentleman caller will be passing for me anytime now," she answered.

"Oh."

She blew smoke at an upward angle, her face aloof and flat-sided in the shadows.

"Mattie?"

"Yes?"

"Weldon's out back. Can he come in the house?"

"Little mice always return where the cheese is," she said.

I hated her. I wanted something terrible to happen to her. I could feel my fingernails knifing into my palms.

She turned around, her palm supporting one elbow, her cigarette an inch from her mouth, her hair wreathed in smoke. "Do you have a reason for staring through the screen at me?" she asked.

"No," I said.

"When you're bigger, you'll get to do what's on your mind. In the meantime, don't let your thoughts show on your face. You're a lewd little boy."

Her suggestion repelled me and made water well up in my eyes. I backed away from the screen, then turned and ran through the rear of the house and out into the backyard where Weldon, Lyle, and Drew sat against the barn wall, fireflies lighting in the wisteria over their heads.

No one came for Mattie that evening. She sat in the stuffed chair in her room, putting on layers of lipstick until her mouth had the crooked, bright red shape of a clown's. She smoked a whole package of Chesterfields, constantly wiping the ashes off her dark blue skirt with a hand towel soaked in dry-cleaning fluid; then she drank herself unconscious.

It was hot that night, and dry lightning leaped from the horizon to the top of the blue-black vault of sky over the Gulf. Weldon sat on the side of his bed in the dark, his shoulders hunched, his fists between his white thighs. His burr haircut looked like duck down on his head in the flicker of lightning through the window. When I was almost asleep he shook both me and Lyle awake and said, "We got to get rid of her. You know we got to do it."

I put my pillow over my head and rolled away from him, as though I could drop away into sleep and rise in the morning into a sun-spangled and different world.

But in the false dawn I woke to both Lyle's and Weldon's faces close to mine. Weldon's eyes were hollow, his breath rank with funk. The mist was heavy and wet in the pecan trees outside the window.

"She's not gonna hurt Drew again. Are you gonna help or not?" Weldon said.

I followed them into the hallway, my heart sinking at the realization of what I was willing to participate in, my body as numb as if I had been stunned with Novocaine. Mattie was sleeping in the stuffed chair, her hose rolled down over her knees, an overturned jelly glass on the rug next to the can of spot cleaner.

Weldon walked quietly across the rug, unscrewed the cap on the can, laid the can on its side in front of Mattie's feet, then backed away from her. The cleaning fluid spread in a dark circle around her chair, the odor as bright and sharp as a slap across the face.

Weldon slid open a box of kitchen matches and we each took one, raked it across the striker, and, with the sense that our lives at that moment had changed forever, threw them at Mattie's feet. But the burning matches fell outside the wet area. The blood veins in my head dilated with fear, my ears hummed with a sound like the roar of the ocean in a seashell, and I jerked the box from Weldon's hand, clutched a half-dozen matches in my fist, dragged them across the striker, and flung them right on Mattie's feet.

The chair was enveloped in a cone of flame, and she burst out of it with her arms extended, as though she were pushing blindly through a curtain, her mouth and eyes wide with terror. We could smell her hair burning as she raced past us and crashed through the screen door out onto the gallery and into the yard. She beat at her flaming clothes and raked at her hair as though it were swarming with yellow jackets.

I stood transfixed in mortal dread at what I had done.

A Negro man walking to work came out of the mist on the road and knocked her to the ground, slapping the fire out of her dress, pinning her under his spread knees as though he were assaulting her. Smoke rose from her scorched clothes and hair as in a depiction of a damned figure on one of my holy cards.

The Negro rose to his feet and walked toward the gallery, a solitary line of blood running down his cheek where Mattie had scratched him.

"Yo' mama ain't hurt bad. Get some butter or some bacon grease. She gonna be all right, you gonna see. You children don't be worried, no," he said. His gums were purple with snuff when he smiled.

The volunteer firemen bounced across the cattle guard in an old fire truck whose obsolete hand-crank starter still dangled from under the radiator. They coated Mattie's room with foam from a fire extinguisher and packed Mattie off in an ambulance to the charity hospital in Lafayette. Two sheriff's deputies arrived, and before he left, one of the volunteers took them aside in the yard and talked with them, looking over his shoulder at us children, then walked over to us and said, "The fire chief gonna come out here and check it out. Y'all stay out of that bedroom."

His face was narrow and dark with shadow under the brim of his big rubber fireman's hat. I felt a fist squeeze my heart.

But suddenly Sister Roberta was in the midst of everything. Someone had carried word to the school about the fire, and she'd had one of the brothers drive her out to the house. She talked with the deputies, helped us fix cereal at the kitchen table, and made telephone calls to find a place for us to stay besides the welfare shelter. Then she looked in Mattie's bedroom door and studied the interior for what seemed a long time. When she came back in the kitchen, her eyes peeled the skin off our faces. I looked straight down into my cereal bowl.

She placed her small hand on my shoulder. I could feel her fingers tapping on the bone, as though she were processing her own thoughts. Then she said, "Well, what should we do here today? I think we should clean up first. Where's the broom?"

Without waiting for an answer she pulled the broom out of the closet and went to work in Mattie's room, sweeping the spilled and unstruck matches as well as the burned ones in a pile by a side door that gave onto the yard. The soot and blackened threads from the rug swirled up in a cloud around her veils and wings and smudged her starched wimple.

One of the deputies put his hand on the broomstick. "There ain't been an investigation yet. You can't do that till the fire chief come out and see, Sister," he said.

"You always talked like a fool, Gaspard," she said. "Now that you have a uniform, you talk like a bigger one. This house smells like an incinerator. Now get out of the way." With one sweep of the broom she raked all the matches out into the yard.

We were placed in foster homes, and over the years I lost contact with Sister Roberta. But later I went to work in the oil fields, and I think perhaps I talked with my father in a nightclub outside of Morgan City. An enormous live oak tree grew through the floor and roof, and he was leaning against the bar that had been built in a circle around the tree. His face was puckered with white scar tissue, his ears burned into stubs, his right hand atrophied and frozen against his chest like a broken bird's foot. But beyond the layers of mutilated skin I could see my father's face, like the image in a photographic negative held up against a light.

"Is your name Sonnier?" I asked.

He looked at me curiously.

"Maybe. You want to buy me a drink?" he said.

"Yeah, I can do that," I said.

He ordered a shot of Beam with a frosted schooner of Jax on the side.

"Are you Verise Sonnier from New Iberia?" I asked.

He grinned stiffly when he took the schooner of beer away from his mouth. "Why you want to know?" he said.

"I think I'm your son. I'm Billy Bob."

His turquoise eyes wandered over my face, then they lost interest.

"I had a son. But you ain't him. Buy me another shot?" he said.

"Why not?" I replied.

Sometimes he comes to me in my dreams, and I wonder if ironically all our stories were written on his skin back there in Texas City in 1947. Or maybe that's just a poetic illusion purchased by time. But even in the middle of an Indian summer's day, when the sugarcane is beaten with purple and gold light in the fields and the sun is both warm and cool on your skin at the same time, when I know that the earth is a fine place after all, I have to mourn just a moment for those people of years ago who lived lives they did not choose, who carried burdens that were not their own, whose invisible scars were as private as the scarlet beads of Sister Roberta's rosary wrapped across the back of her small hand, as bright as drops of blood ringed round the souls of little people.

1993

HARLAN ELLISON

MEFISTO IN ONYX

Harlan Ellison (1934–) was born in Cleveland, Ohio, and had various jobs, mostly blue collar, in all parts of the country before settling in New York to become a full-time writer. Within the next two years, he produced and sold more than one hundred stories and articles before being drafted into the Army. Soon after his discharge, he moved to Chicago to work as an editor at *Rogue* magazine and Regency Books. His prolific writing career continued when he moved to California to write for motion pictures (including the 1966 blockbuster *The Oscar*) and, mostly, for television. Ellison supplied scripts for many series, including *Burke's Law, The Flying Nun, Route 66, The Man from U.N.C.L.E., The Outer Limits,* and, most famously, *Star Trek*—his "The City on the Edge of Forever" is regarded as the best episode in the history of that series, named Best Original Teleplay by the Writers Guild of America; his "Demon with a Glass Hand," for *The Outer Limits,* and two other teleplays also won the award. He is among the most honored writers in America, especially among writers of speculative fiction, winning ten Hugos (World Science Fiction Society), including Grand Master; four Nebulas (Science Fiction and Fantasy Writers of America); five Bram Stoker Awards (Horror Writers Association), including lifetime achievement; and two Edgar Allan Poe Awards (Mystery Writers of America) for his memorable short stories "The Whimper of Whipped Dogs" and "Soft Monkey"; among many other genre and nongenre honors.

It is uncommon to find fantasy and supernatural elements mixed with crime fiction, but Ellison's work successfully bridges and encompasses those genres frequently, as with this novella. "Mefisto in Onyx" originally appeared in the October 1993 issue of *Omni* magazine; several minor emendations were made for its first publication in book form three months later by the California publisher Mark V. Ziesing. The text for this volume is taken from that publication.

■ ■ ■

Once. I only went to bed with her once. Friends for eleven years—before and since—but it was just one of those things, just one of those crazy flings: the two of us alone on a New Year's Eve, watching rented Marx Brothers videos so we wouldn't have to go out with a bunch of idiots and make noise and pretend we were having a good time when all we'd be doing was getting drunk, whooping like morons, vomiting on slow-moving strangers, and spending more money than we had to waste. And we drank a little too much cheap champagne; and we fell off the sofa laughing at Harpo a few times too many; and we wound up on the floor at the same time; and next thing we knew we had our faces plastered together, and my hand up her skirt, and her hand down in my pants . . .

But it was just the *once,* fer chrissakes! Talk about imposing on a cheap sexual liaison! She *knew* I went mixing in other people's minds only when I absolutely had no other way to make a buck. Or I forgot myself and did it in a moment of human weakness.

It was always foul.

Slip into the thoughts of the best person who ever lived, even Saint Thomas Aquinas, for instance, just to pick an absolutely terrific person you'd think had a mind so clean you could eat off it (to paraphrase my mother), and when you come out — take my word for it — you'd want to take a long, intense shower in Lysol.

Trust me on this: I go into somebody's landscape when there's *nothing else* I can do, no other possible solution . . . or I forget and do it in a moment of human weakness. Such as, say, the IRS holds my feet to the fire; or I'm about to get myself mugged and robbed and maybe murdered; or I need to find out if some specific she that I'm dating has been using somebody else's dirty needle or has been sleeping around without she's taking some extra-heavy-duty AIDS precautions; or a coworker's got it in his head to set me up so I make a mistake and look bad to the boss and I find myself in the unemployment line again; or . . .

I'm a wreck for weeks after.

Go jaunting through a landscape trying to pick up a little insider arbitrage bric-a-brac, and come away no better heeled, but all muddy with the guy's infidelities, and I can't look a decent woman in the eye for days. Get told by a motel desk clerk that they're all full up and he's sorry as hell but I'll just have to drive on for about another thirty miles to find the next vacancy, jaunt into his landscape and find him lit up with neon signs that got a lot of the word *nigger* in them, and I wind up hitting the son of a bitch so hard his grandmother has a bloody nose, and usually have to hide out for three or four weeks after. Just about to miss a bus, jaunt into the head of the driver to find his name so I can yell for him to hold it a minute Tom or George or Willie, and I get smacked in the mind with all the garlic he's been eating for the past month because his doctor told him it was good for his system, and I start to dry-heave, and I wrench out of the landscape, and not only have I missed the bus, but I'm so sick to my stomach I have to sit down on the filthy curb to get my gorge submerged. Jaunt into a potential employer, to see if he's trying to lowball me, and I learn he's part of a massive coverup of industrial malfeasance that's caused hundreds of people to die when this or that cheaply made grommet or tappet or gimbal mounting underperforms and fails, sending the poor souls falling thousands of feet to shrieking destruction. Then just *try* to accept the job, even if you haven't paid your rent in a month. No way.

Absolutely: I listen in on the landscape *only* when my feet are being fried; when the shadow stalking me turns down alley after alley tracking me relentlessly; when the drywall guy I've hired to repair the damage done by my leaky shower presents me with a dopey smile and a bill $360 higher than the estimate. Or in a moment of human weakness.

But I'm a wreck for weeks after. For weeks.

Because you can't, you simply can't, you absolutely *cannot* know what people are truly and really like till you jaunt their landscape. If Aquinas had had my ability, he'd have very quickly gone off to be a hermit, only occasionally visiting the mind of a sheep or a hedgehog. In a moment of human weakness.

That's why in my whole life—and; as best I can remember back, I've been doing it since I was five or six years old, maybe even younger—there have only been eleven, maybe twelve people, of all those who know that I can "read minds," that I've permitted myself to get close to. Three of them never used it against me, or tried to exploit me, or tried to kill me when I wasn't looking. Two of those three were my mother and father, a pair of sweet old black folks who'd adopted me, a late-in-life baby, and were now dead (but probably still worried about me, even on the Other Side), and whom I missed very very much, particularly in moments like this. The other eight, nine were either so turned off by the knowledge that they made sure I never came within a mile of them—one moved to another entire country just to be on the safe side, although her thoughts were a helluva lot more boring and innocent than she thought they were—or they tried to brain me with something heavy when I was distracted—I still have a shoulder separation that kills me for two days before it rains—or they tried to use me to make a buck for them. Not having the common sense to figure it out, that if I was *capable* of using the ability to make vast sums of money, why the hell was I living hand to mouth like some overaged grad student who was afraid to desert the university and go become an adult?

Now *they* was some dumb-ass muthuhfugguhs.

Of the three who never used it against me — my mom and dad — the last was Allison Roche. Who sat on the stool next to me, in the middle of May, in the middle of a Wednesday afternoon, in the middle of Clanton, Alabama, squeezing ketchup onto her All-American Burger, imposing on the memory of that one damned New Year's Eve sexual interlude, with Harpo and his sibs; the two of us all alone except for the fry cook; and she waited for my reply.

"I'd sooner have a skunk spray my pants leg," I replied.

She pulled a napkin from the chrome dispenser and swabbed up the red that had overshot the sesame-seed bun and redecorated the Formica countertop. She looked at me from under thick, lustrous eyelashes; a look of impatience and violet eyes that must have been a killer when she unbottled it at some truculent witness for the defense. Allison Roche was a chief deputy district attorney in and for Jefferson County, with her office in Birmingham, Alabama. Where near we sat, in Clanton, having a secret meeting, having All-American Burgers; three years after having had quite a bit of champagne, 1930s black-and-white video-rental comedy, and black-and-white sex. One extremely stupid New Year's Eve.

Friends for eleven years. And once, just once; as a prime example of what happens in a moment of human weakness. Which is not to say that it wasn't terrific, because it was; absolutely terrific; but we never did it again; and we never brought it up again after the next morning when we opened our eyes and looked at each other the way you look at an exploding can of sardines, and both of us said *Oh Jeezus* at the same time. Never brought it up again until this memorable afternoon at the greasy spoon where I'd joined Ally, driving up from Montgomery to meet her halfway, after her peculiar telephone invitation.

Can't say the fry cook, Mr. All-American, was particularly happy at the pigmentation arrangement at his counter. But I stayed out of his head and let him think what he wanted. Times change on the outside, but the inner landscape remains polluted.

"All I'm asking you to do is go have a chat with him," she said. She gave me that look. I have a hard time with that look. It isn't entirely honest, neither is it entirely disingenuous. It plays on my remembrance of that one night we spent in bed. And is just *dis*honest enough to play on the part of that night we spent on the floor, on the sofa, on the coffee counter between the dining room and the kitchenette, in the bathtub, and about nineteen minutes crammed among her endless pairs of shoes in a walk-in clothes closet that smelled strongly of cedar and virginity. She gave me that look, and wasted no part of the memory.

"I don't *want* to go have a chat with him. Apart from he's a piece of human shit and I have better things to do with my time than to go on down to Atmore and take a jaunt through this crazy son of a bitch's diseased mind, may I remind you that of the 160, 70 men who have died in that electric chair, including the original 'Yellow Mama' they scrapped in 1990, about 130 of them were gentlemen of color, and I do not mean you to picture any color of a shade much lighter than that cuppa coffee you got sittin' by your left hand right this minute, which is to say that I, being an inordinately well-educated African American who values the full measure of living negritude in his body, am not crazy enough to want to visit a racist '*co*-rectional center' like Holman Prison, thank you very much."

"Are you finished?" she asked, wiping her mouth.

"Yeah. I'm finished. Case closed. Find somebody else."

She didn't like that. "There *isn't* anybody else."

"There has to be. Somewhere. Go check the research files at Duke University. Call the Fortean Society. Mensa. *Jeopardy.* Some 900-number astrology psychic hotline. Ain't there some semi-senile senator with a full-time paid assistant who's been trying to get legislation through one of the statehouses for the last five years to fund this kind of bullshit research? What about the Russians . . . now that the Evil Empire's fallen, you ought to be able to get some word about their success with Kirlian auras or whatever those assholes were working at. Or you could —"

She screamed at the top of her lungs. *"Stop it, Rudy!"*

The fry cook dropped the spatula he'd been using to scrape off the grill. He picked it up, looking at us, and his face (I didn't read his mind) said *If that white bitch makes one more noise I'm callin' the cops.*

I gave him a look he didn't want, and he went back to his chores, getting ready for the after-work crowd. But the stretch of his back and angle of his head told me he wasn't going to let this pass.

I leaned in toward her, got as serious as I could, and just this quietly, just this softly, I said, "Ally, good pal, listen to me. You've been one of the few friends I could count on, for a long time now. We have history between us, and you've *never,* not once, made me feel like a freak. So OK, I trust you. I trust you with something about me that causes immeasurable goddamn pain. A thing about me that could get me killed. You've never betrayed me, and you've never tried to use me.

"Till now. This is the first time. And you've got to admit that it's not even as rational as you maybe saying to me that you've gambled away every cent you've got and you owe the mob a million bucks and would I mind taking a trip to Vegas or Atlantic City and taking a jaunt into the minds of some high-pocket poker players so I could win you enough to keep the goons from shooting you. Even *that,* as creepy as it would be if you said it to me, even *that* would be easier to understand than *this!*"

She looked forlorn. "There isn't anybody else, Rudy. *Please.*"

"What the hell is this all about? Come on, tell me. You're hiding something, or holding something back, or lying about —"

"I'm not lying!" For the second time she was suddenly, totally, extremely pissed at me. Her voice spattered off the white tile walls. The fry cook spun around at the sound, took a step toward us, and I jaunted into his landscape, smoothed down the rippled AstroTurf, drained away the storm clouds, and suggested in there that he go take a cigarette break out back. Fortunately, there were no other patrons at the elegant All-American Burger that late in the afternoon, and he went.

"Calm fer chrissakes down, will you?" I said.

She had squeezed the paper napkin into a ball.

She was lying, hiding, holding something back. Didn't have to be a telepath to figure *that* out. I waited, looking at her with a slow, careful distrust, and finally she sighed, and I thought, *Here it comes.*

"Are you reading my mind?" she asked.

"Don't insult me. We know each other too long."

She looked chagrined. The violet of her eyes deepened. "Sorry."

But she didn't go on. I wasn't going to be outflanked. I waited.

After a while she said, softly, very softly, "I think I'm in love with him. I *know* I believe him when he says he's innocent."

I never expected that. I couldn't even reply.

It was unbelievable. Unfuckingbelievable. She was the chief deputy DA who had prosecuted Henry Lake Spanning for murder. Not just one murder, one random slaying, a heat-of-the-moment Saturday-night killing regretted deeply on Sunday morning but punishable by electrocution in the Sovereign State of Alabama nonetheless, but a string of the vilest, most sickening serial slaughters in Alabama history, in the history of the Glorious South, in the history of the United States. Maybe even in the history of the entire wretched human universe that went wading hip-deep in the wasted spilled blood of innocent men, women, and children.

Henry Lake Spanning was a monster, an ambulatory disease, a killing machine without conscience or any discernible resemblance to a thing we might call decently human. Henry Lake Spanning had butchered his way across a half-dozen states; and they had caught up to him in Huntsville, in a garbage Dumpster behind a supermarket, doing something so vile and inhuman to what was left of a sixty-five-year-old cleaning woman that not even the tabloids would get more explicit than *unspeakable;* and somehow he got away from the cops; and somehow he evaded their dragnet; and somehow he found out where the police lieutenant in charge of the manhunt lived; and somehow he slipped into that neighborhood when the lieutenant was out creating roadblocks — and he gutted the man's wife and two kids. Also the family cat. And then he killed a couple of more times in Birmingham and Decatur, and by then had gone so completely out of his mind that they got him again, and the second time they hung on to him, and they brought him to trial. And Ally had prosecuted this bottom-feeding monstrosity.

And oh, what a circus it had been. Though he'd been *caught,* the second time, and this time for keeps, in Jefferson County, scene of three of his most sickening jobs, he'd murdered (with such a disgustingly similar MO that it was obvious he was the perp) in twenty-two of the sixty-seven counties; and every last one of them wanted him to stand trial in that venue. Then there were the other five states in which he had butchered, to a total body count of fifty-six. Each of *them* wanted him extradited.

So, here's how smart and quick and smooth an attorney Ally is: she somehow managed to coze up to the attorney general, and somehow managed to unleash those violet eyes on him, and somehow managed to get and keep his ear long enough to con him into setting a legal precedent. Attorney General of the State of Alabama allowed Allison Roche to consolidate, to secure a multiple bill of indictment that forced Spanning to stand trial on all twenty-nine Alabama murder counts at once. She meticulously documented to the state's highest courts that Henry Lake Spanning presented such a clear and present danger to society that the prosecution was willing to take a chance (big chance!) of trying in a winner-take-all consolidation of venues. Then she managed to smooth the feathers of all those other vote-hungry prosecutors in those twenty-one other counties, and she put on a case that dazzled everyone, including Spanning's defense attorney, who had screamed about the legality of the multiple bill from the moment she'd suggested it.

And she won a fast jury verdict on all twenty-nine counts. Then she got *really* fancy in the penalty phase after the jury verdict, and proved up the *other* twenty-seven murders with their flagrantly identical trademarks, from those other five states, and there was nothing left but to sentence Spanning — essentially for all fifty-six — to the replacement for the "Yellow Mama."

Even as pols and power brokers throughout the state were murmuring Ally's name for higher office, Spanning was slated to sit in that new electric chair in Holman Prison, built by the Fred A. Leuchter Associates of Boston, Massachusetts, that delivers 2,640 volts of pure sparklin' death in $^{1}/_{240}$th of a second, six times faster than the $^{1}/_{40}$th of a second that it takes for the brain to sense it, which is — if you ask me — much too humane an exit line, more than three times the 700-volt-jolt lethal dose that destroys a brain, for a pus-bag like Henry Lake Spanning.

But if we were lucky — and the scheduled day of departure was very nearly upon us — if we were lucky, if there was a God and Justice and Natural Order and all that good stuff, then Henry Lake Spanning, this foulness, this corruption, this thing that lived only to ruin . . . would end up as a pile of fucking ashes somebody might use to sprinkle over a flower garden, thereby providing this ghoul with his single opportunity to be of some use to the human race.

That was the guy that my pal Allison Roche wanted me to go and "chat" with, down to Holman Prison, in Atmore, Alabama. There, sitting on death row, waiting to get his demented head tonsured, his pants legs slit, his tongue fried black as the inside of a sheep's belly . . . down there at Holman my pal Allison wanted me to go "chat" with one of the most awful creatures made for killing this side of a hammerhead shark, which creature had an infinitely greater measure of human decency than Henry Lake Spanning had ever demonstrated. Go chitchat, and enter his landscape, and read his mind, Mr. Telepath, and use the marvelous mythic power of extrasensory perception: this nifty swell ability that has made me a bum all my life, well, not *exactly* a bum: I do have a decent apartment, and I do earn a decent, if sporadic, living; and I try to follow Nelson Algren's warning never to get involved with a woman whose troubles are bigger than my own; and sometimes I even have a car of my own, even though at that moment such was not the case, the Camaro having been repo'd, and not by Harry Dean Stanton or Emilio Estevez, lemme tell you; but a bum in the sense of — how does Ally put it? — oh yeah — I don't "realize my full and forceful potential" — a bum in the sense that I can't hold a job, and I get rotten breaks, and all of this despite a Rhodes scholarly education so far above what a poor nigrahlad such as myself could expect that even Rhodes hisownself would've been chest-out proud as hell of me. A bum, mostly, despite an *outstanding* Rhodes Scholar education and a pair of kind, smart, loving parents—even for foster parents—shit, *especially* for being foster parents—who died knowing the certain sadness that their only child would spend his life as a wandering freak unable to make a comfortable living or consummate a normal marriage or raise children without the fear of passing on this special personal horror . . . this astonishing ability fabled in song and story that I possess . . . that no one else seems to possess, though I know there must have been others, somewhere, sometime, somehow! Go, Mr. Wonder of Wonders, shining black Cagliostro of the modern world, go with this super nifty swell ability that gullible idiots and flying-saucer assholes have been trying to prove exists for at least fifty years, that no one has been able to isolate the way I, me, the only one has been isolated, let me tell you about *isolation,* my brothers; and here I was, here was I, Rudy Pairis . . . just a guy, making a buck every now and then with nifty swell impossible ESP, resident of thirteen states and twice that many cities so far in his mere thirty years of landscape-jaunting life, here was I, Rudy Pairis, Mr. I-Can-Read-Your-Mind, being asked to go and walk through the mind of a killer who scared half the people in the world. Being asked by the only living person, probably, to whom I could not say no. And, oh, take me at my word here: I *wanted* to say no. *Was,* in fact, saying no at every breath. What's that? Will I do it? Sure, yeah sure, I'll go on down to Holman and jaunt through this sick bastard's mind landscape. Sure I will. You got two chances: slim, and none.

All of this was going on in the space of one greasy double cheeseburger and two cups of coffee.

The worst part of it was that Ally had somehow gotten involved with him. *Ally!* Not some bimbo bitch . . . but *Ally.* I couldn't believe it.

Not that it was unusual for women to become mixed up with guys in the joint, to fall under their "magic spell" and to start corresponding with them, visiting them, taking them candy and cigarettes, having conjugal visits, playing mule for them and smuggling in dope where the tampon never shine, writing them letters that got steadily more exotic, steadily more intimate, steamier and increasingly dependent emotionally. It wasn't that big a deal; there exist entire psychiatric treatises on the phenomenon; right alongside the papers about women who go stud-crazy for cops. No big deal indeed: hundreds of women every year find themselves writing to these guys, visiting these guys, building dream castles with these guys, fucking these guys, pretending that even the worst of these guys, rapists and woman-beaters and child molesters, repeat pedophiles of the lowest pustule sort, and murderers and stickup punks who crush old ladies' skulls for food stamps, and terrorists and bunco barons . . . that one sunny might-be, gonna-happen pink cloud day these demented creeps will emerge from behind the walls, get back in the wind, become upstanding nine-to-five Brooks Bros. Galahads. Every year hundreds of women marry these guys, finding themselves in a hot second snookered by the wily, duplicitous, motherfuckin' lying greaseball addictive behavior of guys who had spent their sporadic years, their intermittent freedom on the outside, doing *just that:* roping people in, ripping people off, bleeding people dry, conning them into being tools, taking them for their every last cent, their happy home, their sanity, their ability to trust or love ever again.

But this wasn't some poor illiterate naive woman-child. This was *Ally.* She had damned near pulled off a legal impossibility, come *that* close to Bizarro Jurisprudence by putting the attorneys general of five other states in a maybe frame of mind where she'd have been able to consolidate a multiple bill of indictment *across state lines!* Never been done; and now, probably, never ever would be. But she could have possibly pulled off such a thing. Unless you're a stone court-bird, you can't know what a mountaintop that is!

So, now, here's Ally, saying this shit to me. Ally, my best pal, stood up for me a hundred times; not some dip, but the steely-eyed Sheriff of Suicide Gulch, the over-forty, past-the-age-of-innocence, no-nonsense woman who had seen it all and come away tough but not cynical, hard but not mean.

"I think I'm in love with him." She had said.

"I *know* I believe him when he says he's innocent." She had said.

I looked at her. No time had passed. It was still the moment the universe decided to lie down and die. And I said, "So if you're certain this paragon of the virtues *isn't* responsible for fifty-six murders — that we *know* about — and who the hell knows how many more we *don't* know about, since he's apparently been at it since he was twelve years old — remember the couple of nights we sat up and you *told* me all this shit about him, and you said it with your skin crawling, *remember?* — then if you're so damned positive the guy you spent eleven weeks in court sending to the chair is innocent of butchering half the population of the planet — then why do you need me to go to Holman, drive all the way to Atmore, just to take a jaunt in this sweet peach of a guy?

"Doesn't your 'woman's intuition' tell you he's squeaky clean? Don't 'true love' walk yo' sweet young ass down the primrose path with sufficient surefootedness?"

"Don't be a smartass!" she said.

"Say again?" I replied, with disfuckingbelief.

"I said: don't be such a high-verbal goddamned smart aleck!"

Now *I* was steamed. "No, I shouldn't be a smartass: I should be your pony, your show dog, your little trick bag mind-reader freak! Take a drive over to Holman, Pairis; go right on into Rednecks from Hell; sit your ass down on death row with the rest of the niggers and have a chat with the one white boy who's been in a cell up there for the past three years or so; sit down nicely with the king of the fucking vampires, and slide inside his garbage dump of a brain—and what a joy *that's* gonna be, I can't believe you'd ask me to do this—and read whatever piece of boiled shit in there he calls a brain, and see if he's jerking you around. *That's* what I ought to do, am I correct? Instead of being a smartass. Have I got it right? Do I properly pierce your meaning, pal?"

She stood up. She didn't even say *Screw you, Pairis!*

She just slapped me as hard as she could.

She hit me a good one straight across the mouth.

I felt my upper teeth bite my lower lip. I tasted the blood. My head rang like a church bell. I thought I'd fall off the goddamn stool.

When I could focus, she was just standing there, looking ashamed of herself, and disappointed, and mad as hell, and worried that she'd brained me. All of that, all at the same time. Plus, she looked as if I'd broken her choo-choo train.

"OK," I said wearily, and ended the word with a sigh that reached all the way back into my hip pocket. "OK, calm down. I'll see him. I'll do it. Take it easy."

She didn't sit down. "Did I hurt you?"

"No, of course not," I said, unable to form the smile I was trying to put on my face. "How could you possibly hurt someone by knocking his brains into his lap?"

She stood over me as I clung precariously to the counter, turned halfway around on the stool by the blow. Stood over me, the balled-up paper napkin in her fist, a look on her face that said she was nobody's fool, that we'd known each other a long time, that she hadn't asked this kind of favor before, that if we were buddies and I loved her, that I would see she was in deep pain, that she was conflicted, that she needed to know, *really* needed to know without a doubt, and in the name of God—in which she believed, though I didn't, but either way what the hell—that I do this thing for her, that I just *do it* and not give her any more crap about it.

So I shrugged, and spread my hands like a man with no place to go, and I said, "How'd you get into this?"

She told me the first fifteen minutes of her tragic, heartwarming, never-to-be-ridiculed story still standing. After fifteen minutes I said, "Fer chrissakes, Ally, at least *sit down!* You look like a damned fool standing there with a greasy napkin in your mitt."

A couple of teenagers had come in. The four-star chef had finished his cigarette out back and was reassuringly in place, walking the duckboards and dishing up All-American arterial cloggage.

She picked up her elegant attaché case and, without a word, with only a nod that said let's get as far from them as we can, she and I moved to a double against the window to resume our discussion of the varieties of social suicide available to an unwary and foolhardy gentleman of the colored persuasion if he allowed himself to be swayed by a cagey and cogent, clever and concupiscent female of another color entirely.

See, what it is, is this:

Look at that attaché case. You want to know what kind of an Ally this Allison Roche is? Pay heed, now.

In New York, when some wannabe junior ad exec has smooched enough butt to get tossed a bone account, and he wants to walk his colors, has a need to signify, has got to demonstrate to everyone that he's got the juice, first thing he does, he hies his ass downtown to Barney's, West Seventeenth and Seventh, buys hisself a Burberry, loops the belt casually *behind,* leaving the coat open to suh*wing,* and he circumnavigates the office.

In Dallas, when the wife of the CEO has those six or eight upper-management husbands and wives over for an *intime, faux*-casual dinner, sans place cards, sans *entrée* fork, *sans cérémonie,* and we're talking the kind of woman who flies Virgin Air instead of the Concorde, she's so in charge she don't got to use the Orrefors, she can put out the Kosta Boda and say *give a fuck.*

What it is, kind of person so in charge, so easy with they own self, they don't *have* to laugh at your poor dumb struttin' Armani suit, or your bedroom done in Laura Ashley, or that you got a gig writing articles for *TV Guide.* You see what I'm sayin' here? The sort of person Ally Roche is, you take a look at that attaché case, and it'll tell you everything you need to know about how strong she is, because it's an Atlas. Not a Hartmann. Understand: she could *afford* a Hartmann, that gorgeous imported Canadian belting leather, top of the line, somewhere around 950 bucks maybe, equivalent of Orrefors, a Burberry, breast of guinea hen and Mouton Rothschild 1492 or 1066 or whatever year is the most expensive, drive a Rolls instead of a Bentley and the only difference is the grille . . . but she doesn't *need* to signify, doesn't *need* to suh*wing*, so she gets herself this Atlas. Not some dumb chickenshit Louis Vuitton or Mark Cross all the divorcée real estate ladies carry, but an Atlas. Irish hand leather. Custom-tanned cowhide. Hand-tanned in Ireland by out-of-work IRA bombers. Very classy. Just a state understated. See that attaché case? That tell you why I said I'd do it?

She picked it up from where she'd stashed it, right up against the counter wall by her feet, and we went to the double over by the window, away from the chef and the teenagers, and she stared at me till she was sure I was in a right frame of mind, and she picked up where she'd left off.

The next twenty-three minutes by the big greasy clock on the wall she related from a sitting position. Actually, a series of sitting positions. She kept shifting in her chair like someone who didn't appreciate the view of the world from that window, someone hoping for a sweeter horizon. The story started with a gang rape at the age of thirteen and moved right along: two broken foster-home families, a little casual fondling by surrogate papas, intense studying for perfect school grades as a substitute for happiness, working her way through John Jay College of Law, a truncated attempt at wedded bliss in her late twenties, and the long miserable road of legal success that had brought her to Alabama. There could have been worse places.

I'd known Ally for a long time, and we'd spent totals of weeks and months in each other's company. Not to mention the New Year's Eve of the Marx Brothers. But I hadn't heard much of this. Not much at all.

Funny how that goes. Eleven years. You'd think I'd've guessed or suspected or *some*thing. What the hell makes us think we're friends with *any*body, when we don't know the first thing about them, not really?

What are we, walking around in a dream? That is to say: what the fuck are we *thinking!?!*

And there might never have been a reason to hear *any* of it, all this Ally that was the real Ally, but now she was asking me to go somewhere I didn't want to go, to do something that scared the shit out of me; and she wanted me to be as fully informed as possible.

It dawned on me that those same eleven years between us hadn't really given her a full, laser-clean insight into the why and wherefore of

Rudy Pairis, either. I hated myself for it. The concealing, the holding back, the giving up only fragments, the evil misuse of charm when honesty would have hurt. I was facile, and a very quick study; and I had buried all the equivalents to Ally's pains and travails. I could've matched her, in spades; or blacks, or just plain nigras. But I remained frightened of losing her friendship. I've never been able to believe in the myth of unqualified friendship. Too much like standing hip-high in a fast-running, freezing river. Standing on slippery stones.

Her story came forward to the point at which she had prosecuted Spanning; had amassed and winnowed and categorized the evidence so thoroughly, so deliberately, so flawlessly; had orchestrated the case so brilliantly; that the jury had come in with guilty on all twenty-nine, soon — in the penalty phase — fifty-six. Murder in the first. Premeditated murder in the first. Premeditated murder with special ugly circumstances in the first. On each and every of the twenty-nine. Less than an hour it took them. There wasn't even time for a lunch break. Fifty-one minutes it took them to come back with the verdict guilty on all charges. Less than a minute per killing. Ally had done that.

His attorney had argued that no direct link had been established between the fifty-sixth killing (actually, only his twenty-ninth in Alabama) and Henry Lake Spanning. No, they had not caught him down on his knees eviscerating the shredded body of his final victim — ten-year-old Gunilla Ascher, a parochial-school girl who had missed her bus and been picked up by Spanning just about a mile from her home in Decatur — no, not down on his knees with the can opener still in his sticky red hands, but the MO was the same, and he was there in Decatur, on the run from what he had done in Huntsville, what they had *caught* him doing in Huntsville, in that Dumpster, to that old woman. So they *couldn't* place him with his smooth, slim hands inside dead Gunilla Ascher's still-steaming body. So what? They could not have been surer he was the serial killer, the monster, the ravaging nightmare whose methods were so vile the newspapers hadn't even *tried* to cobble up some smart-aleck name for him like the Strangler or the Backyard Butcher. The jury had come back in fifty-one minutes, looking sick, looking as if they'd try and try to get everything they'd seen and heard out of their minds, but knew they never would, and wishing to God they could've managed to get out of their civic duty on this one.

They came shuffling back in and told the numbed court: hey, put this slimy excuse for a maggot in the chair and cook his ass till he's fit only to be served for breakfast on cinnamon toast. This was the guy my friend

Ally told me she had fallen in love with. The guy she now believed to be innocent.

This was seriously crazy stuff.

"So how did you get, er, uh, how did you . . . ?"

"How did I fall in love with him?"

"Yeah. That."

She closed her eyes for a moment, and pursed her lips as if she had lost a flock of wayward words and didn't know where to find them. I'd always known she was a private person, kept the really important history to herself—hell, until now I'd never known about the rape, the ice mountain between her mother and father, the specifics of the seven-month marriage—I'd known there'd been a husband briefly; but not what had happened; and I'd known about the foster homes; but again, not how lousy it had been for her—even so, getting *this* slice of steaming craziness out of her was like using your teeth to pry the spikes out of Jesus's wrists.

Finally, she said, "I took over the case when Charlie Whilborg had his stroke . . ."

"I remember."

"He was the best litigator in the office, and if he hadn't gone down two days before they caught"—she paused, had trouble with the name, went on,—"before they caught Spanning in Decatur, and if Morgan County hadn't been so worried about a case this size, and bound Spanning over to us in Birmingham . . . all of it so fast nobody really had a chance to talk to him . . . I was the first one even got *near* him, everyone was so damned scared of him, of what they *thought* he was . . ."

"Hallucinating, were they?" I said, being a smartass.

"Shut up.

"The office did most of the donkeywork after that first interview I had with him. It was a big break for me in the office; and I got obsessed by it. So after the first interview, I never spent much actual time with Spanky, never got too close, to see what kind of a man he *really* . . ."

I said: "Spanky? Who the hell's 'Spanky'?"

She blushed. It started from the sides of her nostrils and went out both ways toward her ears, then climbed to the hairline. I'd seen that happen only a couple of times in eleven years, and one of those times had been when she'd farted at the opera. *Lucia di Lammermoor.*

I said it again: "Spanky? You're putting me on, right? You call him *Spanky?*" The blush deepened. "Like the fat kid in *The Little Rascals* . . . c'mon, I don't fuckin' *believe* this!"

She just glared at me.

I felt the laughter coming.

My face started twitching.

She stood up again. "Forget it. Just forget it, OK?" She took two steps away from the table, toward the street exit. I grabbed her hand and pulled her back, trying not to fall apart with laughter, and I said, "OK OK OK . . . I'm *sorry* . . . I'm really and truly, honest to goodness, may I be struck by a falling space lab no kidding 100 percent absolutely sorry . . . but you gotta admit . . . catching me unawares like that . . . I mean, come *on,* Ally . . . *Spanky!?!* You call this guy who murdered at least fifty-six people Spanky? Why not Mickey, or Froggy, or Alfalfa . . . ? I can understand not calling him Buckwheat, you can save that one for me, but *Spanky???*"

And in a moment *her* face started to twitch; and in another moment she was starting to smile, fighting it every micron of the way; and in another moment she was laughing and swatting at me with her free hand; and then she pulled her hand loose and stood there falling apart with laughter; and in about a minute she was sitting down again. She threw the balled-up napkin at me.

"It's from when he was a kid," she said. "He was a fat kid, and they made fun of him. You know the way kids are . . . they corrupted Spanning into 'Spanky' because *The Little Rascals* was on television and . . . oh, shut *up,* Rudy!"

I finally quieted down, and made conciliatory gestures.

She watched me with an exasperated wariness till she was sure I wasn't going to run any more dumb gags on her, and then she resumed. "After Judge Fay sentenced him, I handled Spa . . . *Henry's* case from our office, all the way up to the appeals stage. I was the one who did the pleading against clemency when Henry's lawyers took their appeal to the Eleventh Circuit in Atlanta.

"When he was denied a stay by the appellate, three to nothing, I helped prepare the brief when Henry's counsel went to the Alabama Supreme Court; then when the Supreme Court refused to hear his appeal, I thought it was all over. I knew they'd run out of moves for him, except maybe the governor; but that wasn't ever going to happen. So I thought *that's that.*

"When the Supreme Court wouldn't hear it three weeks ago, I got a letter from him. He'd been set for execution next Saturday, and I couldn't figure out why he wanted to see *me.*"

I asked, "The letter . . . it got to you how?"

"One of his attorneys."

"I thought they'd given up on him."

"So did I. The evidence was so overwhelming; half a dozen counselors found ways to get themselves excused; it wasn't the kind of case that would bring any litigator good publicity. Just the number of eyewitnesses in the parking lot of that Winn-Dixie in Huntsville . . . must have been fifty of them, Rudy. And they all saw the same thing, and they all identified Henry in lineup after lineup, twenty, thirty, could have been fifty of them if we'd needed that long a parade. And all the rest of it . . ."

I held up a hand. *I know,* the flat hand against the air said. She had told me all of this. Every grisly detail, till I wanted to puke. It was as if I'd done it all myself, she was so vivid in her telling. Made my jaunting nausea pleasurable by comparison. Made me so sick I couldn't even think about it. Not even in a moment of human weakness.

"So the letter comes to you from the attorney . . ."

"I think you know this lawyer. Larry Borlan; used to be with the ACLU; before that he was senior counsel for the Alabama Legislature down to Montgomery; stood up, what was it, twice, three times, before the Supreme Court? Excellent guy. And not easily fooled."

"And what's *he* think about all this?"

"He thinks Henry's absolutely innocent."

"Of all of it?"

"Of everything."

"But there were fifty disinterested random eyewitnesses at one of those slaughters. Fifty, you just said it. Fifty, you could've had a parade. All of them nailed him cold, without a doubt. Same kind of kill as all the other fifty-five, including that schoolkid in Decatur when they finally got him. And Larry Borlan thinks he's not the guy, right?"

She nodded. Made one of those sort of comic pursings of the lips, shrugged, and nodded. "Not the guy."

"So the killer's still out there?"

"That's what Borlan thinks."

"And what do *you* think?"

"I agree with him."

"Oh Jeezus, Ally, my aching boots and saddle! You got to be workin' some kind of off-time! The killer is still out here in the mix, but there hasn't been a killing like those Spanning slaughters for the three years that he's been in the joint. Now *what* do that say to you?"

"It says whoever the guy *is,* the one who killed all those people, he's *days* smarter than all the rest of us, and he set up the perfect freefloater to take the fall for him, and he's either long far gone in some other state, working his way, or he's sitting quietly right here in Alabama, waiting and watching. And smiling." Her face seemed to sag with misery. She started to tear up, and said, "In four days he can stop smiling."

Saturday night.

"OK, take it easy. Go on, tell me the rest of it. Borlan comes to you, and he begs you to read Spanning's letter and . . . ?"

"He didn't beg. He just gave me the letter, told me he had no idea what Henry had written, but he said he'd known me a long time, that he thought I was a decent, fair-minded person, and he'd appreciate it in the name of our friendship if I'd read it."

"So you read it."

"I read it."

"Friendship. Sounds like you an' him was *good* friends. Like maybe you and I were good friends?"

She looked at me with astonishment.

I think *I* looked at me with astonishment.

"Where the hell did *that* come from?" I said.

"Yeah, really," she said, right back at me, "where the hell *did* that come from?" My ears were hot, and I almost started to say something about how if it was OK for *her* to use our Marx Brothers indiscretion for a lever, why wasn't it OK for me to get cranky about it? But I kept my mouth shut; and for once knew enough to move along. "Must've been *some* letter," I said.

There was a long moment of silence during which she weighed the degree of shit she'd put me through for my stupid remark, after all this was settled; and having struck a balance in her head, she told me about the letter.

It was perfect. It was the only sort of come-on that could lure the avenger who'd put you in the chair to pay attention. The letter had said that fifty-six was not the magic number of death. That there were many, *many* more unsolved cases, in many, *many* different states; lost children, runaways, unexplained disappearances, old people, college students hitchhiking to Sarasota for spring break, shopkeepers who'd carried their day's take to the night deposit drawer and never gone home for dinner, hookers left in pieces in Hefty bags all over town, and death death death unnumbered and unnamed. Fifty-six, the letter had said, was just the start. And if she, her, no one else, Allison Roche, my pal Ally, would come on down to Holman, and talk to him, Henry Lake Spanning would help her close all those open files. National rep. Avenger of the unsolved. Big-time mysteries revealed. "So you read the letter, and you went . . ."

"Not at first. Not immediately. I was sure he was guilty, and I was pretty certain at that moment, three years and more, dealing with the case, I was pretty sure if he said he could fill in all the blank spaces, that he could do it. But I just didn't like the idea. In court, I was always twitchy when I got near him at the defense table. His eyes, he never took them off me. They're blue, Rudy, did I tell you that . . . ?"

"Maybe. I don't remember. Go on."

"Bluest blue you've ever seen . . . well, to tell the truth, he just plain *scared* me. I wanted to win that case so badly, Rudy, you can never know . . . not just for me or the career or for the idea of justice or to avenge all those people he'd killed, but just the thought of him out there on the street, with those blue eyes, so blue, never stopped looking at me from the moment the trial began . . . the *thought* of him on the loose drove me to whip that case like a howling dog. I *had* to put him away!"

"But you overcame your fear."

She didn't like the edge of ridicule on the blade of that remark. "That's right. I finally 'overcame my fear' and I agreed to go see him."

"And you saw him."

"Yes."

"And he didn't know shit about no other killings, right?"

"Yes."

"But he talked a good talk. And his eyes was blue, so blue."

"Yes, you asshole."

I chuckled. Everybody is somebody's fool.

"Now let me ask you this — very carefully — so you don't hit me again: the moment you discovered he'd been shuckin' you, lyin', that he *didn't* have this long, unsolved crime roster to tick off, why didn't you get up, load your attaché case, and hit the bricks?"

Her answer was simple. "He begged me to stay awhile."

"That's it? He *begged* you?"

"Rudy, he has no one. He's *never* had anyone." She looked at me as if I were made of stone, some basalt thing, an onyx statue, a figure carved out of melanite, soot and ashes fused into a monolith. She feared she could not, in no way, no matter how piteously or bravely she phrased it, penetrate my rocky surface.

Then she said a thing that I never wanted to hear.

"Rudy . . ."

Then she said a thing I could never have imagined she'd say. Never in a million years.

"Rudy . . ."

Then she said the most awful thing she could say to me, even more awful than that she was in love with a serial killer.

"Rudy . . . go inside . . . read my mind . . . I need you to know, I need you to understand . . . Rudy . . ."

The look on her face killed my heart.

I tried to say no, oh God no, not that, please, no, not that, don't ask me to do that, please *please.* I don't want to go inside, we mean so much to each other, I don't *want* to know your landscape. Don't make me feel filthy, I'm no peeping-tom, I've *never* spied on you, never stolen a look when you were coming out of the shower, or undressing, or when you were being sexy . . . I never invaded your privacy, I wouldn't *do* a thing like that . . . we're friends, I don't need to know it all, I don't *want* to go in there. I can go inside anyone, and it's always awful . . . please don't make me see things in there I might not like, you're my friend, please don't steal that from me . . .

"Rudy, *please.* Do it."

Oh JeezusJeezusJeezus, again, she said it again!

We sat there. And we sat there. And we sat there longer. I said, hoarsely, in fear, "Can't you just . . . just *tell* me?"

Her eyes looked at stone. A man of stone. And she tempted me to do what I could do casually, tempted me the way Faust was tempted by Mefisto, Mephistopheles, Mefistofele, Mephostopilis. Black rock Dr. Faustus, possessor of magical mind-reading powers, tempted by thick, lustrous eyelashes and violet eyes and a break in the voice and an imploring movement of hand to face and a tilt of the head that was pitiable and the begging word *please* and all the guilt that lay between us that was mine alone. The seven chief demons. Of whom Mefisto was the one "not loving the light."

I knew it was the end of our friendship. But she left me nowhere to run. Mefisto in onyx.

So I jaunted into her landscape.

I stayed in there less than ten seconds. I didn't want to know everything I could know; and I definitely wanted to know *nothing* about how she really thought of me. I couldn't have borne seeing a caricature of a bug-eyed, shuffling, thick-lipped darkie in there. Mandingo man. Steppin Porchmonkey Rudy Pair . . .

Oh God, what was I thinking!

Nothing in there like that. Nothing! Ally wouldn't *have* anything like that in there. I was going nuts, going absolutely fucking crazy, in there, back out in less than ten seconds. I want to block it, kill it, void it, waste it, empty it, reject it, squeeze it, darken it, obscure it, wipe it, do away with it like it never happened. Like the moment you walk in on your mama and papa and catch them fucking, and you want never to have known that.

But at least I understood.

In there, in Allison Roche's landscape, I saw how her heart had responded to this man she called Spanky, not Henry Lake Spanning. She did not call him, in there, by the name of a monster; she called him a honey's name. I didn't know if he was innocent or not, but *she* knew he was innocent. At first she had responded to just talking with him, about being brought up in an orphanage, and she was able to relate to his stories of being used and treated like chattel, and how they had stripped him of his dignity, and made him afraid all the time. She knew what that was like. And how he'd always been on his own. The running away. The being captured like a wild thing, and put in this home or that lockup or the orphanage "for his own good." Washing stone steps with a tin bucket full of gray water, with a horsehair brush and a bar of lye soap, till the tender folds of skin between the fingers were furiously red and hurt so much you couldn't make a fist.

She tried to tell me how her heart had responded, with a language that has never been invented to do the job. I saw as much as I needed, there in that secret landscape, to know that Spanning had led a miserable life, but that somehow he'd managed to become a decent human being. And it showed through enough when she was face to face with him, talking to him without the witness box between them, without the adversarial thing, without the tension of the courtroom and the gallery and those parasite creeps from the tabloids sneaking around taking pictures of him, that she identified with his pain. Hers had been not the same, but similar; of a kind, if not of identical intensity.

She came to know him a little.

And came back to see him again. Human compassion. In a moment of human weakness.

Until, finally, she began examining everything she had worked up as evidence, trying to see it from *his* point of view, using *his* explanations of circumstantiality. And there were inconsistencies. Now she saw them. Now she did not turn her prosecuting attorney's mind from them, recasting them in a way that would railroad Spanning; now she gave him just the barest possibility of truth. And the case did not seem as incontestable.

By that time, she had to admit to herself, she had fallen in love with him. The gentle quality could not be faked; she'd known fraudulent kindness in her time.

I left her mind gratefully. But at least I understood.

"Now?" she asked.

Yes, now. Now I understood. And the fractured glass in her voice told me. Her face told me. The way she parted her lips in expectation, waiting for me to reveal what my magic journey had conveyed by way of truth. Her palm against her cheek. All that told me. And I said, "Yes."

Then, silence, between us.

After a while she said, "I didn't feel anything."

I shrugged. "Nothing to feel. I was in for a few seconds, that's all."

"You didn't see everything?"

"No."

"Because you didn't want to?"

"Because . . ."

She smiled. "I understand, Rudy."

Oh, do you? Do you really? That's just fine. And I heard me say, "You made it with him yet?"

I could have torn off her arm; it would've hurt less.

"That's the second time today you've asked me that kind of question. I didn't like it much the first time, and I like it less *this* time."

"You're the one wanted me to go into your head. I didn't buy no ticket for the trip."

"Well, you were in there. Didn't you look around enough to find out?'

"I didn't look for that."

"What a chickenshit, wheedling, lousy and *cowardly* . . ."

"I haven't heard an answer, Counselor. Kindly restrict your answers to a simple yes or no."

"Don't be ridiculous! He's on death row!"

"There are ways."

"How would *you* know?"

"I had a friend. Up at San Rafael. What they call Tamal. Across the bridge from Richmond, a little north of San Francisco."

"That's San Quentin."

"That's what it is, all right."

"I thought that *friend* of yours was at Pelican Bay?"

"Different friend."

"You seem to have a lot of old chums in the joint in California."

"It's a racist nation."

"I've heard that."

"But Q ain't Pelican Bay. Two different states of being. As hard time as they pull at Tamal, it's worse up to Crescent City. In the Shoe."

"You never mentioned 'a friend' at San Quentin."

"I never mentioned a lotta shit. That don't mean I don't know it. I am large, I contain multitudes."

We sat silently, the three of us: me, her, and Walt Whitman. *We're fighting,* I thought. Not make-believe, dissin' some movie we'd seen and disagreed about; this was nasty. Bone nasty and memorable. No one ever forgets this kind of fight. Can turn dirty in a second, say some trash you can never take back, never forgive, put a canker on the rose of friendship for all time, never be the same look again.

I waited. She didn't say anything more; and I got no straight answer; but I was pretty sure Henry Lake Spanning had gone all the way with her. I felt a twinge of emotion I didn't even want to look at, much less analyze, dissect, and name. *Let it be,* I thought. Eleven years. Once, just once. *Let it just lie there and get old and withered and die a proper death like all ugly thoughts.*

"OK. So I go on down to Atmore," I said. "I suppose you mean in the very near future, since he's supposed to bake in four days. Sometime very soon: like today."

She nodded.

I said, "And how do I get in? Law student? Reporter? Tag along as Larry Borlan's new law clerk? Or do I go in with you? What am I, friend of the family, representative of the Alabama State Department of Corrections; maybe you could set me up as an inmate's rep from Project Hope."

"I can do better than that," she said. The smile. "Much."

"Yeah, I'll just bet you can. Why does that worry me?"

Still with the smile, she hoisted the Atlas onto her lap. She unlocked it, took out a small manila envelope, unsealed but clasped, and slid it across the table to me. I pried open the clasp and shook out the contents.

Clever. Very clever. And already made up, with my photo where necessary, admission dates stamped for tomorrow morning, Thursday, absolutely authentic and foolproof.

"Let me guess," I said. "Thursday mornings, the inmates of death row have access to their attorneys?"

"On death row, family visitation Monday and Friday. Henry has no family. Attorney visitations Wednesdays and Thursdays, but I couldn't count on today. It took me a couple of days to get through to you . . ."

"I've been busy."

". . . but inmates consult with their counsel on Wednesday and Thursday mornings."

I tapped the papers and plastic cards. "This is very sharp. I notice my name and my handsome visage already here, already sealed in plastic. How long have you had these ready?"

"Couple of days."

"What if I'd continued to say no?"

She didn't answer. She just got that look again.

"One last thing," I said. And I leaned in very close, so she would make no mistake that I was dead serious. "Time grows short. Today's Wednesday. Tomorrow's Thursday. They throw those computer-controlled twin switches Saturday night midnight. What if I jaunt into him and find out you're right, that he's absolutely innocent? What then? They going to listen to me? Fiercely high-verbal black boy with the magic mind-read power?

"I don't think so. Then what happens, Ally?"

"Leave that to me." Her face was hard. "As you said: there are ways. There are roads and routes and even lightning bolts, if you know where to shop. The power of the judiciary. An election year coming up. Favors to be called in."

I said, "And secrets to be wafted under sensitive noses?"

"You just come back and tell me Spanky's telling the truth" — and she smiled as I started to laugh — "and I'll worry about the world one minute after midnight Sunday morning."

I got up and slid the papers back into the envelope, and put the envelope under my arm. I looked down at her and I smiled as gently as I could, and I said, "Assure me that you haven't stacked the deck by telling Spanning I can read minds."

"I wouldn't do that."

"Tell me."

"I haven't told him you can read minds."

"You're lying."

"Did you . . . ?"

"Didn't have to. I can see it in your face, Ally."

"Would it matter if he knew?"

"Not a bit. I can read the son of a bitch cold or hot, with or without. Three seconds inside and I'll know if he did it all, if he did part of it, if he did none of it."

"I think I love him, Rudy."

"You told me that."

"But I wouldn't set you up. I need to know . . . that's why I'm asking you to do it."

I didn't answer. I just smiled at her. She'd told him. He'd know I was coming. But that was terrific. If she hadn't alerted him, I'd have asked her to call and let him know. The more aware he'd be, the easier to scorch his landscape.

I'm a fast study, king of the quick learners: Vulgate Latin in a week; standard apothecary's pharmacopoeia in three days; Fender bass on a weekend; Atlanta Falcons' playbook in an hour; and, in a moment of human weakness, what it feels like to have a very crampy, heavy-flow menstrual period, two minutes flat.

So fast, in fact, that the more somebody tries to hide the boiling pits of guilt and the crucified bodies of shame, the faster I adapt to their landscape. Like a man taking a polygraph test gets nervous, starts to sweat, ups the galvanic skin response, tries to duck and dodge, gets himself hinky and more hinky and hinkier till his upper lip could water a truck garden, the more he tries to hide from me . . . the more he reveals . . . the deeper inside I can go.

There is an African saying: *Death comes without the thumping of drums.*

I have no idea why that one came back to me just then.

Last thing you expect from a prison administration is a fine sense of humor. But they got one at the Holman facility.

They had the bloody monster dressed like a virgin.

White duck pants, white short-sleeve shirt buttoned up to the neck, white socks. Pair of brown ankle-high brogans with crepe soles, probably neoprene, but they didn't clash with the pale, virginal apparition that came through the security door with a large, black brother in Alabama Prison Authority uniform holding on to his right elbow.

Didn't clash, those work shoes, and didn't make much of a tap on the white tile floor. It was as if he floated. Oh yes, I said to myself, oh yes indeed: I could see how this messianic figure could wow even as tough a cookie as Ally. *Oh my, yes.*

Fortunately, it was raining outside.

Otherwise, sunlight streaming through the glass, he'd no doubt have a halo. I'd have lost it. Right there, a laughing jag would *not* have ceased. Fortunately, it was raining like a son of a bitch.

Which hadn't made the drive down from Clanton a possible entry on any deathbed list of Greatest Terrific Moments in My Life. Sheets of aluminum water, thick as misery, like a never-ending shower curtain that I could drive through for an eternity and never really penetrate. I went into the ditch off the I-65 half a dozen times. Why I never plowed down and buried myself up to the axles in the sucking goo running those furrows, never be something I'll understand.

But each time I skidded off the interstate, even the twice I did a complete 360 and nearly rolled the old Fairlane I'd borrowed from John the C Hepworth, even then I just kept digging, slewed like an epileptic seizure, went sideways and climbed right up the slippery grass and weeds and running, sucking red Alabama goo, right back onto that long black anvil pounded by rain as hard as roofing nails. I took it then, as I take it now, to be a sign that Destiny was determined the mere heavens and earth would not be permitted to fuck me around. I had a date to keep, and Destiny was on top of things.

Even so, even living charmed, which was clear to me, even so: when I got about five miles north of Atmore, I took the 57 exit off the I-65 and a left onto 21, and pulled in at the Best Western. It wasn't my intention to stay overnight that far south—though I knew a young woman with excellent teeth down in Mobile—but the rain was just hammering and all I wanted was to get this thing done and go fall asleep. A drive that long, humping something as lame as that Fairlane, hunched forward to scope the rain . . . with Spanning in front of me . . . all I desired was surcease. A touch of the old oblivion.

I checked in, stood under the shower for half an hour, changed into the three-piece suit I'd brought along, and phoned the front desk for directions to the Holman facility.

Driving there, a sweet moment happened for me. It was the last sweet moment for a long time thereafter, and I remember it now as if it were still happening. I cling to it.

In May, and on into early June, the yellow lady's slipper blossoms. In the forests and the woodland bogs, and often on some otherwise undistinguished slope or hillside, the yellow and purple orchids suddenly appear.

I was driving. There was a brief stop in the rain. Like the eye of the hurricane. One moment sheets of water, and the next, absolute silence before the crickets and frogs and birds started complaining; and darkness on all sides, just the idiot staring beams of my headlights poking into nothingness; and cool as a well between the drops of rain; and I was driving. And suddenly, the window rolled down so I wouldn't fall asleep, so I could stick my head out when my eyes started to close, suddenly I smelled the delicate perfume of the sweet May-blossoming lady's slipper. Off to my left, off in the dark somewhere on a patch of hilly ground, or deep in a stand of invisible trees, *Cypripedium calceolus* was making the night world beautiful with its fragrance.

I neither slowed, nor tried to hold back the tears.

I just drove, feeling sorry for myself; for no good reason I could name.

Way, way down—almost to the corner of the Florida Panhandle, about three hours south of the last truly imperial barbecue in that part of the world, in Birmingham—I made my way to Holman. If you've never been inside the joint, what I'm about to say will resonate about as clearly as Chaucer to one of the gentle Tasaday.

The stones call out.

That institution for the betterment of the human race, the Organized Church, has a name for it. From the fine folks at Catholicism, Lutheranism, Baptism, Judaism, Islamism, Druidism . . . Ismism . . . the ones who brought you Torquemada, several spicy varieties of Inquisition, original sin, holy war, sectarian violence, and something called "pro-lifers" who bomb and maim and kill . . . comes the catchy phrase Damned Places.

Rolls off the tongue like *God's on Our Side,* don't it?

Damned Places.

As we say in Latin, the *situs* of malevolent shit. The *venue* of evil happenings. *Locations* forever existing under a black cloud, like residing in a rooming house run by Jesse Helms or Strom Thurmond. The big slams are like that. Joliet, Dannemora, Attica, Rahway State in Jersey, that hellhole down in Louisiana called Angola, old Folsom—not the new one, the old Folsom—Q, and Ossining. Only people who read about it call it "Sing Sing." Inside, the cons call it Ossining. The Ohio State pen in Columbus. Leavenworth, Kansas. The ones they talk about among themselves when they talk about doing hard time. The Shoe at Pelican Bay State Prison. In there, in those ancient structures mortared with guilt and depravity and no respect for human life and just plain meanness on both sides, cons and screws, in there where the walls and floors have absorbed all the pain and loneliness of a million men and women for decades . . . in there, the stones call out.

Damned Places. You can feel it when you walk through the gates and go through the metal detectors and empty your pockets on counters and open your briefcase so that thick fingers can rumple the papers. You feel it. The moaning and thrashing, and men biting holes in their own wrists so they'll bleed to death.

And I felt it worse than anyone else.

I blocked out as much as I could. I tried to hold on to the memory of the scent of orchids in the night. The last thing I wanted was to jaunt into somebody's landscape at random. Go inside and find out what he had done, what had *really* put him here, not just what they'd got him for. And I'm not talking about Spanning; I'm talking about every one of them. Every guy who had kicked to death his girlfriend because she brought him bratwurst instead of spicy Cajun sausage. Every pale, wormy Bible-reciting psycho who had stolen, butt-fucked, and sliced up an altar boy in the name of secret voices that "tole him to g'wan *do* it!" Every amoral druggie who'd shot a pensioner for her food stamps. If I let down for a second, if I didn't keep that shield up, I'd be tempted to send out a scintilla and touch one of them. In a moment of human weakness.

So I followed the trusty to the warden's office, where his secretary checked my papers, and the little plastic cards with my face encased in them, and she kept looking down at the face, and up at my face, and down at my face, and up at the face in front of her, and when she couldn't restrain herself a second longer she said, "We've been expecting you, Mr. Pairis. Uh. Do you *really* work for the president of the United States?"

I smiled at her. "We go bowling together."

She took that highly, and offered to walk me to the conference room where I'd meet Henry Lake Spanning. I thanked her the way a well-mannered gentleman of color thanks a civil servant who can make life easier or more difficult, and I followed her along corridors and in and out of guarded steel-riveted doorways, through Administration and the segregation room and the main hall, to the brown-paneled, stained-walnut, white-tile-over-cement-floored, roll-out-security-windowed, white-draperied, drop-ceiling-with-two-inch-acoustical-Celotex-squared conference room, where a security officer met us. She bid me fond adieu, not yet fully satisfied that such a one as I had come, that morning, on Air Force One, straight from a 7-10 split with the president of the United States.

It was a big room.

I sat down at the conference table; about twelve feet long and four feet wide; highly polished walnut, maybe oak. Straight-back chairs: metal tubing with a light yellow upholstered cushion. Everything quiet, except for the sound of matrimonial rice being dumped on a connubial tin roof. The rain had not slacked off. Out there on the I-65 some luck-lost bastard was being sucked down into red death.

"He'll be here," the security officer said.

"That's good," I replied. I had no idea why he'd tell me that, seeing as how it was the reason I was there in the first place. I imagined him to be the kind of guy you dread sitting in front of at the movies, because he always explains everything to his date. Like a bracero laborer with a valid green card interpreting a Woody Allen movie line-by-line to his illegal-alien cousin Humberto, three weeks under the wire from Matamoros. Like one of a pair of Beltone-wearing octogenarians on the loose from a rest home for a wild Saturday afternoon at the mall, plonked down in the third-level multiplex, one of them describing whose ass Clint Eastwood is about to kick, and why. All at the top of her voice.

"Seen any good movies lately?" I asked him.

He didn't get a chance to answer, and I didn't jaunt inside to find out, because at that moment the steel door at the far end of the conference room opened, and another security officer poked his head in, and called across to Officer Let-Me-State-the-Obvious, "Dead man walking!"

Officer Self-Evident nodded to him, the other head poked back out, the door slammed, and my companion said, "When we bring one down from death row, he's gotta walk through the Ad Building and Segregation and the Main Hall. So everything's locked down. Every man's inside. It takes some time, y'know."

I thanked him.

"Is it true you work for the president, yeah?" He asked it so politely I decided to give him a straight answer; and to hell with all the phony credentials Ally had worked up. "Yeah," I said, "we're on the same bocce ball team."

"Izzat so?" he said, fascinated by sports stats.

I was on the verge of explaining that the president was, in actuality, of Italian descent, when I heard the sound of the key turning in the security door, and it opened outward, and in came this messianic apparition in white, being led by a guard who was seven feet in any direction.

Henry Lake Spanning, sans halo, hands and feet shackled, with the chains cold-welded into a wide anodized-steel belt, shuffled toward me; and his neoprene soles made no disturbing cacophony on the white tiles.

I watched him come the long way across the room, and he watched me right back. I thought to myself, *Yeah, she told him I can read minds. Well, let's see which method you use to try and keep me out of the landscape.* But I couldn't tell from the outside of him, not just by the way he shuffled and looked, if he had fucked Ally. But I knew it had to've been. Somehow. Even in the big lockup. Even here.

He stopped right across from me, with his hands on the back of the chair, and he didn't say a word, just gave me the nicest smile I'd ever gotten from anyone, even my mama. *Oh, yes,* I thought, *oh my goodness, yes.* Henry Lake Spanning was either the most masterfully charismatic person I'd ever met, or so good at the charm con that he could sell a slashed throat to a stranger.

"You can leave him," I said to the great black behemoth brother.

"Can't do that, sir."

"I'll take full responsibility."

"Sorry, sir; I was told someone had to be right here in the room with you and him, all the time."

I looked at the one who had waited with me. "That mean you, too?"

He shook his head. "Just one of us, I guess."

I frowned. "I need absolute privacy. What would happen if I were this man's attorney of record? Wouldn't you have to leave us alone? Privileged communication, right?"

They looked at each other, this pair of security officers, and they looked back at me, and they said nothing. All of a sudden Mr. Plain-As-the-Nose-on-Your-Face had nothing valuable to offer; and the sequoia with biceps "had his orders."

"They tell you who I work for? They tell you who it was sent me here to talk to this man?" Recourse to authority often works. They mumbled yessir yessir a couple of times each, but their faces stayed right on the mark of *sorry, sir, but we're not supposed to leave anybody alone with this man.* It wouldn't have mattered if they'd believed I'd flown in on Jehovah One.

So I said to myself *fuckit* I said to myself, and I slipped into their thoughts, and it didn't take much rearranging to get the phone wires restrung and the underground cables rerouted and the pressure on their bladders something fierce.

"On the other hand . . ." the first one said.

"I suppose we could . . ." the giant said.

And in a matter of maybe a minute and a half one of them was entirely gone, and the great one was standing outside the steel door, his back filling the double-pane chickenwire-embedded security window. He effectively sealed off the one entrance or exit to or from the conference room; like the three hundred Spartans facing the tens of thousands of Xerxes' army at the Hot Gates.

Henry Lake Spanning stood silently watching me.

"Sit down," I said. "Make yourself comfortable."

He pulled out the chair, came around, and sat down.

"Pull it closer to the table," I said.

He had some difficulty, hands shackled that way, but he grabbed the leading edge of the seat and scraped forward till his stomach was touching the table.

He was a handsome guy, even for a white man. Nice nose, strong cheekbones, eyes the color of that water in your toilet when you toss in a tablet of 2000 Flushes. Very nice-looking man. He gave me the creeps.

If Dracula had looked like Shirley Temple, no one would've driven a stake through his heart. If Harry Truman had looked like Freddy Krueger, he would never have beaten Tom Dewey at the polls. Joe Stalin and Saddam Hussein looked like sweet, avuncular friends of the family, really nice-looking, kindly guys — who just incidentally happened to slaughter millions of men, women, and children. Abe Lincoln looked like an ax murderer, but he had a heart as big as Guatemala.

Henry Lake Spanning had the sort of face you'd trust immediately if you saw it in a TV commercial. Men would like to go fishing with him, women would like to squeeze his buns. Grannies would hug him on sight, kids would follow him straight into the mouth of an open oven. If he could play the piccolo, rats would gavotte around his shoes.

What saps we are. Beauty is only skin deep. You can't judge a book by its cover. Cleanliness is next to godliness. Dress for success. What saps we are.

So what did that make my pal Allison Roche?

And why the hell didn't I just slip into his thoughts and check out the landscape? Why was I stalling?

Because I was scared of him.

This was fifty-six verified, gruesome, disgusting murders sitting forty-eight inches away from me, looking straight at me with blue eyes and soft, gently blond hair. Neither Harry nor Dewey would've had a prayer.

So why was I scared of him? Because; that's why.

This was damned foolishness. I had all the weaponry, he was shackled, and I didn't for a second believe he was what Ally *thought* he was: innocent. Hell, they'd caught him, literally, red-handed. Bloody to the armpits, fer chrissakes. Innocent, my ass! *OK, Rudy,* I thought, *get in there and take a look around.* But I didn't. I waited for him to say something.

He smiled tentatively, a gentle and nervous little smile, and he said, "Ally asked me to see you. Thank you for coming."

I looked *at* him, but not *into* him.

He seemed upset that he'd inconvenienced me. "But I don't think you can do me any good, not in just three days."

"You scared, Spanning?"

His lips trembled. "Yes I am, Mr. Pairis. I'm about as scared as a man can be." His eyes were moist.

"Probably gives you some insight into how your victims felt, whaddaya think?"

He didn't answer. His eyes were moist.

After a moment just looking at me, he scraped back his chair and stood up. "Thank you for coming, sir. I'm sorry Ally imposed on your time." He turned and started to walk away. I jaunted into his landscape.

Oh my God, I thought. He was innocent.

Never done any of it. None of it. Absolutely no doubt, not a shadow of a doubt. Ally had been right. I saw every bit of that landscape in there, every fold and crease; every bolt hole and rat run; every gully and arroyo; all of his past, back and back and back to his birth in Lewistown, Montana, near Great Falls, thirty-six years ago; every day of his life right up to the minute they arrested him leaning over that disemboweled cleaning woman the real killer had tossed into the Dumpster.

I saw every second of his landscape; and I saw him coming out of the Winn-Dixie in Huntsville; pushing a cart filled with grocery bags of food for the weekend. And I saw him wheeling it around the parking lot toward the Dumpster area overflowing with broken-down cardboard boxes and fruit crates. And I heard the cry for help from one of those Dumpsters; and I saw Henry Lake Spanning stop and look around, not sure he'd heard anything at all. Then I saw him start to go to his car, parked right there at the edge of the lot beside the wall because it was a Friday evening and everyone was stocking up for the weekend, and there weren't any spaces out front; and the cry for help, weaker this time, as pathetic as a crippled kitten; and Henry Lake Spanning stopped cold, and he looked around; and we *both* saw the bloody hand raise itself above the level of the open Dumpster's filthy green steel side. And I saw him desert his groceries without a thought to their cost, or that someone might run off with them if he left them unattended, or that he only had eleven dollars left in his checking account, so if those groceries were snagged by someone he wouldn't be eating for the next few days . . . and I watched him rush to the Dumpster and look into the crap filling it . . . and I felt his nausea at the sight of that poor old woman, what was left of her . . . and I was with him as he crawled up onto the Dumpster and dropped inside to do what he could for that mass of shredded and pulped flesh.

And I cried with him as she gasped, with a bubble of blood that burst in the open ruin of her throat, and she died. But though *I* heard the scream of someone coming around the corner, Spanning did not; and so he was still there, holding the poor mass of stripped skin and black bloody clothing, when the cops screeched into the parking lot. And only *then,* innocent of anything but decency and rare human compassion, did Henry Lake Spanning begin to understand what it must look like to middle-aged hausfraus, sneaking around Dumpsters to pilfer cardboard boxes, who see what they think is a man murdering an old woman.

I was with him, there in that landscape within his mind, as he ran and ran and dodged and dodged. Until they caught him in Decatur, seven miles from the body of Gunilla Ascher. But they had him, and they had positive identification, from the Dumpster in Huntsville; and all the rest of it was circumstantial, gussied up by bedridden, recovering Charlie Whilborg and the staff in Ally's office. It looked good on paper — so good that Ally had brought him down on twenty-nine-*cum*-fifty-six counts of murder in the vilest extreme.

But it was all bullshit.

The killer was still out there.

Henry Lake Spanning, who looked like a nice, decent guy, was exactly that. A nice, decent, goodhearted, but most of all *innocent* guy.

You could fool juries and polygraphs and judges and social workers and psychiatrists and your mommy and your daddy, but you could *not* fool Rudy Pairis, who travels regularly to the place of dark where you can go but not return.

They were going to burn an innocent man in three days.

I had to do something about it.

Not just for Ally, though that was reason enough; but for this man who thought he was doomed, and was frightened, but didn't have to take no shit from a wiseguy like me.

"Mr. Spanning," I called after him.

He didn't stop.

"Please," I said. He stopped shuffling, the chains making their little charm-bracelet sounds, but he didn't turn around.

"I believe Ally is right, sir," I said. "I believe they caught the wrong man; and I believe all the time you've served is wrong; and I believe you ought not die."

Then he turned slowly, and stared at me with the look of a dog that has been taunted with a bone. His voice was barely a whisper. "And why is that, Mr. Pairis? Why is it that you believe me when nobody else but Ally and my attorney believed me?"

I didn't say what I was thinking. What I was thinking was that I'd been *in* there, and I *knew* he was innocent. And more than that, I knew that he truly loved my pal Allison Roche.

And there wasn't much I wouldn't do for Ally.

So what I said was: "I know you're innocent, because I know who's guilty."

His lips parted. It wasn't one of those big moves where someone's mouth flops open in astonishment; it was just a parting of the lips. But he was startled; I knew that as I knew the poor son of a bitch had suffered too long already.

He came shuffling back to me, and sat down.

"Don't make fun, Mr. Pairis. Please. I'm what you said, I'm scared. I don't want to die, and I surely don't want to die with the world thinking I did those . . . those things."

"Makin' no fun, Captain. I know who ought to burn for all those murders. Not six states, but eleven. Not fifty-six dead, but an even seventy. Three of them little girls in a day nursery, and the woman watching them, too."

He stared at me. There was horror on his face. I know that look real good. I've seen it at least seventy times.

"I know you're innocent, Cap'n, because *I'm* the man they want. *I'm* the guy who put your ass in here."

In a moment of human weakness. I saw it all. What I had packed off to live in that place of dark where you can go but not return. The wall-safe in my drawing room. The four-foot-thick walled crypt encased in concrete and sunk a mile deep into solid granite. The vault whose composite laminate walls of judiciously sloped extremely thick blends of steel and plastic, the equivalent of 600–700 mm of homogenous depth protection approached the maximum toughness and hardness of crystaliron, that iron grown with perfect crystal structure and carefully controlled quantities of impurities that in a modern combat tank can shrug off a hollow charge warhead like a spaniel shaking himself dry. The Chinese puzzle box. The hidden chamber. The labyrinth. The maze of the mind where I'd sent all seventy to die, over and over and over, so I wouldn't hear their screams, or see the ropes of bloody tendon, or stare into the pulped sockets where their pleading eyes had been.

When I had walked into that prison, I'd been buttoned up totally. I was safe and secure, I knew nothing, remembered nothing, suspected nothing.

But when I walked into Henry Lake Spanning's landscape, and I could not lie to myself that he was the one, I felt the earth crack. I felt the tremors and the upheavals, and the fissures started at my feet and ran to the horizon; and the lava boiled up and began to flow. And the steel walls melted, and the concrete turned to dust, and the barriers dissolved; and I looked at the face of the monster.

No wonder I had such nausea when Ally had told me about this or that slaughter ostensibly perpetrated by Henry Lake Spanning, the man she was prosecuting on twenty-nine counts of murders I had committed. No wonder I could picture all the details when she would talk to me about the barest description of the murder site. No wonder I fought so hard against coming to Holman.

In there, in his mind, his landscape open to me, I saw the love he had for Allison Roche, for my pal and buddy with whom I had once, just once . . .

Don't try tellin' me that the Power of Love can open the fissures. I don't want to hear that shit. I'm telling *you* that it was a combination, a buncha things that split me open, and possibly maybe one of those things was what I saw between them.

I don't know that much. I'm a quick study, but this was in an instant. A crack of fate. A moment of human weakness. That's what I told myself in the part of me that ventured to the place of dark: that I'd done what I'd done in moments of human weakness.

And it was those moments, not my "gift," and not my blackness, that had made me the loser, the monster, the liar that I am.

In the first moment of realization, I couldn't believe it. Not me, not good old Rudy. Not likable Rudy Pairis never done no one but hisself wrong his whole life.

In the next second I went wild with anger, furious at the disgusting thing that lived on one side of my split brain. Wanted to tear a hole through my face and yank the killing thing out, wet and putrescent, and squeeze it into pulp.

In the next second I was nauseated, actually wanted to fall down and puke, seeing every moment of what I had done, unshaded, unhidden, naked to this Rudy Pairis who was decent and reasonable and law-abiding, even if such a Rudy was little better than a well-educated fuckup. But not a killer . . . I wanted to puke.

Then, finally, I accepted what I could not deny.

For me, never again would I slide through the night with the scent of the blossoming yellow lady's slipper. I recognized that perfume now.

It was the odor that rises from a human body cut wide open, like a mouth making a big, dark yawn.

The other Rudy Pairis had come home at last.

They didn't have half a minute's worry. I sat down at a little wooden writing table in an interrogation room in the Jefferson County DA's offices, and I made up a graph with the names and dates and locations. Names of as many of the seventy as I actually knew. (A lot of them had just been on the road, or in a men's toilet, or taking a bath, or lounging in the back row of a movie, or getting some cash from an ATM, or just sitting around doing nothing but waiting for me to come along and open them up, and maybe have a drink off them, or maybe just something to snack on . . . down the road.) Dates were easy, because I've got a good memory for dates. And the places where they'd find the ones they didn't know about, the fourteen with exactly the same MO as the other fifty-six, not to mention the old-style rip-and-pull can opener I'd used on that little Catholic bead-counter Gunilla Whatsername, who did Hail Mary this and Sweet Blessed Jesus that all the time I was opening her up, even at the last, when I held up parts of her insides for her to look at, and tried to get her to lick them, but she died first. Not half a minute's worry for the State of Alabama. All in one swell foop they corrected a tragic miscarriage of justice, nobbled a maniac killer, solved fourteen more murders than they'd counted on (in five additional states, which made the police departments of those five additional states extremely pleased with the law enforcement agencies of the Sovereign State of Alabama), and made first spot on the evening news on all three major networks, not to mention CNN, for the better part of a week. Knocked the Middle East right out of the box. Neither Harry Truman nor Tom Dewey would've had a prayer.

Ally went into seclusion, of course. Took off and went somewhere down on the Florida coast, I heard. But after the trial, and the verdict and Spanning being released, and me going inside, and all like that, well, oo-poppa-dow as they used to say, it was all reordered properly. *Sat cito si sat bene,* in Latin. "It is done quickly enough if it is done well." A favorite saying of Cato. The Elder Cato.

And all I asked, all I begged for, was that Ally and Henry Lake Spanning, who loved each other and deserved each other, and whom I had almost fucked up royally, that the two of them would be there when they jammed my weary black butt into that new electric chair at Holman.

Please come, I begged them.

Don't let me die alone. Not even a shit like me. Don't make me cross over into that place of dark, where you can go, but not return — without the face of a friend. Even a former friend. And as for you, Captain, well, hell didn't I save your life so you could enjoy the company of the woman you love? Least you can do. Come on now; be there or be square!

I don't know if Spanning talked her into accepting the invite, or if it was the other way around; but one day about a week prior to the event of cooking up a mess of fried Rudy Pairis, the warden stopped by my commodious accommodations on death row and gave me to understand that it would be SRO for the barbecue, which meant Ally my pal, and her boyfriend, the former resident of the row where now I dwelt in durance vile.

The things a guy'll do for love.

Yeah, that was the key. Why would a very smart operator who had gotten away with it, all the way free and clear, why would such a smart operator suddenly pull one of those hokey courtroom "I did it, I did it!" routines, and as good as strap himself into the electric chair?

Once. I only went to bed with her once.

The things a guy'll do for love.

When they brought me into the death chamber from the holding cell where I'd spent the night before and all that day, where I'd had my last meal (which had been a hot roast beef sandwich, double meat, on white toast, with very crisp French fries, and hot brown country gravy poured over the whole thing, apple sauce, and a bowl of Concord grapes), where a representative of the Holy Roman Empire had tried to make amends for destroying most of the gods, beliefs, and cultures of my black forebears, they held me between security officers, neither one of whom had been in attendance when I'd visited Henry Lake Spanning at this very same correctional facility slightly more than a year before.

It hadn't been a bad year. Lots of rest; caught up on my reading, finally got around to Proust and Langston Hughes, I'm ashamed to admit, so late in the game; lost some weight; worked out regularly; gave up cheese and dropped my cholesterol count. Ain't nothin' to it, just to do it.

Even took a jaunt or two or ten, every now and awhile. It didn't matter none. I wasn't going anywhere, neither were they. I'd done worse than the worst of them; hadn't I confessed to it? So there wasn't a lot that could ice me, after I'd copped to it and released all seventy of them out of my unconscious, where they'd been rotting in shallow graves for years. No big thang, Cuz.

Brought me in, strapped me in, plugged me in.

I looked through the glass at the witnesses.

There sat Ally and Spanning, front row center. Best seats in the house. All eyes and crying, watching, not believing everything had come to this, trying to figure out when and how and in what way it had all gone down without her knowing anything at all about it. And Henry Lake Spanning sitting close beside her, their hands locked in her lap. True love.

I locked eyes with Spanning.

I jaunted into his landscape.

No, I *didn't.*

I *tried* to, and couldn't squirm through. Thirty years, or less, since I was five or six, I'd been doing it; without hindrance, all alone in the world the only person who could do this listen-in-on-the-landscape trick; and for the first time I was stopped. Absolutely no fuckin' entrance. I went wild! I tried running at it full-tilt, and hit something khaki-colored, like beach sand, and only slightly giving, not hard, but resilient. Exactly like being inside a ten-foot-high, fifty-foot-diameter paper bag, like a big shopping bag from a supermarket, that stiff butcher's paper kind of bag, and that color, like being inside a bag that size, running straight at it, thinking you're going to bust through . . . and being thrown back. Not hard, not like bouncing on a trampoline, just shunted aside like the fuzz from a dandelion hitting a glass door. Unimportant. Khaki-colored and not particularly bothered.

I tried hitting it with a bolt of pure blue lightning mental power, like someone out of a Marvel comic, but that wasn't how mixing in other people's minds works. You don't think yourself in with a psychic battering-ram. That's the kind of arrant foolishness you hear spouted by unattractive people on public-access cable channels, talking about the Power of Love and the Power of the Mind and the ever-popular toe-tapping Power of a Positive Thought. Bullshit; I don't be home to *that* folly!

I tried picturing myself in there, but that didn't work, either. I tried blanking my mind and drifting across, but it was pointless. And at that moment it occurred to me that I didn't really know *how* I jaunted. I just . . . did it. One moment I was snug in the privacy of my own head, and the next I was over there in someone else's landscape. It was instantaneous, like teleportation, which also is an impossibility, like telepathy.

But now, strapped into the chair, and them getting ready to put the leather mask over my face so the witnesses wouldn't have to see the smoke coming out of my eye sockets and the little sparks as my nose hairs burned, when it was urgent that I get into the thoughts and landscape of Henry Lake Spanning, I was shut out completely. And right *then,* that moment, I was scared!

Presto, without my even opening up to him, there he was: inside my head.

He had jaunted into *my* landscape.

"You had a nice roast beef sandwich, I see."

His voice was a lot stronger than it had been when I'd come down to see him a year ago. A *lot* stronger inside my mind.

"Yes, Rudy, I'm what you knew probably existed somewhere. Another one. A shrike." He paused. "I see you call it 'jaunting in the landscape.' I just called myself a shrike. A butcherbird. One name's as good as another. Strange, isn't it; all these years; and we never met anyone else? There *must* be others, but I think — now I can't prove this, I have no real data, it's just a wild idea I've had for years and years — I think they don't know they can do it."

He stared at me across the landscape, those wonderful blue eyes of his, the ones Ally had fallen in love with, hardly blinking.

"Why didn't you let me know before this?"

He smiled sadly. "Ah, Rudy. Rudy, Rudy, Rudy; you poor benighted pickaninny.

"Because I needed to suck you in, kid. I needed to put out a bear trap, and let it snap closed on your scrawny leg, and send you over. Here, let me clear the atmosphere in here . . ." And he wiped away all the manipulation he had worked on me, way back a year ago, when he had so easily covered his own true thoughts, his past, his life, the real panorama of what went on inside his landscape — like bypassing a surveillance camera with a continuous-loop tape that continues to show a placid scene while the joint is being actively burgled — and when he convinced me not only that he was innocent, but that the real killer was someone who had blocked the hideous slaughters from his conscious mind and had lived an otherwise exemplary life. He wandered around my landscape — and all of this in a second or two, because time has no duration in the landscape, like the hours you can spend in a dream that are just thirty seconds long in the real world, just before you wake up — and he swept away all the false memories and suggestions, the logical structure of sequential events that he had planted that would dovetail with my actual existence, my true memories, altered and warped and rearranged so I would believe that I had done all seventy of those ghastly murders . . . so that I'd believe, in a moment of horrible realization, that I was the demented psychopath who had ranged state to state to state, leaving piles of ripped flesh at every stop. Blocked it all, submerged it all, sublimated it all, me. Good old Rudy Pairis, who never killed anybody. I'd been the patsy he was waiting for.

"There, now, kiddo. See what it's really like?

"You didn't do a thing.

"Pure as the driven snow, nigger. That's the truth. And what a find you were. Never even suspected there was another like me, till Ally came to interview me after Decatur. But there you were, big and black as a Great White Hope, right there in her mind. Isn't she fine, Pairis? Isn't she something to take a knife to? Something to split open like a nice piece of fruit warmed in a summer sunshine field, let all the steam rise off her . . . maybe have a picnic . . ."

He stopped.

"I wanted her right from the first moment I saw her.

"Now, you know, I could've done it sloppy, just been a shrike to Ally, that first time she came to the holding cell to interview me; just jump into her, that was my plan. But what a noise that Spanning in the cell would've made, yelling it wasn't a man, it was a woman, not Spanning, but Deputy DA Allison Roche . . . too much noise, too many complications. But I *could* have done it, jumped into her. Or a guard, and then slice her at my leisure, stalk her, find her, let her steam . . .

"You look distressed, Mr. Rudy Pairis. Why's that? Because you're going to die in my place? Because I could have taken you over at any time, and didn't? Because after all this time of your miserable, wasted, lousy life you finally find someone like you, and we don't even have the convenience of a chat? Well, that's sad, that's really sad, kiddo. But you didn't have a chance."

"You're stronger than me, you kept me out," I said.

He chuckled.

"Stronger? Is that all you think it is? Stronger? You still don't get it, do you?" His face, then, grew terrible. "You don't even understand now, right now that I've cleaned it all away and you can *see* what I did to you, do you?

"Do you think I stayed in a jail cell, and went through that trial, all of that, because I couldn't do anything about it? You poor jig slob. I could have jumped like a shrike any time I wanted to. But the first time I met your Ally I saw *you*."

I cringed. "And you waited . . . ? For me, you spent all that time in prison, just to get to me . . . ?"

"At the moment when you couldn't do anything about it, at the moment you couldn't shout 'I've been taken over by someone else, I'm Rudy Pairis here inside this Henry Lake Spanning body, help me, help me!' Why stir up noise when all I had to do was bide my time, wait a bit, wait for Ally, and let Ally go for you."

I felt like a drowning turkey, standing idiotically in the rain, head tilted up, mouth open, water pouring in. "You can . . . leave the mind . . . leave the body . . . go out . . . jaunt, jump permanently . . ."

Spanning sniggered like a schoolyard bully.

"You stayed in jail three years just to get *me*?"

He smirked. Smarter than thou.

"Three years? You think that's some big deal to me? You don't think I could have someone like you running around, do you? Someone who can 'jaunt' as I do? The only other shrike I've ever encountered. You think I wouldn't sit in here and wait for you to come to me?"

"But three *years* . . ."

"You're what, Rudy . . . thirty-one, is it? Yes, I can see that. Thirty-one. You've never jumped like a shrike. You've just entered, jaunted, gone into the landscapes, and never understood that it's more than reading minds. You can change domiciles, black boy. You can move out of a house in a bad neighborhood — such as strapped into the electric chair — and take up residence in a brand-spanking-new housing complex of million-and-a-half-buck condos, like Ally."

"But you have to have a place for the other one to go, don't you?" I said it just flat, no tone, no color to it at all. I didn't even think of the place of dark, where you can go . . .

"Who do you think I am, Rudy? Just who the hell do you think I was when I started, when I learned to shrike, how to jaunt, what I'm telling you now about changing residences? You wouldn't know my first address. I go a long way back.

"But I can give you a few of my more famous addresses. Gilles de Rais, France, 1440; Vlad Tepes, Romania, 1462; Elizabeth Bathory, Hungary, 1611; Catherine DeShayes, France, 1680; Jack the Ripper, London, 1888; Henri Désiré Landru, France, 1915; Albert Fish, New York City, 1934; Ed Gein, Plainfield, Wisconsin, 1954; Myra Hindley Manchester,

1963; Albert DeSalvo, Boston, 1964; Charles Manson, Los Angeles, 1969; John Wayne Gacy, Norwood Park Township, Illinois, 1977.

"Oh, but how I do go on. And on. And on and on and on, Rudy, my little porch monkey. That's what I do. I go on. And on and on. Shrike will nest where it chooses. If not in your beloved Allison Roche, then in the cheesy fucked-up black boy, Rudy Pairis. But don't you think that's a waste, kiddo? Spending however much time I might have to spend in your socially unacceptable body, when Henry Lake Spanning is such a handsome devil? Why should I have just switched with you when Ally lured you to me, because all it would've done is get you screeching and howling that you weren't Spanning, you were this nigger son who'd had his head stolen . . . and then you might have manipulated some guards or the warden . . .

"Well, you see what I mean, don't you?

"But now that the mask is securely in place, and now that the electrodes are attached to your head and your left leg, and now that the warden has his hand on the switch, well, you'd better get ready to do a lot of drooling."

And he turned around to jaunt back out of me, and I closed the perimeter. He tried to jaunt, tried to leap back to his own mind, but I had him in a fist. Just that easy. Materialized a fist, and turned him to face me.

"Fuck you, Jack the Ripper. And fuck you twice, Bluebeard. And on and on and on fuck you Manson and Boston Strangler and any other dipshit warped piece of sick crap you been in your years. You sure got some muddy-shoes credentials there, boy.

"What I care about all those names, Spanky my brother? You really think I don't know those names? I'm an educated fellah, Mistuh Rippuh, Mistuh Mad Bomber. You missed a few. Were you also, did you inhabit, hast thou possessed Winnie Ruth Judd and Charlie Starkweather and Mad Dog Coll and Richard Speck and Sirhan Sirhan and Jeffrey Dahmer? You the boogieman responsible for *every* bad number the human race ever played? You ruin Sodom and Gomorrah, burned the Great Library of Alexandria, orchestrated the Reign of Terror *dans Paree,* set up the Inquisition, stoned and drowned the Salem witches, slaughtered unarmed women and kids at Wounded Knee, bumped off John Kennedy?

"I don't think so.

"I don't even think you got so close as to share a pint with Jack the Ripper. And even if you did, even if you *were* all those maniacs, you were small potatoes, Spanky. The least of us human beings outdoes you, three times a day. How many lynch ropes you pulled tight, M'sieur Landru?

"What colossal egotism you got, makes you blind, makes you think you're the only one, even when you find out there's someone else, you can't get past it. What makes you think I didn't know what you can do? What makes you think I didn't let you do it, and sit here waiting for you like you sat there waiting for me, till this moment when you can't do shit about it?

"You so goddamn stuck on yourself, Spankyhead, you never give it the barest that someone else is a faster draw than you.

"Know what your trouble is, Captain? You're old, you're *real* old, maybe hundreds of years who gives a damn old. That don't count for shit, old man. You're old, but you never got smart. You're just mediocre at what you do.

"You moved from address to address. You didn't have to be Son of Sam or Cain slayin' Abel, or whoever the fuck you been . . . you could've been Moses or Galileo or George Washington Carver or Harriet Tubman or Sojourner Truth or Mark Twain or Joe Louis. You could've been Alexander Hamilton and helped found the Manumission Society in New York. You could've discovered radium, carved Mount Rushmore, carried a baby out of a burning building. But you got old real fast, and you never got any smarter. You didn't need to, did you, Spanky? You had it all to yourself, all this 'shrike' shit, just jaunt here and jaunt there, and bite off someone's hand or face like the old, tired, boring, repetitious, no-imagination stupid shit that you are.

"Yeah, you got me good when I came here to see your landscape. You got Ally wired up good. And she suckered me in, probably not even knowing she was doing it . . . you must've looked in her head and found just the right technique to get her to make me come within reach. Good, m' man; you were excellent. But I had a year to torture myself. A year to sit here and think about it. About how many people I'd killed, and how sick it made me, and little by little I found my way through it.

"Because . . . and here's the big difference 'tween us, dummy:

"I unraveled what was going on . . . it took time, but I learned. Understand, asshole? *I* learn! *You* don't.

"There's an old Japanese saying — I got lots of these, Henry, m' man — I read a whole lot — and what it says is, 'Do not fall into the error of the artisan who boasts of twenty years' experience in his craft while in fact he has had only one year of experience — twenty times.'" Then I grinned back at him.

"Fuck you, sucker," I said, just as the warden threw the switch and I jaunted out of there and into the landscape and mind of Henry Lake Spanning.

I sat there getting oriented for a second; it was the first time I'd done more than a jaunt . . . this was . . . *shrike;* but then Ally beside me gave a little sob for her old pal Rudy Pairis, who was baking like a Maine lobster, smoke coming out from under the black cloth that covered my, his, face; and I heard the vestigial scream of what had been Henry Lake Spanning and thousands of other monsters, all of them burning, out there on the far horizon of my new landscape; and I put my arm around her, and drew her close, and put my face into her shoulder and hugged her to me; and I heard the scream go on and on for the longest time, I think it was a long time, and finally it was just wind . . . and then gone . . . and I came up from Ally's shoulder, and I could barely speak.

"Shhh, honey, it's OK," I murmured. "He's gone where he can make right for his mistakes. No pain. Quiet, a real quiet place; and all alone forever. And cool there. And dark."

I was ready to stop failing at everything, and blaming everything. Having fessed up to love, having decided it was time to grow up and be an adult — not just a very quick study who learned fast, extremely fast, a lot faster than anybody could imagine an orphan like me could learn, than *any*body could imagine — I hugged her with the intention that Henry Lake Spanning would love Allison Roche more powerfully, more responsibly, than anyone had ever loved anyone in the history of the world. I was ready to stop failing at everything.

And it would be just a whole lot easier as a white boy with great big blue eyes.

Because — get on this now — all my wasted years didn't have as much to do with blackness or racism or being overqualified or being unlucky or being high-verbal or even the curse of my "gift" of jaunting, as they did with one single truth I learned waiting in there, inside my own landscape, waiting for Spanning to come and gloat:

I have always been one of those miserable guys who *couldn't get out of his own way.*

Which meant I could, at last, stop feeling sorry for that poor nigger, Rudy Pairis. Except, maybe, in a moment of human weakness.

1995

ED GORMAN

OUT THERE IN THE DARKNESS

Ed Gorman (1941–) was born in Cedar Rapids, Iowa, and graduated from Coe College in Iowa (1963). He worked in advertising as a copywriter and freelance writer for twenty years, then became a full-time writer, mainly of fiction. While most of his work has been in the mystery genre, he has also written many other types of fiction, including horror (he was nominated for Bram Stoker Awards from the Horror Writers Association for his short story collections *Cages* [1995] and *The Dark Fantastic* [2001]) and westerns (he won a Spur Award from the Western Writers of America for Best Short Fiction, for "The Face" in 1992), under both his own name and the pen names E. J. Gorman and Daniel Ransom. He has been nominated for two Edgar Allan Poe Awards by the Mystery Writers of America, for Best Short Story, for "Prisoners" (1991), and (with others) Best Biographical/Critical Work, for *The Fine Art of Murder* (1994). He was also honored with MWA's Ellery Queen Award in 2003, given primarily for his numerous works of mystery fiction, his long editorship of *Mystery Scene Magazine*, a fanzine, and his many anthologies.

Among his many novels are the first in the six-volume Jack Dwyer series, *Rough Cut* (1985); *The Day the Music Died* (1999), the first of more than a half-dozen Sam McCain novels; and *The Poker Club* (1999), which was made into a feature film directed by Tim McCann in 2008. *The Poker Club* is an expansion of the short story "Out There in the Darkness," which was first published in a limited-edition (five hundred copies) chapbook by Subterranean Press, in 1995.

▪ ▪ ▪

1

The night it all started, the whole strange spiral, we were having our usual midweek poker game — four fortyish men who work in the financial business getting together for beer and bawdy jokes and straight poker. No wildcard games. We hate them.

This was summer, and vacation time, and so it happened that the game was held two weeks in a row at my house. Jan had taken the kids to see her Aunt Wendy and Uncle Verne at their fishing cabin, and so I offered to have the game at my house this week, too. With nobody there to supervise, the beer could be laced with a little bourbon, and the jokes could get even bawdier. With the wife and kids in the house, you're always at least a little bit intimidated.

Mike and Bob came together, bearing gifts, which in this case meant the kind of sexy magazines our wives did not want in the house in case the kids might stumble across them. At least that's what they say. I think they sense, and rightly, that the magazines might give their spouses bad ideas about taking the secretary out for a few after-work drinks, or stopping by a singles bar some night.

We got the chips and cards set up at the table, we got the first beers open (Mike chasing a shot of bourbon with his beer), and we started passing the dirty magazines around with tenth-grade glee. The magazines compensated, I suppose, for the balding head, the bloating belly, the stooping shoulders. Deep in the heart of every hundred-year-old man is a horny fourteen-year-old boy.

All this, by the way, took place up in the attic. The four of us got to know one another when we all moved into what city planners called a "transitional neighborhood." There were some grand old houses that could be renovated with enough money and real care. The city designated a ten-square-block area as one it wanted to restore to shiny new luster. Jan and I chose a crumbling Victorian. You wouldn't recognize it today. And that includes the attic, which I've turned into a very nice den.

"Pisses me off," Mike O'Brien said. "He's always late."

And that was true. Neil Solomon *was* always late. Never by that much but always late nonetheless.

"At least tonight he has a good excuse," Bob Genter said.

"He does?" Mike said. "He's probably swimming in his pool." Neil recently got a bonus that made him the first owner of a full-size outdoor pool in our neighborhood.

"No, he's got patrol. But he's stopping at nine. He's got somebody trading with him for next week."

"Oh, hell," Mike said, obviously sorry that he'd complained. "I didn't know that."

Bob Genter's handsome black head nodded solemnly.

Patrol is something we all take very seriously in this newly restored "transitional neighborhood." Eight months ago, the burglaries started, and they've gotten pretty bad. My house has been burglarized once and vandalized once. Bob and Mike have had curb-sitting cars stolen. Neil's wife, Sarah, was surprised in her own kitchen by a burglar. And then there was the killing four months ago, man and wife who'd just moved into the neighborhood, savagely stabbed to death in their own bed. The police caught the guy a few days later trying to cash some of the traveler's checks he'd stolen after killing his prey. He was typical of the kind of man who infested this neighborhood after sundown: a twentyish junkie stoned to the point of psychosis on various street drugs, and not at all averse to murdering people he envied and despised. He also knew a whole hell of a lot about fooling burglar alarms.

After the murders there was a neighborhood meeting, and that's when we came up with the patrol, something somebody'd read about being popular back east. People think that a nice middle-sized Midwestern city like ours doesn't have major crime problems. I invite them to walk many of these streets after dark. They'll quickly be disabused of that notion. Anyway, the patrol worked this way: each night, two neighborhood people got in the family van and patrolled the ten-block area that had been restored. If they saw anything suspicious, they used their cellular phones and called police. We jokingly called it the Baby-Boomer Brigade. The patrol had one strict rule: you were never to take direct action unless somebody's life was at stake. Always, always use the cellular phone and call the police.

Neil had patrol tonight. He'd be rolling in here in another half hour. The patrol had two shifts: early, eight to ten; late, ten to twelve.

Bob said, "You hear what Evans suggested?"

"About guns?" I said.

"Yeah."

"Makes me a little nervous," I said.

"Me, too," Bob said. For somebody who'd grown up in the worst area of the city, Bob Genter was a very polished guy. Whenever he joked that he was the token black, Neil always countered with the fact that he was the token Jew, just as Mike was the token Catholic and I was the token Methodist. We were friends of convenience, I suppose, but we all really did like one another, something that was demonstrated when Neil had a cancer scare a few years back. Bob, Mike, and I were in his hospital room twice a day, all eight days running.

"I think it's time," Mike said. "The bad guys have guns, so the good guys should have guns."

"The good guys are the cops," I said. "Not us."

"People start bringing guns on patrol," Bob said, "somebody innocent is going to get shot."

"So some night one of us here is on patrol and we see a bad guy and he sees us and before the cops get there, the bad guy shoots us? You don't think that's going to happen?"

"It *could* happen, Mike," I said, "but I just don't think that justifies carrying guns."

The argument gave us something to do while we waited for Neil.

"Sorry I'm late," Neil Solomon said after he followed me up to the attic and came inside.

"We already drank all the beer," Mike O'Brien said loudly.

Neil smiled. "That gut you're carrying lately, I can believe that *you* drank all the beer."

Mike always enjoyed being put down by Neil, possibly because most people were a bit intimidated by him—he had that angry Irish edge—and he seemed to enjoy Neil's skilled and fearless handling of him. He laughed with real pleasure.

Neil sat down, I got him a beer from the tiny fridge I keep up here, cards were dealt, seven-card stud was played.

Bob said, "How'd patrol go tonight?"

Neil shrugged. "No problems."

"I still say we should carry guns," Mike said.

"You're not going to believe this, but I agree with you," Neil said.

"Seriously?" Mike said.

"Oh, great," I said to Bob Genter. "Another beer-commercial cowboy."

Bob smiled. "Where I come from, we didn't have cowboys, we had 'mothas.'" He laughed. "Mean mothas, let me tell you. And practically *all* of them carried guns."

"That mean you're siding with them?" I said.

Bob looked at his cards again, then shrugged. "Haven't decided yet, I guess."

I didn't think the antigun people were going to lose this round. But I worried about the round after it, a few months down the line, when the subject of carrying guns came up again. All the TV coverage violence gets in this city, people are more and more developing a siege mentality.

"Play cards," Mike said, "and leave the debate-society crap till later."

Good idea.

We played cards.

In forty-five minutes, I lost $63.82. Mike and Neil always played as if their lives were at stake. All you had to do was watch their faces. Gunfighters couldn't have looked more serious or determined.

The first pit stop came just after ten o'clock, and Neil took it. There was a john on the second floor between the bedrooms, and another john on the first floor.

Neil said, "The good Dr. Gottesfeld had to give me a finger-wave this afternoon, gents, so this may take a while."

"You should trade that prostate of yours in for a new one," Mike said.

"Believe me, I'd like to."

While Neil was gone, the three of us started talking about the patrol again, and whether we should go armed.

We made the same old arguments. The passion was gone. We were just marking time waiting for Neil, and we knew it.

Finally, Mike said, "Let me see some of those magazines again."

"You got some identification?" I said.

"I'll show you some identification," Mike said.

"Spare me," I said. "I'll just give you the magazines."

"You mind if I use the john on the first floor?" Bob said.

"Yeah, it would really piss me off," I said.

"Really?"

That was one thing about Bob. He always fell for deadpan humor.

"No, not really," I said. "Why would I care if you used the john on the first floor?"

He grinned. "Thought maybe they were segregated facilities or something."

He left.

Mike said, "We're lucky, you know that?"

"You mean me and you?"

"Yeah."

"Lucky how?"

"Those two guys. They're great guys. I wish I had them at work." He shook his head. "Treacherous bastards. That's all I'm around all day long."

"No offense, but I'll bet you can be pretty treacherous yourself."

He smiled. "Look who's talking."

The first time I heard it, I thought it was some kind of animal noise from outside, a dog or a cat in some kind of discomfort maybe. Mike, who was dealing himself a hand of solitaire, didn't even look up from his cards.

But the second time I heard the sound, Mike and I both looked up. And then we heard the exploding sound of breaking glass.

"What the hell is that?" Mike said.

"Let's go find out."

Just about the time we reached the bottom of the attic steps, we saw Neil coming out of the second-floor john. "You hear that?"

"Sure as hell did," I said.

We reached the staircase leading to the first floor. Everything was dark. Mike reached for the light switch, but I brushed his hand away.

I put a *sssh*ing finger to my lips and then showed him the Louisville Slugger I'd grabbed from Tim's room. He's my nine-year-old, and his most devout wish is to be a good baseball player. His mother has convinced him that just because I went to college on a baseball scholarship, I was a good player. I wasn't. I was a lucky player.

I led the way downstairs, keeping the bat ready at all times.

"You son of a bitch!"

The voice belonged to Bob.

More smashing glass.

I listened to the passage of the sound. Kitchen. Had to be the kitchen.

In the shadowy light from the street, I saw their faces, Mike's and Neil's. They looked scared.

I hefted the bat some more and then started moving fast to the kitchen.

Just as we passed through the dining room, I heard something heavy hit the kitchen floor. Something human and heavy.

I got the kitchen light on.

He was at the back door. White. Tall. Blond shoulder-length hair. Filthy tan T-shirt. Greasy jeans. He had grabbed one of Jan's carving knives from the huge iron rack that sits atop the butcher-block island. The one curious thing about him was the eyes: there was a malevolent iridescence to the blue pupils, an angry but somehow alien intelligence, a silver glow.

Bob was sprawled face-down on the tile floor. His arms were spread wide on either side of him. He didn't seem to be moving. Chunks and fragments of glass were strewn everywhere across the floor. My uninvited guest had smashed two or three of the colorful pitchers we'd bought the winter before in Mexico.

"Run!" the burglar cried to somebody on the back porch.

He turned, waving the butcher knife back and forth to keep us at bay.

Footsteps out the back door.

The burglar held us off a few more moments, but then I gave him a little bit of tempered Louisville Slugger wood right across the wrist. The knife went clattering.

By this time, Mike and Neil were pretty crazed. They jumped him, hurled him back against the door, and then started putting in punches wherever they'd fit.

"Hey!" I said, and tossed Neil the bat. "Just hold this. If he makes a move, open up his head. Otherwise leave him alone."

They really were crazed, like pit bulls who'd been pulled back just as a fight was starting to get good.

"Mike, call the cops and tell them to send a car."

I got Bob up and walking. I took him into the bathroom and sat him down on the toilet lid. I found a lump the size of an egg on the back of his head. I soaked a clean washcloth with cold water and pressed it against the lump. Bob took it from there.

"You want an ambulance?" I said.

"An ambulance? Are you kidding? You must think I'm a ballet dancer or something."

I shook my head. "No. I know better than that. I've got a male cousin who's a ballet dancer, and he's one tough son of a bitch, believe me. You—" I smiled. "You aren't that tough, Bob."

"I don't need an ambulance. I'm fine."

He winced and tamped the washcloth tighter against his head. "Just a little headache is all." He looked young suddenly, the aftershock of fear in his brown eyes. "Scared the hell out of me. Heard something when I was leaving the john. Went out to the kitchen to check it out. He jumped me."

"What'd he hit you with?"

"No idea."

"I'll go get you some whiskey. Just sit tight."

"I love sitting in bathrooms, man."

I laughed. "I don't blame you."

When I got back to the kitchen, they were gone. All three of them. Then I saw the basement door. It stood open a few inches. I could see dusty light in the space between door and frame. The basement was our wilderness. We hadn't had the time or money to really fix it up yet. We were counting on this year's Christmas bonus from the Windsor Financial Group to help us set it right.

I went down the stairs. The basement is one big, mostly unused room except for the washer and dryer in the corner. All the boxes and odds and ends that should have gone to the attic instead went down here. It smells damp most of the time. The idea is to turn it into a family room for when the boys are older. These days it's mostly inhabited by stray waterbugs.

When I reached the bottom step, I saw them. There are four metal support poles in the basement, near each corner. They had him lashed to a pole in the east quadrant, lashed his wrists behind him with rope found in the tool room. They also had him gagged with what looked like a pillowcase. His eyes were big and wide. He looked scared, and I didn't blame him. I was scared, too.

"What the hell are you guys doing?"

"Just calm down, Papa Bear," Mike said. That's his name for me whenever he wants to convey to people that I'm kind of this old fuddy-duddy. It so happens that Mike is two years older than I am, and it also happens that I'm not a fuddy-duddy. Jan has assured me of that, and she's completely impartial.

"Knock off the Papa Bear bullshit. Did you call the cops?"

"Not yet," Neil said. "Just calm down a little, all right?"

"You haven't called the cops. You've got some guy tied up and gagged in my basement. You haven't even asked how Bob is. And you want me to calm down."

Mike came up to me then. He still had that air of pit-bull craziness about him, frantic, uncontrollable, alien.

"We're going to do what the cops *can't* do, man," he said. "We're going to sweat this son of a bitch. We're going to make him tell us who he was with tonight, and then we're going to make him give us every single name of every single bad guy who works this neighborhood. And then we'll turn all the names over to the cops."

"It's just an extension of the patrol," Neil said. "Just keeping our neighborhood safe is all."

"You guys are nuts," I said, and turned back toward the steps. "I'm going up and call the cops."

That's when I realized just how crazed Mike was. "You aren't going anywhere, man. You're going to stay here and help us break this bastard down. You're going to do your goddamned neighborhood *duty*."

He'd grabbed my sleeve so hard that he'd torn it at the shoulder. We both discovered this at the same time.

I expected him to look sorry. He didn't. In fact, he was smirking at me. "Don't be such a wimp, Aaron," he said.

2

Mike led the charge getting the kitchen cleaned up. I think he was feeling guilty about calling me a wimp with such angry exuberance. Now I understood how lynch mobs got formed. One guy like Mike stirring people up by alternately insulting them and urging them on.

After the kitchen was put back in order, and after I'd taken inventory to find that nothing had been stolen, I went to the refrigerator and got beers for everybody. Bob had drifted back to the kitchen, too.

"All right," I said. "Now that we've all calmed down, I want to walk over to that yellow kitchen wall phone there and call the police. Any objections?"

"I think blue would look better in here than yellow," Neil said.

"Funny," I said.

They looked like themselves now, no feral madness on the faces of Mike and Neil, no winces on Bob's.

I started across the floor to the phone.

Neil grabbed my arm. Not with the same insulting force Mike had used on me. But enough to get the job done.

"I think Mike's right," Neil said. "I think we should grill that bastard a little bit."

I shook my head, politely removed his hand from my forearm, and proceeded to the phone.

"This isn't just your decision alone," Mike said.

He'd finally had his way. He'd succeeded in making me angry. I turned around and looked at him. "This is my house, Mike. If you don't like my decisions, then I'd suggest you leave."

We both took steps toward each other. Mike would no doubt win any battle we had, but I'd at least be able to inflict a little damage, and right now that's all I was thinking about.

Neil got between us.

"Hey," he said. "For God's sake, you two, c'mon. We're friends, remember?"

"This is my house," I said, my words childish in my ears.

"Yeah, but we live in the same neighborhood, Aaron," Mike said, "which makes this 'our' problem."

"He's right, Aaron," Bob said from the breakfast nook. There's a window there where I sometimes sit to watch all the animals on sunny days. I saw a mother raccoon and four baby raccoons one day, marching single-file across the grass. My grandparents were the last generation to live on the farm. My father came to town here and ultimately became a vice president of a ball-bearing company. Raccoons are a lot more pleasant to gaze upon than people.

"He's not right," I said to Bob. "He's wrong. We're not cops, we're not bounty hunters, we're not trackers. We're a bunch of goddamned guys who peddle stocks and bonds. Mike and Neil shouldn't have tied him up downstairs — that happens to be illegal, at least the way they went about it — and now I'm going to call the cops."

"Yes, that poor thing," Mike said. "Aren't we just picking on him, though? Tell you what, why don't we make him something to eat?"

"Just make sure we have the right wine to go with it," Neil said. "Properly chilled, of course."

"Maybe we could get him a chick," Bob said.

"With bombers out to here," Mike said, indicating with his hands where "here" was.

I couldn't help it. I smiled. They were all being ridiculous. A kind of fever had caught them.

"You really want to go down there and question him?" I said to Neil.

"Yes. We can ask him things the cops can't."

"Scare the bastard a little," Mike said. "So he'll tell us who was with him tonight, and who else works this neighborhood." He came over and put his hand out. "God, man, you're one of my best friends. I don't want you mad at me."

Then he hugged me, which is something I've never been comfortable with men doing, but to the extent I could, I hugged him back.

"Friends?" he said.

"Friends," I said. "But I still want to call the cops."

"And spoil our fun?" Neil said.

"And spoil your fun."

"I say we take it to a vote," Bob said.

"This isn't a democracy," I said. "It's my house and I'm the king. I don't want to have a vote."

"Can we ask him one question?" Bob said.

I sighed. They weren't going to let go. "One question?"

"The names of the guys he was with tonight."

"And that's it?"

"That's it. That way we get him and his pals off the street."

"And then I call the cops?"

"Then," Mike said, "you call the cops."

"One question," Neil said.

While we finished our beers, we argued a little more, but they had a lot more spirit left than I did. I was tired now and missing Jan and the kids and feeling lonely. These three guys had become strangers to me tonight. Very old boys eager to play at boy games once again.

"One question," I said. "Then I call the cops."

I led the way down, sneezing as I did so.

There's always enough dust floating around in the basement to play hell with my sinuses.

The guy was his same sullen self, glaring at us as we descended the stairs and then walked over to him. He smelled of heat and sweat and city grime. The long bare arms sticking out of his filthy T-shirt told tattoo tales of writhing snakes and leaping panthers. The arms were joined in the back with rope. His jaw still flexed, trying to accommodate the intrusion of the gag.

"Maybe we should castrate him," Mike said, walking up close to the guy. "You like that, scumbag? If we castrated you?"

If the guy felt any fear, it wasn't evident in his eyes. All you could see there was the usual contempt.

"I'll bet this is the jerk who broke into the Donaldsons' house a couple weeks ago," Neil said.

Now he walked up to the guy. But he was more ambitious than Mike had been. Neil spat in the guy's face.

"Hey," I said, "cool it."

Neil glared at me. "Yeah, I wouldn't hurt his feelings, would I?"

Then he suddenly turned back on the guy, raised his fist, and started to swing. All I could do was shove him. That sent his punch angling off to the right, missing our burglar by about half a foot.

"You asshole," Neil said, turning back on me now.

But Mike was there, between us.

"You know what we're doing? We're making this jerk happy. He's gonna have some nice stories to tell all his criminal friends."

He was right. The burglar was the one who got to look all cool and composed. We looked like squabbling brats. As if to confirm this, a hint of amusement played in the burglar's blue eyes.

"Oh, hell, Aaron, I'm sorry," Neil said, putting his hand out. This was like a political convention, all the handshaking going on.

"So am I, Neil," I said. "That's why I want to call the cops and get this over with."

And that's when he chose to make his move, the burglar. As soon as I mentioned the cops, he probably realized that this was going to be his last opportunity.

He waited until we were just finishing up with the handshake, when we were all focused on one another. Then he took off running. We could see that he'd slipped the rope. He went straight for the stairs, angling out around us like a running back seeing daylight. He even stuck his long, tattooed arm out as if he were trying to repel a tackle.

"Hey!" Bob shouted. "He's getting away."

He was at the stairs by the time we could gather ourselves enough to go after him. But when we moved, we moved fast, and in virtual unison.

By the time I got my hand on the cuff of his left jeans leg, he was close enough to the basement door to open it.

I yanked hard and ducked out of the way of his kicking foot. By now I was as crazy as Mike and Neil had been earlier. There was adrenaline, and great anger. He wasn't just a burglar, he was all burglars, intent not merely on stealing things from me but on hurting my family, too. He hadn't had time to take the gag from his mouth.

This time, I grabbed booted foot and leg and started hauling him back down the stairs. At first he was able to hold on to the door, but when I wrenched his foot rightward, he tried to scream behind the gag. He let go of the doorknob.

The next half minute is still unclear in my mind. I started running down the stairs, dragging him with me. All I wanted to do was get him on the basement floor again, turn him over to the others to watch, and then go call the cops.

But somewhere in those few seconds when I was hauling him back down the steps, I heard edge of stair meeting back of skull. The others heard it, too, because their shouts and curses died in their throats.

When I turned around, I saw the blood running fast and red from his nose. The blue eyes no longer held contempt. They were starting to roll up white in the back of his head.

"God," I said. "He's hurt."

"I think he's a lot more than hurt," Mike said.

"Help me carry him upstairs."

We got him on the kitchen floor. Mike and Neil rushed around soaking paper towels. We tried to revive him. Bob, who kept wincing from his headache, tried the guy's wrist, ankle, and throat for a pulse. None. His nose and mouth were bloody. Very bloody.

"No way you could die from hitting your head like that," Neil said.

"Sure you could," Mike said. "You hit it just the right way."

"He can't be dead," Neil said. "I'm going to try his pulse again."

Bob, who obviously took Neil's second opinion personally, frowned and rolled his eyes. "He's dead, man. He really is."

"Bullshit."

"You a doctor or something?" Bob said.

Neil smiled nervously. “No, but I play one on TV.”

So Neil tried the pulse points. His reading was exactly what Bob’s reading had been.

“See,” Bob said.

I guess none of us was destined to ever quite be an adult.

“Man,” Neil said, looking down at the long, cold, unmoving form of the burglar. “He’s really dead.”

“What the hell’re we gonna do?” Mike said.

“We’re going to call the police,” I said, and started for the phone.

“The hell we are,” Mike said. “The hell we are.”

3

Maybe half an hour after we laid him on the kitchen floor, he started to smell. We’d looked for identification and found none. He was just the Burglar.

We sat at the kitchen table, sharing a fifth of Old Grand-Dad and innumerable beers.

We’d taken two votes, and they’d come up ties. Two for calling the police, Bob and I; two for not calling the police, Mike and Neil.

“All we have to tell them,” I said, “is that we tied him up so he wouldn’t get away.”

“And then they say,” Mike said, “so why didn’t you call us before now?”

“We just lie about the time a little,” I said. “Tell them we called them within twenty minutes.”

“Won’t work,” Neil said.

“Why not?” Bob said.

“Medical examiner can fix the time of death,” Neil said.

“Not that close.”

“Close enough so that the cops might question our story,” Neil said. “By the time they get here, he’ll have been dead at least an hour, hour and a half.”

“And then we get our names in the paper for not reporting the burglary or the death right away,” Mike said. “Brokerages just love publicity like that.”

“I’m calling the cops right now,” I said, and started up from the table.

“Think about Tomlinson a minute,” Neil said.

Tomlinson was my boss at the brokerage. “What about him?”

“Remember how he canned Dennis Bryce when Bryce’s ex-wife took out a restraining order on him?”

“This is different,” I said.

"The hell it is," Mike said. "Neil's right, none of our bosses will like publicity like this. We'll all sound a little—crazy—you know, keeping him locked up in the basement. And then killing him when he tried to get away."

They all looked at me.

"You bastards," I said. "I was the one who wanted to call the police in the first place. And I sure as hell didn't try to kill him on purpose."

"Looking back on it," Neil said, "I guess you were right, Aaron. We should've called the cops right away."

"Now's a great time to realize that," I said.

"Maybe they've got a point," Bob said softly, glancing at me, then glancing nervously away.

"Oh, great. You, too?" I said.

"They just might kick my black ass out of there if I had any publicity that involved somebody getting killed," Bob said.

"He was a frigging burglar," I said.

"But he's dead," Neil said.

"And we killed him," Mike said.

"I appreciate you saying 'we,'" I said.

"I know a good place," Bob said.

I looked at him carefully, afraid of what he was going to say next.

"Forget it," I said.

"A good place for what?" Neil said.

"Dumping the body," Bob said.

"No way," I said.

This time, when I got up, nobody tried to stop me. I walked over to the yellow wall telephone.

I wondered if the cozy kitchen would ever feel the same to me now that a dead body had been laid upon its floor.

I had to step over him to reach the phone. The smell was even more sour now.

"You know how many bodies get dumped in the river that never wash up?" Bob said.

"No," I said, "and you don't either."

"Lots," he said.

"There's a scientific appraisal for you. 'Lots.'"

"Lots and lots, probably," Neil said, taking up Bob's argument.

Mike grinned. "Lots and lots and *lots.*"

"Thank you, Professor," I said.

I lifted the receiver and dialed 0.

"Operator."

"The Police Department, please."

"Is this an emergency?" asked the young woman. Usually, I would have spent more time wondering if the sweetness of her voice was matched by the sweetness of her face and body. I'm still a face man. I suppose it's my romantic side. "Is this an emergency?" she repeated.

"No; no, it isn't."

"I'll connect you," she said.

"You think your kids'll be able to handle it?" Neil said.

"No mind games," I said.

"No mind games at all," he said. "I'm asking you a very realistic question. The police have some doubts about our story and then the press gets ahold of it, and bam. We're the lead story on all three channels. 'Did four middle-class men murder the burglar they captured?' The press even goes after the kids these days. 'Do *you* think your daddy murdered that burglar, son?'"

"Good evening. Police Department."

I started to speak, but I couldn't somehow. My voice wouldn't work. That's the only way I can explain it.

"The six o'clock news five nights running," Neil said softly behind me. "And the DA can't endorse any kind of vigilante activity, so he nails us on involuntary manslaughter."

"Hello? This is the Police Department," said the black female voice on the phone.

Neil was there then, reaching me as if by magic.

He took the receiver gently from my hand and hung it back up on the phone again.

"Let's go have another drink and see what Bob's got in mind, all right?"

He led me, as if I were a hospital patient, slowly and carefully back to the table, where Bob, over more whiskey, slowly and gently laid out his plan.

The next morning, three of us phoned in sick. Bob went to work because he had an important meeting.

Around noon—a sunny day when a softball game and a cold six-pack of beer sounded good—Neil and Mike came over. They looked as bad as I felt, and no doubt looked, myself.

We sat out on the patio eating the Hardee's lunch they'd bought. I'd need to play softball to work off some of the calories I was eating.

Birdsong and soft breezes and the smell of fresh-cut grass should have made our patio time enjoyable. But I had to wonder if we'd ever enjoy anything again. I just kept seeing the body momentarily arced above the roaring waters of the dam, and dropping into white, churning turbulence.

"You think we did the right thing?" Neil said.

"Now's a hell of a time to ask that," I said.

"Of course we did the right thing," Mike said. "What choice did we have? It was either that or get our asses arrested."

"So you don't have any regrets?" Neil said.

Mike sighed. "I didn't say that. I mean, I wish it hadn't happened in the first place."

"Maybe Aaron was right all along," Neil said.

"About what?"

"About going to the cops."

"Goddamn," Mike said, sitting up from his slouch. We all wore button-down shirts without ties and with the sleeves rolled up. Somehow there was something profane about wearing shorts and T-shirts on a workday. We even wore pretty good slacks. We were those kind of people. "Goddamn."

"Here he goes," Neil said.

"I can't believe you two," Mike said. "We should be happy that everything went so well last night—and what're we doing? Sitting around here pissing and moaning."

"That doesn't mean it's over," I said.

"Why the hell not?" Mike said.

"Because there's still one left."

"One what?"

"One burglar."

"So?"

"So you don't think he's going to get curious about what the hell happened to his partner?"

"What's he gonna do?" Mike said. "Go to the cops?"

"Maybe."

"Maybe? You're crazy. He goes to the cops, he'd be setting himself up for a robbery conviction."

"Not if he tells them we murdered his pal."

Neil said, "Aaron's got a point. What if this guy goes to the cops?"

"He's not going to the cops," Mike said. "No way he's going to the cops at all."

4

I was dozing on the couch, a Cubs game on the TV set, when the phone rang around nine that evening. I hadn't heard from Jan yet, so I expected it would be her. Whenever we're apart, we call each other at least once a day.

The phone machine picks up on the fourth ring, so I had to scramble to beat it.

"Hello?"

Nothing. But somebody was on the line. Listening.

"Hello?"

I never play games with silent callers. I just hang up. I did so now.

Two innings later, having talked to Jan, having made myself a tuna fish sandwich on rye, found a package of potato chips I thought we'd finished off at the poker game, and gotten myself a new can of beer, I sat down to watch the last inning. The Cubs had a chance of winning. I said a silent prayer to the god of baseball.

The phone rang.

I mouthed several curses around my mouthful of tuna sandwich and went to the phone.

"Hello?" I said, trying to swallow the last of the bite.

My silent friend again.

I slammed the phone.

The Cubs got two more singles. I started on the chips, and I had polished off the beer and was thinking of getting another one when the phone rang again.

I had a suspicion of who was calling and then saying nothing — but I didn't really want to think about it.

Then I decided there was an easy way to handle this situation. I'd just let the phone machine take it. If my anonymous friend wanted to talk to a phone machine, good for him.

Four rings. The phone machine took over, Jan's pleasant voice saying that we weren't home but would be happy to call you back if you'd just leave your number.

I waited to hear dead air and then a click.

Instead, a familiar female voice said, "Aaron, it's Louise. Bob —" Louise was Bob's wife. She was crying. I ran from the couch to the phone machine in the hall.

"Hello, Louise. It's Aaron."

"Oh, Aaron. It's terrible."

"What happened, Louise?"

"Bob—" More tears. "He electrocuted himself tonight out in the garage." She said that a plug had accidentally fallen into a bowl of water, according to the fire captain on the scene, and Bob hadn't noticed this and put the plug into the outlet and—

Bob had a woodcraft workshop in his garage, a large and sophisticated one. He knew what he was doing. "He's dead, Aaron. He's dead."

"Oh, God, Louise. I'm sorry."

"He was so careful with electricity, too. It's just so hard to believe—"

Yes, I thought. Yes, it was hard to believe. I thought of last night. Of the burglars—one who'd died, one who'd gotten away.

"Why don't I come over?"

"Oh, thank you, Aaron, but I need to be alone with the children. But if you could call Neil and Mike—"

"Of course."

"Thanks for being such good friends, you and Jan."

"Don't be silly, Louise. The pleasure's ours."

"I'll talk to you tomorrow. When I'm—you know."

"Good night, Louise."

Mike and Neil were at my place within twenty minutes. We sat in the kitchen again, where we were last night.

I said, "Either of you get any weird phone calls tonight?"

"You mean just silence?" Neil said.

"Right."

"I did," Mike said. "Tracy was afraid it was that pervert who called all last winter."

"I did, too," Neil said. "Three of them."

"Then a little while ago, Bob dies out in his garage," I said. "Some coincidence."

"Hey, Aaron," Mike said. "Is that why you got us over here? Because you don't think it was an accident?"

"I'm sure it wasn't an accident," I said. "Bob knew what he was doing with his tools. He didn't notice a plug that had fallen into a bowl of water?"

"He's coming after us," Neil said.

"Oh, God," Mike said. "Not you, too."

"He calls us, gets us on edge," I said. "And then he kills Bob. Making it look like an accident."

"These are pretty bright people," Mike said sarcastically.

"You notice the burglar's eyes?" Neil said.

"I did," I said. "He looked very bright."

"And spooky," Neil said. "Never saw eyes like that before."

"I can shoot your theory right in the butt," Mike said.

"How?" I said.

He leaned forward, sipped his beer. I'd thought about putting out some munchies, but somehow that seemed wrong given poor Bob's death and the phone calls. The beers we had to have. The munchies were too festive.

"Here's how. There are two burglars, right? One gets caught, the other runs. And given the nature of burglars, keeps on running. He wouldn't even know who was in the house last night, except for Aaron, and that's only because he's the owner and his name would be in the phone book. But he wouldn't know anything about Bob or Neil or me. No way he'd have been able to track down Bob."

I shook my head. "You're overlooking the obvious."

"Like what?"

"Like he runs off last night, gets his car, and then parks in the alley to see what's going to happen."

"Right," Neil said. "Then he sees us bringing his friend out wrapped in a blanket. He follows us to the dam and watches us throw his friend in."

"And," I said, "everybody had his car here last night. Very easy for him to write down all the license numbers."

"So he kills Bob," Neil said. "And starts making the phone calls to shake us up."

"Why Bob?"

"Maybe he hates black people," I said.

Mike looked first at me and then at Neil. "You know what this is?"

"Here he goes," Neil said.

"No; no, I'm serious here. This is Catholic guilt."

"How can it be Catholic guilt when I'm Jewish?" Neil said.

"In a culture like ours, everybody is a little bit Jewish and a little bit Catholic, anyway," Mike said. "So you guys are in the throes of Catholic guilt. You feel bad about what we had to do last night — and we did have to do it, we really didn't have any choice — and the guilt starts to prey on your mind. So poor Bob electrocutes himself accidentally, and you immediately think it's the second burglar."

"He followed him," Neil said.

"What?" Mike said.

"That's what he did, I bet. The burglar. Followed Bob around all day trying to figure out what was the best way to kill him. You know, the best way that would look like an accident. So then he finds out about the workshop and decides it's perfect."

"That presumes," Mike said, "that one of us is going to be next."

"Hell, yes," Neil said. "That's why he's calling us. Shake us up. Sweat us out. Let us know that he's out there somewhere, just waiting. And that we're next."

"I'm going to follow you to work tomorrow, Neil," I said. "And Mike's going to be with me."

"You guys are having breakdowns. You really are," Mike said.

"We'll follow Neil tomorrow," I said. "And then on Saturday, you and Neil can follow me. If he's following *us* around, then we'll see it. And then we can start following him. We'll at least find out who he is."

"And then what?" Mike said. "Suppose we do find out where he lives? Then what the hell do we do?"

Neil said, "I guess we worry about that when we get there, don't we?"

In the morning, I picked Mike up early. We stopped off for doughnuts and coffee. He's like my brother, not a morning person. Crabby. Our conversation was at a minimum, though he did say, "I could've used the extra hour's sleep this morning. Instead of this crap, I mean."

As agreed, we parked half a block from Neil's house. Also as agreed, Neil emerged exactly at 7:35. Kids were already in the wide suburban streets on skateboards and rollerblades. No other car could be seen, except for a lone silver BMW in a driveway far down the block.

We followed him all the way to work. Nobody else followed him. Nobody.

When I dropped Mike off at his office, he said, "You owe me an hour's sleep."

"Two hours," I said.

"Huh?"

"Tomorrow, you and Neil follow me around."

"No way," he said.

There are times when only blunt anger will work with Mike. "It was your idea not to call the police, remember? I'm not up for any of your sulking, Mike. I'm really not."

He sighed. "I guess you're right."

I drove for two and a half hours Saturday morning. I hit a hardware store, a lumberyard, and a Kmart. At noon, I pulled into a McDonald's. The three of us had some lunch.

"You didn't see anybody even suspicious?"

"Not even suspicious, Aaron," Neil said. "I'm sorry."

"This is all bullshit. He's not going to follow us around."

"I want to give it one more chance," I said.

Mike made a face. "I'm not going to get up early, if that's what you've got in mind."

I got angry again. "Bob's dead, or have you forgotten?"

"Yeah, Aaron," Mike said. "Bob *is* dead. He got electrocuted. Accidentally."

I said, "You really think it was an accident?"

"Of course I do," Mike said. "When do you want to try it again?"

"Tonight. I'll do a little bowling."

"There's a fight on I want to watch," Mike said.

"Tape it," I said.

"'Tape it,'" he mocked. "Since when did you start giving us orders?"

"Oh, for God's sake, Mike, grow up," Neil said. "There's no way that Bob's electrocution was an accident or a coincidence. He's probably not going to stop with Bob either."

The bowling alley was mostly teenagers on Saturday night. There was a time when bowling was mostly a working-class sport. Now it's come to the suburbs and the white-collar people. Now the bowling lane is a good place for teenage boys to meet teenage girls.

I bowled two games, drank three beers, and walked back outside an hour later.

Summer night. Smell of dying heat, car exhaust, cigarette smoke, perfume. Sound of jukebox, distant loud mufflers, even more distant rushing train, lonely baying dogs.

Mike and Neil were gone.

I went home and opened myself a beer.

The phone rang. Once again, I was expecting Jan.

"Found the bastard," Neil said. "He followed you from your house to the bowling alley. Then he got tired of waiting and took off again. This time we followed *him*."

"Where?"

He gave me an address. It wasn't a good one.

"We're waiting for you to get here. Then we're going up to pay him a little visit."

"I need twenty minutes."

"Hurry."

Not even the silver touch of moonlight lent the blocks of crumbling stucco apartment houses any majesty or beauty. The rats didn't even bother to hide. They squatted red-eyed on the unmown lawns, amid beer cans, broken bottles, wrappers from Taco John's, and used condoms that looked like deflated mushrooms.

Mike stood behind a tree.

"I followed him around back," Mike said. "He went up the fire escape on the back. Then he jumped on this veranda. He's in the back apartment on the right side. Neil's in the backyard, watching for him."

Mike looked down at my ball bat. "That's a nice complement," he said. Then he showed me his handgun. "To this."

"Why the hell did you bring that?"

"Are you kidding? You're the one who said he killed Bob."

That I couldn't argue with.

"All right," I said, "but what happens when we catch him?"

"We tell him to lay off us," Mike said.

"We need to go to the cops."

"Oh, sure. Sure we do." He shook his head. He looked as if he were dealing with a child. A very slow one. "Aaron, going to the cops now won't bring Bob back. And it's only going to get us in trouble."

That's when we heard the shout. Neil; it sounded like Neil.

Maybe five feet of rust-colored grass separated the yard from the alley that ran along the west side of the apartment house.

We ran down the alley, having to hop over an ancient drooping picket fence to reach the backyard, where Neil lay sprawled, face-down, next to a twenty-year-old Chevrolet that was tireless and up on blocks. Through the windshield, you could see the huge gouges in the seats where the rats had eaten their fill.

The backyard smelled of dog shit and car oil.

Neil was moaning. At least we knew he was alive.

"The son of a bitch," he said when we got him to his feet. "I moved over to the other side, back of the car there, so he wouldn't see me if he tried to come down that fire escape. I didn't figure there was another fire escape on the side of the building. He must've come around there and snuck up on me. He tried to kill me, but I had this—"

In the moonlight, his wrist and the switchblade he held in his fingers were wet and dark with blood. "I got him a couple of times in the arm. Otherwise, I'd be dead."

"We're going up there," Mike said.

"How about checking Neil first?" I said.

"I'm fine," Neil said. "A little headache from where he caught me on the back of the neck." He waved his bloody blade. "Good thing I had this."

The landlord was on the first floor. He wore Bermuda shorts and no shirt. He looked eleven or twelve months pregnant, with little male titties and enough coarse black hair to knit a sweater with. He had a plastic-tipped cigarillo in the left corner of his mouth.

"Yeah?"

"Two-F," I said.

"What about it?"

"Who lives there?"

"Nobody."

"Nobody?"

"If you were the law, you'd show me a badge."

"I'll show you a badge," Mike said, making a fist.

"Hey," I said, playing good cop to bad cop. "You just let me speak to this gentleman."

The guy seemed to like my reference to him as a gentleman. It was probably the only name he'd never been called.

"Sir, we saw somebody go up there."

"Oh," he said. "The vampires."

"Vampires?"

He sucked down some cigarillo smoke. "That's what we call 'em, the missus and me. They're street people, winos and homeless and all like that. They know that sometimes some of these apartments ain't rented for a while, so they sneak up there and spend the night."

"You don't stop them?"

"You think I'm gonna get my head split open for something like that?"

"I guess that makes sense." Then: "So nobody's renting it now?"

"Nope, it ain't been rented for three months. This fat broad lived there then. Man, did she smell. You know how fat people can smell sometimes? *She* sure smelled." He wasn't svelte.

Back on the front lawn, trying to wend my way between the mounds of dog shit, I said, "'Vampires.' Good name for them."

"Yeah, it is," Neil said. "I just keep thinking of the one who died. His weird eyes."

"Here we go again," Mike said. "You two guys love to scare the shit out of each other, don't you? They're a couple of nickel-dime crooks, and that's *all* they are."

"All right if Mike and I stop and get some beer and then swing by your place?"

"Sure," I said. "Just as long as Mike buys Bud and none of that generic crap."

"Oh, I forgot." Neil laughed. "He does do that when it's his turn to buy, doesn't he?"

"Yeah," I said, "he certainly does."

I was never sure what time the call came. Darkness. The ringing phone seemed part of a dream from which I couldn't escape. Somehow I managed to lift the receiver before the phone machine kicked in.

Silence. That special *kind* of silence.

Him. I had no doubt about it. The vampire, as the landlord had called him. The one who'd killed Bob. I didn't say so much as hello. Just listened, angry, afraid, confused.

After a few minutes, he hung up.

Darkness again; deep darkness, the quarter moon in the sky a cold golden scimitar that could cleave a head from a neck.

5

About noon on Sunday, Jan called to tell me that she was staying a few days extra. The kids had discovered archery, and there was a course at the Y they were taking and wouldn't she please please *please* ask good old Dad if they could stay. I said sure.

I called Neil and Mike to remind them that at nine tonight we were going to pay a visit to that crumbling stucco apartment house again.

I spent an hour on the lawn. My neighbors shame me into it. Lawns aren't anything I get excited about. But they sort of shame you into it. About halfway through, Byrnes, the chunky advertising man who lives next door, came over and clapped me on the back. He was apparently pleased that I was a real human being and taking a real-human-being interest in my lawn. As usual, he wore an expensive T-shirt with one of his clients' products on it and a pair of Bermuda shorts. As usual, he tried hard to be the kind of winsome neighbor you always had in sitcoms of the 1950s. But I knew somebody who knew him. Byrnes had fired his number two man so he wouldn't have to keep paying the man's insurance. The man was unfortunately dying of cancer. Byrnes was typical of all the ad people I'd met. Pretty treacherous people who spent most of their time cheating clients out of their money and putting on awards banquets so they could convince themselves that advertising was actually an endeavor that was of consequence.

Around four, *Hombre* was on one of the cable channels, so I had a few beers and watched Paul Newman doing the best acting of his career. At least that was my opinion.

I was just getting ready for the shower when the phone rang.

He didn't say hello. He didn't identify himself. "Tracy call you?"

It was Neil. Tracy was Mike's wife. "Why should she call me?"

"He's dead. Mike."

"What?"

"You remember how he was always bitching about that elevator at work?"

Mike worked in a very old building. He made jokes about the antiquated elevators. But you could always tell the joke simply hid his fears. He'd gotten stuck innumerable times, and it was always stopping several feet short of the upcoming floor.

"He opened the door and the car wasn't there. He fell eight floors."

"Oh, God."

"I don't have to tell you who did it, do I?"

"Maybe it's time—"

"I'm way ahead of you, Aaron. I'll pick you up in half an hour. Then we go to the police. You agree?"

"I agree."

Late Sunday afternoon, the Second Precinct parking lot is pretty empty. We'd missed the shift change. Nobody came or went.

"We ask for a detective," Neil said. He was dark-sportcoat, white-shirt, necktie earnest. I'd settled for an expensive blue sportshirt Jan had bought me for my last birthday.

"You know one thing we haven't considered?"

"You're not going to change my mind."

"I'm not *trying* to change your mind, Neil, I'm just saying that there's one thing we haven't considered."

He sat behind his steering wheel, his head resting on the back of his seat.

"A lawyer."

"What for?"

"Because we may go in there and say something that gets us in very deep shit."

"No lawyers," he said. "We'd just look like we were trying to hide something from the cops."

"You sure about that?"

"I'm sure."

"You ready?" I said.

"Ready."

The interior of the police station was quiet. A muscular bald man in a dark uniform sat behind a desk with a sign that read INFORMATION.

He said, "Help you?"

"We'd like to see a detective," I said.

"Are you reporting a crime?"

"Uh, yes," I said.

"What sort of crime?" he said.

I started to speak but once again lost my voice. I thought about all the reporters, about how Jan and the kids would be affected by it all. How my job would be affected. Taking a guy down to the basement and tying him up and then accidentally killing him—

Neil said: "Vandalism."

"Vandalism?" the cop said. "You don't need a detective, then. I can just give you a form." Then he gave us a leery look, as if he sensed we'd just changed our minds about something.

"In that case, could I just take it home with me and fill it out there?" Neil said.

"Yeah, I guess." The cop still watched us carefully now.

"Great."

"You sure that's what you wanted to report? Vandalism?"

"Yeah; yeah, that's exactly what we wanted to report," Neil said. "Exactly."

"Vandalism?" I said when we were back in the car.

"I don't want to talk right now."

"Well, maybe *I* want to talk."

"I just couldn't do it."

"No kidding."

He looked over at me. "You could've told him the truth. Nobody was stopping you."

I looked out the window. "Yeah, I guess I could've."

"We're going over there tonight. To the vampire's place."

"And do what?"

"Ask him how much he wants."

"How much he wants for what?" I said.

"How much he wants to forget everything. He goes on with his life, we go on with ours."

I had to admit, I'd had a similar thought myself. Neil and I didn't know how to do any of this. But the vampire did. He was good at stalking, good at harassing, good at violence.

"We don't have a lot of money to throw around."

"Maybe he won't *want* a lot of money. I mean, these guys aren't exactly sophisticated."

"They're sophisticated enough to make two murders look like accidents."

"I guess that's a point."

"I'm just not sure we should pay him anything, Neil."

"You got any better ideas?"

I didn't, actually. I didn't have any better ideas at all.

6

I spent an hour on the phone with Jan that afternoon. The last few days I'd been pretty anxious, and she'd sensed it, and now she was making sure that everything was all right with me. In addition to being wife and lover, Jan's also my best friend. I can't kid her. She always knows when something's wrong. I'd put off telling her about Bob and Mike dying. I'd been afraid that I might accidentally say more than I should and make her suspicious. But now I had to tell her about their deaths. It was the only way I could explain my tense mood.

"That's awful," she said. "Their poor families."

"They're handling it better than you might think."

"Maybe I should bring the kids home early."

"No reason to, hon. I mean, realistically there isn't anything any of us can do."

"Two accidents in that short a time. It's pretty strange."

"Yeah, I guess it is. But that's how it happens sometimes."

"Are you going to be all right?"

"Just need to adjust is all." I sighed. "I guess we won't be having our poker games anymore."

Then I did something I hadn't intended. I started crying, and the tears caught in my throat.

"Oh, honey," Jan said. "I wish I was there so I could give you a big hug."

"I'll be OK."

"Two of your best friends."

"Yeah." The tears were starting to dry up now.

"Oh, did I tell you about Tommy?" Tommy was our six-year-old.

"No, what?"

"Remember how he used to be so afraid of horses?"

"Uh-huh."

"Well, we took him out to this horse ranch where you can rent horses?"

"Uh-huh."

"And they found him a little Shetland pony and let him ride it, and he loved it. He wasn't afraid at all." She laughed. "In fact, we could barely drag him home." She paused. "You're probably not in the mood for this, are you? I'm sorry, hon. Maybe you should do something to take your mind off things. Is there a good movie on?"

"I guess I could check."

"Something light, that's what you need."

"Sounds good," I said. "I'll go get the newspaper and see what's on."

"Love you."

"Love you, too, sweetheart," I said.

I spent the rest of the afternoon going through my various savings accounts and investments. I had no idea what the creep would want to leave us alone. We could always threaten him with going to the police, though he might rightly point out that if we really wanted to do that, we would already have done it.

I settled in the five-thousand-dollar range. That was the maximum cash I had to play with. And even then I'd have to borrow a little from one of the mutual funds we had earmarked for the kids and college.

Five thousand dollars. To me, it sounded like an enormous amount of money, probably because I knew how hard I'd had to work to get it.

But would it be enough for our friend the vampire?

Neil was there just at dark. He parked in the drive and came in. Meaning he wanted to talk.

We went in the kitchen. I made us a couple of highballs, and we sat there and discussed finances.

"I came up with six thousand," he said.

"I've got five."

"That's eleven grand," he said. "It's got to be more cash than this creep has ever seen."

"What if he takes it and comes back for more?"

"We make it absolutely clear," Neil said, "that there is no more. That this is it. Period."

"And if not?"

Neil nodded. "I've thought this through. You know the kind of lowlife we're dealing with? A, he's a burglar, which means, these days, that he's a junkie. B, if he's a junkie, then that means he's very susceptible to AIDS. So between being a burglar and shooting up, this guy is probably going to have a very short lifespan."

"I guess I'd agree."

"Even if he wants to make our life miserable, he probably won't live long enough to do it. So I think we'll be making just the one payment. We'll buy enough time to let nature take its course — his nature."

"What if he wants more than the eleven grand?"

"He won't. His eyes'll pop out when he sees this."

I looked at the kitchen clock. It was going on nine now.

"I guess we could drive over there."

"It may be a long night," Neil said.

"I know."

"But I guess we don't have a hell of a lot of choice, do we?"

As we'd done the last time we'd been here, we split up the duties. I took the backyard, Neil the apartment door. We'd waited until midnight. The rap music had died by now. Babies cried and mothers screamed; couples fought. TV screens flickered in dark windows.

I went up the fire escape slowly and carefully. We'd talked about bringing guns, then decided against it. We weren't exactly marksmen, and if a cop stopped us for some reason, we could be arrested for carrying unlicensed firearms. All I carried was a flashlight in my back pocket.

As I grabbed the rungs of the ladder, powdery rust dusted my hands. I was chilly with sweat. My bowels felt sick. I was scared. I just wanted it to be over with. I wanted him to say yes, he'd take the money, and then that would be the end of it.

The stucco veranda was filled with discarded toys — a tricycle, innumerable games, a space helmet, a Wiffle bat and ball. The floor was crunchy with dried animal feces. At least, I hoped the feces belonged to animals and not human children.

The door between veranda and apartment was open. Fingers of moonlight revealed an overstuffed couch and chair and a floor covered with the debris of fast food, McDonald's sacks, Pizza Hut wrappers and cardboards, Arby's wrappers, and what seemed to be five or six dozen empty beer cans. Far toward the hall that led to the front door, I saw four red eyes watching me, a pair of curious rats.

I stood still and listened. Nothing. No sign of life. I went inside. Tiptoeing.

I went to the front door and let Neil in. There in the murky light of the hallway, he made a face. The smell *was* pretty bad.

Over the next ten minutes, we searched the apartment. And found nobody.

"We could wait here for him," I said.

"No way."

"The smell?"

"The smell, the rats. God. Don't you just feel unclean?"

"Yeah, guess I do."

"There's an empty garage about halfway down the alley. We'd have a good view of the back of this building."

"Sounds pretty good."

"Sounds better than this place, anyway."

This time, we both went out the front door and down the stairway. Now the smells were getting to me as they'd earlier gotten to Neil. Unclean. He was right.

We got in Neil's Buick, drove down the alley that ran along the west side of the apartment house, backed up to the dark garage, and whipped inside.

"There's a sack in back," Neil said. "It's on your side."

"A sack?"

"Brewskis. Quart for you, quart for me."

"That's how my old man used to drink them," I said. I was the only blue-collar member of the poker club. "Get off work at the plant and stop by and pick up two quart bottles of Hamms. Never missed."

"Sometimes I wish I would've been born into the working class," Neil said.

I was the blue-collar guy, and Neil was the dreamer, always inventing alternative realities for himself.

"No, you don't," I said, leaning over the seat and picking up the sack damp from the quart bottles. "You had a damned nice life in Boston."

"Yeah, but I didn't learn anything. You know I was eighteen before I learned about cunnilingus?"

"Talk about cultural deprivation," I said.

"Well, every girl I went out with probably looks back on me as a pretty lame lover. They went down on me, but I never went down on them. How old were you when you learned about cunnilingus?"

"Maybe thirteen."

"See?"

"I learned about it, but I didn't do anything about it."

"I was twenty years old before I lost my cherry," Neil said.

"I was seventeen."

"Bullshit."

"Bullshit what? I was seventeen."

"In sociology, they always taught us that blue-collar kids lost their virginity a lot earlier than white-collar kids."

"That's the trouble with sociology. It tries to particularize from generalities."

"Huh?" He grinned. "Yeah, I always thought sociology was full of shit, too, actually. But you were really seventeen?"

"I was really seventeen."

I wish I could tell you that I knew what it was right away, the missile that hit the windshield and shattered and starred it, and then kept right on tearing through the car until the back window was also shattered and starred.

But all I knew was that Neil was screaming and I was screaming and my quart bottle of Miller's was spilling all over my crotch as I tried to hunch down behind the dashboard. It was a tight fit because Neil was trying to hunch down behind the steering wheel.

The second time, I knew what was going on: somebody was shooting at us. Given the trajectory of the bullet, he had to be right in front of us, probably behind the two Dumpsters that sat on the other side of the alley.

"Can you keep down and drive this son of a bitch at the same time?"

"I can try," Neil said.

"If we sit here much longer, he's going to figure out we don't have guns. Then he's gonna come for us for sure."

Neil leaned over and turned on the ignition. "I'm going to turn left when we get out of here."

"Fine. Just get moving."

"Hold on."

What he did was kind of slump over the bottom half of the wheel, just enough so he could sneak a peek at where the car was headed.

There were no more shots.

All I could hear was the smooth-running Buick motor.

He eased out of the garage, ducking down all the time.

When he got a chance, he bore left.

He kept the lights off.

Through the bullet hole in the windshield, I could see an inch or so of starry sky.

It was a long alley, and we must have gone a quarter block before he said, “I’m going to sit up. I think we lost him.”

“So do I.”

“Look at the frigging windshield.”

Not only was the windshield a mess, the car reeked of spilled beer.

“You think I should turn on the headlights?”

“Sure,” I said. “We’re safe now.”

We were still crawling at maybe ten miles per hour when he pulled the headlights on.

That’s when we saw him, silver of eye, dark of hair, crouching in the middle of the alley waiting for us. He was a good fifty yards ahead of us, but we were still within range.

There was no place we could turn around.

He fired.

This bullet shattered whatever had been left untouched of the windshield. Neil slammed on the brakes.

Then he fired a second time.

By now, both Neil and I were screaming and cursing again.

A third bullet.

“Run him over!” I yelled, ducking behind the dashboard.

“What?” Neil yelled back.

“Floor it!”

He floored it. He wasn’t even sitting up straight. We might have gone careening into one of the garages or Dumpsters. But somehow the Buick stayed in the alley. And very soon it was traveling eighty-five miles per hour. I watched the speedometer peg it.

More shots, a lot of them now, side windows shattering, bullets ripping into fender and hood and top.

I didn’t see us hit him, but I *felt* us hit him, the car traveling that fast, the creep so intent on killing us he hadn’t bothered to get out of the way in time.

The front of the car picked him up and hurled him into a garage near the head of the alley.

We both sat up, watched as his entire body was broken against the edge of the garage, and he then fell smashed and unmoving to the grass.

“Kill the lights,” I said.

“What?”

"Kill the lights, and let's go look at him."

Neil punched off the headlights.

We left the car and ran over to him.

A white rib stuck bloody and brazen from his side. Blood poured from his ears, nose, mouth. One leg had been crushed and also showed white bone. His arms had been broken, too.

I played my flashlight beam over him.

He was dead, all right.

"Looks like we can save our money," I said. "It's all over now."

"I want to get the hell out of here."

"Yeah," I said. "So do I."

We got the hell out of there.

7

A month later, just as you could smell autumn on the summer winds, Jan and I celebrated our twelfth wedding anniversary. We drove up to Lake Geneva, in Wisconsin, and stayed at a very nice hotel and rented a Chris-Craft for a couple of days. This was the first time I'd been able to relax since the thing with the burglar had started.

One night when Jan was asleep, I went up on the deck of the boat and just watched the stars. I used to read a lot of Edgar Rice Burroughs when I was a boy. I always remembered how John Carter felt—that the stars had a very special destiny for him and would someday summon him to that destiny. My destiny, I decided that night there on the deck, was to be a good family man, a good stockbroker, and a good neighbor. The bad things were all behind me now. I imagined Neil was feeling pretty much the same way. Hot bitter July seemed a long way behind us now. Fall was coming, bringing with it football and Thanksgiving and Christmas. July would recede even more with snow on the ground.

The funny thing was, I didn't see Neil much anymore. It was as if the sight of each other brought back a lot of bad memories. It was a mutual feeling, too. I didn't want to see him any more than he wanted to see me. Our wives thought this was pretty strange. They'd meet at the supermarket or shopping center and wonder why "the boys" didn't get together anymore. Neil's wife, Sarah, kept inviting us over to "sit around the pool and watch Neil pretend he knows how to swim." September was summer hot. The pool was still the centerpiece of their life.

Not that I made any new friends. The notion of a midweek poker game had lost all its appeal. There was work and my family and little else.

Then, one sunny Indian-summer afternoon, Neil called and said, "Maybe we should get together again."

"Maybe."

"It's over, Aaron. It really is."

"I know."

"Will you at least think about it?"

I felt embarrassed. "Oh, hell, Neil. Is that swimming pool of yours open Saturday afternoon?"

"As a matter of fact, it is. And as a matter of fact, Sarah and the girls are going to be gone to a fashion show at the club."

"Perfect. We'll have a couple of beers."

"You know how to swim?"

"No," I said, laughing. "And from what Sarah says, you don't either."

I got there about three, pulled into the drive, walked to the back where the gate in the wooden fence led to the swimming pool. It was eighty degrees, and even from here I could smell the chlorine.

I opened the gate and went inside and saw him right away. The funny thing was, I didn't have much of a reaction at all. I just watched him. He was floating. Face-down. He looked pale in his red trunks. This, like the others, would be judged an accidental death. Of that I had no doubt at all.

I used the cellular phone in my car to call 911.

I didn't want Sarah and the girls coming back to see an ambulance and police cars in the drive and them not knowing what was going on.

I called the club and had her paged.

I told her what I'd found. I let her cry. I didn't know what to say. I never do.

In the distance, I could hear the ambulance working its way toward the Neil Solomon residence.

I was just about to get out of the car when my cellular phone rang. I picked up. "Hello?"

"There were three of us that night at your house, Mr. Bellini. You killed two of us. I recovered from when your friend stabbed me, remember? Now I'm ready for action. I really am, Mr. Bellini."

Then the emergency people were there, and neighbors, too, and then wan, trembling Sarah. I just let her cry some more. Gave her whiskey and let her cry.

8

He knows how to do it, whoever he is.

He lets a long time go between late-night calls. He lets me start to think that maybe he changed his mind and left town. And then he calls.

Oh, yes, he knows just how to play this little game.

He never says anything. He doesn't need to. He just listens. And then hangs up.

I've considered going to the police, of course, but it's way too late for that. Way too late.

Or I could ask Jan and the kids to move away to a different city with me. But he knows who I am, and he'd find me again.

So all I can do is wait and hope that I get lucky, the way Neil and I got lucky the night we killed the second of them.

Tonight I can't sleep.

It's after midnight.

Jan and I wrapped presents until well after eleven. She asked me again if anything was wrong. We don't make love as much as we used to, she said; and then there are the nightmares. "Please tell me if something's wrong, Aaron. Please."

I stand at the window watching the snow come down. Soft and beautiful snow. In the morning, a Saturday, the kids will make a snowman and then go sledding and then have themselves a good old-fashioned snowball fight, which invariably means that one of them will come rushing in at some point and accuse the other of some terrible misdeed.

I see all this from the attic window.

Then I turn back and look around the poker table. Four empty chairs. Three of them belong to dead men.

I look at the empty chairs and think back to summer.

I look at the empty chairs and wait for the phone to ring.

I wait for the phone to ring.

1996

JAMES CRUMLEY

HOT SPRINGS

James (Arthur) Crumley (1939–2008) was born in Three Rivers, Texas, and grew up in south Texas. After serving in the Army in the Philippines, he received his BA in history (1964) from the Texas College of Arts and Industries, to which he had received a football scholarship, then got his Master of Fine Arts in creative writing (1966) from the University of Iowa, where he began his first novel, *One to Count Cadence,* as his master's thesis; it was published in 1969.

After that Vietnam War novel, he turned to mystery fiction with *The Wrong Case* (1975), introducing the first of his two private eye characters, Milo Milodragovich, who also appeared in *Dancing Bear* (1983) and *The Final Country* (2001). His tougher PI, C. W. Sughrue, made his debut in *The Last Good Kiss* (1978), which many contemporary mystery writers, such as George Pelecanos, Michael Connelly, and Dennis Lehane, regard as among the most influential crime novels of the second half of the twentieth century. This memorable novel opens with one of the most famous and perfect first lines in crime fiction: "When I finally caught up with Abraham Trahearne, he was drinking beer with an alcoholic bulldog named Fireball Roberts in a ramshackle joint just outside Sonoma, California, drinking the heart right out of a fine spring afternoon." Sughrue also appeared in *The Mexican Tree Duck* (1993), *The Right Madness* (2005), and *Bordersnakes* (1996), in which Milo also features. Inexplicably, and to its everlasting shame, the Mystery Writers of America never gave Crumley any award, or even nominated him for one — a seemingly impossible scenario when one considers the power and importance of his work, as well as the nearly overwhelming beauty of his prose.

"Hot Springs" was first published in the anthology *Murder for Love* (New York: Delacorte, 1996).

▪ ▪ ▪

At night, even in the chill mountain air, Mona Sue insisted on cranking the air conditioner all the way up. Her usual temperature always ran a couple of degrees higher than normal, and she claimed that the baby she carried made her constant fever even worse. She kept the cabin cold enough to hang meat. During the long, sleepless nights, Benbow spooned to her naked, burning skin, trying to stay warm.

In the mornings, too, Mona Sue forced him into the cold. The modern cabin sat on a bench in the cool shadow of Mount Nihart, and they broke their fast with a room-service breakfast on the deck, a robe wrapped loosely about her naked body while Benbow bundled into both sweats and a robe. She ate furiously, stoking a furnace, and recounted her dreams as if they were gospel, effortlessly consuming most of the spread of exotic cheeses and expensively unseasonable fruits, a loaf of sourdough toast, and four kinds of meat, all the while aimlessly babbling through the events of her internal night, the dreams of a teenage girl, languidly symbolic and vaguely frightening. She dreamed of her mother, young and lovely, devouring her litter of barefoot boys in the dark Ozark hollows. And her father, home from a Tennessee prison, his crooked member dangling against her smooth cheek.

Benbow suspected she left the best parts out and did his best to listen to the soft southern cadences without watching her face. He knew what happened when he watched her talk, watched the soft moving curve of her dark lips, the wise slant of her gray eyes. So he picked at his breakfast and tried to focus his stare downslope at the steam drifting off the large hot-water pool behind the old shagbark lodge.

But then she switched to her daydreams about their dubious future, which were as deadly specific as a .45 slug in the brainpan: after the baby, they could flee to Canada; nobody would follow them up there. He listened and watched with the false patience of a teenage boy involved in his first confrontation with pure lust and hopeless desire.

Mona Sue ate with the precise and delicate greed of a heart surgeon, the pad of her spatulate thumb white on the handle of her spoon as she carved a perfect curled ball from the soft orange meat of her melon. Each bite of meat had to be balanced with an equal weight of toast before being crushed between her tiny white teeth. Then she examined each strawberry poised before her darkly red lips as if it might be a jewel of great omen and she some ancient oracle, then sank her shining teeth into the fleshy fruit as if it were the mortal truth. Benbow's heart rolled in his chest as he tried to fill his lungs with the cold air to fight off the heat of her body.

Fall had come to the mountains, now. The cottonwoods and alders welcomed the change with garish mourning dress, and in the mornings a rime of ice covered the windshield of the gray Taurus he had stolen at the Denver airport. New snow fell each night, moving slowly down the ridges from the high distant peaks of the Hard Rock Range, and slipped closer each morning down the steep ridge behind them. Below the bench the old lodge seemed to settle more deeply into the narrow canyon, as if hunkering down for eons of snow, and the steam from the hot springs mixed with wood smoke and lay flat and sinuous among the yellow creek willows.

Benbow suspected, too, that the scenery was wasted on Mona Sue. Her dark eyes seemed turned inward to a dreamscape of her life, her husband, R. L. Dark, the pig farmer, his bull-necked son, Little R. L., and the lumpy Ozark offal of her large worthless family.

"Coach," she'd say — she thought it funny to call him Coach — interrupting the shattered and drifting narrative of her dreams. Then she would sweep back the thick black Indian hair from her face, tilt her narrow head on the slender column of her neck, and laugh. "Coach, that ol' R. L., he's a-comin'. You stole somethin' belonged to him, and you can bet he's on his way. Lit'l R. L., too, prob'ly, 'cause he tol' me once he'd like to string your guts on a bob-wire fence," she recited like a sprightly but not very bright child.

"Sweetheart, R. L. Dark can just barely cipher the numbers on a dollar bill or the spots on a card," Benbow answered, as he had each morning for the six months they'd been on the run. "He can't read a map that he hasn't drawn himself, and by noon he's too drunk to fit his ass in a tractor seat and find his hog pens . . ."

"You know, Puddin', an ol' boy's got enough a them dollar bills, or stacks a them Franklins like we do," she added, laughing, "he can hire-out that readin' part, and the map part too. So he's a-comin'. You can put that in your mama's piggy bank."

This was a new wrinkle in their morning ritual, and Benbow caught himself glancing down at the parking lot behind the lodge and at the single narrow road up Hidden Springs Canyon, but he shook it off quickly. When he made the fateful decision to take Mona Sue and the money, he vowed to go for it, never glancing over his shoulder, living in the moment.

And this was it. Once more. Leaving his breakfast untouched, again, he slipped his hand through the bulky folds of Mona Sue's terry cloth robe to cradle the warm ripening fullness of her breasts and the long, thick nipples, already rock-hard before his touch, and he kissed her mouth, sweet with strawberry and melon. Once again, he marveled at the deep passionate growl from the base of her throat as he pressed his lips into the hollow, then Benbow lifted her small frame — she nestled the baby high under the smooth vault of her rib cage and even at seven months the baby barely showed — and carried her to the bedroom.

Benbow knew, from recent experience, that the horse wrangler who doubled as room-service waiter would be waiting to clear the picnic table when they came out of the house to finish the coffee. The wrangler might have patience with horses but not with guests who spent their mornings in bed. But he would wait for long minutes, silent as a Sioux scout, as Mona Sue searched her robe for his tip, occasionally exposing the rising contour of a breast or the clean scissoring of her long legs. Benbow had given him several hard looks, which the wrangler ignored as if the blunt stares were spoken in a foreign tongue. But nothing helped. Except to take the woman inside and avoid the wrangler altogether.

This morning Benbow laid Mona Sue on the featherbed like a gift, opened her robe, kissed the soft curve of her swollen belly, then blew softly on her feathery pubic hair. Mona Sue sobbed quickly, coughed as if she had a catfish bone caught in her throat, her long body arching. Benbow sobbed, too, his hunger for her more intense than the hunger growling in his empty stomach.

While Mona Sue had swelled through her pregnancy, Benbow had shed twenty-seven pounds from his blocky frame. Sometimes, just after they made love, it seemed as if her burning body had stolen the baby from his own muscled flesh, something stolen during the tangle of love, something growing hard and tight in her smooth, slim body.

As usual, they made love, then finished the coffee, ordered a fresh pot, tipped the wrangler, then made love again before her morning nap.

While Mona Sue slept, usually Benbow would drink the rest of the coffee as he read the day-old Meriwether newspaper, then slip into his sweats and running shoes, and jog down the switchbacks to the lodge to laze in the hot waters of the pools. He loved it there, floating in the water that seemed heavier than normal, thicker but cleaner, clearer. He almost felt whole there, cleansed and healthy and warm, taking the waters like some rich foreign prince, fleeing his failed life.

Occasionally, Benbow wished Mona Sue would interrupt her naps to join him, but she always said it might hurt the baby and she was already plenty hot with her natural fevers. As the weeks passed, Benbow learned to treasure his time alone in the hot pool and stopped asking her.

So their days wound away routinely, spooling like silk ribbons through their fingers, as placid as the deeply still waters of the pool.

But this noon, exhausted from the run and the worry, the lack of sleep and food, Benbow slipped effortlessly into the heated gravity of Mona

Sue's sleeping body and slept, only to wake suddenly, sweating in spite of the chill, when the air conditioner was switched off.

R. L. Dark stood at the foot of their bed. Grinning. The old man stretched his crinkled neck, sniffing the air like an ancient snapping turtle, testing the air for food or fun, since he had no natural enemies except for teenage boys with .22s. R. L. had dressed for the occasion. He wore a new Carhart tin coat and clean bib overalls with the old Webley .455 revolver hanging on a string from his neck and bagging the bib pocket.

Two good ol' boys flanked him, one bald and the other wildly hirsute, both huge and dressed in Kmart flannel plaid. The bald one held up a small ball-peen hammer like a trophy. They weren't grinning. A skinny man in a baggy white suit shifted from foot to foot behind them, smiling weakly like a gun-shy pointer pup.

"Well, piss on the fire, boys, and call the dogs," R. L. Dark said, hustling the extra .455 rounds in his pocket as if they were his withered privates, "this hunt's done." The old man's cackle sounded like the sunrise cry of a cannibalistic rooster. "Son, they say you coulda been some kinda football coach, and I know you're one hell of a poker player, but I'd a never thought you'd come to this sorry end—a simple-minded thief and a chickenfuckin' wife stealer." Then R. L. brayed like one of the old plow mules he kept in the muddy bottoms of the White. "But you can run right smart, son. Gotta say that. Sly as an old boar coon. We might still be a-lookin' if'n Baby Doll there ain't a called her mama. Collect. To brag 'bout the baby."

Jesus, Benbow thought. Her mother. A toothless woman, now shaped like a potato dumpling, topped with greasy hair, seasoned with moles.

Mona Sue woke, rubbing her eyes like a child, murmuring, "How you been, Daddy Honey?"

And Benbow knew he faced a death even harder than his unlucky life, knew even before the monster on the right popped him behind the ear with the ball-peen hammer and jerked his stunned body out of bed as if he were a child and handed him to his partner, who wrapped him in a full nelson. The bald one flipped the hammer and rapped his nuts smartly with it, then flipped it again and began breaking the small bones of Benbow's right foot with the round knob of the hammerhead.

Before Benbow fainted, harsh laughter raked his throat. Maybe this was the break he had been waiting for all his life.

Actually, it had all been Little R. L.'s fault. Sort of. Benbow had spotted the hulking bowlegged kid with the tiny ears and the thick neck three years earlier, when the downward spiral of his football coaching career had led him to Alabamphilia, a small town on the edge of the Ozarks, a town without hope or dignity or even any convincing religious fervor, a town that smelled of chicken guts, hog manure, and rampant incest, which seemed to be the three main industries.

Benbow first saw Little R. L. in a pickup touch-football game played on the hardscrabble playground, and knew from the first moment that the boy had the quick grace of a deer, combined with the strength of a wild boar. This kid was one of the best natural running backs he'd ever seen. Benbow also found out just as quickly that Little R. L. was one of the redheaded Dark boys, and the Dark boys didn't play football.

Daddy R. L. thought football was a silly game, a notion with which Benbow agreed, and too much like work not to draw wages, with which once again Benbow agreed, and if'n his boys were going to work for free, they were damn well going to work for him and his hog operation, not some dirt-poor pissant washed-up football bum. Benbow had to agree with that, too, right to R. L.'s face, had to eat the old man's shit to get to the kid. Because this kid could be Benbow's ticket out of this Ozark hell, and he intended to have him. This was the one break Benbow needed to save his life. Once again.

It had always been that way for Benbow, needing that one break that never seemed to come. During his senior year at the small high school in western Nebraska, after three and a half years of mostly journeyman work as a blocking back in a pass-crazy offense, Benbow's mother had worked double shifts at the truck-stop café — his dad had been dead so long nobody really remembered him — so they could afford to put together a videotape of his best efforts as a running back and pass receiver to send down to the university coaches in Lincoln. Once they had agreed to send a scout up for one game, Benbow had badgered his high school coach into a promise to let him carry the ball at least twenty times that night.

But the weather screwed him. On what should have been a lovely early October Friday night, a storm raced in from Canada, days early, and its icy wind blew Benbow's break right out of the water. Before the game it rained two hard inches, then the field froze. During the first half it rained again, then hailed, and at the end of the second quarter it became a blinding snow squall.

Benbow had gained sixty yards, sure, but none of it pretty. And at halftime the Nebraska scout came by to apologize but if he was to get home in this weather, he had to start now. The lumpy old man invited

Benbow to try a walk-on. Right, Benbow thought. Without a scholarship, he didn't have the money to register for fall semester. *Damn,* Benbow thought as he kicked the water cooler, and *damn it to hell,* he thought as his big toe shattered and his senior season ended.

So he played football for some pissant Christian college in the Dakotas where he didn't bother to take a degree. With his fused toe, he had lost a step in the open field and his cuts lost their precision, so he haunted the weight room, forced thick muscle over his running back's body, and made himself into a solid if small fullback, but good enough to wrangle an invitation to one of the postseason senior bowl games. Then the first-string fullback, who was sure to be drafted by the pros, strained his knee in practice and refused to play. *Oh, God,* Benbow thought, *another break.*

But God foxed this one. The backfield coach was a born-again fundamentalist named Culpepper, and once he caught Benbow neither bowing his head nor even bothering to close his eyes during a lengthy team prayer, the coach became determined to convert the boy. Benbow played along, choking on his anger at the self-righteous bastard until his stomach cramped, swallowing the anger until he was throwing up three times a day, twice during practice and once before lights-out. By game day he'd lost twelve pounds and feared he wouldn't have the strength to play.

But he did. He had a first half to praise the football gods, if not the Christian one: two rushing touchdowns, one three yards dragging a linebacker and a corner, the other thirty-nine yards of fluid grace and power; and one receiving, twenty-two yards. But the quarterback had missed the handoff at the end of the first half, jammed the ball against Benbow's hip, and a blitzing linebacker picked it out of the air, then scored.

In the locker room at halftime, Culpepper was all over him like stink on shit. *Pride goeth before a fall!* he shouted. *We're never as tall as we are on our knees before Jesus!* And all the other soft-brain clichés. Benbow's stomach knotted like a rawhide rope, then rebelled. Benbow caught that bit of vomit and swallowed it. But the second wave was too much. He turned and puked into a nearby sink. Culpepper went mad. Accused him of being out of shape, of drinking, smoking, and fornicating. When Benbow denied the charges, Culpepper added another, screamed *Prevaricator!* his foamy spittle flying into Benbow's face. And that was that.

Culpepper lost an eye from the single punch and nearly died during the operation to rebuild his cheekbone. Everybody said Benbow was lucky not to do time, like his father, who had killed a corrupt weighmaster down in Texas with his tire thumper, and was then killed himself by a bad Houston drug dealer down in the Ellis Unit at Huntsville when Benbow was six. Benbow was lucky, he guessed, but marked "Uncoachable" by the pro scouts and denied tryouts all over the league. Benbow played three years in Canada, then destroyed his knee in a bar fight with a Chinese guy in Vancouver. Then he was out of the game. Forever.

Benbow drifted west, fighting fires in the summers and dealing poker in the winter, taking the occasional college classes until he finally finished a PE teaching degree at Northern Montana and garnered an assistant coach's job at a small town in the Sweetgrass Hills, where he discovered he had an unsuspected gift for coaching, as he did for poker: a quick mind and no fear. A gift, once discovered, that became an addiction to the hard work, long hours, loving the game, and paying the price to win.

Head coach in three years, then two state championships, and a move to a larger school in Washington State. Where his mother came to live with him. Or die with him, as it were. The doctors said it was her heart, but Benbow knew that she died of truck-stop food, cheap whiskey, and long-haul drivers whose souls were as full of stale air as their tires.

But he coached a state championship team the next year and was considering offers from a football power down in northern California when he was struck down by a scandalous lawsuit. His second-string quarterback had become convinced that Benbow was sleeping with his mother, which of course he was. When the kid attacked Benbow at practice with his helmet, Benbow had to hit the kid to keep him off. He knew this part of his life was over when he saw the kid's eye dangling out of its socket on the grayish pink string of the optic nerve.

Downhill, as they say, from there. Drinking and fighting as often as coaching, low-rent poker games and married women, usually married to school-board members or dumb-shit administrators. Downhill all the way to Alabamphilia.

Benbow came back to this new world propped in a heap on the couch in the cottage's living room, with a dull ache behind his ear and a thousand sharp pains in his foot, which was propped in a white cast on the coffee table, the fresh cast the size of a watermelon. Benbow didn't have to ask what purpose it served. The skinny man sat beside him, a syringe in hand. Across the room, R. L.'s bulk stood black against a fiery sunset, Mona Sue sitting curled in a chair in his shadow, slowly filing her nails.

Through the window, Benbow could see the Kmart twins walking slow guard tours back and forth across the deck.

"He's comin' out of it, Mr. Dark," the old man said, his voice as sharp as his pale nose.

"Well, give him another dose, Doc," R. L. said without turning. "We don't want that boy a-hurtin' none. Not yet."

Benbow didn't understand what R. L. meant as the doctor stirred beside him, releasing a thin, dry stench like a limestone cavern or an open grave. Benbow had heard that death supposedly hurt no more than having a tooth pulled, and he wondered who had brought back that bit of information as the doctor hit him in the shoulder with a blunt needle, then he slipped uneasily into an enforced sleep like a small death.

When he woke again, Benbow found little changed but the light. Mona Sue still curled in her chair, sleeping now, below her husband's hulk against the full dark sky. The doctor slept, too, leaning the fragile bones of his skull against Benbow's sore arm. And Benbow's leg was also asleep, locked in position by the giant cast resting on the coffee table. He sat very still for as long as he could, waiting for his mind to clear, willing his dead leg to awaken, and wondering why he wasn't dead, too.

"Don't be gettin' no ideas, son," R. L. said without turning.

Of all the things Benbow had hated during the long Sundays shoveling pig shit or dealing cards for R. L. Dark — that was the trade he and the old man had made for Little R. L.'s football services — he hated the bastard calling him "son."

"I'm not your son, you fucking old bastard."

R. L. ignored him, didn't even bother to turn. "How hot's that there water?" he asked calmly as the doctor stirred.

Benbow answered without thinking. "Somewhere between 98 and 102. Why?"

"How 'bout half a dose, Doc?" R. L. said, turning now. "And see 'bout makin' that boy's cast waterproof. I'm thinkin' that hot water might take the edge off my rheumatism and I for sure want the coach there to keep me company . . ."

Once again Benbow found the warm, lazy path back to the darkness at the center of his life, half listening to the old man and Mona Sue squabble over the air conditioner.

After word of his bargain with R. L. Dark for the gridiron services of his baby son spread throughout every tuck and hollow of the county, Benbow could no longer stop after practice for even a single quiet beer at any one of the rank honky-tonks that surrounded the dry town without hearing snickers as he left. It seemed that whatever he might have gained in sympathy, he surely lost in respect. And the old man treated him worse than a farting joke.

On the Saturdays that first fall, when Benbow began his days exchanging his manual labor for Little R. L.'s rushing talents, the old man dogged him all around the hog farm on a small John Deere tractor, endlessly pointing out Benbow's total ignorance of the details of trading bacon for bread and his general inability to perform hard work, complaining at great length, then cackling wildly and jacking the throttle on the tractor as if this was the funniest thing he'd ever seen. Even knowing that Little R. L. was lying on the couch in front of the television and soothing his sore muscles with a pint jar of 'shine couldn't make Benbow even begin to resent his bargain, and he never even bothered to look at the old man, knowing that this was his only escape.

Sundays, though, the old man left him alone. Sunday was Poker Day. Land-rich farmers, sly country lawyers with sharp eyes and soft hands, and small-town bankers with the souls of slave traders came from as far away as West Memphis, St. Louis, and Fort Smith to gather in R. L.'s double-wide for a table stakes hold 'em game, a game famous in at least four states, and occasionally in northern Mexico.

On the sabbath he was on his own, except for the surly, lurking presence of Little R. L., who seemed to blame his coach for every ache and pain, and the jittery passage of a slim, petulant teenage girl who slopped past him across the muddy farmyard in a shapeless feed-sack dress and oversized rubber boots, trailing odd, throaty laughter, the same laughter she had when one of the sows decided to dine on her litter. Benbow should have listened.

But these seemed minor difficulties when balanced against the fact that Little R. L. gained nearly a hundred yards a game his freshman year.

The next fall, the shit-shoveling and the old man's attitude seemed easier to bear. Then when Benbow casually let slip that he had once dealt and played poker professionally, R. L.'s watery blue eyes suddenly glistened with greed, and the Sunday portion of Benbow's bargain became both easier and more complicated. Not that the old man needed him to cheat. R. L. Dark always won. The only times the old man signaled him to deal seconds was to give hands to his competitors to keep them in the game so the old man could skin them even deeper.

The brutal arid dangerous monotony of Benbow's life continued, controlled and hopeful until the fall of Little R. L.'s junior year, when everything came apart. Then back together with a terrible rush. A break, a dislocation, and a connection.

On the Saturday afternoon after Little R. L. broke the state rushing record the night before, the teenage girl stopped chuckling long enough to ask a question. "How long you have to go to college, Coach, to figure out how to scoot pig shit off concrete with a fire hose?"

When she laughed, Benbow finally asked, "Who the fuck are you, honey?"

"Mrs. R. L. Dark, Senior," she replied, the perfect arch of her nose in the air, "that's who." And Benbow looked at her for the first time, watched the thrust of her hard, marvelous body naked beneath the thin fabric of her cheap dress.

Then Benbow tried to make conversation with Mona Sue, made the mistake of asking Mona Sue why she wore rubber boots. "Hookworms," she said, pointing at his sockless feet in old Nikes. *Jesus,* he thought. Then *Jesus wept* that night as he watched the white worms slither through his dark, bloody stool. Now he knew what the old man had been laughing about.

On Sunday a rich Mexican rancher tried to cover one of R. L.'s raises with a Rolex, then the old man insisted on buying the fifteen-thousand-dollar watch with five K cash, and when he opened the small safe set in the floor of the trailer's kitchen, Benbow glimpsed the huge pile of banded stacks of one-hundred-dollar bills that filled the safe.

The next Friday night Little R. L. broke his own rushing record with more than a quarter left in the game, which was good because in the fourth quarter the turf gave way under his right foot, which then slid under a pursuing tackle. Benbow heard the *pop* all the way from the sidelines as the kid's knee dislocated.

Explaining to R. L. that a bargain was a bargain, no matter what happened with the kid's knee, the next day Benbow went about his chores just long enough to lure Mona Sue into a feed shed and out of her dress. But not her rubber boots. Benbow didn't care. He just fucked her. The revenge he planned on R. L. Dark a frozen hell in his heart. But the soft hunger of her mouth and the touch of her astonishing body — diamond-hard nipples, fast-twitch cat muscle slithering under human skin, her cunt like a silken bag of rich, luminous seed pearls suspended in heavenly fucking fire — destroyed his hope of vengeance. Now he simply wanted her. No matter the cost.

Two months later, just as her pregnancy began to show, Benbow cracked the safe with a tablespoon of nitro, took all the money, and they ran.

Although he was sure Mona Sue still dreamed, she'd lost her audience. Except for the wrangler, who still watched her as if she were some heathen idol. But every time she tried to talk to the dark cowboy, the old man pinched her thigh with horny fingers so hard it left blood blisters.

Their mornings were much different now. They all went to the hot water. The doctor slept on a poolside bench behind Mona Sue, who sat on the side of the pool, her feet dangling in the water, her blotched thighs exposed, and her eyes as vacant as her half-smile. R. L. Dark, Curly, and Bald Bill, wearing cutoffs and cheap T-shirts, stood neck-deep in the steamy water, loosely surrounding Benbow, anchored by his plastic-shrouded cast, which loomed like a giant boulder under the heavy water.

A vague sense of threat, like an occasional sharp sniff of sulfur, came off the odd group and kept the other guests at a safe distance, and the number of guests declined every day as the old man rented each cabin and room at the lodge as it came empty. The rich German twins who owned the place didn't seem to care who paid for their cocaine.

During the first few days, nobody had much bothered to speak to Benbow, not even to ask where he had hidden the money. The pain in his foot had retreated to a dull ache, but the itch under the cast had become unbearable. One morning, the doctor had taken pity on him and searched the kitchen drawers for something for Benbow to use to scratch beneath the cast, finally corning up with a cheap shish kebab skewer. Curly and Bald Bill had examined the thin metal stick as if it might be an Arkansas toothpick or a bowie knife, then laughed and let Benbow have it. He kept it holstered in his cast, waiting, scratching the itch. And a deep furrow in the rear of the cast.

Then one morning as they stood silent and safe in the pool, a storm cell drifted slowly down the mountain to fill the canyon with swirling squalls of thick, wet snow, and the old man raised his beak into the flakes and finally spoke: "I always meant to come back to this country," he said.

"What?"

Except for the wrangler slowly gathering damp towels and a dark figure in a hooded sweatshirt and sunglasses standing inside the bar, the pool and the deck had emptied when the snow began. Benbow had been watching the snow gather in the dark waves of Mona Sue's hair as she tried to catch a spinning flake on her pink tongue. Even as he faced death, she still stirred the banked embers glowing in Benbow's crotch.

"During WW Two," the old man said softly, "I got in some trouble over at Fort Chaffee — stuck a noncom with a broomstick — so the Army sent me up here to train with the Tenth Mountain. Stupid assholes thought it was some kinda punishment. Always meant to come back someday . . ."

But Benbow watched the cold wind ripple the stolid surface of the hot water as the snowflakes melted into it. The rising steam became a thick fog.

"I always liked it," Benbow said, glancing up at the mountain as it appeared and disappeared behind the roiling clouds of snow. "Great hunting weather," he added. "There's a little herd of elk bedded just behind that first ridge." As his keepers' eyes followed his upslope, he drifted slowly through the fog toward Mona Sue's feet aimlessly stirring the water. "If you like it so much, you old bastard, maybe you should buy it."

"Watch your tongue, boy," Curly said as he cuffed Benbow on the head. Benbow stumbled closer to Mona Sue.

"I just might do that, son," the old man said, cackling, "just to piss you off. Not that you'll be around to be pissed off."

"So what the fuck are we hanging around here for?" Benbow asked, turning on the old man, which brought him even closer to Mona Sue.

The old man paused as if thinking. "Well, son, we're waitin' for that baby. If'n that baby has red hair and you tell us where you hid the money, we'll just take you home, kill you easy, then feed you to the hogs."

"And if it doesn't have red hair, since I'm not about to tell you where to find the money?"

"We'll just find a hungry sow, son, and feed you to her," the old man said, "startin' with your good toes."

Everybody laughed then: R. L. Dark threw back his head and howled; the hulks exchanged high-fives and higher giggles; and Benbow collapsed underwater. Even Mona Sue chuckled deep in her throat. Until Benbow jerked her off the side of the pool. Then she choked. The poor girl had never learned to swim.

Before either the old man or his bodyguards could move, though, the dark figure in the hooded sweatshirt burst through the bar door in a quick, limping dash and dove into the pool, then lifted the struggling girl onto the deck and knelt beside her while enormous amounts of steaming water poured from her nose and mouth before she began breathing. Then the figure swept the hood from the flaming red hair and held Mona Sue close to his chest.

"Holy shit, boy," the old man asked unnecessarily as Bald Bill helped him out of the pool. "What the fuck you doin' here?"

"Goddammit, baby, lemme go," Mona Sue screamed. "It's a-comin'!"

Which roused the doctor from his sleepy rest. And the wrangler from his work. Both of them covered the wide wooden bench with dry towels, upon which Little R. L. gently placed Mona Sue's racked body. Curly scrambled out of the pool, warning Benbow to stay put, and joined the crowd of men around her sudden and violent contractions. Bald Bill helped the old man into his overalls and the pistol's thong as Little R. L. helped the doctor hold Mona Sue's body, arched with sudden pain, on the bench.

"Oh, Lordy me!" she screamed. "It's tearin' me up!"

"Do somethin', you pissant," the old man said to the wiry doctor, then slapped him soundly.

Benbow slapped to the side of the pool, holding on to the edge with one hand as he dug frantically at the cast with the other. Bits of plaster of Paris and swirls of blood rose through the hot water. Then it was off, and the skewer in his hand. He planned to roll out of the pool, drive the sliver of metal through the old man's kidney, then grab the Webley. After that, he'd call the shots.

But life should have taught him not to plan.

As Bald Bill helped his boss into the coat, he noticed Benbow at the edge of the pool and stepped over to him. Bald Bill saw the bloody cast floating at Benbow's chest. "What the fuck?" he said, kneeling down to reach for him.

Benbow drove the thin shaft of metal with the strength of a lifetime of disappointment and rage into the bottom of Bald Bill's jaw, up through the root of his tongue, then up through his soft palate, horny brainpan, mushy gray matter, and the thick bones of his skull. Three inches of the skewer poked like a steel finger bone out of the center of his bald head.

Bald Bill didn't make a sound. Just blinked once dreamily, smiled, then stood up. After a moment, swaying, he began to walk in small airless circles at the edge of the deck until Curly noticed his odd behavior.

"Bubba?" he said as he stepped over to his brother.

Benbow leaped out of the water; one hand grabbed an ankle and the other dove up the leg of Curly's trunks to grab his nut sack and jerk the giant toward the pool. Curly's grunt and the soft clunk of his head against the concrete pool edge was lost as Mona Sue delivered the child with a deep sigh, and the old man shouted boldly, "Goddamn, it's a girl! A black-headed girl!"

Benbow had slithered out of the pool and limped halfway to the old man's back as he watched the doctor lay the baby on Mona Sue's heaving chest. "Shit fire and save the matches," the old man said, panting deeply as if the labor had been his.

Little R. L. turned and jerked his father toward him by the front of his coat, hissing, "Shut the fuck up, old man." Then he shoved him violently away, smashing the old man's frail body into Benbow's shoulder. Something cracked inside the old man's body, and he sank to his knees, snapping at the cold air with his bloody beak like a gut-shot turtle. Benbow grabbed the pistol's thong off his neck before the old man tumbled dead into the water.

Benbow cocked the huge pistol with a soft metallic click, then his sharp bark of laughter cut through the snowy air like a gunshot. Everything slowed to a stop. The doctor finished cutting the cord. The wrangler's hands held a folded towel under Mona Sue's head. Little R. L. held his gristled body halfway into a mad charge. Bald Bill stopped his aimless circling long enough to fall into the pool. Even Mona Sue's cooing sighs died. Only the cold wind moved, whipping the steamy fog across the pool as the snowfall thickened.

Then Mona Sue screamed, "No!" and broke the frozen moment

The bad knee gave Benbow time to get off a round. The heavy slug took Little R. L. in the top of his shoulder, tumbled through his chest, and exited just above his kidney in a shower of blood, bone splinters, and lung tissue, and dropped him like a side of beef on the deck. But the round had already gone on its merry way through the sternum of the doctor as if he weren't there. Which, in moments, he wasn't.

Benbow threw the pistol joyfully behind him, heard it splash in the pool, and hurried to Mona Sue's side. As he kissed her blood-spattered face, she moaned softly. He leaned closer, but only mistook her moans for passion until he understood what she was saying. Over and over. The way she once called his name. And Little R. L.'s. Maybe even the old man's. "Cowboy, Cowboy, Cowboy," she whispered.

Benbow wasn't even mildly surprised when he felt the arm at his throat or the blade tickle his short ribs. "I took you for a backstabber," he said, "the first time I laid eyes on your sorry ass."

"Just tell me where the money is, *old man,*" the wrangler whispered, "and you can die easy."

"You can have the money," Benbow sobbed, trying for one final break, "just leave me the woman." But the flash of scorn in Mona Sue's eyes was the only answer he needed. "Fuck it," Benbow said, almost laughing, "let's do it the hard way."

Then he fell backward onto the hunting knife, driving the blade to the hilt above his short ribs before the wrangler could release the handle. He stepped back in horror as Benbow stumbled toward the hot waters of the pool.

At first, the blade felt cold in Benbow's flesh, but the flowing blood quickly warmed it. Then he eased himself into the hot water and lay back against its compassionate weight like the old man the wrangler had called him. The wrangler stood over Benbow, his eyes like coals glowing through the fog and thick snow. Mona Sue stepped up beside the wrangler, Benbow's baby whimpering at her chest, snow melting on her shoulders.

"Fuck it," Benbow whispered, drifting now, "it's in the air conditioner."

"Thanks, old man," Mona Sue said, smiling.

"Take care," Benbow whispered, thinking, *This is the easy part,* then leaned farther back into the water, sailing on the pool's wind-riffled, snow-shot surface, eyes closed, happy in the hot, heavy water, moving his hands slightly to stay afloat, his fingers tangled in dark, bloody streams, the wind pushing him toward the cool water at the far end of the pool, blinking against the soft cold snow, until his tired body slipped, unwatched, beneath the hot water to rest.

1996

JEFFERY DEAVER

THE WEEKENDER

JEFFERY DEAVER (1950–) was born outside Chicago and received a journalism degree from the University of Missouri, becoming a newspaperman, then received a law degree from Fordham University, practicing law for several years. A poet, he wrote his own songs and performed them across the country.

One of the most prominent and consistently excellent suspense writers in the world, Deaver is the author of twenty-three novels and two short story collections. He has been translated into twenty-five languages and is a perennial bestseller in America and elsewhere. Among his many honors are six nominations for Edgar Allan Poe Awards (twice for Best Paperback Original, four times for Best Short Story); three Ellery Queen Readers' Awards for Best Short Story of the Year; the 2001 W. H. Smith Thumping Good Read Award for *The Empty Chair;* and the 2004 Ian Fleming Steel Dagger Award from the British Crime Writers' Association for *Garden of Beasts.* In 2009 he was the guest editor of *The Best American Mystery Stories of the Year.* He has written about a dozen standalone novels, but is most famous for his series about Lincoln Rhyme, the brilliant quadriplegic detective who made his debut in *The Bone Collector* (1997), which was filmed by Universal in 1999 and starred Denzel Washington and Angelina Jolie. Other Rhyme novels are *The Coffin Dancer* (1998), *The Empty Chair* (2000), *The Stone Monkey* (2002), *The Vanished Man* (2003), *The Twelfth Card* (2005), *The Cold Moon* (2006), and *The Broken Window* (2008). His nonseries novel *A Maiden's Grave* (1995) was adapted for an HBO movie titled *Dead Silence* (1997) and starred James Garner and Marlee Matlin.

"The Weekender" was first published in the December 1996 issue of *Alfred Hitchcock's Mystery Magazine;* it was selected for *The Best American Mystery Stories 1997.*

▪ ▪ ▪

I LOOKED IN the rearview mirror and didn't see any lights, but I knew they were after us and it was only a matter of time till I'd see the cops.

Toth started to talk, but I told him to shut up and got the Buick up to eighty. The road was empty, nothing but pine trees for miles around.

"Oh brother," Toth muttered. I felt his eyes on me, but I didn't even want to look at him, I was so mad.

They were never easy, drugstores.

Because, just watch sometime, when cops make their rounds they cruise drugstores more often than anyplace else. Because of the prescription drugs.

You'd think they'd stake out convenience stores. But those're a joke, and with the closed-circuit TV you're going to get your picture took, you just are. So nobody who knows the business, I mean really *knows* it, hits them. And banks, forget banks. Even ATMs. I mean, how much can you clear? Three, four hundred tops? And around here the Fast Cash button gives you twenty bucks. Which tells you something. So why even bother?

No. We wanted cash and that meant a drugstore, even though they can be tricky. Ardmore Drugs. Which is a big store in a little town. Liggett Falls. Sixty miles from Albany and a hundred or so from where Toth and me lived, farther west into the mountains. Liggett Falls is a poor place. You'd think it wouldn't make sense to hit a store there. But that's exactly why—because like everywhere else people there need medicine and hairspray and makeup, only they don't have credit cards. Except maybe a Sears or Penney's. So they pay cash.

"Oh brother," Toth whispered again. "Look."

And he made me even madder, him saying that. I wanted to shout, Look at what, you son of a bitch? But then I could see what he was talking about, and I didn't say anything. Up ahead. It was like just before dawn, light on the horizon. Only this was red, and the light wasn't steady. It was like it was pulsing, and I knew that they'd got the roadblock up already. This was the only road to the interstate from Liggett Falls. So I should've guessed.

"I got an idea," Toth said. Which I didn't want to hear but I also wasn't going to go through another shootout. Sure not at a roadblock where they was ready for us.

"What?" I snapped.

"There's a town over there. See those lights? I know a road'll take us there."

Toth's a big guy, and he looks calm. Only he isn't really. He gets shook easy, and he now kept turning around, skittish, looking in the back seat. I wanted to slap him and tell him to chill.

"Where's it?" I asked. "This town?"

"About four, five miles. The turnoff, it ain't marked. But I know it."

This was that lousy upstate area where everything's green. But dirty green, you know. And all the buildings're gray. These gross little shacks, pickups on blocks. Little towns without even a 7-Eleven. And full of hills they call mountains but aren't.

Toth cranked down the window and let this cold air in and looked up at the sky. "They can find us with those, you know, satellite things."

"What're you talking about?"

"You know, they can see you from miles up. I saw it in a movie."

"You think the state cops do that? Are you nuts?"

This guy, I don't know why I work with him. And after what happened at the drugstore, I won't again.

He pointed out where to turn, and I did. He said the town was at the base of the Lookout. Well, I remembered passing that on the way to Liggett Falls that afternoon. It was this huge rock a couple of hundred feet high. Which if you looked at it right looked like a man's head, like a profile, squinting. It'd been some kind of big deal to the Indians around here. Blah, blah, blah. He told me, but I didn't pay no attention. It was spooky, that weird face, and I looked once and kept on driving. I didn't like it. I'm not really superstitious, but sometimes I am.

"Winchester," he said now, meaning what the name of the town was. Five, six thousand people. We could find an empty house, stash the car in a garage, and just wait out the search. Wait till tomorrow afternoon — Sunday — when all the weekenders were driving back to Boston and New York and we'd be lost in the crowd.

I could see the Lookout up ahead, not really a shape, mostly this blackness where the stars weren't. And then the guy on the floor in the back started to moan all of a sudden and just about give me a heart attack.

"You. Shut up back there." I slapped the seat, and the guy in the back went quiet.

What a night.

We'd got to the drugstore fifteen minutes before it closed. Like you ought to do. 'Cause mosta the customers're gone and a lot've the clerks've left and people're tired, and when you push a Glock or Smitty into their faces, they'll do just about anything you ask.

Except tonight.

We had our masks down and walked in slow. Toth getting the manager out of his little office, a fat guy started crying and that made me mad, a grown man doing that. He kept a gun on the customers and the clerks, and I was telling the cashier, this kid, to open the tills and, Jesus, he had an attitude. Like he'd seen all of those Steven Seagal movies or something. A little kiss on the cheek with the Smitty and he changed his mind and started moving. Cussing me out, but he was moving. I was counting the bucks as we were going along from one till to the next, and sure enough, we were up to about three thousand when I heard this noise and turned around and what it was, Toth was knocking a rack of chips over. I mean, Jesus. He's getting Doritos!

I look away from the kid for just a second, and what's he do? He pitches this bottle. Only not at me. Out the window. Bang, it breaks. There's no alarm I can hear, but half of them are silent anyway and I'm really pissed. I could've killed him. Right there. Only I didn't. Toth did.

He shoots the kid, blam, blam, blam. And everybody else is scattering and he turns around and shoots another one of the clerks and a customer, just bang, not thinking or nothing. Just for no reason. Hit this girl clerk in the leg, but this guy, this customer, well, he was dead. You could see. And I'm going, What're you doing, what're you doing? And he's going, Shut up, shut up, shut up . . . And we're like we're swearing at each other when we figured out we hadta get outa there.

So we left. Only what happens is, there's a cop outside. That's why the kid threw the bottle. And he's outa his car. So we grab another customer, this guy by the door, and we use him like a shield and get outside. And there's the cop, he's holding his gun up, looking at the customer we've got, and the cop, he's saying, It's OK, it's OK, just take it easy.

And I couldn't believe it, Toth shot him, too. I don't know whether he killed him, but there was blood so he wasn't wearing a vest it didn't look like, and I could've killed Toth there on the spot. Because why'd he do that? He didn't have to.

We threw the guy, the customer, into the back seat and tied him up with tape. I kicked out the taillights and burned rubber outa there. We made it out of Liggett Falls.

That was all just a half hour ago, but it seems like weeks.

And now we were driving down this highway through a million pine trees. Heading right for the Lookout.

Winchester was dark.

I don't get why weekenders come to places like this. I mean, my old man took me hunting a long time ago. A couple of times, and I liked it. But coming to places like this just to look at leaves and buy furniture they call antiques but's really just busted-up crap . . . I don't know.

We found a house a block off Main Street with a bunch of newspapers in front, and I pulled into the drive and put the Buick behind it just in time. Two state police cars went shooting by. They'd been behind us not more than a half mile, without the lightbars going. Only they hadn't seen us 'causa the broke taillights, and they went by in a flash and were gone, going into town.

Toth got into the house, and he wasn't very clean about it, breaking a window in the back. It was a vacation place, pretty empty and the refrigerator shut off and the phone, too, which was a good sign — there wasn't anybody coming back soon. Also, it smelled pretty musty and had stacks of old books and magazines from the summer.

We took the guy inside, and Toth started to take the hood off this guy's head and I said, "What the hell're you doing?"

"He hasn't said anything. Maybe he can't breathe."

This was a man talking who'd just laid a cap on three people back there, and he was worried about this guy *breathing?* Man. I just laughed. Disgusted, I mean. "Like maybe we don't want him to see us?" I said. "You think of that?" See, we weren't wearing our ski masks anymore.

It's scary when you have to remind people of stuff like that. I was thinking Toth knew better. But you never know.

I went to the window and saw another squad car go past. They were going slower now. They do that. After like the first shock, after the rush, they get smart and start cruising slow, really looking for what's funny — what's *different,* you know? That's why I didn't take the papers up from the front yard. Which would've been different from how the yard looked that morning. Cops really do that Columbo stuff. I could write a book about cops.

"Why'd you do it?"

It was the guy we took.

"Why?" he whispered again.

The customer. He had a low voice, and it sounded pretty calm, I mean considering. I'll tell you, the first time I was in a shootout I was totally freaked for a day afterwards. And I had a gun.

I looked him over. He was wearing a plaid shirt and jeans. But he wasn't a local. I could tell because of the shoes. They were rich-boy shoes, the kind you see all the yuppies wear in TV shows about Connecticut. I couldn't see his face because of the mask, but I pretty much remembered it. He wasn't young. Maybe in his forties. Kind of wrinkled skin. And he was skinny, too. Skinnier'n me, and I'm one of those people can eat what I want and I don't get fat. I don't know why. It just works that way.

"Quiet," I said. There was another car going by.

He laughed. Soft. Like he was saying, What? So they can hear me all the way outside?

Kind of laughing *at* me, you know? I didn't like that at all. And sure, I guess you *couldn't* hear anything out there, but I didn't like him giving me any crap so I said, "Just shut up. I don't want to hear your voice."

He did for a minute and just sat back in the chair where Toth put him. But then he said again, "Why'd you shoot them? You didn't have to."

"Quiet!"

"Just tell me why."

I took out my knife and snapped that sucker open, then threw it down so it stuck in a tabletop. Sort of a *thunk* sound. "You hear that? That was a eight-inch Buck knife. Carbon tempered. With a locking blade. It'd cut clean through a metal bolt. So you be quiet. Or I'll use it on you."

And he gave this laugh again. Maybe. Or it was just a snort of air. But I was thinking it was a laugh. I wanted to ask him what he meant by that, but I didn't.

"You got any money on you?" Toth asked, and took the wallet out of the guy's back pocket. "Lookit," Toth said, and pulled out what must've been five or six hundred. Man.

Another squad car went past, moving slow. It had a spotlight and the cop turned it on the driveway, but he just kept going. I heard a siren across town. And another one, too. It was a weird feeling, knowing those people were out there looking for us.

I took the wallet from Toth and went through it.

Randall C. Weller Jr. He lived in Boston. A weekender. Just like I thought. He had a bunch of business cards that said he was vice president of this big computer company. One that was in the news, trying to take over IBM or something. All of a sudden I had this thought. We could hold him for ransom. I mean, why not? Make a half million. Maybe more.

"My wife and kids'll be sick worrying," Weller said. It spooked me, hearing that. First, 'cause you don't expect somebody with a hood over his head to say anything. But mostly 'cause there I was, looking right at a picture in his wallet. And what was it of? His wife and kids.

"I ain't letting you go. Now, just shut up. I may need you."

"Like a hostage, you mean? That's only in the movies. They'll shoot you when you walk out, and they'll shoot me, too, if they have to. That's the way they do it. Just give yourself up. At least you'll save your life."

"Shut up!" I shouted.

"Let me go and I'll tell them you treated me fine. That the shooting was a mistake. It wasn't your fault."

I leaned forward and pushed the knife against his throat, not the blade 'cause that's real sharp, but the blunt edge, and I told him to be quiet.

Another car went past, no light this time but it was going slower, and all of a sudden I got to thinking what if they do a door-to-door search?

"Why did he do it? Why'd he kill them?"

And funny, the way he said *he* made me feel a little better 'cause it was like he didn't blame me for it. I mean, it was Toth's fault. Not mine.

Weller kept going. "I don't get it. That man by the counter? The tall one. He was just standing there. He didn't do anything. He just shot him down."

But neither of us said nothing. Probably Toth because he didn't know why he'd shot them. And me because I didn't owe this guy any answers. I had him in my hand. Completely, and I had to let him know that. I didn't have to talk to him.

But the guy, Weller, he didn't say anything else. And I got this weird sense. Like this pressure building up. You know, because nobody was answering his damn stupid question. I felt this urge to say something. Anything. And that was the last thing I wanted to do. So I said, "I'm gonna move the car into the garage." And I went outside to do it.

I was a little spooked after the shootout. And I went through the garage pretty good. Just to make sure. But there wasn't nothing inside except tools and an old Snapper lawnmower. So I drove the Buick inside and closed the door. And went back into the house.

And then I couldn't believe what happened. I mean, Jesus . . .

When I walked into the living room, the first thing I heard was Toth saying, "No way, man. I'm not snitching on Jack Prescot."

I just stood there. And you should've seen the look on his face. He knew he'd blown it big.

Now this Weller guy knew my name.

I didn't say anything. I didn't have to. Toth started talking real fast and nervous. "He said he'd pay me some big bucks to let him go." Trying to turn it around, make it Weller's fault. "I mean, I wasn't going to. I wasn't even thinking 'bout it, man. I told him forget it."

"I figured that," I said. "So? What's that got to do with tellin' him my name?"

"I don't know, man. He confused me. I wasn't thinking."

I'll say he wasn't. He hadn't been thinking all night.

I sighed to let him know I wasn't happy, but I just clapped him on the shoulder. "OK," I said. "S'been a long night. These things happen."

"I'm sorry, man. Really."

"Yeah. Maybe you better go spend the night in the garage or something. Or upstairs. I don't want to see you around for a while."

"Sure."

And the funny thing was, it was that Weller gave this little snicker or something. Like he knew what was coming. How'd he know that? I wondered.

Toth went to pick up a couple of magazines and the knapsack with his gun in it and extra rounds.

Normally, killing somebody with a knife is a hard thing to do. I say normally even though I've only done it one other time. But I remember it, and it was messy and hard work. But tonight, I don't know, I was all filled up with this . . . feeling from the drugstore. Mad. I mean, really. Crazy, too, a little. And as soon as Toth turned his back, I went to work, and it wasn't three minutes later it was over. I drug his body behind the couch and then — why not — I pulled Weller's hood off. He already knew my name. He might as well see my face.

He was a dead man. We both knew it.

"You were thinking of holding me for ransom, right?"

I stood at the window and looked out. Another cop car went past, and there were more flashing lights bouncing off the low clouds and off the face of the Lookout, right over our heads. Weller had a thin face and short hair, cut real neat. He looked like every ass-kissing businessman I'd ever met. His eyes were dark and calm, and it made me even madder he wasn't shook up looking at that big bloodstain on the rug and floor.

"No," I told him.

He looked at the pile of stuff I'd taken from his wallet and kept going like I hadn't said anything. "It won't work. A kidnapping. I don't have a lot of money, and if you saw my business card and're thinking I'm an executive at the company, they have about five hundred vice presidents. They won't pay diddly for me. And you see those kids in the picture? It was taken twelve years ago. They're both in college now."

"Where," I asked, sneering. "Harvard?"

"One's at Harvard," he said, like he was snapping at me. "And one's at Northwestern. So the house's mortgaged to the hilt. Besides, kidnapping somebody by yourself? No, you couldn't bring that off."

He saw the way I looked at him, and he said, "I don't mean you personally. I mean somebody by himself. You'd need partners."

And I figured he was right. The ransom thing was looking, I don't know, tricky.

That silence again. Nobody saying nothing and it was like the room was filling up with cold water. I walked to the window and the floors creaked under my feet, and that only made things worse. I remember one time my dad said that a house had a voice of its own, and some houses were laughing houses and some were forlorn. Well, this was a forlorn house. Yeah, it was modern and clean and the *National Geographics* were all in order, but it was still forlorn.

Just when I felt like shouting because of the tension, Weller said, "I don't want you to kill me."

"Who said I was going to kill you?"

He gave me this funny little smile. "I've been a salesman for twenty-five years. I've sold pets and Cadillacs and typesetters, and lately I've been selling mainframe computers. I know when I'm being handed a line. You're going to kill me. It was the first thing you thought of when you heard him" — nodding toward Toth — "say your name."

I just laughed at him. "Well, that's a damn handy thing to be, sorta a walking lie detector," I said, and I was being sarcastic.

But he just said, "Damn handy," like he was agreeing with me.

"I don't want to kill you."

"Oh, I know you don't *want* to. You didn't want your friend to kill anybody back there at the drugstore either. I could see that. But people *got* killed, and that ups the stakes. Right?"

And those eyes of his, they just dug into me, and I couldn't say anything.

"But," he said, "I'm going to talk you out of it."

He sounded real certain and that made me feel better. 'Cause I'd rather kill a cocky son of a bitch than a pathetic one. And so I laughed. "Talk me out of it?"

"I'm going to try."

"Yeah? How you gonna do that?"

Weller cleared his throat a little. "First, let's get everything on the table. I've seen your face, and I know your name. Jack Prescot. Right? You're, what? about five-nine, 150 pounds, black hair. So you've got to assume I can identify you. I'm not going to play any games and say I didn't see you clearly or hear who you were. Or anything like that. We all squared away on that, Jack?"

I nodded, rolling my eyes like this was all a load of crap. But I gotta admit I was kinda curious what he had to say.

"My promise," he said, "is that I won't turn you in. Not under any circumstances. The police'll never learn your name from me. Or your description. I'll never testify against you."

Sounding honest as a priest. Real slick delivery. Well, he was a salesman, and I wasn't going to buy it. But he didn't know I was onto him. Let him give me his pitch, let him think I was going along. When it came down to it, after we'd got away and were somewhere in the woods upstate, I'd want him relaxed. Thinking he was going to get away. No screaming, no hassles. Just two fast cuts and that'd be it.

"You understand what I'm saying?"

I tried to look serious and said, "Sure. You're thinking you can talk me out of killing you. Which I'm not inclined to do anyway. Kill you, I mean."

And there was that weird little smile again.

I said, "You think you can talk me out of it. You've got reasons?"

"Oh, I've got reasons, you bet. One in particular. One that you can't argue with."

"Yeah? What's that?"

"I'll get to it in a minute. Let me tell you some of the practical reasons you should let me go. First, you think you've got to kill me because I know who you are, right? Well, how long you think your identity's going to be a secret? Your buddy shot a cop back there. I don't know police stuff except what I see in the movies. But they're going to be looking at tire tracks and witnesses who saw plates and makes of cars and gas stations you might've stopped at on the way here."

He was just blowing smoke. The Buick was stolen. I mean, I'm not stupid.

But he went on, looking at me real coy. "Even if your car was stolen, they're going to check down every lead. Every shoeprint around where you or your friend found it, talk to everybody in the area around the time it vanished."

I kept smiling like it was nuts what he was saying. But this was true, shooting the cop part. You do that and you're in big trouble. Trouble that sticks with you. They don't stop looking till they find you.

"And when they identify your buddy" — he nodded toward the couch where Toth's body was lying — "they're going to make some connection to you."

"I don't know him that good. We just hung around together the past few months."

Weller jumped on this. "Where? A bar? A restaurant? Anybody ever see you in public?"

I got mad, and I shouted, "So? What're you saying? They gonna bust me anyway, then I'll just take you out with me. How's that for an argument?"

Calm as could be he said, "I'm simply telling you that one of the reasons you want to kill me doesn't make sense. And think about this — the shooting at the drugstore? It wasn't premeditated. It was, what do they call it? Heat of passion. But you kill me, that'll be first degree. You'll get the death penalty when they find you."

When they find you. Right. I laughed to myself. Oh, what he said made sense, but the fact is, killing isn't a making-sense kind of thing. Hell, it *never* makes sense, but sometimes you just have to do it. But I was kind of having fun now. I wanted to argue back. "Yeah, well, I killed Toth. That wasn't heat of passion. I'm going to get the needle anyway for that."

"But nobody gives a damn about him," he came right back. "They don't care if he killed *himself* or got hit by a car accidentally. You can take that piece of garbage out of the equation altogether. They care if you kill *me*. I'm the 'Innocent Bystander' in the headlines. I'm the 'Father of Two.' You kill me, you're as good as dead."

I started to say something, but he kept going.

"Now, here's another reason I'm not going to say anything about you. Because you know my name, and you know where I live. You know I have a family, and you know how important they are to me. If I turn you in, you could come after us. I'd never jeopardize my family that way. Now let me ask you something. What's the worst thing that could happen to you?"

"Keep listening to you spout on and on."

Weller laughed hard at that. I could see he was surprised I had a sense of humor. After a minute he said, "Seriously. The worst thing."

"I don't know. I never thought about it."

"Lose a leg? Go deaf? Lose all your money? Go blind . . . Hey, that looked like it hit a nerve. Going blind?"

"Yeah, I guess. That'd be the worst thing I could think of."

That *was* a pretty damn scary thing, and I'd thought on it before. 'Cause that was what happened to my old man. And it wasn't not seeing anymore that got to me. No, it was that I'd have to depend on somebody else for, Christ, for everything, I guess.

"OK, think about this," he said. "The way you feel about going blind's the way my family'd feel if they lost me. It'd be that bad for them. You don't want to cause them that kind of pain, do you?"

I didn't want to, no. But I knew I *had* to. I didn't want to think about it anymore. I asked him, "So what's this last reason you're telling me about?"

"The last reason," he said, kind of whispering. But he didn't go on. He looked around the room, you know, like his mind was wandering.

"Yeah?" I asked. I was pretty curious. "Tell me."

But he just asked, "You think these people, they have a bar?"

And I'd just been thinking I could use a drink, too. I went into the kitchen, and of course they didn't have any beer in the fridge on account of the house being all closed up and the power off. But they did have scotch, and that'd be my first choice anyway.

I got a couple of glasses and took the bottle back to the living room. Thinking this was a good idea. When it came time to do it, it'd be easier for him and for me both if we were kinda tanked. I shoved my Smitty into his neck and cut the tape his hands were tied with, then taped them in front of him. I sat back and kept my knife near, ready to go, in case he tried something. But it didn't look like he was going to be a hero or anything. He read over the scotch bottle, kind of disappointed it was cheap. And I agreed with him there. One thing I learned a long time ago, you going to rob, rob rich.

I sat back where I could keep an eye on him.

"The last reason. OK, I'll tell you. I'm going to *prove* to you that you should let me go."

"You are?"

"All those other reasons — the practical ones, the humanitarian ones . . . I'll concede you don't care much about those — you don't look very convinced. All right? Then let's look at the one reason you should let me go."

I figured this was going to be more crap. But what he said was something I never would've expected, and it made me laugh.

"For your own sake."

"For me? What're you talking about?"

"See, Jack, I don't think you're lost."

"Whatta you mean, lost?"

"I don't think your soul's beyond redemption."

I laughed at this, laughed out loud, because I just had to. I expected a hell of a lot better from a hotshot vice president salesman like him. "Soul? You think I got a soul?"

"Well, everybody has a soul," he said, and what was crazy was, he said it like he was surprised that I didn't think so. It was like I'd said, Wait a minute, you mean the earth ain't flat? or something.

"Well, if I got a soul it's taken the fast lane to hell." Which was this line I heard in this movie and I tried to laugh, but it sounded flat. Like Weller was saying something deep and I was just kidding around. It made me feel cheap. I stopped smiling and looked down at Toth, lying there in the corner, those dead eyes of his just staring, staring, and I wanted to stab him again I was so mad.

"We're talking about your soul."

I snickered and sipped the liquor. "Oh yeah, I'll bet you you're the sort that reads those angel books they got all over the place now."

"I go to church, but no, I'm not talking about all that silly stuff. I don't mean magic. I mean your conscience. What Jack Prescot's all about."

I could tell him about social workers and youth counselors and all those guys who don't know nothing about the way life works. They think they do. But it's the words they use. You can tell they don't know a thing. Some counselors or somebody'll talk to me and they say, Oh, you're maladjusted, you're denying your anger, things like that. When I hear that, I know they don't know nothing about souls or spirits.

"Not the afterlife," Weller was going on. "Not mortality. I'm talking about life here on earth that's important. Oh sure, you look skeptical. But listen to me. I really believe if you have a connection with somebody, if you trust them, if you have faith in them, then there's hope for you."

"Hope? What does that mean? Hope for what?"

"That you'll become a real human being. Lead a real life."

Real . . . I didn't know what he meant, but he said it like what he was saying was so clear that I'd have to be an idiot to miss it. So I didn't say nothing.

He kept going. "Oh, there're reasons to steal, and there're reasons to kill. But on the whole, don't you really think it's better not to? Just think about it: why do we put people in jail if it's all right for them to murder? Not just us but all societies."

"So, what? I'm gonna give up my evil ways?" I laughed at him.

And he just lifted his eyebrow and said, "Maybe. Tell me, Jack, how'd you feel when your buddy — what's his name?"

"Joe Roy Toth."

"Toth, when he shot that guy by the counter? How'd you feel?"

"I don't know."

"He just turned around and shot him. For no reason. You knew that wasn't right, didn't you?" And I started to say something. But he said, "No, don't answer me. You'd be inclined to lie. And that's all right. It's an instinct in your line of work. But I don't want you *believing* any lies you tell me. OK? I want you to look into your heart and tell me if you didn't think something was real wrong about what Toth did. Think about that, Jack. You knew something wasn't right."

All right, I did. But who wouldn't? Toth screwed everything up. Everything went sour. And it was all his fault.

"It dug at you, right, Jack? You wished he hadn't done it."

I didn't say nothing but just drank some more scotch and looked out the window and watched the flashing lights around the town. Sometimes they seemed close, and sometimes they seemed far away.

"If I let you go, you'll tell 'em."

Like everybody else. They all betrayed me. My father — even after he went blind, the son of a bitch turned me in. My first PO, the judges. Sandra . . . My boss, the one I knifed.

"No, I won't," Weller said. "We're talking about an agreement. I don't break deals. I promised I won't tell a soul about you, Jack. Not even my wife." He leaned forward, cupping the booze between his hands. "You let me go, it'll mean all the difference in the world to you. It'll mean that you're not hopeless. I guarantee your life'll be different. That one act — letting me go — it'll change you forever. Oh, maybe not this year. Or for five years. But you'll come around. You'll give up all this, everything that happened back there in Liggett Falls. All the crime, the killing. You'll come around. I know you will."

"You just expect me to believe you won't tell anybody?"

"Ah," Weller said, and lifted his taped-up hands to drink more scotch. "Now we get down to the big issue."

Again that silence, and finally I said, "And what's that?"

"Faith."

There was this burst of siren outside, and I told him to shut up and pushed the gun against his head. His hands were shaking, but he didn't do anything stupid and a few minutes later, after I sat back, he started talking again. "Faith. That's what I'm talking about. A man who has faith is somebody who can be saved."

"Well, I don't have any goddamn faith," I told him.

But he kept right on talking. "If you believe in another human being, you have faith."

"Why the hell do you care whether I'm saved or not?"

"Because life's hard, and people're cruel. I told you I'm a churchgoer. A lot of the Bible's crazy. But some of it I believe. And one of the things I believe is that sometimes we're put in these situations to make a difference. I think that's what happened tonight. That's why you and I both happened to be at the drugstore at the same time. You've felt that, haven't you? Like an omen? Like something happens and is telling you you ought do this or shouldn't do that."

Which was weird 'cause the whole time we were driving up to Liggett Falls I kept thinking, something funny's going on. I don't know what it is, but this job's gonna be different.

"What if," he said, "everything tonight happened for a purpose? My wife had a cold, so I went to buy NyQuil. I went to that drugstore instead of 7-Eleven to save a buck or two. You happened to hit that store at just that time. You happened to have your buddy" — he nodded toward Toth's body — "with you. The cop car just happened by at that particular moment. And the clerk behind the counter just happened to see him. That's a lot of coincidences. Don't you think?"

And then — this sent a damn chill right down my spine — he said, "Here we are in the shadow of that big rock, that face."

Which is 100 percent what I was thinking. Exactly the same — about the Lookout, I mean. I don't know why I was. But I happened to be looking out the window and thinking about it at that exact same instant. I tossed back the scotch and had another and, oh man, I was pretty freaked out.

"Like he's looking at us, waiting for you to make a decision. Oh, don't think it was just you, though. Maybe the purpose was to affect everybody's life there. That customer at the counter Toth shot. Maybe it was just his time to go — fast, you know, before he got cancer or had a stroke. Maybe that girl, the clerk, had to get shot in the leg so she'd get her life together, maybe get off drugs or give up drinking."

"And you? What about you?"

"Well, I'll tell you about me. Maybe you're the good deed in my life. I've spent years thinking only about making money. Take a look at my wallet. There. In the back."

I pulled it open. There were a half-dozen of these little cards, like certificates. RANDALL WELLER — SALESMAN OF THE YEAR. EXCEEDED TARGET TWO YEARS STRAIGHT. BEST SALESMAN OF 1992.

Weller kept going. "There are plenty of others back in my office. And trophies, too. And in order for me to win those, I've had to neglect people. My family and friends. People who could maybe use my help. And that's not right. Maybe you kidnapping me, it's one of those signs to make me turn my life around."

The funny thing was this made sense. Oh, it was hard to imagine not doing heists. And I couldn't see myself, if it came down to a fight, not going for my Buck or my Smitty to take the other guy out. That turning the other cheek stuff, that's only for cowards. But maybe I *could* see a day when my life'd be just straight time. Living with some woman, maybe a wife, living in a house. Doing what my father and mother, whatever she was like, never did.

"If I was to let you go," I said, "you'd have to tell 'em something."

He shrugged. "I'll say you locked me in the trunk and then tossed me out somewhere near here. I wandered around, looking for a house or something, and got lost. It could take me a day to find somebody. That's believable."

"Or you could flag down a car in an hour."

"I could. But I won't."

"You keep saying that. But how do I *know?*"

"That's the faith part. You don't know. No guarantees."

"Well, I guess I don't have any faith."

"Then *I'm* dead. And *your* life's never gonna change. End of story." He sat back, and it was crazy but he looked calm, smiling a little.

That silence again, but it was like it was really this roar all around us, and it kept going till the whole room was filled up with the sound of a siren.

"You just want . . . what do you want?"

He drank more scotch. "Here's a proposal. Let me walk outside."

"Oh, right. Just let you stroll out for some fresh air or something?"

"Let me walk outside and I promise you I'll walk right back again."

"Like a test?"

He thought about this for a second. "Yeah. A test."

"Where's this faith you're talking about? You walk outside, you try to run and I'd shoot you in the back."

"No, what you do is you put the gun someplace in the house. The kitchen or someplace. Somewhere you couldn't get it if I ran. You stand at the window, where we can see each other. And I'll tell you up front. I can run like the wind. I was lettered track and field in college, and I still jog every day of the year."

"You know if you run and bring the cops back everything's gonna get bloody. I'll kill the first five troopers come through that door. Nothing'll stop me, and that blood'll be on your hands."

"Of course I know that," he said. "But if this's going to work, you can't think that way. You've got to assume the worst is going to happen. That if I run I'll tell the cops everything. Where you are and that there're no hostages here and that you've only got one or two guns. And they're going to come in and blow you to hell. And you're not going to take a single one down with you. You're going to die and die painfully 'cause of a few lousy hundred bucks . . . But, but, but . . ." He held up his hands and stopped me from saying anything. "You gotta understand, faith means risk."

"That's stupid."

"I think it's just the opposite. It'd be the smartest thing you ever did in your life."

"What'll it prove?" I asked. But I was just stalling. And he knew it. He said patiently, "That I'm a man of my word. That you can trust me."

"And what do I get out of it?"

And then this son of a bitch smiled that weird little smile of his. "I think you'll be surprised."

I tossed back another scotch and had to think about this.

Weller said, "I can see it there already. Some of that faith. It's there. Not a lot. But some."

And yeah, maybe there was a little. 'Cause I was thinking about how mad I got at Toth and the way he ruined everything. I didn't want anybody to get killed tonight. I *was* sick of it. Sick of the way my life had gone. Sometimes it was good, being alone and all. Not answering to anybody. But sometimes it was real bad. And this guy, Weller, it was like he was showing me something different.

"So," I said. "You just want me to put the gun down?"

He looked around. "Put it in the kitchen. You stand in the doorway or window. All I'm gonna do is walk down to the street and walk back."

I looked out the window. It was maybe fifty feet down the driveway. There were these bushes on either side of it. He could just take off, and I'd never find him.

All through the sky I could see lights flickering.

"Naw, I ain't gonna. You're nuts."

And I expected begging or something. Or getting pissed off, more likely — which is what happens to me when people don't do what I tell them. Or don't do it fast enough. But, naw, he just nodded. "OK, Jack. You thought about it. That's a good thing. You're not ready yet. I respect that." He sipped a little more scotch, looking at the glass. And that was the end of it.

Then all of a sudden these searchlights started up. They was some ways away, but I still got spooked and backed away from the window.

Pulled my gun out. Only then I saw that it wasn't nothing to do with the robbery. It was just a couple of big spotlights shining on the Lookout. They must've gone on every night, this time.

I looked up at it. From here it didn't look like a face at all. It was just a rock. Gray and brown and these funny pine trees growing sideways out of cracks.

Watching it for a minute or two. Looking out over the town, and something that guy was saying went into my head. Not the words, really. Just the *thought.* And I was thinking about everybody in that town. Leading normal lives. There was a church steeple and the roofs of small houses. A lot of little yellow lights in town. You could just make out the hills in the distance. And I wished for a minute I was in one of them houses. Sitting there. Watching TV with a wife next to me. Like Sandy or somebody.

I turned back from the window and I said, "You'd just walk down to the road and back? That's it?"

"That's all. I won't run off, you don't go get your gun. We trust each other. What could be simpler?"

Listening to the wind. Not strong but a steady hiss that was comforting in a funny way even though any other time I'da thought it sounded cold and raw. It was like I heard a voice. I don't know from where. Something in me said I ought to do this.

I didn't say nothing else 'cause I was right on the edge and I was afraid he'd say something that'd make me change my mind. I just took the Smith & Wesson and looked at it for a minute, then put it on the kitchen table. I came back with the Buck and cut his feet free. Then I figured if I was going to do it I ought go all the way. So I cut his hands free, too. Weller seemed surprised I did that. But he smiled like he knew I was playing the game. I pulled him to his feet and held the blade to his neck and took him to the door.

"You're doing a good thing," he said.

I was thinking, Oh man, I can't believe this. It's crazy.

I opened the door and smelled cold fall air and woodsmoke and pine, and I heard the wind in the rocks and trees above our heads.

"Go on," I told him.

Weller didn't look back to check up on me . . . Faith, I guess. He kept walking real slow down toward the road.

I felt funny, I'll tell you, and a couple of times when he went past some real shadowy places in the driveway and could disappear I was like, oh man, this is all messed up. I'm crazy.

I almost panicked a few times and bolted for the Smitty but I didn't. When Weller got down near the sidewalk, I was actually holding my breath. I expected him to go, I really did. I was looking for that moment—when people tense up, when they're gonna swing or draw down on you or bolt. It's like their bodies're shouting what they're going to be doing before they do it. Only Weller wasn't doing none of that. He walked down to the sidewalk real casual. And he turned and looked up at the face of the Lookout, like he was just another weekender. Then he turned around. He nodded at me. Which is when the car came by. It was a state trooper. Those're the dark cars, and he didn't have the lightbar going. So he was almost on us before I knew it. I guess I was looking at Weller so hard I didn't see nothing else.

There it was, two doors away, and Weller saw it the same time I did.

And I thought, That's it. Oh, hell.

But when I was turning to get the gun, I saw this like flash of motion down by the road. And I stopped cold.

Could you believe it? Weller'd dropped onto the ground and rolled underneath a tree. I closed the door real fast and watched from the window. The trooper stopped and turned his light on the driveway. The beam—it was real bright—it moved up and down and hit all the bushes and the front of the house, then back to the road. But it was like Weller was digging down into the pine needles to keep from being seen. I mean, he was *hiding* from those sons of bitches. Doing whatever he could to stay out of the way of the light.

Then the car moved on, and I saw the lights checking out the house next door and then it was gone. I kept my eyes on Weller the whole time, and he didn't do nothing stupid. I seen him climb out from under the trees and dust himself off. Then he came walking back to the house. Easy, like he was walking to a bar to meet some buddies.

He came inside and shook his head. Gave this little sigh, like relief. And laughed. Then he held his hands out. I didn't even ask him to.

I taped 'em up again with adhesive tape, and he sat down in the chair, picked up his scotch, and sipped it.

And damn, I'll tell you something. The God's truth. I felt good. Naw, naw, it wasn't like I'd seen the light or anything like that. But I was thinking that of all the people in my life—my dad or Sandy or Toth or anybody else—I never did really trust them. I'd never let myself go all the way. And here, tonight, I did. With a stranger and somebody who had the power to do me some harm. It was a pretty scary feeling, but it was also a good feeling.

It was a little thing, real little. But maybe that's where stuff like this starts. I realized then that I'd been wrong. I could let him go. Oh, I'd keep him tied up here. Gagged. It'd be a day or so before he'd get out. But he'd agree to that. I knew he would. And I'd write his name and address down, let him know I knew where him and his family lived. But that was only part of why I was thinking I'd let him go. I wasn't sure what the rest of it was. But it was something about what'd just happened, something between me and him.

"How you feel?" he asked.

I wasn't going to give too much away. No, sir. But I couldn't help saying, "I thought I was gone then. But you did right by me."

"And you did right, too, Jack." And then he said, "Pour us another round."

I filled the glasses to the top. We tapped 'em.

"Here's to you, Jack. And to faith."

"To faith."

I tossed back the whiskey, and when I lowered my head, sniffing air through my nose to clear my head, well, that was when he got me. Right in the face.

He was good, that son of a bitch. Tossed the glass low so that even when I ducked, automatically, the booze caught me in the eyes, and man, that stung like nobody's business. I couldn't believe it. I was howling in pain and going for the knife. But it was too late. He had it all planned out, exactly what I was going to do. How I was gonna move. He brought his knee up into my chin and knocked a couple of teeth out, and I went over onto my back before I could get the knife out my pocket. Then he dropped down on my belly with his knee — I remembered I'd never bothered to tape his feet up again — and he knocked the wind out, and there I was lying, like I was paralyzed, trying to breathe and all. Only I couldn't. And the pain was incredible, but what was worse was the feeling that he didn't trust me.

I was whispering, "No, no, no. I was going to, man. You don't understand. I was going to let you go."

I couldn't see nothing and couldn't really hear nothing either, my ears were roaring so much. I was gasping, "You don't understand you don't understand."

Man, the pain was so bad. So bad . . .

Weller must've got the tape off his hands, chewed through it, I guess, 'cause he was rolling me over. I felt him tape my hands together, then grab me and drag me over to a chair, tape my feet to the legs. He got some water and threw it in my face to wash the whiskey out of my eyes.

He sat down in a chair in front of me. And he just stared at me for a long time while I caught my breath. He picked up his glass, poured more scotch. I shied away, thinking he was going to throw it in my face again, but he just sat there, sipping it and staring at me.

"You . . . I was going to let you go. I *was.*"

"I know," he said. Still calm.

"You know?"

"I could see it in your face. I've been a salesman for twenty-five years, remember? I know when I've closed a deal."

I'm a pretty strong guy, 'specially when I'm mad, and I tried real hard to break through that tape but there was no doing it. "Goddamn you!" I shouted. "You said you weren't going to turn me in. You, all your goddamn talk about faith . . ."

"Shhhh," Weller whispered. And he sat back, crossing his legs. Easy as could be. Looking me up and down. "That fellow your friend shot back at the drugstore. The customer at the counter?"

I nodded slowly.

"He was my friend. It's his place my wife and I are staying at this weekend. With all our kids."

I just stared at him. His friend? What was he saying?

"I didn't know—"

"Be quiet," he said, real soft. "I've known him for years. Gerry was one of my best friends."

"I didn't want nobody to die. I—"

"But somebody did die. And it was your fault."

"Toth . . ."

He whispered, "It was your fault."

"All right, you tricked me. Call the cops. Get it over with, you goddamn liar."

"You really don't understand, do you?" He shook his head. Why was he so calm? His hands weren't shaking. He wasn't looking around, nervous and all. Nothing like that. He said, "If I'd wanted to turn you in, I would just've flagged down that squad car a few minutes ago. But I said I wouldn't do that. And I won't. I gave you my word I wouldn't tell the cops a thing about you. And I won't."

"Then what do you want?" I shouted. "Tell me." Trying to bust through that tape. And as he unfolded my Buck knife with a click, I was thinking of something I told him.

Oh man, no . . . Oh, no.

"Yeah, being blind, I guess. That'd be the worst thing I could think of."

"What're you going to do?"

"What'm I going to do, Jack?" Weller said. He cut the last bit of tape off his wrists with the Buck, then looked up at me. "Well, I'll tell you. I spent a good bit of time tonight proving to you that you shouldn't kill me. And now . . ."

"What, man? What?"

"Now I'm going to spend a good bit of time proving to you that you should've."

Then, real slow, Weller finished his scotch and stood up. And he walked toward me, that weird little smile on his face.

1997

JOYCE CAROL OATES

FAITHLESS

Joyce Carol Oates (1938–) was born and raised in rural upstate New York and graduated valedictorian of her class at Syracuse University (where she won the 1959 college short story contest sponsored by *Mademoiselle*). She received her MA at the University of Wisconsin at Madison, where she met her future husband of forty-seven years, Raymond Smith. After teaching at the University of Detroit and the University of Windsor (Ontario), she became a professor of creative writing at Princeton University in 1978, a position she still holds.

She wrote relentlessly from the age of fourteen, producing novels and then throwing them away as she honed her talent. Her first novel, *With Shuddering Fall* (1964), has been followed by more than fifty others, as well as more than thirty short story collections, ten volumes of poetry, a dozen collections of essays and criticism, eight novellas, eight collections of plays, and eight books for children and young adults. Although some critics fault her for her prolificacy (as they might have Dickens in another era), few cavil with her excellence. She has been a deserving candidate for the Nobel Prize for a quarter century, only her lack of strident political views denying it to her. She has been nominated for an astonishing six National Book Awards, winning for the novel *them* in 1970. Generally regarded as among her greatest works are *A Garden of Earthly Delights* (1967); *Black Water* (1992), a fictional version of the Chappaquiddick incident, in which Senator Ted Kennedy caused the death of a campaign aide; *We Were the Mulvaneys* (1996), a national bestseller when it was picked for Oprah's Book Club; and *Blonde* (2000), a fictional account of the life of Marilyn Monroe. Her book-length essay *On Boxing* (1987) has been called the best writing on any sport by anyone. Much of Oates's work deals with crime and violence, notably the psychological suspense novels written under the pen names Rosamond Smith and Lauren Kelly.

"Faithless" was originally published in the winter 1997 issue of *Kenyon Review*. It was selected for *The Best American Mystery Stories 1998* and served as the title story for Oates's 2001 collection *Faithless: Tales of Transgression*.

▪ ▪ ▪

1

THE LAST TIME my mother Cornelia Nissenbaum and her sister Constance saw their mother was the day before she vanished from their lives forever, April 11, 1923.

It was a rainy-misty morning. They'd been searching for their mother because something was wrong in the household; she hadn't come downstairs to prepare breakfast so there wasn't anything for them except what their father gave them, glutinous oatmeal from the previous morning hastily reheated on the stove sticking to the bottom of the pan and tasting of scorch. Their father had seemed strange to them, smiling but not-seeing in that way of his like Reverend Dieckman too fierce in his pulpit Sunday mornings, intoning the Word of God. His eyes were threaded with blood and his face was still pale from the winter but flushed, mottled. In those days he was a handsome man but stern-looking and severe. Gray-grizzled side-whiskers and a spade-shaped beard, coarse and grizzled too with gray, but thick springy-sleek black hair brushed back from his forehead in a crest. The sisters were fearful of their father without their mother to mediate among them, it was as if none of them knew who they were without her.

Connie chewed her lip and worked up her nerve to ask where was Momma? and their father said, hitching up his suspenders, on his way outside, "Your mother's where you'll find her."

The sisters watched their father cross the mud-puddled yard to where a crew of hired men was waiting in the doorway of the big barn. It was rye-planting season and always in spring in the Chautauqua Valley there was worry about rain: too much rain and the seed would be washed away or rot in the soil before it could sprout. My mother Cornelia would grow to adulthood thinking how blessings and curses fell from the sky with equal authority, like hard-pelting rain. There was God, who set the world in motion, and who intervened sometimes in the affairs of men, for reasons no one could know. If you lived on a farm there was weather, always weather, every morning was weather and every evening at sundown calculating the next day's, the sky's moods meant too much. Always casting your glance upward, outward, your heart set to quicken.

That morning. The sisters would never forget that morning. We knew something was wrong, we thought Momma was sick. The night before having heard—what, exactly? Voices. Voices mixed with dreams, and the wind. On that farm, at the brink of a ten-mile descent to the Chautauqua River, it was always windy—on the worst days the wind could literally suck your breath away! — like a ghost, a goblin. An invisible being pushing up close beside you, sometimes even inside the house, even in your bed, pushing his mouth (or muzzle) to yours and sucking out the breath.

Connie thought Nelia was silly, a silly-baby, to believe such. She was eight years old and skeptical-minded. Yet maybe she believed it, too? Liked to scare herself, the way you could almost tickle yourself, with such wild thoughts.

Connie, who was always famished, and after that morning would be famished for years, sat at the oilcloth-covered table and ate the oatmeal her father had spooned out for her, devoured it, scorch-clots and all, her head of fair-frizzy braids lowered and her jaws working quickly. Oatmeal sweetened with top-milk on the very edge of turning sour, and coarse brown sugar. Nelia, who was fretting, wasn't able to swallow down more than a spoon or two of hers so Connie devoured that, too. She would remember that part of the oatmeal was hot enough to burn her tongue and other parts were icebox-cold. She would remember that it was all delicious.

The girls washed their dishes in the cold-water sink and let the oatmeal pan soak in scummy soapsuds. It was time for Connie to leave for school but both knew she could not go, not today. She could not leave to walk two miles to the school with that feeling *something is wrong,* nor could she leave her little sister behind. Though when Nelia snuffled and wiped her nose on both her hands Connie cuffed her on the shoulder and scolded, "Piggy-*piggy.*"

This, a habit of their mother's when they did something that was only mildly disgusting.

Connie led the way upstairs to the big bedroom at the front of the house that was Momma and Pappa's room and that they were forbidden to enter unless specifically invited; for instance if the door was open and Momma was cleaning inside, changing bedclothes so she'd call out *Come in, girls!* smiling in her happy mood so it was all right and they would not be scolded. *Come in, give me a hand,* which turned into a game shaking out sheets, fluffing out pillowcases to stuff heavy goose-feather pillows inside, Momma and Connie and Nelia laughing together. But this morning the door was shut. There was no sound of Momma inside. Connie dared to turn the doorknob, push the door open slowly, and they saw, yes, to their surprise there was their mother lying on top of the unmade bed, partly dressed, wrapped in an afghan. My God, it was scary to see Momma like that, lying down at such an hour of the morning! Momma, who was so brisk and capable and who routed them out of bed if they lingered, Momma with little patience for Connie's lazy-tricks as she called them or for Nelia's sniffles, tummyaches, and baby-fears.

"Momma?" — Connie's voice was cracked.

"Mom-ma?" — Nelia whimpered.

Their mother groaned and flung an arm across one of the pillows lying crooked beside her. She was breathing hard, like a winded horse, her chest rising and falling so you could see it and her head was flung back on a pillow and she'd placed a wetted cloth across her eyes mask-like so half her face was hidden. Her dark-blond hair was disheveled, unplaited, coarse and lusterless as a horse's mane, unwashed for days. That rich rank smell of Momma's hair when it needed washing. You remember such smells, the sisters would say, some of them not-so-nice smells, all your life. And the smell in their parents' forbidden room of — was it talcum powder, sweaty armpits, a sourish-sweet fragrance of bedclothes that no matter how frequently laundered with detergent and bleach were never truly fresh. A smell of bodies. Adult bodies. Yeasty, stale. Pappa's tobacco (he rolled his own crude paper cigarettes, he chewed tobacco in a thick tarry-black wad) and Pappa's hair oil and that special smell of Pappa's shoes, the black Sunday shoes always kept polished. (His work boots, etc., he kept downstairs in the closed-in porch by the rear door called the "entry.") In the step-in closet close by the bed, behind an unhemmed length of chintz, was a blue-speckled porcelain chamber pot with a detachable lid and a rim that curled neatly under it, like a lip.

The sisters had their own chamber pot — their potty, as it was called. There was no indoor plumbing in John Nissenbaum's farmhouse as in any farmhouse in the Chautauqua Valley well into the 1930s and in poorer homes well into the 1940s, and even beyond. One hundred yards behind the house, beyond the silo, was the outhouse, the latrine, the "privy." But you would not want to make that trip in cold weather or in rain or in the pitch-black of night, not if you could help it.

Of course the smell of urine and a fainter smell of excrement must have been everywhere, the sisters conceded, years later. As adults, reminiscing. But it was masked by the barnyard smell, probably. Nothing worse than pig manure, after all!

At least, we weren't *pigs*.

Anyway, there was Momma, on the bed. The bed that was so high from the floor you had to raise a knee to slide up on it, and grab on to whatever you could. And the horsehair mattress, so hard and ungiving. The cloth over Momma's eyes she hadn't removed and beside Momma in the rumpled bedclothes her Bible. Face-down. Pages bent. That Bible her mother-in-law Grandma Nissenbaum had given her for a wedding present, seeing she hadn't one of her own. It was smaller than the heavy black family Bible and it was made of limp ivory-leather covers and had onionskin pages the girls were allowed to examine but not to turn without Momma's supervision; the Bible that would disappear with Gretel Nissenbaum, forever.

The girls begged, whimpered. "Momma? Momma, are you sick?"

At first there was no answer. Just Momma's breath coming quick and hard and uneven. And her olive-pale skin oily with heat like fever. Her legs were tangled in the afghan, her hair was strewn across the pillow. They saw the glint of Momma's gold cross on a thin gold chain around her neck, almost lost in her hair. (Not only a cross but a locket, too: when Momma opened it there was, inside, a tiny strand of silver hair once belonging to a woman the sisters had never known, Momma's own grandmother she'd loved so when she was a little girl.) And there were Momma's breasts, almost exposed! — heavy, lush, beautiful almost spilling out of a white eyelet slip, rounded like sacs holding warm liquid, and the nipples dark and big as eyes. You weren't supposed to stare at any part of a person's body but how could you help it? — especially Connie who was fascinated by such, guessing how one day she'd inhabit a body like Momma's. Years ago she'd peeked at her mother's big milk-swollen breasts when Nelia was still nursing, jealous, awed. Nelia was now five years old and could not herself recall nursing at all; would come one day to believe, stubborn and disdainful, that she had never nursed, had only been bottle-fed.

At last Momma snatched the cloth off her face. "You! Damn you! What do you want?" She stared at the girls as if, clutching hands and gaping at her, they were strangers. Her right eye was bruised and swollen and there were raw red marks on her forehead and first Nelia then Connie began to cry and Momma said, "Constance, why aren't you in school? Why can't you let me alone? God help me — always 'Momma' — 'Momma' — 'Momma.'" Connie whimpered, "Momma, did you hurt yourself?" and Nelia moaned, sucking a corner of the afghan like a deranged baby and Momma ignored the question, as Momma often ignored questions she thought nosy, none of your business; her hand lifted as if she meant to slap them but then fell wearily, as if this had happened many times before, this exchange, this emotion, and it was her fate that it would happen many times again. A close sweet-stale blood-odor lifted from Momma's lower body, out of the folds of the soiled afghan, that odor neither of the little girls could have identified except in retrospect, in adolescence at last detecting it in themselves: shamed, discomforted, the secret of their bodies at what was called, invariably in embarrassed undertones, *that certain time of the month.*

So: Gretel Nissenbaum, at the time she disappeared from her husband's house, was having her period.

Did that mean something, or nothing?

Nothing, Cornelia would say sharply.

Yes, Constance would insist, it meant our mother was *not* pregnant. She wasn't running away with any lover because of *that.*

That morning, what confusion in the Nissenbaum household! However the sisters would later speak of the encounter in the big bedroom, what their mother had said to them, how she'd looked and behaved, it had not been precisely that way, of course. Because how can you speak of confusion, where are the words for it? How to express in adult language the wild fibrillation of children's minds, two child-minds beating against each other like moths, how to know what had truly happened and what was only imagined! Connie would swear that their mother's eye looked like a nasty dark-rotted egg, so swollen, but she could not say which eye it was, right or left; Nelia, shrinking from looking at her mother's bruised face, wanting only to burrow against her, to hide and be comforted, would come in time to doubt that she'd seen a *hurt eye* at all; or whether she'd been led to believe she saw it because Connie, who was so bossy, claimed she had.

Connie would remember their mother's words, Momma's rising desperate voice, "Don't touch me — I'm afraid! I might be going somewhere but I'm not ready — oh God, I'm so afraid!" — and on and on, saying she was going away, she was afraid, and Connie trying to ask where? where was she going? and Momma beating at the bedclothes with her fists. Nelia would remember being hurt at the way Momma yanked the spittle-soaked corner of the afghan out of her mouth, so roughly! Not Momma but *bad-Momma, witch-Momma* who scared her.

But then Momma relented, exasperated. "Oh come on, you damn little babies! Of course 'Momma' loves you."

Eager then as starving kittens the sisters scrambled up onto the high, hard bed, whimpering, snuggling into Momma's arms, her damp snarled hair, those breasts. Connie and Nelia burrowing, crying themselves to sleep like nursing babies, Momma drew the afghan over the three of them as if to shield them. That morning of April 11, 1923.

And next morning, early, before dawn. The sisters would be awakened by their father's shouts, "Gretel? Gretel!"

2

. . . never spoke of her after the first few weeks. After the first shock. We learned to pray for her and to forgive her and to forget her. We didn't miss her. So Mother said, in her calm judicious voice. A voice that held no blame.

But Aunt Connie would take me aside. The older, wiser sister. *It's true we never spoke of Momma when any grownups were near, that was forbidden. But, God! we missed her every hour of every day all the time we lived on that farm.*

I was Cornelia's daughter but it was Aunt Connie I trusted.

No one in the Chautauqua Valley knew where John Nissenbaum's young wife Gretel had fled, but all knew, or had an opinion of, why she'd gone.

Faithless, she was. A *faithless woman.* Had she not *run away with a man: abandoned her children.* She was twenty-seven years old and too young for John Nissenbaum and she wasn't a Ransomville girl, her people lived sixty miles away in Chautauqua Falls. Here was a wife who'd committed *adultery,* was an *adulteress.* (Some might say a *tramp,* a *whore,* a *slut.*) Reverend Dieckman, the Lutheran minister, would preach amazing sermons in her wake. For miles through the valley and for years well into the 1940s there would be scandalized talk of Gretel Nissenbaum: a woman who left her faithful Christian husband and her two little girls with no warning! no provocation! disappearing in the middle of a night taking with her only a single suitcase and, as every woman who ever spoke of the episode liked to say, licking her lips, *the clothes on her back.*

(Aunt Connie said she'd grown up imagining she had actually seen her mother, as in a dream, walking stealthily up the long drive to the road, a bundle of clothes, like laundry, slung across her back. Children are so damned impressionable, Aunt Connie would say, laughing wryly.)

For a long time after their mother disappeared, and no word came from her, or of her, so far as the sisters knew, Connie couldn't seem to help herself teasing Nelia saying "Mommy's coming home!" — for a birthday of Nelia's, or Christmas, or Easter. How many times Connie thrilled with wickedness deceiving her baby sister and silly-baby that she was, Nelia believed.

And how Connie would laugh, laugh at her.

Well, it *was* funny. Wasn't it?

Another trick of Connie's: poking Nelia awake in the night when the wind was rattling the windows, moaning in the chimney like a trapped animal. Saying excitedly, *Momma is outside the window, listen! Momma is a ghost trying to get YOU!*

Sometimes Nelia screamed so, Connie had to straddle her chest and press a pillow over her face to muffle her. If they'd wakened Pappa with such nonsense there'd sure have been hell to pay.

Once, I might have been twelve, I asked if my grandfather had spanked or beaten them.

Aunt Connie, sitting in our living room on the high-backed mauve-brocade chair that was always hers when she came to visit, ignored me. Nor did Mother seem to hear. Aunt Connie lit one of her Chesterfields with a fussy flourish of her pink-frosted nails and took a deep satisfied puff and said, as if it were a thought only now slipping into her head, and like all such thoughts deserving of utterance, "I was noticing the other day, on TV, how brattish and idiotic children are, and we're supposed to think they're cute. Pappa wasn't the kind to tolerate children carrying on for a single minute." She paused, again inhaling deeply. "None of the men were, back there."

Mother nodded slowly, frowning. These conversations with my aunt seemed always to give her pain, an actual ache behind the eyes, yet she could no more resist them than Aunt Connie. She said, wiping at her eyes, "Pappa was a man of pride. After she left us as much as before."

"Hmmm!" Aunt Connie made her high humming nasal sound that meant she had something crucial to add, but did not want to appear pushy. "Well — maybe more, Nelia. More pride. After." She spoke insinuatingly, with a smile and a glance toward me.

Like an actress who has strayed from her lines, Mother quickly amended, "Yes, of course. Because a weaker man would have succumbed to — shame and despair —"

Aunt Connie nodded briskly. "— might have cursed God —"

"— turned to drink —"

"— so many of 'em *did,* back there —"

"— but not Pappa. He had the gift of faith."

Aunt Connie nodded sagely. Yet still with that strange almost-teasing smile.

"Oh indeed, Pappa did. That was his gift to us, Nelia, wasn't it? — his faith."

Mother was smiling her tight-lipped smile, her gaze lowered. I knew that, when Aunt Connie left, she would go upstairs to lie down, she would take two aspirins and draw the blinds, and put a damp cold cloth over her eyes and lie down and try to sleep. In her softening middle-aged face, the hue of putty, a young girl's face shone rapt with fear. "Oh yes! His faith."

Aunt Connie laughed heartily. Laugh, laugh. Dimples nicking her cheeks and a wink in my direction.

Years later, numbly sorting through Mother's belongings after her death, I would discover, in a lavender-scented envelope in a bureau drawer, a single strand of dry, ash-colored hair. On the envelope, in faded purple ink *Beloved Father John Allard Nissenbaum 1872–1957.*

3

By his own account, John Nissenbaum, the wronged husband, had not had the slightest suspicion that his strong-willed young wife had been discontent, restless. Certainly not that she'd had a secret lover! So many local women would have dearly wished to change places with her, he'd been given to know when he was courting her, his male vanity, and his Nissenbaum vanity, and what you might call common sense suggested otherwise.

For the Nissenbaums were a well-regarded family in the Chautauqua Valley. Among the lot of them they must have owned thousands of acres of prime farmland.

In the weeks, months, and eventually years that followed the scandalous departure, John Nissenbaum, who was by nature, like most of the male Nissenbaums, reticent to the point of arrogance, and fiercely private, came to make his story—*his side of it*—known. As the sisters themselves gathered (for their father never spoke of their mother to them after the first several days following the shock), this was not a single coherent history but one that had to be pieced together like a giant quilt made of a myriad of fabric-scraps.

He did allow that Gretel had been missing her family, an older sister with whom she'd been especially close, and cousins and girlfriends she'd gone to high school with in Chautauqua Falls; he understood that the two-hundred-acre farm was a lonely place for her, their next-door neighbors miles away, and the village of Ransomville seven miles. (Trips beyond Ransomville were rare.) He knew, or supposed he knew, that his wife had harbored what his mother and sisters called *wild imaginings*, even after nine years of marriage, farm life, and children: she had asked several times to be allowed to play the organ at church, but had been refused; she reminisced often wistfully and perhaps reproachfully of long-ago visits to Port Oriskany, Buffalo, and Chicago, before she'd gotten married at the age of eighteen to a man fourteen years her senior . . . in Chicago she'd seen stage plays and musicals, the sensational dancers Irene and Vernon Castle in Irving Berlin's *Watch Your Step.* It wasn't just Gretel wanting to take over the organ at Sunday services (and replacing the elderly male organist whose playing, she said, sounded like a cat in heat), it was her general attitude toward Reverend Dieckman and his wife. She resented having to invite them to an elaborate Sunday dinner every few weeks, as the Nissenbaums insisted; she allowed her eyes to roam the congregation during Dieckman's sermons, and stifled yawns behind her gloved hand; she woke in the middle of the night, she said, wanting to argue about damnation, hell, the very concept of grace. To the minister's astonished face she declared herself "not able to *fully accept* the teachings of the Lutheran Church."

If there were other more intimate issues between Gretel and John Nissenbaum, or another factor in Gretel's emotional life, of course no one spoke of it at the time.

Though it was hinted — possibly more than hinted? — that John Nissenbaum was disappointed with only daughters. Naturally he wanted sons, to help him with the ceaseless work of the farm; sons to whom he could leave the considerable property, just as his married brothers had sons.

What was generally known was: John woke in the pitch-dark an hour before dawn of that April day, to discover that Gretel was gone from their bed. Gone from the house? He searched for her, called her name, with growing alarm, disbelief. "Gretel? Gret-el!" He looked in all the upstairs rooms of the house including the bedroom where his sleep-dazed, frightened daughters were huddled together in their bed; he looked in all the downstairs rooms, even the damp, dirt-floor cellar into which he descended with a lantern. "Gretel? Where are you?" Dawn came dull, porous and damp, and with a coat yanked on in haste over his nightclothes, and his bare feet jammed into rubber boots, he began a frantic yet methodical search of the farm's outbuildings — the privy, the cow barn and the adjoining stable, the hay barn and the corncrib where rats rustled at his approach. In none of these save perhaps the privy was it likely that Gretel might be found, still John continued his search with growing panic, not knowing what else to do. From the house his now terrified daughters observed him moving from building to building, a tall, rigid, jerkily moving figure with hands cupped to his mouth shouting, "Gretel! Gret-el! Do you hear me! Where are you! Gret-el!" The man's deep, raw voice pulsing like a metronome, ringing clear, profound, and, to his daughters' ears, as terrible as if the very sky had cracked open and God himself was shouting.

(What did such little girls, eight and five, know of God — in fact, as Aunt Connie would afterward recount, quite a bit. There was Reverend Dieckman's baritone impersonation of the God of the Old Testament, the expulsion from the Garden, the devastating retort to Job, the spectacular burning bush where fire itself cried *HERE I AM!* — such had already been imprinted irrevocably upon their imaginations.)

Only later that morning — but this was a confused, anguished account — did John discover that Gretel's suitcase was missing from the closet. And there were garments conspicuously missing from the clothes rack. And Gretel's bureau drawers had been hastily ransacked — underwear, stockings were gone. And her favorite pieces of jewelry, of which she was childishly vain, were gone from her cedarwood box; gone, too, her heirloom, faded-cameo hairbrush, comb, and mirror set. And her Bible.

What a joke, how people would chuckle over it — Gretel Nissenbaum taking her Bible with her!

Wherever in hell the woman went.

And was there no farewell note, after nine years of marriage? — John Nissenbaum claimed he'd looked everywhere, and found nothing. Not a word of explanation, not a word of regret even to her little girls. *For that alone we expelled her from our hearts.*

During this confused time while their father was searching and calling their mother's name, the sisters hugged each other in a state of numbness beyond shock, terror. Their father seemed at times to be rushing toward them with the eye-bulging blindness of a runaway horse — they hurried out of his path. He did not see them except to order them out of his way, not to trouble him now. From the rear entry door they watched as he hitched his team of horses to his buggy and set out shuddering for Ransomville along the winter-rutted Post Road, leaving the girls behind, erasing them from his mind. As he would tell afterward, in rueful self-disgust, with the air of an enlightened sinner, he'd actually believed he would overtake Gretel on the road — convinced she'd be there, hiking on the grassy shoulder, carrying her suitcase. Gretel was a wiry-nervous woman, stronger than she appeared, with no fear of physical exertion. A woman capable of anything!

John Nissenbaum had the idea that Gretel had set out for Ransomville, seven miles away, there to catch the midmorning train to Chautauqua Falls, another sixty miles south. It was his confused belief that they must have had a disagreement, else Gretel would not have left; he did not recall any disagreement in fact, but Gretel was after all an *emotional woman,* a *highly strung woman;* she'd insisted upon visiting the Hausers, her family, despite his wishes, was that it? — she was lonely for them, or lonely for something. She was angry they hadn't visited Chautauqua Falls for Easter, hadn't seen her family since Christmas. Was that it? *We were never enough for her. Why were we never enough for her?*

But in Ransomville, in the cinderblock Chautauqua & Buffalo depot, there was no sign of Gretel, nor had the lone clerk seen her.

"This woman would be about my height," John Nissenbaum said, in his formal, slightly haughty way. "She'd be carrying a suitcase, her feet would maybe be muddy. Her boots."

The clerk shook his head slowly. "No sir, nobody looking like that."

"A woman by herself. A" — a hesitation, a look of pain — "good-looking woman, young. A kind of a, a way about her — a way of" — another pause — "making herself known."

"Sorry," the clerk said. "The 8:20 just came through, and no woman bought a ticket."

It happened then that John Nissenbaum was observed, stark-eyed, stiff-springy black hair in tufts like quills, for the better part of that morning, April 12, 1923, wandering up one side of Ransomville's single main street, and down the other. Hatless, in farm overalls and boots but wearing a suit coat — somber, gunmetal-gray, of "good" wool — buttoned crooked across his narrow muscular torso. Disheveled and ravaged with the grief of a betrayed husband too raw at this time for manly pride to intervene, pathetic some said as a kicked dog, yet eager too, eager as a puppy he made inquiries at Meldron's Dry Goods, at Elkin & Sons Grocers, at the First Niagara Trust, at the law office of Rowe & Nissenbaum (this Nissenbaum, a young cousin of John's), even in the Five & Dime where the salesgirls would giggle in his wake. He wandered at last into the Ransomville Hotel, into the gloomy public room where the proprietor's wife was sweeping sawdust-strewn floorboards. "Sorry, sir, we don't open till noon," the woman said, thinking he was a drunk, dazed and swaying-like on his feet, then she looked more closely at him: not knowing his first name (for John Nissenbaum was not one to patronize local taverns) but recognizing his features. For it was said the male Nissenbaums were either born looking alike, or came in time to look alike. "Mr. Nissenbaum? Is something wrong?" In a beat of stymied silence Nissenbaum blinked at her, trying to smile, groping for a hat to remove but finding none, murmuring, "No ma'am, I'm sure not. It's a misunderstanding, I believe. I'm supposed to meet Mrs. Nissenbaum somewhere here. My wife."

Shortly after Gretel Nissenbaum's disappearance there emerged, from numerous sources, from all points of the compass, certain tales of the woman. How rude she'd been, more than once, to the Dieckmans! — to many in the Lutheran congregation! A *bad wife. Unnatural mother.* It was said she'd left her husband and children in the past, running back to her family in Chautauqua Falls, or was it Port Oriskany; and poor John Nissenbaum having to fetch her home again. (This was untrue, though in time, even to Constance and Cornelia, it would come to seem true. As an elderly woman Cornelia would swear she remembered "both times" her mother ran off.) A shameless hussy, a tramp who *had an eye* for men. *Had the hots* for men. *Anything in pants.* Or was she *stuck-up, snobby.* Marrying into the Nissenbaum family, a man almost old enough to be her father, no mystery there! Worse yet she could be sharp-tongued, profane. Heard to utter such words as *damn, goddamn, hell.* Yes and *horseballs, bullshit.* Standing with her hands on her hips fixing her eyes on you, that loud laugh. And showing her teeth that were too big for her mouth. She was *too smart for her own good,* that's for sure. She was *scheming, faithless.* Everybody knew she flirted with her husband's hired hands, she did a hell of a lot more than flirt with them, ask around. Sure she had a *boyfriend,* a *lover.* Sure she was an *adulteress.* Hadn't she run off with a man? She'd run off and where was she to go, where was a woman to go, except *run off with a man?* Whoever he was.

In fact, he'd been sighted: a tower operator for the Chautauqua & Buffalo railroad, big redheaded guy living in Shaheen, twelve miles away. Or was he a carpet-sweeper salesman, squirrelly little guy with a mustache and a smooth way of talking, who passed through the valley every few months but, after April 12, 1923, was never seen there again.

Another, more attractive rumor was that Gretel Nissenbaum's lover was a thirty-year-old Navy officer stationed at Port Oriskany. He'd been transferred to a base in North Carolina, or was it Pensacola, Florida, and Gretel had no choice but run away with him, she loved him so. *And three months pregnant with his child.*

There could have been no romance in the terrible possibility that Gretel Nissenbaum had fled on foot, alone, not to her family but simply to escape from her life; in what exigency of need, what despondency of spirit, no name might be given it by any who have not experienced it.

But, in any case, where had she *gone?*

Where? Disappeared. Over the edge of the world. To Chicago, maybe. Or that Army base in North Carolina, or Florida.

We forgave, we forgot. We didn't miss her.

The things Gretel Nissenbaum left behind in the haste of her departure.

Several dresses, hats. A shabby cloth coat. Rubberized "galoshes" and boots. Undergarments, mended stockings. Knitted gloves. In the parlor of John Nissenbaum's house, in cut-glass vases, bright yellow daffodils she'd made from crepe paper; hand-painted fans, teacups; books she'd brought with her from home — *A Golden Treasury of Verse,* Mark Twain's *Joan of Arc,* Fitzgerald's *This Side of Paradise,* missing its jacket cover. Tattered programs for musical shows, stacks of popular piano music from the days Gretel had played in her childhood home. (There was no piano in Nissenbaum's house, Nissenbaum had no interest in music.)

These meager items, and some others, Nissenbaum unceremoniously dumped into cardboard boxes fifteen days after Gretel disappeared, taking them to the Lutheran church, for the "needy fund"; without inquiring if the Hausers might have wanted anything, or whether his daughters might have wished to be given some mementos of their mother.

Spite? Not John Nissenbaum. He was a proud man even in his public humiliation. It was the Lord's work he was thinking of. Not mere *human vanity,* at all.

That spring and summer Reverend Dieckman gave a series of grim, threatening, passionate sermons from the pulpit of the First Lutheran Church of Ransomville. It was obvious why, what the subject of the sermons was. The congregation was thrilled.

Reverend Dieckman, whom Connie and Nelia feared, as much for his fierce smiles as his stern, glowering expression, was a short, bulky man with a dull-gleaming dome of a head, eyes like ice water. Years later when they saw a photograph of him, inches shorter than his wife, they laughed in nervous astonishment — was that the man who'd intimidated them so? Before whom even John Nissenbaum stood grave and downgazing.

Yet: that ringing, vibrating voice of the God of Moses, the God of the

Old Testament, you could not shut out of consciousness even hours, days later. Years later. Pressing your hands against your ears and shutting your eyes tight, tight.

"'Unto the WOMAN He said, I will GREATLY MULTIPLY thy sorrow and thy conception; IN SORROW shalt thou bring forth children: and thy desire shall be to THY HUSBAND, and he shall RULE OVER THEE. And unto Adam He said, Because thou hast harkened unto the voice of THY WIFE, and has eaten of THE TREE, of which I commanded thee saying, THOU SHALT NOT EAT OF IT: cursed is the ground for thy sake; in sorrow shall thou eat of it all the days of thy life: THORNS ALSO AND THISTLES shall it bring forth to thee; and thou shalt eat the herb of the field; in the SWEAT OF THY FACE shalt thou eat bread, till thou return to the ground; for out of it thou wast taken: for DUST THOU ART, and UNTO DUST SHALT THOU RETURN.'" Reverend Dieckman paused to catch breath like a man running uphill. Greasy patches gleamed on his solid face like coins. Slowly his ice-eyes searched the rows of worshipers until as if by chance they came to rest on the upturned yet cowering faces of John Nissenbaum's daughters, who sat in the family pew, directly in front of the pulpit in the fifth row, between their rigid-backed father in his clothes somber as mourning and their Grandmother Nissenbaum also in clothes somber as mourning though badly round-shouldered, with a perceptible hump, this cheerless dutiful grandmother who had come to live with them now that their mother was gone.

(Their other grandparents, the Hausers, who lived in Chautauqua Falls and whom they'd loved, the sisters would never see again. It was forbidden even to speak of these people, *Gretel's people.* The Hausers were to blame somehow for Gretel's desertion. Though they claimed, would always claim, they knew nothing of what she'd done and in fact feared something had happened to her. But the Hausers were a forbidden subject. Only after Constance and Cornelia were grown, no longer living in their father's house, did they see their Hauser cousins; but still, as Cornelia confessed, she felt guilty about it. Father would have been so hurt and furious if he'd known. *Consorting with the enemy* he would deem it. *Betrayal.*)

In Sunday school, Mrs. Dieckman took special pains with little Constance and little Cornelia. They were regarded with misty-eyed pity, like child lepers. Fattish little Constance prone to fits of giggling, and hollow-eyed little Cornelia prone to sniffles, melancholy. Both girls had chafed, reddened faces and hands because their Grandmother Nissenbaum scrubbed them so, with strong gray soap, never less than twice a day. Cornelia's dun-colored hair was strangely thin. When the other children trooped out of the Sunday school room, Mrs. Dieckman kept the sisters behind, to pray with them. She was very concerned about them, she said. She and Reverend Dieckman prayed for them constantly. Had their mother contacted them, since leaving? Had there been any . . . hint of what their mother was planning to do? Any strangers visiting the farm? Any . . . unusual incidents? The sisters stared blankly at Mrs. Dieckman. She frowned at their ignorance, or its semblance. Dabbed at her watery eyes and sighed as if the world's weight had settled on her shoulders. She said half-chiding, "You should know, children, it's for a reason that your mother left you. It's God's will. God's plan. He is testing you, children. You are special in his eyes. Many of us have been special in his eyes and have emerged stronger for it, and not weaker." There was a breathy pause. The sisters were invited to contemplate how Mrs. Dieckman with her soft-wattled face, her stout-corseted body and fattish legs encased in opaque support hose, was a stronger and not a weaker person, by God's special plan. "You will learn to be stronger than girls with mothers, Constance and Cornelia—" (these words *girls with mothers* enunciated oddly, contemptuously). "You are already learning: feel God's strength coursing through you!" Mrs. Dieckman seized the girls' hands, squeezing so quick and hard that Connie burst into frightened giggles and Nelia shrieked as if she'd been burned, and almost wet her panties.

Nelia acquired pride, then. Instead of being ashamed, publicly humiliated (at the one-room country schoolhouse, for instance: where certain of the other children were ruthless), she could be proud, like her father. *God had a special feeling for me. God cared about me. Jesus Christ, his only son, was cruelly tested, too. And exalted. You can bear any hurt and degradation. Thistles and thorns. The flaming sword, the cherubims guarding the garden.*

Mere *girls with mothers,* how could they know?

4

Of course, Connie and Nelia had heard their parents quarreling. In the weeks, months before their mother disappeared. In fact, all their lives. Had they been queried, had they had the language, they might have said *This is what is done, a man, a woman—isn't it?*

Connie, who was three years older than Nelia, knew much that Nelia would not ever know. Not words exactly, these quarrels, and of a tone different from their father shouting out instructions to his farm hands. Not words but an eruption of voices. Ringing through the floorboards if the quarrel came from downstairs. Reverberating in the windowpanes where wind thinly whistled. In bed, Connie would hug Nelia tight, pretending Nelia was Momma. Or Connie was herself Momma. If you shut your eyes tight enough. If you shut your ears. Always after the voices there came silence. If you wait. Once, crouched at the foot of the stairs it was Connie? — or Nelia? — gazing upward astonished as Momma descended the stairs swaying like a drunk woman, her left hand groping against the railing, face dead-white and a bright crimson rosebud in the corner of her mouth glistening as she wiped, wiped furiously at it. And quick-walking in that way of his that made the house vibrate, heavy-heeled behind her, descending from the top of the stairs a man whose face she could not see. Fiery, and blinding. God in the burning bush. God in thunder. *Bitch! Get back up here! If I have to come get you, if you won't be a woman, a wife!*

It was a fact the sisters learned, young: if you wait long enough, run away and hide your eyes, shut your ears, there comes a silence vast and rolling and empty as the sky.

There was the mystery of the letters my mother and Aunt Connie would speak of, though never exactly discuss in my presence, into the last year of my mother's life.

Which of them first noticed, they couldn't agree. Or when it began, exactly — no earlier than the fall, 1923. It would happen that Pappa went to fetch the mail, which he rarely did, and then only on Saturdays; and, returning, along the quarter-mile lane, he would be observed (by accident? the girls weren't spying) with an opened letter in his hand, reading; or was it a postcard; walking with uncharacteristic slowness, this man whose step was invariably brisk and impatient. Connie recalled he'd sometimes slip into the stable to continue reading, Pappa had a liking for the stable which was for him a private place where he'd chew tobacco, spit into the hay, run his callused hands along a horse's flanks, think his own thoughts. Other times, carrying whatever it was, letter, postcard, the rarity of an item of personal mail, he'd return to the kitchen and his place at the table. There the girls would find him (by accident, they *were not* spying) drinking coffee laced with top-milk and sugar, rolling one of his clumsy cigarettes. And Connie would be the one to inquire, "Was there any mail, Pappa?" keeping her voice low, unexcited. And Pappa would shrug and say, "Nothing." On the table where he'd dropped them indifferently might be a few bills, advertising flyers, the *Chautauqua Valley Weekly Gazette.* Nelia never inquired about the mail at such times because she would not have trusted her voice. But, young as ten, Connie could be pushy, reckless. "Isn't there a letter, Pappa? What *is* that, Pappa, in your pocket?"

And Pappa would say calmly, staring her full in the face, "When your father says *nothing,* girl, he means *nothing.*"

Sometimes his hands shook, fussing with the pouch of Bugler and the stained cigarette-roller.

Since the shame of losing his wife, and everybody knowing the circumstances, John Nissenbaum had aged shockingly. His face was creased, his skin reddened and cracked, finely stippled with what would be diagnosed (when finally he went to a doctor) as skin cancer. His eyes, pouched in wrinkled lids like a turtle's, were often vague, restless. Even in church, in a row close to Reverend Dieckman's pulpit, he had a look of wandering off. In what he called his earlier life he'd been a rough, physical man, intelligent but quick-tempered; now he tired easily, could not keep up with his hired men whom he more and more mistrusted. His beard, once so trim and shapely, grew ragged and uneven and was entirely gray-grizzled, like cobwebs. And his breath — it smelled of tobacco juice, wet, rank, sickish, rotted.

Once, seeing the edge of the letter in Pappa's pocket, Connie bit her lip and said, "It's from *her,* isn't it!"

Pappa said, still calmly, "I said it's *nothing,* girl. From *nobody.*"

Never in their father's presence did either of the sisters allude to their missing mother except as *her, she.*

Later when they searched for the letter, even for its envelope, of course they found nothing. Pappa had burned it in the stove probably. Or torn it into shreds, tossed into the garbage. Still, the sisters risked their father's wrath by daring to look in his bedroom (the stale-smelling room he'd moved to, downstairs at the rear of the house) when he was out; even, desperate, knowing it was hopeless, poking through fresh-dumped garbage. (Like all farm families of their day, the Nissenbaums dumped raw garbage down a hillside, in the area of the outhouse.) Once Connie scrambled across fly-buzzing mounds of garbage holding her nose, stooping to snatch up — what? A card advertising a fertilizer sale, that had looked like a picture postcard.

"Are you crazy?" Nelia cried. "I hate you!"

Connie turned to scream at her, eyes brimming tears. "Go to hell, horse's ass, I hate *you!*"

Both wanted to believe, or did in fact believe, that their mother was not writing to their father but to them. But they would never know. For years, as the letters came at long intervals, arriving only when their father fetched the mail, they would not know.

This might have been a further element of mystery: why the letters, arriving so infrequently, arrived only when their father got the mail. Why, when Connie, or Nelia, or Loraine (John's younger sister, who'd come to live with them) got the mail, there would never be one of the mysterious letters. *Only when Pappa got the mail.*

After my mother's death in 1981, when I spoke more openly to my Aunt Connie, I asked why they hadn't been suspicious, just a little. Aunt Connie lifted her penciled eyebrows, blinked at me as if I'd uttered something obscene — "Suspicious? Why?" Not once did the girls (who were in fact intelligent girls, Nelia a straight-A student in the high school in town) calculate the odds: how the presumed letter from their mother could possibly arrive only on those days (Saturdays) when their father got the mail; one day out of six mail-days, yet never any day except that particular day (Saturday). But as Aunt Connie said, shrugging, it just seemed that that was how it was — they would never have conceived of even the possibility of any situation in which the odds wouldn't have been against them, and in favor of Pappa.

5

The farmhouse was already old when I was first brought to visit it: summers, in the 1950s. Part red brick so weathered as to seem without color and part rotted wood, with a steep shingled roof, high ceilings, and spooky corners; a perpetual odor of woodsmoke, kerosene, mildew, time. A perpetual draft passed through the house from the rear, which faced north, opening out onto a long incline of acres, miles, dropping to the Chautauqua River ten miles away like an aerial scene in a movie. I remember the old wash room, the machine with a hand-wringer; a door to the cellar in the floor of that room, with a thick metal ring as a handle. Outside the house, too, was another door, horizontal and not vertical. The thought of what lay beyond those doors, the dark, stone-smelling cellar where rats scurried, filled me with a childish terror.

I remember Grandfather Nissenbaum as always old. A lean, sinewy, virtually mute old man. His finely cracked, venous-glazed skin, red-stained as if with earth; narrow rheumy eyes whose pupils seemed, like the pupils of goats, horizontal black slats. How they scared me! Deafness had made Grandfather remote and strangely imperial, like an old almost-forgotten king. The crown of his head was shinily bald and a fringe of coarse hair bleached to the color of ash grew at the sides and back. Where once, my mother lamented, he'd been careful in his dress, especially on Sundays, for churchgoing, he now wore filth-stained overalls and in all months save summer long gray-flannel underwear straggling at his cuffs like a loose, second skin. His breath stank of tobacco juice and rotted teeth, the knuckles of both his hands were grotesquely swollen. My heart beat quickly and erratically in his presence. "Don't be silly," Mother whispered nervously, pushing me toward the old man, "—your grandfather *loves you.*" But I knew he did not. Never did he call me by my name, Bethany, but only "girl" as if he hadn't troubled to learn my name.

When Mother showed me photographs of the man she called Pappa, some of these scissored in half, to excise my missing grandmother, I stared, and could not believe he'd once been so handsome! Like a film actor of some bygone time. "You see," Mother said, incensed, as if the two of us had been quarreling, "—this is who John Nissenbaum really *is.*"

I grew up never really knowing Grandfather, and I certainly didn't love him. He was never "Grandpa" to me. Visits to Ransomville were sporadic, sometimes canceled at the last minute. Mother would be excited, hopeful, apprehensive—then, who knows why, the visit would be canceled, she'd be tearful, upset, yet relieved. Now, I can guess that Mother and her family weren't fully welcomed by my grandfather; he was a lonely and embittered old man, but still proud—he'd never forgiven her for leaving home, after high school, just like her sister Connie; going to the teachers' college at Elmira instead of marrying a local man worthy of working and eventually inheriting the Nissenbaum farm. By the time I was born, in 1951, the acreage was being sold off; by the time Grandfather Nissenbaum died, in 1972, in a nursing home in Yewville, the two hundred acres had been reduced to a humiliating seven acres, now the property of strangers.

In the hilly cemetery behind the First Lutheran Church of Ransomville, New York, there is a still-shiny black granite marker at the edge of rows of Nissenbaum markers, JOHN ALLARD NISSENBAUM 1872–1957. Chiseled into the stone is *How long shall I be with you? How long shall I suffer you?* Such angry words of Jesus Christ's! I wondered who had chosen them — not Constance or Cornelia, surely. It must have been John Nissenbaum himself.

Already as a girl of eleven, twelve, I was pushy and curious, asking my mother about my missing grandmother. *Look, Mother, for God's sake where did she go? Didn't anybody try to find her?* Mother's replies were vague, evasive. As if rehearsed. That sweet-resolute stoic smile. Cheerful resignation, Christian forgiveness. For thirty-five years she taught high school English in the Rochester public schools, and especially after my father left us, and she became a single, divorced woman, the manner came easily to her of brisk classroom authority, that pretense of the skilled teacher of weighing others' opinions thoughtfully before reiterating one's own.

My father, an education administrator, left us when I was fourteen, to remarry. I was furious, heartbroken. Dazed. *Why? How could he betray us?* But Mother maintained her Christian fortitude, her air of subtly wounded pride. *This is what people will do, Bethany. Turn against you, turn faithless. You might as well learn, young.*

Yet I pushed. Up to the very end of her life, when Mother was so ill. You'd judge me harsh, heartless — people did. But for God's sake I wanted to know: what happened to my Grandmother Nissenbaum, why did nobody seem to care she'd gone away? Were the letters my mother and Connie swore their father received authentic, or had he been playing a trick of some kind? And if it had been a trick, what was its purpose? *Just tell me the truth for once, Mother. The truth about anything.*

I'm forty-four years old, I still want to know.

But Mother, the intrepid schoolteacher, the good Christian, was impenetrable. Inscrutable as her pappa. Capable of summing up her entire childhood *back there* (this was how she and Aunt Connie spoke of Ransomville, their pasts: *back there*) by claiming that such *hurts* are God's will, God's plan for each of us. A test of our faith. A test of our inner strength. I said, disgusted, what if you don't believe in God, what are you left with then? — and Mother said matter-of-factly, "You're left with yourself, of course, your inner strength. Isn't that enough?"

That final time we spoke of this, I lost patience, I must have pushed Mother too far. In a sharp, stinging voice, a voice I'd never heard from her before, she said, "Bethany, what do you want me to tell you? About my mother? — my father? Do you imagine I ever knew them? Either of them? My mother left Connie and me when we were little girls, left us with *him*, wasn't that her choice? Her selfishness? Why should anyone have gone looking for her? She was trash, she was *faithless.* We learned to forgive, and to forget. Your aunt tells you a different story, I know, but it's a lie — I was the one who was hurt, I was the youngest. Your heart can be broken only once — you'll learn! Our lives were busy, busy like the lives of us grown women today, women who have to work, women who don't have time to moan and groan over their hurt feelings, you can't know how Connie and I worked on that farm, in that house, like grown women when we were girls. Father tried to stop both of us going to school beyond eighth grade — imagine! We had to walk two miles to get a ride with a neighbor, to get to the high school in Ransomville; there weren't school buses in those days. Everything you've had you've taken for granted and wanted more, but we weren't like that. We hadn't money for the right school clothes, all our textbooks were used, but we went to high school. I was the only 'farm girl' — that's exactly what I was known as, even by my teachers — in my class to take math, biology, physics, Latin. I was memorizing Latin declensions milking cows at five in the morning, winter mornings. I was laughed at, Nelia Nissenbaum was *laughable.* But I accepted it. All that mattered was that I win a scholarship to a teachers' college so I could escape the country, and I did win a scholarship and I never returned to Ransomville to live. Yes, I loved Pappa — I still love him. I loved the farm, too. You can't not love any place that's taken so much from you. But I had my own life, I had my teaching jobs, I had my faith, my belief in God, I had my destiny. I even got married — that was extra, unexpected. I've worked for everything I ever got and I never had time to look back, to feel sorry for myself. Why then should I think about *her?* — why do you torment me about *her?* A woman who abandoned me when I was five years old! In 1923! I made my peace with the past, just like Connie in her different way. We're happy women, we've been spared a lifetime of bitterness. *That* was God's gift to us." Mother paused, breathing quickly. There was in her face the elation of one who has said too much, that can never be retracted; I was stunned into silence. She plunged on, now contemptuously, "What are you always wanting me to admit, Bethany? That you know something I don't know? What is your generation always pushing for, from ours? Isn't it enough we gave birth to you, indulged you, must we be sacrificed to you, too? What do you want us to tell you — that life is cruel and purposeless? that there is no loving God, and never was, only accident? Is that what you want to hear, from your mother? That I married your father because he was a weak man, a man I couldn't feel much for, who wouldn't, when it came time, hurt me?"

And then there was silence. We stared at each other, Mother in her glisten of fury, daughter Bethany so shocked she could not speak. Never again would I think of my mother in the old way.

What Mother never knew: In April 1983, two years after her death, a creek that runs through the old Nissenbaum property flooded its banks, and several hundred feet of red clayey soil collapsed overnight into the creek bed, as in an earthquake. And in the raw, exposed earth there was discovered a human skeleton, decades old but virtually intact. It had been apparently buried, less than a mile behind the Nissenbaum farmhouse.

There had never been anything so newsworthy — so sensational — in the history of Chautauqua County.

State forensic investigators determined that the skeleton had belonged to a woman, apparently killed by numerous blows to the head (a hammer, or the blunt edge of an ax) that shattered her skull like a melon. Dumped into the grave with her was what appeared to have been a suitcase, now rotted, its contents — clothes, shoes, underwear, gloves — scarcely recognizable from the earth surrounding it. There were a few pieces of jewelry and, still entwined around the skeleton's neck, a tarnished gold cross on a chain. Most of the woman's clothing had long ago rotted away and almost unrecognizable too was a book — a leather-bound Bible? — close beside her. About the partly detached, fragile wrist and ankle bones were loops of rusted baling wire that had fallen loose, coiled in the moist red clay like miniature sleeping snakes.

1998

TOM FRANKLIN

POACHERS

TOM (THOMAS GERALD) FRANKLIN (1962–) was born and raised in the tiny town of Dickinson, Alabama, before his family moved to Mobile. He received a BA in English from the University of South Alabama, working his way through school with jobs in a hospital morgue, a factory, and cleaning up waste at a chemical plant. He received his MFA from the University of Arkansas, where he met his future wife, the poet Beth Ann Fennelly. He taught at South Alabama and Selma University, then held the Philip Roth Residence in Creative Writing at Bucknell University, was writer in residence at Knox College, the John and Renée Grisham Writer in Residence at the University of Mississippi, and the Tennessee Williams Fellow at the University of the South. He was also awarded a Guggenheim Fellowship. Franklin's short story "Poachers" won the Edgar Allan Poe Award in 1999 and was the centerpiece for his first book, *Poachers: Stories* (1999). His first novel, *Hell at the Breech* (2003), is a fictionalized version of a violent episode near the author's home in post–Civil War Alabama. When an aspiring politician is murdered, members of his constituency, mostly poor cotton farmers, form a secret society called Hell at the Breech. They wear hoods, swear an oath of loyalty, and terrorize the people they believe were responsible for the killing. When their victims retaliate, a great deal of blood is spilled. The book was called the best novel to come out of the South since Charles Frazier's *Cold Mountain.* Franklin's second novel, equally praised, was *Smonk* (2006).

"Poachers" was originally published in the spring 1998 issue of *Texas Review.* It was selected for *The Best American Mystery Stories 1999* and for *The Best American Mystery Stories of the Century.*

▪ ▪ ▪

AT DAWN, ON THE first day of April, the three Gates brothers banked their ten-foot aluminum boat in a narrow slough of dark water. They tied their hounds, strapped on their rifles, and stepped out, ducking black magnolia branches heavy with rain and Spanish moss. The two thin younger brothers, denim overalls tucked into their boots, lugged between them a styrofoam cooler of iced fish and coons and possums. The oldest brother—bearded, heavyset, twenty years old—carried a Sunbeam Bread sack of eels in his coat pocket. Hooked over his left shoulder was the pink body of a fawn they'd shot and skinned, and, over the right, a stray dog to which they'd done the same. With the skins and heads gone and the dog's tail chopped off, they were difficult to tell apart.

The Gateses climbed the hill, clinging to vines and saplings, slipping in the red clay, their boots coated and enormous by the time they stepped out of the woods. For a moment they stood in the road, looking at the gray sky, the clouds piling up. The two younger ones, Scott and Wayne, set the cooler down. Kent, the oldest, removed his limp cap and squeezed the water from it. He nodded and his brothers picked up the cooler. They rounded a curve and crossed a one-lane bridge, stopping to piss over the rail into creek water high from all the rain, then went on, passing houses on either side: dark warped boards with knotholes big enough to look through and cement blocks for steps. Black men appeared in doors and windows to watch them go by—to most of these people they were something not seen often, something nocturnal and dangerous. Along this stretch of the Alabama River, everyone knew that the brothers' father, Boo Gates, had married a girl named Anna when he was thirty and she was seventeen, and that the boys had been born in quick succession, with less than a year between them.

But few outside the family knew that a fourth child—a daughter, unnamed—had been stillborn, and that Boo had buried her in an unmarked grave in a clearing in the woods behind their house. Anna died the next day and the three boys, dirty and naked, watched their father's stoop-shouldered descent into the earth as he dug her grave. By the time he'd finished it was dark and the moon had come up out of the trees and the boys lay asleep upon each other in the dirt like wolf pups.

The name of this community, if it could be called that, was Lower Peachtree, though as far as anybody knew there'd never been an Upper Peachtree. Scattered along the leafy banks of the river were ragged houses, leaning and drafty, many empty, caving in, so close to the water they'd been built on stilts. Each April floods came and the crumbling land along the riverbank would disappear and each May, when the floodwaters receded, a house or two would be gone.

Upriver, near the lock and dam, stood an old store, a slanting building with a steep, rusty tin roof and a stovepipe in the back. Behind the store the mimosa trees sagged, waterlogged. In front, beside the gas pump, long green steps led up to the door, where a red sign said OPEN. Inside to the right, like a bar, a polished maple counter covered the entire wall. Behind the counter hung a rack with wire pegs for tools, hardware, fishing tackle. The condoms, bullets, and tobacco products, the rat poison and the Old Timer knife display were beneath the counter.

The store owner, Old Kirxy, had bad knees, and this weather settled around his joints like rot. For most of his life he'd been married and lived in a nice house on the highway. Two-story. Fireplaces in every bedroom. A china cabinet. But when his wife died two years ago, cancer, he found it easier to avoid the house, to keep the bills paid and the grass mowed but the door locked, to spend nights in the store, to sleep in the back room on the Army cot and to warm his meals of corned beef and beef stew on a hot plate. He didn't mind that people had all but stopped coming to the store. As long as he served a few long-standing customers, he thought he'd stick around. He had his radio and one good station, WJDB of Thomasville, and money enough. He liked the area, knew his regulars weren't the kind to drive an hour to the nearest town. For those few people, Kirxy would go once a week to Grove Hill to shop for goods he'd resell, marking up the price just enough for a reasonable profit. He didn't need the money, it was just good business.

Liquor-wise, the county was dry, but that didn't stop Kirxy from selling booze. For his regulars, he would serve plastic cups of the cheap whiskey he bought in the next county or bottles of beer he kept locked in the old refrigerator in back. For these regulars, he would break packages of cigarettes and keep them in a cigar box and sell them for a dime apiece, a nickel stale. Aspirins were seven cents each, Tylenol tablets nine. He would open boxes of shotgun shells or cartridges and sell them for amounts that varied, according to caliber, and he'd been known to find specialty items—paperback novels, explosives, and, once, a rotary telephone.

At Euphrates Morrisette's place, the Gates brothers pounded on the back door. In his yard a cord of wood was stacked between two fence-posts and covered by a green tarp, brick halves holding the tarp down. A tire swing, turning slowly and full of rainwater, hung from a white oak. When Morrisette appeared—he was a large, bald black man—Kent held out the fawn and dog. Morrisette put on glasses and squinted at both. "Hang back," he said, and closed the door. Kent sat on the porch edge and his brothers on the steps.

The door opened and Morrisette came out with three pint jars of homemade whiskey. Each brother took a jar and unscrewed its lid, sniffed the clear liquid. Morrisette set his steaming coffee cup on the windowsill. He fastened his suspenders, looking at the carcasses hanging over the rail. The brothers were already drinking.

"Where's that girl?" Kent asked, his face twisted from the sour whiskey.

"My stepdaughter, you mean?" Morrisette's Adam's apple pumped in his throat. "She inside." Far away a rooster crowed.

"Get her out here," Kent said. He drank again, shuddered.

"She ain't but fifteen."

Kent scratched his beard. "Just gonna look at her."

When they left, the stepdaughter was standing on the porch in her white nightgown, barefoot, afraid, and rubbing the sleep from her eyes. The brothers backed away clanking with hardware and grinning at her, Morrisette's jaw clenched.

Sipping from their jars, they took the bag of eels down the road to the half-blind conjure woman who waited on her porch. Her house, with its dark drapes and empty parrot cages dangling from the eaves, seemed to be slipping off into the gully. She snatched the eels from Kent, squinting into the bag with her good eye. Grunting, she paid them from a dusty cloth sack on her apron and muttered to herself as they went up the dirt road. Wayne, the youngest, looked back, worried that she'd put a hex on them.

They peddled the rest of the things from their cooler, then left through the dump, stumbling down the ravine in the rain, following the water's edge to their boat. In the back, Kent wedged his jar between his thighs and ran the silent trolling motor with his foot. His brothers leaned against the walls of the boat, facing opposite banks, no sound but rain and the low hum of the motor. They drank silently, holding the burning whiskey in their mouths before gathering the will to swallow. Along the banks, fallen trees held thick strands of cottonmouth, black sparkling creatures dazed and slow from winter, barely able to move. If not for all the rain, they might still be hibernating, comatose in the banks of the river or beneath the soft yellow underbellies of rotten logs.

Rounding a bend, the brothers saw a small boat downriver, its engine clear, loud, and unfamiliar. Heading this way. The man in the boat lifted a hand in greeting. He wore a green poncho and a dark hat covered with plastic. Kent shifted his foot, turning the trolling motor, and steered them toward the bank, giving the stranger a wide berth. He felt for their outboard's crank rope while Scott and Wayne faced forward and sat on the boat seats. The man drawing closer didn't look much older than Kent. He cut his engine and coasted up beside them, smiling.

"Morning, fellows," he said, showing a badge. "New district game warden."

The brothers looked straight ahead, as if he wasn't there. The warden's engine was steaming, a flock of geese passed overhead. Wayne slipped his hands inside the soft leather collars of two dogs, who'd begun to growl.

"You fellows oughta know," the warden said, pointing his long chin to the rifle in Scott's hands, "that it's illegal to have those guns loaded on the river. I'm gonna have to check 'em. I'll need to see some licenses, too."

When he stood, the dogs jumped forward, toenails scraping aluminum. Wayne pulled them back, glancing at his brothers.

Kent spat into the brown water. He met the warden's eyes, and in an instant knew the man had seen the telephone in the floor of their boat.

"Pull to the bank!" the warden yelled, drawing a pistol. "Y'all are under arrest for poaching!"

The Gateses didn't move. One of the dogs began to claw the hull and the others joined him. A howl arose.

"Shut those dogs up!" The warden's face had grown blotchy and red.

The spotted hound broke free and sprang over the gunnel, slobber strung from its teeth, and the man most surprised by the game warden's shot was the game warden himself. His face drained of color as the noise echoed off the water and died in the bent black limbs and the cattails. The bullet had passed through the front dog's neck and smacked into the bank behind them, missing Wayne by inches. The dog collapsed, and there was an instant of silence before the others, now loose, clattered overboard into the water, red-eyed, tangled in their leashes, trying to swim.

"Pull to the goddamn bank!" the warden yelled. "Right now!"

Scowling, Kent leaned and spat. He laid his .30-30 aside. Using the shoulders of his brothers for balance, he made his way to the prow. Scott, flecked with dog blood, moved to the back to keep the boat level. At the front, Kent reached into the water and took the first dog by its collar, lifted the kicking form, and set it streaming and shivering behind him. His brothers turned their faces away as it shook off the water, rocking the whole boat. Kent grabbed the rope that led to the big three-legged hound and pulled it in hand over hand until he could work his fingers under its collar. He gave Wayne a sidelong look and together they hauled it in. Then Kent grabbed for the smaller bitch while Wayne got the black and tan.

The warden watched them, his hips swaying with the rise and fall of the current. Rain fell harder now, spattering against the aluminum boats. Kneeling among the dogs, Kent unsnapped the leash and tossed the spotted hound overboard. It sank, then resurfaced and floated on its side, trailing blood. Kent's lower lip twitched. Wayne whispered to the dogs and placed his hands on two of their heads to calm them — they were retching and trembling and rolling their eyes fearfully at the trees.

Scott stood up with his hands raised, as if to surrender. When the man looked at him, Kent jumped from his crouch into the other boat, his big fingers closing around the game warden's neck.

Later that morning, Kirxy had just unlocked the door and hung out the OPEN sign when he heard the familiar rattle of the Gates truck. He sipped his coffee and limped behind the counter, sat on his stool. The boys came several times a week, usually in the afternoon, before they started their evenings of hunting and fishing. Kirxy would give them the supplies they needed — bullets, fishing line, socks, a new cap to replace one lost in the river. They would fill their truck and cans with gas. Eighteen-year-old Wayne would get the car battery from the charger near the wood-burning stove and replace it with the drained one from their boat's trolling motor. Kirxy would serve them coffee or Cokes — never liquor, not to minors — and they'd eat whatever they chose from the shelves, usually candy bars or potato chips, ignoring Kirxy's advice that they ought to eat healthier: Vienna sausages, Dinty Moore, or Chef Boyardee.

Today they came in looking a little spooked, Kirxy thought. Scott stayed near the door, peering out, the glass fogging by his face. Wayne went to the candy aisle and selected several Hershey bars. He left a trail of muddy boot prints behind him. Kirxy would mop later.

"Morning, boys," he said. "Coffee?"

Wayne nodded. Kirxy filled a styrofoam cup, then grinned as the boy loaded it with sugar.

"You take coffee with your sweet'ner?" he said.

Kent leaned on the counter, inspecting the hardware items on their pegs, a hacksaw, a set of Allen wrenches. A gizmo with several uses, knife, measuring tape, awl. Kirxy could smell the booze on the boys.

"Y'all need something?" he asked.

"That spotted one you give us?" Kent said. "Won't bark no more."

"She won't?"

"Naw. Tree 'em fine, but won't bark nary a time. Gonna have to shoot her, I expect."

His mouth full of chocolate, Wayne looked at Kirxy. By the door, Scott unfolded his arms. He kept looking outside.

"No," Kirxy said. "Ain't no need to shoot her, Kent. Do what that conjure woman recommends. Go out in the woods, find you a locust shell stuck to a tree. This is the time of year for 'em, if I'm not mistaken."

"Locust shell?" Kent asked.

"Yeah. Bring it back home and crunch it up in the dog's scraps, and that'll make her bark like she ought to."

Kent nodded to Kirxy and walked to the door. He went out, his brothers following.

"See you," Kirxy called.

Wayne waved with a Hershey bar and closed the door.

Kirxy stared after them for a time. It had been a year since they'd paid him anything, but he couldn't bring himself to ask for money; he'd even stopped writing down what they owed.

He got his coffee and limped from behind the counter to the easy chair by the stove. He shook his head at the muddy footprints on the candy aisle. He sat slowly, tucked a blanket around his legs, took out his bottle and added a splash to his coffee. Sipping, he picked up a novel—Louis L'Amour, *Sackett's Land*—and reached in his apron pocket for his glasses.

Though she had been once, the woman named Esther wasn't much of a regular in Kirxy's store these days. She lived two miles upriver in a shambling white house with magnolia trees in the yard. The house had a wraparound porch, and when it flooded you could fish from the back, sitting in the tall white rocking chairs, though you weren't likely to catch anything. A baby alligator maybe, or sometimes bullfrogs. Owls nested in the trees along her part of the river, but in this weather they seemed quiet; she missed their hollow calling.

Esther was fifty. She'd had two husbands and six children who were gone and had ill feelings toward her. She'd had her female parts removed in an operation. Now she lived alone and, most of the time, drank alone. If the Gates boys hadn't passed out in their truck somewhere in the woods, they might stop by after a night's work. Esther would make them strong coffee and feed them salty fried eggs and greasy link sausages, and some mornings, like today, she would get a faraway look in her eyes and take Kent's shirt collar in her fingers and lead him upstairs and watch him close the bathroom door and listen to the sounds of his bathing.

She smiled, knowing these were the only baths he ever took.

When he emerged, his long hair stringy, his chest flat and hard, she led him down the hall past the telephone nook to her bedroom. He crawled into bed and watched her take off her gown and step out of her underwear. Bending, she looked in the mirror to fluff her hair, then climbed in beside him. He was gentle at first, curious, then rougher, the way she liked him to be. She closed her eyes, the bed frame rattling and bumping, her father's old pocket watch slipping off the nightstand. Water gurgled in the pipework in the walls as the younger brothers took baths, too, hoping for a turn of their own, which had never happened. At least not yet.

"Slow, baby," Esther whispered in Kent's ear. "It's plenty of time . . ."

On April third it was still raining. Kirxy put aside his crossword to answer the telephone.

"Can you come on down to the lock and dam?" Goodloe asked. "We got us a situation here."

Kirxy disliked smart-assed Goodloe, but something in the sheriff's voice told him it was serious. On the news, he'd heard that the new game warden had been missing for two days. The authorities had dragged the river all night and had three helicopters in the air. Kirxy sat forward in his chair, waiting for his back to loosen a bit. He added a shot of whiskey to his coffee and gulped it down as he shrugged into his denim jacket, zipping it up to his neck because he stayed cold when it rained. He put cotton balls in his ears and set his cap on his bald head, took his walking cane from beside the door.

In his truck, the four-wheel-drive engaged and the defroster on high, he sank and rose in the deep ruts, gobs of mud flying past his windows, the wipers swishing across his view. The radio announcer said it was sixty degrees, more rain on the way. Conway Twitty began to sing. A mile from the lock and dam Kirxy passed the Grove Hill ambulance, axle-deep in mud. A burly black paramedic wedged a piece of two-by-four beneath one of the rear tires while the bored-looking driver sat behind the wheel, smoking and racing the engine.

Kirxy slowed and rolled down his window. "Y'all going after a live one or a dead one?"

"Dead, Mr. Kirxy," the black man answered.

Kirxy nodded and sped up. At the lock and dam, he could see a crowd of people and umbrellas and beyond them he saw the dead man, lying on the ground under a black raincoat. Some onlooker had begun to direct traffic. Goodloe and three deputies in yellow slickers stood near the body with their hands in their pockets.

Kirxy climbed out and people nodded somberly and parted to let him through. Goodloe, who'd been talking to his deputies, ceased as Kirxy approached and they stood looking at the raincoat.

"Morning, Sugarbaby," Kirxy said, using the childhood nickname Goodloe hated. "Is this who I think it is?"

"Yep," Goodloe muttered. "Rookie game warden of the year."

With his cane, Kirxy pulled back the raincoat to reveal the white face. "Young fellow," he said.

There was a puddle beneath the dead man. Twigs in his hair and a clove of moss in his breast pocket. With the rubber tip of his cane, Kirxy brushed a leech from the man's forehead. He bent and looked into the warden's left eye, which was partly open. He noticed his throat, the dark bruises there.

Goodloe unfolded a handkerchief and blew his nose, then wiped it. "Don't go abusing the evidence, Kirxy." He stuffed the handkerchief into his back pocket.

"Evidence? Now, Sugarbaby."

Goodloe exhaled and looked at the sky. "Don't shit me, Kirxy. You know good and well who done this. I expect they figure the law don't apply up here on this part of the river, the way things is been all these years. Them other wardens scared of 'em. But I reckon that's fixing to change." He paused. "I had to place me a call to the capital this morning. To let 'em know we was all outa game wardens. And you won't believe who they patched me through to."

Kirxy adjusted the cotton in his right ear.

"Old Frank David himself," the sheriff said. "Ain't nothing ticks him off more than this kind of thing."

A dread stirred in Kirxy's belly. "Frank David. Was he a relation of this fellow?"

"Teacher," Goodloe said. "Said he's been giving lessons to young game wardens over at the forestry service. He asked me a whole bunch of questions. Regular interrogation. Said this here young fellow was the cream of the crop. Best new game warden there was."

"Wouldn't know it from this angle," Kirxy said.

Goodloe grunted.

A photographer from the paper was studying the corpse. He glanced at the sky as if gauging the light. When he snapped the first picture, Kirxy was in it, like a sportsman.

"What'd you want from me?" he asked Goodloe.

"You tell them boys I need to ask 'em some questions, and I ain't fixing to traipse all over the county. I'll drop by the store this evening."

"If they're there, they're there," Kirxy said. "I ain't their damn father."

Goodloe followed him to the truck. "You might think of getting 'em a lawyer," he said through the window.

Kirxy started the engine. "Shit, Sugarbaby. Them boys don't need a lawyer. They just need to stay in the woods, where they belong. Folks oughta know to let 'em alone by now."

Goodloe stepped back from the truck. He smacked his lips. "I don't reckon anybody got around to telling that to the deceased."

Driving, Kirxy turned off the radio. He remembered the Gates brothers when they were younger, before their father shot himself. He pictured the three blond heads in the front of Boo's boat as he motored upriver past the store, lifting a solemn hand to Kirxy where he stood with a broom on his little back porch. After Boo's wife and newborn daughter had died, he'd taught those boys all he knew about the woods, about fishing, tracking, hunting, killing. He kept them in his boat all night as he telephoned catfish and checked his trotlines and jugs and shot things on the bank. He'd given each of his sons a specific job to do, one dialing the rotary phone, another netting the stunned catfish, the third adjusting the chains which generated electricity from a car battery into the water. Boo would tie a piece of clothesline around each of his sons' waists and loop the other end to his own ankle in case one of the boys fell overboard. Downriver, Kent would pull in the trotlines while Wayne handed him a cricket or cockroach or catalpa worm for the hook. Scott took the bass, perch, or catfish Kent gave him and slit its soft cold belly with a fillet knife and ran two fingers up into the fish and drew out its palmful of guts and dumped them overboard. Sometimes on warm nights cottonmouths or young alligators would follow them, drawn by blood. A danger was catching a snake or snapping turtle on the trotline, and each night Boo whispered for Kent to be careful, to lift the line with a stick and see what he had there instead of using his bare hand.

During the morning they would leave the boat tied and the boys would follow their father through the trees from trap to trap, stepping when he stepped, not talking. Boo emptied the traps and rebaited them while behind him Kent put the carcass in his squirrel pouch. In the afternoons, they gutted and skinned what they'd brought home. What time was left before dark they spent sleeping in the feather bed in the cabin where their mother and sister had died.

After Boo's suicide, Kirxy had tried to look after the boys, their ages twelve, thirteen, and fourteen — just old enough, Boo must've thought, to raise themselves. For a while Kirxy let them stay with him and his wife, who'd never had a child. He tried to send them to school, but they were past learning to read and write and got expelled the first day for fighting, ganging up on a black kid. They were past the kind of life Kirxy's wife was used to living. They scared her, the way they watched her with eyes narrowed into black lines, the way they ate with their hands. The way they wouldn't talk. What she didn't know was that from those years of wordless nights on the river and silent days in the woods they had developed a kind of language of their own, a language of the eyes, of the fingers, of the way a shoulder moved, a nod of the head.

Because his wife's health wasn't good in those days, Kirxy had returned the boys to their cabin in the woods. He spent most Saturdays with them, trying to take up where Boo had left off, bringing them food and milk, clothes and new shoes, reading them books, teaching them things and telling stories. He'd worked out a deal with Esther, who took hot food to them in the evenings and washed and mended their clothes.

Slowing to let two buzzards hop away from a dead deer, Kirxy lit a cigarette and wiped his foggy windshield with the back of his hand. He thought of Frank David, Alabama's legendary game warden. There were dozens of stories about the man — Kirxy had heard and told them for years, had repeated them to the Gates boys, even made some up to scare them. Now the true ones and the fictions were confused in his mind. He remembered one: A dark, moonless night, and two poachers use a spotlight to freeze a buck in the darkness and shoot it. They take hold of its wide rack of horns and struggle to drag the big deer when suddenly they realize that now three men are pulling. The first poacher jumps and says, "Hey, it ain't supposed to be but two of us dragging this deer!"

And Frank David says, "Ain't supposed to be none of y'all dragging it."

The Gates boys came in the store just before closing, smelling like the river. Nodding to Kirxy, they went to the shelves and began selecting cans of things to eat. Kirxy poured himself a generous shot of whiskey. He'd stopped by their cabin earlier and, not finding them there, left a quarter on the steps. An old signal he hadn't used in years.

"Goodloe's coming by tonight," he said to Kent. "Wants to ask if y'all know anything about that dead game warden."

Kent shot the other boys a look.

"Now I don't know if y'all've ever even seen that fellow," Kirxy said, "and I'm not asking you to tell me." He paused, in case they wanted to. "But that's what old Sugarbaby's gonna want to know. If I was y'all, I just wouldn't tell him anything. Just say I was at home, that I don't know nothing about any dead game warden. Nothing at all."

Kent shrugged and walked down the aisle he was on and stared out the back window, though there wasn't anything to see except the trees, ghostly and bent, when the lightning came. His brothers took seats by the stove and began to eat. Kirxy watched them, remembering when he used to read to them, *Tarzan of the Apes* and *The Return of Tarzan*. The boys had wanted to hear the books over and over—they loved the jungle, the elephants, rhinos, gorillas, the anacondas thirty feet long. They would listen intently, their eyes bright in the light of the stove, Wayne holding in his small dirty hand the Slinky Kirxy had given him as a Christmas present, his lips moving along with Kirxy's voice, mouthing some of the words: *the great apes; Numa the lion; La, Queen of Opar, the Lost City.*

They had listened to his Frank David stories the same way: the game warden appearing beside a tree on a night when there wasn't a moon, a tracker so keen he could see in the dark, could follow a man through the deepest swamp by smelling the fear in his sweat, by the way the water swirled; a bent-over shadow slipping between the beaver lairs, the cypress trees, the tangle of limb and vine, parting the long wet bangs of Spanish moss with his rifle barrel, creeping toward the glowing windows of the poacher's cabin, the deer hides nailed to the wall. The gator pelts. The fish with their grim smiles hooked to a clothesline, turtle shells like army helmets drying on the windowsills. Any pit bull or mutt meant to guard the place lying with its throat slit behind him, Frank David slips out of the fog with fog still clinging to the brim of his hat. He circles the cabin, peers in each window, mounts the porch. Puts his shoulder through the front door. Stands with wood splinters landing on the floor at his feet. A hatted man of average height, clean-shaven: no threat until the big hands come up, curl into fists, the knuckles scarred, blue, sharp.

Kirxy finished his drink and poured another. It burned pleasantly in his belly. He looked at the boys, occupied by their bags of corn curls. A Merle Haggard song ended on the radio and Kirxy clicked it off, not wanting the boys to hear the evening news.

In the quiet, Kirxy heard Goodloe's truck. He glanced at Kent, who'd probably been hearing it for a while. Outside, Goodloe slammed his door. He hurried up the steps and tapped on the window. Kirxy exaggerated his limp and took his time letting him in.

"Evening," Goodloe said, shaking the water from his hands. He took off his hat and hung it on the nail by the door, then hung up his yellow slicker.

"Evening, Sugarbaby," Kirxy said.

"It's a wet one out there tonight," Goodloe said.

"Yep." Kirxy went behind the counter and refilled his glass. "You just caught the tail end of happy hour. That is, if you're off the wagon again. Can I sell you a tonic? Warm you up?"

"You know we're a dry county, Kirxy."

"Would that be a no?"

"It's a watch your ass." Goodloe looked at the brothers. "Just wanted to ask these boys some questions."

"Have at it, Sugarbaby."

Goodloe walked to the Lance rack and detached a package of Nip-Cheese crackers. He opened it, offered the pack to each of the boys. Only Wayne took one. Smiling, Goodloe bit a cracker in half and turned a chair around and sat with his elbows across its back. He looked over toward Kent, half-hidden by shadow. He chewed slowly. "Come on out here so I can see you, boy. I ain't gonna bite nothing but these stale-ass cheese crackers."

Kent moved a step closer.

Goodloe took out a notepad and addressed Kent. "Where was y'all between the hours of four and eight A.M. two days ago?"

Kent looked at Scott. "Asleep."

"Asleep," Scott said.

Goodloe snorted. "Now come on, boys. The whole dern county knows y'all ain't slept a night in your life. Y'all was out on the river, wasn't you? Making a few telephone calls?"

"You saying he's a liar?" Kirxy asked.

"I'm posing the questions here." Goodloe chewed another cracker. "Hell, everybody knows the other game wardens has been letting y'all get away with all kinds of shit. I reckon this new fellow had something to prove."

"Sounds like he oughta used a life jacket," Kirxy said, wiping the counter.

"It appears" — Goodloe studied Kent — "that he might've been strangled. You got a alibi, boy?"

Kent looked down.

Goodloe sighed. "I mean — Christ — is there anybody can back up what you're saying?"

The windows flickered.

"Yeah," Kirxy said. "I can."

Goodloe turned and faced the storekeeper. "You."

"That's right. They were here with me. Here in the store."

Goodloe looked amused. "They was, was they. OK, Mr. Kirxy. How come you didn't mention that to me this morning? Saved us all a little time?"

Kirxy sought Kent's eyes but saw nothing there, no understanding, no appreciation. No fear. He went back to wiping the counter. "Well, I guess because they was passed out drunk, and I didn't want to say anything, being as I was, you know, giving alcohol to young'uns."

"But now that it's come down to murder, you figured you'd better just own up."

"Something like that."

Goodloe stared at Kirxy for a long time, neither would look away. Then the sheriff turned to the boys. "Y'all ever heard of Frank David?"

Wayne nodded.

"Well," Goodloe said. "Looks like he's aiming to be this district's game warden. I figure he pulled some strings, what he did."

Kirxy came from behind the counter. "That all your questions? It's past closing and these young'uns need to go home and get some sleep." He went to the door and opened it, stood waiting.

"All righty then," the sheriff said, standing. "I expect I oughta be getting back to the office anyhow." He winked at Kirxy. "See you or these boys don't leave the county for a few days. This ain't over yet." He put the crackers in his coat. "I expect y'all might be hearing from Frank David, too," he said, watching the boys' faces. But there was nothing to see.

Alone later, Kirxy put out the light and bolted the door. He went to adjust the stove and found himself staring out the window, looking into the dark where he knew the river was rising and swirling, tires and plastic garbage can lids and deadwood from upriver floating past. He struck a match and lit a cigarette, the glow of his ash reflected in the window, and he saw himself years ago, telling the boys those stories.

How Frank David would sit so still in the woods waiting for poachers that dragonflies would perch on his nose, gnats would walk over his eyeballs. Nobody knew where he came from, but Kirxy had heard that he'd been orphaned as a baby in a fire and found half-starved in the swamp by a Cajun woman. She'd raised him on the slick red clay banks of the Tombigbee River, among lean black poachers and white-trash moonshiners. He didn't even know how old he was, people said. And they said he was the best poacher ever, the craftiest, the meanest. That he cut a drunk logger's throat in a juke joint knife-fight one night. That he fled south and, underage, joined the Marines in Mobile and wound up in Korea, the infantry, where because of his shooting ability and his stealth they made him a sniper. Before he left that country, he'd registered over a hundred kills, communists half a world away who never saw him coming.

Back home in Alabama, he disappeared for a few years, then showed up at the state game warden's office, demanding a job. Some people heard that in the intervening time he'd gotten religion.

"What makes you think I ought to hire you?" the head warden asked.

"Because I spent ten years of my life poaching right under your goddamn nose," Frank David said.

The Gates boys' pickup was the same old Ford their father had shot himself in several years earlier. The bullet hole in the roof had rusted out but was now covered with a strip of duct tape from Kirxy's store. Spots of the truck's floor were rusted away, too, so things in the road often flew up into their laps: rocks, cans, a king snake they were trying to run over. The truck was older than any of them, only one thin prong left of the steering wheel and the holes of missing knobs in the dash. It was a three-speed, a column shifter, the gear-stick covered with a buck's dried ball sack. The windows and windshield, busted or shot out years before, hadn't been replaced because most of their driving took them along back roads after dark or in fields, and the things they came upon were easier shots without glass.

Though he'd never had a license, Kent drove, he'd been doing this since he was eight. Scott rode shotgun. Tonight both were drinking, and in the back Wayne stood holding his rifle and trying to keep his balance. Below the soles of his boots the floor was soft, a tarry black from the blood of all the animals they'd killed. You could see spike antlers, forelegs, and hooves of deer. Teeth, feathers, and fur. The brittle beaks and beards of turkeys and the delicate, hinged leg bone of something molded in the sludge like a fossil.

Just beyond a NO TRESPASSING sign, Kent swerved off the road and they bounced and slid through a field in the rain, shooting at rabbits.

Then they split up, the younger boys checking traps — one on each side of the river — and Kent in the boat rebaiting their trotlines the way his father had shown him.

They met at the truck just before midnight, untied the dogs, and tromped down a steep logging path, Wayne on one end of four leashes and the lunging hounds on the other. When they got to the bottomland, he unclipped the leashes and loosed the dogs and the brothers followed the baying ahead in the dark, aiming their flashlights into the black mesh of trees where the eyes of coons and possums gleamed like rubies. The hounds bayed and frothed, clawed the trunks of trees and leaped into the air and landed and leaped again, their sides pumping, ribs showing, hounds that, given the chance, would never stop eating.

When the Gateses came to the river two hours later, the dogs were lapping water and panting. Wayne bent and rubbed their ears and let them lick his cheeks. His brothers rested and drank, belching at the sky. After a time, they leashed the hounds and staggered downstream to the live oak where their boat was tied. They loaded the dogs and shoved off into the fog and trolled over the still water.

In the middle, Scott lowered the twin chains beside the boat and began dialing the old telephone. Wayne netted the stunned catfish — you couldn't touch them with your hand or they'd come to — and threw them into the cooler, where in a few seconds the waking fish would begin to thrash. In the rear, Kent fingered his rifle and watched the bank in case a coyote wandered down, hunting bullfrogs.

They climbed up out of the woods into a dirt road in the misty dawn, plying through the muddy yards and pissing by someone's front porch in plain sight of the black face inside. A few houses down, Morrisette didn't come to his door, and when Kent tried the handle it was locked. He looked at Scott, then put his elbow through the glass and reached in and unlocked it.

While his brothers searched for the liquor, Wayne ate the biscuits he found wrapped in tin foil on the stove. He found a box of Corn Flakes in a cabinet and ate most of them, too. He ate a plate of cold fried chicken liver. Scott was in a bedroom looking under the bed. In the closet. He was going through drawers, his dirty fingers among the white cloth. In the back of the house Kent found a door, locked from the inside. He jimmied it open with his knife, and when he came into the kitchen, he had a gallon jar of whiskey under his arm and Euphrates' stepdaughter by the wrist.

Wayne stopped chewing, crumbs falling from his mouth. He approached the girl and put his hand out to touch her, but Kent pushed him hard, into the wall. Wayne stayed there, a clock ticking beside his head, a string of spit linking his two opened lips, watching as his brother ran his rough hands up and down the girl's trembling body, over the nipples that showed through the thin cloth. Her eyes were closed, lips moving in prayer. Looking down, Kent saw the puddle spreading around her bare feet.

"Shit," he said, a hand cupping her breast. "Pissed herself."

He let her go and she shrank back against the wall, behind the door. She was still there, along with a bag of catfish on the table, when her stepfather came back half an hour later, ten gallons of whiskey under the tarp in his truck.

On that same Saturday Kirxy drove to the chicken fights, held in Heflin Bradford's bulging barn, deep in woods cloudy with mosquitoes. He passed the hand-painted sign that'd been there forever, as long as he could remember, nailed to a tree. It said JESUS IS NOT COMING.

Kirxy climbed out of his truck and buttoned his collar, his ears full of cotton. Heflin's wife worked beneath a rented awning, grilling chicken and sausages, selling Cokes and beer. Gospel music played from a portable tape player by her head. Heflin's grandson Nolan took the price of admission at the barn door and stamped the backs of white hands and the cracked pink palms of black ones. Men in overalls and baseball caps that said CAT DIESEL POWER or STP stood at the tailgates of their pickups, smoking cigarettes, stooping to peer into the dark cages where roosters paced. The air was filled with windy rain spits and the crowing of roosters, the ground littered with limp, dead birds.

A group of men discussed Frank David, and Kirxy paused to listen.

"He's the one caught that bunch over in Warshington County," one man said. "Them alligator poachers."

"Sugarbaby said two of 'em wound up in the intensive care," another claimed. "Said they pulled a gun and old Frank David went crazy with an ax handle."

Kirxy moved on and paid the five-dollar admission. In the barn, there were bleachers along the walls and a big circular wooden fence in the center, a dome of chicken wire over the top. Kirxy found a seat at the bottom next to the back door, near a group of mean old farts he'd known for forty years. People around them called out bets and bets were accepted. Cans of beer lifted. Kirxy produced a thermos of coffee and a dented tin cup. He poured the coffee, then added whiskey from a bottle that went back into his coat pocket. The tin cup warmed his fingers as he squinted through his bifocals to see which bird to bet on.

In separate corners of the barn, two bird handlers doused their roosters' heads and asses with rubbing alcohol to make them fight harder. They tightened the long steel curved spurs. When the referee in the center of the ring indicated it was time, the handlers entered the pen, each cradling his bird in his arms. They flashed the roosters at one another until their feathers had ruffled with bloodlust and rage, the roosters pedaling the air, stretching their necks toward each other. The handlers kept them a breath apart for a second, then withdrew them to their corners, whispering in their ears. When the referee tapped the ground three times with his stick, the birds were unleashed on each other. They charged and rose in the center of the ring, gouging with spur and beak, the handlers circling the fight like crabs, blood on their forearms and faces, ready to seize their roosters at the referee's cry of "Handle!"

A clan of Louisiana Cajuns watched. They'd emerged red-eyed from a van in a marijuana cloud: skinny, shirtless men with oily ponytails and goatees and tattoos of symbols of black magic. Under their arms, they carried thick white hooded roosters to pit against the reds and blacks of the locals. Their women had stumbled out of the van behind them, high yellow like Gypsies, big-lipped, big-chested girls in halter-tops tied at their bellies and miniskirts and red heels.

In the ring the Cajuns kissed their birds on the beaks, and one tall, completely bald Cajun wearing gold earrings in both ears put his bird's whole head in his mouth. His girl, too, came barefoot into the ring, tattoo of a snake on her shoulder, and took the bird's head into her mouth.

"Bet on them white ones," a friend whispered to Kirxy. "These ones around here ain't ever seen a white rooster. They don't know what they're fighting."

That evening, checking traps in the woods north of the river, Wayne kept hearing things. Little noises. Leaves. Twigs.

Afraid, he forced himself to go on so his brothers wouldn't laugh at him. Near dark, in a wooden trap next to an old fencerow, he was surprised to find the tiny white fox they'd once seen cross the road in front of their truck. He squatted before the trap and poked a stick through the wire at the thin snout, his hand steady despite the way the fox snapped at the stick and bit off the end. Would the witch woman want this alive? At the thought of her he looked around. It felt like she was watching him, as if she were hiding in a tree in the form of some animal, a possum, a swamp rat. He stood and dragged the trap through the mud and over the land while the fox jumped in circles, growling.

A mile upstream, Scott had lost a boot to the mud and was hopping back one-footed to retrieve it. It stood alone, buried to the ankle. He wrenched it free, then sat with his back against a sweet gum to scrape off the mud. He'd begun to lace the boot when he saw a hollow tree stump, something moving inside. With his rifle barrel, he rolled the thing out — it was most of the body of a dead catfish, the movement from the maggots devouring it. When he kicked it, they spilled from the fish like rice pellets and lay throbbing in the mud.

Downstream, as night came and the rain fell harder, Kent trolled their boat across the river, flashlight in his mouth, using a stick to pull up a trotline length by length and removing the fish or turtles and rebaiting the hooks and dropping them back into the water. Near the bank, approaching the last hook, he heard something. He looked up with the flashlight in his teeth to see the thing untwirling in the air. It wrapped around his neck like a rope, and for an instant he thought he was being hanged. He grabbed the thing. It flexed and tightened, then his neck burned and went numb and he felt dizzy, his fingertips buzzing, legs weak, a tree on the bank distorting, doubling, tripling into a whole line of fuzzy shapes, turning sideways, floating.

Kent blinked. Felt his eyes bulging, his tongue swelling. His head about to explode. Then a bright light.

His brothers found the boat at dawn, four miles downstream, lodged on the far side in a fallen tree. They exchanged a glance, then looked back across the river. A heavy gray fog hooded the water and the boat appeared and dissolved in the ghostly limbs around it. Scott sat on a log and took off his boots and left them standing by the log. He removed his coat and laid it over the boots. He handed his brother his rifle without looking at him, left him watching as he climbed down the bank and, hands and elbows in the air like a believer, waded into the water.

Wayne propped the second rifle against a tree and stood on the bank holding his own gun, casting his frightened eyes up and down the river. From far away a woodpecker drummed. Crows began to collect in a pecan tree downstream. After a while Wayne squatted, thinking of their dogs, tied to the bumper of their truck. They'd be under the tailgate, probably, trying to keep dry.

Soon Scott had trolled the boat back across. Together they pulled it out of the water and stood looking at their brother who lay across the floor among the fish and turtles he'd caught. One greenish terrapin, still alive, a hook in its neck, stared back. They both knew what they were supposed to think—the blood and the sets of twin fang marks, the black bruises and shriveled skin, the neck swollen like mumps, the purple bulb of tongue between his lips. They were supposed to think *cottonmouth.* Kent's hands were squeezed into fists and they'd hardened that way, the skin wrinkled. His eyes half open. His rifle lay unfired in the boat, as if indeed a snake had done this.

But it wasn't the tracks of a snake they found when they went to get the white fox. The fox was gone, though, the trap empty, its catch sprung. Scott knelt and ran his knuckles along the rim of a boot print in the mud—not a very wide track, not very far from the next one. He put his finger in the black water that'd already begun to fill the track: not too deep. He looked up at Wayne. The print of an average-sized man. In no hurry. Scott rose and they began.

Above them, the sky cracked and flickered.

Silently, quickly—no time to get the dogs—they followed the trail back through the woods, losing it once, twice, backtracking, working against the rain that fell and fell harder, that puddled blackly and crept up their legs, until they stood in water to their calves, rain beading on the brims of their caps. They gazed at the ground, the sky, at the rain streaming down each other's muddy face.

At the truck, Wayne jumped in the driver's seat and reached for the keys. Scott appeared in the window, shaking his head. When Wayne didn't scoot over, the older boy hit him in the jaw, then slung open the door and pulled Wayne out, sent him rolling over the ground. Scott climbed in and had trouble getting the truck choked. By the time he had the hang of it, Wayne had gotten into the back and sat among the wet dogs, staring at his dead brother.

At their cabin, they carried Kent into the woods. They laid him on the ground and began digging near where their sister, mother, and father were buried in their unmarked graves. For three hours they worked, the dogs coming from under the porch and sniffing around Kent and watching the digging, finally slinking off and crawling back under the porch, out of the rain. An hour later the dogs came boiling out again and stood in a group at the edge of the yard, baying. The boys paused but saw or heard nothing. When the dogs kept making noise, Scott got his rifle and fired into the woods several times. He nodded to his brother and they went back to digging. By the time they'd finished, it was late afternoon and the hole was full of slimy water and they were black with mud. They each took off one of Kent's boots and Scott got the things from his pockets. They stripped off his shirt and pants and lowered him into the hole. When he bobbed to the top of the water, they got stones and weighted him down. Then shoveled mud into the grave.

They showed up at Esther's, black as tar.

"Where's Kent?" she asked, holding her robe closed at her throat.

"We buried him," Scott said, moving past her into the kitchen. She put a hand over her mouth, and as Scott told her what they'd found she slumped against the door, looking outside. An owl flew past in the floodlights. She thought of calling Kirxy but decided to wait until morning—the old bastard thought she was a slut and a corruption. For tonight she'd just keep them safe in her house.

Scott went to the den. He turned on the TV, the reception bad because of the weather. Wayne, a bruise on his left cheek, climbed the stairs. He went into one of the bedrooms and closed the door behind him. It was chilly in the room and he noticed pictures of people on the wall, children, and a tall man and a younger woman he took to be Esther. She'd been pretty then. He stood dripping on the floor, looking into her black and white face, searching for signs of the woman he knew now. Soon the door opened behind him and she came in. And though he still wore his filthy wet clothes, she steered him to the bed and guided him down onto it. She unbuckled his belt, removed his hunting knife, and stripped the belt off. She unbuttoned his shirt and rubbed her fingers across his chest, the hair just beginning to thicken there. She undid his pants and ran the zipper down its track. She worked them over his thighs, knees, and ankles and draped them across the back of a chair. She pulled off his boots and socks. Pried a finger beneath the elastic of his underwear, felt that he'd already come.

He looked at her face. His mouth opened. Esther touched his chin, the scratch of whiskers, his breath on her hand.

"Hush now," she said, and watched him fall asleep.

Downstairs, the TV went off.

When Goodloe knocked, Esther answered, a cold sliver of her face in the cracked door. "The hell you want?"

"Good evening to you, too. The Gateses here?"

"No."

Goodloe glanced behind him. "I believe that's their truck. It's kinda hard to mistake, especially for us trained lawmen."

She tried to close the door but Goodloe had his foot in it. He glanced at the three deputies who stood importantly by the Blazer. They dropped their cigarettes and crushed them out. They unsnapped their holsters and strode across the yard, standing behind Goodloe with their hands on their revolvers and their legs apart like TV deputies.

"Why don't y'all just let 'em alone?" Esther said. "Ain't they been through enough?"

"Tell 'em I'd like to see 'em," Goodloe said. "Tell 'em get their boots."

"You just walk straight to hell, mister."

Wayne appeared behind her, naked, lines from the bed linen on his face.

"Whoa, Nellie," Goodloe said. "Boy, you look plumb terrible. Why don't you let us carry you on down to the office for a little coffee? Little cake." He glanced back at one of the deputies. "We got any of that cinnamon roll left, Dave?"

"You got a warrant for their arrest?" Esther asked.

"No, I ain't got a warrant for their arrest. They ain't under arrest. They fixing to get questioned, is all. Strictly informal." Goodloe winked. "You reckon you could do without 'em for a couple of hours?"

"Fuck you, Sugarbaby."

The door slammed. Goodloe nodded down the side of the house and two deputies went to make sure nobody escaped from the back. But in a minute Wayne came out dressed, his hands in his pockets, and followed Goodloe down the stairs, the deputies watching him closely, and watching the house.

"Where's your brothers?" Goodloe asked.

He looked down.

Goodloe nodded to the house and two deputies went in, guns drawn. They came out a few minutes later, frowning.

"Must've heard us coming," Goodloe said. "Well, we got this one. We'll find them other two tomorrow." They got into the Blazer and Goodloe looked at Wayne, sitting in the back.

"Put them cuffs on him," Goodloe said.

Holding his rifle, Scott came out of the woods when the Blazer was gone. He returned to the house.

"They got Wayne," Esther said. "Why didn't you come tell him they was out there?"

"He got to learn," Scott said. He went to the cabinet where she kept the whiskey and took the bottle. She watched him go to the sofa and sit down in front of the blank TV. Soon she joined him, bringing glasses. He filled both, and when they emptied them he filled them again.

They spent the night like that, and at dawn they were drunk. Wearing her robe, Esther began clipping her fingernails, a cigarette smoking in the ashtray beside her. She'd forgotten about calling Kirxy.

Scott was telling her about the biggest catfish they'd ever called up: 100 pounds, he swore, 150. "You could of put your whole head in that old cat's mouth," he said, sipping his whiskey. "Back fin long as your damn arm."

He stood. Walked to the front window. There were toads in the yard — with the river swelling they were everywhere. In the evenings there were rainfrogs. The yard had turned into a pond and each night the rainfrogs sang. It was like no other sound. Esther said it kept her up at night.

"That, and some other things," she said.

Scott heard a fingernail ring the ashtray. He rubbed his hand across his chin, felt the whiskers there. He watched the toads as they huddled in the yard, still as rocks, bloated and miserable-looking.

"That catfish was green," Scott said, sipping. "I swear to God. Green as grass."

"Them goddamn rainfrogs," she said. "I just lay there at night with my hands over my ears."

A clipping rang the ashtray.

He turned and went to her on the sofa. "They was moss growing on his nose," he said, putting his hand on her knee.

"Go find your brother," she said. She got up and walked unsteadily across the floor and went into the bathroom, closed the door. When she came out, he and the bottle were gone.

Without Kent, Scott felt free to do what he wanted, which was to drive very fast. He got the truck started and spun off, aiming for every mud hole he could. He shot past a house with a washing machine on the front porch, two thin black men skinning a hog hanging from a tree. One of the men waved with a knife. Drinking, Scott drove through the mountains of trash at the dump and turned the truck in circles, kicking up muddy roostertails. He swerved past the Negro church and the graveyard where a group of blacks huddled, four warbling poles over an open grave, the wind tearing the preacher's hat out of his hands and a woman's umbrella reversing suddenly.

When he tired of driving, he left the truck in their hiding place, and using trees for balance, stumbled down the hill to their boat. He carried Kent's rifle, which he'd always admired. On the river, he fired up the outboard and accelerated, the boat prow lifting and leveling out, the buzz of the motor rising in the trees. The water was nearly orange from mud, the cypress knees nothing but knobs and tips because of the floods. Nearing the old train trestle, he cut the motor and coasted to a stop. He sat listening to the rain, to the distant barking of a dog, half a mile away. Chasing something, maybe a deer. As the dog charged through the woods, Scott closed his eyes and imagined the terrain, marking where he thought the dog was now, and where he thought it was now. Then the barking stopped, suddenly, as if the dog had run smack into a tree.

Scott clicked on the trolling motor and moved the boat close to the edge of the river, the rifle across his knees. He scanned the banks, and when the rain started to fall harder he accelerated toward the trestle. From beneath the crossties, he smelled creosote and watched the rain as it stirred the river. He looked into the gray trees and thought he would drive into town later, see about getting Wayne. Kent had never wanted to go to Grove Hill—their father had warned them of the police, of jail.

Scott picked up one of the catfish from the night before. It was stiff, as if carved out of wood. He stared at it, watching the green blowflies hover above his fist, then threw it over into the cattails along the bank.

The telephone rig lay under the seat. He lifted the chains quietly, considering what giant catfish might be passing beneath the boat this very second, a thing as large as a man's thigh with eyes the size of ripe plums and skin the color of mud. Catfish, their father had taught them, have long whiskers that make them the only fish you can "call." Kirxy had told Scott and his brothers that if a game warden caught you telephoning, all you needed to do was dump your rig overboard. But, Kirxy warned, Frank David would handcuff you and swim around the bottom of the river until he found your rig.

Scott spat a stream of tobacco into the brown water. Minnows appeared and began to investigate, nibbling at the dark yolk of spit as it elongated and dissolved. With his rifle's safety off, he lowered the chains into the water, a good distance apart. He checked the connections—the battery, the telephone. He lifted the phone and began to dial. "Hello?" he whispered, the thing his father had always said, grinning in the dark. The wind picked up a bit, he heard it rattling in the trees, and he dialed faster, had just seen the first silver body bob to the surface when something landed with a clatter in his boat. He glanced over.

A bundle of dynamite, sparks shooting off the end, fuse already gone. He looked above him, the trestle, but nobody was there. He moved to grab the dynamite, but his cheeks ballooned with hot red wind and his hands caught fire.

When the smoke cleared and the water stopped boiling, silver bodies began to bob to the surface—largemouth bass, bream, gar, suckers, white perch, polliwogs, catfish—some only stunned but others dead, in pieces, pink fruit-like things, the water blooming darkly with mud.

Kirxy's telephone rang for the second time in one day, a rarity that proved what his wife had always said: bad news came over the phone. The first call had been Esther, telling him of Kent's death, Wayne's arrest, Scott's disappearance. This time Kirxy heard Goodloe's voice telling him that somebody—or maybe a couple of somebodies—had been blown up out on the trestle.

"Scott," Kirxy said, sitting.

He arrived at the trestle, and with his cane hobbled over the uneven tracks. Goodloe's deputies and three ambulance drivers in rubber gloves and waders were scraping pieces off the crossties with spoons, dropping the parts in ziplock bags. The boat, two flattened shreds of aluminum, lay on the bank. In the water, minnows darted about, nibbling.

"Christ," Kirxy said. He brought a handkerchief to his lips. Then he went to where Goodloe stood on the bank, writing in his notebook.

"What do you aim to do about this?" Kirxy demanded.

"Try to figure out who it was, first."

"You know goddamn well who it was."

"I expect it's either Kent or Scott Gates."

"It's Scott," Kirxy said.

"How do you know that?"

Kirxy told him that Kent was dead.

"I ain't seen the body," Goodloe said.

Kirxy's blood pressure was going up. "Fuck, Sugarbaby. Are you one bit aware what's going on here?"

"Fishing accident," Goodloe said. "His bait exploded."

From the bank, a deputy called that he'd found most of a boot. "Foot's still in it," he said, holding it up by the lace.

"Tag it," Goodloe said, writing something down. "Keep looking."

Kirxy poked Goodloe in the shoulder with his cane. "You really think Scott'd blow himself up?"

Goodloe looked at his shoulder, the muddy cane print, then at the storekeeper. "Not on purpose, I don't." He paused. "Course, suicide does run in their family."

"What about Kent?"

"What about him?"

"Christ, Sugarbaby—"

Goodloe held up his hand. "Just show me, Kirxy."

They left the ambulance drivers and the deputies and walked the other way without talking. When they came to Goodloe's Blazer, they got in and drove without talking. Soon they stopped in front of the Gateses' cabin. Instantly hounds surrounded the truck, barking viciously and jumping with muddy paws against the glass. Goodloe blew the horn until the hounds slunk away, heads low, fangs bared. The sheriff opened his window and fired several times in the air, backing the dogs up. When he and Kirxy got out, Goodloe had reloaded.

The hounds kept to the edge of the woods, watching.

His eye on them, Kirxy led Goodloe behind the decrepit cabin. Rusty screens covered some windows, rags of drape others. Beneath the house, the dogs paced them. "Back here," Kirxy said, heading into the trees. Esther had said they'd buried Kent, and this was the logical place. He went slowly, careful not to bump a limb and cause a small downpour. Sure enough, there lay the grave. You could see where the dogs had been scratching around it.

Goodloe went over and toed the dirt. "You know the cause of death?"

"Yeah, I know the cause of death. His name's Frank fucking David."

"I meant how he was killed."

"The boys said snakebite. Three times in the neck. But I'd do an autopsy."

"You would." Goodloe exhaled. "OK. I'll send Roy and Avery over here to dig him up. Maybe shoot these goddern dogs."

"I'll tell you what you'd better do first. You better keep Wayne locked up safe."

"I can't hold him much longer," Goodloe said. "Unless he confesses."

Kirxy pushed him from behind, and at the edge of the woods the dogs tensed. Goodloe backed away, raising his pistol, the grave between them.

"You crazy, Kirxy? You been locked in that store too long?"

"Goodloe," Kirxy gasped. The cotton in his left ear had come out and suddenly air was roaring through his head. "Even you can't be this stupid. You let that boy out and he's that cold-blooded fucker's next target—"

"Target, Kirxy? Shit. Ain't nothing to prove anybody killed them damn boys? This one snakebit, you said so yourself. That other one blowing himself up. Them dern Gateses has fished with dynamite their whole life. You oughta know that—you the one gets it for 'em." He narrowed his eyes. "You're about neck deep in this thing, you know. And I don't mean just lying to protect them boys neither. I mean selling explosives illegally, to minors, Kirxy."

"I don't give a shit if I am!" Kirxy yelled. "Two dead boys in two days and you're worried about dynamite? You oughta be out there looking for Frank David."

"He ain't supposed to be here for another week or two," Goodloe said. "Paperwork—"

He fired his pistol then. Kirxy jumped, but the sheriff was looking past him, and when Kirxy followed his eyes he saw the dog that had been creeping in. It lay slumped in the mud, a hind leg kicking, blood coloring the water around it.

Goodloe backed away, smoke curling from the barrel of his pistol.

Around them the other dogs circled, heads low, moving sideways, the hair on their spines sticking up.

"Let's argue about this in the truck," Goodloe said.

At the store Kirxy put out the OPEN sign. He sat in his chair with his coffee and a cigarette. He'd read the same page three times when it occurred to him to phone Montgomery and get Frank David's office on the line. It took a few calls, but he soon got the number and dialed. The snippy young woman who answered told Kirxy that yes, Mr. David *was* supposed to take over the Lower Peachtree district, but that he wasn't starting until next week, she thought.

Where was he now? Kirxy wanted to know.

"Florida?" she said. "No, Louisiana. Fishing." No sir, he couldn't be reached. He preferred his vacations private.

Kirxy slammed down the phone. He lit another cigarette and tried to think.

It was just a matter, he decided, of keeping Wayne alive until Frank David took over the district. There were probably other game wardens who'd testify that Frank David *was* over in Louisiana fishing right now. But once the son of a bitch officially moved here, he'd have motive and his alibi wouldn't be as strong. If Wayne turned up dead, Frank David would be the chief suspect.

Kirxy inhaled smoke deeply and tried to imagine how Frank David would think. How he would act. The noise he would make or not make as he went through the woods. What he would say if you happened upon him. Or he upon you. What he would do if he came into the store. Certainly he wasn't the creature Kirxy had created to scare the boys, not some wild ghostly thing. He was just a man who'd had a hard life and grown bitter and angry. Probably an alcoholic. A man who chose to uphold the law because breaking it was no challenge. A man with no obligation to any other men or a family. Just to himself and his job. To some goddamned game-warden code. His job was to protect the wild things the law had deemed worthy: dove, duck, owls, hawks, turkeys, alligators, squirrels, coons, and deer. But how did the Gates boys fall into the category of trash animal — wildcats or possums or armadillos, snapping turtles, snakes? Things you could kill any time, run over in your truck and not even look at in your mirror to see dying behind you? Christ. Why couldn't Frank David see that he — more than a match for the boys — was of their breed?

Kirxy drove to the highway. The big .30-06 he hadn't touched in years was on the seat next to him, and as he steered he pushed cartridges into the clip, then shoved the clip into the gun's underbelly. He pulled the lever that injected a cartridge into the chamber and took a long drink of whiskey to wash down three of the pills that helped dull the ache in his knees, and the one in his gut.

It was almost dark when he arrived at the edge of a large field. He parked facing the grass. This was a place a few hundred yards from a fairly well-traveled blacktop, a spot no sane poacher would dare use. There were already two or three deer creeping into the open from the woods across the field. They came to eat the tall grass, looking up only when a car passed, their ears swiveling, jaws frozen, sprigs of grass twitching in their lips like the legs of insects.

Kirxy sat watching. He sipped his whiskey and lit a cigarette with a trembling hand. Both truck doors were locked and he knew this was a very stupid thing he was doing. Several times he told himself to go home, let things unfold as they would. Then he saw the faces of the two dead boys. And the face of the live one.

When Boo had killed himself, the oldest two had barely been teenagers, but it was eleven-year-old Wayne who'd found him. That truck still had windows then, and the back windshield had been sprayed red with blood. Flies had gathered at the top of the truck in what Wayne discovered was a twenty-two-caliber hole. Kirxy frowned, thinking of it. Boo's hat still on his head, a small hole through the hat, too. The back of the truck was full of wood Boo'd been cutting, and the three boys had unloaded the wood and stacked it neatly beside the road. Kirxy shifted in his seat, imagining the boys pushing that truck for two miles over dirt roads, somehow finding the leverage or whatever, the goddamn strength, to get it home. To pull their father from inside and bury him. To clean out the truck. Kirxy shuddered and thought of Frank David, then made himself think of his wife instead. He rubbed his biceps and watched the shadows creep across the field, the tree line dim and begin to disappear.

Soon it was full dark. He unscrewed the interior light bulb from the ceiling, pulled the door lock up quietly. Holding his breath, he opened the door. Outside, he propped the rifle on the side mirror, flicked the safety off. He reached through the window, felt along the dash for the headlight switch, pulled it.

The field blazed with the eyes of deer — red hovering dots staring back at him. Kirxy aimed and squeezed the trigger at the first pair of eyes. Not waiting to see if he'd hit the deer, he moved the gun to another pair. He'd gotten off five shots before the eyes began to disappear. When the last echo from the gun faded, at least three deer lay dead or wounded in the glow of his headlights. One doe bleated weakly and bleated again. Kirxy coughed and took the gun back into the truck, closed the door, and reloaded in the dark. Then he waited. The doe kept bleating and things in the woods took shape, detached, and whisked toward Kirxy over the grass like spooks. And the little noises. Things like footsteps. And the stories. Frank David appearing in the bed of somebody's *moving truck* and punching through the back glass, grabbing and breaking the driver's arm. Leaping from the truck and watching while it wrecked.

"Quit it," Kirxy croaked. "You damn schoolgirl."

Several more times that night he summoned his nerve and flicked on the headlights, firing at any eyes he saw or firing at nothing. When he finally fell asleep just after two A.M., his body numb with painkillers and whiskey, he dreamed of his wife on the day of her first miscarriage. The way the nurses couldn't find the vein in her arm, how they'd kept trying with the needle, the way she'd cried and held his fingers tightly, like a woman giving birth.

He started awake, terrified, as if he'd fallen asleep driving.

Caring less for silence, he stumbled from the truck and flicked on the lights and fired at the eyes, though now they were doubling up, floating in the air. He lowered the gun and for no good reason found himself thinking of a time when he'd tried fly-fishing, standing in his yard with his wife watching from the porch, *Tarzan of the Apes* in her lap, him whipping the line in the air, showing off, and then the strange pulling you get when you catch a fish, Betty jumping to her feet, the book falling, and her yelling that he'd caught a bat, for heaven's sake, a *bat!*

He climbed back into the truck. His hands shook so hard he had trouble getting the door locked. He bowed his head, missing her so much that he cried, softly and for a long time.

Dawn found him staring at a field littered with dead does, yearlings, and fawns. One of the deer, only wounded, tried to crawl toward the safety of the trees. Kirxy got out of the truck and vomited colorless water, then stood looking around at the foggy morning. He lifted his rifle and limped into the grass in the drizzle and, a quick hip shot, put the deer out of its misery.

He was sitting on the open tailgate trying to light a cigarette when Goodloe and a deputy passed in their Blazer and stopped.

The sheriff stepped out, signaling for the deputy to stay put. He sat beside Kirxy on the tailgate, the truck dipping with his weight. His stomach was growling and he patted it absently.

"You old fool," Goodloe said, staring at Kirxy and then at the field. "You figured to make Frank David show himself?" He shook his head. "Good Lord Almighty, Kirxy. What'll it take to prove to you there ain't no damn game warden out there? Not yet, anyhow."

Kirxy didn't answer. Goodloe went to the Blazer and told the deputy to pick him up at Kirxy's store. Then he helped the old man into the passenger seat and went around and got in the driver's side. He took the rifle and unloaded it, put its clip in his pocket.

"We'll talk about them deer later," he said. "Now I'd better get you back."

They'd gone a silent mile when Kirxy said, "Would you mind running me by Esther's?"

Goodloe shrugged and turned that way. His stomach made a strangling noise. The rain and wind were picking up, rocking the truck. The sheriff took a bottle of whiskey from his pocket. "Medicinal," he said, handing the bottle to Kirxy. "It's just been two freak accidents, is all, Kirxy. I've seen some strange shit, a lot stranger than this. Them Gateses is just a unlucky bunch. Period. I ain't one to go believing in curses, but I swear to God if they ain't downright snakebit."

Soon Goodloe had parked in front of Esther's and they sat waiting for the rain to slack. Kirxy rubbed his knees and looked out the windows where the trees were half-submerged in the rising floodwaters.

"They say old Esther has her a root cellar," Goodloe said, taking a sip. "Shit. I expect it's full of water this time of year. She's probably got cottonmouths wrapped around her plumbing." He shuddered and offered the bottle. Kirxy took it and sipped. He gave it back and Goodloe took it and drank, then drank again. "Lord if that don't hit the spot.

"When I was in the service," Goodloe went on, "over in Thailand? They had them little bitty snakes, them banded kraits. Poison as cobras, what they told us. Used to hide up under the commode lid. Every time you took you a shit, you had to lift up the lid, see was one there." He drank. "Yep. It was many a time I kicked one off in the water, flushed it down."

"Wait here," Kirxy said. He opened the door, his pants leg darkening as the rain poured in, cold as needles. He set his knee out deliberately, planted his cane in the mud and pulled himself up, stood in water to his ankles. He limped across the yard with his hand blocking the rain. There were two chickens on the front porch, their feathers fluffed out so that they looked strange, menacing. Kirxy climbed the porch steps with the pain so strong in his knees that stars popped near his face by the time he reached the top. He leaned against the house, breathing hard. Touched himself at the throat where a tie might've gone. Then he rapped gently with the hook of his cane. The door opened immediately. Dark inside. She stood there, looking at him.

"How come you don't ever stop by the store anymore?" he asked.

She folded her arms.

"Scott's dead," he said.

"I heard," Esther said. "And I'm leaving. Fuck this place and every one of you."

She closed the door and Kirxy would never see her again.

At the store, Goodloe nodded for the deputy to stay in the Blazer, then he took Kirxy by the elbow and helped him up the steps. He unlocked the door for him and held his hand as the old man sank in his chair.

"Want those boots off?" Goodloe asked, spreading a blanket over Kirxy's lap.

He bent and unlaced the left, then the right.

"Pick up your foot.

"Now the other one."

He set the wet boots by the stove.

"It's a little damp in here. I'll light this thing."

He found a box of kitchen matches on a shelf under the counter among the glass figurines Kirxy's wife had collected. The little deer. The figure skater. The unicorn. Goodloe got a fire going in the stove and stood warming the backs of his legs.

"I'll bring Wayne by a little later," he said, but Kirxy didn't seem to hear.

* * *

Goodloe sat in his office with his feet on the desk, rolling a cartridge between his fingers. Despite himself, he was beginning to think Kirxy might be right. Maybe Frank David *was* out there on the prowl. He stood, put on his pistol belt and walked to the back, pushed open the swinging door and had Roy buzz him through. So far he'd had zero luck getting anything out of Wayne. The boy just sat in his cell wrapped in a blanket, not talking to anybody. Goodloe had told him about his brother's death, and he'd seen no emotion cross the boy's face. Goodloe figured that it wasn't this youngest one who'd killed that game warden, it'd probably been the others. He knew that this boy wasn't carrying a full cylinder, the way he never talked, but he had most likely been a witness. He'd been considering calling in the state psychologist from the Searcy Mental Hospital to give the boy an evaluation.

"Come on," Goodloe said, stopping by Wayne's cell. "I'm fixing to put your talent to some good use."

He kept the boy cuffed as the deputy drove them toward the trestle.

"Turn your head, Dave," Goodloe said, handing Wayne a pint of Old Crow. The boy took it in both hands and unscrewed the lid, began to drink too fast.

"Slow down there, partner," Goodloe said, taking back the bottle. "You need to be alert."

Soon they stood near the trestle, gazing at the flat shapes of the boat on the bank. Wayne knelt and examined the ground. The deputy came up and started to say something, but Goodloe motioned for quiet.

"Just like a goddern bloodhound," he whispered. "Maybe I oughta give him your job."

"Reckon what he's after?" the deputy asked.

Wayne scrabbled up the trestle, and the two men followed. The boy walked slowly over the rails, examining the spaces between the crossties. He stopped, bent down, and peered at something. Picked it up.

"What you got there, boy?" Goodloe called, going and squatting beside him. He took a sip of Old Crow.

When Wayne hit him, two-handed, the bottle flew one way and Goodloe the other. Both landed in the river, Goodloe with his hand clapped to his head to keep his hat on. He came up immediately, bobbing and sputtering. On the trestle, the deputy tackled Wayne and they went down fighting on the crossties. Below, Goodloe dredged himself out of the water. He came ashore dripping and tugged his pistol from its holster. He held it up so that a thin trickle of orange water fell. He took off his hat and looked up to see the deputy disappear belly-first into the face of the river.

Wayne ran down the track, toward the swamp. The deputy came boiling ashore. He had his own pistol drawn and was looking around vengefully.

Goodloe climbed the trestle in time to see Wayne disappear into the woods. The sheriff chased him for a while, ducking limbs and vines, but stopped, breathing hard. The deputy passed him.

Wayne circled back through the woods and went quickly over the soft ground, half-crawling up the sides of hills and sliding down the other sides. Two hollows over, he heard the deputy heading the wrong direction. Wayne slowed a little and just trotted for a long time in the rain, the cuffs rubbing his wrists raw. He stopped once and looked at what he'd been carrying in one hand: a match, limp and black now with water, nearly dissolved. He stood looking at the trees around him, the hanging Spanish moss and the cypress knees rising from the stagnant creek to his left.

The hair on the back of his neck rose. He knelt, tilting his head, closing his eyes, and listened. He heard the rain, heard it hit leaves and wood and heard the puddles lapping at their tiny banks, but beyond those sounds there were other muffled noises. A mockingbird mocking a blue jay. A squirrel barking and another answering. The deputy falling, a quarter mile away. Then another sound, this one close. A match striking. Wayne began to run before opening his eyes and crashed into a tree. He rolled and ran again, tearing through limbs and briars. He leaped small creeks and slipped and got up and kept running. At every turn he expected Frank David, and he was near tears when he finally stumbled into his family graveyard.

The first thing he saw was that Kent had been dug up. Wooden stakes surrounded the hole and fenced it in with yellow tape that had words on it. Wayne approached slowly, hugging himself. Something floated in the grave. With his heart pounding, he peered inside. A dog.

Wary of the trees behind him, he crept toward their backyard, stopping at the edge. He crouched and blew into his hands to warm his cheeks. He gazed at the dark windows of their cabin, then circled the house, keeping to the woods. He saw the pine tree with the low limb they used for stringing up larger animals to clean, the rusty chain hanging and the iron pipe they stuck through the back legs of a deer or the rare wild pig. Kent and Scott had usually done the cleaning while Wayne fed the guts to their dogs and tried to keep the dogs from fighting.

And there, past the tree, lay the rest of the dogs. Shot dead. Partially eaten. Buzzards standing in the mud, staring boldly at him with their heads bloody and their beaks open.

It was dark when Kirxy woke in his chair; he'd heard the door creak. Someone stood there, and the storekeeper was afraid until he smelled the river.

"Hey, boy," he said.

Wayne ate two cans of potted meat with his fingers and a candy bar and a box of saltines. Kirxy gave him a Coke from the red cooler and he drank it and took another one while Kirxy got a hacksaw from the rack of tools behind the counter. He slipped the cardboard wrapping off and nodded for Wayne to sit. The storekeeper pulled up another chair and faced the boy and began sawing the handcuff chain. The match dropped out of Wayne's hand but neither saw it. Wayne sat with his head down and his palms up, his wrists on his knees, breathing heavily, while Kirxy worked and the silver shavings accumulated in a pile between their boots. The boy didn't lift his head the entire time, and he'd been asleep for quite a while when Kirxy finally sawed through. The old man rose, flexing his sore hands, and got a blanket from a shelf. He unfolded it, shook out the dust, and spread it over Wayne. He went to the door and turned the dead bolt.

The phone rang later. It was Goodloe, asking about the boy.

"He's asleep," Kirxy said. "You been lost all this time, Sugarbaby?"

"That I have," Goodloe said, "and we still ain't found old Dave yet."

For a week they stayed there together. Kirxy could barely walk now, and the pain in his side was worse than ever, but he put the boy to work, sweeping, dusting, and scrubbing the shelves. He had Wayne pull a table next to his chair, and Kirxy did something he hadn't done in years: took inventory. With the boy's help, he counted and ledgered each item, marking them in his long green book. The back shelf contained canned soups, vegetables, sardines, and tins of meat. Many of the cans were so old that the labels flaked off in Kirxy's hand, so they were unmarked when Wayne replaced them in the rings they'd made not only in the dust but on the wood itself. In the back of that last shelf, Wayne discovered four tins of Underwood Deviled Ham, and as their labels fell away at Kirxy's touch, he remembered a time when he'd purposely unwrapped the paper from these cans because each label showed several red dancing devils, and some of his Negro customers had refused to buy anything that advertised the devil.

Kirxy now understood that his store was dead, that it no longer provided a service. His Negro customers had stopped coming years before. The same with Esther. For the past few years, except for the rare hunter, he'd been in business for the Gates boys alone. He looked across the room at Wayne, spraying the windows with Windex and wiping at them absently, gazing outside. The boy wore the last of the new denim overalls Kirxy had in stock. Once, when the store had thrived, he'd had many sizes, but for the longest time now the only ones he'd stocked were the boys'.

That night, beneath his standing lamp, Kirxy began again to read his wife's copy of *Tarzan of the Apes* to Wayne. He sipped his whiskey and spoke clearly, to be heard over the rain. When he paused to turn a page, he saw that the boy lay asleep across the row of chairs they'd arranged in the shape of a bed. Looking down through his bifocals, Kirxy flipped to the back of the book to the list of other Tarzan novels — twenty-four in all — and he decided to order them through the mail so Wayne would hear the complete adventures of Tarzan of the Apes.

In the morning, Goodloe called and said that Frank David had officially arrived — the sheriff himself had witnessed the swearing-in — and he was now this district's game warden.

"Pretty nice fellow," Goodloe said. "Kinda quiet. Polite. He asked me how the fishing was."

Then it's over, Kirxy thought.

A week later, Kirxy told Wayne he had to run some errands in Grove Hill. He'd spent the night before trying to decide whether to take the boy with him but had decided not to, that he couldn't watch him forever. Before he left he gave Wayne his .30-06 and told him to stay put, not to leave for anything. For himself, Kirxy took an old .22 bolt action and placed it in the back window rack of his truck. He waved to Wayne and drove off.

He thought that if the boy wanted to run away, it was his own choice. Kirxy owed him the chance, at least.

At the doctor's office the young surgeon frowned and removed his glasses when he told Kirxy that the cancer was advancing, that he'd need to check into the hospital in Mobile immediately. It was way past time. "Just look at your color," the surgeon said. Kirxy stood, thanked the man, put on his hat, and limped outside. He went by the post office and placed his order for the Tarzan books. He shopped for supplies in the Dollar Store and the Piggly Wiggly, had the checkout boys put the boxes in the front seat beside him. Coming out of the drugstore, he remembered that it was Saturday, that there'd be chicken fights today. And possible news about Frank David.

At Heflin's, Kirxy paid his five-dollar admission and let Heflin help him to a seat in the bottom of the stands. He poured some whiskey in his coffee and sat studying the crowd. Nobody had mentioned Frank David, but a few old-timers had offered their sympathies on the deaths of Kent and Scott. Down in the pit the Cajuns were back, and during the eighth match — one of the Louisiana whites versus a local red, the tall bald Cajun stooping and circling the tangled birds and licking his lips as his rooster swarmed the other and hooked it, the barn smoky and dark, rain splattering the tin roof — the door swung open.

Instantly the crowd was hushed. Feathers settled to the ground. Even the Cajuns knew who he was. He stood at the door, unarmed, his hands on his hips. A wiry man. He lifted his chin and people tried to hide their drinks. His giant ears. The hooked nose. The eyes. Bird handlers reached over their shoulders, pulling at the numbered pieces of masking tape on their backs. The two handlers and the referee in the ring sidled out, leaving the roosters.

For a full minute Frank David stood staring. People stepped out the back door. Climbed out windows. Half-naked boys in the rafters were frozen like monkeys hypnotized by a snake.

Frank David's gaze didn't stop on Kirxy but settled instead on the roosters, the white one pecking out the red's eyes. Outside, trucks roared to life, backfiring like gunshots. Kirxy placed his hands on his knees. He rose, turned up his coat collar, and flung his coffee out. Frank David still hadn't looked at him. Kirxy planted his cane and made his way out the back door and through the mud.

Not a person in sight, just tailgates vanishing into the woods.

From inside his truck, Kirxy watched Frank David walk away from the barn and head toward the trees. Now he was just a bowlegged man with white hair. Kirxy felt behind him for the .22 rifle with one hand while rolling down the window with the other. He had a little trouble aiming the gun with his shaky hands. He pulled back the bolt and inserted a cartridge into the chamber. Flicked the safety off. The sight of the rifle wavered between Frank David's shoulders as he walked. As if an old man like Kirxy were nothing to fear. Kirxy ground his teeth: that was why the bastard hadn't come to his deer massacre — an old storekeeper wasn't worth it, wasn't dangerous.

Closing one eye, Kirxy pulled the trigger. He didn't hear the shot, though later he would notice his ears ringing.

Frank David's coat bloomed out to the side and he missed a step. He stopped and put his hand to his lower right side and looked over his shoulder at Kirxy, who was fumbling with the rifle's bolt action. Then Frank David was gone, just wasn't there, there were only the trees, bent in the rain, and shreds of fog in the air. For a moment, Kirxy wondered if he'd even seen a man at all, if he'd shot at something out of his own imagination, if the cancer that had started in his pancreas had inched up along his spine into his brain and was deceiving him, forming men out of the air and walking them across fields, giving them hands and eyes and the power to disappear.

From inside the barn, the rooster crowed. Kirxy remembered Wayne. He hung the rifle in its rack and started his truck, gunned the engine. He banged over the field, flattening saplings and a fence, and though he couldn't feel his toes, he drove very fast.

Not until two days later, in the VA hospital in Mobile, would Kirxy finally begin to piece it all together. Parts of that afternoon were patchy and hard to remember: shooting Frank David, going back to the store and finding it empty, no sign of a struggle, the .30-06 gone, as if Wayne had walked out on his own and taken the gun. Kirxy could remember getting back into his truck. He'd planned to drive to Grove Hill—the courthouse, the game warden's office—and find Frank David, but somewhere along the way he passed out behind the wheel and veered off the road into a ditch. He barely remembered the rescue workers. The sirens. Goodloe himself pulling Kirxy out.

Later that night two coon hunters had stumbled across Wayne, wandering along the river, his face and shirt covered in blood, the .30-06 nowhere to be found.

When Goodloe had told the semiconscious Kirxy what happened, the storekeeper turned silently to the window, where he saw only the reflected face of an old, failed, dying man.

And later still, in the warm haze of morphine, Kirxy lowered his eyelids and let his imagination unravel and retwine the mystery of Frank David: it was as if Frank David himself appeared in the chair where Goodloe had sat, as if the game warden broke the seal on a bottle of Jim Beam and leaned forward on his elbows and touched the bottle to Kirxy's cracked lips and whispered to him a story about boots going over land and not making a sound, about rain washing the blood trail away even as the boots passed. About a tired old game warden taking his hand out of his coat and seeing the blood from Kirxy's bullet there, feeling it trickle down his side. About the boy in the back of his truck, handcuffed, gagged, blindfolded. About driving carefully through deep ruts in the road. Stopping behind Esther's empty house and carrying the kicking boy inside on his shoulder.

When the blindfold is removed, Wayne has trouble focusing but knows where he is because of her smell. Bacon and soap. Cigarettes, dust. Frank David holds what looks like a pillowcase. He comes across the room and puts the pillowcase down. He rubs his eyes and sits on the bed beside Wayne. He opens a book of matches and lights a cigarette. Holds the filtered end to Wayne's lips, but the boy doesn't inhale. Frank David puts the cigarette in his own lips, the embers glow. Then he drops it on the floor, crushes it out with his boot. Picks up the butt and slips it into his shirt pocket. He puts his hand over the boy's watery eyes, the skin of his palm dry and hard. Cool. Faint smell of blood. He moves his fingers over Wayne's nose, lips, chin. Stops at his throat and holds the boy tightly but not painfully. In a strange way Wayne can't understand, he finds it reassuring. His thudding heart slows. Something is struggling beside his shoulder and Frank David takes the thing from the bag. Now the smell in the room changes. Wayne begins to thrash and whip his head from side to side.

"Goddamn, son," Frank David whispers. "I hate to civilize you."

Goodloe began going to the veterans' hospital in Mobile once a week. He brought Kirxy cigarettes from his store. There weren't any private rooms available, and the beds around the storekeeper were filled with dying ex-soldiers who never talked, but Kirxy was beside a window and Goodloe would raise the glass and prop it open with a novel. They smoked together and drank whiskey from paper cups, listening for nurses.

It was the tall mean one.

"One more time, goddamn it," she said, coming out of nowhere and plucking the cigarettes from their lips so quickly they were still puckered.

Sometimes Goodloe would wheel Kirxy down the hall in his chair, the IV rack attached by a stainless steel contraption with a black handle the shape of a flower. They would go to the elevator and ride down three floors to a covered area where people smoked and talked about the weather. There were nurses and black cafeteria workers in white uniforms and hairnets and people visiting other people and a few patients. Occasionally in the halls they'd see some mean old fart Kirxy knew and they'd talk about hospital food or chicken fighting. Or the fact that Frank

David had surprised everyone and decided to retire after only a month of quiet duty, that the new game warden was from Texas. And a nigger to boot.

Then Goodloe would wheel Kirxy back along a long window, out of which you could see the tops of oak trees.

On one visit, Goodloe told Kirxy they'd taken Wayne out of intensive care. Three weeks later he said the boy'd been discharged.

"I give him a ride to the store," Goodloe said. This was in late May and Kirxy was a yellow skeleton with hands that shook.

"I'll stop by and check on him every evening," Goodloe went on. "He'll be OK, the doctor says. Just needs to keep them bandages changed. I can do that, I reckon."

They were quiet then, for a time, just the coughs of the dying men and the soft swishing of nurses' thighs and the hum of IV machines.

"Goodloe," Kirxy whispered, "I'd like you to help me with something."

Goodloe leaned in to hear, an unlit cigarette behind his ear like a pencil.

Kirxy's tongue was white and cracked, his breath awful. "I'd like to change my will," he said, "make the boy beneficiary."

"All right," Goodloe said.

"I'm obliged," whispered Kirxy. He closed his eyes.

Near the end he was delirious. He said he saw a little black creature at the foot of his bed. Said it had him by the toe. In surprising fits of strength, he would throw his water pitcher at it, or his box of tissues, or the *TV Guide.* Restraints were called for. His coma was a relief to everyone, and he died quietly in the night.

In Kirxy's chair in the store, Wayne didn't seem to hear Goodloe's questions. The sheriff had done some looking in the Grove Hill library — "research" was the modern word — and discovered that one species of cobra spat venom at its victim's eyes, but there weren't such snakes in southern Alabama. Anyway, the hospital lab had confirmed that it was the venom of a cottonmouth that had blinded Wayne. The question, of course, was who had put the venom in his eyes. Goodloe shuddered to think of it, how they'd found Wayne staggering about, howling in pain, bleeding from his tear ducts, the skin around his eye sockets dissolving, exposing the white ridges of his skull.

In the investigation, several local blacks including Euphrates Morrisette stated to Goodloe that the youngest Gates boy and his two dead brothers had molested Euphrates' stepdaughter in her own house. There was a rumor that several black men dressed in white sheets with pillowcases for hoods had caught and punished Wayne as he lurked along the river, peeping in folks' windows and doing unwholesome things to himself. Others suggested that the conjure woman had cast a spell on the Gateses, that she'd summoned a swamp demon to chase them to hell. And still others attributed the happenings to Frank David. There were a few occurrences of violence between some of the local whites and the blacks — some fires, a broken jaw — but soon it died down and Goodloe filed the deaths of Kent and Scott Gates as accidental.

But he listed Wayne's blinding as unsolved. The snake venom had bleached his pupils white, and the skin around his eye sockets had required grafts. The doctors had had to use skin from his buttocks, and because his buttocks were hairy, the skin around his eyes grew hair, too.

In the years to come, the loggers who clear-cut the land along the river would occasionally stop in the store, less from a need to buy something than from a curiosity to see the hermit with the milky, hairy eyes. The store smelled horrible, like the inside of a bear's mouth, and dust lay thick and soft on the shelves. Because they'd come in, the loggers would feel obligated to buy something, but every item was moldy or stale beyond belief, except for the things in cans, which were all unlabeled so they never knew what they'd get. Nothing was marked as to price either, and the blind man wouldn't talk. He just sat by the stove. So the loggers paid more than what they thought a can was worth, leaving the money on the counter by the telephone, which hadn't been connected in years. When plumper, grayer Goodloe came by on the occasional evening, he'd take the bills and coins and put them in Kirxy's cash drawer. He was no longer sheriff, having lost several elections back to one of his deputies, Roy or Dave. Now he drove a Lance truck, his routes including the hospitals in the county.

"Dern, boy," he cracked once. "This store's doing a better business now than it ever has. You sure you don't want a cracker rack?"

When Goodloe left, Wayne listened to the sound of the truck as it faded. "Sugarbaby," he whispered.

And many a night for years after, until his own death in his sleep, Wayne would rise from the chair and move across the floor, taking Kirxy's cane from where it stood by the coat rack. He would go outside, down the stairs like a man who could see, his beard nearly to his chest, and he would walk soundlessly the length of the building, knowing the woods even better now as he crept down the rain-rutted gullyside toward the river whose smell never left the caves of his nostrils and the roof of his mouth. At the riverbank, he would stop and sit with his back against a small pine, and lifting his white eyes to the sky, he would listen to the clicks and hum and thrattle of the woods, seeking out each noise at its source and imagining it: an acorn nodding, detaching, falling, its thin ricochet and the way it settles into the leaves. A bullfrog's bubbling throat and the things it says. The soft movement of the river over rocks and around the bases of cattails and cypress knees and through the wet hanging roots of trees. And then another sound, familiar. The soft, precise footsteps of Frank David. Downwind. Not coming closer, not going away. Circling. The striking of a match and the sizzle of ember and the fall of ash. The ascent of smoke. A strange and terrifying comfort for the rest of Wayne Gates's life.

1998

LAWRENCE BLOCK

LIKE A BONE IN THE THROAT

LAWRENCE BLOCK (1938–) was born and raised in Buffalo, New York. After attending Antioch College in Ohio, he moved to New York City, working as an editor at the Scott Meredith Literary Agency, then at Whitman Publishing Company. His career as a professional writer began early, with his first story, "You Can't Lose," being published in 1957, when he was nineteen, and his first novel, *Death Pulls a Double Cross,* in 1961, when he was twenty-three. As prolific as he is talented and versatile, he can be ranked with such contemporaries as Evan Hunter (Ed McBain) and Donald E. Westlake in all three categories. They all reached the hundred-book mark, under their own names and numerous pseudonyms; Block's pen names include Chip Harrison, Jill Emerson, and Paul Kavanagh. His bibliography illustrates his versatility: his finest work, the hard-boiled mysteries featuring Matthew Scudder; the much softer and funnier series about a bookstore-owner-*cum*-burglar, Bernie Rhodenbarr; espionage stories (as Kavanagh); outlandish humor in the Evan Tanner thrillers; soft-core erotica (as Emerson); fantasy (*Ariel,* 1980); and nonfiction books about the writing craft. His excellence as a writer has resulted in numerous honors, including eleven Edgar Allan Poe Award nominations. He has won the Edgar four times: once for Best Novel, *A Dance at the Slaughterhouse* (1992), and three times for Best Short Story, the only writer to win three times in that category. In 1994 he was named a Grand Master by the Mystery Writers of America, for lifetime achievement.

"Like a Bone in the Throat" was first published in the anthology *Murder for Revenge* (New York: Delacorte, 1998). While it is surely the most noir of his stories (can you imagine a darker one?), readers should also seek "By Dawn's Early Light," which won the Edgar in 1985 and is one of the modern classics of the mystery genre. It was written specifically for the first Private Eye Writers of America anthology, *The Eyes Have It* (New York: Mysterious Press, 1984), but first appeared two months earlier in the August 1984 issue of *Playboy.*

■ ■ ■

THROUGHOUT THE TRIAL, Paul Dandridge did the same thing every day. He wore a suit and tie, and he occupied a seat toward the front of the courtroom, and his eyes, time and time again, returned to the man who had killed his sister.

He was never called upon to testify. The facts were virtually undisputed, the evidence overwhelming. The defendant, William Charles Croydon, had abducted Dandridge's sister at knifepoint as she walked from the college library to her off-campus apartment. He had taken her to an isolated and rather primitive cabin in the woods, where he had subjected her to repeated sexual assaults over a period of three days, at the conclusion of which he had caused her death by manual strangulation.

Croydon took the stand in his own defense. He was a handsome young man who'd spent his thirtieth birthday in a jail cell awaiting trial, and his preppy good looks had already brought him letters and photographs and even a few marriage proposals from women of all ages. (Paul Dandridge was twenty-seven at the time. His sister, Karen, had been twenty when she died. The trial ended just weeks before her twenty-first birthday.)

On the stand, William Croydon claimed that he had no recollection of choking the life out of Karen Dandridge, but allowed as how he had no choice but to believe he'd done it. According to his testimony, the young woman had willingly accompanied him to the remote cabin, and had been an enthusiastic sexual partner with a penchant for rough sex. She had also supplied some particularly strong marijuana with hallucinogenic properties and had insisted that he smoke it with her. At one point, after indulging heavily in the unfamiliar drug, he had lost consciousness and awakened later to find his partner beside him, dead.

His first thought, he'd told the court, was that someone had broken into the cabin while he was sleeping, had killed Karen, and might return to kill him. Accordingly he'd panicked and rushed out of there, abandoning Karen's corpse. Now, faced with all the evidence arrayed against him, he was compelled to believe he had somehow committed this awful crime, although he had no recollection of it whatsoever, and although it was utterly foreign to his nature.

The district attorney, prosecuting this case himself, tore Croydon apart on cross-examination. He cited the bite marks on the victim's breasts, the rope burns indicating prolonged restraint, the steps Croydon had taken in an attempt to conceal his presence in the cabin. "You must be right," Croydon would admit, with a shrug and a sad smile. "All I can say is that I don't remember any of it."

The jury was eleven-to-one for conviction right from the jump, but it took six hours to make it unanimous. *Mr. Foreman, have you reached a verdict? We have, Your Honor. On the sole count of the indictment, murder in the first degree, how do you find? We find the defendant, William Charles Croydon, guilty.*

One woman cried out. A couple of others sobbed. The DA accepted congratulations. The defense attorney put an arm around his client. Paul Dandridge, his jaw set, looked at Croydon.

Their eyes met, and Paul Dandridge tried to read the expression in the killer's eyes. But he couldn't make it out.

Two weeks later, at the sentencing hearing, Paul Dandridge got to testify.

He talked about his sister, and what a wonderful person she had been. He spoke of the brilliance of her intellect, the gentleness of her spirit, the promise of her young life. He spoke of the effect of her death upon him. They had lost both parents, he told the court, and Karen was all the family he'd had in the world. And now she was gone. In order for his sister to rest in peace, and in order for him to get on with his own life, he urged that her murderer be sentenced to death.

Croydon's attorney argued that the case did not meet the criteria for the death penalty, that while his client possessed a criminal record he had never been charged with a crime remotely of this nature, and that the rough-sex-and-drugs defense carried a strong implication of mitigating circumstances. Even if the jury had rejected the defense, surely the defendant ought to be spared the ultimate penalty, and justice would be best served if he were sentenced to life in prison.

The DA pushed hard for the death penalty, contending that the rough-sex defense was the cynical last-ditch stand of a remorseless killer, and that the jury had rightly seen that it was wholly without merit. Although her killer might well have taken drugs, there was no forensic evidence to indicate that Karen Dandridge herself had been under the influence of anything other than a powerful and ruthless murderer. Karen Dandridge needed to be avenged, he maintained, and society needed to be assured that her killer would never, ever, be able to do it again.

Paul Dandridge was looking at Croydon when the judge pronounced the sentence, hoping to see something in those cold blue eyes. But as the words were spoken — *death by lethal injection* — there was nothing for Paul to see. Croydon closed his eyes.

When he opened them a moment later, there was no expression to be seen in them.

They made you fairly comfortable on death row. Which was just as well, because in this state you could sit there for a long time. A guy serving a life sentence could make parole and be out on the street in a lot less time than a guy on death row could run out of appeals. In that joint alone, there were four men with more than ten years apiece on death row, and one who was closing in on twenty.

One of the things they'd let Billy Croydon have was a typewriter. He'd never learned to type properly, the way they taught you in typing class, but he was writing enough these days so that he was getting pretty good at it, just using two fingers on each hand. He wrote letters to his lawyer, and he wrote letters to the women who wrote to him. It wasn't too hard to keep them writing, but the trick lay in getting them to do what he wanted. They wrote plenty of letters, but he wanted them to write really hot letters, describing in detail what they'd done with other guys in the past, and what they'd do if by some miracle they could be in his cell with him now.

They sent pictures, too, and some of them were good-looking and some of them were not. "That's a great picture," he would write back, "but I wish I had one that showed more of your physical beauty." It turned out to be surprisingly easy to get most of them to send increasingly revealing pictures. Before long he had them buying Polaroid cameras with timers and posing in obedience to his elaborate instructions. They'd do anything, the bitches, and he was sure they got off on it, too.

Today, though, he didn't feel like writing to any of them. He rolled a sheet of paper into the typewriter and looked at it, and the image that came to him was the grim face of that hard-ass brother of Karen Dandridge's. What was his name, anyway? Paul, wasn't it?

"Dear Paul," he typed, and frowned for a moment in concentration. Then he started typing again.

"Sitting here in this cell waiting for the day to come when they put a needle in my arm and flush me down God's own toilet, I found myself thinking about your testimony in court. I remember how you said your sister was a goodhearted girl who spent her short life bringing pleasure to everyone who knew her. According to your testimony, knowing this helped you rejoice in her life at the same time that it made her death so hard to take.

"Well, Paul, in the interest of helping you rejoice some more, I thought I'd tell you just how much pleasure your little sister brought to me. I've got to tell you that in all my life I never got more pleasure from anybody. My first look at Karen brought me pleasure, just watching her walk across campus, just looking at those jiggling tits and that tight little ass and imagining the fun I was going to have with them.

"Then when I had her tied up in the back seat of the car with her mouth taped shut, I have to say she went on being a real source of pleasure. Just looking at her in the rearview mirror was enjoyable, and from time to time I would stop the car and lean into the back to run my hands over her body. I don't think she liked it much, but I enjoyed it enough for the both of us.

"Tell me something, Paul. Did you ever fool around with Karen yourself? I bet you did. I can picture her when she was maybe eleven, twelve years old, with her little titties just beginning to bud out, and you'd have been seventeen or eighteen yourself, so how could you stay away from her? She's sleeping and you walk into her room and sit on the edge of her bed . . ."

He went on, describing the scene he imagined, and it excited him more than the pictures or letters from the women. He stopped and thought about relieving his excitement but decided to wait. He finished the scene as he imagined it and went on:

"Paul, old buddy, if you didn't get any of that you were missing a good thing. I can't tell you the pleasure I got out of your sweet little sister. Maybe I can give you some idea by describing our first time together." And he did, recalling it all to mind, savoring it in his memory, reliving it as he typed it out on the page.

"I suppose you know she was no virgin," he wrote, "but she was pretty new at it all the same. And then when I turned her face-down, well, I can tell you she'd never done *that* before. She didn't like it much, either. I had the tape off her mouth and I swear I thought she'd wake the neighbors, even though there weren't any. I guess it hurt her some, Paul, but that was just an example of your darling sister sacrificing everything to give pleasure to others, just like you said. And it worked, because I had a hell of a good time."

God, this was great. It really brought it all back.

"Here's the thing," he wrote. "The more we did it, the better it got. You'd think I would have grown tired of her, but I didn't. I wanted to keep on having her over and over again forever, but at the same time I felt this urgent need to finish it, because I knew that would be the best part.

"And I wasn't disappointed, Paul, because the most pleasure your sister ever gave anybody was right at the very end. I was on top of her, buried in her to the hilt, and I had my hands wrapped around her neck. And the ultimate pleasure came with me squeezing and looking into her eyes and squeezing harder and harder and going on looking into those eyes all the while and watching the life go right out of them."

He was too excited now. He had to stop and relieve himself. Afterward he read the letter and got excited all over again. A great letter, better than anything he could get any of his bitches to write to him, but he couldn't send it, not in a million years.

Not that it wouldn't be a pleasure to rub the brother's nose in it. Without the bastard's testimony, he might have stood a good chance to beat the death sentence. With it, he was sunk.

Still, you never knew. Appeals would take a long time. Maybe he could do himself a little good here.

He rolled a fresh sheet of paper in the typewriter. "Dear Mr. Dandridge," he wrote. "I'm well aware that the last thing on earth you want to read is a letter from me. I know that in your place I would feel no different myself. But I cannot seem to stop myself from reaching out to you. Soon I'll be strapped down onto a gurney and given a lethal injection. That frightens me horribly, but I'd gladly die a thousand times over if only it would bring your sister back to life. I may not remember killing her, but I know I must have done it, and I would give anything to undo it. With all my heart, I wish she were alive today."

Well, that last part was true, he thought. He wished to God she were alive, and right there in that cell with him, so that he could do her all over again, start to finish.

He went on and finished the letter, making it nothing but an apology, accepting responsibility, expressing remorse. It wasn't a letter that sought anything, not even forgiveness, and it struck him as a good opening shot. Probably nothing would ever come of it, but you never knew.

After he'd sent it off, he took out the first letter he'd written and read it through, relishing the feelings that coursed through him and strengthened him. He'd keep this, maybe even add to it from time to time. It was really great the way it brought it all back.

Paul destroyed the first letter.

He opened it, unaware of its source, and was a sentence or two into it before he realized what he was reading. It was, incredibly, a letter from the man who had killed his sister.

He felt a chill. He wanted to stop reading but he couldn't stop reading. He forced himself to stay with it all the way to the end.

The nerve of the man. The unadulterated gall.

Expressing remorse. Saying how sorry he was. Not asking for anything, not trying to justify himself, not attempting to disavow responsibility.

But there had been no remorse in the blue eyes, and Paul didn't believe there was a particle of genuine remorse in the letter, either. And what difference did it make if there was?

Karen was dead. Remorse wouldn't bring her back.

His lawyer had told him they had nothing to worry about, they were sure to get a stay of execution. The appeal process, always drawn out in capital cases, was in its early days. They'd get the stay in plenty of time, and the clock would start ticking all over again.

And it wasn't as though it got to the point where they were asking him what he wanted for a last meal. That happened sometimes, there was a guy three cells down who'd had his last meal twice already, but it didn't get that close for Billy Croydon. Two and a half weeks to go and the stay came through.

That was a relief, but at the same time he almost wished it had run out a little closer to the wire. Not for his benefit, but just to keep a couple of his correspondents on the edges of their chairs.

Two of them, actually. One was a fat girl who lived at home with her mother in Burns, Oregon, the other a sharp-jawed old maid employed as a corporate librarian in Philadelphia. Both had displayed a remarkable willingness to pose as he specified for their Polaroid cameras, doing interesting things and showing themselves in interesting ways. And, as the countdown had continued toward his date with death, both had proclaimed their willingness to join him in heaven.

No joy in that. In order for them to follow him to the grave, he'd have to be in it himself, wouldn't he? They could cop out and he'd never even know it.

Still, there was great power in knowing they'd even made the promise. And maybe there was something here he could work with.

He went to the typewriter. "My darling," he wrote. "The only thing that makes these last days bearable is the love we have for each other. Your pictures and letters sustain me, and the knowledge that we will be together in the next world draws much of the fear out of the abyss that yawns before me.

"Soon they will strap me down and fill my veins with poison, and I will awaken in the void. If only I could make that final journey knowing you would be waiting there for me! My angel, do you have the courage to make the trip ahead of me? Do you love me that much? I can't ask so great a sacrifice of you, and yet I am driven to ask it, because how dare I withhold from you something that is so important to me?"

He read it over, crossed out "sacrifice" and penciled in "proof of love." It wasn't quite right, and he'd have to work on it some more. Could either of the bitches possibly go for it? Could he possibly get them to do themselves for love?

And, even if they did, how would he know about it? Some hatchet-faced dame in Philly slashes her wrists in the bathtub, some fat girl hangs herself in Oregon, who's going to know to tell him so he can get off on it? *Darling, do it in front of a video cam, and have them send me the tape.* Be a kick, but it'd never happen.

Didn't Manson get his girls to cut *X*s on their foreheads? Maybe he could get his to cut themselves a little, where it wouldn't show except in the Polaroids. Would they do it? Maybe, if he worded it right.

Meanwhile, he had other fish to fry.

"Dear Paul," he typed. "I've never called you anything but 'Mr. Dandridge,' but I've written you so many letters, some of them just in the privacy of my mind, that I'll permit myself this liberty. And for all I know you throw my letters away unread. If so, well, I'm still not sorry I've spent the time writing them. It's a great help to me to get my thoughts on paper in this manner.

"I suppose you already know that I got another stay of execution. I can imagine your exasperation at the news. Would it surprise you to know that my own reaction was much the same? I don't want to die, Paul, but I don't want to live like this either, while lawyers scurry around just trying to postpone the inevitable. Better for both of us if they'd just killed me right away.

"Though I suppose I should be grateful for this chance to make my peace, with you and with myself. I can't bring myself to ask for your forgiveness, and I certainly can't summon up whatever is required for me to forgive myself, but perhaps that will come with time. They seem to be giving me plenty of time, even if they do persist in doling it out to me bit by bit . . ."

* * *

When he found the letter, Paul Dandridge followed what had become standard practice for him. He set it aside while he opened and tended to the rest of his mail. Then he went into the kitchen and brewed himself a pot of coffee. He poured a cup and sat down with it and opened the letter from Croydon.

When the second letter came he'd read it through to the end, then crumpled it in his fist. He hadn't known whether to throw it in the garbage or burn it in the fireplace, and in the end he'd done neither. Instead he'd carefully unfolded it and smoothed out its creases and read it again before putting it away.

Since then he'd saved all the letters. It had been almost three years since sentence was pronounced on William Croydon, and longer than that since Karen had died at his hands. (Literally at his hands, he thought; the hands that typed the letter and folded it into its envelope had encircled Karen's neck and strangled her. The very hands.)

Now Croydon was thirty-three and Paul was thirty himself, and he had been receiving letters at the approximate rate of one every two months. This was the fifteenth, and it seemed to mark a new stage in their one-sided correspondence. Croydon had addressed him by his first name.

"Better for both of us if they'd just killed me right away." Ah, but they hadn't, had they? And they wouldn't, either. It would drag on and on and on. A lawyer he'd consulted had told him it would not be unrealistic to expect another ten years of delay. For God's sake, he'd be forty years old by the time the state got around to doing the job.

It occurred to him, not for the first time, that he and Croydon were fellow prisoners. He was not confined to a cell and not under a sentence of death, but it struck him that his life held only the illusion of freedom. He wouldn't really be free until Croydon's ordeal was over. Until then he was confined in a prison without walls, unable to get on with his life, unable to have a life, just marking time.

He went over to his desk, took out a sheet of letterhead, uncapped a pen. For a long moment he hesitated. Then he sighed gently and touched pen to paper.

"Dear Croydon," he wrote. "I don't know what to call you. I can't bear to address you by your first name or to call you 'Mr. Croydon.' Not that I ever expected to call you anything at all. I guess I thought you'd be dead by now. God knows I wished it . . ."

Once he got started, it was surprisingly easy to find the words.

* * *

An answer from Dandridge.

Unbelievable.

If he had a shot, Paul Dandridge was it. The stays and the appeals would only carry you so far. The chance that any court along the way would grant him a reversal and a new trial was remote at best. His only real hope was a commutation of his death sentence to life imprisonment.

Not that he wanted to spend the rest of his life in prison. In a sense, you lived better on death row than if you were doing life in general prison population. But in another sense the difference between a life sentence and a death sentence was, well, the difference between life and death. If he got his sentence commuted to life, that meant the day would come when he made parole and hit the street. They might not come right out and say that, but that was what it would amount to, especially if he worked the system right.

And Paul Dandridge was the key to getting his sentence commuted.

He remembered how the prick had testified at the presentencing hearing. If any single thing had ensured the death sentence, it was Dandridge's testimony. And, if anything could swing a commutation of sentence for him, it was a change of heart on the part of Karen Dandridge's brother.

Worth a shot.

"Dear Paul," he typed. "I can't possibly tell you the sense of peace that came over me when I realized the letter I was holding was from you . . ."

Dandridge, seated at his desk, uncapped his pen and wrote the day's date at the top of a sheet of letterhead. He paused and looked at what he had written. It was, he realized, the fifth anniversary of his sister's death, and he hadn't been aware of that fact until he'd inscribed the date at the top of a letter to the man who'd killed her.

Another irony, he thought. They seemed to be infinite.

"Dear Billy," he wrote. "You'll appreciate this. It wasn't until I'd written the date on this letter that I realized its significance. It's been exactly five years since the day that changed both our lives forever."

He took a breath, considered his words. He wrote, "And I guess it's time to acknowledge formally something I've acknowledged in my heart some time ago. While I may never get over Karen's death, the bitter hatred that has burned in me for so long has finally cooled. And so I'd like to say that you have my forgiveness in full measure. And now I think it's time for you to forgive yourself . . ."

It was hard to sit still.

That was something he'd had no real trouble doing since the first day the cell door closed with him inside. You had to be able to sit still to do time, and it was never hard for him. Even during the several occasions when he'd been a few weeks away from an execution date, he'd never been one to pace the floor or climb the walls.

But today was the hearing. Today the board was hearing testimony from three individuals. One was a psychiatrist who would supply some professional arguments for commuting his sentence from death to life. Another was his fourth-grade teacher, who would tell the board how rough he'd had it in childhood and what a good little boy he was underneath it all. He wondered where they'd dug her up, and how she could possibly remember him. He didn't remember her at all.

The third witness, and the only really important one, was Paul Dandridge. Not only was he supplying the only testimony likely to carry much weight, but it was he who had spent money to locate Croydon's fourth-grade teacher, he who had enlisted the services of the shrink.

His buddy, Paul. A crusader, moving heaven and earth to save Billy Croydon's life.

Just the way he'd planned it.

He paced, back and forth, back and forth, and then he stopped and retrieved from his locker the letter that had started it all. The first letter to Paul Dandridge, the one he'd had the sense not to send. How many times had he reread it over the years, bringing the whole thing back into focus?

"When I turned her face-down, well, I can tell you she'd never done *that* before." Jesus, no, she hadn't liked it at all. He read and remembered, warmed by the memory.

What did he have these days but his memories? The women who'd been writing him had long since given it up. Even the ones who'd sworn to follow him to death had lost interest during the endless round of stays and appeals. He still had the letters and pictures they'd sent, but the pictures were unappealing, only serving to remind him what a bunch of pigs they all were, and the letters were sheer fantasy with no underpinning of reality. They described, and none too vividly, events that had never happened and events that would never happen. The sense of power to compel them to write those letters and pose for their pictures had faded over time. Now they only bored him and left him faintly disgusted.

Of his own memories, only that of Karen Dandridge held any real flavor. The other two girls, the ones he'd done before Karen, were almost impossible to recall. They were brief encounters, impulsive, unplanned, and over almost before they'd begun. He'd surprised one in a lonely part of the park, just pulled her skirt up and her panties down and went at her, hauling off and smacking her with a rock a couple of times when she wouldn't keep quiet. That shut her up, and when he finished he found out why. She was dead. He'd evidently cracked her skull and killed her, and he'd been thrusting away at dead meat.

Hardly a memory to stir the blood ten years later. The second one wasn't much better, either. He'd been about half drunk, and that had the effect of blurring the memory. He'd snapped her neck afterward, the little bitch, and he remembered that part, but he couldn't remember what it had felt like.

One good thing. Nobody ever found out about either of those two. If they had, he wouldn't have a prayer at today's hearing.

After the hearing, Paul managed to slip out before the press could catch up with him. Two days later, however, when the governor acted on the board's recommendation and commuted William Croydon's sentence to life imprisonment, one persistent reporter managed to get Paul in front of a video camera.

"For a long time I wanted vengeance," he admitted. "I honestly believed that I could only come to terms with the loss of my sister by seeing her killer put to death."

What changed that, the reporter wanted to know.

He stopped to consider his answer. "The dawning realization," he said, "that I could really only recover from Karen's death not by seeing Billy Croydon punished but by letting go of the need to punish. In the simplest terms, I had to forgive him."

And could he do that? Could he forgive the man who had brutally murdered his sister?

"Not overnight," he said. "It took time. I can't even swear I've forgiven him completely. But I've come far enough in the process to realize capital punishment is not only inhumane but pointless. Karen's death was wrong, but Billy Croydon's death would be another wrong, and two wrongs don't make a right. Now that his sentence has been lifted, I can get on with the process of complete forgiveness."

The reporter commented that it sounded as though Paul Dandridge had gone through some sort of religious conversion experience.

"I don't know about religion," Paul said, looking right at the camera. "I don't really consider myself a religious person. But something's happened, something transformational in nature, and I suppose you could call it spiritual."

With his sentence commuted, Billy Croydon drew a transfer to another penitentiary, where he was assigned a cell in general population. After years of waiting to die he was being given a chance to create a life for himself within the prison's walls. He had a job in the prison laundry, he had access to the library and exercise yard. He didn't have his freedom, but he had life.

On the sixteenth day of his new life, three hard-eyed lifers cornered him in the room where they stored the bed linen. He'd noticed one of the men earlier, had caught him staring at him a few times, looking at Croydon the way you'd look at a woman. He hadn't spotted the other two before, but they had the same look in their eyes as the one he recognized.

There wasn't a thing he could do.

They raped him, all three of them, and they weren't gentle about it, either. He fought at first but their response to that was savage and prompt, and he gasped at the pain and quit his struggling. He tried to disassociate himself from what was being done to him, tried to take his mind away to some private place. That was a way old cons had of doing time, getting through the hours on end of vacant boredom. This time it didn't really work.

They left him doubled up on the floor, warned him against saying anything to the hacks, and drove the point home with a boot to the ribs.

He managed to get back to his cell, and the following day he put in a request for a transfer to B Block, where you were locked down twenty-three hours a day. He was used to that on death row, so he knew he could live with it.

So much for making a life inside the walls. What he had to do was get out.

He still had his typewriter. He sat down, flexed his fingers. One of the rapists had bent his little finger back the day before, and it still hurt, but it wasn't one that he used for typing. He took a breath and started in.

Dear Paul . . .

Dear Billy,

As always, it was good to hear from you. I write not with news but just in the hope that I can lighten your spirits and build your resolve for the long road ahead. Winning your freedom won't be an easy task, but it's my conviction that working together we can make it happen . . .

Yours, Paul

Dear Paul,

Thanks for the books. I missed a lot, all those years when I never opened a book. It's funny—my life seems so much more spacious now, even though I'm spending all but one hour a day in a dreary little cell. But it's like that poem that starts, "Stone walls do not a prison make / Nor iron bars a cage." (I'd have to say, though, that the stone walls and iron bars around this place make a pretty solid prison.)

I don't expect much from the parole board next month, but it's a start . . .

Dear Billy,

I was deeply saddened by the parole board's decision, although everything I'd heard had led me to expect nothing else. Even though you've been locked up more than enough time to be eligible, the thinking evidently holds that death row time somehow counts less than regular prison time, and that the board wants to see how you do as a prisoner serving a life sentence before letting you return to the outside world. I'm not sure I understand the logic there . . .

I'm glad you're taking it so well.

Your friend, Paul

Dear Paul,

Once again, thanks for the books. They're a healthy cut above what's available here. This joint prides itself in its library, but when you say "Kierkegaard" to the prison librarian he looks at you funny, and you don't dare try him on Martin Buber.

I shouldn't talk, because I'm having troubles of my own with both of those guys. I haven't got anybody else to bounce this off, so do you mind if I press you into service? Here's my take on Kierkegaard . . .

Well, that's the latest from the Jailhouse Philosopher, who is pleased to be

Your friend, Billy

Dear Billy,

Well, once again it's time for the annual appearance before parole board — or the annual circus, as you call it with plenty of justification. Last year we thought maybe the third time was the charm, and it turned out we were wrong, but maybe it'll be different this year . . .

Dear Paul,

"Maybe it'll be different this time." Isn't that what Charlie Brown tells himself before he tries to kick the football? And Lucy always snatches it away.

Still, some of the deep thinkers I've been reading stress that hope is important even when it's unwarranted. And, although I'm a little scared to admit it, I have a good feeling this time.

And if they never let me out, well, I've reached a point where I honestly don't mind. I've found an inner life here that's far superior to anything I had in my years as a free man. Between my books, my solitude, and my correspondence with you, I have a life I can live with. Of course I'm hoping for parole, but if they snatch the football away again, it ain't gonna kill me . . .

Dear Billy,

. . . Just a thought, but maybe that's the line you should take with them. That you'd welcome parole, but you've made a life for yourself within the walls and you can stay there indefinitely if you have to.

I don't know, maybe that's the wrong strategy altogether, but I think it might impress them . . .

Dear Paul,

Who knows what's likely to impress them? On the other hand, what have I got to lose?

Billy Croydon sat at the end of the long conference table, speaking when spoken to, uttering his replies in a low voice, giving pro forma responses to the same questions they asked him every year. At the end they asked him, as usual, if there was anything he wanted to say.

Well, what the hell, he thought. What did he have to lose?

"I'm sure it won't surprise you," he began, "to hear that I've come before you in the hope of being granted early release. I've had hearings before, and when I was turned down it was devastating. Well, I may not be doing myself any good by saying this, but this time around it won't destroy me if you decide to deny me parole. Almost in spite of myself, I've made a life for myself within prison walls. I've found an inner life, a life of the spirit, that's superior to anything I had as a free man . . ."

Were they buying it? Hard to tell. On the other hand, since it happened to be the truth, it didn't really matter whether they bought it or not.

He pushed on to the end. The chairman scanned the room, then looked at him and nodded shortly.

"Thank you, Mr. Croydon," he said. "I think that will be all for now."

"I think I speak for all of us," the chairman said, "when I say how much weight we attach to your appearance before this board. We're used to hearing the pleas of victims and their survivors, but almost invariably they come here to beseech us to deny parole. You're virtually unique, Mr. Dandridge, in appearing as the champion of the very man who . . ."

"Killed my sister," Paul said levelly.

"Yes. You've appeared before us on prior occasions, Mr. Dandridge, and while we were greatly impressed by your ability to forgive William Croydon and by the relationship you've forged with him, it seems to me that there's been a change in your own sentiments. Last year, I recall, while you pleaded on Mr. Croydon's behalf, we sensed that you did not wholeheartedly believe he was ready to be returned to society."

"Perhaps I had some hesitation."

"But this year . . ."

"Billy Croydon's a changed man. The process of change has been completed. I know that he's ready to get on with his life."

"There's no denying the power of your testimony, especially in light of its source." The chairman cleared his throat. "Thank you, Mr. Dandridge. I think that will be all for now."

"Well?" Paul said. "How do you feel?"

Billy considered the question. "Hard to say," he said. "Everything's a little unreal. Even being in a car. Last time I was in a moving vehicle was when I got my commutation and they transferred me from the other prison. It's not like Rip Van Winkle, I know what everything looks like from television, cars included. Tell the truth, I feel a little shaky."

"I guess that's to be expected."

"I suppose." He tugged his seatbelt to tighten it. "You want to know how I feel, I feel vulnerable. All those years I was locked down twenty-three hours out of twenty-four. I knew what to expect, I knew I was safe. Now I'm a free man, and it scares the crap out of me."

"Look in the glove compartment," Paul said.

"Jesus, Johnnie Walker Black."

"I figured you might be feeling a little anxious. That ought to take the edge off."

"Yeah, Dutch courage," Billy said. "Why Dutch, do you happen to know? I've always wondered."

"No idea."

He weighed the bottle in his hand. "Been a long time," he said. "Haven't had a taste of anything since they locked me up."

"There was nothing available in prison?"

"Oh, there was stuff. The jungle juice cons made out of potatoes and raisins, and some good stuff that got smuggled in. But I wasn't in population, so I didn't have access. And anyway it seemed like more trouble than it was worth."

"Well, you're a free man now. Why don't you drink to it? I'm driving or I'd join you."

"Well . . ."

"Go ahead."

"Why not?" he said, and uncapped the bottle and held it to the light. "Pretty color, huh? Well, here's to freedom, huh?" He took a long drink, shuddered at the burn of the whiskey. "Kicks like a mule," he said.

"You're not used to it."

"I'm not." He put the cap on the bottle and had a little trouble screwing it back on. "Hitting me hard," he reported. "Like I was a little kid getting his first taste of it. Whew."

"You'll be all right."

"Spinning," Billy said, and slumped in his seat.

Paul glanced over at him, looked at him again a minute later. Then, after checking the mirror, he pulled the car off the road and braked to a stop.

Billy was conscious for a little while before he opened his eyes. He tried to get his bearings first. The last thing he remembered was a wave of dizziness after the slug of scotch hit bottom. He was still sitting upright, but it didn't feel like a car seat, and he didn't sense any movement. No, he was in some sort of chair, and he seemed to be tied to it.

That didn't make any sense. A dream? He'd had lucid dreams before and knew how real they were, how you could be in them and wonder if you were dreaming and convince yourself you weren't. The way you broke the surface and got out of it was by opening your eyes. You had to force yourself, had to open your real eyes and not just your eyes in the dream, but it could be done . . . There!

He was in a chair, in a room he'd never seen before, looking out a window at a view he'd never seen before. An open field, woods behind it.

He turned his head to the left and saw a wall paneled in knotty cedar. He turned to the right and saw Paul Dandridge, wearing boots and jeans and a plaid flannel shirt and sitting in an easy chair with a book. He said, "Hey!" and Paul lowered the book and looked at him.

"Ah," Paul said. "You're awake."

"What's going on?"

"What do you think?"

"There was something in the whiskey."

"There was indeed," Paul agreed. "You started to stir just as we made the turn off the state road. I gave you a booster shot with a hypodermic needle."

"I don't remember."

"You never felt it. I was afraid for a minute there that I'd given you too much. That would have been ironic, wouldn't you say? 'Death by lethal injection.' The sentence carried out finally after all these years, and you wouldn't have even known it happened."

He couldn't take it in. "Paul," he said, "for God's sake, what's it all about?"

"What's it about?" Paul considered his response. "It's about time."

"Time?"

"It's the last act of the drama."

"Where are we?"

"A cabin in the woods. Not the cabin. That would be ironic, wouldn't it?"

"What do you mean?"

"If I killed you in the same cabin where you killed Karen. Ironic, but not really feasible. So this is a different cabin in different woods, but it will have to do."

"You're going to kill me?"

"Of course."

"For God's sake, why?"

"Because that's how it ends, Billy. That's the point of the whole game. That's how I planned it from the beginning."

"I can't believe this."

"Why is it so hard to believe? We conned each other, Billy. You pretended to repent and I pretended to believe you. You pretended to reform and I pretended to be on your side. Now we can both stop pretending."

Billy was silent for a moment. Then he said, "I was trying to con you at the beginning."

"No kidding."

"There was a point where it turned into something else, but it started out as a scam. It was the only way I could think of to stay alive. You saw through it?"

"Of course."

"But you pretended to go along with it. Why?"

"Is it that hard to figure out?"

"It doesn't make any sense. What do you gain by it? My death? If you wanted me dead all you had to do was tear up my letter. The state was all set to kill me."

"They'd have taken forever," Paul said bitterly. "Delay after delay, and always the possibility of a reversal and a retrial, always the possibility of a commutation of sentence."

"There wouldn't have been a reversal, and it took you working for me to get my sentence commuted. There would have been delays, but there'd already been a few of them before I got around to writing to you. It couldn't have lasted too many years longer, and it would have added up to a lot less than it has now, with all the time I spent serving life and waiting for the parole board to open the doors. If you'd just let it go, I'd be dead and buried by now."

"You'll be dead soon," Paul told him. "And buried. It won't be much longer. Your grave's already dug. I took care of that before I drove to the prison to pick you up."

"They'll come after you, Paul. When I don't show up for my initial appointment with my parole officer —"

"They'll get in touch, and I'll tell them we had a drink and shook hands and you went off on your own. It's not my fault if you decided to skip town and violate the terms of your parole."

He took a breath. He said, "Paul, don't do this."

"Why not?"

"Because I'm begging you. I don't want to die."

"Ah," Paul said. "*That's* why."

"What do you mean?"

"If I left it to the state," he said, "they'd have been killing a dead man. By the time the last appeal was denied and the last request for a stay of execution turned down, you'd have been resigned to the inevitable. They'd strap you to a gurney and give you a shot, and it would be just like going to sleep."

"That's what they say."

"But now you want to live. You adjusted to prison, you made a life for yourself in there, and then you finally made parole, icing on the cake, and now you genuinely want to live. You've really got a life now, Billy, and I'm going to take it away from you."

"You're serious about this."

"I've never been more serious about anything."

"You must have been planning this for years."

"From the very beginning."

"Jesus, it's the most thoroughly premeditated crime in the history of the world, isn't it? Nothing I can do about it, either. You've got me tied tight and the chair won't tip over. Is there anything I can say that'll make you change your mind?"

"Of course not."

"That's what I thought." He sighed. "Get it over with."

"I don't think so."

"Huh?"

"This won't be what the state hands out," Paul Dandridge said. "A minute ago you were begging me to let you live. Before it's over you'll be begging me to kill you."

"You're going to torture me."

"That's the idea."

"In fact you've already started, haven't you? This is the mental part."

"Very perceptive of you, Billy."

"For all the good it does me. This is all because of what I did to your sister, isn't it?"

"Obviously."

"I didn't do it, you know. It was another Billy Croydon that killed her, and I can barely remember what he was like."

"That doesn't matter."

"Not to you, evidently, and you're the one calling the shots. I'm sure Kierkegaard had something useful to say about this sort of situation, but I'm damned if I can call it to mind. You knew I was conning you, huh? Right from the jump?"

"Of course."

"I thought it was a pretty good letter I wrote you."

"It was a masterpiece, Billy. But that didn't mean it wasn't easy to see through."

"So now you dish it out and I take it," Billy Croydon said, "until you get bored and end it, and I wind up in the grave you've already dug for me. And that's the end of it. I wonder if there's a way to turn it around."

"Not a chance."

"Oh, I know I'm not getting out of here alive, Paul, but there's more than one way of turning something around. Let's see now. You know, the letter you got wasn't the first one I wrote to you."

"So?"

"The past is always with you, isn't it? I'm not the same man as the guy who killed your sister, but he's still there inside somewhere. Just a question of calling him up."

"What's that supposed to mean?"

"Just talking to myself, I guess. I was starting to tell you about that first letter. I never sent it, you know, but I kept it. For the longest time I held on to it and read it whenever I wanted to relive the experience. Then it stopped working, or maybe I stopped wanting to call up the past, but whatever it was I quit reading it. I still held on to it, and then one day I realized I didn't want to own it anymore. So I tore it up and got rid of it."

"That's fascinating."

"But I read it so many times I bet I can bring it back word for word." His eyes locked with Paul Dandridge's, and his lips turned up in the slightest suggestion of a smile. He said, "'Dear Paul, Sitting here in this cell waiting for the day to come when they put a needle in my arm and flush me down God's own toilet, I found myself thinking about your testimony in court. I remember how you said your sister was a good-hearted girl who spent her short life bringing pleasure to everyone who knew her. According to your testimony, knowing this helped you rejoice in her life at the same time that it made her death so hard to take.

"'Well, Paul, in the interest of helping you rejoice some more, I thought I'd tell you just how much pleasure your little sister brought to me. I've got to tell you that in all my life I never got more pleasure from anybody. My first look at Karen brought me pleasure, just watching her walk across campus, just looking at those jiggling tits and that tight little ass and imagining the fun I was going to have with them.'"

"Stop it, Croydon!"

"You don't want to miss this, Paulie. 'Then when I had her tied up in the back seat of the car with her mouth taped shut, I have to say she went on being a real source of pleasure. Just looking at her in the rearview mirror was enjoyable, and from time to time I would stop the car and lean into the back to run my hands over her body. I don't think she liked it much, but I enjoyed it enough for the both of us.'"

"You're a son of a bitch."

"And you're an asshole. You should have let the state put me out of everybody's misery. Failing that, you should have let go of the hate and sent the new William Croydon off to rejoin society. There's a lot more to the letter, and I remember it perfectly." He tilted his head, resumed quoting from memory. "'Tell me something, Paul. Did you ever fool around with Karen yourself? I bet you did. I can picture her when she was maybe eleven, twelve years old, with her little titties just beginning to bud out, and you'd have been seventeen or eighteen yourself, so how could you stay away from her? She's sleeping and you walk into her room and sit on the edge of her bed.'" He grinned. "I always liked that part. And there's lots more. You enjoying your revenge, Paulie? Is it as sweet as they say it is?"

1999

JAMES W. HALL

CRACK

JAMES W. HALL was born in Hopkinsville, Kentucky, but has lived in Florida most of his adult life. He received a BA in literature in 1969 from Florida Presbyterian College (now Eckerd College), an MA in creative writing from Johns Hopkins University (1970), and a PhD in literature from the University of Utah (1977). A full professor, he has taught literature and creative writing at Florida International University for more than three decades.

His writing career began with four books of poetry and several short stories in such literary journals as *Georgia Review* and *Kenyon Review* before he turned to the mystery genre with *Under Cover of Daylight* (1986), which introduced the character Thorn. Thorn, a cranky middle-aged loner who earns a modest living tying fishing flies, finds himself unexpectedly involved in mysteries when he'd rather be left alone to fish, but he cannot turn his back on friends, relatives, and neighbors who need his help. He is reminiscent of John D. MacDonald's Travis McGee, but without the charm. He has appeared in ten novels, one of which, *Blackwater Sound* (2002), won the Shamus Award for Best PI Novel from the Private Eye Writers of America. The author's writing, both in the Thorn series and in his six nonseries novels, is clearly influenced by the hard-boiled style of Ernest Hemingway, Dashiell Hammett, and Ross Macdonald. Most of his books are set in Florida and often involve serious issues such as illegal animal smuggling and fish farming, but Thorn (and Hall) never gets on a soapbox.

"Crack" was first published in the anthology *Murder and Obsession* (New York: Mysterious Press, 1999); it was nominated for an Edgar Allan Poe Award by the Mystery Writers of America and was selected for the 2000 edition of *The Best American Mystery Stories.*

▪ ▪ ▪

WHEN I FIRST saw the slit of light coming through the wall, I halted abruptly on the stairway, and instantly my heart began to thrash with a giddy blend of dread and craving.

At the time, I was living in Spain, a section named Puerto Viejo, or the Old Port, in the small village of Algorta just outside the industrial city of Bilbao. It was a filthy town, a dirty region, with a taste in the air of old pennies and a patina of grime dulling every bright surface. The sunlight strained through perpetual clouds that had the density and monotonous luster of lead. It was to have been my year of *flamenco y sol*, but instead I was picked to be the Fulbright fellow of a dour Jesuit university in Bilbao on the northern coast where the umbrellas were pocked by ceaseless acid rain and the customary dress was black—shawls, dresses, berets, raincoats, shirts, and trousers. It was as if the entire Basque nation was in perpetual mourning.

The night I first saw the light I was drunk. All afternoon I had been swilling Rioja on the balcony overlooking the harbor, celebrating the first sunny day in a month. It was October and despite the brightness and clarity of the light, my wife had been darkly unhappy all day, even unhappier than usual. At nine o'clock she was already in bed paging aimlessly through month-old magazines and sipping her sherry. I finished with the dishes and double-checked all the locks and began to stumble up the stairs of our 250-year-old stone house that only a few weeks before our arrival in Spain had been subdivided into three apartments.

I was midway up the stairs to the second floor when I saw the slim line of the light shining through a chink in the new mortar. There was no debate, not even a millisecond of equivocation about the propriety of my actions. In most matters I considered myself a scrupulously moral man. I had always been one who could be trusted with other people's money or their most damning secrets. But like so many of my fellow puritans I long ago had discovered that when it came to certain libidinous temptations I was all too easily swept off my safe moorings into the raging currents of erotic gluttony.

I immediately pressed my eye to the crack.

It took me a moment to get my bearings, to find the focus. And when I did, my knees softened and my breath deserted me. The view was beyond anything I might have hoped for. The small slit provided a full panorama of my neighbors' second story. At knee-high level I could see their master bathroom and a few feet to the left their king-size brass bed.

That first night the young daughter was in the bathroom with the door swung open. If the lights had been off in their apartment or the bathroom door had been closed I might never have given the peephole another look. But that girl was standing before the full-length mirror and she was lifting her fifteen-year-old breasts that had already developed quite satisfactorily, lifting them both at once and reshaping them with her hands to meet some standard that only she could see. After a while she released them from her grip, then lifted them on her flat palms as though offering them to her image in the mirror. They were beautiful breasts, with small nipples that protruded nearly an inch from the aureole, and she handled them beautifully, in a fashion that was far more mature and knowing than one would expect from any ordinary fifteen-year-old.

I did not know her name. I still don't, though certainly she is the most important female who ever crossed my path. Far more crucial in my life's trajectory than my mother or either of my wives. Yet it seems appropriate that I should remain unaware of her name. That I should not personalize her in any way. That she should remain simply an abstraction — simply the girl who destroyed me.

In the vernacular of that year in Spain, she was known as a *niña pera,* or pear girl. One of hundreds of shapely and succulent creatures who cruised about the narrow, serpentine roads of Algorta and Bilbao on loud mopeds, their hair streaming in their wake. She was as juicy as any of them. More succulent than most, as I had already noticed from several brief encounters as we exited from adjacent doors onto the narrow alley-streets of the Old Port. On these two or three occasions, I remember fumbling through my Spanish greetings and taking a stab at small talk while she, with a patient but faintly disdainful smile, suffered my clumsy attempts at courtesy. Although she wore the white blouse and green plaid skirts of all the other Catholic schoolgirls, such prosaic dress failed to disguise her pearness. She was achingly succulent, blindingly juicy. At the time I was twice her age. Double the fool and half the man I believed I was.

That first night, after a long, hungering look, I pulled away from the crack of light and with equal measures of reluctance and urgency, I marched back down the stairs and went immediately to the kitchen and found the longest and flattest knife in the drawer and brought it back to the stairway, and with surgical precision I inserted the blade into the soft mortar and as my pulse throbbed, I painstakingly doubled the size of my peephole.

When I withdrew the blade and applied my eye again to the slit, I now could see my *niña pera* from her thick black waist-length hair to her bright pink toenails. While at the same time I calculated that if my neighbors ever detected the lighted slit from their side and dared to press an eye to the breach, they would be rewarded with nothing more than a static view of the 250-year-old stones of my rented stairwell.

I knew little about my neighbors except that the father of my pear girl was a vice consul for that South American country whose major role in international affairs seemed to be to supply America with her daily dose of granulated ecstasy.

He didn't look like a gangster. He was tall and elegant, with wavy black hair that touched his shoulders and an exquisitely precise beard. He might have been a maestro of a European symphony or a painter of romantic landscapes. And his young wife could easily have been a slightly older sister to my succulent one. She was in her middle thirties and had the wide and graceful hips, the bold, uplifting breasts, the gypsy features and black unfathomable eyes that seemed to spring directly from the archetypal pool of my carnality. In the Jungian parlance of my age, the wife was my anima, while the daughter was the anima of my adolescent self. They were perfect echoes of the dark secret female who glowed like uranium in the bowels of my psyche.

That first night when the bedsprings squeaked behind me, and my wife padded across the bedroom floor for her final visit to the bathroom, I allowed myself one last draft of the amazing sight before me. The *niña* was now stooped forward and was holding a small hand mirror to her thicket of pubic hair, poking and searching with her free hand through the dense snarl as if she were seeking that tender part of herself she had discovered by touch but not yet by sight.

Trembling and breathless, I pressed my two hands flat against the stone wall and shoved myself away and with my heart in utter disarray, I carried my lechery up the stairs to bed.

The next day I set about learning my neighbors' schedule and altering mine accordingly. My wife had taken a job as an English teacher in a nearby *instituto* and was occupied every afternoon and through the early evening. My duties at the university occupied me Monday, Wednesday, and Friday. I was expected to offer office hours before and after my classes on those days. However, I immediately began to curtail these sessions because I discovered that my *niña pera* returned from school around three o'clock, and on many days she showered and changed into casual clothes, leaving her school garb in a heap on the bathroom floor as she fled the apartment for an afternoon of boy-watching in the Algorta pubs.

To my department chairman's dismay, I began to absent myself from the university hallways immediately after my last class of the day, hurrying with my umbrella along the five blocks to the train station so I could be home by 2:55. In the silence of my apartment, hunched breathless at my hole, I watched her undress. I watched the steam rise from her shower, and I watched her towel herself dry. I watched her on the toilet and I watched her using the sanitary products she preferred. I watched her touch the flawless skin of her face with her fingertips, applying makeup or wiping it away. On many afternoons I watched her examine herself in the full-length mirror. Running her hands over that seamless flesh, trying out various seductive poses while an expression played on her face that was equal parts exultation and shame — that peculiar adolescent emotion I so vividly recalled.

These were the times when I would have touched myself were I going to do so. But these moments at the peephole, while they were intensely sexual, were not the least masturbatory. Instead, they had an almost spiritual component. As though I were worshiping at the shrine of hidden mysteries, allowed by divine privilege to see beyond the walls of my own paltry life. In exchange for this gift I was cursed to suffer a brand of reverential horniness I had not imagined possible. I lusted for a vision that was forever intangible, a girl I could not touch, nor smell, nor taste. A girl who was no more than a scattering of light across my retina.

Although I never managed to establish a definite pattern to her mother's schedule, I did my best to watch her as well. At odd unpredictable hours, she appeared in my viewfinder and I watched the elder *niña pera* bathe in a tub of bubbles, and even when her house was empty, I watched her chastely close the bathroom door whenever she performed her toilette. I watched her nap on the large brass bed. And three times that fall in the late afternoons, I watched her slide her hand inside her green silk robe and touch herself between the legs, hardly moving the hand at all, giving herself the subtlest of touches until she rocked her head back into the pillow and wept.

I kept my eye to the wall during the hours when I should have been preparing for my classes and grading my students' papers and writing up their weekly exams. Instead, I stationed myself at the peephole, propping myself up with pillows, finding the best alignment for nose and cheek against the rough cool rock. I breathed in the sweet grit of mortar, trained my good right eye on the bathroom door and the bed, scanning the floor for shadows, primed for any flick of movement, always dreadfully alert for the sound of my wife's key in the front door.

After careful study, I had memorized her homecoming ritual. Whenever she entered our apartment, it took her two steps to reach the foyer and put down her bag. She could then choose to turn right into the kitchen or take another step toward the stairway. If she chose the latter, almost instantly she would be able to witness me perched at the peephole, and my clandestine life would be exposed. In my leisure, I clocked a normal entry and found that on average I had almost a full twenty seconds from the moment her key turned the tumblers till she reached the bottom of the stairs, twenty seconds to toss the pillows back into the bedroom and absent myself from the hole.

I briefly toyed with the idea of revealing the peephole to her. But I knew her sense of the perverse was far short of my own. She was constitutionally gloomy, probably a clinical depressive. Certainly a passive-aggressive, who reveled in bitter nonresponse, bland effect, withdrawing into maddening hours of silence whenever I blundered across another invisible foul line she had drawn.

I watched the father too, the vice consul. On many occasions I saw him strip off his underwear and climb into the shower, and I saw him dry himself and urinate and brush his teeth. Once I saw him reach down and retrieve a pair of discarded briefs and bring the crotch to his nose before deciding they were indeed fresh enough to wear again. He had the slender and muscular build of a long-distance runner. Even in its slackened state his penis was formidable.

On one particular Sunday morning, I watched with grim fascination as he worked his organ to an erection, all the while gazing at the reflection of his face. And a few moments later as the spasms of his pleasure shook him and he was bending forward to ejaculate into the sink, the *niña pera* appeared at the doorway of the bathroom. She paused briefly to watch the vice consul's last strokes, then passed behind him and stepped into the shower with a nonchalance that I found more shocking than anything I had witnessed to that point.

Late in November, the chairman of my department called me into his office and asked me if I was happy in Spain, and I assured him that I most certainly was. He smiled uncomfortably and offered me a glass of scotch and as we sipped, he told me that the students had been complaining that I was not making myself sufficiently available to them. I feigned shock, but he simply shook his head and waved off my pretense. Not only had I taken to missing office hours, I had failed to return a single set of papers or tests. The students were directionless and confused and in a unified uproar. And because of their protests, much to his regret, the chairman was going to have to insist that I begin holding my regular office hours immediately. If I failed to comply, he would have no choice but to act in his students' best interest by calling the Fulbright offices in Madrid and having my visiting professorship withdrawn for the second semester. I would be shipped home in disgrace.

I assured him that I would not disappoint him again.

Two days later after my last class of the day as I walked back to my office, all I could think of was my *niña pera* stripping away her Catholic uniform and stepping into the shower, then stepping out again wet and naked and perfectly succulent. I turned from my office door and the five scowling students waiting there and hurried out of the building. I caught the train just in time and was home only seconds before she arrived.

And this was the day it happened.

Breathless from my jog from the train station, I clambered up the stairs and quickly assumed my position at the slit, but was startled to see that it was not my *niña pera* beyond the wall, but her father, the diplomat in his dark suit, home at that unaccustomed hour. He was pacing back and forth in front of the bathroom, where a much shorter and much less elegant man was holding the head of a teenage boy over the open toilet bowl. The young man had long stringy hair and was dressed in a black T-shirt and blue jeans. The thug who was gripping him by the ears above the bowl was also dressed in black, a bulky black sweatshirt with the sleeves torn away and dark jeans and a black Basque beret. His arms were as gnarled as oak limbs, and the boy he held was unable to manage even a squirm.

The vice consul stopped his pacing and spat out a quick, indecent bit of Spanish. Even though the wall muffled most conversation, I heard and recognized the phrase. While my conversational skills were limited, I had mastered a dozen or so of the more useful and colorful Spanish curses. The vice consul had chosen to brand the boy as a pig's bastard child. Furthermore, a pig covered in its own excrement.

Though my disappointment at missing my daily appointment with the *niña pera* deflated my spirits, witnessing such violence and drama was almost fair compensation. My assumption was that my neighbor was disciplining the young man for some botched assignment — the most natural guess being that he was a courier who transported certain highly valued pharmaceutical products that happened also to be the leading export of the vice consul's country. The other possibility, of course, and one that gave me a particularly nasty thrill, was that the boy was guilty of some impropriety with the diplomat's daughter, my own *niña pera,* and now was suffering the dire consequences of his effrontery.

I watched as the vice consul came close to the boy and bent to whisper something to him, then tipped his head up by the chin and gave some command to the thug. The squat man let go of the boy's right ear, and with a gesture so quick I only caught the end of it, he produced a knife and slashed the boy's right ear away from his head.

I reeled back from the slit in the wall and pressed my back against the banister and tried to force the air into my lungs.

At that moment I should have rushed downstairs, gotten on the phone, and called the militia to report the outrage beyond my wall. And I honestly considered doing so. For surely it would have been the moral, virtuous path. But I could not move. And as I considered my paralysis, the utter selfishness of my inaction filled me with acid self-contempt. I reviled myself even as I kept my place. I could not call for help because I did not dare to upset the delicate equipoise of my neighbors' lives. The thought of losing my *niña pera* to the judicial process, or even worse to extradition, left me lifeless on the stairway. Almost as terrifying was the possibility that if I called for the militia, a further investigation would expose the slit in the wall and I would be hauled out into the streets for a public thrashing.

For a very long while I did not move.

Finally, when I found the courage to bring my eye back to the crack in the wall, I saw that the thug had lifted the boy to a standing position before the toilet, and the vice consul had unzipped him and was gripping the tip of his penis, holding it out above the bloody porcelain bowl, a long steak knife poised a few inches above the pale finger of flesh.

The vice consul's arm quivered and began its downward slash.

"No!" I cried out, then louder, "No!"

My neighbor aborted his savage swipe and spun around. I watched him take a hesitant step my way, then another. His patent-leather shoes glowed in the eerie light beyond the wall. Then in an unerring path he marched directly to the wall where I was perched.

I pulled away, scooted backward up the stairs, and held my breath.

I waited.

I heard nothing but the distant siren wail of another supertanker coming into port.

I was just turning to tiptoe up to the bedroom when the blade appeared. It slid through the wall and glittered in the late-afternoon light, protruding a full five inches into my apartment. He slipped it back and forth as if he, too, were trying to widen the viewing hole, then drew it slowly out of sight. For a second I was in real danger of toppling forward down the flight of stairs, but I found a grip on the handrail and restrained myself on the precarious landing.

Though it was no longer visible, the knife blade continued to vibrate in my inner sight. I realized it was not a steak knife at all, but a very long fillet knife with a venomous tapered blade that shone with the brilliance of a surgical tool. I had seen similar knives many times along the Algorta docks, for this was the sort of cutlery that saw service gutting the abundant local cod.

And while I held my place on the stairs, the point of the knife shot through the wall again and remained there, very still, as eloquent and vile a threat as I had ever experienced. And a moment later in the vice consul's apartment I heard a wet piercing noise followed by a heavy thunk, as if a sack of cement had been broken open with the point of a shovel.

A second later my wife's key turned in the front-door lock and she entered the apartment, shook her umbrella, and stripped off her rain gear and took her standard fifteen seconds to reach the bottom of the stairs. She gazed up and saw me frozen on the landing and the knife blade still shimmering through the wall of this house she had come to despise. For it was there in those four walls that I had fatally withdrawn from her as well as my students, where I had begun to match her obdurate silences with my own. In these last few months I had become so devoted to my *niña pera* that I had established a bond with this unknown juvenile beyond the wall that was more committed and passionate than any feelings I had ever shown my wife.

And when she saw the knife blade protruding from the wall, she knew all this and more. More than I could have told her if I had fallen to my knees and wallowed in confession. Everything was explained to her, my vast guilt, my repellent preoccupation, the death of our life together. Our eyes interlocked, and whatever final molecules of adhesion still existed between us dissolved in those silent seconds.

She turned and strode to the foyer. As I came quickly down the stairs, she picked up her raincoat and umbrella and opened the heavy door of our apartment and stepped out into the narrow alley-street of the Old Port. I hurried after her, calling out her name, pleading with her, but she shut the door behind her with brutal finality.

As I rushed to catch her, pushing open the door, I nearly collided with my succulent young neighbor coming home late from school. She graced me with a two-second smile and entered her door, and I stood on the stoop for a moment looking down the winding, rain-slicked street after my wife. Wretched and elated, I swung around and shut myself in once more with my utter depravity.

I mounted the stairs.

There was nothing in my heart, nothing in my head. Simply the raging current of blood that powered my flesh. I knelt at the wall and felt the magnetic throb of an act committed a thousand times and rewarded almost as often, the Pavlovian allure, a need beyond need, a death-hungering wish to see, to know, to live among that nefarious family who resided only a knife blade away.

I pressed my eye to the hole and she was there, framed in the bathroom doorway wearing her white blouse, her green plaid skirt. Behind her I could see that the toilet bowl had been wiped clean of blood. My *niña pera*'s hands hung uneasily at her sides and she was staring across the room at the wall we shared, her head canted to the side, her eyes focused on the exact spot where I pressed my face into the stone and drank her in. My pear girl, my succulent child, daughter of the devil.

And though I was certain that the glimmer of my eye was plainly visible to her and anyone else who stood on that side of the wall, I could not pull myself from the crack, for my *niña pera* had begun to lift her skirt, inch by excruciating inch, exposing those immaculate white thighs. And though there was no doubt she was performing under duress and on instructions from her father, I pressed my face still harder against the wall and drank deep of the vision before me.

Even when my succulent one cringed and averted her face, giving me a second or two of ample warning of what her father was about to do, I could not draw my eye away from the lush expanse of her thighs.

A half second later her body disappeared and a wondrous flash of darkness swelled inside me and exploded. I was launched into utter blankness, riding swiftly out beyond the edges of the visible world, flying headlong into a bright galaxy of pain.

And yet, if I had not passed out on the stairway, bleeding profusely from my ruined eye, if somehow I had managed to stay conscious for only a few seconds more, I am absolutely certain that after I suffered the loss of sight in my right eye, I would have used the last strength I had to reposition myself on the stairway and resume my vigil with my left.

In the following months of recuperation and repair, I came to discover that a man can subsist with one eye as readily as with one hand or leg. For apparently nature anticipated that some of us would commit acts of such extreme folly and self-destructiveness that we would require such anatomical redundancy if we were to survive. And in her wisdom, she created us to be two halves cojoined. So that even with one eye, a man can still see, just as with only a single hand he may still reach out and beckon for his needs. And yes, even halfheartedly, he may once again know love.

1999

DENNIS LEHANE

RUNNING OUT OF DOG

DENNIS LEHANE (1965–) was born and raised, and still lives much of the year, in the Boston area, where most of his work is set. He is a graduate of Eckerd College in Florida and the graduate writing program at Florida International University. His first book, *A Drink before the War* (1994), introduced a pair of private eyes, Patrick Kenzie and Angela Gennaro, who appeared in the author's next four books: *Darkness, Take My Hand* (1996), *Sacred* (1997), *Gone, Baby, Gone* (1998), and *Prayers for Rain* (1999). His next book, *Mystic River* (2001), attained bestseller status and firmly established Lehane as one of the country's foremost crime writers. It was bought for Hollywood by Clint Eastwood, who directed it and made it into an Academy Award–winning film in 2003, starring Sean Penn, Tim Robbins, and Kevin Bacon. *Gone, Baby, Gone* was also a successful film in 2007, directed by Ben Affleck and starring Casey Affleck and Michelle Monaghan as Kenzie and Gennaro. Lehane's seventh novel, *Shutter Island* (2003), was also adapted for film, with Martin Scorsese directing and Leonardo DiCaprio as the star. *The Given Day* (2008), Lehane's most recent novel, is a huge history of post–World War I Boston, focusing on the police riots that had such enormous influence on the American labor movement. It is the first volume of what may eventually turn out to be a trilogy.

"Running Out of Dog" was first published in the anthology *Murder and Obsession* (New York: Delacorte, 1999). It was selected for *The Best American Mystery Stories 2000* and *The Best American Mystery Stories of the Century.*

▪ ▪ ▪

THIS THING WITH *Blue and the dogs and Elgin Bern happened a while back, a few years after some of our boys — like Elgin Bern and Cal Sears — came back from Vietnam, and a lot of others — like Eddie Vorey and Carl Joe Carol, the Stewart cousins — didn't. We don't know how it worked in other towns, but that war put something secret in our boys who returned. Something quiet and untouchable. You sensed they knew things they'd never say, did things on the sly you'd never discover. Great card players, those boys, able to bluff with the best, let no joy show in their face no matter what they were holding.*

A small town is a hard place to keep a secret, and a small Southern town with all that heat and all those open windows is an even harder place than most. But those boys who came back from overseas, they seemed to have mastered the trick of privacy. And the way it's always been in this town, you get a sizable crop of young, hard men coming up at the same time, they sort of set the tone.

So, not long after the war, we were a quieter town, a less trusting one (or so some of us seemed to think), and that's right when tobacco money and textile money reached a sort of critical mass and created construction money and pretty soon there was talk that our small town should maybe get a little bigger, maybe build something that would bring in more tourist dollars than we'd been getting from fireworks and pecans.

That's when some folks came up with this Eden Falls idea—a big carnival-type park with roller coasters and water slides and such. Why should all those Yankees spend all their money in Florida? South Carolina had sun too. Had golf courses and grapefruit and no end of KOA campgrounds.

So now a little town called Eden was going to have Eden Falls. We were going to be on the map, people said. We were going to be in all the brochures. We were small now, people said, but just you wait. Just you wait.

And that's how things stood back then, the year Perkin and Jewel Lut's marriage hit a few bumps and Elgin Bern took up with Shelley Briggs and no one seemed able to hold on to their dogs.

The problem with dogs in Eden, South Carolina, was that the owners who bred them bred a lot of them. Or they allowed them to run free where they met up with other dogs of opposite gender and achieved the same result. This wouldn't have been so bad if Eden weren't so close to I-95, and if the dogs weren't in the habit of bolting into traffic and fucking up the bumpers of potential tourists.

The mayor, Big Bobby Vargas, went to a mayoral conference up in Beaufort, where the governor made a surprise appearance to tell everyone how pissed off he was about this dog thing. Lot of money being poured into Eden these days, the governor said, lot of steps being taken to change her image, and he for one would be goddamned if a bunch of misbehaving canines was going to mess all that up.

"Boys," he'd said, looking Big Bobby Vargas dead in the eye, "they're starting to call this state the Devil's Kennel 'cause of all them pooch corpses along the interstate. And I don't know about you all, but I don't think that's a real pretty name."

Big Bobby told Elgin and Blue he'd never heard anyone call it the Devil's Kennel in his life. Heard a lot worse, sure, but never that. Big Bobby said the governor was full of shit. But, being the governor and all, he was sort of entitled.

The dogs in Eden had been a problem going back to the 1920s and a part-time breeder named J. Mallon Ellenburg who, if his arms weren't up to their elbows in the guts of the tractors and combines he repaired for a living, was usually lashing out at something—his family when they weren't quick enough, his dogs when the family was. J. Mallon Ellenburg's dogs were mixed breeds and mongrels and they ran in packs, as did their offspring, and several generations later, those packs still moved through the Eden night like wolves, their bodies stripped to muscle and gristle, tense and angry, growling in the dark at J. Mallon Ellenburg's ghost.

Big Bobby went to the trouble of measuring exactly how much of 95 crossed through Eden, and he came up with 2.8 miles. Not much really, but still an average of .74 dog a day or 4.9 dogs a week. Big Bobby wanted the rest of the state funds the governor was going to be doling out at year's end, and if that meant getting rid of five dogs a week, give or take, then that's what was going to get done.

"On the QT," he said to Elgin and Blue, "on the QT, what we going to do, boys, is set up in some trees and shoot every canine who gets within barking distance of that interstate."

Elgin didn't much like this "we" stuff. First place, Big Bobby'd said "we" that time in Double O's four years ago. This was before he'd become mayor, when he was nothing more than a county tax assessor who shot pool at Double O's every other night, same as Elgin and Blue. But one night, after Harlan and Chub Uke had roughed him up over a matter of some pocket change, and knowing that neither Elgin nor Blue was too fond of the Uke family either, Big Bobby'd said, "We going to settle those boys' asses tonight," and started running his mouth the minute the brothers entered the bar.

Time the smoke cleared, Blue had a broken hand, Harlan and Chub were curled up on the floor, and Elgin's lip was busted. Big Bobby, meanwhile, was hiding under the pool table, and Cal Sears was asking who was going to pay for the pool stick Elgin had snapped across the back of Chub's head.

So Elgin heard Mayor Big Bobby saying "we" and remembered the ten dollars it had cost him for that pool stick, and he said, "No, sir, you can count me out this particular enterprise."

Big Bobby looked disappointed. Elgin was a veteran of a foreign war, former Marine, a marksman. "Shit," Big Bobby said, "what good are you, you don't use the skills Uncle Sam spent good money teaching you?"

Elgin shrugged. "Damn, Bobby. I guess not much."

But Blue kept his hand in, as both Big Bobby and Elgin knew he would. All the job required was a guy didn't mind sitting in a tree who liked to shoot things. Hell, Blue was home.

Elgin didn't have the time to be sitting up in a tree anyway. The past few months, he'd been working like crazy after they'd broke ground at Eden Falls — mixing cement, digging postholes, draining swamp water to shore up the foundation — with the real work still to come. There'd be several more months of drilling and bilging, spreading cement like cake icing, and erecting scaffolding to erect walls to erect facades. There'd be the hump-and-grind of rolling along in the dump trucks and drill trucks, the forklifts and cranes and industrial diggers, until the constant heave and jerk of them drove up his spine or into his kidneys like a corkscrew.

Time to sit up in a tree shooting dogs? Shit. Elgin didn't have time to take a piss some days.

And then on top of all the work, he'd been seeing Drew Briggs's ex-wife, Shelley, lately. Shelley was the receptionist at Perkin Lut's Auto Emporium, and one day Elgin had brought his Impala in for a tire rotation and they'd got to talking. She'd been divorced from Drew over a year, and they waited a couple of months to show respect, but after a while they began showing up at Double O's and down at the IHOP together.

Once they drove clear to Myrtle Beach together for the weekend. People asked them what it was like, and they said, "Just like the postcards." Since the postcards never mentioned the price of a room at the Hilton, Elgin and Shelley didn't mention that all they'd done was drive up and down the beach twice before settling in a motel a bit west in Conway. Nice, though; had a color TV and one of those switches turned the bathroom into a sauna if you let the shower run. They'd started making love in the sauna, finished up on the bed with the steam coiling out from the bathroom and brushing their heels. Afterward, he pushed her hair back off her forehead and looked in her eyes and told her he could get used to this.

She said, "But wouldn't it cost a lot to install a sauna in your trailer?" then waited a full thirty seconds before she smiled.

Elgin liked that about her, the way she let him know he was still just a man after all, always would take himself too seriously, part of his nature. Letting him know she might be around to keep him apprised of that fact every time he did. Keep him from pushing a bullet into the breech of a .30-06, slamming the bolt home, firing into the flank of some wild dog.

Sometimes, when they'd shut down the site early for the day—if it had rained real heavy and the soil loosened near a foundation, or if supplies were running late—he'd drop by Lut's to see her. She'd smile as if he'd brought her flowers, say, "Caught boozing on the job again?" or some other smart-ass thing, but it made him feel good, as if something in his chest suddenly realized it was free to breathe.

Before Shelley, Elgin had spent a long time without a woman he could publicly acknowledge as his. He'd gone with Mae Shiller from fifteen to nineteen, but she'd gotten lonely while he was overseas, and he'd returned to find her gone from Eden, married to a boy up in South of the Border, the two of them working a corn-dog concession stand, making a tidy profit, folks said. Elgin dated some, but it took him a while to get over Mae, to get over the loss of something he'd always expected to have, the sound of her laugh and an image of her stepping naked from Cooper's Lake, her pale flesh beaded with water, having been the things that got Elgin through the jungle, through the heat, through the ticking of his own death he'd heard in his ears every night he'd been over there.

About a year after he'd come home, Jewel Lut had come to visit her mother, who still lived in the trailer park where Jewel had grown up with Elgin and Blue, where Elgin still lived. On her way out, she'd dropped by Elgin's and they'd sat out front of his trailer in some folding chairs, had a few drinks, talked about old times. He told her a bit about Vietnam, and she told him a bit about marriage. How it wasn't what you expected, how Perkin Lut might know a lot of things but he didn't know a damn sight about having fun.

There was something about Jewel Lut that sank into men's flesh the way heat did. It wasn't just that she was pretty, had a beautiful body, moved in a loose, languid way that made you picture her naked no matter what she was wearing. No, there was more to it. Jewel, never the brightest girl in town and not even the most charming, had something in her eyes that none of the women Elgin had ever met had; it was a capacity for living, for taking moments—no matter how small or inconsequential—and squeezing every last thing you could out of them.

Jewel gobbled up life, dove into it like it was a cool pond cut in the shade of a mountain on the hottest day of the year.

That look in her eyes — the one that never left — said, Let's have fun, goddammit. Let's eat. Now.

She and Elgin hadn't been stupid enough to do anything that night, not even after Elgin caught that look in her eyes, saw it was directed at him, saw she wanted to eat.

Elgin knew how small Eden was, how its people loved to insinuate and pry and talk. So he and Jewel worked it out, a once-a-week thing mostly that happened down in Carlyle, at a small cabin had been in Elgin's family since before the War Between the States. There, Elgin and Jewel were free to partake of each other, squeeze and bite and swallow and inhale each other, to make love in the lake, on the porch, in the tiny kitchen.

They hardly ever talked, and when they did it was about nothing at all, really — the decline in quality of the meat at Billy's Butcher Shop, rumors that parking meters were going to be installed in front of the courthouse, if McGarrett and the rest of Five-O would ever put the cuffs on Wo Fat.

There was an unspoken understanding that he was free to date any woman he chose and that she'd never leave Perkin Lut. And that was just fine. This wasn't about love; it was about appetite.

Sometimes, Elgin would see her in town or hear Blue speak about her in that puppy-dog-love way he'd been speaking about her since high school, and he'd find himself surprised by the realization that he slept with this woman. That no one knew. That it could go on forever, if both of them remained careful, vigilant against the wrong look, the wrong tone in their voices when they spoke in public.

He couldn't entirely put his finger on what need she satisfied, only that he needed her in that lakefront cabin once a week, that it had something to do with walking out of the jungle alive, with the ticking of his own death he'd heard for a full year. Jewel was somehow reward for that, a fringe benefit. To be naked and spent with her lying atop him and seeing that look in her eyes that said she was ready to go again, ready to gobble him up like oxygen. He'd earned that by shooting at shapes in the night, pressed against those damp foxhole walls that never stayed shored up for long, only to come home to a woman who couldn't wait, who'd discarded him as easily as she would a once-favored doll she'd grown beyond, looked back upon with a wistful mix of nostalgia and disdain.

He'd always told himself that when he found the right woman, his passion for Jewel, his need for those nights at the lake, would disappear. And, truth was, since he'd been with Shelley Briggs, he and Jewel had cooled it. Shelley wasn't Perkin, he told Jewel; she'd figure it out soon enough if he left town once a week, came back with bite marks on his abdomen.

Jewel said, "Fine. We'll get back to it whenever you're ready."

Knowing there'd be a next time, even if Elgin wouldn't admit it to himself.

So Elgin, who'd been so lonely in the year after his discharge, now had two women. Sometimes, he didn't know what to think of that. When you were alone, the happiness of others boiled your insides. Beauty seemed ugly. Laughter seemed evil. The casual grazing of one lover's hand into another was enough to make you want to cut them off at the wrist. *I will never be loved,* you said. *I will never know joy.*

He wondered sometimes how Blue made it through. Blue, who'd never had a girlfriend he hadn't rented by the half hour. Who was too ugly and small and just plain weird to evoke anything in women but fear or pity. Blue, who'd been carrying a torch for Jewel Lut since long before she married Perkin and kept carrying it with a quiet fever Elgin could only occasionally identify with. Blue, he knew, saw Jewel Lut as a queen, as the only woman who existed for him in Eden, South Carolina. All because she'd been nice to him, pals with him and Elgin, back about a thousand years ago, before sex, before breasts, before Elgin or Blue had even the smallest clue what that thing between their legs was for, before Perkin Lut had come along with his daddy's money and his nice smile and his bullshit stories about how many men he'd have killed in the war if only the draft board had seen fit to let him go.

Blue figured if he was nice enough, kind enough, waited long enough — then one day Jewel would see his decency, need to cling to it.

Elgin never bothered telling Blue that some women didn't want decency. Some women didn't want a nice guy. Some women, and some men too, wanted to get into a bed, turn out the lights, and feast on each other like animals until it hurt to move.

Blue would never guess that Jewel was that kind of woman, because she was always so sweet to him, treated him like a child really, and with every friendly hello she gave him, every pat on the shoulder, every "What you been up to, old bud?" Blue pushed her further and further up the pedestal he'd built in his mind.

"I seen him at the Emporium one time," Shelley told Elgin. "He just come in for no reason anyone understood and sat reading magazines until Jewel came in to see Perkin about something. And Blue, he just stared at her. Just stared at her talking to Perkin in the showroom. When she finally looked back, he stood up and left."

Elgin hated hearing about, talking about, or thinking about Jewel when he was with Shelley. It made him feel unclean and unworthy.

"Crazy love," he said to end the subject.

"Crazy something, babe."

Nights sometimes, Elgin would sit with Shelley in front of his trailer, listen to the cicadas hum through the scrawny pine, smell the night and the rock salt mixed with gravel; the piña colada shampoo Shelley used made him think of Hawaii though he'd never been, and he'd think how their love wasn't crazy love, wasn't burning so fast and furious it'd burn itself out they weren't careful. And that was fine with him. If he could just get his head around this Jewel Lut thing, stop seeing her naked and waiting and looking back over her shoulder at him in the cabin, then he could make something with Shelley. She was worth it. She might not be able to fuck like Jewel, and, truth be told, he didn't laugh as much with her, but Shelley was what you aspired to. A good woman, who'd be a good mother, who'd stick by you when times got tough. Sometimes he'd take her hand in his and hold it for no other reason but the doing of it. She caught him one night, some look in his eyes, maybe the way he tilted his head to look at her small white hand in his big brown one.

She said, "Damn, Elgin, if you ain't simple sometimes." Then she came out of her chair in a rush and straddled him, kissed him as if she were trying to take a piece of him back with her. She said, "Baby, we ain't getting any younger. You know?"

And he knew, somehow, at that moment why some men build families and others shoot dogs. He just wasn't sure where he fit in the equation.

He said, "We ain't, are we?"

Blue had been Elgin's best buddy since either of them could remember, but Elgin had been wondering about it lately. Blue'd always been a little different, something Elgin liked, sure, but there was more to it now. Blue was the kind of guy you never knew if he was quiet because he didn't have anything to say or, because what he had to say was so horrible, he knew enough not to send it out into the atmosphere.

When they'd been kids, growing up in the trailer park, Blue used to be out at all hours because his mother was either entertaining a man or had gone out and forgotten to leave him the key. Back then, Blue had this thing for cockroaches. He'd collect them in a jar, then drop bricks on them to test their resiliency. He told Elgin once, "That's what they are—resilient. Every generation, we have to come up with new ways to kill 'em because they get immune to the poisons we had before." After a while, Blue took to dousing them in gasoline, lighting them up, seeing how resilient they were then.

Elgin's folks told him to stay away from the strange, dirty kid with the white-trash mother, but Elgin felt sorry for Blue. He was half Elgin's size even though they were the same age; you could place your thumb and forefinger around Blue's biceps and meet them on the other side. Elgin hated how Blue seemed to have only two pairs of clothes, both usually dirty, and how sometimes they'd pass his trailer together and hear the animal sounds coming from inside, the grunts and moans, the slapping of flesh. Half the time you couldn't tell if Blue's old lady was in there fucking or fighting. And always the sound of country music mingled in with all that animal noise, Blue's mother and her man of the moment listening to it on the transistor radio she'd given Blue one Christmas.

"*My* fucking radio," Blue said once and shook his small head, the only time Elgin ever saw him react to what went on in that trailer.

Blue was a reader—knew more about science and ecology, about anatomy and blue whales and conversion tables than anyone Elgin knew. Most everyone figured the kid for a mute—hell, he'd been held back twice in fourth grade—but with Elgin he'd sometimes chat up a storm while they puffed smokes together down at the drainage ditch behind the park. He'd talk about whales, how they bore only one child, who they were fiercely protective of, but how if another child was orphaned, a mother whale would take it as her own, protect it as fiercely as she did the one she gave birth to. He told Elgin how sharks never slept, how electrical currents worked, what a depth charge was. Elgin, never much of a talker, just sat and listened, ate it up, and waited for more.

The older they got, the more Elgin became Blue's protector, till finally, the year Blue's face exploded with acne, Elgin got in about two fights a day until there was no one left to fight. Everyone knew—they were brothers. And if Elgin didn't get you from the front, Blue was sure to take care of you from behind, like that time a can of acid fell on Roy Hubrist's arm in shop, or the time someone hit Carnell Lewis from behind with a brick, then cut his Achilles tendon with a razor while he lay out cold. Everyone knew it was Blue, even if no one actually saw him do it.

Elgin figured with Roy and Carnell, they'd had it coming. No great loss. It was since Elgin'd come back from Vietnam, though, that he'd noticed some things and kept them to himself, wondered what he was going to do the day he'd know he had to do something.

There was the owl someone had set afire and hung upside down from a telephone wire, the cats who turned up missing in the blocks that surrounded Blue's shack off Route 11. There were the small pink panties Elgin had seen sticking out from under Blue's bed one morning when he'd come to get him for some cleanup work at a site. He'd checked the missing-persons reports for days, but it hadn't come to anything, so he'd just decided Blue had picked them up himself, fed a fantasy or two. He didn't forget, though, couldn't shake the way those panties had curled upward out of the brown dust under Blue's bed, seemed to be pleading for something.

He'd never bothered asking Blue about any of this. That never worked. Blue just shut down at times like that, stared off somewhere as if something you couldn't hear was drowning out your words, something you couldn't see was taking up his line of vision. Blue, floating away on you, until you stopped cluttering up his mind with useless talk.

One Saturday, Elgin went into town with Shelley so she could get her hair done at Martha's Unisex on Main. In Martha's, as Dottie Leeds gave Shelley a shampoo and rinse, Elgin felt like he'd stumbled into a chapel of womanhood. There was Jim Hayder's teenage daughter, Sonny, getting one of those feathered cuts was growing popular these days and several older women who still wore beehives, getting them reset or plastered or whatever they did to keep them up like that. There was Joylene Covens and Lila Sims having their nails done while their husbands golfed and the black maids watched their kids, and Martha and Dottie and Esther and Gertrude and Hayley dancing and flitting, laughing and chattering among the chairs, calling everyone "Honey," and all of them—the young, the old, the rich, and Shelley—kicking back like they did this every day, knew each other more intimately than they did their husbands or children or boyfriends.

When Dottie Leeds looked up from Shelley's head and said, "Elgin, honey, can we get you a sports page or something?" the whole place burst out laughing, Shelley included. Elgin smiled though he didn't feel like it and gave them all a sheepish wave that got a bigger laugh, and he told Shelley he'd be back in a bit and left.

He headed up Main toward the town square, wondering what it was those women seemed to know so effortlessly that completely escaped him, and saw Perkin Lut walking in a circle outside Dexter Isley's Five &

Dime. It was one of those days when the wet, white heat was so overpowering that unless you were in Martha's, the one place in town with central air-conditioning, most people stayed inside with their shades down and tried not to move much.

And there was Perkin Lut walking the soles of his shoes into the ground, turning in circles like a little kid trying to make himself dizzy.

Perkin and Elgin had known each other since kindergarten, but Elgin could never remember liking the man much. Perkin's old man, Mance Lut, had pretty much built Eden, and he'd spent a lot of money keeping Perkin out of the war, hid his son up in Chapel Hill, North Carolina, for so many semesters even Perkin couldn't remember what he'd majored in. A lot of men who'd gone overseas and come back hated Perkin for that, as did the families of most of the men who hadn't come back, but that wasn't Elgin's problem with Perkin. Hell, if Elgin'd had the money, he'd have stayed out of that shitty war too.

What Elgin couldn't abide was that there was something in Perkin that protected him from consequence. Something that made him look down on people who paid for their sins, who fell without a safety net to catch them.

It had happened more than once that Elgin had found himself thrusting in and out of Perkin's wife and thinking, Take that, Perkin. Take that.

But this afternoon, Perkin didn't have his salesman's smile or aloof glance. When Elgin stopped by him and said, "Hey, Perkin, how you?" Perkin looked up at him with eyes so wild they seemed about to jump out of their sockets.

"I'm not good, Elgin. Not good."

"What's the matter?"

Perkin nodded to himself several times, looked over Elgin's shoulder. "I'm fixing to do something about that."

"About what?"

"About that." Perkin's jaw gestured over Elgin's shoulder.

Elgin turned around, looked across Main and through the windows of Miller's Laundromat, saw Jewel Lut pulling her clothes from the dryer, saw Blue standing beside her, taking a pair of jeans from the pile and starting to fold. If either of them had looked up and over, they'd have seen Elgin and Perkin Lut easily enough, but Elgin knew they wouldn't. There was an air to the two of them that seemed to block out the rest of the world in that bright Laundromat as easily as it would in a dark bedroom. Blue's lips moved and Jewel laughed, flipped a T-shirt on his head.

"I'm fixing to do something right now," Perkin said.

Elgin looked at him, could see that was a lie, something Perkin was repeating to himself in hopes it would come true. Perkin was successful in business, and for more reasons than just his daddy's money, but he wasn't the kind of man who did things; he was the kind of man who had things done.

Elgin looked across the street again. Blue still had the T-shirt sitting atop his head. He said something else and Jewel covered her mouth with her hand when she laughed.

"Don't you have a washer and dryer at your house, Perkin?"

Perkin rocked back on his heels. "Washer broke. Jewel decides to come in town." He looked at Elgin. "We ain't getting along so well these days. She keeps reading those magazines, Elgin. You know the ones? Talking about liberation, leaving your bra at home, shit like that." He pointed across the street. "Your friend's a problem."

Your friend.

Elgin looked at Perkin, felt a sudden anger he couldn't completely understand, and with it a desire to say, That's my friend and he's talking to my fuck-buddy. Get it, Perkin?

Instead, he just shook his head and left Perkin there, walked across the street to the Laundromat.

Blue took the T-shirt off his head when he saw Elgin enter. A smile, half frozen on his pitted face, died as he blinked into the sunlight blaring through the windows.

Jewel said, "Hey, we got another helper!" She tossed a pair of men's briefs over Blue's head, hit Elgin in the chest with them.

"Hey, Jewel."

"Hey, Elgin. Long time." Her eyes dropped from his, settled on a towel.

Didn't seem like it at the moment to Elgin. Seemed almost as if he'd been out at the lake with her as recently as last night. He could taste her in his mouth, smell her skin damp with a light sweat.

And standing there with Blue, it also seemed like they were all three back in that trailer park, and Jewel hadn't aged a bit. Still wore her red hair long and messy, still dressed in clothes seemed to have been picked up, wrinkled, off her closet floor and nothing fancy about them in the first place, but draped over her body, they were sexier than clothes other rich women bought in New York once a year.

This afternoon, she wore a crinkly, paisley dress that might have been on the pink side once but had faded to a pasty newspaper color after years of washing. Nothing special about it, not too high up her thigh or down her chest, and loose — but something about her body made it appear like she might just ripen right out of it any second.

Elgin handed the briefs to Blue as he joined them at the folding table. For a while, none of them said anything. They picked clothes from the large pile and folded, and the only sound was Jewel whistling.

Then Jewel laughed.

"What?" Blue said.

"Aw, nothing." She shook her head. "Seems like we're just one happy family here, though, don't it?"

Blue looked stunned. He looked at Elgin. He looked at Jewel. He looked at the pair of small, light blue socks he held in his hands, the monogram *JL* stitched in the cotton. He looked at Jewel again.

"Yeah," he said eventually, and Elgin heard a tremor in his voice he'd never heard before. "Yeah, it does."

Elgin looked up at one of the upper dryer doors. It had been swung out at eye level when the dryer had been emptied. The center of the door was a circle of glass, and Elgin could see Main Street reflected in it, the white posts that supported the wood awning over the Five & Dime, Perkin Lut walking in circles, his head down, heat shimmering in waves up and down Main.

The dog was green.

Blue had used some of the money Big Bobby'd paid him over the past few weeks to upgrade his target scope. The new scope was huge, twice the width of the rifle barrel, and because the days were getting shorter, it was outfitted with a light-amplification device. Elgin had used similar scopes in the jungle, and he'd never liked them, even when they'd saved his life and those of his platoon, picked up Charlie coming through the dense flora like icy gray ghosts. Night scopes — or LADs as they'd called them over there — were just plain unnatural, and Elgin always felt like he was looking through a telescope from the bottom of a lake. He had no idea where Blue would have gotten one, but hunters in Eden had been showing up with all sorts of weird Marine or Army surplus shit these last few years; Elgin had even heard of a hunting party using grenades to scare up fish — blowing 'em up into the boat already half-cooked, all you had to do was scale 'em.

The dog was green, the highway was beige, the top of the tree line was yellow, and the trunks were the color of Army fatigues.

Blue said, "What you think?"

They were up in the tree house Blue'd built. Nice wood, two lawn chairs, a tarp hanging from the branch overhead, a cooler filled with Coors. Blue'd built a railing across the front, perfect for resting your elbows when you took aim. Along the tree trunk, he'd mounted a huge klieg light plugged to a portable generator, because while it was illegal to "shine" deer, nobody'd ever said anything about shining wild dogs. Blue was definitely home.

Elgin shrugged. Just like in the jungle, he wasn't sure he was meant to see the world this way — faded to the shades and textures of old photographs. The dog, too, seemed to sense that it had stepped out of time somehow, into this seaweed circle punched through the landscape. It sniffed the air with a misshapen snout, but the rest of its body was tensed into one tight muscle, leaning forward as if it smelled prey.

Blue said, "You wanna do it?"

The stock felt hard against Elgin's shoulder. The trigger, curled under his index finger, was cold and thick, something about it that itched his finger and the back of his head simultaneously, a voice back there with the itch in his head saying, "Fire."

What you could never talk about down at the bar to people who hadn't been there, to people who wanted to know, was what it had been like firing on human beings, on those icy gray ghosts in the dark jungle. Elgin had been in fourteen battles over the course of his twelve-month tour, and he couldn't say with certainty that he'd ever killed anyone. He'd shot some of those shapes, seen them go down, but never the blood, never their eyes when the bullets hit. It had all been a cluster-fuck of swift and sudden noise and color, an explosion of white lights and tracers, green bush, red fire, screams in the night. And afterward, if it was clear, you walked into the jungle and saw the corpses, wondered if you'd hit this body or that one or any at all.

And the only thing you were sure of was that you were too fucking hot and still — this was the terrible thing, but oddly exhilarating too — deeply afraid.

Elgin lowered Blue's rifle, stared across the interstate, now the color of seashell, at the dark mint tree line. The dog was barely noticeable, a soft dark shape amid other soft dark shapes.

He said, "No, Blue, thanks," and handed him the rifle.

Blue said, "Suit yourself, buddy." He reached behind them and pulled the beaded string on the klieg light. As the white light erupted across the highway and the dog froze, blinking in the brightness, Elgin found himself wondering what the fucking point of a LAD scope was when you were just going to shine the animal anyway.

Blue swung the rifle around, leaned into the railing, and put a round in the center of the animal, right by its rib cage. The dog jerked inward, as if someone had whacked it with a bat, and as it teetered on wobbly legs, Blue pulled back on the bolt, drove it home again, and shot the dog in the head. The dog flipped over on its side, most of its skull gone, back leg kicking at the road like it was trying to ride a bicycle.

"You think Jewel Lut might, I dunno, like me?" Blue said.

Elgin cleared his throat. "Sure. She's always liked you."

"But I mean . . ." Blue shrugged, seemed embarrassed suddenly. "How about this: You think a girl like that could take to Australia?"

"Australia?"

Blue smiled at Elgin. "Australia."

"Australia?" he said again.

Blue reached back and shut off the light. "Australia. They got some wild dingoes there, buddy. Could make some real money. Jewel told me the other day how they got real nice beaches. But dingoes too. Big Bobby said people're starting to bitch about what's happening here, asking where Rover is and such, and anyway, ain't too many dogs left dumb enough to come this way anymore. Australia," he said, "they never run out of dog. Sooner or later, here, I'm gonna run out of dog."

Elgin nodded. Sooner or later, Blue would run out of dog. He wondered if Big Bobby'd thought that one through, if he had a contingency plan, if he had access to the National Guard.

"The boy's just, what you call it, zealous," Big Bobby told Elgin.

They were sitting in Phil's Barbershop on Main. Phil had gone to lunch, and Big Bobby'd drawn the shades so people'd think he was making some important decision of state.

Elgin said, "He ain't zealous, Big Bobby. He's losing it. Thinks he's in love with Jewel Lut."

"He's always thought that."

"Yeah, but now maybe he's thinking she might like him a bit too."

Big Bobby said, "How come you never call me Mayor?"

Elgin sighed.

"All right, all right. Look," Big Bobby said, picking up one of the hair-tonic bottles on Phil's counter and sniffing it, "so Blue likes his job a little bit."

Elgin said, "There's more to it and you know it."

Playing with combs now. "I do?"

"Bobby, he's got a taste for shooting things now."

"Wait." He held up a pair of fat, stubby hands. "Blue always liked to shoot things. Everyone knows that. Shit, if he wasn't so short and didn't have six or seven million little health problems, he'd a been the first guy in this town to go to the 'Nam. 'Stead, he had to sit back here while you boys had all the fun."

Calling it the 'Nam. Like Big Bobby had any idea. Calling it fun. Shit.

"Dingoes," Elgin said.

"Dingoes?"

"Dingoes. He's saying he's going to Australia to shoot dingoes."

"Do him a world of good too." Big Bobby sat back down in the barber's chair beside Elgin. "He can see the sights, that sort of thing."

"Bobby, he ain't going to Australia and you know it. Hell, Blue ain't never stepped over the county line in his life."

Big Bobby polished his belt buckle with the cuff of his sleeve. "Well, what you want me to do about it?"

"I don't know. I'm just telling you. Next time you see him, Bobby, you look in his fucking eyes."

"Yeah. What'll I see?"

Elgin turned his head, looked at him. "Nothing."

Bobby said, "He's your buddy."

Elgin thought of the small panties curling out of the dust under Blue's bed. "Yeah, but he's your problem."

Big Bobby put his hands behind his head, stretched in the chair. "Well, people getting suspicious about all the dogs disappearing, so I'm going to have to shut this operation down immediately anyway."

He wasn't getting it. "Bobby, you shut this operation down, someone's gonna get a world's worth of that nothing in Blue's eyes."

Big Bobby shrugged, a man who'd made a career out of knowing what was beyond him.

The first time Perkin Lut struck Jewel in public was at Chuck's Diner.

Elgin and Shelley were sitting just three booths away when they heard a racket of falling glasses and plates, and by the time they came out of their booth, Jewel was lying on the tile floor with shattered glass and chunks of bone china by her elbows and Perkin standing over her, his arms shaking, a look in his eyes that said he'd surprised himself as much as anyone else.

Elgin looked at Jewel, on her knees, the hem of her dress getting stained by the spilled food, and he looked away before she caught his eye, because if that happened he just might do something stupid, fuck Perkin up a couple-three ways.

"Aw, Perkin," Chuck Blade said, coming from behind the counter to help Jewel up, wiping gravy off his hands against his apron.

"We don't respect that kind of behavior 'round here, Mr. Lut," Clara Blade said. "Won't have it neither."

Chuck Blade helped Jewel to her feet, his eyes cast down at his broken plates, the half a steak lying in a soup of beans by his shoe. Jewel had a welt growing on her right cheek, turning a bright red as she placed her hand on the table for support.

"I didn't mean it," Perkin said.

Clara Blade snorted and pulled the pen from behind her ear, began itemizing the damage on a cocktail napkin.

"I didn't." Perkin noticed Elgin and Shelley. He locked eyes with Elgin, held out his hands. "I swear."

Elgin turned away and that's when he saw Blue coming through the door. He had no idea where he'd come from, though it ran through his head that Blue could have just been standing outside looking in, could have been standing there for an hour.

Like a lot of small guys, Blue had speed, and he never seemed to walk in a straight line. He moved as if he were constantly sidestepping tackles or land mines — with sudden, unpredictable pivots that left you watching the space where he'd been, instead of the place he'd ended up.

Blue didn't say anything, but Elgin could see the determination for homicide in his eyes and Perkin saw it too, backed up, and slipped on the mess on the floor and stumbled back, trying to regain his balance as Blue came past Shelley and tried to lunge past Elgin.

Elgin caught him at the waist, lifted him off the ground, and held on tight because he knew how slippery Blue could be in these situations. You'd think you had him and he'd just squirm away from you, hit somebody with a glass.

Elgin tucked his head down and headed for the door, Blue flopped over his shoulder like a bag of cement mix, Blue screaming, "You see me, Perkin? You see me? I'm a last face you see, Perkin! Real soon."

Elgin hit the open doorway, felt the night heat on his face as Blue screamed, "Jewel! You all right? Jewel?"

Blue didn't say much back at Elgin's trailer.

He tried to explain to Shelley how pure Jewel was, how hitting something that innocent was like spitting on the Bible.

Shelley didn't say anything, and after a while Blue shut up too.

Elgin just kept plying him with Beam, knowing Blue's lack of tolerance for it, and pretty soon Blue passed out on the couch, his pitted face still red with rage.

"He's never been exactly right in the head, has he?" Shelley said.

Elgin ran his hand down her bare arm, pulled her shoulder in tighter against his chest, heard Blue snoring from the front of the trailer. "No, ma'am."

She rose above him, her dark hair falling to his face, tickling the corners of his eyes. "But you've been his friend."

Elgin nodded.

She touched his cheek with her hand. "Why?"

Elgin thought about it a bit, started talking to her about the little, dirty kid and his cockroach flambés, of the animal sounds that came from his mother's trailer. The way Blue used to sit by the drainage ditch, all pulled into himself, his body tight. Elgin thought of all those roaches and cats and rabbits and dogs, and he told Shelley that he'd always thought Blue was dying, ever since he'd met him, leaking away in front of his eyes.

"Everyone dies," she said.

"Yeah." He rose up on his elbow, rested his free hand on her warm hip. "Yeah, but with most of us it's like we're growing toward something and then we die. But with Blue, it's like he ain't never grown toward nothing. He's just been dying real slowly since he was born."

She shook her head. "I'm not getting you."

He thought of the mildew that used to soak the walls in Blue's mother's trailer, of the mold and dust in Blue's shack off Route 11, of the rotting smell that had grown out of the drainage ditch when they were kids. The way Blue looked at it all — seemed to be at one with it — as if he felt a bond.

Shelley said, "Babe, what do you think about getting out of here?"

"Where?"

"I dunno. Florida. Georgia. Someplace else."

"I got a job. You too."

"You can always get construction jobs other places. Receptionist jobs too."

"We grew up here."

She nodded. "But maybe it's time to start our life somewhere else."

He said, "Let me think about it."

She tilted his chin so she was looking in his eyes. "You've *been* thinking about it."

He nodded. "Maybe I want to think about it some more."

In the morning, when they woke up, Blue was gone.

Shelley looked at the rumpled couch, over at Elgin. For a good minute they just stood there, looking from the couch to each other, the couch to each other.

An hour later, Shelley called from work, told Elgin that Perkin Lut was in his office as always, no signs of physical damage.

Elgin said, "If you see Blue . . ."

"Yeah?"

Elgin thought about it. "I dunno. Call the cops. Tell Perkin to bail out a back door. That sound right?"

"Sure."

Big Bobby came to the site later that morning, said, "I go over to Blue's place to tell him we got to end this dog thing and—"

"Did you tell him it was over?" Elgin asked.

"Let me finish. Let me explain."

"Did you tell him?"

"Let me finish." Bobby wiped his face with a handkerchief. "I was gonna tell him, but—"

"You didn't tell him."

"But Jewel Lut was there."

"What?"

Big Bobby put his hand on Elgin's elbow, led him away from the other workers. "I said Jewel was there. The two of them sitting at the kitchen table, having breakfast."

"In Blue's place?"

Big Bobby nodded. "Biggest dump I ever seen. Smells like something I-don't-know-what. But bad. And there's Jewel, pretty as can be in her summer dress and soft skin and makeup, eating Eggos and grits with Blue, big brown shiner under her eye. She smiles at me, says, 'Hey, Big Bobby,' and goes back to eating."

"And that was it?"

"How come no one ever calls me Mayor?"

"And that was it?" Elgin repeated.

"Yeah. Blue asks me to take a seat, I say I got business. He says him too."

"What's that mean?" Elgin heard his own voice, hard and sharp.

Big Bobby took a step back from it. "Hell do I know? Could mean he's going out to shoot more dog."

"So you never told him you were shutting down the operation."

Big Bobby's eyes were wide and confused. "You hear what I told you? He was in there with Jewel. Her all doll-pretty and him looking, well, ugly as usual. Whole situation was too weird. I got out."

"Blue said he had business too."

"He said he had business too," Bobby said, and walked away.

The next week, they showed up in town together a couple of times, buying some groceries, toiletries for Jewel, boxes of shells for Blue.

They never held hands or kissed or did anything romantic, but they were together, and people talked. Said, Well, of all things. And I never thought I'd see the day. How do you like that? I guess this is the day the cows actually come home.

Blue called and invited Shelley and Elgin to join them one Sunday afternoon for a late breakfast at the IHOP. Shelley begged off, said something about coming down with the flu, but Elgin went. He was curious to see where this was going, what Jewel was thinking, how she thought her hanging around Blue was going to come to anything but bad.

He could feel the eyes of the whole place on them as they ate.

"See where he hit me?" Jewel tilted her head, tucked her beautiful red hair back behind her ear. The mark on her cheekbone, in the shape of a small rain puddle, was faded yellow now, its edges roped by a sallow beige.

Elgin nodded.

"Still can't believe the son of a bitch hit me," she said, but there was no rage in her voice anymore, just a mild sense of drama, as if she'd pushed the words out of her mouth the way she believed she should say them. But the emotion she must have felt when Perkin's hand hit her face, when she fell to the floor in front of people she'd known all her life — that seemed to have faded with the mark on her cheekbone.

"Perkin Lut," she said with a snort, then laughed.

Elgin looked at Blue. He'd never seemed so . . . fluid in all the time Elgin had known him. The way he cut into his pancakes, swept them off his plate with a smooth dip of the fork tines; the swift dab of the napkin against his lips after every bite; the attentive swivel of his head whenever Jewel spoke, usually in tandem with the lifting of his coffee mug to his mouth.

This was not a Blue Elgin recognized. Except when he was handling weapons, Blue moved in jerks and spasms. Tremors rippled through his limbs and caused his fingers to drop things, his elbows and knees to move too fast, crack against solid objects. Blue's blood seemed to move too quickly through his veins, made his muscles obey his brain after a quarter-second delay and then too rapidly, as if to catch up on lost time.

But now he moved in concert, like an athlete or a jungle cat.

That's what you do to men, Jewel: you give them a confidence so total it finds their limbs.

"Perkin," Blue said, and rolled his eyes at Jewel and they both laughed.

She not as hard as he did, though.

Elgin could see the root of doubt in her eyes, could feel her loneliness in the way she fiddled with the menu, touched her cheekbone, spoke too loudly, as if she wasn't just telling Elgin and Blue how Perkin had mistreated her, but the whole IHOP as well, so people could get it straight that she wasn't the villain, and if after she returned to Perkin she had to leave him again, they'd know why.

Of course she was going back to Perkin.

Elgin could tell by the glances she gave Blue—unsure, slightly embarrassed, maybe a bit repulsed. What had begun as a nighttime ride into the unknown had turned cold and stale during the hard yellow lurch into morning.

Blue wiped his mouth, said, "Be right back," and walked to the bathroom with surer strides than Elgin had ever seen on the man.

Elgin looked at Jewel.

She gripped the handle of her coffee cup between the tips of her thumb and index finger and turned the cup in slow revolutions around the saucer, made a soft scraping noise that climbed up Elgin's spine like a termite trapped under the skin.

"You ain't sleeping with him, are you?" Elgin said quietly.

Jewel's head jerked up and she looked over her shoulder, then back at Elgin. "What? God, no. We're just . . . He's my pal. That's all. Like when we were kids."

"We ain't kids."

"I know. Don't you know I know?" She fingered the coffee cup again. "I miss you," she said softly. "I miss you. When you coming back?"

Elgin kept his voice low. "Me and Shelley, we're getting pretty serious."

She gave him a small smile that he instantly hated. It seemed to know him; it seemed like everything he was and everything he wasn't was caught in the curl of her lips. "You miss the lake, Elgin. Don't lie."

He shrugged.

"You ain't ever going to marry Shelley Briggs, have babies, be an upstanding citizen."

"Yeah? Why's that?"

"Because you got too many demons in you, boy. And they need me. They need the lake. They need to cry out every now and then."

Elgin looked down at his own coffee cup. "You going back to Perkin?"

She shook her head hard. "No way. Uh-uh. No way."

Elgin nodded, even though he knew she was lying. If Elgin's demons needed the lake, needed to be unbridled, Jewel's needed Perkin. They needed security. They needed to know the money'd never run out, that she'd never go two full days without a solid meal, like she had so many times as a child in the trailer park.

Perkin was what she saw when she looked down at her empty coffee cup, when she touched her cheek. Perkin was at their nice home with his feet up, watching a game, petting the dog, and she was in the IHOP in the middle of a Sunday when the food was at its oldest and coldest, with one guy who loved her and one who fucked her, wondering how she got there.

Blue came back to the table, moving with that new sure stride, a broad smile in the wide swing of his arms.

"How we doing?" Blue said. "Huh? How we doing?" And his lips burst into a grin so huge Elgin expected it to keep going right off the sides of his face.

Jewel left Blue's place two days later, walked into Perkin Lut's Auto Emporium and into Perkin's office, and by the time anyone went to check, they'd left through the back door, gone home for the day.

Elgin tried to get a hold of Blue for three days—called constantly, went by his shack and knocked on the door, even staked out the tree house along I-95 where he fired on the dogs.

He'd decided to break into Blue's place, was fixing to do just that, when he tried one last call from his trailer that third night and Blue answered with a strangled "Hello."

"It's me. How you doing?"

"Can't talk now."

"Come on, Blue. It's me. You OK?"

"All alone," Blue said.

"I know. I'll come by."

"You do, I'll leave."

"Blue."

"Leave me alone for a spell, Elgin. OK?"

That night Elgin sat alone in his trailer, smoking cigarettes, staring at the walls.

Blue'd never had much of anything his whole life—not a job he enjoyed, not a woman he could consider his—and then between the dogs and Jewel Lut he'd probably thought he'd got it all at once. Hit pay dirt.

Elgin remembered the dirty little kid sitting down by the drainage ditch, hugging himself. Six, maybe seven years old, waiting to die.

You had to wonder sometimes why some people were even born. You had to wonder what kind of creature threw bodies into the world, expected them to get along when they'd been given no tools, no capacity to get any either.

In Vietnam, this fat boy, name of Woodson from South Dakota, had been the least popular guy in the platoon. He wasn't smart, he wasn't athletic, he wasn't funny, he wasn't even personable. He just was. Elgin had been running beside him one day through a sea of rice paddies, their boots making sucking sounds every step they took, and someone fired a hell of a round from the other side of the paddies, ripped Woodson's head in half so completely all Elgin saw running beside him for a few seconds was the lower half of Woodson's face. No hair, no forehead, no eyes. Just half the nose, a mouth, a chin.

Thing was, Woodson kept running, kept plunging his feet in and out of the water, making those sucking sounds, M-15 hugged to his chest, for a good eight or ten steps. Kid was dead, he's still running. Kid had no reason to hold on, but he don't know it, he keeps running.

What spark of memory, hope, or dream had kept him going?

You had to wonder.

In Elgin's dream that night, a platoon of ice-gray Vietcong rose in a straight line from the center of Cooper's Lake while Elgin was inside the cabin with Shelley and Jewel. He penetrated them both somehow, their separate torsos branching out from the same pair of hips, their four legs clamping at the small of his back, this Shelley-Jewel creature crying out for more, more, more.

And Elgin could see the VC platoon drifting in formation toward the shore, their guns pointed, their faces hidden behind thin wisps of green fog.

The Shelley-Jewel creature arched her backs on the bed below him, and Woodson and Blue stood in the corner of the room watching as their dogs padded across the floor, letting out low growls and drooling.

Shelley dissolved into Jewel as the VC platoon reached the porch steps and released their safeties all at once, the sound like the ratcheting of a thousand shotguns. Sweat exploded in Elgin's hair, poured down his body like warm rain, and the VC fired in concert, the bullets shearing the walls of the cabin, lifting the roof off into the night. Elgin looked above him at the naked night sky, the stars zipping by like tracers, the yellow moon full and mean, the shivering branches of birch trees. Jewel rose and straddled him, bit his lip, and dug her nails into his back, and the bullets danced through his hair, and then Jewel was gone, her writhing flesh having dissolved into his own.

Elgin sat naked on the bed, his arms stretched wide, waiting for the bullets to find his back, to shear his head from his body the way they'd sheared the roof from the cabin, and the yellow moon burned above him as the dogs howled and Blue and Woodson held each other in the corner of the room and wept like children as the bullets drilled holes in their faces.

Big Bobby came by the trailer late the next morning, a Sunday, and said, "Blue's a bit put out about losing his job."

"What?" Elgin sat on the edge of his bed, pulled on his socks. "You picked now — now, Bobby — to fire him?"

"It's in his eyes," Big Bobby said. "Like you said. You can see it."

Elgin had seen Big Bobby scared before, plenty of times, but now the man was trembling.

Elgin said, "Where is he?"

Blue's front door was open, hanging half down the steps from a busted hinge. Elgin said, "Blue."

"Kitchen."

He sat in his Jockeys at the table, cleaning his rifle, each shiny black piece spread in front of him on the table. Elgin's eyes watered a bit because there was a stench coming from the back of the house that he felt might strip his nostrils bare. He realized then that he'd never asked Big Bobby or Blue what they'd done with all those dead dogs.

Blue said, "Have a seat, bud. Beer in the fridge if you're thirsty."

Elgin wasn't looking in that fridge. "Lost your job, huh?"

Blue wiped the bolt with a shammy cloth. "Happens." He looked at Elgin. "Where you been lately?"

"I called you last night."

"I mean in general."

"Working."

"No, I mean at night."

"Blue, you been" — he almost said "playing house with Jewel Lut" but caught himself — "up in a fucking tree, how do you know where I been at night?"

"I don't," Blue said. "Why I'm asking."

Elgin said, "I've been at my trailer or down at Doubles, same as usual."

"With Shelley Briggs, right?"

Slowly, Elgin said, "Yeah."

"I'm just asking, buddy. I mean, when we all going to go out? You, me, your new girl."

The pits that covered Blue's face like a layer of bad meat had faded some from all those nights in the tree.

Elgin said, "Anytime you want."

Blue put down the bolt. "How 'bout right now?" He stood and walked into the bedroom just off the kitchen. "Let me just throw on some duds."

"She's working now, Blue."

"At Perkin Lut's? Hell, it's almost noon. I'll talk to Perkin about that Dodge he sold me last year, and when she's ready we'll take her out someplace nice." He came back into the kitchen wearing a soiled brown T-shirt and jeans.

"Hell," Elgin said, "I don't want the girl thinking I've got some serious love for her or something. We come by for lunch, next thing she'll expect me to drop her off in the mornings, pick her up at night."

Blue was reassembling the rifle, snapping all those shiny pieces together so fast, Elgin figured he could do it blind. He said, "Elgin, you got to show them some affection sometimes. I mean, Jesus." He pulled a thin brass bullet from his T-shirt pocket and slipped it in the breech, followed it with four more, then slid the bolt home.

"Yeah, but you know what I'm saying, bud?" Elgin watched Blue nestle the stock in the space between his left hip and ribs, let the barrel point out into the kitchen.

"I know what you're saying," Blue said. "I know. But I got to talk to Perkin about my Dodge."

"What's wrong with it?"

"What's wrong with it?" Blue turned to look at him, and the barrel swung level with Elgin's belt buckle. "What's wrong with it, it's a piece of shit, what's wrong with it, Elgin. Hell, you know that. Perkin sold me a lemon. This is the situation." He blinked. "Beer for the ride?"

Elgin had a pistol in his glove compartment. A .32. He considered it.

"Elgin?"

"Yeah?"

"Why you looking at me funny?"

"You got a rifle pointed at me, Blue. You realize that?"

Blue looked at the rifle, and its presence seemed to surprise him. He dipped it toward the floor. "Shit, man, I'm sorry. I wasn't even thinking. It feels like my arm sometimes. I forget. Man, I am sorry." He held his arms out wide, the rifle rising with them.

"Lotta things deserve to die, don't they?"

Blue smiled. "Well, I wasn't quite thinking along those lines, but now you bring it up . . ."

Elgin said, "Who deserves to die, buddy?"

Blue laughed. "You got something on your mind, don't you?" He hoisted himself up on the table, cradled the rifle in his lap. "Hell, boy, who you got? Let's start with people who take two parking spaces."

"OK." Elgin moved the chair by the table to a position slightly behind Blue, sat in it. "Let's."

"Then there's DJs talk through the first minute of a song. Fucking Guatos coming down here these days to pick tobacco, showing no respect. Women wearing all those tight clothes, look at you like you're a pervert when you stare at what they're advertising." He wiped his forehead with his arm. "Shit."

"Who else?" Elgin said quietly.

"OK. OK. You got people like the ones let their dogs run wild into the highway, get themselves killed. And you got dishonest people, people who lie and sell insurance and cars and bad food. You got a lot of things. Jane Fonda."

"Sure." Elgin nodded.

Blue's face was drawn, gray. He crossed his legs over each other like he used to down at the drainage ditch. "It's all out there." He nodded and his eyelids drooped.

"Perkin Lut?" Elgin said. "He deserve to die?"

"Not just Perkin," Blue said. "Not just. Lots of people. I mean, how many you kill over in the war?"

Elgin shrugged. "I don't know."

"But some. Some. Right? Had to. I mean, that's war—someone gets on your bad side, you kill them and all their friends till they stop bothering you." His eyelids drooped again, and he yawned so deeply he shuddered when he finished.

"Maybe you should get some sleep."

Blue looked over his shoulder at him. "You think? It's been a while."

A breeze rattled the thin walls at the back of the house, pushed that thick dank smell into the kitchen again, a rotting stench that found the back of Elgin's throat and stuck there. He said, "When's the last time?"

"I slept? Hell, a while. Days maybe." Blue twisted his body so he was facing Elgin. "You ever feel like you spend your whole life waiting for it to get going?"

Elgin nodded, not positive what Blue was saying, but knowing he should agree with him. "Sure."

"It's hard," Blue said. "Hard." He leaned back on the table, stared at the brown water marks in his ceiling.

Elgin took in a long stream of that stench through his nostrils. He kept his eyes open, felt that air entering his nostrils creep past into his corneas, tear at them. The urge to close his eyes and wish it all away was as strong an urge as he'd ever felt, but he knew now was that time he'd always known was coming.

He leaned in toward Blue, reached across him, and pulled the rifle off his lap.

Blue turned his head, looked at him.

"Go to sleep," Elgin said. "I'll take care of this a while. We'll go see Shelley tomorrow. Perkin Lut too."

Blue blinked. "What if I can't sleep? Huh? I've been having that problem, you know. I put my head on the pillow and I try to sleep and it won't come and soon I'm just bawling like a fucking child till I got to get up and do something."

Elgin looked at the tears that had just then sprung into Blue's eyes, the red veins split across the whites, the desperate, savage need in his face that had always been there if anyone had looked close enough, and would never, Elgin knew, be satisfied.

"I'll stick right here, buddy. I'll sit here in the kitchen and you go in and sleep."

Blue turned his head and stared up at the ceiling again. Then he slid off the table, peeled off his T-shirt, and tossed it on top of the fridge. "All right. All right. I'm gonna try." He stopped at the bedroom doorway. "'Member—there's beer in the fridge. You be here when I wake up?"

Elgin looked at him. He was still so small, probably so thin you could still wrap your hand around his biceps, meet the fingers on the other side. He was still ugly and stupid-looking, still dying right in front of Elgin's eyes.

"I'll be here, Blue. Don't you worry."

"Good enough. Yes, sir."

Blue shut the door and Elgin heard the bedsprings grind, the rustle of pillows being arranged. He sat in the chair, with the smell of whatever decayed in the back of the house swirling around his head. The sun had hit the cheap tin roof now, heating the small house, and after a while he realized the buzzing he'd thought was in his head came from somewhere back in the house too.

He wondered if he had the strength to open the fridge. He wondered if he should call Perkin Lut's and tell Perkin to get the hell out of Eden for a bit. Maybe he'd just ask for Shelley, tell her to meet him tonight with her suitcases. They'd drive down 95 where the dogs wouldn't disturb them, drive clear to Jacksonville, Florida, before the sun came up again. See if they could outrun Blue and his tiny, dangerous wants, his dog corpses, and his smell; outrun people who took two parking spaces and telephone solicitors and Jane Fonda.

Jewel flashed through his mind then, an image of her sitting atop him, arching her back and shaking that long red hair, a look in her green eyes that said this was it, this was why we live.

He could stand up right now with this rifle in his hands, scratch the itch in the back of his head, and fire straight through the door, end what should never have been started.

He sat there staring at the door for quite a while, until he knew the exact number of places the paint had peeled in teardrop spots, and eventually he stood, went to the phone on the wall by the fridge, and dialed Perkin Lut's.

"Auto Emporium," Shelley said, and Elgin thanked God that in his present mood he hadn't gotten Glynnis Verdon, who snapped her gum and always placed him on hold, left him listening to Muzak versions of the Shirelles.

"Shelley?"

"People gonna talk, you keep calling me at work, boy."

He smiled, cradled the rifle like a baby, leaned against the wall. "How you doing?"

"Just fine, handsome. How 'bout yourself?"

Elgin turned his head, looked at the bedroom door. "I'm OK."

"Still like me?"

Elgin heard the springs creak in the bedroom, heard weight drop on the old floorboards. "Still like you."

"Well, then, it's all fine then, isn't it?"

Blue's footfalls crossed toward the bedroom door, and Elgin used his hip to push himself off the wall.

"It's all fine," he said. "I gotta go. I'll talk to you soon."

He hung up and stepped away from the wall.

"Elgin," Blue said from the other side of the door.

"Yeah, Blue?"

"I can't sleep. I just can't."

Elgin saw Woodson sloshing through the paddy, the top of his head gone. He saw the pink panties curling up from underneath Blue's bed and a shaft of sunlight hitting Shelley's face as she looked up from behind her desk at Perkin Lut's and smiled. He saw Jewel Lut dancing in the night rain by the lake and that dog lying dead on the shoulder of the interstate, kicking its leg like it was trying to ride a bicycle.

"Elgin," Blue said. "I just can't sleep. I got to do something."

"Try," Elgin said and cleared his throat.

"I just can't. I got to . . . do something. I got to go . . ." His voice cracked, and he cleared his throat. "I can't sleep."

The doorknob turned and Elgin raised the rifle, stared down the barrel.

"Sure, you can, Blue." He curled his finger around the trigger as the door opened. "Sure you can," he repeated and took a breath, held it in.

The skeleton of Eden Falls still sits on twenty-two acres of land just east of Brimmer's Point, covered in rust thick as flesh. Some say it was the levels of iodine an environmental inspector found in the groundwater that scared off the original investors. Others said it was the downswing of the state economy or the governor's failed reelection bid. Some say Eden Falls was just plain a dumb name, too biblical. And then, of course, there were plenty who claimed it was Jewel Lut's ghost scared off all the workers.

They found her body hanging from the scaffolding they'd erected by the shell of the roller coaster. She was naked and hung upside down from a rope tied around her ankles. Her throat had been cut so deep the coroner said it was a miracle her head was still attached when they found her. The coroner's assistant, man by the name of Chris Gleason, would claim when he was in his cups that the head had fallen off in the hearse as they drove down Main toward the morgue. Said he heard it cry out.

This was the same day Elgin Bern called the sheriff's office, told them he'd shot his buddy Blue, fired two rounds into him at close range, the little guy dead before he hit his kitchen floor. Elgin told the deputy he was still sitting in the kitchen, right where he'd done it a few hours before. Said to send the hearse.

Due to the fact that Perkin Lut had no real alibi for his whereabouts when Jewel passed on and owing even more to the fact there'd been some very recent and very public discord in their marriage, Perkin was arrested and brought before a grand jury, but that jury decided not to indict. Perkin and Jewel had been patching things up, after all; he'd bought her a car (at cost, but still . . .).

Besides, we all knew it was Blue had killed Jewel. Hell, the Simmons boy, a retard ate paint and tree bark, could have told you that. Once all that stuff came out about what Blue and Big Bobby'd been doing with the dogs around here, well, that just sealed it. And everyone remembered how that week she'd been separated from Perkin, you could see the dream come alive in Blue's eyes, see him allow hope into his heart for the first time in his sorry life.

And when hope comes late to a man, it's quite a dangerous thing. Hope is for the young, the children. Hope in a full-grown man — particularly one with as little acquaintanceship with it or prospect for it as Blue — well, that kind of hope burns as it dies, boils blood white, and leaves something mean behind when it's done.

Blue killed Jewel Lut.

And Elgin Bern killed Blue. And ended up doing time. Not much, due to his war record and the circumstances of who Blue was, but time just the same. Everyone knew Blue probably had it coming, was probably on his way back into town to do to Perkin or some other poor soul what he'd done to Jewel. Once a man gets that look in his eyes — that boiled look, like a dog searching out a bone who's not going to stop until he finds it — well, sometimes he has to be put down like a dog. Don't he?

And it was sad how Elgin came out of prison to find Shelley Briggs gone, moved up North with Perkin Lut of all people, who'd lost his heart for the car business after Jewel died, took to selling home electronics imported from Japan and Germany, made himself a fortune. Not long after he got out of prison, Elgin left too, no one knows where, just gone, drifting.

See, the thing is — no one wanted to convict Elgin. We all understood. We did. Blue had to go. But he'd had no weapon in his hand when Elgin, standing just nine feet away, pulled that trigger. Twice. Once we might been able to overlook, but twice, that's something else again. Elgin offered no defense, even refused a fancy lawyer's attempt to get him to claim he'd suffered something called posttraumatic stress disorder, which we're hearing a lot more about these days.

"I don't have that," Elgin said. "I shot a defenseless man. That's the long and the short of it, and that's a sin."

And he was right:

In the world, case you haven't noticed, you usually pay for your sins.

And in the South, always.

2000

WILLIAM GAY

THE PAPERHANGER

WILLIAM GAY (1941–) was born in the rural town of Hohenwald, Tennessee, and after joining the Navy and serving in the Vietnam War, he lived in New York and Chicago before returning permanently to his hometown in 1978. He did not receive a formal college education, but read voraciously and began writing at the age of fifteen. He earned a living in the construction trade as a drywall hanger, painter, carpenter — "whatever worked," as he once stated it. For an author of such singular talent, it is astonishing to note that Gay did not sell any of his literary output until 1998, when literary magazines bought two of his stories.

The following year, his novel *The Long Home* was published to outstanding reviews and won the James A. Michener Memorial Prize. Like his other work, it is clearly in the Southern Gothic tradition of William Faulkner, Flannery O'Connor, and Cormac McCarthy. He also was influenced by the works of such great American crime writers as Raymond Chandler and Ross Macdonald, though his stories are not set in California, as theirs are, but are placed in the rural South, their dark, weird, violent landscapes populated by seemingly ordinary working-class people. He also published *Provinces of Night* (2000), a short story collection, *I Hate to See That Evening Sun Go Down* (2002), and *Twilight* (2006).

"The Paperhanger" grew out of a story Gay had heard years before he wrote it, told to him by a plumber. It was first published in the February 2000 issue of *Harper's Magazine.* It was selected for *The Best American Mystery Stories 2001, The O. Henry Prize Stories 2001,* and *The Best American Mystery Stories of the Century.*

▪ ▪ ▪

THE VANISHING OF the doctor's wife's child in broad daylight was an event so cataclysmic that it forever divided time into the then and the now, the before and the after. In later years, fortified with a pitcher of silica-dry vodka martinis, she had cause to replay the events preceding the disappearance. They were tawdry and banal but in retrospect freighted with menace, a foreshadowing of what was to come, like a footman or a fool preceding a king into a room.

She had been quarreling with the paperhanger. Her four-year-old daughter, Zeineb, was standing directly behind the paperhanger where he knelt smoothing air bubbles out with a wide plastic trowel. Zeineb had her fingers in the paperhanger's hair. The paperhanger's hair was shoulder length and the color of flax and the child was delighted with it. The paperhanger was accustomed to her doing this and he did not even turn around. He just went on with his work. His arms were smooth and brown and corded with muscle and in the light that fell upon the paperhanger through stained-glass panels the doctor's wife could see that they were lightly downed with fine golden hair. She studied these arms bemusedly while she formulated her thoughts.

You tell me so much a roll, she said. The doctor's wife was from Pakistan and her speech was still heavily accented. I do not know single-bolt rolls and double-bolt rolls. You tell me double-bolt price but you are installing single-bolt rolls. My friend has told me. It is cost me perhaps twice as much.

The paperhanger, still on his knees, turned. He smiled up at her. He had pale blue eyes. I did tell you so much a roll, he said. You bought the rolls. The child, not yet vanished, was watching the paperhanger's eyes. She was a scaled-down clone of the mother, the mother viewed through the wrong end of a telescope, and the paperhanger suspected that as she grew neither her features nor her expression would alter, she would just grow larger, like something being aired up with a hand pump.

And you are leave lumps, the doctor's wife said, gesturing at the wall. I do not leave lumps, the paperhanger said. You've seen my work before. These are not lumps. The paper is wet. The paste is wet. Everything will shrink down and flatten out. He smiled again. He had clean even teeth. And besides, he said, I gave you my special cockteaser rate. I don't know what you're complaining about.

Her mouth worked convulsively. She looked for a moment as if he'd slapped her. When words did come they came in a fine spray of spit. You are trash, she said. You are scum.

Hands on knees, he was pushing erect, the girl's dark fingers trailing out of his hair. Don't call me trash, he said, as if it were perfectly all right to call him scum, but he was already talking to her back. She had whirled on her heels and went twisting her hips through an arched doorway into the cathedraled living room. The paperhanger looked down at the child. Her face glowed with a strange constrained glee, as if she and the paperhanger shared some secret the rest of the world hadn't caught on to yet.

In the living room the builder was supervising the installation of a chandelier that depended from the vaulted ceiling by a long golden chain. The builder was a short bearded man dancing about, showing her the features of the chandelier, smiling obsequiously. She gave him a flat angry look. She waved a dismissive hand toward the ceiling. Whatever, she said.

She went out the front door onto the porch and down a makeshift walkway of two-by-tens into the front yard where her car was parked. The car was a silver-gray Mercedes her husband had given her for their anniversary. When she cranked the engine its idle was scarcely perceptible.

She powered down the window. Zeineb, she called. Across the razed earth of the unlandscaped yard a man in a grease-stained T-shirt was booming down the chains securing a backhoe to a lowboy hooked to a gravel truck. The sun was low in the west and blood-red behind this tableau and man and tractor looked flat and dimensionless as something decorative stamped from tin. She blew the horn. The man turned, raised an arm as if she'd signaled him.

Zeineb, she called again.

She got out of the car and started impatiently up the walkway. Behind her the gravel truck started, and truck and backhoe pulled out of the drive and down toward the road.

The paperhanger was stowing away his T-square and trowels in his wooden toolbox. Where is Zeineb? the doctor's wife asked. She followed you out, the paperhanger told her. He glanced about, as if the girl might be hiding somewhere. There was nowhere to hide.

Where is my child? she asked the builder. The electrician climbed down from the ladder. The paperhanger came out of the bathroom with his tools. The builder was looking all around. His elfin features were touched with chagrin, as if this missing child were just something else he was going to be held accountable for.

Likely she's hiding in a closet, the paperhanger said. Playing a trick on you.

Zeineb does not play tricks, the doctor's wife said. Her eyes kept darting about the huge room, the shadows that lurked in corners. There was already an undercurrent of panic in her voice and all her poise and self-confidence seemed to have vanished with the child.

The paperhanger set down his toolbox and went through the house, opening and closing doors. It was a huge house and there were a lot of closets. There was no child in any of them.

The electrician was searching upstairs. The builder had gone through the French doors that opened onto the unfinished veranda and was peering into the backyard. The backyard was a maze of convoluted ditch excavated for the septic tank field line and beyond that there was just woods. She's playing in that ditch, the builder said, going down the flagstone steps.

She wasn't, though. She wasn't anywhere. They searched the house and grounds. They moved with jerky haste. They kept glancing toward the woods where the day was waning first. The builder kept shaking his head. She's got to be *somewhere,* he said.

Call someone, the doctor's wife said. Call the police.

It's a little early for the police, the builder said. She's got to be here.

You call them anyway. I have a phone in my car. I will call my husband.

While she called, the paperhanger and the electrician continued to search. They had looked everywhere and were forced to search places they'd already looked. If this ain't the goddamnedest thing I ever saw, the electrician said.

The doctor's wife got out of the Mercedes and slammed the door. Suddenly she stopped and clasped a hand to her forehead. She screamed. The man with the tractor, she cried. Somehow my child is gone with the tractor man.

Oh Jesus, the builder said. What have we got ourselves into here?

The high sheriff that year was a ruminative man named Bellwether. He stood beside the county cruiser talking to the paperhanger while deputies ranged the grounds. Other men were inside looking in places that had already been searched numberless times. Bellwether had been in the woods and he was picking cockleburs off his khakis and out of his socks. He was watching the woods, where dark was gathering and seeping across the field like a stain.

I've got to get men out here, Bellwether said. A lot of men and a lot of lights. We're going to have to search every inch of these woods.

You'll play hell doing it, the paperhanger said. These woods stretch all the way to Lawrence County. This is the edge of the Harrikan. Down in there's where all those old mines used to be. Allens Creek.

I don't give a shit if they stretch all the way to Fairbanks, Alaska, Bellwether said. They've got to be searched. It'll just take a lot of men.

The raw earth yard was full of cars. Doctor Jamahl had come in a sleek black Lexus. He berated his wife. Why weren't you watching her? he asked. Unlike his wife's, the doctor's speech was impeccable. She covered her face with her palms and wept. The doctor still wore his green surgeon's smock and it was flecked with bright dots of blood as a butcher's smock might be.

I need to feed a few cows, the paperhanger said. I'll feed my stock pretty quick and come back and help hunt.

You don't mind if I look in your truck, do you?

Do what?

I've got to cover my ass. If that little girl don't turn up damn quick this is going to be over my head. TBI, FBI, network news. I've got to eliminate everything.

Eliminate away, the paperhanger said.

The sheriff searched the floorboard of the paperhanger's pickup truck. He shined his huge flashlight under the seat and felt behind it with his hands.

I had to look, he said apologetically.

Of course you did, the paperhanger said.

Full dark had fallen before he returned. He had fed his cattle and stowed away his tools and picked up a six-pack of San Miguel beer and he sat in the back of the pickup truck drinking it. The paperhanger had been in the Navy and stationed in the Philippines and San Miguel was the only beer he could drink. He had to go out of town to buy it, but he figured it was worth it. He liked the exotic labels, the dark bitter taste on the back of his tongue, the way the chilled bottles felt held against his forehead.

A motley crowd of curiosity seekers and searchers thronged the yard. There was a vaguely festive air. He watched all this with a dispassionate eye, as if he were charged with grading the participants, comparing this with other spectacles he'd seen. Coffee urns had been brought in and set up on tables, sandwiches prepared and handed out to the weary searchers. A crane had been hauled in and the septic tank reclaimed from the ground. It swayed from a taut cable while men with lights searched the impacted earth beneath it for a child, for the very trace of a child. Through the far dark woods lights crossed and recrossed, darted to and fro like fireflies. The doctor and the doctor's wife sat in folding camp chairs looking drained, stunned, waiting for their child to be delivered into their arms.

The doctor was a short portly man with a benevolent expression. He had a moon-shaped face, with light and dark areas of skin that looked swirled, as if the pigment coloring him had not been properly mixed. He had been educated at Princeton. When he had established his practice he had returned to Pakistan to find a wife befitting his station. The woman he had selected had been chosen on the basis of her beauty. In retrospect, perhaps more consideration should have been given to other qualities. She was still beautiful but he was thinking that certain faults might outweigh this. She seemed to have trouble keeping up with her children. She could lose a four-year-old child in a room no larger than six hundred square feet and she could not find it again.

The paperhanger drained his bottle and set it by his foot in the bed of the truck. He studied the doctor's wife's ravaged face through the deep blue light. The first time he had seen her she had hired him to paint a bedroom in the house they were living in while the doctor's mansion was being built. There was an arrogance about her that cried out to be taken down a notch or two. She flirted with him, backed away, flirted again. She would treat him as if he were a stain on the bathroom rug and then stand close by him while he worked until he was dizzy with the smell of her, with the heat that seemed to radiate off her body. She stood by him while he knelt painting baseboards and after an infinite moment leaned carefully the weight of a thigh against his shoulder. You'd better move it, he thought. She didn't. He laughed and turned his face into her groin. She gave a strangled cry and slapped him hard. The paintbrush flew away and speckled the dark rose walls with antique white. You filthy beast, she said. You are some kind of monster. She stormed out of the room and he could hear her slamming doors behind her.

Well, I was looking for a job when I found this one. He smiled philosophically to himself.

But he had not been fired. In fact now he had been hired again. Perhaps there was something here to ponder.

At midnight he gave up his vigil. Some souls more hardy than his kept up the watch. The earth here was worn smooth by the useless traffic of the searchers. Driving out, he met a line of pickup trucks with civil-defense tags. Grim-faced men sat aligned in their beds. Some clutched rifles loosely by their barrels, as if they would lay waste whatever monster, man or beast, would snatch up a child in its slaverous jaws and vanish, prey and predator, in the space between two heartbeats.

Even more dubious reminders of civilization as these fell away. He drove into the Harrikan, where he lived. A world so dark and forlorn light itself seemed at a premium. Whippoorwills swept red-eyed up from the roadside. Old abandoned foundries and furnaces rolled past, grim and dark as forsaken prisons. Down a ridge here was an abandoned graveyard, if you knew where to look. The paperhanger did. He had dug up a few of the graves, examined with curiosity what remained, buttons, belt buckles, a cameo brooch. The bones he laid out like a child with a Tinkertoy, arranging them the way they went in jury-rigged resurrection.

He braked hard on a curve, the truck slewing in the gravel. A bobcat had crossed the road, graceful as a wraith, fierce and lantern-eyed in the headlights, gone so swiftly it might have been a stage prop swung across the road on wires.

Bellwether and a deputy drove to the backhoe operator's house. He lived up a gravel road that wound through a great stand of cedars. He lived in a board-and-batten house with a tin roof rusted to a warm umber. They parked before it and got out, adjusting their gun belts.

Bellwether had a search warrant with the ink scarcely dry. The operator was outraged.

Look at it this way, Bellwether explained patiently. I've got to cover my ass. Everything has got to be considered. You know how kids are. Never thinking. What if she run under the wheels of your truck when you was backing out? What if quicklike you put the body in your truck to get rid of somewhere?

What if quicklike you get the hell off my property, the operator said.

Everything has to be considered, the sheriff said again. Nobody's accusing anybody of anything just yet.

The operator's wife stood glowering at them. To have something to do with his hands, the operator began to construct a cigarette. He had huge red hands thickly sown with brown freckles. They trembled. I ain't got a thing in this round world to hide, he said.

Bellwether and his men searched everywhere they could think of to look. Finally they stood uncertainly in the operator's yard, out of place in their neat khakis, their polished leather.

Now get the hell off my land, the operator said. If all you think of me is that I could run over a little kid and then throw it off in the bushes like a dead cat or something then I don't even want to see your goddamn face. I want you gone and I want you by God gone now.

Everything had to be considered, the sheriff said.

Then maybe you need to consider that paperhanger.

What about him?

That paperhanger is one sick puppy.

He was still there when I got there, the sheriff said. Three witnesses swore nobody ever left, not even for a minute, and one of them was the child's mother. I searched his truck myself.

Then he's a sick puppy with a damn good alibi, the operator said.

* * *

That was all. There was no ransom note, no child that turned up two counties over with amnesia. She was a page turned, a door closed, a lost ball in the high weeds. She was a child no larger than a doll, but the void she left behind her was unreckonable. Yet there was no end to it. No finality. There was no moment when someone could say, turning from a mounded grave, Well, this has been unbearable, but you've got to go on with your life. Life did not go on.

At the doctor's wife's insistence an intensive investigation was focused on the backhoe operator. Forensic experts from the FBI examined every millimeter of the gravel truck, paying special attention to its wheels. They were examined with every modern crime-fighting device the government possessed, and there was not a microscopic particle of tissue or blood, no telltale chip of fingernail, no hair ribbon.

Work ceased on the mansion. Some subcontractors were discharged outright, while others simply drifted away. There was no one to care if the work was done, no one to pay them. The half-finished veranda's raw wood grayed in the fall, then winter, rains. The ditches were left fallow and uncovered and half-filled with water. Kudzu crept from the woods. The hollyhocks and oleanders the doctor's wife had planted grew entangled and rampant. The imported windows were stoned by double-dared boys who whirled and fled. Already this house where a child had vanished was acquiring an unhealthy, diseased reputation.

The doctor and his wife sat entombed in separate prisons replaying real and imagined grievances. The doctor felt that his wife's neglect had sent his child into the abstract. The doctor's wife drank vodka martinis and watched talk shows where passed an endless procession of vengeful people who had not had children vanish, and felt, perhaps rightly, that the fates had dealt her from the bottom of the deck, and she prayed with intensity for a miracle.

Then one day she was just gone. The Mercedes and part of her clothing and personal possessions were gone too. He idly wondered where she was, but he did not search for her.

Sitting in his armchair cradling a great marmalade cat and a bottle of J&B and observing with bemused detachment the gradations of light at the window, the doctor remembered studying literature at Princeton. He had particular cause to reconsider the poetry of William Butler Yeats. For how surely things fell apart, how surely the center did not hold.

His practice fell into a ruin. His colleagues made sympathetic allowances for him at first, but there are limits to these things. He made erroneous diagnoses, prescribed the wrong medicines not once or twice but as a matter of course.

Just as there is a deepening progression to misfortune, so too there is a point beyond which things can only get worse. They did. A middle-aged woman he was operating on died.

He had made an incision to remove a ruptured appendix and the incised flesh was clamped aside while he made ready to slice it out. It was not there. He stared in drunken disbelief. He began to search under things, organs, intestines, a rising tide of blood. The appendix was not there. It had gone into the abstract, atrophied, been removed twenty-five years before, he had sliced through the selfsame scar. He was rummaging through her abdominal cavity like an irritated man fumbling through a drawer for a clean pair of socks, finally bellowing in rage and wringing his hands in bloody vexation while nurses began to cry out, another surgeon was brought on the run as a closer, and he was carried from the operating room.

Came then days of sitting in the armchair while he was besieged by contingency lawyers, action news teams, a long line of process servers. There was nothing he could do. It was out of his hands and into the hands of the people who are paid to do these things. He sat cradling the bottle of J&B with the marmalade cat snuggled against his portly midriff. He would study the window, where the light drained away in a process he no longer had an understanding of, and sip the scotch and every now and then stroke the cat's head gently. The cat purred against his breast as reassuringly as the hum of an air conditioner.

He left in the middle of the night. He began to load his possessions into the Lexus. At first he chose items with a great degree of consideration. The first thing he loaded was a set of custom-made monogrammed golf clubs. Then his stereo receiver, Denon AC3, $1,750. A copy of *This Side of Paradise* autographed by Fitzgerald that he had bought as an investment. By the time the Lexus was half full he was just grabbing things at random and stuffing them into the back seat, a half-eaten pizza, half a case of cat food, a single brocade house shoe.

He drove west past the hospital, the country club, the city limit sign. He was thinking no thoughts at all, and all the destination he had was the amount of highway the headlights showed him.

In the slow rains of late fall the doctor's wife returned to the unfinished mansion. She used to sit in a camp chair on the ruined veranda and drink chilled martinis she poured from the pitcher she carried in a foam ice chest. Dark fell early these November days. Raincrows husbanding some far cornfield called through the smoky autumn air. The sound was fiercely evocative, reminding her of something but she could not have said what.

She went into the room where she had lost the child. The light was failing. The high corners of the room were in deepening shadow but she could see the nests of dirt daubers clustered on the rich flocked wallpaper, a spider swing from a chandelier on a strand of spun glass. Some animal's dried blackened stool curled like a slug against the baseboards. The silence in the room was enormous.

One day she arrived and was surprised to find the paperhanger there. He was sitting on a yellow four-wheeler drinking a bottle of beer. He made to go when he saw her but she waved him back. Stay and talk with me, she said.

The paperhanger was much changed. His pale locks had been shorn away in a makeshift haircut as if scissored in the dark or by a blind barber and his cheeks were covered with a soft curly beard.

You have grow a beard.

Yes.

You are strange with it.

The paperhanger sipped from his San Miguel. He smiled. I was strange without it, he said. He arose from the four-wheeler and came over and sat on the flagstone steps. He stared across the mutilated yard toward the tree line. The yard was like a funhouse maze seen from above, its twistings and turnings bereft of mystery.

You are working somewhere now?

No. I don't take so many jobs anymore. There's only me, and I don't need much. What has become of the doctor?

She shrugged. Many things have change, she said. He has gone. The banks have foreclose. What is that you ride?

An ATV. A four-wheeler.

It goes well in the woods?

It was made for that.

You could take me in the woods. How much would you charge me?

For what?

To go in the woods. You could drive me. I will pay you.

Why?

To search for my child's body.

I wouldn't charge anybody anything to search for a child's body, the paperhanger said. But she's not in these woods. Nothing could have stayed hidden, the way these woods were searched.

Sometimes I think she just kept walking. Perhaps just walking away from the men looking. Far into the woods.

Into the woods, the paperhanger thought. If she had just kept walking in a straight line with no time out for eating or sleeping, where would she be? Kentucky, Algiers, who knew.

I'll take you when the rains stop, he said. But we won't find a child.

The doctor's wife shook her head. It is a mystery, she said. She drank from her cocktail glass. Where could she have gone? How could she have gone?

There was a man named David Lang, the paperhanger said. Up in Galletin, back in the late 1800s. He was crossing a barn lot in full view of his wife and two children and he just vanished. Went into thin air. There was a judge in a wagon turning into the yard and he saw it too. It was just like he took a step in this world and his foot came down in another one. He was never seen again.

She gave him a sad smile, bitter and one-cornered. You make fun with me.

No. It's true. I have it in a book. I'll show you.

I have a book with dragons, fairies. A book where hobbits live in the middle earth. They are lies. I think most books are lies. Perhaps all books. I have prayed for a miracle but I am not worthy of one. I have prayed for her to come from the dead, then just to find her body. That would be a miracle to me. There are no miracles.

She rose unsteadily, swayed slightly, leaning to take up the cooler. The paperhanger watched her. I have to go now, she said. When the rains stop we will search.

Can you drive?

Of course I can drive. I have drive out here.

I mean are you capable of driving now. You seem a little drunk.

I drink to forget but it is not enough, she said. I can drive.

After a while he heard her leave in the Mercedes, the tires spinning in the gravel drive. He lit a cigarette. He sat smoking it, watching the rain string off the roof. He seemed to be waiting for something. Dusk was falling like a shroud, the world going dark and formless the way it had begun. He drank the last of the beer, sat holding the bottle, the foam bitter in the back of his mouth. A chill touched him. He felt something watching him. He turned. From the corner of the ruined veranda a child was watching him. He stood up. He heard the beer bottle break on the flagstones. The child went sprinting past the hollyhocks toward the brush at the edge of the yard, tiny sepia child with an intent sloe-eyed face, real as she had ever been, translucent as winter light through dirty glass.

The doctor's wife's hands were laced loosely about his waist as they came down through a thin stand of sassafras, edging over the ridge where the ghost of a road was, a road more sensed than seen that faced into a half acre of tilting stones and fading granite tablets. Other graves marked only by their declivities in the earth, folk so far beyond the pale even the legibility of their identities had been leached away by the weathers.

Leaves drifted, huge poplar leaves veined with amber so golden they might have been coin of the realm for a finer world than this one. He cut the ignition of the four-wheeler and got off. Past the lowering trees the sky was a blue of an improbable intensity, a fierce cobalt blue shot through with dense golden light.

She slid off the rear and steadied herself a moment with a hand on his arm. Where are we? she asked. Why are we here?

The paperhanger had disengaged his arm and was strolling among the gravestones reading such inscriptions as were legible, as if he might find forebear or antecedent in this moldering earth. The doctor's wife was retrieving her martinis from the luggage carrier of the ATV. She stood looking about uncertainly. A graven angel with broken wings crouched on a truncated marble column like a gargoyle. Its stone eyes regarded her with a blind benignity. Some of these graves have been rob, she said.

You can't rob the dead, he said. They have nothing left to steal.

It is a sacrilege, she said. It is forbidden to disturb the dead. You have done this.

The paperhanger took a cigarette pack from his pocket and felt it, but it was empty, and he balled it up and threw it away. The line between grave robbing and archaeology has always looked a little blurry to me, he said. I was studying their culture, trying to get a fix on what their lives were like.

She was watching him with a kind of benumbed horror. Standing hip-slung and lost like a parody of her former self. Strange and anomalous in her fashionable but mismatched clothing, as if she'd put on the first garment that fell to hand. Someday, he thought, she might rise and wander out into the daylit world wearing nothing at all, the way she had come into it. With her diamond watch and the cocktail glass she carried like a used-up talisman.

You have break the law, she told him.

I got a government grant, the paperhanger said contemptuously.

Why are we here? We are supposed to be searching for my child.

If you're looking for a body the first place to look is the graveyard, he said. If you want a book don't you go to the library?

I am paying you, she said. You are in my employ. I do not want to be here. I want you to do as I say or carry me to my car if you will not.

Actually, the paperhanger said, I had a story to tell you. About my wife.

He paused, as if leaving a space for her comment, but when she made none he went on. I had a wife. My childhood sweetheart. She became a nurse, went to work in one of these drug rehab places. After she was there a while she got a faraway look in her eyes. Look at me without seeing me. She got in tight with her supervisor. They started having meetings to go to. Conferences. Sometimes just the two of them would confer, generally in a motel. The night I watched them walk into the Holiday Inn in Franklin I decided to kill her. No impetuous spur-of-the-moment thing. I thought it all out and it would be the perfect crime.

The doctor's wife didn't say anything. She just watched him.

A grave is the best place to dispose of a body, the paperhanger said. The grave is its normal destination anyway. I could dig up a grave and then just keep on digging. Save everything carefully. Put my body there and fill in part of the earth, and then restore everything the way it was. The coffin, if any of it was left. The bones and such. A good settling rain and the fall leaves and you're home free. Now that's eternity for you.

Did you kill someone, she breathed. Her voice was barely audible.

Did I or did I not, he said. You decide. You have the powers of a god. You can make me a murderer or just a heartbroke guy whose wife quit him. What do you think? Anyway, I don't have a wife. I expect she just walked off into the abstract like that Lang guy I told you about.

I want to go, she said. I want to go where my car is.

He was sitting on a gravestone watching her out of his pale eyes. He might not have heard.

I will walk.

Just whatever suits you, the paperhanger said. Abruptly, he was standing in front of her. She had not seen him arise from the headstone or stride across the graves, but like a jerky splice in a film he was before her, a hand cupping each of her breasts, staring down into her face.

Under the merciless weight of the sun her face was stunned and vacuous. He studied it intently, missing no detail. Fine wrinkles crept from the corners of her eyes and mouth like hairline cracks in porcelain.

Grime was impacted in her pores, in the crepe flesh of her throat. How surely everything had fallen from her: beauty, wealth, social position, arrogance. Humanity itself, for by now she seemed scarcely human, beleaguered so by the fates that she suffered his hands on her breasts as just one more cross to bear, one more indignity to endure.

How far you've come, the paperhanger said in wonder. I believe you're about down to my level now, don't you?

It does not matter, the doctor's wife said. There is no longer one thing that matters.

Slowly and with enormous lassitude her body slumped toward him, and in his exultance it seemed not a motion in itself but simply the completion of one begun long ago with the fateful weight of a thigh, a motion that began in one world and completed itself in another one.

From what seemed a great distance he watched her fall toward him like an angel descending, wings spread, from an infinite height, striking the earth gently, tilting, then righting itself.

The weight of moonlight tracking across the paperhanger's face awoke him from where he took his rest. Filigrees of light through the gauzy curtains swept across him in stately silence like the translucent ghosts of insects. He stirred, lay still then for a moment getting his bearings, a fix on where he was.

He was in his bed, lying on his back. He could see a huge orange moon poised beyond the bedroom window, ink-sketch tree branches that raked its face like claws. He could see his feet bookending the San Miguel bottle that his hands clasped erect on his abdomen, the amber bottle hard edged and defined against the pale window, dark atavistic monolith reared against a harvest moon.

He could smell her. A musk compounded of stale sweat and alcohol, the rank smell of her sex. Dissolution, ruin, loss. He turned to study her where she lay asleep, her open mouth a dark cavity in her face. She was naked, legs outflung, pale breasts pooled like cooling wax. She stirred restively, groaned in her sleep. He could hear the rasp of her breathing. Her breath was fetid on his face, corrupt, a graveyard smell. He watched her in disgust, in a dull self-loathing.

He drank from the bottle, lowered it. Sometimes, he told her sleeping face, you do things you can't undo. You break things you just can't fix. Before you mean to, before you know you've done it. And you were right, there are things only a miracle can set to rights.

He sat clasping the bottle. He touched his miscut hair, the soft down of his beard. He had forgotten what he looked like, he hadn't seen his reflection in a mirror for so long. Unbidden, Zeineb's face swam into his memory. He remembered the look on the child's face when the doctor's wife had spun on her heel: spite had crossed it like a flicker of heat lightning. She stuck her tongue out at him. His hand snaked out like a serpent and closed on her throat and snapped her neck before he could call it back, sloe eyes wild and wide, pink tongue caught between tiny seed-pearl teeth like a bitten-off rosebud. Her hair swung sidewise, her head lolled onto his clasped hand. The tray of the toolbox was out before he knew it, he was stuffing her into the toolbox like a ragdoll. So small, so small, hardly there at all.

He arose. Silhouetted naked against the moon-drenched window, he drained the bottle. He looked about for a place to set it, leaned and wedged it between the heavy flesh of her upper thighs. He stood in silence, watching her. He seemed philosophical, possessed of some hard-won wisdom. The paperhanger knew so well that while few are deserving of a miracle, fewer still can make one come to pass.

He went out of the room. Doors opened, doors closed. Footsteps softly climbing a staircase, descending. She dreamed on. When he came back into the room he was cradling a plastic-wrapped bundle stiffly in his arms. He placed it gently beside the drunk woman. He folded the plastic sheeting back like a caul.

What had been a child. What the graveyard earth had spared the freezer had preserved. Ice crystals snared in the hair like windy snowflakes whirled there, in the lashes. A doll from a madhouse assembly line.

He took her arm, laid it across the child. She pulled away from the cold. He firmly brought the arm back, arranging them like mannequins, madonna and child. He studied this tableau, then went out of his house for the last time. The door closed gently behind him on its keeper spring.

The paperhanger left in the Mercedes, heading west into the open country, tracking into wide-open territories he could infect like a malignant spore. Without knowing it, he followed the selfsame route the doctor had taken some eight months earlier, and in a world of infinite possibilities where all journeys share a common end, perhaps they are together, taking the evening air on a ruined veranda among the hollyhocks and oleanders, the doctor sipping his scotch and the paperhanger his San Miguel, gentlemen of leisure discussing the vagaries of life and pondering deep into the night not just the possibility but the inevitability of miracles.

2001

F. X. TOOLE

MIDNIGHT EMISSIONS

F. X. TOOLE, the pseudonym of Jerry Boyd (1930–2002), was the son of Irish immigrants. He had a varied background, working in such jobs as shoeshine boy, bartender, and cement truck driver. After reading Ernest Hemingway's nonfiction work about bullfighting, Death in the Afternoon, he moved to Mexico to learn how to be a matador. After his bullfighting career ended, he moved to Los Angeles, getting into shape at boxing gyms and eventually becoming a trainer and cutman, who attends to a fighter's injuries between rounds.

After trying unsuccessfully for forty years, he finally sold his first short story to a literary journal, *Zyzzyva,* in 1999. Once he was published, he chose a pseudonym, an amalgam of Francis Xavier, the sixteenth-century philosopher, teacher, and saint, and his favorite actor, Peter O'Toole. A collection of his short stories, *Rope Burns: Stories from the Corner,* was published in 2000. Incidents from several of these stories were adapted for the screenplay of *Million Dollar Baby* (2004); the film won four Academy Awards, for Best Picture, Best Director (Clint Eastwood, who also starred), Best Actress (Hilary Swank), and Best Supporting Actor (Morgan Freeman). Many of the stories were based on the real-life exploits of Boyd's friend Dub Huntley, who taught him to box. Four years after Toole's death, his long novel, *Pound for Pound,* was published to outstanding reviews. In 2007 the AMC cable channel announced a series of one-hour boxing dramas based on Toole's short stories.

"Midnight Emissions" was first published in the anthology *Murder on the Ropes* (Los Angeles: New Millennium, 2001); it was selected for the 2002 edition of *The Best American Mystery Stories.*

■ ■ ■

BUTCHERIN' WAS DONE while the deceased was still alive," Junior said.

See, we was at the gym and I'd been answering a few things. Old Junior's a cop, and his South Texas twang was wide and flat like mine. 'Course he was dipping, and he let a stream go into the Coke bottle he was carrying in the hand that wasn't his gun hand. His blue eyes was paler than a washed-out work shirt.

"Hail," he said, "one side of the mouth'd been slit all the way to the earring."

See, when the police find a corpse in Texas, their first question ain't who done it, it's what did the dead do to deserve it?

Billy Clancy'd been off the police force a long time before Kenny Coyle come along, but he had worked for the San Antonia Police Department a spell there after boxing. He made some good money for himself on the side — down in dark town, if you know what I'm saying? That's after I trained him as a heavyweight in the old *El Gallo,* or Fighting Cock gym off Blanco Road downtown. We worked together maybe six years all told, starting off when he was a amateur. Billy Clancy had all the Irish heart in the world. At six-three and two-twenty-five, he had a fine frame on him, most of his weight upstairs. He had a nice clean style, too, and was quick as a sprinter. But after he was once knocked out for the first time? He had no chin after that. He'd be kicking ass and taking names, but even in a rigged fight with a bum, if he got caught, down he'd go like a longneck at a ice house.

He was a big winner in the amateurs, Billy was, but after twelve pro fights, he had a record of eight and four, with his nose broke once — that's eight wins by KO, but he lost four times by KO, so that's when he hung 'em up. For a long time, he went his way and I went mine. But then Billy Clancy opened Clancy's Pub with his cop money. That was his big break. There was Irish night with Mick music, corned beef and cabbage, and Caffery's Ale on tap and Harp Lager from Dundalk. And he had Messkin night with *mariachis* and folks was dancin' *corridos* and the band was whooping out *rancheras* and they'd get to playing some of that *norteña* polka music that'd have you laughing and crying at the same time. For shrimp night, all you can eat, Billy trucked in fresh Gulf shrimp sweeter than plum jelly straight up from Matamoros on the border. There was kicker, and hillbilly night, and on weekends there was just about the best jazz and blues you ever did hear. B. B. King did a whole week there one time. It got to be a hell of a deal for Billy, and then he opened up a couple of more joints till he had six in three towns, and soon Billy Clancy was somebody all the way from San Antonia up to Dallas, and down to Houston. Paid all his taxes, obeyed all the laws, treated folks like they was ladies and gentlemen, no matter how dusty the boots, how faded the dress, or if a suit was orange and purple and green.

By then he had him a home in the historic old Monte Vista section of San Antonia. His wife had one of them home-decorating businesses on her own, and she had that old place looking so shiny that it was like going back a hundred years. His kids was all in private school, all of them geared to go to UT up Austin, even though the dumb young one saw himself as a Aggie.

So one day Billy called me for some "Q" down near the river, knew I was a whore for baby back ribs. Halfway through, he just up and said, "Red, I want back in."

See, he got to missing the smell of leather and sweat, and the laughter of men — he missed the action, is what, and got himself back into the game the only way he could, managing fighters. He was good at it, too. By then he was better'n forty, and myself I was getting on — old's when you sit on the crapper and you have to hold your nuts up so they don't get wet. But what with my rocking-chair money every month, and the money I made off Billy's fighters, it got to where I was doing pretty good. Even got me some ostrich boots and a El Patron 30x beaver Stetson, *yip!*

What Billy really wanted was a heavyweight. With most managers, it's only the money, 'cause heavies is what brings in them stacks of green fun-tickets. Billy wanted fun-tickets, too, but with Billy it was more like he wanted to get back something what he had lost. 'Course, finding the right heavyweight's like finding a cherry at the high school prom.

Figure it, with only twenty, twenty-five good wins, 'specially if he can crack, a heavy can fight for a title's worth millions. There's exceptions, but most little guys'll fight forever and never crack maybe two hundred grand. One of the reason's 'cause there's so many of them. Other reason's 'cause they's small. Fans like seeing heavyweights hit the canvas.

But most of today's big guys go into the other sports where you don't get hit the way you do in the fights. It ain't held against you in boxing if you're black nowadays, but if you're a white heavy it makes it easier to pump paydays, and I could tell that it wouldn't make Billy sad if I could get him a white boy — Irish or Italian would be desired. But working with the big guys takes training to a level that can break your back and your heart, and I wasn't all that sure a heavy was what I wanted, what with me being the one what's getting broke up.

See, training's a hard row to hoe. It ain't only the physical and mental parts for the fighter what's hard, but it's hard for the trainer, too. Fighters can drive you crazy, like maybe right in the middle of a fight they're *winning*, when they forget everything what you taught them? And all of a sudden they can't follow instructions from the corner? Pressure, pain, and being out of gas will make fighters go flat brain-dead on you. Your fighter's maybe sweated off six or eight pounds in there, his body's breaking down, and the jungle in him is yelling quick to get him some gone. Trainers come to know how that works, so you got to hang with your boy when he's all alone out there in the canvas part of the world. He takes heart again, 'cause he knows with you there he's still got a fighting chance to go for the titties of the win. 'Course, that means cutting grommets, Red Ryder.

Everyone working corners knows you'll more'n likely lose more'n you'll ever win, that boxing for most is refried beans and burnt tortillas. But winning is what makes your birdie chirp, so you got to always put in your mind that losing ain't nothing but a hitch in the git-along.

Working with the big guys snarls your task. How do you tell a heavyweight full-up on his maleness to use his mind instead of his sixty-pound dick? How do you teach someone big as a garage that it ain't the fighter with the biggest brawn what wins, but it's the one what gets there first with deadly force? How do you make him see that hitting hard ain't the problem, but that hitting *right* is? How do you get through to him that you don't have to be mad at someone to knock him out, same as you don't have to be in a frenzy to kill with a gun? Heavyweights got that upper-body strength what's scary, it's what they'd always use to win fights at school and such, so it's their way to work from the waist up. That means they throw arm punches, but arm punches ain't good enough. George Foreman does it, but he's so strong, and don't hardly miss, so he most times gets away with punching wrong. 'Course he didn't get away with it in Zaire with Mr. Ali.

So the big deal with heavies is getting them to work from the waist down as well as from the waist up. And they got to learn that the last thing that happens is when the punch lands. A thousand things got to happen before that can happen. Those things begin on the floor with balance. But how do you get across that he's got to work hard, but not so hard that he harms himself? How do you do that in a way what don't threaten what he already knows and has come to depend on? How do you do it so's it don't jar how he has come to see himself and his fighting style? And most of all, how do you do it so when the pressure's on he don't go back to his old ways?

After they win a few fights by early knockout, some heavies get to where they try to control workouts, will balk at new stuff what they'll need as they step up in class. When they pick up a few purses and start driving that new car, lots get lazy and spend their time chasing poon, of which there is a large supply when there is evidence of a quantity of hundred-dollar bills. Some's hop heads, but maybe they fool you and you don't find that out till it's too late. Now you got to squeeze as many paydays out of your doper that you can. Most times, you love your fighter like he's kin, but with a goddamn doper you get to where you couldn't give a bent nail.

Why shouldn't I run things? the heavy's eyes will glare. His nose is flared, his socks is soggy with sweat, his heart's banging at his rib cage like it's trying to bust out of jail. It's 'cause he don't understand that he can't be the horse and the jockey. *How could anyone as big and handsome and powerful and smart as me be wrong about anything?* he will press. Under his breath he's saying, *And who's big enough to tell me I'm wrong?*

When that happens, your boy's attitude is moving him to the streets, and you may have to let him go.

Not many fight fans ever see the inside of fight gyms, so they get to wondering what's the deal with these big dummies who get all sweaty and grunty and beat on each other. Well, sir, they ain't big dummies when you think big money. Most big guys in team sports figure there's more gain and less pain than in fights, even if they have to play a hundred fifty games a year or more, and even if they have to get those leg and back operations that go with them. Some starting-out heavies get to thinking they ought to get the same big payday as major-league pitchers from the day they walk into the gym. Some see themselves as first-round draft picks in the NBA before they ever been hit. What they got to learn is that you got to be a hungry fighter before you can become a championship fighter, a fighter who has learned and survived all the layers of work and hurt the fight game will put on you. Good heavyweights're about as scarce as black cotton.

There're less white heavies than black, and the whites can be even goofier than blacks about quick money. Some whites spout off that 'cause they're white, as in White Hope, that they should be getting easy fights up to and including the one for the title. If you're that kind — and there's black ones same as white — you learn right quick that he don't have the tit or the brains to be a winner under them bright lights.

Though heavies may have the same look, they're as different from each other as zebras when it comes to mental desire, chin, heart, and *huevos* — *huevos* is eggs, but in Messkin it means "balls." Getting heavies into shape is another problem, keeping them in shape is a even bigger one, 'cause they got these bottomless pits for stomachs. So you work to keep them in at least decent shape all the time — but not in punishing *top shape,* the kind that peaks just before a fight. Fighter'd go wild-pig crazy if he had to live at top shape longer than a few days, his nerves all crawly and hunger eating him alive. And then there's that blood-clotting wait to the first bell. See, the job of molding flesh and bone into a fighting machine that meets danger instead of hightailing from it is as tricky as the needlework what goes into one of them black, lacy deals what Spanish ladies wear on their heads. Fighting's easy, cowboy, it's training what's hard.

But once a trainer takes a heavy on, there's all that thump. First of all, when the heavy moves, you got to move with him — up in the ring, on the hardwood, around the big bag. You're there to guide him like a mama bear, and to stay on his ass so's he don't dog it. All fighters'll dog it after they been in the game a while, but the heavies can be the worst. They got all that weight to transport, and being human, they'll look for a place to hide. A good piece of change'll usually goad them. But always there is more training than fighting, and the faith and the fever it takes to be a champ will drop below ninety-eight-point-six real quick unless your boy eats and sleeps fight. 'Course, no fighter can do that one hundred percent. Besides, there's the pussy factor. Which is part of where the punch mitts come in. They'll make him sharp with his punches, but they're also there to help tire him into submission come bedtime.

The big bag they can fake if you don't stay on them, but a trainer with mitts, calling for combination after combination, see that's for the fighter like he's wearing a wire jock. But for the trainer, the mitts mean you're catching punches thrown by a six-foot-five longhorn, and the punches carry force enough to drop a horse. And the trainer takes this punishment round after round, day after day, the *thump* pounding through him like batting practice and he's the ball. I can't much work the mitts like I once did, only when I'm working on moves, or getting ready for a set date. But even bantamweights can make your eyes pop.

Part of the payoff for all this is sweeter'n whipped cream on top of strawberry pie. It's when your fighter comes to see himself from the outside instead of just from the in. It's when all of a sudden he can see how to use his feet to control that other guy in the short pants. It's how a fighter'll smile like a shy little boy when he understands that all his moves're now offense *and* defense, and that he suddenly has the know-how to beat the other guy with his mind, that he no longer has to be just some bull at the watering hole looking to gore. And that's when, Lordy, that you just maybe got yourself a piece of somebody what can change sweat and hurt into gold and glory.

Getting a boy ready for a fight is the toughest time of all for trainers.

After a session with the mitts, your fingers'll curl into the palms of your hands for a hour or so, and driving home in your Jimmy pickup means your hands'll be claws on the steering wheel. The muscles in the middle of your back squeeze your shoulders up around your ears. Where your chest hooks into your shoulders, you go home feeling there's something tore down in there. Elbows get sprung, and groin pulls hobble you. In my case, I've got piano wire holding my chest and ribs together, so when I leave the gym shock keeps on twanging through me. By the time I'm heading home, I'm thinking hard on a longneck bottle of Lone Star. The only other thing I'm thinking on is time in the prone position underneath Granny's quilt.

See, what we're talking about here is signing on to be a cripple, 'cause when you get down to it, trainers in their way get hit more than fighters, only we do it for nickels and dimes, compared. So what's the rest of the deal for the trainer? Well, sir, after getting through all the training and hurting, you live with the threat that you could work years with a heavy only to have him quit on you for somebody who's dangling money at him now that you've done the job that changed a lump of fear and doubt into a fighter. But like I say, a good heavy these days only has to win a few fights for a shot at the title. If he wins that, he's suddenly drinking from solid gold teacups. As the champ, he will defend his title as little as once. But the payoff can be *mucho* if he can defend a few times. So when the champ gets a ten-million-dollar payday, the trainer gets ten percent off the top — that's a one-million-dollar bill. That can make you forget crippled backs and hands.

'Course the downside can be there, too. That's when your heart goes out to your fighter as you watch helpless sometimes as he takes punches to the head that can hack into his memory forever. And your gut will turn against you when one day you see your boy's eyes wander all glassy when he tries to find a word that he don't have in his mouth no more. You feel rotten deep down, but you also love your fighter for having the heart to roll the dice of his life on a dream. And above all, you see clear that no matter how rotten you feel, that your boy never had nothing else but his life to roll, and that you was the lone one who ever cared enough to give him the only shot he would ever have.

Yet the real lure, when you love the fights with everything that's left of your patched-up old heart, is to be part of the great game — a game where the dues are so high that once paid they take you to the Mount Everest of the Squared Circle, to that highest of places, where fire and ice are one and where only the biggest and best can play, *yip!*

Trainers know going in that the odds against you are a ton to one.

So why do I risk the years, why do I take shots that stun my heart? Why am I part of the spilt blood? Why do I take trips to Leipzig or Johannesburg that take me two weeks to recover from? B. B. King sings my answer for me, backs it up with that big old guitar. *"I got a bad case of love."*

Anyway, all I was able to get Billy was what was out there, mostly Messkins, little guys wringing wet at a hundred twenty-four and three quarters, what with us being in San Antonia. But there was some black fighters, too, a welter or a middleweight, now and then. Billy treated all his fighters like they was champs, no matter that they was prelim boys hanging between hope and fear, and praying hard the tornado don't touch down. If they was to show promise, he'd outright sponsor them good, give them a deuce a week minimum, no paybacks, a free room someplace decent, and eats in one of his pubs, whatever they wanted as long as they kept their weight right. If a boy wasn't so good, Billy'd give 'em work, that way if the kid didn't catch in boxing, leastways he always had a job. People loved Billy Clancy.

See, he'd start boys as a dishwasher, but then he'd move 'em up, make waiters and bartenders of them. He had Messkin managers what started as busboys. He was godfather to close to two dozen Messkin babies, and he never forgot a birthday or Christmas. His help would invite him to their weddings, sometimes deep into Mexico, and damned if he wouldn't go. Eyes down there would bug out when this big *gringo*'d come driving through a dusty *pueblo* in one of his big old silver Lincoln Town Cars what he ordered made special. Billy'd join right in, *yip!,* got to where he could talk the lingo passable-good enough to where he could tell jokes and make folks laugh in their own tongue.

Billy Clancy'd be in the middle of it, but he never crossed the line, never messed with any of the gals, though he could have had any or all of 'em. The priests would always take a shine to him, too, want to talk baseball. He never turned one down who come to him about somebody's grandma what needed a decent burial, instead of being dropped down a hole in a bag.

One time I asked Billy why he didn't try on one of them Indian-eyed honeys down there. Respect, is what he said, for the older folks, and 'specially for the young men, you don't want to take a man's pride.

"When you're invited to a party," said Billy, "act like you care to be invited back."

That was Billy Clancy; you don't shit where you eat.

* * *

My deal with Billy was working in the gym with his fighters for ten percent of the purse off the top. No fights, no money. I didn't see him for days unless it was getting up around fight time. But he'd stop by, not to check up on me, but just to let his boys know he cared about them. Most times he was smoother than gravy on a biscuit, but I could always tell when something was pestering him. 'Course he wouldn't talk about it much. Billy didn't feel the need to talk, or he saw fit not to.

I know there was this one time when the head manager of all Billy's joints in San Antonia took off with Billy's cash. Billy come into his private office one Monday expecting to see deposit slips for the money what come in over a big weekend. Well, sir, there was no money, and no keys, and no manager, but that same manager had held a gun on Billy's little Messkin office gal so's she'd open the safe. The manager had whipped on the little gal, taped her to a chair with duct tape to where she'd peed herself, and she was near hysteric.

Billy had some of his help make a few phone calls, and damned if the boy what did Billy didn't head for his hometown on the island of Isla Mujeres way down at the tip of Mexico, where he thought he'd be safe. Billy waited a week, then took a plane to Mérida in the Yucatán. He rented him a big car with a good AC and drove on over to the dried-out, palmy little town of Puerto Juárez on the coast that's just lick across the water from what's called Women's Island.

He hung out a day or so in Puerto Juárez, until he got a feel for the place, and so the local police could get a good look at him. Then he just pulled up in front of their peach-colored shack, half its palm-leaf roof hanging loose. He took his time getting out of his rental car, and walked slow inside. Stood a foot taller than most. He talked Spanish and told the captain of the local *federales* his deal, made it simple. All he wanted was his keys back, *and* he wanted both the manager's balls. The captain was to keep what was left of the money.

That night late, the captain brought forty-six keys on three key rings to Billy's blistered motel. He showed Polaroids of the manager's corpse what was dumped to cook in the hot water off the island, and he also brought in the manager's two *huevos* — his two eggs, each wrapped in a corn tortilla. Billy Clancy fed them to the wild dogs on the other side of the adobe back fence.

Billy checked out some of the Mayan ruins down around those parts, giving local folks time to call the news back to San Antonia. Billy got back, nobody said nothing. Didn't have no more problems with the help stealing now he'd made clear what was his was his.

* * *

There was only one other deal about Billy I ever knew about, this time with one of his ex-fighters, a failed middleweight, a colored boy Billy'd made a cook in one of his places. Nice boy, worked hard, short hair, all the good stuff. First off, he worked as a bar-back. But then the bartenders found out the kid was sneaking their tips. They cornered him in a storeroom. They had him turned upside down, was ready to break his hands for him, but then he started squealing they was only doing it 'cause he's black. Billy heard it from upstairs and called off his bartenders, piecing them off with a couple of C-notes each. He listened to the boy's story, and 'cause he couldn't prove the boy was dirty, he moved him to a different joint, and that's where he made a fry cook out of him. The kid was good at cooking, worked overtime anytime the head cook wanted. But then word come down the kid was dealing drugs outta the kitchen. Billy knew dead bang this time and he had one of his cop friends make a buy on the sly.

See, Billy always tried to take care of his own business, unless when it was something like down in Mexico. Billy said when he took care of things himself, there was nobody could tell a story different from the one he told. So he waited for the boy outside the boy's mama's house one night late, slashed two of his tires. Boy comes out and goes shitting mad when he sees his tires cut, starts waving his arms like a crawdad.

Billy comes up with a baseball bat alongside his leg, said, "Boy, I come to buy some of that shit you sell."

Boy pissed the boy off something awful, but he knew better than to challenge Billy on it. So the boy tried to run. He showed up dead, is what happened, his legs broke, his balls in his mouth. No cop ever knocked on Billy Clancy's door, but drugs didn't happen in any of Billy's places after that neither.

It was a couple years after that when Dee-Cee Swans collared me about this heavyweight he'd been working with over at the Brown Bomber Gym in Houston. I said I wasn't going to no Houston — even if it was to look at the real Brown Bomber himself. Dee-Cee said there wasn't no need.

Henrilee "Dark Chocolate" Swans was from Louisiana, his family going back to Spanish slave times, the original name was Cisneros. Family'd brought him as a boy to Houston during World War Two, where they'd come to better themself. Henrilee's fighting days started on the streets of the Fifth Ward. He said things was so tough in his part of town that when a wino died, his dog ate him. Dee-Cee was a pretty good lightweight in his time, now a'course he weighs more. Fight guys got to calling him Dee-Cee instead of Dark Chocolate, to make things short. Dee-Cee said call him anything you want, long as you called him to dinner.

He wore a cap 'cause he was baldheaded except for the white fringe around his ears and neck. He wore glasses, but one lens had a crack in it. He had a bad back and a slight limp, so he walked with a polished, homemade old mesquite walking stick. It was thick as your wrist and was more like a knobby club than a cane. But old Dee-Cee still had the moves. The time, between now and back when he was still Dark Chocolate, disappeared when Dee-Cee had need to move. Said he never had no trouble on no bus in no part of town, not with that stick between his legs. Dee-Cee had them greeny-blue eyes what some coloreds gets, and when he looked at you square, you was looked at.

Way me and him hooked up was chancy, like everything else in fights. 'Course we knew each other going way back. Both of us liked stand-up style of fighters, so we always had a lot to talk about, things like moves, slips, and counters. Like me, he knew that a fighter's feet are his brains —that they're what tell you what punches to throw and when to do it. Since there was more colored fighters in Dallas and Houston, that's where Dee-Cee operated out of most. But he had folks in San Antonia, too. He showed up again, him and a white heavyweight, big kid, a Irish boy from L.A. calling himself "KO" Kenny Coyle. What wasn't chancy was that Dee-Cee knew I was connected with Billy Clancy.

Dee-Cee got together with Coyle, trained him a while in Houston after working the boy's corner twice as a pickup cutman in a Alabama casino. The way the boy was matched, he was supposed to lose. See, he hadn't fought in a while. But he won both fights by early KOs, and his record got to be seventeen and one, with fifteen knockouts. Coyle could punch with both hands at six-foot-five, two hundred forty-five pounds, size sixteen shoe. His only loss came a few years back from a bad cut to his left eyelid up Vancouver, Canada.

The boy'd also worked as sparring partner for big-time heavyweights, going to camp sometimes for weeks at a time. That's a lot of high-level experience, but it's a lot of punishment, even when you're bone strong, and sometimes you could tell that Coyle'd lose a word. Except for the bad scar on his eyelid, and his nose being a little flat, he didn't look much busted up, so that made you think he maybe had some smarts. He was in shape, too. That made you like him right off.

Dee-Cee was slick. He always put one hand up to his mouth when he talked, said he didn't want spies to read his lips, said some had telescopes. He was known to be a bad man, Dee-Cee, but that didn't mean he didn't have a sense of right and wrong. Back before he had to use a cane, we got to drinking over Houston after a afternoon fight — it was at a fair where we both lost. Half drunk, we went to a fish shack in dark town for some catfish. Place was jam-packed. The lard-ass owner had one of them muslim-style gold teeth — the slip-on kind with a star cut-out that shows white from the white enamel underneath? Wouldn't you know it, he took one look at my color and flat said they didn't serve no food. Dee-Cee was fit to be tied — talked nigga, talked common, said Allah was going to send his black ass to the pit along with his four handkerchief-head ho's. Old muslim slid off the tooth quick as a quail when Dee-Cee tapped his pocket and said he was going to cut that tooth out or break it off.

We headed for a liquor store, bought some jerky, and ended up out at one of them baseball-pitching park deals drinking rock and rye and falling down in the dirt from swinging and missing pitches. People got to laughing like we was Richard Pryor. Special loud was the hustler running a three-card monte game next to the stands, a little round dude with fuzzy-wuzzy hair. He worked off a old lettuce crate and cheated people for nickels and dimes. Not one of them ever broke the code, but old Dee-Cee had broke it from the git. He watched sly from the fence as the monte-guy took even pennies from the raggedy kids what made a few cents chasing down balls in the outfield.

Dee-Cee put on his Louisiana country-boy act, bet a dollar, and pointed to one of the cards after the monte-guy moved the three cards all around. 'Course Dee-Cee didn't choose right, *couldn't* choose right, so he went head-on and lost another twenty, thirty dollars. Then he bet fifty, like he was trying to get his money back. The dealer did more slick business with his cards, and Dee-Cee chose the one in the middle — only this time, instead of just pointing to it and waiting for the dealer to turn it face-up like before, Dee-Cee held it down hard with two fingers and told monte-man to flip the other two cards over first. Dee-Cee said he'd turn his card over *last,* said he wanted to eyeball *all* the cards. See, there was no way for nobody to win. The dealer knew he'd been caught cheating, and tried to slide. Dee-Cee cracked him in the shins a few times with a piece of pipe he carried those days, and pretty soon — wouldn't you know it? — the monte-man got to begging Dee-Cee to take *all* his money. Dee-Cee took it all, too. 'Course he kept his own money, what was natural, but he gave the rest to the ragamuffins in the field — at which juncture the little guys all took the rest of the night off.

* * *

Dee-Cee got me off to the side one day, his hand over his mouth, said did I want to work with him and Coyle? He told me Coyle maybe had a ten-round fight coming up at one of the Mississippi casinos, and I figured Dee-Cee wanted me as cutman for the fight, him being the trainer and chief second. I say why not? some extra cash to go along with my rocking chair, right?

But Dee-Cee said, "Naw, Red, not just cutman, I want you wit' me full-time training Coyle."

I say to myself, *A heavyweight what can crack, a big old white Irish one!*

Dee-Cee says he needs he'p 'cause as chief second he can't hardly get up the ring steps and through the ropes quick enough no more. 'Course with me working inside the ring, that makes me chief second *and* cutman. I'd done that before, hell.

Dee-Cee says he chose me 'cause he don't trust none of what he called the niggas and the beaners in the gym. Said he don't think much of the rednecks neither. See, that's the way Dee-Cee *talked,* not the way he *acted* toward folks. Dee-Cee always had respect.

He said, "See, you'n me knows that a fighter's feet is his brains. My white boy's feet ain't right, and you good wit' feet. We split the trainer's ten percent, even."

Five percent of a heavyweight can mount.

Dee-Cee said, "Yeah, and maybe you could bring in Billy Clancy."

Like I said, Dee-Cee's slick. So I ask myself if this is something I want bad enough to kiss a spider for? See, when a fan sees the pros and the amateurs, he sees them as a sport. But the pros is a business, too. It's maybe more a business than a sport. I liked the business part like everybody else, but heavyweights can hurt you like nobody else. So I'm thinking, do I want to chance sliding down that dark hole a heavyweight can dig? Besides, do I want to risk my good name on KO Kenny Coyle with Billy Clancy? I told Dee-Cee I'd wait a spell before I'd do that.

Dee-Cee said, "No, no, you right, hail yeah!"

See, I'm slick, too.

What it was is, Coyle was quirky. He'd gone into the Navy young and started fighting as a service fighter, started knocking everybody out. He won all of the fleet and other service titles, and most of the civilian amateur tournaments, and people was talking Olympics. But the Olympics was maybe three years away, and he wanted to make some money right now. Couldn't make no big money or train full-time in the Navy, so one day Coyle up and walks straight into the ship's captain's face. Damned if Coyle don't claim he's queer as a three-dollar bill. See, the service folks these days ain't supposed to ask, and you ain't supposed to tell, but here was Coyle telling what he really wanted was to be a woman and dance the ballet. Captain hit the overhead, was ready to toss him in the brig, but Coyle threatened to suck off all the Marine guards, and to contact the president himself about sexual harassment. Didn't take more'n a lick, and the captain made Coyle a ex-Navy queer. Coyle laughed his snorty laugh when he told the story, said wasn't he equal smart as he was big? Guys said he sure was, but all knew Coyle wasn't smart as Coyle thought he was—'specially when he got to bragging about how he stung some shyster lawyers what had contacted him while he was still a amateur. See, they started funneling him money, and got him to agree to sign with them when he turned pro. He knew up front that nobody was supposed to be buzzing amateurs, and he got them for better'n twenty big ones before he pulled his sissy stunt on the Navy. When they come to him with a pro contract, he told them to stick it, told them no contract with a amateur was valid, verbal or written, and that he had bigger plans. He had them shysters by the ying-yang, he said, and them shysters knew it. Coyle laughed about that one, too.

Too bad I didn't hear about the lawyer deal until we was already into the far turn with Coyle. By the time I did, I already knew Kenny was too big for his britches, and that he was a liar no different from my cousin Royal. If it was four o'clock, old Royal'd say it was four-thirty. Couldn't help himself.

Coyle's problem as a fighter was he'd not been trained right, but he was smart enough to know it. His other trainers depended on his reach and power, and that he could take a shot. The problem with that is that you end up fighting with your face. What I worked on with him was the angles of the game, distance, and how to get in and out of range with the least amount of work. The big fellows got to be careful not to waste gas. But where I started Coyle first was with the *bitch*. See, the bitch is what I call the jab, that's the one'll get a crowd up and cheering, you do it pretty. *Bing! Bing!* Man, there ain't nothing like the bitch. And Coyle took to it good, him being fed up with getting hit. With the bitch, you automatic got angles. You got the angle, you got the opening. *Bang!* Everything comes off the bitch. I got him to moving on the balls of his feet, and soon he was coming off that right toe behind the bitch like he was a great white going for a seal pup. *Whooom!*

See, when you got the bitch working for you is when you got the other guy blinking, and on his heels going backward, and you can knock a man down with the bitch, even knock him out if you can throw a one-two-one combination right. Coyle picking up the bitch like he did is what got me to think serious on him, 'specially when I saw how hard he worked day in, day out. On time every day, nary a balk. Dee-Cee and me both started counting fun-tickets in our sleep but both of us agreed to pass on the ten-round Mississippi fight until I could get Coyle's feet right.

Moving with Coyle, like with the other heavies, is easy for me even now. 'Cause of their weight, they get their feet tangled when they ain't trained right, and I know how to back them to the ropes or into a corner. I don't kid myself, they could knock me out with the bitch alone if we was fighting, but what we're up to ain't fighting. What we're up to is what makes fighting boxing.

Billy Clancy got wind of Coyle and called me in, wanted to know why I was keeping my white boy secret. I told him Coyle wasn't no secret, said it was too soon.

"Who's feedin' him?"

"Me and Dee-Cee."

Billy peeled off some hundreds. I'd later split the six hundred with Dee-Cee.

Billy said, "Tell him to start eatin' at one of my joints, as much as he wants. But no drinks and no partyin' in the place. When'll Coyle be ready?"

"Gimme six weeks. If he can stand up to what I put on him, then we'll see."

"Will he fight?"

"He better."

Once I got Coyle's feet slick, damn if he didn't come along as if he was champion already. When I told Billy, he put a eight-round fight together at one of the Indian reservations on the Mississippi. We went for eight so's not to put too much pressure on Coyle, what with me being a new trainer to him. We fought for only seventy-five hundred — took the fight just to get Coyle on the card. When I told Coyle about it, he said book it, didn't even ask who's the opponent. See, Coyle was broke and living in dark town with Dee-Cee, and hoping to impress Billy 'cause Dee-Cee'd told him about Billy Clancy having money.

Well, sir, halfway through the fifth round with Marcellus Ellis, Coyle got himself head-butted in the same eye where he'd been cut up in Vancouver. Ellis was a six-foot-seven colored boy weighing two-seventy, but he couldn't do nothing with Coyle, 'cause of the bitch. So Ellis hoped to save his big ass with a head-butt. Referee didn't see the butt, and wouldn't take our word it was intentional, so the butt wasn't counted. Cut was so bad I skipped adrenaline and went direct to Thrombin, the ten-thousand-unit bovine coagulant deal. Thrombin stopped the blood quicker'n morphine'll stop the runs, but the cut was in the eyelid, and the fight shoulda been stopped in truth. But we was in Mississippi and the casino wanted happy gamblers, so the ref let it go on with a warning that he'd stop the fight in the next round if the cut got worse.

Dee-Cee got gray-looking, said he was ready to go over and whip on Ellis's nappy head with his cane.

I told Coyle the only thing I could tell him. "They'll stop this fight on us and we could lose, so you got to get into Ellis's ass with the bitch and then drop your right hand on him and get *respect!*"

All Coyle did was to nod. He went out there serious as a diamond-back. Six hard jabs busted up Ellis so bad that he couldn't think nothing but the bitch. That's when Coyle got the angle and, *Bang!* he hit Ellis with a straight right that was like the right hand of God. Lordy, Ellis was out for five minutes. He went down stiff like a tree and bounced on his face, and then one leg went all jerk and twitchy. We went to whooping and hugging. That right hand was lightning in human form. But what it was that did it for me wasn't Coyle's big right hand, it was the way he stuck the *bitch,* and the way Coyle *listened* to me in the corner.

Billy wanted to sign him right then, but I said wait, even though I knew Coyle was antsy to get him a place of his own. Besides, we had to wait a month and more to see if the eye'd heal complete. It took longer than we thought, so Billy started paying the boy three hundred a week walking-around money. Folks at the casino was so wild about that right hand coming outta a white boy that Billy was able to get twenty-five thousand for Coyle's next fight soon's a doctor'd clear his eye. And sure enough, Coyle was right back in the gym when the doctor gave him the OK. But he had some kind of funny look to him, so I told him to go home and rest. But no, Coyle kept showing up saying he wanted to get back to that casino. How do you reach the brain of a pure-strain male hormone when he's eighteen and one, with sixteen KOs? But one morning when me and Dee-Cee was out with him doing his road work, we got a surprise. Coyle started pressing his chest and had to stop running. Damn if he didn't look half-blue and ready to go down. Me and Dee-Cee walked him back to the car, both holding him by a arm. I thought maybe it was a heart attack. We hauled ass over to Emergency. They checked him all over, hooked him up to all the machines, checked his blood for enzymes. Said it wasn't no heart attack, said it was maybe some kind of quick virus going around that could knock folks down. Coyle wanted to know when he'd be able to fight again in Mississippi, and I told him to forget Mississippi till he was well. On our way out, the doctor got me to the side to tell me he wasn't positive Coyle was sick.

I said, "What does that mean?"

Doc said, "I'm not sure. Just thought you might want to know."

After a couple of days' rest Coyle was back in the gym, but then he had to stop his road work outta weakness again. He looked like a whipped pup, so I figured he had to have something wrong. He said, "But I can't fight if I don't run, you said it yourself."

I said, "You can't fight if you ain't got gas in your tank, that's what that means. Right now, you got a hole in your tank."

"I need dough, Red."

He was a hungry fighter; it's what you dream about. And there he'd be the next day, even if he coughed till he gagged. You never saw anybody push himself like him. But by then, the fool could hardly punch, much less run. But he still wanted to train, said he didn't want us to think he didn't have no heart.

I said, "Hail, boy, I'm worried about your brain, not heart. You got money from the last fight. Rest."

He said, "I sent all but a thousand to my brother for an operation. He's a cripple."

Well, later on I learned he'd pissed all the money away on pussy and pool, and there wasn't no cripple. But at that time I was so positive Coyle had the heart it takes that I just grabbed the bull by the horns and told Billy it was time. Billy could see the weak state Coyle was in, but on my good word it was a virus, Billy signed Coyle up to a four-year contract. On top of that, he gave Coyle a one-bedroom poolside apartment in one of his units for free. Said he'd give Coyle twenty-five hundred a month, that he'd put it in the contract, no payback, until Coyle started clearing thirty thousand a year. Said he'd give Coyle sixty thousand dollars under the table as a signing bonus soon's he was well enough to get back in the gym. Coyle wanted a hundred thousand, but settled for sixty.

Billy said, "That's cash, Kenny. So you don't have to pay no taxes on it."

"I'll get you the title, Mr. Clancy."

"Billy."

I looked at Dee-Cee, knew the head of his dick was glowing same as mine. Damned if Coyle wasn't back in the gym working hard and doing road work in only three days. Billy's word was good, and I was there when he paid Coyle off in stacks of hundreds. Money smells bad when you get a gang of it all together.

Wouldn't you know it? Old stinky-head went right out and spent the whole shiteree on one of them new BMW four-wheel-drive deals what goes for better than fifty thousand. Coyle got to bragging about the sports package, the killer sound system, how much horsepower it had. Who gives a rap when you can't afford tires and battery? Buying them boogers is easy, keeping them up what's hard.

Besides, it was about that time that Coyle's knees went to flap like butterfly wings. See, the ladies took one look at Coyle and thought they had the real deal, what with him having that big car and flashing hundreds in the clubs.

Dee-Cee said, "How many times you get you nut this week?"

Coyle said, "That's personal."

Dee-Cee said, "So you been gettin' you nut every night."

Coyle said, "No, I ain't."

Dee-Cee said, "You is, too. If it was one or none, or even two times, you'da said so."

Coyle looked at me like he'd never heard such talk.

I said, "He's sayin' when your legs get to wobblin', you been doin' it too much. He's saying that when your legs're weak that your brain gets to wonderin' why's it so hard to keep itself from fallin' down. That's when your brain is so busy keeping you on your feet that it don't pay attention to fightin'. Son, you got to have your legs right so your mind can work quicker than light, or you end up as a opponent talkin' through your nose, and the do-gooders wants to blame us trainers. No good, it's you and your dick what's doin' wrong."

Coyle said, "I'm a fighter livin' like a fighter."

Dee-Cee said, "Way you goin', you won't be for long."

I said, "Dee-Cee ain't wrong, Kenny."

Dee-Cee said, "Boy, you can fuck you white ass black, but that ain't never gonna make you champ of nothin'."

Coyle snorted, said, "I'll be champ of the bitches."

Dee-Cee said, "You go out, screw a thousand bitches, you think you somethin'? Sheeuh, you don't screw no thousand bitches, a thousand bitches screw you—and there go you title shot, fool."

Coyle said, "Fighters need release."

Dee-Cee said, "Say *what?* All you got to do is wait some. You midnight emissions'll natural take care of you goddamn release!"

I said, "Look, we're tryin' to get you around the track and across the finish line first, but you're headin' into the rail on us."

"Yeah," said Dee-Cee, "workin' wit' you be like holdin' water in one hand."

Coyle thought about that and seemed to nod, but next day when he come in his knees were flapping same as before.

Come to find out, Coyle wasn't worth the powder to blow him to hell. Billy found out Coyle had been with three gals in the stall of the men's toilet at one of his hot spots — that they'd been smoking weed hunched around the stool, *yip!* Billy didn't jump Coyle. But instead of seeing him as a long-lost White Hope in shining armor, he saw him same as me and Dee-Cee'd come to — like a peach what had gone part bad. So, do you cut out the bad part and keep the good? Or do you shit-can the whole deal? Billy decided to save what he could as long as he could.

Billy told Coyle to flat take his partying somewhere else, like he was first told. If I know Billy, there was more he wanted to say, but didn't. 'Course big old Coyle didn't take it too good, and wanted to dispute with Billy. So Billy said not to mistake kindness for weakness. Coyle got the message looked like, and was back in the gym working hard again — he wanted that twenty-five hundred a month. We figured the bullshit was over, leastways the in-public bullshit. But who could tell about weed? And who knew what else Coyle was messing with? By then, I got to feeling like I was a cat trapped in a sock drawer.

I told Coyle that what he'd pulled on Billy wasn't the right way to do business.

Coyle said, "He's makin' money off me."

I said, "Not yet he ain't."

That's when things got so squirrelly you'd think Coyle had a tail.

First thing what come up was that stink with the plain-Jane cop's daughter who said Coyle knocked her up — said Coyle'd gave her some of this GHB stuff that's floating around that'll make a gal pass out so deep she's a corpse. Cop's daughter said the last thing she remembered was that she was in Coyle's pool playing kissy face. Next thing she knew she was bare-ass on the floor and Coyle was fixing to do her. She said she jumped up and fled.

Coyle claimed that he'd already done her twice, said she was crying for more.

See, it wasn't until it come out she was pregnant that she told her daddy, who was a detective sergeant of the San Antonia P.D. She was a only child, and Daddy had them squinty blue eyes set in a face wide in the cheekbones what the Polacks brought into Texas. That good old boy got to rampaging like a rodeo bull, and right about then his neighbors got to thinking about calling Tom Bodette and checking into a Motel 6.

Once Daddy'd killed a half bottle of Jim Beam, he loaded up a old .44 six-gun, put on his boots and hat, and went on over to shoot Coyle dead.

Coyle told Daddy he loved plain-Jane more than his life itself, said that he wanted to marry her.

Cop was one of them fundamentals and figured marrying was better'n killing, so he let Coyle off.

Arrangements was made quick so the girl could wear white to the altar and not show. But then Coyle ups and says he'd have to wait till after the kid was born, that he wanted a blood test to prove he was the real daddy. The cop went to rampaging again and was fixing to hunt Coyle down, but he was took off the scent when his daughter stuck something up herself. Killed the baby, and liked to killed herself. The family was in such grief that Daddy started to drink full-time. The girl was sent off to live with a aunt up Nacogdoches. The cop had to go into one of them anger management deals or get fired from the force. 'Course Coyle slapped his thigh.

Second deal was about sparring, and was way worse for me'n Dee-Cee than the cop-daughter deal. All of a sudden Coyle started sparring like he never done it before. Everybody was hitting him — middleweights we had in with him to work speed, high school linemen in the gym on a dare, grunts for God's sake. The eye puffed up again, and we had to take off more time. All of a sudden Coyle's moving on his heels instead of his toes, and now he can't jump rope without stumbling into a wall. A amateur light heavy knocked him down hard enough to make him go pie-eyed, and Dee-Cee called the session off. Most times like that, a fighter's pride will make him want to keep on working, but not Coyle. He was happy to get his ass outta there. Billy heard about it and quick got Coyle that second Mississippi fight for seventy-five thousand. Got Coyle ten rounds with a dead man just to see what was what.

The opponent was six foot tall, three hundred twenty-eight pounds, a big old black country boy from Lake Charles, Louisiana, who couldn't hardly scrawl his own name. But in the first round, with his damn eyes closed, he hit Coyle high on the head with an overhand right and knocked him on his ass. Me and Dee-Cee couldn't figure how he didn't see the punch coming, it was so high and wide. Coyle jumped up, and to his credit, he went right to work.

Bang! Three bitches to the eyes, right hand to the chin, left hook to the body, all the punches quick and pretty. The black boy settled like a dead whale to the bottom, and white folks was dancing in the aisles and waving the Stars and Bars. It was pitiful, but Coyle strutted like he just knocked out Jack Johnson. Me and Dee-Cee was pissed, and our peters had lost their glow. Dressing room afterward was quiet as a gray dawn.

Coyle took time off, not that he needed the rest. He came back for a few days, then it got so he wasn't coming in at all. If he did, he'd lie around and bullshit instead of work. You could smell weed on him, and his hair got greasy. Now all our fighters started going flaky. Sweat got scarcer and scarcer. There was other times Coyle'd come in so fluffy from screwing you wished he didn't come in at all. Gym got to be a goddamned social club what looked full of boy whores and Social Security socialites. What with Coyle lying around like a pet poodle, Billy's other fighters started doing the same. Some begged off fights that were sure wins for them. You never want a fighter to fight if he's not ready, but when they're being paid to be in shape, they're supposed to be in shape, not Butterball goddamn turkeys.

I tried to get Coyle to get serious, but he kept saying, "I'm cool, I'm cool."

I said, "Tits on a polar bear's what's cool."

That went on for three months, but I wasn't big enough to choke sense into him. Besides, no trainer worth a damn would want to. Fighters come in on their own, or they don't come in. Billy wanted a answer, but I didn't have one. How do you figure it when a ten-round fighter hungry for money pulls out of fights 'cause of a sore knuckle, or a sprung thumb, or a bad elbow? 'Course old Coyle didn't volunteer for no cut in pay.

One day he was lounging in his velour sweatsuit looking at tittie magazines. He said to turn up the lights. I said they was turned up. He said to turn them up again, and I said they was up again. Coyle yelled at me the first and last time.

"Turn 'em all the goddamn fuck up!"

"Boy," I said, and then I said it again real quiet. "Boy, lights is all the goddamn fuck up."

He looked up. "Oh, uh-huh, yeah, Red, thanks."

About then I figure Kenny don't know shit from Shinola.

Vegas called Billy for a two-hundred-thousand-dollar fight with some African fighting outta France. He had big German money behind him, and he was a tough sumbitch, but he didn't have no punch like Kenny Coyle. Coyle said he'd go for the two-hundred-thousand fight in a heartbeat.

I knew there had to be some fun in all this pain. We whip the Afro-Frenchie and win the next couple of fights, and we're talking three, maybe five hundred thousand a fight. Even if he loses, Billy's got all his money back and more, and me and Dee-Cee's doing right good, too. If we win big, we'll be talking title fight, 'cause word'll be out that there's some big white boy who could be the one to win boxing back from the coloreds. The only coloreds me and Dee-Cee gave a rap about was them colored twenties, and fifties, and hundreds that'd make us proud standing in the bank line instead of meek. Like I say, the amateurs and the pros ain't alike, and Billy's figuring to get his money out of Coyle while he can. Me and Dee-Cee's for that, 'specially me, since it gets me off the hook.

But neither one of us could figure what had happened with Coyle, so we got Billy to bring in some tough sparring partners for the Frenchie fight to test what Coyle had. Same-oh same-oh, with Coyle getting hit. But when he hit them, *damn!* they'd go *down!* A gang of them took off when Coyle threw what that writer guy James Ellroy calls *body rockets* that tore up short ribs and squashed livers. But it was almost like Coyle was swinging blind. Usual-like, you don't care about the sparring partners, they're paid to get hit. But the problem was that Coyle was getting hit, and going *down,* too. He'd take a shot and his knees would do the old butterfly. We figured he'd been smoking weed, or worse — being up all night in toilets with hoochies.

Dee-Cee said, "Can't say I didn't tell him 'bout midnight emissions, but no, he won't listen a me."

But Coyle wasn't short on wind, and he looked strong. Me'n Dee-Cee'd never seen nothing like it, a top guy gets to be a shot fighter so quick like that, 'specially with him doing his road work every dawn? Hell, come to find out he wasn't even smoking weed, just having a beer after a workout so's he could relax and sleep.

Seeing all our work fall apart, I figured we was Cinderella at midnight. Me and Dee-Cee both knew it, but we still couldn't make out why. Then Dee-Cee come to me, his hand over his mouth.

Dee-Cee said, "Coyle's blind in that bad eye."

I said, "What? Bullshit, the commission doctors passed him."

"He's blind, Red, in that hurt eye, I'm tellin' you. I been wavin' a white towel next to it two days now, and he don't blink on the bad-eye side. Watch."

Between rounds sparring next day, with me greasing and watering Coyle, Dee-Cee kind of waved the tip of the towel next to Coyle's good eye and Coyle blinked automatic. Between the next round, Dee-Cee was on the other side. He did the same waving deal with the towel. But Coyle's bad eye didn't blink 'cause he never saw the towel. That's when I understood why he was taking all them shots, that's when I knew he was moving on his heels 'cause he couldn't see the floor clear. And that's why he was getting rocked like it was the first time he was ever hit, 'cause shots was surprising him that he couldn't tell was coming. And it's when I come to know why he was pulling out of fights—he knew he'd lose 'cause he couldn't see. He went for the two-hundred-thousand fight knowing he'd lose, but he took it for the big money. I wanted to shoot the bastard, what with him taking Billy's money and not saying the eye'd gone bad and making a chump outta me.

The rule is if you can't see, then you can't fight. I told Dee-Cee we got to tell Billy. See, Billy's close to being my own kin, and it's like I stuck a knife in his back if I don't come clean.

Dee-Cee said to wait, that it was the commission doctor's fault, not ours, let them take the heat. He said maybe Vegas won't find out, and maybe the fight will fuck Coyle up so bad he'll have to retire anyhow. Billy'll still get most of his money back, Dee-Cee said, so Billy won't have cause to be mad with us. That made sense.

But what happened to mess up our deal permanent was that the Vegas Boxing Commission faxed in its forms for the AIDS blood test, said they wanted a current neuro exam, and they sent forms for a eye exam that had to be done by a ophthalmologist, not some regular doctor with a eye chart. Damned if Coyle wasn't sudden all happy. He couldn't wait once he heard about the eye test. Me and Dee-Cee was wondering how can he want a eye test, what with what we know about that eye?

Sure enough, when the eye test comes in, it says that Coyle's close to stone blind in the bad eye, the one what got cut in Canada. The neuro showed Coyle's balance was off from being hit too much in training camps, which is why he couldn't jump rope, and why he'd shudder when he got popped. The eye exam proved what me and Dee-Cee already knew, which is why Coyle was taking shots what never shoulda landed. What it come down to was the two-hundred-thousand-dollar fight was off, and Coyle's fighting days for big money was over. It also come down to Billy taking it in the ass for sixty grand in signing money that was all my fault. And that ain't saying nothing about all the big purses Coyle coulda won if he had been fit.

Turns out that the fight in Vancouver where Coyle got cut caused his eye to first go bad. The reason why word didn't get loose on him is 'cause Coyle didn't tell the Canadian doctors he was a fighter, and 'cause it was done on that Canadian free health deal they got up there. The eye doc said the operation was seventy percent successful, but told Coyle to be careful, 'cause trauma to the eye could mess it up permanent. What with him dropping out of boxing for a couple of years the way fighters'll do when they lose, people wasn't thinking on him. And the way Coyle passed the eye test in Alabama and Mississippi was to piece off with a hundred-dollar bill the crooked casino croakers what's checking his eyes. When later on he told me how he did it, he laughed the same snorty way as when he told how he played his game on the Navy.

That's when I worked out what was Coyle's plan. See, he knew right after the Marcellus Ellis fight that the eye had gone bad on him again, but he kept that to himself instead of telling anyone about it, thinking his eye operation in Canada won't come out. That way, he could steal Billy's signing money, and pick up the twenty-five hundred a month chasing-pussy money, too. I wondered how long he'd be laughing.

Only now what am I supposed to say to Billy? After all, it was my name on Coyle what clinched the deal. It got to be where my shiny, big old white boy was tarnished as a copper washtub. I talked with Dee-Cee about it.

Dee-Cee said, "You right. That why the schemin' muhfuh come down South from the front!"

See, we surprised Coyle. He didn't know the tests had come back, so me and Dee-Cee just sat him down on the ring apron. Starting out, he was all fluffy.

Dee-Cee said, "Why didn't you tell us about the eye?"

Coyle lied, said, "What eye?"

Dee-Cee said, "Kenny, the first rule's don't shit a shitter. The eye what's fucked up."

Coyle said, "Ain't no eye fucked up."

"You got a fucked-up eye, don't bullshit," said Dee-Cee.

"It ain't bad, it's just blurry."

"Just *blurry* means you ain't fightin' Vegas, that's what's muthuhfuckin' blurry," Dee-Cee said, muscles jumping along his jaw. "I'm quittin' you right now, hyuh? Don't want no truck with no punk playin' me."

Coyle's eyes started to bulge and his neck got all swole up and red. "You're the punk, old man!"

Coyle shoved Dee-Cee hard in the chest. Dee-Cee went down, but he took the fall rolling on his shoulder, and was up like a bounced ball.

Dee-Cee said, "Boy, second rule's don't hit a hitter."

Coyle moved as if to kick Dee-Cee. I reached for my Buck, but before it cleared my back pocket, Dee-Cee quick as a dart used his cane *bap! bap! bap!* to crack Coyle across one knee and both shins. Coyle hit the floor like a sack full of cats.

"I'll kill you, old man. I'll beat your brains out with that stick."

Dee-Cee said, "Muhfuh, you best don't be talking no *kill* shit wit' Dark Chocolate."

Coyle yelled, "Watch your back, old man!"

Dee-Cee said, "Boy, you diggin' you a hole."

Dee-Cee hobbled off, leaning heavy on his cane. Coyle made to go after Dee-Cee again, but by then I'd long had my one-ten out and open.

I said, "Y'all ever see someone skin a live dog?"

I had to get Coyle outta there, thought to quick get him to the Texas Ice House over on Blanco, where we could have some longnecks like good buds and maybe calm down. Texas Ice House's open three hundred sixty-five days a year, sign out front says GO COWBOYS.

Coyle said, "Got my own Texas shit beer at home."

Texas and *shit* in the same breath ain't something us Texans cotton to, but I went on over to Coyle's place later on 'cause I had to. I knocked, and through the door I heard a shotgun shell being jacked into the chamber.

I said, "It's me, Red."

Coyle opened up, then limped out on the porch looking for Dee-Cee.

Coyle said, "I'm gonna kill him, you tell him."

Inside, there was beer cans all over the floor, and the smell of weed and screwing. Coyle and a half-sleepy tittie-club blond gal was lying around half bare-ass. She never said a word throughout. I got names backing me like Geraghty and O'Kelly, but when I got to know what a sidewinder Coyle was, it made me ashamed of belonging to the same race.

I said, "When did the eye go bad?"

Coyle was still babying his legs. "It was perfect before that Marcellus Ellis butted me at the casino. But with you training me, hey baby, I can still fight down around here."

"You go back to chump change you fight down around here."

"My eye is OK, it's just blurry, that's all, don't you start on me, fuck!"

"It's you's what's startin'."

"This happened time before last in Mississippi, OK? And it was gettin' better all by itself, OK?"

I stayed quiet, so did he. Then I said, "Don't you get it? You fail the eye test, no fights in Vegas, or no place where there's money. Only trainer you'll get now's a blood sucker."

Coyle shrugged, even laughed a little. That's when I asked him the one question he didn't never want to hear, the one that would mean he'd have to give back Billy's money if he told the truth.

I said, "Why didn't you tell us about the eye before you signed Billy's contract?"

Coyle got old. He looked off in a thousand-yard stare for close to a minute. He stuttered twice, and then said, "Everybody knew about my eye."

I said, "Not many in Vancouver, and for sure none in San Antonia."

Coyle said, "Vegas coulda checked."

I said, "We ain't Vegas."

Coyle stood up. He thought he wanted to hit me, but he really wanted to hide. Instead, he moved the shotgun so's it was pointing at my gut.

He said, "I don't want you to train me no more."

I said, "Next time you want to fuck somebody, fuck your mama in her casket. She can't fuck you back."

That stood him straight up, and I knew it was time to git. As the door closed behind me, I could hear Coyle and the tittie-club blonde start to laugh.

I said to myself, "Keep laughin', punk cocksucker — point a gun at me and don't shoot."

I drove my pickup over to Billy's office next day, told him the whole thing. It wasn't far from my place but it was the longest ride I ever took. I was expecting to be told to get my redneck ass out of Texas. He just listened, then lit up a Montecristo contraband Havana robusto with a gold Dunhill. He took his time, poured us both some Hennessy XO.

He could see I felt lowdown and thought I'd killed his friendship.

I said, "I'm sorry, Billy, you know I'd never wrong you on purpose."

Billy said, "You couldn't see the future, Red. Only women can, and that's 'cause they know when they're gonna get fucked."

Billy put the joke in there to save me from myself, damned if he didn't. I was ready to track Coyle and gut him right then. But Billy said to calm down, said he'd go over to Coyle's place later on. I wanted to go, said I'd bring along Mr. Smith and Mr. Wesson.

"Naw," said Billy, "there won't be no shootin'."

When Billy got to Coyle's, Kenny was smoking weed again, had hold of a big-assed, stainless steel .357 Mag Ruger with a six-inch barrel. Billy didn't blink, said could he have some iced tea like Coyle was drinking. Coyle said it was Snapple Peach, not diet, but Billy said go on'n hook one up. Things got friendly, but Coyle kept ahold of the Ruger.

Billy said, "Way I see it, you didn't set out to do it."

Coyle said, "That's right. Ellis did it."

Billy said, "But you still got me for sixty large."

Coyle said, "Depends on how you look at it." He laughed at his joke. "Besides, nobody asked about my eye, so I told no lie. Hey, I can rhyme like Ali, that's me, hoo-ee."

Billy said, "Coyle, there's sins of commission and there's sins of omission. This one's a sixty-thousand-dollar omission."

Coyle said, "You got no proof. It was all cash like you wanted, no taxes."

Billy said, "I want my sixty back. You can forget the free rent and the twenty-five hundred you got off me every month, but I want the bonus money."

Coyle said, "Ain't got it to give back."

Billy said, "You got the BMW free and clear. Sign it over and we're square."

Coyle said, "You ain't gettin' my Beamer. Bought that with my signing money."

Billy said, "You takin' it knowin' your eye was shot, that was humbug."

Coyle said, "I'm stickin' with the contract and my lawyer says you still owe me twenty-five hundred for this month, and maybe for three years to come. He says you're the one that caused it all when you put me in with the wrong opponent."

Billy'd put weight on around the belly, and Coyle was saying he wasn't dick afraid of him.

Billy didn't press for the pink, and didn't argue about the twenty-five hundred a month, didn't say nothing about the lost projected income.

"Then tell me this," Billy said, "when do you plan on gettin' out of my building and givin' back my keys?"

Coyle laughed his laugh. "When you evict me, that's when, and you can't do that for a while 'cause my eye means I'm disabled, I checked."

Billy laughed with Coyle, and Billy shook Coyle's left hand with his right before taking off, 'cause Coyle kept the Ruger in his right hand.

Billy said, "Well, let me know if you change your mind."

"Not hardly," said Coyle. "I'm thinkin' on marrying that cop's daughter. This here's our love nest."

Me and Dee-Cee was cussing Coyle twenty-four hours a day, but Billy never let on he cared. About a week later, he said his wife and kids was heading down to Orlando Disney World for a few days. On Thursday he gave me and Dee-Cee the invite to come on down to Nuevo Laredo with him Friday night for the weekend.

Billy said, "We'll have a few thousand drinks at the Cadillac Bar to wash the taste of Coyle out of our mouths."

He sweetened the pot, said how about spending some quality time in the cat houses of Boys Town, all on him? I said my old root'll still do the job with the right inspiration, so did Dee-Cee. But he said his back was paining him bad since the deal with Coyle, and that he had to go on over Houston where he had this Cuban *Santería* woman. She had some kind of mystic rubjuice made with rooster blood he said was the only thing what'd cure him.

Dee-Cee said, "I hate to miss the trip with y'all, but I got to see my Cuban."

I told Billy he might as well ride with me in my Jimmy down to Nuevo Laredo. See, it's on the border some three hours south of San Antonia. I had a transmission I been wanting to deliver to my cousin Royal in Dilley, which is some seventy-eighty miles down from San Antonia on Highway 35 right on our way. Billy said he had stuff to do in the morning, but that he'd meet me at the Cadillac Bar at six o'clock next day. That left just me heading south alone and feeling busted up inside for doing the right thing by a skunk.

I left early so's I could listen to Royal lie, and level out with some of his Jack Daniel's. When I pulled up in front of the Cadillac Bar at ten of six, I saw Billy's bugged-up Town Car parked out front. He was inside, a big smile on him. With my new hat and boots, I felt fifty again, and screw Kenny Coyle and the BMW he rode in on. We was laughing like Coyle didn't matter to us, but underneath, we knew he did.

Billy got us nice rooms in a brand-new motel once we had quail and Dos Equis for dinner, and finished off with fried ice cream in the Messkin style. Best I can recollect, we left our wheels at the motel and took a cab to Boys Town. We hit places like the Honeymoon Hotel, the Dallas Cowboys, and the New York Yankey. Hell, I buried myself in brown titties, even ended up with a little Chink gal I wanted to smuggle home in my hat. Spent two nights with her and didn't never want to go home.

I ain't sure, but seems to me I went back to the motel once on Saturday just to check on Billy. His car was gone, and there was a message for me blinking on the phone in my room, and five one-hundred-dollar bills on my pillow. Billy's message said he had to go on over to Matamoros 'cause the truck for his shrimps had busted down, and he had to rent another one for shrimp night. So I had me a mess of Messkin scrambled eggs and rice and beans and a few thousand bottles of Negra Modelo. I headed on back for my China doll still shaky, but I hadn't lost my boots or my *El Patrón* so I'm thinking I was a tall dog in short grass.

There seems like there were times when I must a blanked out there. But somewhere along the line, I remember wandering the streets over around Boys Town when I come up on a little park that made me stop and watch. It happens in parks all over Mexico. The street lights ain't nothing but hanging bare bulbs with swarms of bugs and darting bats. Boys and girls of fourteen to eighteen'n more'd make the nightly *paseo* — that's like a stroll on the main drag, 'cause there ain't no TV or nothing, and the *paseo*'s what they do to get out from the house to flirt. In some parts, the young folks form circles in the park. The boys' circle'd form outside the girls' circle and each circle moves slow in opposite directions so's the boys and the girls can be facing each other as they pass. The girls try to squirt cheap perfume on a boy they fancy. The boys try to pitch a pinch of confetti into a special girl's month. Everybody gets to laughing and spitting and holding their noses but inside their knickers they're fixing to explode. It's how folks get married down there.

'Course, getting married wasn't on my mind. Something else was, and I did my best to satisfy my mind with some more of that authentic Chinee sweet and sour.

Billy was asleep the next day, Sunday, when I come stumbling back, so I crapped out, too. I remember right, we headed home separate on Sunday night late. Both of us crippled and green but back in Laredo Billy's car was washed and spanky clean except for a cracked rear window. Billy said some Matamoros drunk had made a failed try to break in. He showed me his raw knuckles to prove it.

Billy said, "I can still punch like you taught me, Reddy."

Driving myself home alone, I was all bowlegged, and my heart was leaping sideways. But when it's my time to go to sleep for the last time, I want to die in Boys Town teasing the girls and learning Chinee.

I was still hung over on Monday, and had to lay around all pale and shaky until I could load up on biscuits and gravy, fresh salsa, fried grits, a near pound of bacon, three or four tomatoes, and a few thousand longnecks. I guess I slept most of the time 'cause I don't remember no TV.

It wasn't until when I got to the gym on Tuesday that I found out about Kenny Coyle. Hunters found him dead in the dirt. He was beside his torched BMW in the mesquite on the outside of town. They found him Sunday noon, and word was he'd been dead some twelve hours, which meant he'd been killed near midnight Saturday night. Someone at the gym said the cops had been by to see me. Hell, me'n Billy was in Mexico, and Dee-Cee was in Houston.

The inside skinny was that Coyle'd been hogtied with them plastic cable-tie deals that cops'll sometimes use instead of handcuffs. One leg'd been knee-capped with his own Ruger someplace else, and later his head was busted in by blunt force with a unknown object. His brains was said to hang free, and looked like a bunch of grapes. His balls was in his mouth, and his mouth had been slit to the ear so's both balls'd fit. The story I got was that the cops who found him got to laughing, said it was funny seeing a man eating his own mountain oysters. See, police right away knew it was business.

When the cops stopped by the gym Tuesday morning, I was still having coffee and looking out the storefront window. I didn't have nothing to hide, so I stayed sipping my joe right where I was. I told them the same story I been telling you, starting off with stopping by to see old Royal in Dilley. See, the head cop was old Junior, and old Junior was daddy to that plain-Jane gal.

I told him me and Billy had been down Nuevo Laredo when the tragedy occurred. Told him about the Cadillac Bar, and about drinking tequila and teasing the girls in Boys Town. 'Course, I left out a few thousand details I didn't think was any of his business. Old Junior's eyes got paler still, and his jaw was clenched up to where his lips didn't hardly move when he talked. He didn't ask but two or three questions, and looked satisfied with what I answered.

Fixing to leave, Junior said, "Seems like some's got to learn good sense the hard way."

Once Junior'd gone, talk started up in the gym again and ropes got jumped. Fight gyms from northern Mexico all up through Texas knew what happened to Coyle. Far as I know, the cops never knocked on Billy Clancy's door, but I can tell you that none of Billy's fighters never had trouble working up a sweat no more, or getting up for a fight neither.

I was into my third cup of coffee when I saw old Dee-Cee get off the bus. He was same as always, except this time he had him a knobby new walking stick. It was made of mesquite like the last one. But as he come closer, I could see that the wood on this new one was still green from the tree.

I said, "You hear about Coyle?"

"I jus' got back," said Dee-Cee, "what about him?" One of the colored boys working out started to snicker. Dee-Cee gave that boy a look with those greeny-blue eyes. And that was the end of that.

2002

ELMORE LEONARD

WHEN THE WOMEN COME OUT TO DANCE

Elmore Leonard (1925–) was born in New Orleans and educated at the University of Detroit, where he received a PhD in 1950. He worked in advertising for the next sixteen years before becoming a full-time writer. He wrote numerous short stories, mostly westerns, for men's magazines, and his earliest novels were in that genre, including *The Bounty Hunters* (1953), *Escape from Five Shadows* (1956), and *Hombre* (1961), which became a successful 1967 film starring Paul Newman, Fredric March, and Richard Boone. When mystery stories superseded westerns as the preferred fiction, Leonard switched genres to become one of the greatest crime writers in history.

His earliest work included *The Big Bounce* (1969), filmed disastrously—twice; *The Moonshine War* (1970), filmed the same year with Richard Widmark and Patrick McGoohan; *Fifty-two Pickup* (1974), filmed in 1986 with Roy Scheider and Ann-Margret; *Cat Chaser* (1982), filmed (1990) with his own screenplay; and *Stick* (1983), filmed in 1985 with Burt Reynolds starring. His later work, much of which has also been filmed, notably the excellent *Get Shorty* (1990), filmed in 1995 with John Travolta, has been less plot-driven, more character-based. Leonard is justly regarded as the modern master of dialogue, with never an extraneous or superfluous word, his vivid characters engaging in what appears to be normal speech patterns for them, their easy acceptance of understated threats of violence and retribution making their positions utterly realistic. Critics and reviewers failed to appreciate, or even discover, Leonard until he won the Edgar Allan Poe Award for Best Novel in 1984 for *La Brava;* since then he has been among the most beloved crime writers of our time—both by critics and by the readers who have made his books perennial bestsellers. He was given the Grand Master Award in 1992 by the Mystery Writers of America for lifetime achievement.

A cautionary tale about being careful what you wish for, "When the Women Come Out to Dance" was first published in the author's short story collection of that name (2002); it was selected for *The Best American Mystery Stories 2003*.

▪ ▪ ▪

Lourdes became Mrs. Mahmood's personal maid when her friend Viviana quit to go to L.A. with her husband. Lourdes and Viviana were both from Cali in Colombia and had come to South Florida as mail-order brides. Lourdes's husband, Mr. Zimmer, worked for a paving contractor until his death, two years from the time they were married.

She came to the home on Ocean Drive, only a few blocks from Donald Trump's, expecting to not have a good feeling for a woman named Mrs. Mahmood, wife of Dr. Wasim Mahmood, who altered the faces and breasts of Palm Beach ladies and aspirated their areas of fat. So it surprised Lourdes that the woman didn't look like a Mrs. Mahmood, and that she opened the door herself: this tall redheaded woman in a little green two-piece swimsuit, sunglasses on her nose, opened the door and said, "Lourdes, as in Our Lady of?"

"No, ma'am, Lour-des, the Spanish way to say it," and had to ask, "You have no help here to open the door?"

The redheaded Mrs. Mahmood said, "They're in the laundry room watching soaps." She said, "Come on in," and brought Lourdes into this home of marble floors, of statues and paintings that held no meaning, and out to the swimming pool, where they sat at a patio table beneath a yellow and white umbrella.

There were cigarettes, a silver lighter, and a tall glass with only ice left in it on the table. Mrs. Mahmood lit a cigarette, a long Virginia Slim, and pushed the pack toward Lourdes, who was saying, "All I have is this, Mrs. Mahmood," Lourdes bringing a biographical data sheet, a printout, from her straw bag. She laid it before the redheaded woman showing her breasts as she leaned forward to look at the sheet.

"'Your future wife is in the mail'?"

"From the Latina introduction list for marriage," Lourdes said. "The men who are interested see it on their computers. Is three years old, but what it tells of me is still true. Except of course my age. Now it would say thirty-five."

Mrs. Mahmood, with her wealth, her beauty products, looked no more than thirty. Her red hair was short and reminded Lourdes of the actress who used to be on TV at home, Jill St. John, with the same pale skin. She said, "That's right, you and Viviana were both mail-order brides," still looking at the sheet. "Your English is good—that's true. You don't smoke or drink."

"I drink now sometime, socially."

"You don't have e-mail."

"No, so we wrote letters to correspond, before he came to Cali, where

I lived. They have parties for the men who come and we get—you know, we dress up for it."

"Look each other over."

"Yes, is how I met Mr. Zimmer in person."

"Is that what you called him?"

"I didn't call him anything."

"Mrs. Zimmer," the redheaded woman said. "How would you like to be Mrs. Mahmood?"

"I wouldn't think that was your name."

She was looking at the printout again. "You're virtuous, sensitive, hardworking, optimistic. Looking for a man who's a kind, loving person with a good job. Was that Mr. Zimmer?"

"He was OK except when he drank too much. I had to be careful what I said or it would cause him to hit me. He was strong, too, for a guy his age. He was fifty-eight."

"When you married?"

"When he died."

"I believe Viviana said he was killed?" The woman sounding like she was trying to recall whatever it was Viviana had told her. "An accident on the job?"

Lourdes believed the woman already knew about it, but said, "He was disappeared for a few days until they find his mix truck out by Hialeah, a pile of concrete by it but no reason for the truck to be here since there's no job he was pouring. So the police have the concrete broken open and find Mr. Zimmer."

"Murdered," the redheaded woman said.

"They believe so, yes, his hands tied behind him."

"The police talk to you?"

"Of course. He was my husband."

"I mean did they think you had anything to do with it."

She knew. Lourdes was sure of it.

"There was a suspicion that friends of mine here from Colombia could be the ones did it. Someone who was their enemy told this to the police."

"It have anything to do with drugs?"

The woman seeing all Colombians as drug dealers.

"My husband drove a cement truck."

"But why would anyone want to kill him?"

"Who knows?" Lourdes said. "This person who finked, he told the police I got the Colombian guys to do it because my husband was always beating me. One time he hit me so hard," Lourdes said, touching the strap of her blue sundress that was faded almost white from washing, "it separated my shoulder, the bones in here, so I couldn't work."

"Did you tell the Colombian guys he was beating you?"

"Everyone knew. Sometime Mr. Zimmer was brutal to me in public, when he was drinking."

"So maybe the Colombian guys did do it." The woman sounding like she wanted to believe it.

"I don't know," Lourdes said, and waited to see if this was the end of it. Her gaze moved out to the sunlight, to the water in the swimming pool lying still, and beyond to red bougainvillea growing against white walls. Gardeners were weeding and trimming, three of them Lourdes thought at first were Latino. No, the color of their skin was different. She said, "Those men . . ."

"Pakistanis," Mrs. Mahmood said.

"They don't seem to work too hard," Lourdes said. "I always have a garden at home, grow things to eat. Here, when I was married, I worked for Miss Olympia. She call her service Cleaning with Biblical Integrity. I wasn't sure what it means, but she would say things to us from the Holy Bible. We cleaned offices in buildings in Miami. What I do here Viviana said would be different, personal to you. See to your things, keep your clothes nice?"

Straighten her dresser drawers. Clean her jewelry. Mrs. Mahmood said she kicked her shoes off in the closet, so Lourdes would see they were paired and hung in the shoe racks. Check to see what needed to be dry-cleaned. Lourdes waited as the woman stopped to think of other tasks. See to her makeup drawers in the bathroom. Lourdes would live here, have Sundays off, a half day during the week. Technically she would be an employee of Dr. Mahmood's.

Oh? Lourdes wasn't sure what that meant. Before she could ask, Mrs. Mahmood wanted to know if she was a naturalized citizen. Lourdes told her she was a permanent resident, but now had to get the papers to become a citizen.

"I say who I work for I put Dr. Wasim Mahmood?"

The redheaded wife said, "It's easier that way. You know, to handle what's taken out. But I'll see that you clear at least three-fifty a week."

Lourdes said that was very generous. "But will I be doing things also for Dr. Mahmood?"

The redheaded woman smoking her cigarette said, "What did Viviana tell you about him?"

"She say only that he didn't speak to her much."

"Viviana's a size twelve. Woz likes them young and as lean as snakes. How much do you weigh?"

"Less than one hundred twenty-five pounds."

"But not much — you may be safe. You cook?"

"Yes, of course."

"I mean for yourself. We go out or order in from restaurants. I won't go near that fucking stove and Woz knows it."

Lourdes said, "Wos?"

"Wasim. He thinks it's because I don't know how to cook, which I don't, really, but that's not the reason. The two regular maids are Filipina and speak English. In fact, they have less of an accent than you. They won't give you any trouble, they look at the ground when they talk to anyone. And they leave at four, thank God. Woz always swims nude — don't ask me why, it might be a Muslim thing — so if they see him in the pool they hide in the laundry room. Or if I put on some southern hip-hop and they happen to walk in while I'm bouncing to Dirty South doing my aerobics, they run for the laundry room." She said without a pause, "What did Viviana say about me?"

"Oh, how nice you are, what a pleasure to work here."

"Come on — I know she told you I was a stripper."

"She say you were a dancer before, yes."

"I started out in a dump on Federal Highway, got discovered and jumped to Miami Gold on Biscayne, valet parking. I was one of the very first, outside of black chicks, to do southern hip-hop, and I mean Dirty South raw and uncut, while the other girls are doing Limp Bizkit, even some old Bob Seeger and Bad Company — and that's OK, whatever works for you. But in the meantime I'm making more doing laptops and private gigs than any girl at the Gold and I'm twenty-seven at the time, older than any of them. Woz would come in with his buddies, all suits and ties, trying hard not to look Third World. The first time he waved a fifty at me I gave him some close-up tribal strip-hop. I said, 'Doctor, you can see better if you put your eyeballs back in your head.' He loved that kind of talk. About the fourth visit I gave him what's known as the million-dollar hand job and became Mrs. Mahmood."

She told this sitting back, relaxed, smoking her Virginia Slim cigarette, Lourdes nodding, wondering at times what she was talking about, Lourdes saying "I see" in a pleasant voice when the woman paused.

Now she was saying, "His first wife stayed in Pakistan while he was here in med school. Right after he finished his residency and opened his practice, she died." The woman said, "Let's see . . . You won't have to wear a uniform unless Woz wants you to serve drinks. Once in a while he has some of his ragtop buddies over for cocktails. Now you see these guys in their Nehru outfits and hear them chattering away in Urdu. I walk in, 'Ah, Mrs. Mahmood,' in that semi-British singsongy way they speak, 'what a lovely sight you are to my eyes this evening.' Wondering if I'm the same chick he used to watch strip."

She took time to light another cigarette, and Lourdes said, "Do I wear my own clothes working here?"

"At first, but I'll get you some cool outfits. What are you, about an eight?"

"My size? Yes, I believe so."

"Let's see — stand up."

Lourdes rose and moved away from the table in the direction Mrs. Mahmood waved her hand. Now the woman was staring at her. She said, "I told you his first wife died?"

"Yes, ma'am, you did."

"She burned to death."

Lourdes said, "Oh?"

But the redheaded woman didn't tell her how it happened. She smoked her cigarette and said, "Your legs are good, but you're kinda short-waisted, a bit top-heavy. But don't worry, I'll get you fixed up. What's your favorite color?"

"I always like blue, Mrs. Mahmood."

She said, "Listen, I don't want you to call me that anymore. You can say ma'am in front of Woz to get my attention, but when it's just you and I? I'd rather you called me by my own name."

"Yes?"

"It's Ginger. Well, actually it's Janeen, but all of my friends call me Ginger. The ones I have left."

Meaning, Lourdes believed, since she was married to the doctor, friends who also danced naked, or maybe even guys.

Lourdes said, "Ginger?"

"Not Yinyor. Gin-ger. Try it again."

"Gin-gar?"

"That's close. Work on it."

But she could not make herself call Mrs. Mahmood Ginger. Not yet. Not during the first few weeks. Not on the shopping trip to Worth Avenue where Mrs. Mahmood knew everyone, all the salesgirls, and some of them did call her Ginger. She picked out for Lourdes casual summer dresses that cost hundreds of dollars each and some things from Resort

Wear, saying, "This is cute," and would hand it to the salesgirl to put aside, never asking Lourdes her opinion, if she liked the clothes or not. She did, but wished some of them were blue. Everything was yellow or yellow and white or white with yellow. She didn't have to wear a uniform, no, but now she matched the yellow and white patio, the cushions, the umbrellas, feeling herself part of the decor, invisible.

Sitting out here in the evening several times a week when the doctor didn't come home, Mrs. Mahmood trying hard to make it seem they were friends, Mrs. Mahmood serving daiquiris in round crystal goblets, waiting on her personal maid. It was nice to be treated this way, and it would continue, Lourdes believed, until Mrs. Mahmood finally came out and said what was on her mind, what she wanted Lourdes to do for her.

The work was nothing, keep the woman's clothes in order, water the houseplants, fix lunch for herself—and the maids, once they came in the kitchen sniffing her spicy seafood dishes. Lourdes had no trouble talking to them. They looked right at her face telling her things. Why they avoided Dr. Mahmood. Because he would ask very personal questions about their sexual lives. Why they thought Mrs. Mahmood was crazy. Because of the way she danced in just her underwear.

And in the evening the woman of the house would tell Lourdes of being bored with her life, not able to invite her friends in because Woz didn't approve of them.

"What do I do? I hang out. I listen to music. I discuss soap operas with the gook maids. Melda stops me. 'Oh, missus, come quick.' They're in the laundry room watching *As the World Turns*. She goes, 'Dick follows Nikki to where she is to meet Ryder, and it look like he was going to hurt her. But Ryder came there in time to save Nikki from a violent Dick.'"

Mrs. Mahmood would tell a story like that and look at her without an expression on her face, waiting for Lourdes to smile or laugh. But what was funny about the story?

"What do I do?" was the question she asked most. "I exist, I have no life."

"You go shopping."

"That's all."

"You play golf."

"You've gotta be kidding."

"You go out with your husband."

"To an Indian restaurant and I listen to him talk to the manager. How many times since you've been here has he come home in the evening?

He has a girlfriend," the good-looking redheaded woman said. "He's with her all the time. Her or another one, and doesn't care that I know. He's rubbing it in my face. All guys fool around at least once in a while. Woz and his buddies live for it. It's accepted over there, where they're from. A guy gets tired of his wife in Pakistan? He burns her to death. Or has it done. I'm not kidding, he tells everyone her *dupatta* caught fire from the stove."

Lourdes said, "Ah, that's why you don't cook."

"Among other reasons. Woz's from Rawalpindi, a town where forty women a *month* show up at the hospital with terrible burns. If the woman survives . . . Are you listening to me?"

Lourdes was sipping her daiquiri. "Yes, of course."

"If she doesn't die, she lives in shame because her husband, this prick who tried to burn her to death, kicked her out of the fucking house. And he gets away with it. Pakistan, India, thousands of women are burned every year 'cause their husbands are tired of them, or they didn't come up with a big enough dowry."

"You say the first wife was burn to death."

"Once he could afford white women — like, what would he need her for?"

"You afraid he's going to burn you?"

"It's what they do, their custom. And you know what's ironic? Woz comes here to be a plastic surgeon, but over in Pakistan, where all these women are going around disfigured? There are no plastic surgeons to speak of." She said, "Some of them get acid thrown in their face." She said, "I made the biggest mistake of my life marrying a guy from a different culture, a towelhead."

Lourdes said, "Why did you?"

She gestured. "This . . ." Meaning the house and all that went with it.

"So you have what you want."

"I won't if I leave him."

"Maybe in the divorce he let you keep the house."

"It's in the prenup, I get zip. And at thirty-two I'm back stripping on Federal Highway, or working in one of those topless doughnut places. You have tits, at least you can get a job. Woz's favorite, I'd come out in a nurse's uniform, peel everything off but the perky little cap?" The woman's mind moving to this without pausing. "Woz said the first time he saw the act he wanted to hire me. I'd be the first topless surgical nurse."

Lourdes imagined this woman dancing naked, men watching her, and thought of Miss Olympia warning the cleaning women with her Biblical Integrity: no singing or dancing around while cleaning the offices, or they might catch the eye of men working late. She made it sound as if they were lying in wait. "Read the Book of Judges," Miss Olympia said, "the twenty-first verse." It was about men waiting for women, the daughters of Shiloh, to come out to dance so they could take them, force the women to be their wives. Lourdes knew of cleaning women who sang while they worked, but not ones who danced. She wondered what it would be like to dance naked in front of men.

"You don't want to be with him," Lourdes said, "but you want to live in this house."

"There it is," the woman who didn't look at all like a Mrs. Mahmood said.

Lourdes sipped her daiquiri, put the glass down, and reached for the pack of Virginia Slims on the table.

"May I try one of these?"

"Help yourself."

She lit the cigarette, sucking hard to get a good draw. She said, "I use to smoke. The way you do it made me want to smoke again. Even the way you hold the cigarette."

Lourdes believed the woman was very close to telling what she was thinking about. Still, it was not something easy to talk about with another person, even for a woman who danced naked. Lourdes decided this evening to help her.

She said, "How would you feel if a load of wet concrete fell on your husband?"

Then wondered, sitting in the silence, not looking at the woman, if she had spoken too soon.

The redheaded woman said, "The way it happened to Mr. Zimmer? How did you feel?"

"I accepted it," Lourdes said, "with a feeling of relief, knowing I wouldn't be beaten no more."

"Were you ever happy with him?"

"Not for one day."

"You picked him, you must've had some idea."

"He picked me. At the party in Cali? There were seven Colombian girls for each American. I didn't think I would be chosen. We married . . . In two years I had my green card and was tired of him hitting me."

The redheaded Mrs. Mahmood said, "You took a lot of shit, didn't you?" and paused this time before saying, "How much does a load of concrete cost these days?"

Lourdes, without pausing, said, "Thirty thousand."

Mrs. Mahmood said, "Jesus Christ," but was composed, sitting back in her yellow cushions. She said, "You were ready. Viviana told you the situation and you decided to go for it."

"I think it was you hired me," Lourdes said, "because of Mr. Zimmer — you so interested in what happen to him. Also I could tell, from the first day we sat here, you don't care for your husband."

"You can understand why, can't you? I'm scared to death of catching on fire. He lights a cigar, I watch him like a fucking hawk."

Giving herself a reason, an excuse.

"We don't need to talk about him," Lourdes said. "You pay the money, all of it before, and we don't speak of this again. You don't pay, we still never speak of it."

"The Colombian guys have to have it all up front?"

"The what guys?"

"The concrete guys."

"You don't know what kind of guys they are. What if it looks like an accident and you say oh, they didn't do nothing, he fell off his boat."

"Woz doesn't have a boat."

"Or his car was hit by a truck. You understand? You not going to know anything before."

"I suppose they want cash."

"Of course."

"I can't go to the bank and draw that much."

"Then we forget it."

Lourdes waited while the woman thought about it smoking her Virginia Slim, both of them smoking, until Mrs. Mahmood said, "If I give you close to twenty thousand in cash, today, right now, you still want to forget it?"

Now Lourdes had to stop and think for a moment.

"You have that much in the house?"

"My getaway money," Mrs. Mahmood said, "in case I ever have to leave in a hurry. What I socked away in tips getting guys to spot their pants and that's the deal, twenty grand. You want it or not? You don't, you might as well leave, I don't need you anymore."

So far in the few weeks she was here, Lourdes had met Dr. Mahmood face-to-face with reason to speak to him only twice. The first time, when he came in the kitchen and asked her to prepare his breakfast, the smoked snook, a fish he ate cold with tea and whole wheat toast. He asked her to have some of the snook if she wished, saying it wasn't as good as kippers but would do. Lourdes tried a piece; it was full of bones but she told him yes, it was good. They spoke of different kinds of fish from the ocean they liked and he seemed to be a pleasant, reasonable man.

The second time Lourdes was with him face-to-face he startled her, coming out of the swimming pool naked as she was watering the plants on the patio. He called to her to bring him his towel from the chair. When she came with it he said, "You were waiting for me?"

"No, sir, I didn't see you."

As he dried his face and his head, the hair so short it appeared shaved, she stared at his skin, at his round belly and his strange black penis, Lourdes looking up then as he lowered the towel.

He said, "You are a widow?" She nodded yes and he said, "When you married, you were a virgin?"

She hesitated, but then answered because she was telling a doctor, "No, sir."

"It wasn't important to your husband?"

"I don't think so."

"Would you see an advantage in again being a virgin?"

She had to think — it wasn't something ever in her mind before — but didn't want to make the doctor wait, so she said, "No, not at my age."

The doctor said, "I can restore it if you wish."

"Make me a virgin?"

"Surgically, a few sutures down there in the tender dark. It's becoming popular in the Orient with girls entering marriage. Also for prostitutes. They can charge much more, often thousands of dollars for that one night." He said, "I'm thinking of offering the procedure. Should you change your mind, wish me to examine you, I could do it in your room."

Dr. Mahmood's manner, and the way he looked at her that time, made Lourdes feel like taking her clothes off.

He didn't come home the night Lourdes and Mrs. Mahmood got down to business. Or the next night. The morning of the following day, two men from the Palm Beach County sheriff's office came to the house. They showed Lourdes their identification and asked to see Mrs. Mahmood.

She was upstairs in her bedroom trying on a black dress, looking at herself in the full-length mirror and then at Lourdes's reflection appearing behind her.

"The police are here," Lourdes said.

Mrs. Mahmood nodded and said, "What do you think?" turning to pose in the dress, the skirt quite short.

Lourdes read the story in the newspaper that said Dr. Wasim Mahmood, prominent etc., etc., had suffered gunshot wounds during an apparent carjacking on Flagler near Currie Park and was pronounced dead on arrival at Good Samaritan. His Mercedes was found abandoned on the street in Delray Beach.

Mrs. Mahmood left the house in her black dress. Later, she phoned to tell Lourdes she had identified the body, spent time with the police, who had no clues, nothing at all to go on, then stopped by a funeral home and arranged to have Woz cremated without delay. She said, "What do you think?"

"About what?" Lourdes said.

"Having the fucker burned."

She said she was stopping to see friends and wouldn't be home until late.

One A.M., following an informal evening of drinks with old friends, Mrs. Mahmood came into the kitchen from the garage and began to lose her glow.

What was going on here?

Rum and mixes on the counter, limes, a bowl of ice. A Latin beat coming from the patio. She followed the sound to a ring of burning candles, to Lourdes in a green swimsuit moving in one place to the beat, hands raised, Lourdes grinding her hips in a subtle way.

The two guys at the table smoking cigarettes saw Mrs. Mahmood, but made no move to get up.

Now Lourdes turned from them and saw her, Lourdes smiling a little as she said, "How you doing? You look like you feeling no pain."

"You have my suit on," Mrs. Mahmood said.

"I put on my yellow one," Lourdes said, still moving in that subtle way, "and took it off. I don't wear yellow no more, so I borrow one of yours. Is OK, isn't it?"

Mrs. Mahmood said, "What's going on?"

"This is *cumbia*, Colombian music for when you want to celebrate. For a wedding, a funeral, anything you want. The candles are part of it. *Cumbia,* you should always light candles."

Mrs. Mahmood said, "Yeah, but what is going on?"

"We having a party for you, Ginger. The Colombian guys come to see you dance."

2002

SCOTT WOLVEN

CONTROLLED BURN

Scott Wolven (1965–) was born in Fort Riley, Kentucky, where his father was stationed before going to Vietnam. He grew up in Saugerties and Catskill, New York. After earning a certificate in creative writing from Columbia University, he studied in the MFA program at Columbia. He worked as a logger, a project manager, and an instructor at Binghamton University (SUNY), and was a visiting writer at Indiana University and the University of Chicago.

Wolven has the remarkable distinction of having appeared in seven consecutive editions of *The Best American Mystery Stories.* His first book, *Controlled Burn: Stories of Prison, Crime, and Men* (2005), collected several of these stories, as well as others, and was one of the most enthusiastically published books of the year. Among those who heaped praise on Wolven's debut are Richard Ford ("Wolven has turned raw, unreconciled life into startling, evocative, and very good short stories. He draws on a New England different from Updike's and even Dubus,' but his fictive lives — no less than theirs — render the world newly, and full of important consequences"); Nelson DeMille ("*Controlled Burn* is good. Very good. Remarkable, actually. Tough, gritty, and honest — reminiscent of Hemingway with a little bit of John Steinbeck"); and George Pelecanos (". . . tough, unsentimental, and completely earned. This is the most exciting, authentic collection of short stories I have read in years"). It had a starred review in *Publishers Weekly;* was named a "A Book to Remember" by the New York Public Library; and Amazon, Borders, and Barnes & Noble all selected it as a top ten fiction debut.

Almost any story in *Controlled Burn* would fit comfortably between the covers of this book, but the lives depicted in this story, of people who chose "an easy way to make a hard living," as the author once described it, are especially deserving.

"Controlled Burn" was originally published in the winter 2002 issue of *Harpur Palate,* and was selected for *The Best American Mystery Stories 2003.*

▪ ▪ ▪

IT WAS A BAD winter and a worse spring. It was the summer Bill Allen lived and died, the sweltering summer I landed a job cutting trees for Robert Wilson's scab-logging outfit near Orford, New Hampshire. June boiled itself away into the heavy steam of July. Heat devils rose in waves off the blacktop as timber trucks rolled in. By the end of July, we switched gears and started cutting stove wood. I was cutting eight cords a day while Robert worked the hydraulic splitter. Then we'd deliver it in one of our dump trucks. Some men drove to the woodlot to pick up their own. Some of them had white salt marks on their boots and jackets from sweat — some of them smelled like beer. Most of them smelled like gasoline. They didn't say much, just paid for their wood and left with it in their pickup trucks. They were either busy working or busy living their lies, which is work in itself. I knew about that. The hard work crushed one empty beer can day after another, adding to my lifetime pile of empties. Summer moved on, gray in spite of the bright sun.

That Friday, I was Bill Allen. I was Bill Allen all that summer. Bill Allen was what caused me to jump every time the phone rang. I was Bill Allen from Glens Falls, New York, and I was taking a summer off from college. I repeated that story as often and as loudly as possible. And each ring of the phone might be someone asking me to prove I was Bill Allen, which was out of the question. Back in December, in the middle of another, different lie, I tried to rob a gas station near Cape May, New Jersey. It was off-season then, nobody around, and I thought it would be easy. It fit the person I'd lied about being. A high school girl was behind the counter. I wore a ski mask and carried a cheap, semiautomatic pistol. I must have touched the trigger, because the gun went off. Maybe she lived. I really couldn't say. I left fast. My brain was on fire, I hadn't meant to shoot her. But it was too late for that. I took a roll of bills and ended up at Robert's. Robert paid cash at the end of the week, didn't bother with Uncle Sam, didn't ask for references, and had plenty of backbreaking work that needed doing, without his son around to help him. Bill Allen was just the man for the job, and every day I was Bill Allen to the best of my ability. It didn't help — my grim yesterdays cast the longest shadows in the Connecticut River Valley. I watched every car, studied every face. Bill Allen never knew a peaceful day. If it hadn't been for the marathon workload Robert demanded, Bill Allen never would have slept. I'd have probably shot Bill Allen myself if I hadn't been working so hard to keep him going. Some days, he lives on with different names. Allen Williams, Al Wilson, Bill Roberts. Bill Allen probably died in a fire that summer. Leave it at that, with questions about Bill Allen.

* * *

The phone at the woodlot rang around noon that Friday. I heard it, had been hearing it most of August. Robert's son John was in jail in Concord, awaiting trial for murderous assault, so there were a lot of phone calls. Robert had rigged the phone with two speakers—one bolted to the stovepipe that stuck out of the roof of our headquarters shack and the other attached by some baling wire to the sick elm on the end of the lot. The sudden scream of the phone spiked my heart rate at least twice a day. Echoing in the alleys between the giant piles of long logs. The woodlot sat surrounded by low, field-grass hills and trees in a natural bowl, just off the highway north of Hanover. Robert's house was on the top of the hill, built with its back to the woodlot, facing a farm field. On a still day, the beauty of the Connecticut River drifted the quarter mile over the farm field and quietly framed all the other sounds, the birds, the trees in the breeze. I was never a part of those days.

The phone rang over the diesel roar of my yellow Maxi-lift, the near-dead cherry picker we kept around to police up the yard. I was working, sweating in the sun, busy shifting a full twelve-ton load of New Hampshire rock maple to the very back of the drying mountains of timber, heat against next year's winter. The phone rang again, not that anyone wanted to talk to me. Most times I'd shut the equipment down, run across the yard, slam into the shed, pick up, and get "Robert there?" and they'd hang up when I said no. Or they wouldn't say anything, just hang up when they knew I wasn't Robert. And I could breathe again, because it wasn't someone looking for me. Just locals, as if I couldn't take a wood order. Or it would be the mechanical jail operator, would I please accept a collect call from inmate John Wilson at the Merrimack Correctional Facility. Then I'd say yes and have to go get Robert anyway. Nobody wanted to talk to me, and I didn't want to talk to anyone, so I let it ring. Robert would get it. Or he wouldn't. They know where to find me, he'd say. Working in the same place for thirty years, if they can't find me, what the hell would I want to talk to them for, he'd say. Must be stupid if they can't get hold of me. Robert's voice was a ton of gravel coming off a truck, years of cigarettes mucking up the inside of his barrel chest. There was no sign at the dirt road entrance to the woodlot. It was Robert Wilson's woodlot, and everyone knew without asking.

Robert came out of the shed and waved at me to shut the cherry picker down. I flipped a switch, turned the keys back a click, and cranked the brake on. I walked over to the shed. Robert had his jean coveralls on. He squinted against the sun, nodded, and spoke.

"That was Frank Lord. He wants his wood tomorrow." Robert took twenty-five dollars out of his pocket and handed it to me. That was our deal—fifty dollars if I had to work on Saturday, twenty-five up front. "You can fix his load today."

I nodded. "What does he get?"

"Two cord, plus half a cord of kiln-dried."

Robert had converted an old singlewide trailer into a kiln and most of his customers ordered mixed loads of both air- and kiln-dried. Kiln-dried wood burns hotter than air-dried. Mixing a kiln-dried log in with every fire produces more heat, allows the air-dried wood to burn more efficiently. People with woodstoves got as much heat out of two air-dried cords mixed with half a cord of kiln-dried as people who burned four straight cords. When a single woodstove is the primary heat source for a whole house, each log has to do its job. Robert charged more for the kiln-dried and nobody kicked about the price.

I took my Texaco ball cap off. "If you don't want it mixed, we'll have to take two trucks." Lord's farm was thirty-five miles north and slightly west, just on the Vermont side of the Connecticut River, near Newbury. The river came straight down through the Northeast Kingdom, and just past Wells River, it made an oxbow, flowing briefly north in a U-shaped collar before returning to its southern course. Lord's farm encompassed all of the oxbow, stretching from Route 5 all the way east to the river, which was the Vermont–New Hampshire border. It was the most beautiful spot on earth, the most amazing fields and woods and sky that Bill Allen had ever seen. Robert and I had driven past once that summer, on the way to Wells River to pick up a chain saw. Looking out of the truck as we drove up Route 5 and seeing Lord's white farm buildings and fields, I thought maybe I could make it through Bill Allen and still have a life, somewhere. On the way back, the view of the green fields sweeping out into the bend of the river made everything stop. I didn't hear the engine of the truck, nor the gears. We floated along the road as my mind took picture after picture, of the farm and the fields and the blue sky with the sun setting. That bend in the river. I came alive for a minute, and as the farm slowly passed by I died again, back into the zombie lie of Bill Allen.

Robert was talking to me, shaking his head. "He's got some extra work. Stobe can drive the small rig."

Stobik lived south of the woodlot, in White River Junction, and did odd jobs for Robert. Stobik's wife was as big as the house they lived in. He didn't have a phone—if Robert needed him for something, I'd drive down first thing in the morning and pick him up. Just pulled my beat-up Bronco into his dooryard and sat there till he came out. Sometimes, a thin, white hand would appear in the dirty window, waving me away. Too drunk to work. He lived in a culvert on the woodlot for about a month when things got tough with his wife. He was skinny as a rail, hadn't showered in about a week, month, year. His teeth were broken brown stumps and his fingers were stained from tobacco. But he could cut and stack firewood faster than two men, and at half the price.

"I'll pick him up in the morning," I said.

"That's OK. I'll get him tonight and let him sleep on the porch," Robert said. "I want to make sure he can work tomorrow." He walked back inside the shed. I fixed Frank Lord's load of wood for the next day and went to the loft of a barn I called home.

Next morning, I was at the woodlot at five-thirty. It was pitch black. Robert was already there, sitting in his pickup truck, drinking coffee and eating a hard-boiled egg. He had the running lights on. I drove slowly over to the open driver's side window.

"Thought you overslept," he said.

I climbed out of the Bronco and got into the big white rig. Stobik got behind the wheel of the small one. Robert was driving the big rig.

The floor of the white rig was taken up with logging chains. The last job Robert had used it for was a semicommercial haul, and he'd left the chains in. He had a whole barn full of them up by his house. He'd load them in the truck and then get weighed, toss them out at the job and then leave them there. The customer paid the difference. How many people paid for those chains, only God knows. The fuse box was open on the passenger's side, so that any metal that jumped up during the ride could cause a spark or worse. It made for a tense ride.

We started the drive up to North Haverhill on the New Hampshire side of the Connecticut River. It was beautiful. The sun began to shine. The truck could only make thirty-five fully loaded. Stobik was always right behind us, with the flashers on. Robert wrestled the gears up a hill. Then he lit a cigarette and spoke.

"When I was fifteen, I ran away and ended up on Frank Lord's farm." He looked over at me.

"I didn't know that," I answered.

"Frank Lord worked me so hard I thought I was going to drop. But it straightened me out. Best thing that ever happened to me."

"What was wrong with you?" I asked.

"Bad temper," Robert answered. "Bad temper and drinking." We passed a broken-down barn.

"At fifteen?"

Robert nodded. "Back then, fifteen was like thirty-five. You had a job, a car — they made you live life back then, and if you didn't like it, get the fuck out." He took a drag off his cigarette. He was silent, smoking, for the rest of the ride.

Frank Lord was standing in his driveway as we pulled up. He looked as though we'd just been there yesterday. He had an oxygen mask on and a green tank marked OXYGEN in white letters standing next to him. The fields stretched out behind him all the way to the river. The big white farmhouse behind him needed a coat of paint. There were a couple of barns and buildings. They needed paint too. Parked alongside the main house was a brand-new pickup truck. On top of the main house was a black wrought iron weather vane, the silhouette of a big black stallion. The weather vane pointed north.

"What are you going to do, make something out of yourself or what?" His voice was muffled behind the clear plastic mask. His breath made it fill with mist. He pointed over toward the nearest barn. "Put it over there," he said through the mask. "Don't mix it together." He and Robert walked slowly toward the main house and sat on the porch in kitchen chairs. Stobik and I unloaded and stacked the wood. Stobik worked fast. His stacks were the straightest I've ever seen. His face seemed frozen in a perpetual grin as we worked in silence. The stacks came out perfectly. We went back over to Robert and Frank on the porch. It was just around noon.

"We've got some other work to do," Frank said. He held out a piece of paper.

"What's that?" I asked.

"Yesterday, in the morning, Judge Harris stopped over here. Unofficially. I've known his family for probably, oh, fifty years." The breeze tossed the tops of the corn. "He told me that the state police got a tip I was growing marijuana. They were trying to get a warrant to search my house and my fields." He held out the paper. "Harris dropped this off." I read the paper. It was a one-day special permit for a controlled burn.

"What do you want us to do?" I asked.

"Burn it, all of it. Right back to the river. I don't want a single thing left alive." He stared at the porch and then looked straight at Stobik and me. "Just in case there's a little Mexican hay that got mixed in with my corn somehow."

Robert came down off the porch to supervise. He and I rigged up a sprayer with some gas and soaked a good portion of the front field. We left a wide strip in the middle completely dry. Then we drove the tractor through a thin line of trees, and there was a huge cornfield that stretched all the way to the river. In the middle of the field, probably six hundred yards away, was a small white shack. Robert spoke up.

"That's where my first wife and I lived." He looked at it.

I looked over at him. "I never think about you being married."

He nodded. "Well I was, for a while." He pointed his chin at the shack. "People that live in places like that don't very often stay married." He stared at the white shack. "I had a bad temper then."

I nodded. "Should we burn it?"

"Oh yeah." Robert wiped his forehead with a red kerchief. Sweat had run down from his forehead and got into his eyes and on his chin.

"What if there are people in it?" I looked over at the shack.

"Then fuck 'em, let 'em burn. Their name isn't Lord and they don't belong on this property." Robert spit into the field. "Frank said burn it, and that's what we're going to do." He looked across the rows of corn toward the river. "Hotter than Hades." He looked over at me. "You'll never be cold again, after this." He started to drive the tractor toward the white shack with me on the back of his seat. "Here, watch this," he shouted over the tractor.

We pulled up next to the shack. The windows on the one side had been broken, but the chicken wire in the glass remained, rusted from the weather. I heard a faint hum.

"Watch this," Robert said. He took the nozzle from the gas sprayer and aimed a fine stream at the window. I saw some wasps beginning to fly out of the broken window. Robert pointed his chin at them and talked above the noise of the tractor. "Wasps," he said. "They're the worst." Some moved slowly, clinging to the chicken wire. I could see their insect heads, sectioned bodies, and stingers. They were getting soaked with gas. "Throw a match," Robert said.

"No," I said. "It'll explode." I pointed at the sprayer and the tank of gas on the tractor.

"Gas doesn't burn," Robert said. "It's wet—nothing that's wet can burn. It's the fumes that burn." He took a wood match out of his pocket and struck it on the tractor, then tossed the small flame into the gas spray.

The air groaned and came alive with fire. The wasps were flying full-bore out of the broken window now, right into the wall of flame and through it. Their wings were on fire, still beating, the air currents lifting them up in the heat even as they burned to nothing. A flaming wasp landed on my work shirt and I smacked it into the corn. Now they were all over, burning and flying. Stinging anything they touched. One lost a wing and kept flying, a coin-sized flaming circle into the corn. I watched one come out of the window whole, coated shiny with gas. It flew over the corn, its wings caught fire and kept beating as the body burned to a cinder, the wings still going until they vanished in tiny ash. Robert smacked some wasps off his arm and backed the tractor up, driving over to the river.

We soaked the corn next to the river and then sprayed it a little thinner up on the bank. "The fire will seek the gas," Robert said. "That patch we left in the middle will burn slower than the rest. We'll be all set."

We decided that the best way to do it would be to have Stobik drive the truck around to the New Hampshire side of the oxbow. Then I'd light the fire from the riverbank too, so that the onrushing flames wouldn't somehow jump the river. Robert drove the tractor back through the field, leaving me standing right on the bend in the river with a box of matches. I could barely see the white shack over the corn. The river ran behind me, softly laughing its way over the rocks. Everything was still, and my heart almost stopped panting for the first time in a long time. Bill Allen stood on the riverbank and knew he needed to die. He knew he had to go back to the place he was born and answer for the crime that fathered him. I heard the airhorn blow from the big rig, Robert's signal to me that he was clear of the fields. As I lit the corn on fire, Bill Allen decided to throw himself into the blaze.

The flames grew fast, and I jumped out into the Connecticut River. It must have been cool, but I didn't feel it. The heat from the fire seemed to reach across the oxbow and right through the water. I climbed up on the bank on the other side just in time to see Robert's white wedding shack take the flames full force. The walls and roof caught like they were made of rice paper, and in the next instant the shack was gone. The fire was so hot, so intense, I couldn't look at it. I walked farther up on the bank and Stobik was there with the small truck. I got in and we started to drive back toward Vermont. A black cloud grew in the air of the beautiful blue horizon and we watched it for miles. It seemed as if we'd permanently smudged the sky.

When we got back to Lord's farm, Robert was busy fending off several local volunteer fire companies, who had arrived with sirens and lights going. He just kept showing them the permit Judge Harris had given to Frank. Stobik and I stayed in the small truck. At one point, I swear the flames in the field were higher than the farmhouse. Stobik backed the truck up so the windshield wouldn't crack. I finally got out and sat alone in the passenger's side of the big rig. I fell asleep. It was late that night when Robert climbed in to drive and slammed his door, bringing me straight up in my seat. The fields were still burning and all I could smell was smoke. We drove slowly back to the woodlot and I slept there in my Bronco. The next day—Sunday—I was going to drive all day and turn myself in. Bill Allen was dead.

The screaming echo of the phone over the woodlot woke me. I saw Robert go into the headquarters shack to answer it. He came back out shortly, still in his coveralls, and walked over to the Bronco. I got out. He handed me a styrofoam cup of coffee and pointed his chin at the Bronco.

"Comfy in there last night?" he asked. I nodded and he went on. "That was John on the phone. He's going to plead out tomorrow and take two years." Robert shook his head. "Anyway, you've got tomorrow off. I'm going up to Concord to be at the sentencing." He reached in his pocket and pulled out a roll of bills. He handed it to me.

"What's this for?" I said.

Robert narrowed his eyes and looked at me. "Do you need it or not?" His voice was the hardest love I'd ever felt. I nodded. He turned around and started walking back to the shed. I watched him close the door. I climbed back in the Bronco and headed out onto the highway. I drove north, and crossed over into Vermont. There was still a huge black cloud in the sky over the oxbow. I drove up Route 5 and looked out over the burnt fields, still smoldering, scorched dead. Lord's farm looked gray from the smoke. I drove up into the Northeast Kingdom. I never did find the courage to turn myself in, and things got worse. I spent the winter at a logging camp in Quebec.

I called once, when I hit a jam out in North Dakota. I called from a phone booth outside a diner. I recognized John's voice the second he spoke. I hung up. Later, much later, in another life, with another name, we were driving and someone handed me a road atlas. I flipped through it and found Vermont and New Hampshire were together on the same page. I started tracing their shared border, the Connecticut River, north toward Canada. I dropped the atlas when my finger reached the oxbow. For just that split second, right on the tip of my finger, the surface of the map was scorching hot. I heard the roar of the fire, the little white house burning. The air rushing to be eaten by the flames. I smelled the gasoline. Riding across the top of the fire on a black horse was Bill Allen.

Three dark shapes followed swiftly after him, the burning wasps in their long black hair, chasing him. Catching him and dragging him down into the fire, screaming.

Years later, on the security ward at Western State Hospital near Tacoma, I saw a man in a straitjacket, strapped to a gurney. I walked over to him and spoke.

"I didn't know they used straitjackets anymore."

He could barely move his head. "Well, they do." The smell of ether was everywhere. He was quiet as a white-jacketed doctor walked by. "Say, Mac, scratch my shoulder, will you?"

I slowly reached down and began scratching the outside of the thick canvas that bound him. Solid steel mesh covered the ward windows.

"Harder," he said. "I can barely feel it." He looked up at me. "I think they're trying to save on the heat. Aren't you cold?" I shook my head. "I'm cold all the time," he said.

I dug my nails into the canvas on his right shoulder. "My name is John Wilson," I said.

He looked at me, his eyes wide. "That's my name," he said softly.

I stopped scratching the straitjacket. "What's your middle name?" I asked.

He shook his head slightly and closed his eyes. "Same as yours," he said. He shivered. It was cold. But my paper gown was soaked with dry sweat and my face was hot. I could smell smoke.

2003

CHRISTOPHER COAKE

ALL THROUGH THE HOUSE

Christopher Coake (1971–) is a native of Indiana who always wanted to be a writer. He received his BA in creative writing from Miami University of Ohio and his MFA from Ohio State University. His stories have appeared in such literary periodicals as the *Journal, Gettysburg Review, Epoch,* and *Southern Review.* His early stories, all written while a student at Ohio State, were collected in *We're in Trouble* (2005), which earned him the Robert Bingham Fellowship from the PEN American Center, awarded to a fiction writer whose debut work shows great promise. In 2007 the British magazine *Granta* named him one of twenty "Best Young American Novelists," an unusually flattering accolade considering Coake is still working on his first novel. He currently teaches creative writing at the University of Nevada, Reno.

"All Through the House" successfully tells a story backward in time, a process the author compared to an archaeological excavation: "If I kept digging in the same place," he wondered, "what would I find?" This is an exceptionally difficult literary form which has become something of a cliché following the success of the 2000 film *Memento,* mostly with predictably poor results. It is unlikely that any story in this collection will offer a greater surprise in its narration than this one.

"All Through the House" was first published in the summer 2003 issue of *Gettysburg Review.* It was first published in book form in *The Best American Mystery Stories 2004* and was collected in *We're in Trouble.*

■ ■ ■

Now

Here is an empty meadow, circled by bare autumn woods.

The trees of the wood — oak, maple, locust — grow through a mat of tangled scrub, rusty leaves, piles of brittle deadfall. Overhead is a rich blue sky, a few high, translucent clouds, moving quickly, but the trees are dense enough to shelter everything below, and the meadow too. And here, leading into the trees from the meadow's edge, is a gravel track, twin ruts now grown over, switching back and forth through the woods and away.

The meadow floor is overrun by tall yellow grass, thorny vines, the occasional sapling — save for at the meadow's center. Here is a wide rectangular depression. The broken remains of a concrete foundation shore up its sides. The bottom is crumbled concrete and cinder, barely visible beneath the thin netting of weeds. A blackened wooden beam angles down from the rim, its underside soft and fibrous. Two oaks lean over the foundation, charred on the sides that face it.

Sometimes deer browse in the meadow. Raccoons and rabbits are always present; they have made their own curving trails across the meadow floor. A fox, rusty and quick, lives in the nearby trees. His den, twisting among tree roots, is pressed flat and smooth by his belly.

Sometimes automobiles crawl slowly along the gravel track and park at the edge of the meadow. The people inside sometimes get out and walk into the grass. They take photographs or draw pictures or read from books. Sometimes they climb down into the old foundation. A few camp overnight, huddling close to fires.

Whenever these people come, a policeman arrives soon after, fat and gray-haired. Sometimes the people speak with him — and sometimes they shout — but always they depart, loading their cars while the policeman watches. When they depart he follows them down the track in his slow, rumbling cruiser. When he comes at night, the spinning of his red and blue lights causes the trees to jump and dance.

Sometimes the policeman arrives alone:

He stops the cruiser and climbs out. He walks slowly into the meadow. He sits on the broken concrete at the rim of the crater, looking into it, looking at the sky, closing his eyes.

When he makes noise the woods grow quiet. All the animals crouch low, flicking their ears at the man's barks and howls.

He does not stay long.

After his cruiser has rolled away down the track, the woods and the meadow remain, for a time, silent. But before long what lives there sniffs the air and, in fits and starts, emerges. Noses press to the ground and into the burrows of mice. Things eat and are eaten.

Here memories are held in muscles and bellies, not in minds. The policeman and the house and all the people who have come and gone here are not forgotten.

They are, simply, never remembered.

1987

Sheriff Larry Thompkins tucked his chin against the cold and, his back to his idling cruiser, unlocked the cattle gate that blocked access to the Sullivan woods. The gate swung inward, squealing, and the cruiser's headlights shone a little ways down the gravel track before it curled off into the trees. Larry straightened, then glanced right and left, down the paved county road behind him. He saw no other cars — not even on the distant interstate. The sky was clouded over — snow was a possibility — and the fields behind him were almost invisible in the dark.

Larry sank back behind the wheel, grateful for the warmth and the spits of static from his radio. He nosed the cruiser through the gate and onto the track, then switched to his parking lights. The trunks of trees ahead faintly glowed, turning orange as he passed. Even though the nearest living soul, old Ned Baker, lived a half mile off, he was an insomniac and often sat in front of his bedroom window watching the Sullivan woods. If Larry used his headlights, Ned would see. Ever since Patricia Pike's book had come out — three months ago now — Ned had watched the gated entrance to the woods like it was a military duty.

Larry had been chasing off trespassers from the Sullivan place ever since the murders, twelve years ago in December. He hated coming out here, but he couldn't very well refuse to do his job — no one else would do it. Almost always the trespassers were kids from the high school, out at the murder house getting drunk or high, and though Larry was always firm with them and made trouble for the bad ones, he knew most kids did stupid things and couldn't blame them that much. Larry had fallen off the roof of a barn, drunk, when he was sixteen. He'd broken his arm in two places, all because he was trying to impress a girl who, in the end, never went out with him.

But activity in the woods had picked up since the Pike woman's book came out. Larry had been out here three times in the last week alone. There were kids, still, more of them than ever — but also people from out of town, some of whom he suspected were mentally ill. Just last weekend Larry had chased off a couple in their twenties, lying on a blanket with horrible screaming music playing on their boom box. They'd told him — calmly, as though he might understand — that they practiced magic and wanted to conceive a child out there. The house, they said, was a place of energy. When they were gone Larry looked up at its empty windows, its stupid, dead house-face, and couldn't imagine anything further from the truth.

The cruiser bounced and shimmied as Larry negotiated the turns through the woods. All his extra visits had deepened the ruts in the track—he'd been cutting through mud and ice all autumn. Now and then the tires spun, and he tried not to think about having to call for a tow, the stories he'd have to make up to explain it. But each time, the cruiser roared and lurched free.

He remembered coming out here with Patricia Pike. He hadn't wanted to, but the mayor told him Pike did a good job with this kind of book, and that—while the mayor was concerned, just like Larry was, about exploiting what had happened—he didn't want the town to get any more of a bad name on account of being uncooperative. So Larry had gone to the library to read one of Pike's other books. *The Beauties and the Beast* was what the book was called, with the close-up of a cat's eye on the front cover. It was about a serial killer in Idaho in the sixties who murdered five women and fed them to his pet cougar. In one chapter Pike wrote that the police had hidden details of the crime from her. Larry could understand why: The killings were brutal, and he was sure the police had a hard time explaining the details to the families of the victims, let alone to ghouls all across the country looking for a thrill.

We're going to get exploited, Larry had told the mayor, waving that book at him.

Look, the mayor said. I know this is difficult for you. But would you rather she wrote it without your help? You knew Wayne better than anybody. Who knows? Maybe we'll finally get to the bottom of things.

What if there's no bottom to get to? Larry asked, but the mayor had looked at him strangely and never answered, just told him to put up with it, that it would be over before he knew it.

Larry wrestled the cruiser around the last bend and then stopped. His parking lights shone dully across what was left of the old driveway turnaround and onto the Sullivan house.

The house squatted, dim and orange. It had never been much to look at, even when new; it was small, unremarkable, square—barely more than a prefab. The garage, jutting off the back, was far too big and made the whole structure look deformed, unbalanced. Wayne had designed the house himself, not long after he and Jenny got married. Most of the paint had chipped off the siding, and the undersized windows were boarded over—the high school kids had broken out all the glass years ago.

Jenny had hated the house even when it was new. She'd told Larry so at her and Wayne's housewarming dinner.

It's bad enough I have to live out here in the middle of nowhere, she'd said under her breath while Wayne chattered to Larry's wife, Emily, in the living room. But at least he could have built us a house you can look at.

He did it because he loves you, Larry whispered. He tried.

Don't remind me, Jenny said, swallowing wine. Why did I ever agree to this?

The house?

The house, the marriage. God, Larry, you name it.

When she'd said it she hadn't sounded bitter. She looked at Larry as though he might have an answer, but he didn't — he'd never been able to see Jenny and Wayne together, from the moment they started dating in college. He remembered telling her, *It'll get better,* and feeling right away as though he'd lied, and Jenny making a face that showed she knew he had, before both of them turned to watch Wayne demonstrate the dimmer switch in the living room for Emily.

The front door, Larry saw now, was swinging open. Some folks he'd chased out two weeks ago had jimmied it, and the lock hadn't worked right afterward. The open door and the black gap behind it made the house look even meaner than it was — like a baby crying. Patricia Pike had said that, at one point. Larry wondered if she'd put it into her book.

She had sent him a copy back in July just before its release. The book was called *All Through the House;* the cover showed a Christmas tree with little skulls as ornaments. Pike had signed it for him: *To Larry, even though I know you prefer fiction. Cheers, Patricia.* He flipped to the index and saw his name with a lot of numbers by it, and then he looked at the glossy plates at the book's center. One was a map of Prescott County, showing the county road and an *X* in the Sullivan woods where the house stood. The next page showed a floor plan of the house, with bodies drawn in outline and dotted lines following Wayne's path from room to room. One plate showed a Sears portrait of the entire family smiling together, plus graduation photos of Wayne and Jenny. Pike had included a picture of Larry, too — taken on the day of the murders — that showed him pointing off to the edge of the picture while EMTs brought one of the boys out the front door, wrapped in a blanket. Larry looked like he was running — his arms were blurry — which was odd. They'd brought no one out of the house alive. He'd have had no need to rush.

The last chapter was titled "Why?" Larry had read that part all the way through. Every rumor and half-baked theory Patricia Pike had heard while in town, she'd included, worded to make it sound like she'd done thinking no one else ever had.

Wayne was in debt. Wayne was jealous because maybe Jenny was sleeping around. Wayne had been seeing a doctor about migraines. Wayne was a man who had never matured past childhood. Wayne lived in a fantasy world inhabited by the perfect family he could never have. *Once again the reluctance of the sheriff's department and the townspeople to discuss their nightmares freely hinders us from understanding a man like Wayne Sullivan, from preventing others from killing as he has killed, from beginning the healing and closure this community so badly needs.*

Larry had tossed his copy in a drawer and hoped everyone else would do the same.

But then the book was a success — all Patricia Pike's books were. And not long after that, the lunatics had started to come out to the house. And then, today, Larry had gotten a call from the mayor.

You're not going to like this, the mayor said.

Larry hadn't. The mayor told him a cable channel wanted to film a documentary based on the book. They were sending out a camera crew at the end of the month, near Christmastime — for authenticity's sake. They wanted to film in the house, and of course they wanted to talk to everybody all over again, Larry first and foremost.

Larry took a bottle of whiskey from underneath the front seat of the cruiser, and watching the Sullivan house through the windshield, he unscrewed the cap and drank a swallow. His eyes watered, but he got it down and drank another. The booze spread in his throat and belly, made him want to sit very still behind the wheel, to keep drinking. Most nights he would. But instead he opened the door and climbed out of the cruiser.

The meadow and the house were mostly blocked from the wind, but the air had a bite to it all the same. He hunched his shoulders, then opened up the trunk and took out one of the gas cans he'd filled up at the station and a few rolls of newspaper. He walked up to the open doorway of the house, his head ducked, careful with his feet in the shadows and the grass.

He smelled the house's insides even before he stepped onto the porch — a smell like the underside of a wet log. He clicked on his flashlight and shone it into the doorway, across the splotched and crumbling walls. He stepped inside. Something living scuttled immediately out of the way: a raccoon or a possum. Maybe even a fox. Wayne had once told him the woods were full of them, but in all the times Larry had been out here, he'd never seen any.

He glanced over the walls. Some new graffiti had appeared: KILL 'EM ALL was spray-painted on the wall where, once, the Christmas tree had leaned. The older messages were still in place. One read, HEY WAYNE, DO MY HOUSE NEXT. Beside a ragged, spackled-over depression in the same wall, someone had painted an arrow and the word BRAINS. Smaller messages were written in marker — the sorts of things high school kids write: initials, graduation years, witless sex puns, pictures of genitalia. And — sitting right there in the corner — was a copy of *All Through the House,* its pages swollen with moisture.

Larry rubbed his temple. The book was as good a place to start as any.

He kicked the book to the center of the living room floor and then splashed it with gas. Nearby was a crevice where the carpet had torn and separated. He rolled the newspapers up and wedged them underneath the carpet, then doused them too. Then he drizzled gasoline in a line from both the book and the papers to the front door. From the edge of the stoop, he tossed arcs of gas onto the door and the jamb until the can was empty.

He stood on the porch, smelling the gas and gasping — he was horribly out of shape. His head was throbbing. He squeezed the lighter in his hand until the pain subsided.

Larry was not much for religion, but he tried a prayer anyway: *Lord, keep them. I know you have been. And please let this work.* But the prayer sounded pitiful in his head, so he stopped it.

He flicked the lighter under a clump of newspaper and, once that had bloomed, touched it to the base of the door.

The fire took the door right away and flickered in a curling line across the carpet to the book and the papers. He could see them burning through the doorway, before thick gray smoke obscured his view. After a few minutes the flames began to gutter. He wasn't much of an arsonist — it was wet in there. He retrieved the other gas can from the trunk and shoved a rolled-up cone of newspaper into the nozzle. He made sure he had a clear throw and then lit the paper and heaved the can inside the house. It exploded right away, with a thump, and orange light bloomed up one of the inside walls. Outside, the flames from the door flared, steadied, then began to climb upward to the siding.

Larry went back to the cruiser and pulled the bottle of whiskey from beneath his seat. He drank from it and thought about Jenny, and then about camping in the meadow as a boy, with Wayne.

Larry had seen this house being built; he'd seen it lived in and died in. He had guessed he might feel a certain joy watching it destroyed, but instead his throat caught. Somewhere down the line, this had gotten to be his house. He'd thought that for a while now: The township owned the Sullivan house, but really, Wayne had passed it on to *him*.

An image of himself drifted into his head — it had come a few times tonight. He saw himself walking into the burning house, climbing up the stairs. In his head he did this without pain, even while fire found his clothing, the bullets in his gun. He would sit upstairs in Jenny's sewing room and close his eyes, and it wouldn't take long.

He sniffled and pinched his nose. That was horseshit. He'd seen people who'd been burned to death. He'd die, all right, but he'd go screaming and flailing. At the thought of it, his arms and legs grew heavy; his skin prickled.

Larry put the cruiser in reverse and backed it slowly away from the house, out of the drive, and onto the track. He watched for ten minutes as the fire grew and tried not to think about anything, to see only the flames. Then he got the call from dispatch.

Sheriff?

Copy, he said.

Ned called in. He says it looks like there's a fire out at the Sullivan place.

A fire?

That's what he said. He sees a fire in the woods.

My my my, Larry said. I'm on old 52 just past Mackey. I'll get out there quick as I can and take a look.

He waited another ten minutes. Flames shot out around the boards on the windows. The downstairs ceiling caught. Long shadows shifted through the trees; the woods came alive, swaying and dancing. Something alive and aflame shot out the front door — a rabbit? It zigged and zagged across the turnaround and then headed toward him. For a moment Larry thought it had shot under his car, and he put his hand on the door handle — but whatever it was cut away for the woods to his right. He saw it come to rest in a patch of scrub; smoke rose from the bush in wisps.

Dispatch? Larry said.

Copy.

I'm at the Sullivan house. It's on fire, all right. Better get the trucks out here.

Twenty minutes later two fire trucks arrived, advancing carefully down the track. The men got out and stood beside Larry, looking over the house, now brightly ablaze from top to bottom. They rolled the trucks past Larry's cruiser and sprayed the grass around the house and the trees nearby. Then all of them watched the house burn and crumble into its foundation, and no one said much of anything.

Larry left them to the rubble just before dawn. He went home and tried to wash the smell of smoke out of his hair and then lay down next to Emily, who didn't stir. He lay awake for a while, trying to convince himself he'd actually done it, and then trying to convince himself he hadn't.

When he finally slept he saw the house on fire, except that in his dream there were people still in it: Jenny Sullivan in the upstairs window, holding her youngest boy to her and shouting Larry's name, screaming it, while Larry sat in his car, tugging at the handle, unable even to shout back to her, to tell her it was locked.

1985

Patricia Pike had known from the start that Sheriff Thompkins was reluctant to work with her. Now, riding in his cruiser with him down empty back roads to the Sullivan house, she wondered if what she'd thought was reticence was actual anger. Thompkins had been civil enough when she spoke with him on the phone a month before, but since meeting him this morning in his small, cluttered office — she'd seen janitors with better quarters — he'd been scowling, sullen, rarely bothering to look her in the eye.

She was used to this treatment from policemen. A lot of them had read her books, two of which had uncovered information the police hadn't found themselves. Her second book — *On a Darkling Plain* — had overturned a conviction. Policemen hated being shown up, even the best of them, and she suspected from the look of Thompkins's office that he didn't operate on the cutting edge of law enforcement.

Thompkins was tall and hunched, perhaps muscular once but going now to fat, with a gray cop's mustache and a single thick fold under his chin. He was only forty — two years younger than she was — but he looked much older. He kept a wedding photo on his desk; in it he had the broad-shouldered, thick-necked look of an offensive lineman. Unsurprising, this; a lot of country cops she spoke to had played football. His wife was a little ghost of a woman, dark-eyed, smiling what Patricia suspected was one of her last big smiles.

Patricia had asked Thompkins a few questions in his office, chatty ones designed to put him at ease. She'd also flirted a little; she was good-looking, and sometimes that worked. But even then Thompkins answered in clipped sentences, in the sort of language police fell back on in their reports. He looked often at his watch, but she wasn't fooled. Kinslow, Indiana, had only six hundred residents, and Thompkins wasn't about to convince her he was a busy man.

Thompkins drove along the interminable gravel roads to the Sullivan woods with one hand on the wheel and the other brushing the corners of his mustache. Finally she couldn't stand it.

Do I make you uncomfortable, Sheriff?

He widened his eyes, and he shifted his shoulders then coughed. He said, Well, I'll be honest. I guess I'd rather not do this.

I can't imagine you would, she said. Best to give him the sympathy he so desperately wanted.

If the mayor wasn't such a fan of yours, I wouldn't be out here.

She smiled at him, just a little. She said, I've talked to Wayne's parents; I know you were close to Wayne and Jenny. It can't be easy to do this.

No, ma'am. That it is not.

Thompkins turned the cruiser onto a smaller paved road. On either side of them was nothing but fields, empty and stubbled with old broken cornstalks and blocky stands of woods so monochrome they could be pencil drawings.

Patricia asked, You all went to high school together, didn't you?

Abington, Class of '64. Jenny was a year behind me and Wayne.

Did you become friends in high school?

That's when I got to know Jenny. Wayne and I knew each other since we were little. Our mothers taught together at the middle school.

Thompkins glanced at Patricia. You know all this already. You drawing out the witness?

She smiled, genuinely grateful. So he had a brain in there after all. It seems I have to, she said.

He sighed — a big man's sigh, long and weary — and said, I have nothing against you personally, Ms. Pike. But I don't like the kind of books you write, and I don't like coming out here.

I do appreciate your help. I know it's hard.

Why this case? he asked her. Why us?

She tried to think of the right words, nothing that would offend him.

Well, I suppose I was just *drawn* to it. My agent sends me clippings about cases, things she thinks I might want to write about. The murders were so . . . brutal, and they happened on Christmas Eve. And since it happened in the country, it never made the news much; people don't know about it — not in the big cities, anyway. There's also kind of a — a fairy-tale quality to it, the house out in the middle of the forest—you know?

Uh-huh, Thompkins said.

And then there's the mystery of *why.* There's a certain type of case I specialize in—crimes with a component of unsolved mystery. I'm intrigued that Wayne didn't leave any notes. You're the only person he gave any information to, and even then—

—He didn't say much.

No. I know, I've read the transcript already. But that's my answer, I suppose: There's a lot to write about.

Thompkins stroked his mustache and turned at a stop sign.

They were to the right of an enormous tract of woods, much larger than the other stands nearby. Patricia had seen it growing on the horizon, almost like a rain cloud, and now, close up, she saw it was at least a mile square. The sheriff slowed and turned off the road, stopping in front of a low metal gate blocking a gravel track that dipped away from the road and into the bare trees. A NO TRESPASSING sign hung from the gate's center. It had been fired upon a number of times; some of the bullet holes had yet to rust. Thompkins said, Excuse me, and got out. He bent over a giant padlock and then swung the gate inward. He got back behind the wheel, drove the cruiser through without shutting his door, then clambered out again and locked the gate behind them.

Keeps the kids out, he told her, shifting the cruiser into gear. Means the only way in is on foot. A lot of them won't walk it, least when it's cold like this.

This is a big woods.

Probably the biggest between Indy and Lafayette. Course no one's ever measured, but that's—that's what Wayne always told me.

Patricia watched his mouth droop when he said this, caught his drop in volume.

The car curved right, then left. The world they were in was almost a sepia-toned old film: bare winter branches, patches of old snow on the ground, pools of black muck. Patricia had grown up in Chicago, had relatives on a farm downstate. She knew what a tangle those woods would be. What a curious place for a house. She opened her notebook and wrote in shorthand.

This land belongs to Wayne's family? she asked.

It used to. Township owns it now. Wayne had put the land up as collateral for the house, and then when he died, his folks didn't pay on the loan. I don't blame them for that. The town might sell it someday, but no one really wants farmland anymore. None of the farmers around here can afford to develop it. An ag company would have to buy it. In the meantime I keep an eye on the place.

Thompkins slowed and the car jounced into and out of a deep rut. He said, Me, I'd like to see the whole thing plowed under. But I don't make those choices.

She wrote his words down.

They rounded a last bend in the track, and there in front of them was a meadow, and in the center of it the Sullivan house. Patricia had seen pictures of it, but here in person it was much smaller than she'd imagined. She pulled her camera out of her bag.

It's ugly, she said.

That's the truth, Thompkins said, and put the car into park.

The house was a two-story of some indeterminate style—closer to a Cape Cod than anything else. The roof was pitched but seemed . . . too small, too flat for the rest of the house. The face suggested by its windows and front door—flanked by faux half-columns—was that of a mongoloid: all chin and mouth, and no forehead. Or like a baby crying. It had been painted an olive color, and now the paint was flaking. The windows had been boarded over with sheets of plywood. The track continued around behind the house, where a two-car garage jutted off at right angles, too big in proportion to the house proper.

Wayne drew up the plans, Thompkins said. He wanted to do it himself.

What did Jenny think of it? Do you know?

She joked about it. Not so Wayne could hear.

Would he have been angry?

No. Sad. He'd wanted a house out here since we were kids. He loved these woods.

Thompkins undid his seatbelt. Then he said, I guess he knew the house was a mess, but he . . . it's hard to say. We all pretended it was fine.

Why?

Some folks, you just want to protect their feelings. He wanted us all to be as excited as he was. It just wouldn't have occurred to us to be . . . blunt with him. You know that type of person? Kind of like a puppy?

Yes.

Well, Thompkins said, that was Wayne. You want to go in?

The interior of the house was dark. Thompkins had brought two electric lanterns; he set one just inside the door and held the other in his hand. He walked inside and then motioned for Patricia to follow.

The inside of the house stank — an old, abandoned smell of mildew and rot. The carpeting — what was left of it, anyway — seemed to be on the verge of becoming mud, or a kind of algae, and held the stink. Patricia had been in morgues and, for one of her books, had accompanied a homicide detective in Detroit to murder sites. She knew what death — dead human beings — smelled like. That smell might have been in the Sullivan house, underneath everything else, but she couldn't be sure. It *ought* to have been.

Patricia could see no furniture. Ragged holes gaped in the ceilings where light fixtures might have been. Behind the sheriff was a staircase, rising up into darkness, and to the right of it an entrance into what seemed to be the kitchen.

Shit, Thompkins said.

What?

He held the lantern close to a wall in the room to the right of the foyer. There was a spot on the wall, a ragged, spackled patch. Someone had spray-painted an arrow pointing at it, and the word BRAINS.

Thompkins turned a circle with the lantern held out. He was looking down, and she followed his gaze. She saw cigarette butts, beer cans.

Kids come in here from Abington, Thompkins said. I run them off every now and then. Sometimes it's adults, even. Have to come out and see for themselves, I guess. Already the kids say it's haunted.

That happens in a lot of places, Patricia said.

Huh, Thompkins said.

She took photos of the rooms, the flashbulb's light dazzling in the dark.

I guess you want the tour, Thompkins said.

I do. She put a hand on his arm, and his eyes widened. She said, as cheerfully as she could, Do you mind if I tape our conversation?

Do you have to? Thompkins asked, looking up from her hand.

It will help me quote you better.

Well. I suppose.

Patricia put a tape into her hand-held recorder, then nodded at him.

Thompkins held the lantern up. The light gleamed off his dark eyes. His mouth hung open, just a little, and when he breathed out it made a thin line of steam in front of the lantern. He looked different — not sad, not anymore. Maybe, Patricia thought, she saw in him what she was feeling, which was a thrill, what a teenaged girl feels in front of a campfire, knowing a scary story is coming. She reminded herself that actual people had died here, that she was in a place of tremendous sadness, but all the same she couldn't help herself. Her books sold well because she wrote them well, with fervency, and she wrote that way because she loved to be in forbidden places like this, she loved learning the secrets no one wanted to say. Just as, she suspected, Sheriff Thompkins wanted deep in his heart to tell them to her. Secrets were too big for people to hold — that was what she found in her research, time after time. Secrets had their own agendas.

Patricia looked at Thompkins, turning a smile into a quick nod.

All right then, the sheriff said. This way.

Here's the kitchen.

Wayne shot Jenny first, in here. But that first shot didn't kill her. You can't tell because of the boards, but the kitchen window looks out over the driveway, just outside the garage. Wayne shot her through the window. Jenny was looking out at Wayne, we know that, because the bullet went in through the front of her right shoulder and out the back, and we know he was outside because the glass was broken and because his footprints were still in the snow when we got there — there was no wind that night. The car was outside the garage. What he did was, he got out of the driver's side door and went around to the trunk and opened it — best guess is the gun was in there; he'd purchased it that night, up at a shop in Muncie. Then he went around to the passenger door and stood there for a while; the snow was all tramped down. We think he was loading the gun. Or maybe he was talking himself into doing it. I don't know.

We figure he braced on the top of the car and shot her from where he stood. The security light over the garage was burnt out when we got here, so from inside, looking out, with the kitchen lights on, Jenny wouldn't have been able to see what he was doing — not very clearly, if at all. I don't know why she was turned around looking out the window at him. Maybe he honked the horn. I also don't know if he aimed to kill her or wound her, but my feeling is he went for a wounding shot. It's about twenty feet from where he stood to where she stood, so it wasn't that hard a shot for him to make, and he made most of his others that night. Now down here —

[The sheriff's pointing to a spot on the linoleum, slightly stained, see photos.]

Excuse me?

[Don't mind me, Sheriff. Just keep talking.]

Oh. All right then.

Well, Jenny — once she was shot, she fell and struggled. There was a lot of blood; we think she probably bled out for seven or eight minutes while

Wayne . . . while Wayne killed the others. She tried to pull herself to the living room; there were . . . ah, smears on the floor consistent with her doing that.

[We're back in the living room; we're facing the front door.]

After he'd shot Jenny, he walked around the east side of the house to the front door here. He could have come in the garage into the kitchen, but he didn't. I'm not sure what happened from there exactly. But here's what I think: The grandmother — Mrs. Murray — and Danny, the four-year-old, were in the living room — in here — next to the tree. She was reading to him; he liked to be read to, and a book of nursery rhymes was open face-down on the couch. The grandmother was infirm — she had diabetes and couldn't walk so well. She was sitting on the couch still when we found her. He shot her once through the head, probably from the doorway.

[We're looking at the graffiti wall, see photos.]

But by this time Jenny would have been . . . she would have been screaming, so we know Wayne didn't catch the rest of them unawares. Jenny might have called out that Daddy was home before Wayne shot her; hell, this place is in the middle of nowhere, and it was nighttime, so they all knew a car had pulled up. What I'm saying is, I'm guessing there was a lot of confusion at this juncture, a lot of shouting. There's a bullet hole at waist height on the wall opposite the front door. My best guess is that Danny ran to the door and was in front of it when Wayne opened it. He could have been looking into the kitchen at his, at his mother, or at the door. I think Wayne took a shot at him from the doorway and missed. Danny ran into the living room, and since Mrs. Murray hadn't tried to struggle to her feet, Wayne shot her next. He took one shot and hit her. Then he shot Danny. Danny was behind the Christmas tree; he probably ran there to hide. Wayne took three shots into the tree, and one of them, or I guess Danny's struggles, knocked it sideways off its base. But he got Danny, shot his own boy in the head just over his left ear.

[We're looking through a door off the dining room; inside is a small room maybe ten by nine, see photos.]

This was a playroom. Mr. Murray and Alex, the two-year-old, were in it. Mr. Murray reacted pretty quick to the shots, for a guy his age, but he was a vet, and he hunted, so he probably would have been moving at the sound of the first gunshot. He opened that window —

[A boarded window on the rear of the house, see photos.]

— which, ah, used to look out behind the garage, and he dropped Alex through it into the snowdrift beneath. Then he got himself through.

Though not without some trouble. The autopsy showed he had a broken wrist, which we figure he broke getting out. But it's still a remarkable thing. I hope you write that. Sam Murray tried his best to save Alex.

[I'll certainly note it. Wayne's parents also mentioned him.]

Well, good. Good.

Sam and Alex got about fifty yards away, toward the woods. Wayne probably went to the doorway of the playroom and saw the window open. He ran back outside, around the west corner of the house, and shot Sam in the back right about where the garden was. There wasn't a lot of light, but the house lights were all on, and if I remember right, the bodies were just about at the limit of what you could see from that corner. So Sam almost made it out of range. But I don't know if he could have got very far once he was in the trees. He was strong for a guy his age, but it was snowy and neither he nor the boy had coats, and it was about ten degrees out that night. Plus Wayne meant to kill everybody, and I think he would have tracked them.

Sam died instantly. Wayne got him in the heart. He fell, and the boy didn't go any farther. Wayne walked about fifty feet out and fired a few shots, and one of them got Alex through the neck. Wayne never went any closer. Either he knew he'd killed them both, or he figured the cold would finish the job for him if he hadn't. Maybe he couldn't look. I don't know.

[We're in the living room again, at the foot of the stairs.]

He went back inside and shut the door behind him. I think he was confronted by the dog, Kodiak, on the stairs, there on the landing. He shot the dog, probably from where you're standing. Then —

[We're looking into the kitchen again.]

Wayne went to the kitchen and shot — he shot Jenny a second time. The killing shot. We found her face-down. Wayne stood over her and fired from a distance of less than an inch. The bullet went in the back of her head just above the neck. He held her down with his boot on her shoulder. We know because she was wearing a white sweater, and he left a bloodstain on it that held the imprint of his boot sole.

He called my house at nine-sixteen. You've seen the transcript.

[How did he sound? On the phone?]

Oh, Jesus. I'd say upset but not hysterical. Like he was out of breath, I guess.

[Will you tell me again what he said?]

Hell. Do you really need me to repeat it?

[If you can.]

. . . Well, he said, Larry, it's Wayne. I said, Hey, Wayne, merry Christ-

mas, or something like that. And then he said, No time, Larry, this is a business call. And I said, What's wrong? And he said, Larry, I killed Jenny and the kids and my in-laws, and as soon as I hang up, I'm going to kill myself. And I said something like, Are you joking? And then he hung up. That's it. I got in the cruiser and drove up here as fast as I could.

[You were first on the scene?]

Yeah. Yeah, I was. I called it in on the way; it took me a while to — to remember. I saw blood through the front windows, and I called for backup as soon as I did. I went inside. I looked around . . . and saw . . . everyone but Sam and Alex. It took me . . .

[Sheriff?]

No, it's all right. I wasn't . . . I wasn't in great shape, which I guess you can imagine, but after a couple of minutes, I found the window open in the playroom. I was out with — with Sam and Alex when the deputies arrived.

[But you found Wayne first?]

Yes. I looked for him right off. For all I knew he was still alive.

[Where was he?]

Down in here.

[We're looking into a door opening off the kitchen; it looks like — the basement?]

Yeah. Wayne killed himself in his workroom. That was his favorite place, where he went for privacy. We used to drink down there, play darts. He sat in a corner and shot himself with a small handgun, which he also purchased that night. It was the only shot he fired from it. He'd shut the basement door behind him.

. . . You want to see down there?

They sat for a while in the cruiser afterward. Thompkins had brought a thermos of coffee, which touched her; the coffee was terrible, but at least it was warm. She held the cup in her hands in front of the dashboard heaters. Thompkins chewed his thumbnail and looked at the house.

Why did he do it? she asked him.

Hm?

Why did Wayne do it?

I don't know.

You don't have any theories?

No.

He said it quickly, an obvious lie. Patricia watched his face and said, I called around after talking with his parents. Wayne was twenty grand behind on his loan payments. If he hadn't worked at the bank already, this place would have been repossessed.

Maybe, Thompkins said and sipped his coffee. But half the farms you see out here are twenty grand in the hole, and no one's slaughtered their entire family over it.

Patricia watched him while he said this. Thompkins kept his big face neutral, but he didn't look at her. His ears were pink with cold.

Wayne's mother, she said, told me she thought that Jenny might have had affairs.

Yeah. I heard that too.

Any truth to it?

Adultery's not against the law. So I don't concern myself with it.

But surely you've heard something.

Well, Ms. Pike, I have the same answer as before. People have been sleeping around on each other out here for a lot longer than I've had this job, and no one ever killed their family over it.

Thompkins put on his seatbelt.

Besides, he said, if you were a man who'd slept with Jenny Sullivan, would *you* say anything about it? You wouldn't, not now. So no, I don't know for sure. And frankly, I wouldn't tell you if I did.

Why?

Because I knew Jenny, and she was a good woman. She was my prom date, for Christ's sake. I stood up at her and Wayne's wedding. Jenny was always straight, and she was smart. If she had an affair, that was her business. But it's not mine, now, and it's not yours.

It would be motive, Patricia said softly.

I took the bodies out of that house, Thompkins said, putting the cruiser into reverse. I took my friends out. I felt their necks to see if they were alive. I saw what Wayne did. There's no reason good enough. No one could have wronged him enough to make him do what he did. I don't care what it was.

He turned the cruiser around; the trees rushed by, and Patricia put both hands around her coffee to keep it from spilling. She'd heard speeches like this before. Someone's brains get opened up, and there's always some backcountry cop who puts his hand to his heart and pretends the poor soul still has any privacy.

There's always a reason, she said.

Thompkins smirked without humor; the cruiser bounced up and down.

Then I'm sure you'll come up with something, he said.

December 25, 1975

In the evening, just past sundown, Larry went out again to the Sullivan house. He and the staties had finished with the scene earlier in the day. There hadn't been much to investigate, really; Wayne had confessed in his phone call, yet Larry had told his deputies to take pictures anyway, to collect what evidence they could. And then all day reporters had come out for pictures, and some of the townspeople had stopped by to gawk or to ask if anything needed to be done, so Larry decided to keep the house under guard. Truth be told, he and the men needed something to do; watching the house was better than fielding questions in town.

When Larry pulled up in front of the house, his deputy, Troy Bowen, was sitting in his cruiser by the garage, reading a paperback behind the wheel. Larry flashed his lights, and Bowen got out and ambled over to Larry's car, hands in his armpits.

Hey, Larry, he said. What're you doing out here?

Slow night, Larry said, which was true enough. He said, I'll take over. Go get dinner. I'll cover until Albie gets here.

That's not till midnight, Bowen said, but his face was open and grateful.

I might as well be out here. It's all I'm thinking about anyway.

Yeah, that's what I thought. But I don't mind saying it gives me the willies. You're welcome to it.

When Bowen's cruiser was gone, Larry stood for a moment on the front stoop, hands in his pockets. Crime scene tape was strung over the doorway in a big haphazard *X;* Bowen had done it after the bodies were removed, still sniffling and red-eyed. It had been his first murder scene. The electricity was still on; the little fake lantern hanging over the door was shining. Larry took a couple of breaths and then fumbled out a copy of the house key. He unlocked the door, ducked under the caution tape, and went inside.

He turned on the living room light, and there everything was, as he'd left it this afternoon. His heart thumped. What else had he expected? That it would all be gone? That it hadn't really happened? It had. Here were the outlines. The bloodstains on the living room carpet and on the landing. The light from the living room just shone into the kitchen; he could see the dark swirls on the linoleum, too. Already a smell was in the air. The furnace was still on, and the blood and the smaller pieces of remains were starting to turn. The place would go bad if Wayne's folks didn't have the house cleaned up soon. Larry didn't want to have that talk with them, but he'd call them tomorrow. He knew a service in Indianapolis that took care of things like this. All the same he turned off the thermostat.

He asked himself why he cared. Surely no one would ever live in this place again. What did it matter?

But it did, somehow.

He walked into the family room. The tree was still canted sideways, knocked partway out of its base. He went to the wall behind it, stepping over stains, careful not to disturb anything. The lights on the tree were still plugged into the wall outlet. He squatted, straddling a collapsing pile of presents, then leaned forward and pulled the cord. The tree might go up, especially with the trunk out of its water.

Larry looked up at the wall and put his hand over his mouth; he'd been trying to avoid looking right at anything, but he'd done it now. Just a few inches in front of him, on the wall, was the spot where Danny had been shot. The bullet had gone right through his head. He'd given Danny a couple of rides in the cruiser, and now here the boy was: matted blood, strands of hair—

He breathed through his fingers and looked down at the presents. He'd seen blood before; he'd seen all kinds of deaths, mostly on the sides of highways, but twice because of bullets to the head. He told himself, *Pretend it's no different.* He tried to focus and made himself pick out words on the presents' tags.

No help there. Wayne had bought them all presents. *To Danny, From Daddy. To Mommy, From Daddy.* All written in Wayne's blocky letters. Jesus H.

Larry knew he should go, just go out and sit in his cruiser until midnight, but he couldn't help it. He took one of Jenny's presents, a small one that had slid almost completely under the couch, and sat down in the dining room with the box on his lap. He shouldn't do this, it was wrong, but really—who was left to know that a present was gone? Larry wasn't family, but he was close enough—he had some rights here. Who, besides him, would ever unwrap them? The presents belonged to Wayne's parents now. Would they? Would they want to see what their son had bought for the family he'd butchered? Not if they had any sense at all.

Larry went into the kitchen, looking down only to step where the rusty smears weren't. Under the sink he found garbage bags; he took one.

He sat back down in the dining room. The gift was only a few inches square, wrapped in gold foil paper. Larry slid a finger under a taped seam. He carefully tore the paper away. Inside was a small, light cardboard box, also taped. He could see Wayne's fingerprint caught in the tape glue before he cut it with a thumbnail. He held the lid lightly between his palms and shook out the container onto his lap.

Wayne had bought Jenny lingerie. A silk camisole and matching panty, in red, folded small.

Jenny liked red. Her skin took to it somehow; she was always a little pink. The bust of the camisole was transparent, lacy. She would look impossible in it. That was Jenny, though. She could slip on a T-shirt and look like your best pal. Or she could put on a little lipstick and do her hair and wear a dress, and she'd look like she ought to be up on a movie screen someplace. Larry ran his fingers over the silk. He wondered if Wayne had touched the lingerie this way, too, and what he might have been thinking when he did. Did he know, when he bought it? When had he found out?

Don't be coy with me, Wayne had said on the phone. He'd called Larry at his house; Emily would have picked up if her hands weren't soapy with dishwater. Larry watched his wife while he listened. I know, Wayne said. I followed you to the motel. I just shot her, Larry. I shot her in the head.

Larry dumped the lingerie and the wrappings into the garbage bag.

He took the bag upstairs with him, turning off the living room light behind him and turning on the one in the stairwell. He had to cling tight to the banister to get past the spot where Wayne had shot the dog, a big husky named Kodiak, rheumy-eyed and arthritic. Kodiak didn't care much for the children, who tried to uncurl his tail, so most of the time he slept in a giant basket in the sewing room upstairs. He must have jumped awake at the sound of gunshots. He would have smelled what was wrong right away. Jenny had gotten him as a puppy during high school. Larry had been dating her then; he remembered sitting on the kitchen floor with her at her parents' house, the dog skidding happily back and forth between them. Kodiak had grown old loving her. He must have stood on the landing and growled and barked at Wayne, and Wayne shot him from the foot of the stairs. Through the head, just like everyone else. Larry had seen dogs driven vicious by bloodshed; it turned on switches in their heads. He hoped Kodiak had at least made a lunge for Wayne before getting shot.

Larry walked into Wayne and Jenny's bedroom. He'd been in it before. Just once. Wayne had gone up to Chicago on business, and the kids were at school, and Jenny called Larry—at the station; she told dispatch she thought she saw someone in the woods, maybe a hunter, and would the sheriff swing by and run him off? That was smart of her. Larry could go in broad daylight and smoke in the living room and drink a cup of coffee, and no one would say boo.

And, as it turned out, Jenny could set his coffee down on the dining room table and then waggle her fingers at him from the foot of the stairs. And he could get hard just at the sight of her doing it, Jenny Sullivan smiling at him in sweatpants and an old T-shirt.

And upstairs she could say, Not the bed.

They'd stood together in front of the mirror over the low bureau, Jenny bent forward, both of them with their pants pulled down mid-thigh, and Larry gritting his teeth just to last a few minutes. Halfway through he took his hat from the bureau top—he'd brought it upstairs with them and couldn't remember why—and set it on her head, and she'd looked up and met his eyes in the mirror, and both of them were laughing when they came. Jenny's laugh turned into something like a shriek. He said, I never heard you sound like that before, and Jenny said, I've never sounded like that before. Not in this room. She said, This house has never heard anything like it. And when she said it, it was like the house was Wayne, like somehow he'd walked in. They both turned serious and sheepish—Jenny's mouth got small and grim—and they'd separated, pulled their clothes up, pulled themselves together.

Now he went through the drawers of the bureau, trying to remember what Jenny wore that day. The blue sweatpants. The Butler Bulldogs shirt. Bright pink socks—he remembered her stumbling around, trying to pull one off. He found a pair that seemed right, rolled tight together. Silk panties, robin's egg blue. He found a fluffy red thing that she used to keep her ponytail together. Little fake ruby earrings in a ceramic seashell. He smelled through the perfumes next to her vanity, found one he liked and remembered, and sprayed it on the clothes, heavily . . . it would fade over time, and if it was too strong now, in ten years it wouldn't be.

He packed all of it into the plastic bag from the kitchen.

Then he sat at the foot of the bed, eyes closed, for a long few minutes. He could hear his own breath. His eyes stung. He looked at the backs of his hands and concentrated on keeping steady. He thought about the sound of Wayne's voice when he called. *I left her sexy for you, Larry.*

That made him feel like doing something other than weeping.

When he was composed he looked through the desks in the bedroom and the drawers of all the bed tables. He glanced at his watch. It was only eight.

He walked down the hall into the sewing room and sat at Jenny's sewing table. The room smelled like Kodiak: an old dog smell, a mixture of the animal and the drops he had to have in his ears. Pictures of the children and Jenny's parents dotted the walls. Wayne's bespectacled head peeped out of a few, too — but not very many, when you looked hard. Larry opened a drawer under the table and rooted through. Then he opened Jenny's sewing box.

He hadn't known what he was looking for, but in the sewing box he found it. He opened a little pillowed silk box full of spare buttons, and inside, pinned to the lid, was a slip of paper. He knew it right away from the green embossment — it was from a stationery pad he'd found at the hotel he and Jenny had sometimes used in Lebanon. He unfolded it. His hands shook, and he was crying now — she'd kept it, she'd kept something.

This was from a year ago, on a Thursday afternoon; Wayne had taken the boys up to see his folks. Larry met Jenny at the hotel after she was done at the school. Jenny wanted to sleep for an hour or two after they made love, but Larry was due home, and it was better for them to come and go separately anyway, so he dressed quietly while she dozed. He'd looked at her asleep for a long time, and then he'd written a note. He remembered thinking at the time: *evidence.* But he couldn't help it. Some things needed to be put down in writing; some things you had to put your name to, if they were going to mean anything at all.

So Larry found the stationery pad and wrote, *My sweet Jenny,* and got teary when he did. He sat on the bed next to her and leaned over and kissed her warm ear. She stirred and murmured without opening her eyes. He finished the note and left it by her hand.

A week later he asked her, Did you get my note?

She said, No. But then she kissed him and smiled and put her warm, small hands on his cheeks. Of course I did, you dummy.

He'd been able to remember the words on the note — he'd run them over and over in his head — but now he opened the folded paper and read them again: *My sweet Jenny, I have trouble with these things but I wouldn't do this if I didn't love you.*

And then he read on. He dropped the note onto the tabletop and stared at it, his hand clamped over his mouth.

He'd signed it *Yours, Larry* — but his name had been crossed out. And over it had been written, in shaky block letters: *Wayne.*

December 24, 1975

If Jenny ever had to tell someone — a stranger, the sympathetic man she imagined coming to the door sometimes, kind of a traveling psychologist and granter of divorces all wrapped up in one — about what it was like to be married to Wayne Sullivan, she would have told him about tonight. She'd say, *Wayne called me at six, after my parents got here for dinner, after I'd gotten the boys into their good clothes for the Christmas picture, to tell me he wouldn't be home for another couple of hours. He had some last-minute shopping, he said.*

Jenny was washing dishes. The leftovers from the turkey had already been sealed in Tupperware and put into the refrigerator. From the living room she could hear Danny with her mother; her father was playing with Alex in the playroom. She could hear Alex squealing every few minutes or shouting nonsense in his two-year-old singsong. It was 8:40. *Almost three hours later,* she told the man in her head, *and no sign of him. And that's Wayne. There's a living room full of presents. All anyone wants of him now is his presence at the table. And he thinks he hasn't done enough, and so our dinner is ruined. It couldn't be more typical.*

Her mother was reading to Danny; she was a schoolteacher too, and Jenny could hear the careful cadences, the little emphasis that meant she was acting out the story with her voice. Her mother had been heroic tonight. She was a master of keeping up appearances, and here, by God, was a time when her gifts were needed. Jenny's father had started to bluster when Jenny announced Wayne was going to be late — Jennifer, I swear to you I think that man does this on purpose — but her mother had gotten up on her cane and gone to her father, put a hand on his shoulder, and said, He's being sweet, dear, he's buying presents. He's doing the best he knows.

Danny of course had asked after his father, and she told him, Daddy will be a little late, and he whined, and Alex picked up on it, and then her mother called both of them over to the couch and let them pick the channel on the television, and for the most part they forgot. Just before dinner was served, her mother hobbled into the kitchen, and Jenny kissed her on the forehead. Thank you, she said.

He's an odd man, her mother said.

You're not telling me anything new.

But loving. He is loving.

Her mother stirred the gravy, a firm smile on her face.

They ate slowly, eyes on the clock — Jenny waited a long time to announce dessert — and at eight o'clock she gave up and cleared the dishes. She put a plate of turkey and potatoes — Wayne wouldn't eat anything else — into the oven.

Jenny scrubbed at the dishes, the same china they'd had since their wedding, even the plates they'd glued together after their first anniversary dinner. She thought, for the hundredth time, what her life would be like if she were in Larry's kitchen now instead of Wayne's.

Larry and Emily had bought a new house the previous spring, on the other side of the county, to celebrate Larry's election as sheriff. Of course Jenny had gone to see it with Wayne and the boys, but she'd been by on her own a couple of times, too. Emily spent two weekends a month visiting her grandmother at a nursing home in Michigan. Jenny had made her visits in summer, when she didn't teach, while Wayne was at work. She dropped the boys at her folks' and parked her car out of sight from the road. It was a nice house, big and bright, with beautiful bay windows that let in the evening sun, filtering it through the leaves of two big maples in the front yard. Larry wouldn't use his and Emily's bed — God, it wouldn't be right, even if I don't love her — so they made love on the guest bed, narrow and squeaky, the same bed Larry had slept on in high school, which gave things a nice nostalgic feel; this was the bed where Larry had first touched her breasts, way back in the mists of time, when she was sixteen. Now she and Larry lay in the guest room all afternoon. They laughed and chattered; when Larry came — with a bellow she would have found funny if it hadn't turned her on so much — it was like a cork popped out from his throat, and he'd talk for hours about the misadventures of the citizens of Kinslow. All the while he'd touch her with his big hands.

I should have slept with you in high school, she told him during one of those afternoons. I would never have gone on to anyone else.

Well, I told you so.

She laughed. But sometimes this was because she tried very hard not to cry in front of Larry. He worried after her constantly, and she wanted him to think as many good thoughts about her as he could.

I married the wrong guy was what she wanted to tell him, but she couldn't. They had just, in a shy way, admitted they were in love, but neither one had been brave enough to bring up what they were going to do about it. Larry had just been elected; even though he was doing what his father had done, he was the youngest sheriff anyone had ever heard of, and a scandal and a divorce would probably torpedo another term. And being sheriff was a job Larry wanted — the only job he'd wanted, why he'd gone into the police force instead of going off to college like her and Wayne. If only he had! She and Wayne had never been friends in high school, but in college they got to know each other because they had Larry in common, because she pined for Larry, and Wayne was good at making her laugh, at making her seem not so lonely.

And then Larry met Emily at church. He called Jenny one night during her sophomore year to tell her he was in love, that he was happy, and that he hoped Jenny would be happy for him, too.

I'm seeing Wayne, she said, blurting it out, relieved she could finally say it.

Really? Larry had paused. *Our* Wayne?

But as much as Jenny now daydreamed about being Larry's wife (which, these days, was often) she knew such a thing was unlikely at best. She could only stand here waiting for the husband she did have —who might as well be a third son—to figure out it was family time, and think of Larry sitting in his living room with Emily. They probably weren't talking, either. Emily would be watching television, Larry sitting in his den, his nose buried in a Civil War book. Or thinking of her. Jenny's stomach thrilled.

But what was she thinking? It was Christmastime at the Thompkins house, too, and Larry's parents were over; her mother was good friends with Mrs. Thompkins and had said something about it earlier. Larry's house would be a lot like hers, except maybe even happier. Larry and his father and brother would be knocking back a special eggnog recipe, and Emily and Mrs. Thompkins, who got along better than Emily and Larry did, would be gossiping over cookie dough in the kitchen. The thought of all that activity and noise made her sad. It was better to think of Larry's house as unhappy; better to think of it as an empty place, too big for Larry, needing her and the children—

She was drying her hands when she heard the car grumbling in the trees. Wayne had been putting off a new muffler. She sighed, then called out: Daddy's home!

Daddy! Danny called. Gramma, finally!

She wished Wayne could hear that.

She looked out the kitchen window and saw Wayne's car pull up in front of the garage, the wide white circles of his headlights getting smaller and more specific on the garage door. He pulled up too close. Jenny had asked him time and time again to give her room to pull the Vega out of the garage if she needed to. She could see Wayne behind the wheel, his Impala's orange dash lights shining onto his face. He had his glasses on; she could see the reflections, little match lights.

She imagined Larry coming home, outside a different kitchen window, climbing out of his cruiser. She imagined her sons calling him Daddy, and the thought made her blush. The fantasy was almost blasphemous, but it made her tingle at the same time. Larry loved the boys, and they loved him; she sometimes stopped at the station house, and Larry would take them for a ride in his cruiser. His marriage to Emily might be different if they could have children of their own. Jenny wasn't supposed to know — no one did — but Emily was infertile. They'd found out just before moving into the new house.

Wayne shut off the engine. The light was out over the garage, and Jenny couldn't see him any longer; the image of the car was replaced by a curved piece of her own reflection in the window. She turned again to putting away the dishes. I think he's bringing presents, she heard her mother say. Danny answered this with shouts, and Alex answered him with a yodel.

Jenny thought about Wayne coming in the front door, forgetting to stamp the snow from his boots. She was going to have to go up and kiss him, pretend she didn't taste the cigarettes on his breath. He would sulk if she didn't. This was what infuriated her most; she could explain and explain (later, when they put the kids to bed), but he wouldn't understand what he'd done wrong. He'd brought the kids presents — he'd probably bought her a present. He'd been moody lately (working long hours was what he'd told her), and — she knew — this was his apology for it. In his head he'd worked it all out; he would make a gesture that far outshone any grumpiness, any silence at the dinner table. He'd come through the door like Santa Claus. She could tell him, *The only gift I wanted was a normal family dinner,* and he'd look hurt, he'd look like she slapped him. *But,* he'd say, and the corners of his mouth would turn down, *I was just trying to* — and then he'd launch into the same story he'd be telling himself right now —

They had done this before, a number of times. Too many times. This was how the rest of the night was going to go. And the thought of it all playing out so predictably —

Jenny set a plate down on the counter. She blinked; her throat stung. The thought of him made her feel ill. Her husband was coming into his house on Christmas Eve, and she couldn't bear it.

About a month ago she'd called in a trespasser while Wayne had the kids at a movie in Indy. This was risky, she knew, but she had gotten weepy like this, and she and Larry wouldn't be able to see each other for weeks yet. She'd asked if the sheriff could come out to the house, and the sheriff came. He looked so happy when she opened the door to him, when he realized Wayne was gone. She took him upstairs, and they did it, and then afterward she said, Now you surprise me, and so he took her out in the cruiser, to a nearby stretch of road, empty for a mile ahead and behind, and he said, Hang on, and floored it. The cruiser seemed almost happy to oblige him. She had her hands on the dashboard, and the road—slightly hilly—lifted her up off the seat, dropped her down again, made her feel like a girl. You're doing one-twenty, Larry said, calm as ever, in between her shrieks. Unfortunately, we're out of road.

At the house she hugged him, kissed his chin. He'd already told her, in a way, but now she told him: I love you. He'd blushed to his ears.

She was going to leave Wayne.

Of course she'd thought about it; she'd been over the possibilities, idly, on and off for the last four years, and certainly since taking up with Larry. But now she knew; she'd crossed some point of balance. She'd been waiting for something to happen with Larry, but she would have to act even sooner. The planning would take a few months at most. She'd have to have a place lined up somewhere else. A job—maybe in Indy, but certainly out of Kinslow. And then she would tell Larry—she'd have to break it to him gently, but she would tell him, once and for all, that she was his for the taking, if he could manage it.

This was it: She didn't love her husband—in fact she didn't much like him—and was never going to feel anything for him again. It had to be done. Larry or no Larry, it had to be done.

Something out the window caught her eye. Wayne had the passenger door of the Impala open and was bent inside; she could see his back under the dome lamp. What was he doing? Maybe he'd spilled his ashtray. She went to the window and put her face close to the glass.

He backed out of the car and stood straight. He stood looking at her for a moment in front of the open car door. He wiped his nose with his gloved hand. Was he crying? She felt a flicker of guilt, as though somehow he'd heard her thoughts. But then he smiled and lifted a finger: *Just a second.*

She did a quick beckon with her hand—*Get your ass in here*—and made a face, eyeballs rolled toward the rest of the house. *Now.*

He shook his head, held the finger up again.

Jenny crossed her arms. She'd see Larry next week; Emily was going to Michigan. She could begin to tell him then.

Wayne bent into the car, then straightened up again. He grinned.

She held her hands out at her sides, palms up: *What? I'm waiting.*

1970

When Wayne had first told her he wanted to blindfold her, Jenny's fear was that he was trying out some kind of sex game, some spice-up-your-love-life idea he'd gotten out of the advice column in *Playboy.* But he promised her otherwise and led her to the car. After fifteen minutes there, arms folded across her chest, and then the discovery that he was serious about guiding her, still blindfolded, through waist-high weeds and clinging spiderwebs, she began to wish sex was on his mind after all.

Wayne, she said, either tell me where we're going or I'm taking this thing off.

It's not far, honey, he said; she could tell from his voice he was grinning. Just bear with me. I'm watching your feet for you.

They were in a woods; that was easy enough to guess. She heard the leaves overhead, and birdcalls; she smelled the thick and cloying smells of the undergrowth. Twice she stumbled, and her hands scraped across tree trunks, furred vines, before Wayne tightened his grip on her arm. They were probably on a path; even blind she knew the going was too easy for them to be headed directly through the bushes. So they were in Wayne's woods, the one his parents owned. Simple enough to figure out; he talked about this place constantly. He'd driven her past it a number of times, but to her it looked like any other stand of trees out in this part of the country: solid green in summertime and dull gray-brown in winter, so thick you couldn't see light shining through from the other side.

I know where we are, she told him.

He gripped her hand and laughed. Maybe, he said, but you don't know *why.*

He had her there. She snagged her skirt on a bush and was tugged briefly between its thorns and Wayne's hand. The skirt ripped and gave. She cursed.

Sorry! Wayne said. Sorry, sorry—not much longer now.

Sunlight flickered over the top of the blindfold, and the sounds around her opened up. She was willing to bet they were in a clearing. A breeze blew past them, smelling of springtime: budding leaves and manure.

OK, Wayne said. Are you ready?

I'm not sure, she said.

Do you love me?

Of course I love you, she said. She reached a hand out in front of her and found he was suddenly absent. OK, she said, enough. Give me your hand or the blindfold's off.

She heard odd sounds — was that metal? Glass?

All right, almost there, he said. Sit down.

On the ground?

No. Just sit.

She sat, his hands on her shoulders, and found, shockingly, a chair underneath her behind. A smooth metal folding chair.

Wayne then unknotted the blindfold. He whipped it away. Happy anniversary! he said.

Jenny squinted in the revealed light, but only for a moment. She opened her eyes wide and saw she was sitting, as she'd thought, in a meadow, maybe fifty yards across, surrounded on all sides by tall green trees, all of them rippling in the wind. In front of her was a card table covered with a red-and-white checked tablecloth. The table was set with dishes — their good china, the plates at least — and two wineglasses, all wedding presents they'd only used once, on her birthday. Wayne sat in a chair opposite her, grinning, eyebrows arched. The wind blew his hair straight up off his head.

A picnic, she said. Wayne, that's lovely, thank you.

She reached her hand across the table and grasped his. He was exasperating sometimes, but no other man she'd met could reach this level of sweetness. He'd lugged all this stuff out into the middle of nowhere for her — *that's* where he must have been all afternoon.

You're welcome, he said. The red spots on his cheeks spread and deepened. He lifted her hand and kissed her knuckles, then her wedding ring. He rubbed the places where he'd kissed with his thumb.

He said, I'm sorry that dinner won't be as fancy as the plates, but I really couldn't get anything but sandwiches out here.

That's fine. She laughed. I've eaten your cooking, and we're better off with sandwiches.

Ouch, he said. He faked a European accent: This kitten, she has the claws. But I have the milk that will tame her.

He bent and rummaged through a paper bag near his chair and produced a bottle of red with a flourish and a cocked eyebrow. She couldn't help but laugh.

Not entirely chilled, he said, but good enough. He uncorked it and poured her a glass.

A toast.

To what?

To the first part of the surprise.

There's more?

He smiled slyly, lifted his glass, then said, After dinner.

He'd won her over; she didn't question it. Jenny lifted her glass, clinked rims with her husband's, and sat back with her legs crossed at the knee. Wayne bent and dug in the bag again, and then came up with sliced wheat bread and cheese and a package of carved roast beef in deli paper. He made her a sandwich, even slicing up a fresh tomato. They ate in the pleasant breeze.

After dinner he leaned back in his chair and rubbed his stomach. When they'd first started dating, she thought he did it to be funny; but really, he did it after eating anything larger than a candy bar. She was willing to bet he'd been doing it since he was a toddler. It meant all was well in the land of Wayne. The gesture made her smile, and she looked away. Since they'd married he'd developed a small wedge of belly; she wondered — not unhappily, not here — if in twenty years he'd have a giant stomach to rub, like his father's.

So I was right? she asked. This is your parents' woods?

Nope, he said, smiling.

It's not?

It was. They don't own it anymore.

They sold it? When? To who?

Yesterday. He was grinning broadly, now. To me. To us.

She sat forward, then back. He glanced around at the trees, his hair tufting in a sudden gust of the wind.

You're serious, she said. Her stomach tightened. This was a feeling she'd had a few times since their wedding — she was learning that the more complicated Wayne's ideas were, the less likely they were to be good ones. A picnic in the woods? Fine. But this?

I'm serious, Wayne said. This is my favorite place in the world — second favorite, I mean. He winked at her, then went on: But either way. Both my favorite places are mine, now. Ours.

She touched a napkin to her lips. So, she said. How much did — did we pay for our woods?

A dollar. He laughed and said, Can you believe it? Dad wanted to give it to us, but I told him, No, Pop, I want to buy it. We ended up compromising.

She could only stare at him. He squeezed her hand and said, We're landowners now, honey. One square mile.

That's —

Dad wanted to sell it off, and I couldn't bear the thought of it going to somebody who was going to plow it all under.

We need to pay your parents more than a dollar, Wayne. That's absurd.

That's what *I* told them. But Dad said no, we needed the money more. But honey — there's something else. That's only part of the surprise.

Jenny twined her fingers together in front of her mouth. A suspicion had formed, and she hoped he wasn't about to do what she guessed. Wayne was digging beside his chair again. He came up with a long roll of paper, blueprint paper, held with a rubber band. He put it on the table between them.

Our paper anniversary, he said.

What is this?

Go ahead. Look at it.

Jenny knew what the plans would show. She rolled the rubber band off the blueprints, her mouth dry. Wayne stood, his hands quick and eager, and spread the prints flat on the tabletop. They were upside down; she went around the table and stood next to him. He put a hand on the small of her back.

The blueprints were for a house. A simple two-story house — the ugliest thing she had ever seen.

I didn't want to tell you too soon, he said, but I got a raise at the bank. Plus, now that I've been there three years, I get a terrific deal on home loans. I got approval three days ago.

A house, she said.

They were living in an apartment in Kinslow, nice enough but bland, sharing a wall with an old woman who complained if they spoke above a whisper or if they played rock 'n' roll records. Jenny put a hand to her hair. Wayne, she said, where is this house going to be?

Here, he said and grinned again. He held his arms out. Right here. The table is on the exact spot. The contractors start digging on Monday. The timing's perfect. It'll be done by the end of summer.

Here . . . in the woods.

Yep.

He laughed, watching her face, and said, We're only three miles from town. The interstate's just on the other side of the field to the south. The county road is paved. All we have to do is have them expand the path in and we'll have a driveway. It'll be our hideaway. Honey?

She sat down in the chair he'd been sitting in. She could barely speak. They had talked about buying a house soon — but one in town. They'd also talked about moving to Indianapolis, about leaving Kinslow—maybe not right away, but within five years.

Wayne, she said. Doesn't this all feel kind of . . . permanent?

Well, he said, it's a house. It's supposed to.

We just talked last month. You wanted to get a job in the city. I want to live in the city. A five-year plan, remember?

Yeah. I do.

He knelt next to her chair and put his arm across her shoulders.

But I've been thinking, he said. The bank is nice, really nice, and the money just got better, and then Dad was talking about getting rid of the land, and I couldn't bear to hear it, and—

And so you went ahead and did it without asking me.

Um, Wayne said, it seemed like such a great deal that—

OK, she told him. OK. It *is* a great deal. If it was just buying the woods, that would be wonderful. But the house is different. What it means is that you're building your dream house right in the spot I want to move away from. I hate to break it to you, but that means it's not quite my dream house.

Wayne removed his hand from her shoulders and clasped his fingers in front of his mouth. She knew that gesture, too.

Wayne—

I really thought this would make you happy, he said.

A house *does* make me happy. But one in Kinslow. One we can sell later and not feel bad about when we move—

She wasn't sure what happened next. Wayne told her it was an accident, that he stood up too fast and hit his shoulder on the table. And it looked that way, sometimes, when she thought back on it. But when it happened she was sure he flung his arm out, that he knocked the table aside, that he did it on purpose. The wineglasses and china plates flew out and disappeared into the clumps of yellow grass; she heard a crash. The blueprints caught in a tangle with the tablecloth and the other folding chair.

Goddammit! Wayne shouted. He walked a quick circle, holding his hand close to his chest.

Jenny was too stunned to move, but after a minute she said Wayne's name.

He shook his head and kept walking the circle. Jenny saw he was crying, and when he saw her looking, he turned his face away. She sat still in her chair, not certain what to say or do. Finally she knelt and tried to assemble the pieces of the broken dishes.

After a minute he said, I think I'm bleeding.

She stood and walked to him and saw that he was. He'd torn a gash in his hand on the meaty outside of his palm. A big one—it would need stitches. His shirt was soaked with blood where he'd cradled his hand.

Come on, she said. We need to get you to the hospital.

No, he said. His voice was low and miserable.

Wayne, don't be silly. This isn't a time to sulk. You're hurt.

No. Hear me out. OK? You always say what you want, and you make me sound stupid for saying what I want. This time I just want to *say* it.

She grabbed some napkins and pressed them against his hand. Jesus, Wayne, she said, seeing blood well up from the cut, across her fingers. OK, OK, say what you need to.

This is my favorite place, he said. I've loved it since I was a kid. I used to come out here with Larry. He and I used to imagine we had a house out here. A hideaway.

Well—

Be quiet. I'm not done yet. His lip quivered, and he said, I know we talked, I know you want to go to Indy. Well, we can. But it looks like we're going to be successful. It looks like I'm going to do well, and you can get a job teaching anywhere. I'll just work hard, and in five years maybe we can have two houses—

Oh, Wayne—

Listen! We can have a house in Indy and then this—this can be our getaway. He sniffled and said, But I want to keep it. Besides you, this is the only thing I want. This house, right out here.

We can talk about it later. You're going to bleed to death if we don't get you to the emergency room.

I wanted you to love it, he said. I wanted you to love it because *I* love it. Is that too much to ask from your wife? I wanted to give you something *special.* I—

It was awful watching him try to talk about this. The spots of red in his cheeks were burning now, and the rims of his eyes were almost the same color. The corners of his mouth turned down in little curls.

Don't worry, she said. We'll talk about it. OK? Wayne? We'll talk. We'll take the blueprints with us to the emergency room. But you need stitches. Let's go.

I love you, he said.

She stopped fussing around his hand. He was looking down at her, tilting his head.

Jenny, just tell me you love me and none of it will matter.

She laughed in spite of herself, shaking her head. Of course, she said. Of course I do.

Say it. I need to hear it.

She kissed his cheek. Wayne, I love you with all my heart. You're my husband. Now move your behind, OK?

He kissed her, dipping his head. Jenny was bending away to pick up the blueprints, and his lips, wet, just grazed her cheek. She smiled at him and gathered their things; Wayne stood and watched her, moist eyed.

She finally took his good hand, and they walked back toward the car, and his kiss, dried slowly by the breeze, felt cool on her cheek. It lingered for a while, and despite everything, she was glad for it.

Then

The boys were first audible only as distant shrieks between the trees.

They were young enough that any time they raised their voices they sounded as though they were in terror. They were chasing each other, their only sounds loud calls, denials, laughter. When they appeared in the meadow — one charging out from a break in a dense thicket of thorned shrubs, the other close behind — they were almost indistinguishable from one another in their squeals, in their red jackets and caps. Late afternoon was shifting into dusky evening. Earlier they had hunted squirrels, unaware of how the sounds of their voices and the pops of their BB guns had traveled ahead of them, sending hundreds of beasts into their dens.

In the center of the meadow, the trailing boy caught up with the fleeing first; he pounced and they wrestled. Caps came off. One boy was blond, the other was mousy brown. The brown-haired boy was smaller. Stop it, he called from the bottom of the pile. Larry! Stop it! I mean it!

Larry laughed and said with a shudder: Wayne, you pussy.

Don't call me that!

Don't be one, pussy!

They flailed and punched until they lay squirming and helpless with laughter.

Later they pitched a tent in the center of the meadow. They had done this before. Near their tent was an old circle of charred stones, ringing a pile of damp ashes and cinders. Wayne wandered out of the meadow and gathered armfuls of deadwood while Larry secured the tent into the soft and unstable earth. They squatted down around the gathered wood and worked at setting it alight. Darkness was coming; beneath the gray overcast sky, light was diffuse anyway, and now it seemed as though the shadows came not from above but from below, shadows pooling and deepening as though they welled up from underground springs. Larry was the first to look nervously into the shadowed trees while Wayne threw matches into the wood. Wayne worked at the fire with his face twisted, mouth pursed. When the fire caught at last, the boys grinned at each other.

I wouldn't want to be out here when it's dark, Larry said, experimentally.

It's dark now.

No, I mean with no fire. Pitch dark.

I have, Wayne said.

No you haven't.

Sure I have. Sometimes I forget what time it is and get back to my bike late. Once it got totally dark. If I wasn't on the path, I would have got lost.

Wayne poked at the fire with a long stick. His parents owned the woods, but their house was two miles away. Larry looked around him, impressed.

Were you scared?

Shit, yeah. Wayne giggled. It was dark. I'm not *dumb.*

Larry looked at him for a while, then said, Sorry I called you a pussy.

Wayne shrugged and said, I should have shot that squirrel.

They'd seen one in a tree, somehow oblivious to them. Wayne was the better shot, and they'd crouched together behind a nearby log, Wayne's BB gun steadied in the crotch of a dead branch. He'd looked at the squirrel for a long time before finally lifting his cheek from the gun. I can't, he'd said.

What do you mean, you can't?

I can't. That's all.

He handed the gun to Larry, and Larry took aim, too fast, and missed.

It's all right, Larry said now, at the fire. Squirrel tastes like shit.

So does baloney, Wayne said, grim.

They pulled sandwiches from their packs. Both took the meat from between the bread, speared it with sticks, and held it over the fire until it charred and sizzled. Then they put it back into the sandwiches. Wayne took a bite first, then squealed and held a hand to his mouth. He spit a hot chunk of meat into his hand, then fumbled it into the fire.

It's *hot,* he said.

Larry looked at him for a long time. Pussy, he said and couldn't hold in his laughter. Wayne ducked his eyes and felt inside his mouth with his fingers.

Later, the fire dimmed. They sat sleepily beside it, talking in low voices. Wayne rubbed his stomach. Things unseen moved in the trees — mostly small animals, from the sound of it, but once or twice larger things.

Deer, probably, Wayne said.

What about wildcats?

No wildcats live around here. I've seen foxes, though.

Foxes aren't that big.

They spread out their sleeping bags inside the tent and opened the flap a bit so they could see the fire.

This is my favorite place, Wayne said, when they zipped into the bags.

The tent?

No. The meadow. I've been thinking about it. I want to have a house here someday.

A house?

Yeah.

What kind of house?

I don't know. Like mine, I guess, but out here. I could come out onto the porch at night, and it would be just like this. But you wouldn't have to pitch a tent. You know what? We could both have it. We'd each get half of the house to do whatever we want in. We wouldn't have to go home before it gets dark, because we'd already be there.

Larry smiled but said, That's dumb. We'll both be married by then. You won't want me in your house all the time.

That's not true.

You won't get married?

No — I mean, yeah, I will. Sure. But you can always come over.

It's not like that, Larry said, laughing.

How do you know?

Because it isn't. Jesus Christ, Wayne. Sometimes I wonder what planet you live on.

You always make my ideas sound dumb.

So don't have dumb ideas.

It isn't a dumb idea to have my friends in my house.

Larry sighed and said, No, it isn't. But marriage is different. You get married, and then the girl you marry is your best friend. That's what being in love is.

My dad has best friends.

Mine too. But who does your dad spend more time with — them or your mom?

Wayne thought for a minute. Oh.

They looked out the tent flap at the fire.

Wayne said, You'll come over when you can, though, right?

Sure, Larry said. You bet.

They lay on their stomachs, and Wayne talked about the house he wanted to build. It would have a tower. It would have a secret hallway built into the walls. It would have a pool table in the basement, better than the one at Vic's Pizza King in town. It would have a garage big enough for three cars.

Four, Larry said. We'll each have two. A sports car and a truck.

Four, Wayne said. A four-car garage. And a pinball machine. I'll have one in the living room, rigged so you don't have to put money in it.

After a while, Wayne heard Larry's breathing soften. He looked out the tent flap at the orange coals of the fire. He was sleepy, but he didn't want to sleep, not yet. He thought about his house and watched the fire fade.

He wished for the house to be here in the meadow now. Larry could have half, Wayne the other. He imagined empty rooms, then rooms full of toys. But that wasn't the way it would be. They'd be grownups. He imagined a long mirror in the bedroom and tried to see himself in it: older, as a man. He'd have rifles, not BB guns. He tried to imagine the rooms full of the things a man would have and a boy wouldn't: bookshelves, closets full of suits and ties.

Then he saw a woman at the kitchen table, wearing a blue dress. Her face kept changing — he couldn't quite see it. But he knew she was pretty. He saw himself open the kitchen door, swinging a briefcase that he put down at his feet. He held out his arms, and the woman stood to welcome him, making a happy girlish sound, and held out her arms too. Then she was close. He smelled her perfume, and she said — in a woman's voice, warm and honeyed — *Wayne,* and he felt a leaping excitement, like he'd just been scared — but better, much better — and he laughed and squeezed her and said into her soft neck and hair, his voice deep: *I'm home.*

2005

THOMAS H. COOK

WHAT SHE OFFERED

THOMAS H(ARPER) COOK (1947–) was born in Fort Payne, Alabama, and received a BA from Georgia State College, a master's in American history from Hunter College in New York, and a master's in philosophy from Columbia University. He worked as a teacher and journalist, including four years as a book reviewer for *Atlanta* magazine, before becoming a full-time writer.

His first novel was a paperback original, *Blood Innocents* (1980), which received the first of his seven Edgar Allan Poe Award nominations from the Mystery Writers of America. He won the Best Novel Edgar in 1997 for *The Chatham School Affair.* He also was nominated by the MWA in 1989 for Best Novel (*Sacrificial Ground*), in 1993 for Best Fact Crime (*Blood Echoes*), in 2005 for Best Paperback Original (*Into the Web*), in 2006 for Best Novel (*Red Leaves*), and in 2007 for Best Short Story ("Rain"). *Red Leaves* was also nominated for an Anthony Award and the (British) Crime Writers' Association's Duncan Lawrie Dagger, and it won the Barry Award and Sweden's Martin Beck Award. Noted for the poetic lyricism of his work, Cook has enjoyed greater success with critics, reviewers, and his fellow mystery writers, who admire the sensitive beauty of his prose, than he has with book buyers, who have thus far failed to place any of his books on the bestseller list. A film of one of his books, the highly suspenseful *Evidence of Blood,* was released in 1998; it was directed by Andrew Mondshein and starred David Strathairn and Mary McDonnell.

"What She Offered" was first published in the anthology *Dangerous Women* (New York: Mysterious Press, 2005).

■ ■ ■

"SOUNDS LIKE A dangerous woman," my friend said. He'd not been with me in the bar the night before, not seen her leave or me follow after her.

I took a sip of vodka and glanced toward the window. Outside, the afternoon light was no doubt as it had always been, but it didn't look the same to me anymore. "I guess she was," I told him.

"So what happened?" my friend asked.

This: I was in the bar. It was two in the morning. The people around me were like tapes from *Mission Impossible,* only without the mission, just that self-destruction warning. You could almost hear it playing in their heads, stark and unyielding as the Chinese proverb: *If you continue down the road you're on, you will get to where you're headed.*

Where were they headed? As I saw it, mostly toward more of the same. They would finish this drink, this night, this week . . . and so on. At some point, they would die like animals after a long, exhausting haul, numb with weariness as they finally slumped beneath the burden. Worse still, according to me, this bar was the world, its few dully buzzing flies no more than stand-ins for the rest of us.

I had written about "us" in novel after novel. My tone was always bleak. In my books, there were no happy endings. People were lost and helpless, even the smart ones . . . especially the smart ones. Everything was vain and everything was fleeting. The strongest emotions quickly waned. A few things mattered, but only because we made them matter by insisting that they should. If we needed evidence of this, we made it up. As far as I could tell, there were basically three kinds of people, the ones who deceived others, the ones who deceived themselves, and the ones who understood that the people in the first two categories were the only ones they were ever likely to meet. I put myself firmly in the third category, of course, the only member of my club, the one guy who understood that to see things in full light was the greatest darkness one could know.

And so I walked the streets and haunted the bars, and was, according to me, the only man on earth who had nothing to learn.

Then suddenly, she walked through the door.

To black, she offered one concession. A string of small white pearls. Everything else, the hat, the dress, the stockings, the shoes, the little purse . . . everything else was black. And so, what she offered at that first glimpse was just the old B movie stereotype of the dangerous woman, the broad-billed hat that discreetly covers one eye, high heels tapping on rain-slicked streets, foreign currency in the small black purse. She offered the spy, the murderess, the lure of a secret past, and, of course, that little hint of erotic peril.

She knows the way men think, I said to myself as she walked to the end of the bar and took her seat. She knows the way they think . . . and she's using it.

"So you thought she was what?" my friend asked.

I shrugged. "Inconsequential."

And so I watched without interest as the melodramatic touches accumulated. She lit a cigarette and smoked it pensively, her eyes opening and closing languidly, with the sort of world-weariness one sees in the heroines of old black-and-white movies.

Yes, that's it, I told myself. She is noir in the worst possible sense, thin as strips of film, and just as transparent at the edges. I looked at my watch. Time to go, I thought, time to go to my apartment and stretch out on the bed and wallow in my dark superiority, congratulate myself that once again I had not been fooled by the things that fool other men.

But it was only two in the morning, early for me, so I lingered in the bar, and wondered, though only vaguely, with no more than passing interest, if she had anything else to offer beyond this little show of being "dangerous."

"Then what?" my friend asked.

Then she reached in her purse, drew out a small black pad, flipped it open, wrote something, and passed it down the bar to me.

The paper was folded, of course. I unfolded it and read what she'd written: *I know what you know about life.*

It was exactly the kind of nonsense I'd expected, so I briskly scrawled a reply on the back of the paper and sent it down the bar to her.

She opened it and read what I'd written: *No, you don't. And you never will.* Then, without so much as looking up, she wrote a lightning-fast response and sent it hurtling back up the bar, quickly gathering her things and heading for the door as it went from hand to hand, so that she'd already left the place by the time it reached me.

I opened the note and read her reply: C+.

My anger spiked. C+? How dare she! I whirled around on the stool and rushed out of the bar, where I found her leaning casually against the little wrought-iron fence that surrounded it.

I waved the note in front of her. "What's this supposed to mean?" I demanded.

She smiled and offered me a cigarette. "I've read your books. They're really dreadful."

I don't smoke, but I took the cigarette anyway. "So, you're a critic?"

She gave no notice to what I'd just said. "The writing is beautiful," she said as she lit my cigarette with a red plastic lighter. "But the idea is really bad."

"Which idea is that?"

"You only have one," she said with total confidence. "That everything ends badly, no matter what we do." Her face tightened. "So, here's the deal. When I wrote, *I know what you know about life,* that wasn't exactly true. I know more."

I took a long draw on the cigarette. "So," I asked lightly. "Is this a date?"

She shook her head, and suddenly her eyes grew dark and somber. "No," she said, "this is a love affair."

I started to speak, but she lifted her hand and stopped me.

"I could do it with you, you know," she whispered, her voice now very grave. "Because you know almost as much as I do, and I want to do it with someone who knows that much."

From the look in her eyes I knew exactly what she wanted to "do" with me. "We'd need a gun," I told her with a dismissing grin.

She shook her head. "I'd never use a gun. It would have to be pills." She let her cigarette drop from her fingers. "And we'd need to be in bed together," she added matter-of-factly. "Naked and in each other's arms."

"Why is that?"

Her smile was soft as light. "To show the world that you were wrong." The smile widened, almost playfully. "That something can end well."

"Suicide?" I asked. "You call that ending well?"

She laughed and tossed her hair slightly. "It's the only way to end well," she said.

And I thought, *She's nuts,* but for the first time in years, I wanted to hear more.

"A suicide pact," my friend whispered.

"That's what she offered, yes," I told him. "But not right away. She said that there was something I needed to do first."

"What?"

"Fall in love with her," I answered quietly.

"And she knew you would?" my friend asked. "Fall in love with her, I mean?"

"Yes, she did," I told him.

But she also knew that the usual process was fraught with trial, a road scattered with pits and snares. So she'd decided to forgo courtship, the tedious business of exchanging mounds of trivial biographical information. Physical intimacy would come first, she said. It was the gate through which we would enter each other.

"So, we should go to my place now," she concluded, after offering her brief explanation of all this. "We need to fuck."

"Fuck?" I laughed. "You're not exactly the romantic type, are you?"

"You can undress me if you want to," she said. "Or, if not, I'll do it myself."

"Maybe you should do it," I said jokingly. "That way I won't dislocate your shoulder."

She laughed. "I get suspicious if a man does it really well. It makes me think that he's a bit too familiar with all those female clasps and snaps and zippers. It makes me wonder if perhaps he's . . . worn it all himself."

"Jesus," I moaned. "You actually think about things like that?"

Her gaze and tone became deadly serious. "I can't handle every need," she said.

There was a question in her eyes, and I knew what the question was. She wanted to know if I had any secret cravings or odd sexual quirks, any "needs" she could not "handle."

"I'm strictly double-vanilla," I assured her. "No odd flavors."

She appeared slightly relieved. "My name is Veronica," she said.

"I was afraid you weren't going to tell me," I said. "That it was going to be one of those things where I never know who you are and vice versa. You know, ships that pass in the night."

"How banal that would be," she said.

"Yes, it would."

"Besides," she added. "I already knew who you were."

"Yes, of course."

"My apartment is just down the block," she said, then offered to take me there.

As it turned out, her place was a bit farther than just down the block, but it didn't matter. It was after two in the morning and the streets were pretty much deserted. Even in New York, certain streets, especially certain Greenwich Village streets, are never all that busy, and once people have gone to and from work, they become little more than country lanes. That night the trees that lined Jane Street swayed gently in the cool autumn air, and I let myself accept what I thought she'd offered, which, for all the "dangerous" talk, would probably be no more than a brief erotic episode, maybe breakfast in the morning, a little light conversation over coffee and scones. Then she would go her way and I would go mine because one of us would want it that way and the other wouldn't care enough to argue the point.

"The vodka's in the freezer," she said as she opened the door to her apartment, stepped inside and switched on the light.

I walked into the kitchen while Veronica headed down a nearby corridor. The refrigerator was at the far end of the room, its freezer door festooned with pictures of Veronica and a short, bald little man who looked to be in his late forties.

"That's Douglas," Veronica called from somewhere down the hall. "My husband."

I felt a pinch of apprehension.

"He's away," she added.

The apprehension fled.

"I should hope so," I said as I opened the freezer door.

Veronica's husband faced me again when I closed it, the ice-encrusted vodka bottle now securely in my right hand. Now I noticed that Douglas was somewhat portly, deep lines around his eyes, graying at the temples. OK, I thought, maybe midfifties. And yet, for all that, he had a boyish face. In the pictures, Veronica towered over him, his bald head barely reaching her broad shoulders. She was in every photograph, his arm always wrapped affectionately around her waist. And in every photograph Douglas was smiling with such unencumbered joy that I knew that all his happiness came from her, from being with her, being her husband, that when he was with her he felt tall and dark and handsome, witty and smart and perhaps even a bit elegant. That was what she offered him, I supposed, the illusion that he deserved her.

"He was a bartender when I met him," she said as she swept into the kitchen. "Now he sells software." She lifted an impossibly long and graceful right arm to the cabinet at her side, opened its plain wooden doors and retrieved two decidedly ordinary glasses, which she placed squarely on the plain Formica counter before turning to face me. "From the beginning, I was always completely comfortable with Douglas," she said.

She could not have said it more clearly. Douglas was the man she had chosen to marry because he possessed whatever characteristics she required to feel utterly at home when she was at home, utterly herself when she was with him. If there had been some great love in her life, she had chosen Douglas over him because with Douglas she could live without change or alteration, without applying makeup to her soul. Because of that, I suddenly found myself vaguely envious of this squat little man, of the peace he gave her, the way she could no doubt rest in the crook of his arm, breathing slowly, falling asleep.

"He seems . . . nice," I said.

Veronica gave no indication that she'd heard me. "You take it straight," she said, referring to the way I took my drink, which was clearly something she'd noticed in the bar.

I nodded.

"Me, too."

She poured our drinks and directed me into the living room. The curtains were drawn tightly together, and looked a bit dusty. The furniture had been chosen for comfort rather than for style. There were a few potted plants, most of them brown at the edges. You could almost hear them begging for water. No dogs. No cats. No goldfish or hamsters or snakes or white mice. When Douglas was away, it appeared, Veronica lived alone.

Except for books, but they were everywhere. They filled shelf after towering shelf, or lay stacked to the point of toppling along the room's four walls. The authors ran the gamut, from the oldest classics to the most recent bestsellers. Stendahl and Dostoyevsky rested shoulder to shoulder with Anne Rice and Michael Crichton. A few of my own stark titles were lined up between Robert Stone and Patrick O'Brian. There was no history or social science in her collection, and no poetry. It was all fiction, as Veronica herself seemed to be, a character she'd made up and was determined to play to the end. What she offered, I believed at that moment, was a well-rounded performance of a New York eccentric.

She touched her glass to mine, her eyes very still. "To what we're going to do," she said.

"Are we still talking about committing suicide together?" I scoffed as I lowered my glass without drinking. "What is this, Veronica? Some kind of *Sweet November* rewrite?"

"I don't know what you mean," she said.

"You know, that stupid movie where the dying girl takes this guy and lives with him for a month and—"

"I would never live with you," Veronica interrupted.

"That's not my point."

"And I'm not dying," Veronica added. She took a quick sip of vodka, placed her glass onto the small table beside the sofa, then rose, as if suddenly called by an invisible voice, and offered her hand to me. "Time for bed," she said.

"Just like that?" my friend asked.

"Just like that."

He looked at me warily. "This is a fantasy, right?" he asked. "This is something you made up."

"What happened next no one could make up."

"And what was that?"

She led me to the bedroom. We undressed silently. She crawled beneath the single sheet and patted the mattress. "This side is yours."

"Until Douglas gets back," I said as I drew in beside her.

"Douglas isn't coming back," she said, then leaned over and kissed me very softly.

"Why not?"

"Because he's dead," she answered lightly. "He's been dead for three years."

And thus I learned of her husband's slow decline, the cancer that began in his intestines and migrated to his liver and pancreas. It had taken six months, and each day Veronica had attended him. She would look in on him on her way to work every morning, then return to him at night, stay at his bedside until she was sure he would not awaken, then, at last, return here, to this very bed, to sleep for an hour or two, three at the most, before beginning the routine again.

"Six months," I said. "That's a long time."

"A dying person is a lot of work," she said.

"Yes, I know," I told her. "I was with my father while he died. I was exhausted by the time he finally went."

"Oh, I don't mean that," she said. "The physical part. The lack of sleep. That wasn't the hard part when it came to Douglas."

"What was?"

"Making him believe I loved him."

"You didn't?"

"No," she said, then kissed me again, a kiss that lingered a bit longer than the first, and gave me time to remember that just a few minutes before she'd told me that Douglas was currently selling software.

"Software," I said, drawing my lips from hers. "You said he sold software now."

She nodded. "Yes, he does."

"To other dead people?" I lifted myself up and propped my head in my hand. "I can't wait for an explanation."

"There is no explanation," she said. "Douglas always wanted to sell software. So, instead of saying that he's in the ground or in heaven, I just say he's selling software."

"So you give death a cute name," I said. "And that way you don't have to face it."

"I say he's selling software because I don't want the conversation that would follow if I told you he was dead," Veronica said sharply. "I hate consolation."

"Then why did you tell me at all?"

"Because you need to know that I'm like you," she answered. "Alone. That no one will mourn."

"So we're back to suicide again," I said. "Do you always circle back to death?"

She smiled. "Do you know what La Rochefoucauld said about death?"

"It's not on the tip of my tongue, no."

"He said that it was like the sun. You couldn't look at it for very long without going blind." She shrugged. "But I think that if you look at it all the time, measure it against living, then you can choose."

I drew her into my arms. "You're a bit quirky, Veronica," I said playfully.

She shook her head, her voice quite self-assured. "No," she insisted. "I'm the sanest person you've ever met."

"And she was," I told my friend.

"What do you mean?"

"I mean she offered more than anyone I'd ever known."

"What did she offer?"

That night she offered the cool, sweet luxury of her flesh, a kiss that so brimmed with feeling I thought her lips would give off sparks.

We made love for a time then, suddenly, she stopped and pulled away. "Time to chat," she said, then walked to the kitchen and returned with another two glasses of vodka.

"Time to chat?" I asked, still disconcerted with how abruptly she'd drawn away from me.

"I don't have all night," she said as she offered me the glass.

I took the drink from her hand. "So we're not going to toast the dawn together?"

She sat on the bed, cross-legged and naked, her body sleek and smooth in the blue light. "You're glib," she said as she clinked her glass to mine. "So am I." She leaned forward slightly, her eyes glowing in the dark. "Here's the deal," she added. "If you're glib, you finally get to the end of what you can say. There are no words left for anything important. Just sleek words. Clever. Glib. That's when you know you've gone as far as you can go, that you have nothing left to offer but smooth talk."

"That's rather harsh, don't you think?" I took a sip of vodka. "And besides, what's the alternative to talking?"

"Silence," Veronica answered.

I laughed. "Veronica, you are hardly silent."

"Most of the time, I am," she said.

"And what does this silence conceal?"

"Anger," she answered without the slightest hesitation. "Fury."

Her face grew taut, and I thought the rage I suddenly glimpsed within her would set her hair ablaze.

"Of course you can get to silence in other ways," she said. She took a quick, brutal drink from her glass. "Douglas got there, but not by being glib."

"How then?"

"By suffering."

I looked for her lip to tremble, but it didn't. I looked for moisture in her eyes, but they were dry and still.

"By being terrified," she added. She glanced toward the window, let her gaze linger there for a moment, then returned to me. "The last week he didn't say a word," she told me. "That's when I knew it was time."

"Time for what?"

"Time for Douglas to get a new job."

I felt my heart stop dead. "In . . . software?" I asked.

She lit a candle, placed it on the narrow shelf above us, then yanked open the top drawer of the small table that sat beside her bed, retrieved a plastic pill case and shook it so that I could hear the pills rattling dryly inside it.

"I'd planned to give him these," she said, "but there wasn't time."

"What do you mean, there wasn't time?"

"I saw it in his face," she answered. "He was living like someone already in the ground. Someone buried and waiting for the air to give out. That kind of suffering, terror. I knew that one additional minute would be too long."

She placed the pills on the table, then grabbed the pillow upon which her head had rested, fluffed it gently, pressed it down upon my face, then lifted it again in a way that made me feel strangely returned to life. "It was all I had left to offer him," she said quietly, then took a long, slow pull on the vodka. "We have so little to offer."

And I thought with sudden, devastating clarity, *Her darkness is real; mine is just a pose.*

"What did you do?" my friend asked.

"I touched her face."

"And what did she do?"

She pulled my hand away almost violently. "This isn't about me," she said.

"Right now, everything is about you," I told her.

She grimaced. "Bullshit."

"I mean it."

"Which only makes it worse," she said sourly. Her eyes rolled upward, then came down again, dark and steely, like the twin barrels of a shotgun. "This is about you," she said crisply. "And I won't be cheated out of it."

I shrugged. "All life is a cheat, Veronica."

Her eyes tensed. "That isn't true and you know it," she said, her voice almost a hiss. "And because of that you're a liar, and all your books are lies." Her voice was so firm, so hard and unrelenting, I felt it like a wind. "Here's the deal," she said. "If you really felt the way you write, you'd kill yourself. If all that feeling was really in you, down deep in you, you wouldn't be able to live a single day." She dared me to contradict her, and when I didn't, she said, "You see everything but yourself. And here's what you don't see about yourself, Jack. You don't see that you're happy."

"Happy?" I asked.

"You are happy," Veronica insisted. "You won't admit it, but you are. And you should be."

Then she offered the elements of my happiness, the sheer good fortune I had enjoyed, health, adequate money, work I loved, little dollops of achievement.

"Compared to you, Douglas had nothing," she said.

"He had you," I said cautiously.

Her face soured again. "If you make it about me," she warned, "you'll have to leave."

She was serious, and I knew it. So I said, "What do you want from me, Veronica?"

Without hesitation she said, "I want you to stay."

"Stay?"

"While I take the pills."

I remembered the line she'd said just outside the bar only a few hours before, *I could do it with you, you know.*

I had taken this to mean that we would do it together, but now I knew that she had never included me. There was no pact. There was only Veronica.

"Will you do it?" she asked somberly.

"When?" I asked quietly.

She took the pills and poured them into her hand. "Now," she said.

"No," I blurted, and started to rise.

She pressed me down hard, her gaze relentlessly determined, so that I knew she would do what she intended, that there was no way to stop her.

"I want out of this noise," she said, pressing her one empty hand to her right ear. "Everything is so loud."

In the fierceness of those words I glimpsed the full measure of her torment, all she no longer wished to hear, the clanging daily vanities and thudding repetitions, the catcalls of the inferior, the trumpeting mediocrities, all of which lifted to a soul-searing roar the unbearable clatter of the wheel. She wanted an end to all of that, a silence she would not be denied.

"Will you stay?" she asked quietly.

I knew that any argument would strike her as just more noise she could not bear. It would clang like cymbals, only add to the mindless cacophony she was so desperate to escape.

And so I said, "All right."

With no further word, she swallowed the pills two at a time, washing them down with quick sips of vodka.

"I don't know what to say to you, Veronica," I told her when she took the last of them and put down the glass.

She curled under my arm. "Say what I said to Douglas," she told me. "In the end it's all anyone can offer."

"What did you say to him?" I asked softly.

"I'm here."

I drew my arm tightly around her. "I'm here," I said.

She snuggled in more closely. "Yes."

"And so you stayed?" my friend asked.

I nodded.

"And she . . . ?"

"In about an hour," I told him. "Then I dressed and walked the streets until I finally came here."

"So right now she's . . ."

"Gone," I said quickly, and suddenly imagined her sitting in the park across from the bar, still and silent.

"You couldn't stop her?"

"With what?" I asked. "I had nothing to offer." I glanced out the front window of the bar. "And besides," I added, "for a truly dangerous woman, a man is never the answer. That's what makes her dangerous. At least, to us."

My friend looked at me oddly. "So what are you going to do now?" he asked.

At the far end of the park a young couple was screaming at each other, the woman's fist in the air, the man shaking his head in violent confusion. I could imagine Veronica turning from them, walking silently away.

"I'm going to keep quiet," I answered. "For a very long time."

Then I got to my feet and walked out into the whirling city. The usual dissonance engulfed me, all the chaos and disarray, but I felt no need to add my own inchoate discord to the rest.

It was a strangely sweet feeling, I realized as I turned and headed home, embracing silence.

From deep within her enveloping calm, Veronica offered me her final words.

I know.

2005

ANDREW KLAVAN

HER LORD AND MASTER

ANDREW KLAVAN (1954–) was born in New York City, the son of popular radio disc jockey and talk show host Gene Klavan. He received a business degree from the University of California, Berkeley, before returning to the New York area to work as a news writer, reporter, book reviewer, and mystery novelist. His first novel, *Face of the Earth* (1980), was published when he was twenty-six, three years after it was completed. He has gone on to write more than twenty additional novels of mystery, crime, horror (*The Uncanny,* 1998), psychological suspense (*Man and Wife,* 2001), and, most recently, international terror (*Empire of Lies,* 2008). He has been nominated for four Edgar Allan Poe Awards by the Mystery Writers of America, winning twice: for *Mrs. White* (1983), coauthored with his brother, the novelist and playwright Laurence Klavan, under the pseudonym Margaret Tracy; and *The Rain* (1988), under the pseudonym Keith Peterson. He was also nominated for Best Novel for *Don't Say a Word* (1991) and for Best Short Story for "Her Lord and Master" (2005). Stephen King once described him as "the most original American novelist of crime and suspense since Cornell Woolrich." Klavan adapted his novel *True Crime* (1995) for a film of the same title that starred and was directed by Clint Eastwood in 1999. Two years later he wrote the screenplay for *Don't Say a Word,* which starred Michael Douglas. He also wrote the screenplay for Simon Brett's *A Shock to the System* (1990).

"Her Lord and Master" was written many years before it was published, his agent refusing to submit it because of its controversial subject matter. It was first published in the anthology *Dangerous Women* (New York: Mysterious Press, 2005), and was selected for *The Best American Mystery Stories 2006.*

▪ ▪ ▪

IT WAS OBVIOUS she'd killed him, but only I knew why. I'd been Jim's friend, and he'd told me everything. It was a shocking story in its way. I found it shocking, at any rate. More than once, when he confided in me, I'd felt the sweat gathering under my collar, on my chest. Goose bumps, and what in a more decorous age we would have called a "stirring in the loins." Nowadays, of course, we're supposed to be able to talk about these things, about anything, in fact. There are so many books and movies and television shows claiming to shatter "the last taboo" that you'd think we were in danger of running out of them.

Well, let's see. Let's just see.

Jim and Susan knew each other at work, and began a relationship after an office party, standard stuff. Jim was Vice President in charge of Entertainment at one of the larger radio networks. "I don't know what my job is," he used to say, "but by gum I must be doing it." Susan was an Assistant Manager in Personnel, which meant she was the secretary in charge of scheduling.

Jim was a tallish, elegant Harvard grad, thirty-five. On the job, he had a slow, thoughtful manner, a way of appearing to consider every word he spoke. Plus a way of boring into your eyes when you spoke, as if every neuron he had was engaged in whatever tedious matter you'd brought before him. After hours, thankfully, he became more satirical, more sardonic. To be honest, I think he considered most people little better than idiots. Which makes him a cockeyed optimist, if you ask me.

Susan was sharp, dark, energetic, in her twenties. A little thin and beaky in the face for my taste, but pretty enough with long, straight, black, black hair. Plus she had a fine figure, small and compact and gracefully, meltingly round at breast and hip. Her attitude was aggressive, funny, challenging: You gonna take me as I am, pal, or what? Which I think disguised a certain defensiveness about her Queens background, her education, maybe even her intelligence. In any case, she could put a charge in your morning, striding by in a short skirt, or drawing her hair from her mouth with one long nail. A Watercooler Fuck, was the general male consensus. In those sociological debates in which gentlemen are prone to discuss how their various female colleagues and acquaintances should be coupled with, Susan was usually voted the girl you'd like to shove against the watercooler and take standing up with the overnight cleaning crew vacuuming down the hall.

So at a party one February at which we celebrated the launch and certain failure of some new moronic management scheme or other, we watched with glee and envy as Jim and Susan stood together, talked together, and eventually left together. And eventually slept together. We didn't watch that part, but I heard all about it later.

I'm a news editor, thirty-eight, once divorced, seven years, two months, and sixteen days ago. Sexually, I think I've pretty much been around the block. But we've all pretty much been around the block these days. They probably ought to widen the lanes around the block to ease the traffic. So, at first, what Jim was telling me brought no more than a mild glaze of lust to my eyes, not to mention the thin line of drool running unattended from the corner of my mouth.

She liked it rough. That's the story. Now it can be told. Our Susan enjoyed the occasional smack with her rumpty-tumpty. Jim, God love him, seemed somewhat disconcerted by this at first. He'd been around the block too, of course, but it was a block in a more sedate neighborhood. And I guess maybe he'd missed that particular address.

Apparently, when they went back to his apartment, Susan had presented Jim with the belt to his terry cloth bathrobe and said, "Tie me." Jim managed to follow these simple instructions and also the ones about grabbing her black, black hair in his fist and forcing her mouth down on what I will politely assume to be his throbbing tumescence. The smacking part came later, after he'd hurled her bellyward onto his bed and was ramming into her from behind. This, too, at her specific request.

"It was kind of kinky," Jim told me.

"Hey, I sympathize," I said. "What does this make you, only the second or third luckiest man on the face of the earth?"

Well, it was a turn-on, Jim admitted that. And it wasn't that he'd never done anything like it before. It was just that, in Jim's experience, you had to get to know a girl a little before you started clobbering her. It was intimate, fantasy stuff, not the sort of thing you did on a first date.

Plus, Jim genuinely liked Susan, He liked the tough, working-stiff jazz of her and the chip-on-the-shoulder wisecracks with the vulnerability underneath. He wanted to get to know her, be with her a while, maybe a long while. And if this was where they started, he wondered, where exactly were they going to go?

But any awkwardness, it turned out, was all on Jim's side. Susan seemed perfectly comfortable when she woke in his arms the next morning. "It was nice last night," she whispered, stretching up to kiss his stubble. And she held his hand as they hailed a cab to take her home for a change of clothes. And she wowed and charmed him with her office etiquette, giving not a clue to the world of their altered state, giving even him only a single token of it when they passed each other, nodding, in the hall, and she murmured, "God, we are *so* professional."

And they had dinner together up on Columbus at the Moroccan and she went on, hilarious, about the management types in her department. And Jim, who usually expressed amusement by narrowing his eyes and smiling thinly, fell back in his chair and laughed with his teeth showing, and had to wipe tears out of his crow's feet with the four fingers of one hand.

That night, she wanted him to thrash her with his leather belt. Jim demurred. "Don't we ever get to do it just the regular way?" he asked.

But she leaned in close and smoldered at him. "Do it. I want you to."

"You know, I'm a little concerned about the noise. The neighbors and everything."

Well, he had a point there. Susan went into the kitchen and returned with a wooden spoon. They don't make quite the crack, apparently. Jim, always the gentleman, proceeded to tie her to the bedposts.

"The woman's killing me, I'm exhausted," he told me a couple of weeks later.

I put my hand under my shirt and moved it up and down so he could see my heart beating for him.

"I mean it," he said. "I mean, I'm up for this stuff sometimes. It's sexy, it's fun. But Jesus. I'd like to see her face from time to time."

"She'll calm down. You're just getting started," I said. "So she digs this stuff. Later, you can gently instruct her in the joys of the missionary position."

We had this conversation at a table in McCord's, the last unspoiled Irish bar on the gentrified West Side. The news team does tend to drift down here of an evening, so we were already speaking in undertones. Now, Jim leaned in toward me even closer. Our foreheads were almost touching and he glanced side to side before he went on.

"The thing is," he said, "I think she's serious."

"What do you mean?"

"I mean, I'm all for fantasy stuff and all that. But I don't think she's kidding around."

"What do you mean?" I said again, more hoarsely and with a bead of sweat forming behind my ear.

It turned out their relationship had now progressed to the point where they were divvying up the household chores. Susan had doled out the assignments and it fell to her to clean Jim's apartment, cook his dinner, and wash the dishes. Naked. Jim's job was to force her to do these things and whip, spank, or rape her if she showed reluctance or made, or pretended to make, some kind of mistake.

Now there's always an element of braggadocio when men complain about their sex lives, but Jim really did seem troubled by this. "I'm not saying it doesn't turn me on. I admit, it's a turn-on. It's just getting kind of . . . ugly at this point. Isn't it?" he said.

I wiped my lips dry and dropped back in my seat. When I could finally stop panting and move my mouth, I said, "I don't know. To each his own. I mean, look, if you don't like it, eject. You know? If it doesn't work for you, hit the button."

Obviously, this thought had occurred to him before. He nodded slowly, as if considering it.

But he didn't eject. In fact, another week or so, and for all intents and purposes Susan was living with him.

At this point, my information becomes less detailed. Obviously, a guy's living with someone, he doesn't go on too much about their sex life. Everyone at the net knew the affair was a happening thing by now, but Susan and Jim remained entirely professional and detached on the job. They'd walk to work together holding hands. They'd kiss once outside the building. And after that, it was business as usual. No low tones in the hallway, no closed office doors. The few times we all went out drinking together after work, they didn't even sit next to each other. Through the bar window, when they left, we'd see Jim put his arm around her. That was all.

The last time Jim and I talked about it before he died was in McCord's again. I came in there one night and there he was sitting at a corner table alone. I knew by the way he was sitting—bolt upright with his eyes half open, staring, glazed—that he was drunk as God on Sunday. I sat down across from him and he made a sloppy gesture with his hand and said, "Drinks are on me." I ordered a scotch.

If I'd been smart, I would've stuck to sports. The Knicks were getting murdered, the Yanks, after a championship season, were struggling to keep pace with Baltimore as the new season got under way. I could've talked about all of that. I should've. But I was curious. If curious is the word I want. Prurient, maybe, is the *mot juste.*

And I said, "So how are things going with Susan?"

And he said, as you will when you're serious about someone, "Fine. Things with Susan are fine." But then he added, "I'm her Lord and Master." Sitting bolt upright. Waving slightly like a lamppost in a gale.

Susan had scripted their routines, but he knew them by heart now and ran through them without prompting. This was apparently more efficient because it left her free to beg him to stop. He would tie her and she would beg him and he would beat her while she begged. He would sodomize her and grab her hair, force her head around so she had to watch him while he did it. "Who's your Lord and Master?" he would say. And she would answer, "You're my Lord and Master. You are." Later she would do the chores, naked or in this lace-and-suspender outfit she'd bought. Usually she'd fumble something or spill something, and he would beat her, which got him ready to take her again.

After he told me this, his eyes sank closed, his lips parted. He seemed to sleep for a few minutes, then woke up with a slight start. But bolt upright always, always straight up and down. Even when he got up to leave, his posture was stiff and perfect. He wafted to the door as if he were one of those old deportment instructors. He was a funny kind of a drunk that way, even more dignified than when he was sober, a sort of exaggerated, comic version of his reserved, dignified sober self.

I watched him leave with a half smile on my face. I miss him.

Susan stabbed him with a kitchen knife, one of those big ones. Just a single convulsive jab but it went straight in, severed the vena cava. He bled out lying on the kitchen floor, staring up at the ceiling while she screamed into the phone for an ambulance.

Jim being a bit of a muck-a-muck, it made the news. Then the feminists got ahold of it, the real bully girls who consider murdering your boyfriend a form of self-expression. They wanted the case dismissed out of hand. And a lot of people agreed they had a point this time. Susan, it was found, had bruises all over her torso, was bleeding from various orifices. And Jim had pretty clearly been wielding a nasty-looking sex store paddle when she went for the knife. According to the political dicta of the day, it was an obvious case of long-term abuse and long-delayed self-defense.

But the cops, for some reason, were not immediately convinced. In general, cops spend enough time in the depths of human depravity to keep a spare suit in the closet there. They know that even the most obvious political axioms don't always cut it when you're dealing with true romance.

So the Manhattan DA's office was caught between the devil and the deep blue sea. Susan had gotten a good lawyer fast and had said nothing to anyone. The police suspected they'd find evidence of consensual rough sex in Susan's life but so far hadn't produced the goods. The press, meanwhile, was starting to link Susan's name with the word "ordeal" a lot, and were running her story next to sidebars on sexual abuse, which was their way of being "objective" while taking Susan's side entirely. Anyway, the last thing the DA wanted was to jail the woman and then release her. So he waffled. Withheld charges for a day or two, pending further investigation. And, in the meantime, the prime suspect was set free.

As for me, all was depression and confusion. Jim wasn't my brother or anything, but he was a good buddy. And I knew I was probably the best friend he had at the network, maybe even in the city, maybe in the world. Still there were moments, watching the feminists on TV, watching Susan's lawyer, when I thought: How do I know? The guy says one thing, the girl says something else. How do I know everything Jim told me wasn't some kind of crazy lie, some sort of justification for the bad stuff he was doing to her?

Of course, all that aside, I called the police the day after the murder, Friday, the first I heard. I phoned a contact of mine in Homicide and told him I had solid information on the case. I think I half-expected to hear the whining sirens of the squad coming for me even as I hung up the phone. Instead, I was given a Monday-morning appointment and asked to wander on by the station house to talk to the detectives in charge.

Which gave me the weekend free. I spent it anchored to the sofa by a leaden nausea. Gazing at the ceiling, arm flung across my brow. Trying to force tears, trying to blame myself, trying not to. The phone rang and rang, but I never answered it. It was just friends—I could hear them on the answering machine—wanting to get in on it: the sympathy, the grief, the gossip. Everybody craving a piece of a murder. I didn't have the energy to play.

Sunday evening, finally, there was a knock at my door. I'm on the top floor of a brownstone so you expect the street buzzer, but this was a knock. I figured it must be one of my neighbors who'd seen the story on TV. I called out as I put my shoes on. Tucked in my shirt as I went to the door. Pulled it open without even looking through the peephole.

And there was Susan.

A lot of things went through my mind in the second I saw her. As she stood there, combative and uncomfortable at once. Chin raised, belligerent; glance sidelong, shy. I thought: Who am I supposed to be here? What am I supposed to be like? Angry? Vengeful? Chilly? Just? Lofty? Compassionate? Christ, it was paralyzing. In the end, I just stood back and let her enter. She walked into the middle of the room and faced me as I closed the door.

Then she shrugged at me. One bare shoulder lifted, one lifted corner of her mouth, a wise-guy smile. She was wearing a pale spring dress, the thin strings tied round her neck in a bow. It showed a lot of her dark flesh. I noticed a crescent of discolor on her thigh beneath the hem.

"I'm not too sure about the etiquette here," I said.

"Yeah. Maybe you could look under 'Entertaining the Girl Who Killed Your Best Friend.'"

I gave her back her wise-guy smile. "Don't say too much, Susan, OK? I gotta go in to see the cops on Monday."

She stopped smiling, nodded, turned away. "So—what? Like, Jim told you everything? About us?" She toyed with the pad on my phone table.

I watched her. My reactions were subtle but intense. It was the way she turned, it was that thing she said. It made me think about what Jim had told me. It made me look, long and slow, down the line of her back. It made my skin feel hot, my stomach cold. An interesting combination.

I moistened my lips and tried to think about my dead friend. "Yeah, that's right," I said gruffly. "He told me pretty much everything."

Susan laughed over her shoulder at me. "Well, that's embarrassing, anyway."

"Hey, don't flirt with me, OK? Don't kill my friend and come over here and flirt with me."

She turned around again, hands primly folded in front of her. I looked so steadily at her face she must've known I was thinking about her breasts. "I'm not flirting with you," she said. "I just want to tell you."

"Tell me what?"

"What he did, that he beat me, that he humiliated me. He was twice my size. Think how you'd like it, think what you would've done if someone was doing that to you."

"Susan!" I spread my hands at her. "You asked him to!"

"Oh, yeah, like, 'She was asking for it,' right? Like you automatically believe that. Your buddy says it so it must be true."

I snorted. I thought about it. I looked at her. I thought about Jim. "Yeah," I said finally. "I do believe it. It was true."

She didn't argue the point. She went right on. "Yeah, well, if it is true, it doesn't make it any better. You know? I mean, you should've seen the way it turned him on. I mean, he could've stopped it. I'd've stopped. He could've changed everything any time, if he wanted to. But he liked it so much . . . And then there he is, hurting me like that, and all turned on by it. How do you think that makes a person feel?"

I am not too proud to admit that I actually scratched my head, dumb as a monkey.

Susan ran one long nail over the phone table pad. She looked down at it. So did I. "Are you really going to the cops?"

"Yeah. Hell, yeah," I said. Then, as if I needed an excuse, "It's not like they won't find someone else. Some other guy you did this stuff with. He'll tell them the same thing."

She shook her head once. "No. There's only you. You're the only one who knows." Which left nothing to say. We stood there silent. She thinking, me just watching her, just watching the lines and colors of her.

Then, finally, she raised her eyes to me, tilted her head. She didn't slink toward me, or tiptoe her fingers up my chest. She didn't nestle under me so I could feel the heat of her breath or smell her perfume. She left that for the movies, for the femme fatales. All she did was stand there like that and give me that Susan look, chin out, dukes up, her soul in the offing, almost trembling in your hand.

"It gives you a lot of power over me, doesn't it?" she said.

"So what?" I said back.

She shrugged again. "You know what I like."

"Get out," I said. I didn't give myself time to start sweating. "Christ. Get the fuck out of here, Susan."

She walked to the door. I watched her go. Yeah, right, I thought. I have power over her. As if. I have power over her until they decide not to charge her, until the headlines disappear. Then where am I? Then I'm her Lord and Master. Just like Jim was.

She passed close to me. Close enough to hear my thoughts. She glanced up, surprised. She laughed at me. "What. You think I'd kill you too?"

"I'd always have to wonder, wouldn't I?" I said.

Still smiling, she jogged her eyebrows comically. "Whatever turns you on," she said.

It was the comedy that did it. I couldn't resist the impulse to wipe that smile off her murdering face. I reached out and grabbed her hair in my fist. Her black, black hair.

It was even softer than I thought it would be.

2006

CHRIS ADRIAN

STAB

Chris Adrian (1970–) received a BA in English from the University of Florida (1993), and an MD from Eastern Virginia Medical School (2001), then completed a pediatric residency at the University of California, San Francisco. He also graduated from the Iowa Writers' Workshop and attended Harvard Divinity School. He is currently a fellow in a pediatric hematology/oncology program in San Francisco.

Although he regards himself primarily as a doctor, Adrian has published two long novels and a short story collection. *Gob's Grief* (2001) is a somewhat surrealistic story set during the Civil War in which a group of people, including Walt Whitman, attempt to build a machine that will abolish death. In *The Children's Hospital* (2006), God brings a second apocalyptic flood to earth, annihilating everyone except the occupants of a single pediatric hospital. His short story collection *A Better Angel* (2008), originally titled *Why Antichrist?*, contains nine stories, including "Stab."

"Stab" was written in 1996, shortly after the death of his older brother, but not published until 2006. While working on his master's thesis, about conjoined twins, Adrian learned that when one twin dies during separation surgery, the survivor always feels a sense of loss, even when the operation occurs in infancy. At about the same time, he had a nightmare in which he was the actress Karen Black being chased by the frightening fetish doll in the 1975 film *Trilogy of Terror,* except that his terrorizer had blond hair. The nightmare, combined with interviews he conducted with survivors of twin-separation surgery, was the inspiration for this strange story.

"Stab" was first published in the summer 2006 issue of *Zoetrope: All-Story.*

▪ ▪ ▪

Someone was murdering the small animals of our neighborhood. We found them in the road outside our houses, and from far away they looked like the victims of careless drivers, but close up you saw that they were plump and round, not flat, and that their bodies were marred by clean-edged rectangular stab wounds. Sometimes they lay in drying pools of blood, and you knew the murder had occurred right there. Other times it was obvious they had been moved from the scene of the crime and arranged in postures, like the two squirrels posed in a hug on Mrs. Chenoweth's doorstep.

Squirrels, then rabbits, then the cats, and dogs in late summer. By that time I had known for months who was doing all the stabbing. I got that information on the first day of June 1979, two years and one month and fourteen days after my brother's death from cancer. I woke up early that morning, a sunny one that broke a chain of rainy days, because my father was taking me to see Spider-Man, who was scheduled to make an appearance at the fourth annual Leukemia Society of America Summer Fair in Washington, D.C. I was eight years old and I thought Spider-Man was very important.

In the kitchen I ate a bowl of cereal while my father spread the paper out before me. "Look at that," he said. On the front page was an article detailing the separation of Siamese twin girls, Lisa and Elisa Johansen from Salt Lake City. They were joined at the thorax, like my brother and I had been, but they shared vital organs, whereas Colm and I never did. There was a word for the way we and they had been joined: thoracopagus. It was still the biggest word I knew.

"Isn't that amazing?" my father said. He was a surgeon, so these sorts of things interested him above all others. "See that? They're just six months old!" Colm and I were separated at eighteen months. I had no clear memories of either the attachment or the operation, though Colm claimed he remembered our heads knocking together all the time, and that he dreamed of monkeys just before we went under from the anesthesia. The Johansen twins were joined side by side; my brother and I were joined back to back. Our parents would hold up mirrors so we could look at each other — that was something I did remember: looking in my mother's silver-handled mirror, over my shoulder at my own face.

Early as it was, on our way out to the car we saw our new neighbor, Molly Matthews, sitting on the front steps of her grandparents' house, reading a book in the morning sun.

"Hello, Molly," said my father.

"Good morning, Dr. Cole," she said. She was unfailingly polite with adults. At school she was already very popular, though she had been there for only two months, and she had a tendency to oppress the other children in our class with her formidable vocabulary.

"Poor girl," said my father, when we were in the car and on our way.

He pitied her because both her parents had died in a car accident. She was in the car with them when they crashed, but she was thrown from the wreck through an open window — this was in Florida, where I supposed everyone always drove around with their windows down and never wore seatbelts.

I turned in my seat so I was upside down. This had long been my habit; I did it so I could look out the window at the trees and telephone wires as we passed them. My mother would never stand for it, but she was flying that day to San Francisco. She was a stewardess. Once my father and I flew with her while she was working and she brought me a cup of Coke with three cherries in it. She put down the drink and leaned over me to open up the window shade, which I had kept closed from the beginning of the flight out of fear. "Look," she said to me. "Look at all that!" I looked and saw sandy mountains that resembled crumpled brown paper bags. I imagined falling from that great height into my brother's arms.

"Spider-Man!" said my father, after we had pulled onto Route 50 and passed a sign that read WASHINGTON, D.C. 29 MILES. "Aren't you excited?" He reached over and rubbed my head with his fist. Had my mother been with me, she would not have spoken at all, but my father talked the whole way, about Spider-Man, about the mall, about the Farrah Fawcett look-alike who was also scheduled to appear; he asked me repeatedly if the prospect of seeing such things didn't make me excited, though he knew I would not answer him. I hadn't spoken a word or uttered a sound since my brother's funeral.

Spider-Man was a great disappointment. When my father brought me close for an autograph, I saw that his Spider-Suit was badly sewn, and glossy in a gross sort of way; his voice, when he said, "Hey there, Spider-Fan," pitched high like a little mouse's. He was an utter fake. I ran away from him, across the mall; my father did not catch me until I had made it all the way to the Smithsonian Castle. He didn't yell at me. It only made him sad when I acted so peculiarly. My mother sometimes lost her temper and would scream out that I was a twisted little fruitcake, and why couldn't I ever make anything easy? She would apologize later, but never with the same ferocity, and so it seemed to me not to count. I always hoped she would burst into my room later on in the night, to wake me by screaming how sorry she was, to slap herself, and maybe me too, because she was so regretful.

"So much for Spider-Man," said my father. He took me to see the topiary buffalo, and for a while we sat in the grass, saying nothing, until he asked me if I wouldn't go back with him. I did, and though we had missed the Farrah Fawcett look-alike's rendition of "Feelings," he got to meet her, because he had connections with the Leukemia Society. She said I was cute and gave me an autographed picture that I later gave to my father because I could tell he wanted it.

When we got home I went up to my room and tossed all my Spider-Man comic books and action figures into the deepest recesses of my closet. Then I took a book out onto the roof. I sat and read *Stuart Little* for the fifth time. Below me, in the yard next door, I could see Molly playing, just as silent as I was. Every once in a while she would look up and catch me looking at her, and she would smile down at her plastic dolls. We had interacted like this before, me reading and her playing, but on this day, for some reason, she spoke to me. She held my gaze for a few moments, then laughed coyly and said, "Would you like to see my bodkin?" I shrugged, then climbed down and followed her into the ravine behind our houses. I did not know what a bodkin was. I thought she was going to make me look inside her panties, like Judy Corcoran had done about three weeks before, trying to make me swear not to tell about the boring thing I had seen.

But what Molly showed me — after we had gone down about thirty feet into the bushes and she had knelt near the arrow-shaped gravestone of our English sheepdog, Gulliver, and after she dug briefly in the dry dirt — was a dagger. It was about a foot long, and ornate, encrusted with what looked like real emeralds and rubies, with a great blue stone set in the pommel, and a rose etched in relief on the upper part of the blade.

"Do you like it?" she asked me. "My father gave it to me. It used to belong to a medieval princess." I did like it. I reached out for it, but she drew it back to her chest and said, "No! You may not touch it." She ran off down the ravine, toward the river; I didn't follow. I sat on Gulliver's stone and thought about all the little dead animals, and I knew — even a little mind could make the connection — that Molly had been murdering them. But I didn't give much thought to it, besides a brief reflection on how sharp the blade must be to make such clean wounds. I walked back to my house and went down to the basement to watch *The Bionic Woman*, my new favorite.

After Colm's death I got into the habit of staring, sometimes for hours at a time, at my image in the mirror. My parents thought it was just another of my new autistic tendencies, and they both discouraged it, even going so far as to remove the mirror from my bedroom. What they didn't know was that the image I was looking at was not really my own; it was Colm's. When I looked in the mirror I saw the face we had shared. We were mirror twins, our faces perfectly symmetrical, the gold flecks in my left eye mirrored in Colm's right, a small flaw at the right edge of his lips mirrored by one at the left edge of mine. So when I looked in the mirror, even the small things that made my face my own made my face into his, and if I waited long enough he would speak to me. He would tell me about heaven, about all sorts of little details, like that nobody ever had to go to the bathroom there. We had both considered that necessity to be a great inconvenience and a bore. He said he was watching me all the time.

There was a connection between us, he often said, even when he was alive, that the surgeons had not broken when we were separated. It was something unseen. We did not have quite two souls between us; it was more that we had one and a half. Sometimes he would hide from me, somewhere in our great big house, and insist that I find him. Usually I couldn't, but he always found me; I couldn't hide from him anywhere in the house, or, I suspected, anywhere on earth.

After he died I found him, not just in mirrors but in every reflective surface. Ponds and puddles or the backs of spoons, anything would do. And invariably the last thing he would say to me was "When are you going to come and be with me again?"

Molly appeared that night at my window. I was still awake when she came. At first I thought she was Colm, until a flash of heat lightning illuminated her and I saw who she was. Glimpsing the dagger flashing in her hand, I was certain she had come to kill me, but when she came over to my bed, she said only, "Do you want to come out with me?" Another flash of lightning lit up the room. The lightning was the reason I had been awake—on hot summer nights Colm and I would stay up for hours watching it flash over the river. Sometimes our parents would let us sleep on the porch, where the view was even better.

She sat down on my bed. "I like your room," she said, looking around. There was light from the hall, enough to make out the general lay of the room. Our father had built it up to look like a ship for Colm and me, complete with sea-blue carpeting and a raised wooden deck with railings and a ship's wheel. Above one bed was an authentic-looking sign that read CAPTAIN'S BUNK; the other bed belonged to the first mate. While he lived we had switched beds every night, in the interest of absolute equality, unless one of us was feeling afraid, in which case we shared the same bed. The last time he slept in the room he had been in the captain's bed, and because the cycle could not go on any longer I had been in the first mate's bed ever since.

Molly pulled my sheets back, and while I dressed she looked around the room for my shoes. When she found them she brought them to me and said, "Come on."

I followed her — out the window, over the roof, and down the blue spruce that grew close to my house. She walked along our road, to the golf course around which part of our community was built. The site, once a Baptist girls' camp, had in the century since its founding turned into a place where well-to-do white people lived in rustic pseudo-isolation. It was called Severna Forest. You couldn't live there if you were Jewish or Italian, and in the summer they made you lock up your dog in a communal kennel. The golf course had only nine holes. It was a very hilly course, bordered by ravines in some places and in others by the Severn River. Molly took me to a wide piece of rough on the fourth hole, only about half a mile from our houses. Though the moon was down, I could see under the starlight that rabbits had gathered in the tall grass and the dandelions. I bent at my knees and picked a stalk. I was about to puff on it and scatter the seeds when Molly held my arm and said, "Don't, you'll frighten them."

For a little while we stood there, she with one hand on my arm and the other on her knife, and we watched the rabbits sitting placidly in the grass, and we waited for them to get used to us. "Aren't they lovely?" she said, letting go of my arm. She began to move, very slowly, toward the nearest one. She moved as slowly as the moon does across the sky. I couldn't tell she was getting any closer to the rabbit unless I looked away for a few minutes; when I looked back she was closer, and the rabbit had not moved. When she was about five feet away she turned and looked at me. It was too dark for me to see her face. I couldn't tell if she smiled. Then she leapt, knife first, at the little creature, and I saw her pierce its body. It thrashed once and was suddenly dead. I realized I was holding my breath, and still holding the dandelion in front of my lips. I blew into it and watched the seeds float toward her, to where she was stabbing the body again and again and again.

In school the next Monday, Molly studiously ignored me. The whole morning long I stared at her, thinking she must give some sign that a special thing had taken place between us, but she never did. I didn't really care if she never spoke to me again; I was used to people experimenting with me as a friend. I let them come and go.

After lunch, when we were all settling down again into our desks, in the silence after Mrs. Wallaby, our teacher, had offered up a post-luncheon prayer for the pope, Molly passed me a note. I opened it up, thinking for some reason that it might say, "I love you," because once a popular girl named Iris had passed me such a note, and when I blushed she and her friends had laughed cruelly. But Molly's note said simply, "You'd better not tell." I supposed she meant I had better not write a letter to the police. She did not really know me at all.

"What's that you've got there, Calvin?" Mrs. Wallaby asked, striding over to me, squinting at me through her glasses. Before she arrived I slipped the piece of paper into my mouth and began to chew.

"What was that?"

I swallowed. She brought her face so close to mine I could read the signature on her designer frame glasses: OSCAR DE LA RENTA.

"What was that?" she asked again. Of course I said nothing. She heaved a great sigh and told me to go sit in "The Judas Chair," which was actually just a desk set aside from the others, facing a corner. She was not a bad woman, but sometimes I brought out the worst in people. Once she saved me at recess from a crowd of girls who were pinching me, trying to make me cry out. She brought me inside and put cold cream from her purse on my welts; then, after she spoke for a while about how I couldn't go on like this, I just couldn't, she gave me a long grave look and pinched me herself. It was not so hard as what the girls were giving me, and it was under my shirt, where no one would see. She looked deep into my eyes as she did it, but I didn't cry out. I didn't even blink.

On the night of the first day of summer vacation, Molly came again and got me from my bed. She said nothing, aside from telling me to get dressed and to follow her. We passed the golf course and I started off to where the rabbits were; she grabbed my collar and pulled me back.

"No," she said. "It's time to move on." We spent the night hunting cats. It wasn't easy. We exhausted ourselves chasing them through the dark. Always they outran us or vanished up trees.

"We need a plan," she said at last. Closer to our houses, we found a neighbor cat named Mr. Charlemagne; we had chased him earlier and he escaped through a cat door into a garage. Molly positioned me in a bush by that door, while Mr. Charlemagne eyed us peacefully. Then she came at him. He took off for his door, but I jumped in front of it. For some reason he leapt right into my arms, looked up in my face, then turned to look at my companion. She had her knife out. He snuggled deeper into my arms, expecting, I think, that I would bring him inside to safety. I threw him down hard on the ground. Molly fell on him and stabbed him through the throat.

The authorities of Severna Forest — the sheriff and the chairman of the community association and the president of the country club — had dismissed the squirrel and rabbit deaths as the gruesome pranks of bored teenagers. When Mr. Charlemagne was discovered, draped along a straight-growing bough of a birch tree, a mildly urgent sense of alarm spread over the community. "Sick!" people muttered to each other while buying vodka and Yoo-hoo at the general store. Not one bit of suspicion fell on Molly or me. Everyone considered me strange and tragic but utterly harmless. Molly was equally tragic yet widely admired, with her manners and her blond hair and her big brown eyes. Sometimes I thought it was only because she stabbed that she could play the part of her sweet, decent self so well.

A few days passed before she came for me again, in the early evening after lacrosse practice. The Severna Forest peewee team practiced every Saturday afternoon. I was one of its best players, because I had absolutely no fear of the ball. Others still ducked when the ball came flying toward them like a little cannon shot, or knocked it away with their sticks. I caught it. If it hit me, I didn't care. I scooped it up and ran with it, often all the way down the field because it rarely occurred to me to pass. I liked to run, and to be exhausted, and I thought one day the ball might fly at me with such force it would burst my head like a rotten pumpkin.

That day I got hit in the eye with the ball. Our coach, a college boy named Sam Corkle, hurled it at me with all his adult strength, thinking I was paying attention. When it struck my eye I saw a great white flash and then a pale afterimage of Colm's face that quickly faded. The blow knocked me down. I looked up at the sky and saw a passing plane and wondered, like I always did when I saw a plane in flight, if my mother was on board, though I knew she was at home that day. Sam came up with the other coach and they asked me all sorts of questions, trying to determine if I was disoriented and might have a concussion. Of course I didn't answer. Someone said I would throw up if I had a concussion, so they sat me on a bench and watched me to see if that would happen.

When it didn't, they let me back onto the field. I went eagerly—though my eyeball was aching and starting to swell—hoping to get hit again, to catch another glimpse of my brother.

"What happened to you?" my mother asked when Sam brought me home. She was sitting at the dining room table, where my father held a package of frozen hamburger to his own swollen purple eye. He had gotten into a fight when someone tried to cut in front of him in a gas line. It was a bad week for gas. Stations were selling their daily allowances before noon. "You too, sport?" he said.

My father examined my eye and said I would be fine. As my mother pressed hamburger against the swelling, there was a knock at the door. Sam answered it, and I heard Molly's voice ask very sweetly, "Can Calvin come out and play?" I jumped from my mother's lap and ran toward the door. She caught me and said, "Take your hamburger with you." I stood at the door while she walked back to the dining room with Sam, and I heard her ask my father, "When did your son get a little girlfriend?"

Molly had an empty mayonnaise jar in her hands. "We're going to catch fireflies," she said, not asking about my eye. I followed her through the dusk to the golf course, dropping my hamburger in a holly bush along the way. We ran around grabbing after bugs. I was delighted she had come for me while there was daylight, thinking that must mean something. I grabbed at her flying blond hair as much as I did the fireflies; she slapped my hands each time.

I thought we were filling the jar so she could crush them mercilessly, or stick them with pins, or distill their glowing parts into some powerful, fluorescent poison with which she could coat her knife. But when it was dark, when about thirty of them were thick in the jar, she took off the lid and went running down the hill to the river, spilling a trail of bright motes that circled around her, rose up, and flew away.

Soon there weren't any cats left for us—not because we had killed them all, but because after the fourth one, a tabby named Vittles, was found stabbed twelve times on the front steps of the general store, people started keeping their cats inside at night. Our hunts were widely spaced, occurring only about once every two weeks, but in between those nights Molly would come to the door for me and take me out to play in the daylight. We did the normal things that children our age were supposed to do, during the day. We swam in the river and played with her dolls and watched television.

In late July Molly decided to change prey again. She took me through the woods, out to the kennel. I could hear the dogs barking in the darkness long before we reached them. They knew we were coming for them.

The kennel was lit by a single streetlamp, stuck in the middle of a clearing in the woods. There was a little service road that ran under the light, out to the main road that led to General's Highway and Annapolis. I watched Molly stalk back and forth in front of the runs. The dogs were all howling and barking at her. It was two A.M. There was nobody around; nobody lived within a mile and a half of the place. The whole point of the kennel was to separate the dogs from the houses between June and September, so their barking wouldn't disturb all the wealthy people in their summer cottages. It was a stupid rule.

Molly had stooped down in front of a poodle. I did not recognize it. It retreated to the back of its run and yipped at her.

"Nice puppy," she said, though it was full grown. She waved me over to her, and then turned me around to take a piece of beef from the Holly Hobbie backpack she had strapped on me at the beginning of our excursion. She took out my lacrosse gloves and told me to put them on.

"Be ready to grab him," she said. She crouched down in front of the bars of the cage and held the meat up in the meager light. "Come on," she said. "Come and get your treat, baby. It's OK." She held on to one end while the poodle nibbled, and with her free hand she scratched its head. She motioned for me to come close beside her. It was the closest I had ever been to a poodle in my life. I tried to imagine the owner, probably a big fat rich lady with white hair, who wore diamonds around her throat while she slept in a giant canopy bed.

"Just about . . . now!" said Molly. I reached through the bars with my thick lacrosse hands and grabbed the dog by a foreleg. Immediately it started to pull away, just a gentle tug. "Don't let it escape!" she said, scrambling in the bag for her knife. The poodle gave me a *What are you doing?* look, and I very nearly lost my hold.

It was an awkward kill, because the bars were in the way, and the poodle was a strong-willed little dog who wanted to live. It bit hard but ineffectively at my hands. It bit at the knife and cut its gums, and its teeth made a ringing sound against the metal. It snarled and yelped and squealed, and all around us the other dogs were all screaming. Molly was saying, "There! There! There!" in a low voice, almost a whisper. When she finally delivered the killing blow to the dog's neck, a gob of hot blood flew out between the bars and hit me in the eye. It burned like the harsh shampoos my parents bought for me, but I didn't cry out.

On the way back I let her walk ahead of me. I watched the glint of her head under the moon as she ducked between bushes and hopped over rotting logs. I felt bad, not about the poodle, which I had hated instantly and absolutely as soon as I had laid eyes upon it, but about the owner, the fat lady who I thought must be named Mrs. Vanderbilt because that was the richest name I knew. I thought about her riding down to the kennel in her limousine with a china bowl full of steak tartare for her Precious, and the way her face would look when she saw the bloody cotton ball on the floor of the cage and could not comprehend that this was the thing she had loved. Molly got farther and farther ahead of me, calling back that I should stop being so poky and hurry up. Eventually all I could see was the moonlight on her head, and on the white bag she had brought for my gloves, promising to clean them.

When we had gone about a mile from the kennel I heard a train whistle sounding. It was still far away, but I knew the tracks ran nearby. I went to them. In the far distance I could see the train light. I lay down in the middle of the tracks and waited. Molly came looking for me — I could hear her calling out, calling me a stupid boy and saying it was late. She was tired. She wanted to go to bed. As the train got nearer, I felt a deep, wonderful hum in the tracks that seemed to pass through my brain and stimulate whatever organ is responsible for generating happiness. I imagined my head flying from my body to land at her feet. Or maybe it would hit her and knock her down. She would, I imagined, give it a calm look, put it in the bag, and take it home, where she would keep it, along with my gloves, under her bed as a souvenir of our acquaintance. The train arrived and passed over me.

I suppose I was too small for it to take off my head. Or maybe it was a different sort of train that did that to Charlie Kelly, a fifteen-year-old who had died the previous summer after a reefer party in the woods when he lay down on the tracks to impress Sam Corkle's sister. The conductor never saw me. The train never slowed. It rushed over me with such a noise — it got louder and louder until I couldn't hear it anymore, until watching the flashes of moon between the boxcars I heard my brother's voice say, "Soon."

All Severna Forest was horrified by the death of the dog, whose name turned out to be Arthur. A guard was posted at the kennel. For the first few nights it was Sheriff Travis himself, but after a week he deputized a teenager he deemed trustworthy; that boy snuck off with his girlfriend to get stoned and listen to loud music in her car. While they were thus occupied we struck again, after two nights of watching and waiting for just such an opportunity. This time it was a Jack Russell terrier named Dreamboat.

After that the kennel was closed and the dogs sent home to owners who locked them indoors, especially at night. Sheriff Travis claimed to be within a hair's breadth of catching the "pervert," but in fact he never came near Molly or me. She never seemed nervous about getting caught. Neither did she gloat about her success. She was silent about it, as she was about why she went around stabbing things in the first place.

But she talked about her parents all summer. When I was not playing lacrosse, I was with her, sailing on the river in the Sunfish her grandparents had bought her in June, or soft-shell crabbing in the muddy flats off Beach Road, or riding around on our banana-seated bicycles. I envied her hers because it had long, multicolored tassels that dangled from the handlebars, and a miniature license plate on the back that read HOT STUFF. Floating in the middle of the river on a calm day, I dangled my hand in the water and listened to her talk about her parents; her father had been a college professor of history, and at night he would tell her stories about ancient princesses and tell her she herself had surely been one in a past life. Didn't she remember? Didn't she recognize this portrait of her antique prince? Didn't she recognize the dagger with which she had slain the beastly suitor who had tried to take her away to live in a black kingdom under the earth? Her mother, a cautious pediatrician, had protested when he gave her the bodkin, though Molly was grave and responsible and not likely to hurt herself or others by accident. "A girl needs to defend herself," her father had said, but he was joking. The knife hung on her wall, along with an ancient tapestry and a number of museum prints of ancient princesses, and she was not supposed to touch them until she was older.

I listened and watched pale sea nettles drift by. Occasionally one would catch my hand with its tentacle and sting me. I wanted to tell her about my brother, about stories we had told each other, about our lighthouse game or our bridge game or our thunder and lightning game, or the fond wish we both had for a flying bed of the sort featured in *Bedknobs and Broomsticks,* except that ours would be equipped with a matter transporter, à la *Star Trek,* so we could hover over our favorite restaurant and beam up pizzas. But nothing could have made me talk, on that day or any of the days that stretched back to Colm's funeral. At the time I didn't know why I would not speak. I think now the reason my throat closed up was that I knew, that day in the funeral parlor, there was nothing I could ever say to equal the occasion of my brother's death. I should have spoken a word that would bring him back, and yet I could not, and so I must say nothing forever.

Molly's birthday came in the first week of August. My mother took me shopping for a present. She spent a lot of time in the Barbie section, agonizing over accessories, but I insisted silently on my own choice: a Bionic Woman combination beauty salon and diagnostic station. It was not the gift I really meant to give Molly, not the gift from my heart. I insisted on it because I knew she would disregard it, and I could then play with it myself. Her real gift from me was a wide, flat stone, taken from the Severn, with which she could sharpen her knife. I wrapped it in the Sunday funnies. When she opened it she smiled with genuine delight and said it was her favorite.

From her grandparents she got a Polaroid camera. Her grandfather, a man who had always believed in buying in bulk, gave her a whole carton of film and flashbulbs. In the evening after her birthday party we sat on my roof and she sent flashes arcing over the ravine, tossing aside the pictures that popped out. They were of nothing, and she was not interested in them. I picked them up and pressed them to my nose because I liked the developing-film smell.

Later that night she came to my window, her backpack on her shoulders. I'd had a feeling she would come and so went to sleep fully dressed, right down to my shoes. To my surprise she removed my shoes, and my socks. While I sat with my feet hanging over the edge of the bed, she took a jar from her pack and scooped out a plum-size dollop of Vaseline, lathering it over my foot and between my toes.

"We have a long walk tonight," she said matter-of-factly. I closed my eyes while she did my other foot, enjoying the feeling. When I put on my socks and shoes and walked on my anointed feet, it was like walking on a pillow or on my father's fat belly, when he would play with Colm and me, all the while yelling, "Oh, oh, the elephants are trampling me!"

We went far past the kennel, three miles from our homes. We walked right out of Severna Forest, past the squat, crumbling brick pillars that marked the entrance to the forest road. We walked past the small black community, right at the edge of the gates, where families lived whose mothers worked as maids in our houses. Molly led me into the fields of a farm whose acreage ran along General's Highway.

"I want a horse," she said, standing still and eyeing the vast expanse of grass before us. In the distance I could see a house and a barn. I had seen the house countless times from my parents' car, when my mother was driving and I had to sit right-side up. I had always imagined it to be inhabited by bonneted women and bare-lipped, bearded men, like the ones in the coffee-table book on the Amish that sat in our living room and was never looked at by anyone but me. Molly started toward the barn. I followed her, looking at the dark house and wondering if some restless person was looking out the bedroom window, watching us coming.

No one challenged us, not even a dog or a cat. I wondered what she would do if a snarling dog came out of the darkness to get us. I did not think she would stab it. I had a theory, entirely unsubstantiated, that she was moving up the class chain, onward from birds to squirrels to cats to dogs and beyond, her destination the fat red heart of a human being, and I knew that once she had finished with an animal class she would not return to it. She was storing the life force of everything she stabbed in the great blue stone in her dagger's hilt, and when she had accumulated enough of it, the stone would glow like the Earth glowed in the space pictures that hung on the wall in our third-grade homeroom, above the motto NOTHING IS IMPOSSIBLE. When the stone glowed like that, I knew, her parents would step from it and be with her again.

If the horse had a name, I never knew it. In the dim light of the stable I might have missed it, carved on the stall somewhere. The horse was a tall Appaloosa. Molly had brought sugar and apples. She fed it and whispered to it. It was the only horse there. The other stalls were empty but looked lived-in. Molly was saying to the horse, "It's OK. It's all right. There's nothing to be afraid of." She smiled at it a truly sweet smile, and it looked at her with its enormous brown eyes, and I could see that it trusted her absolutely, the way unicorns in stories instinctively trust princesses. In her right hand she held the knife, and her left was on the horse's muzzle. "Touch it," she said to me. "It's like velvet." I put my hand on the space just between its eyes. She was right. I closed my eyes and imagined I was touching my mother while she wore her velvet Christmas dress. When I opened them the horse was looking at me with its great eyes, and in them I could see my brother touching the horse, and behind him Molly striking with her dagger. The horse did not even try to pull away until the blade was buried deep in its throat. Then it rose up, jerking the blade out of her hand and trying to hammer us with its hooves, which clattered against the wood of the stall. When it shook its head the knife flew out and landed at my feet. The horse was trying to scream, but because of the wound it could make only spraying, huffing noises.

I watched it jump and then stagger around the stall. I was still and calm until Molly took the first picture — I jumped at the flash. At thirty-second intervals another flash would catch in the horse's eyes. At last it knelt in a wide pool of its blood, and then fell on its side and was dead. All the time our surroundings seemed very quiet, despite the whirring of the Polaroid, and the whooshing and sucking noises of the wound, and the thumping. When those noises stopped I could suddenly hear crickets chirping, and Molly's frantic breathing, and my brother saying, "So soon!"

Molly took me home and made me get in the tub with my pants rolled up. She washed the Vaseline from my feet, and the horse blood from my hair, and then she put me back in my bed, not an hour before the sun came up. I slept and dreamed of horses who bled eternally from their throats, whose eyes held perfect images of Colm, who spoke from their wounds in the voices of old women and said they could take me to him if I would only ride.

A real live police investigation inspired Molly to lie low for a while. While Anne Arundel County police cars cruised the night streets of Severna Forest, we lay most exceedingly low; and even after they were long gone, we still did not emerge. The summer ran out and school started again. Molly mostly ignored me while we were at school, but she still came by occasionally in the afternoons, or on weekends. We sailed in her boat and once went apple picking with her grandparents, in an orchard all the way down in Leonardtown. Outside my bedroom window the leaves dropped from the trees in the ravine, so I got my clear winter view of the river, all the way down to the bay. In the distance I could see the lights of the Naval Academy radio towers, blinking strong and red in the cold. I would watch them and wait for her, my window wide open, but she did not come again until the first snow.

That was in December, just before Christmas break. Earlier that evening, down by the general store, all the children of Severna Forest had gathered under an old spruce, where a false Santa sat on a gold-leafed wooden throne and handed out presents. I knew he was a false Santa, but most of the others there didn't. It was actually Sheriff Travis, handing out presents bought and delivered to him by the parents of all these greedy little kids. He sat in his chair, surrounded by bags of wrapped toys, and made a big fuss over whether or not this or that child had been good throughout the year. When he called my name I went up and dutifully received my present from his rough hands. It was a Fembot doll, the arch nemesis of the Bionic Woman doll that Molly had rejected.

I was in my bed playing with my new toy when she appeared at my window.

"Go down and get your coat," she said. "It's cold out there." I did as she told me. My father had left for the hospital shortly after we got home from seeing Santa, and my mother was asleep in her room, exhausted by an all-night flight from Lima. But almost all the other Severna Forest adults were down at the clubhouse, having their Christmas party. Several of them were famous for getting drunk on the occasion, Sheriff Travis especially. He kept his Santa suit on all night, and people talked about his antics for weeks afterward. They were harmless antics, nothing crass or embarrassing. He sang songs and said sharp, witty things, things he seemed incapable of saying at any other time of the year, drunk or not.

When we left my house, there was already about an inch of snow on the ground. The storm picked up as we climbed a tree outside the clubhouse. We waited there while the party began to die down. I could see my parents' friends dancing with each other, and Sheriff Travis standing on tables and gesticulating, or turning somersaults, or dancing with two ladies at once. Music and laughter drifted through the blowing snow every time someone opened the door. I got sleepy listening to the sounds of adult amusement, just like Colm and I always did when our parents had one of their dinner parties, something they did often back before he died.

I fell asleep in the tree, with my head on Molly's shoulder. We were wedged close to one another, so I was warm. It was snowing heavily when she jabbed me with her elbow and said, "Wake up, it's time to go." She climbed down the tree and hurried off. I jumped down, knocking the accumulated snow from my back and shoulders, and chased after her. She was moving back toward our houses, toward the tee of the seventh hole. When I caught up with her I could see another vague shape stumbling through the snow, about thirty yards before us. We had to get closer before I could make out the distinctive silhouette of the Santa hat.

Sheriff Travis lived down by the river, in a modest cottage that I imagine must have been lonely for all its smallness, because his children were gone and his wife was dead. He was taking a shortcut over the golf course. I knew he would cross through the woods beyond the green to Beach Road. He was singing "Adeste Fideles" in a loud voice and did not hear us come up behind him.

Molly had taken out her dagger and handed me a short length of lead pipe. "Be ready," she said. When we were less than ten yards away, she ran at him, looking slightly ridiculous trying to rush through the deepening snow with her short legs. But there was nothing ridiculous about the blow she struck, just above his wide black belt, about where his kidney would be. He fell to his knees and she struck again, this time at his back, almost right in the middle, and then again at his neck as he collapsed forward. He screamed at the first blow, just like I thought he would, a great, raw scream like the one my father let go in the hospital room when Colm finally stopped breathing. She stabbed him one more time, in the right side of his back. In the dark his blood was black on the snow. He lay on his face and was silent. I stood in the snow, clutching my pipe and wondering if I should hit him with it.

Molly grabbed my hand and dragged me after her. She ran as fast as she could, through the woods, then along Beach Road to a point just below our houses. "I got him," she was saying breathlessly, in a high voice. "I got *Santa.*" Twice we had to crouch down behind tree trunks to escape the passing headlights of the party's last few stragglers. We tore up through the ravine, past Gulliver's headstone, and she gave me a push up the tree by my house, saying only, "Put your coat back downstairs!" before running off to her own house. I did as she said. I would have anyway, and it grated on me that she thought I would be careless. I still had the pipe. I put it deep in my closet, where the Spider-Man toys were piled.

Back in bed I looked out my window at the storm, which was still gaining strength. It would be almost a blizzard by morning. School would be canceled. I lay watching the snow that I knew was covering our child-sized footprints, covering Santa Travis's body. I thought of him dying, the coldness of the snow penetrating in stages through his skin and his muscle and his bone, a dark veil falling over his sight like somebody was wrapping his head in layer after layer of sweet-smelling toilet paper, like Colm and I used to do when we played I Am the Mummy's Bride, or The Plastic Surgeon Just Gave Me a New Face. I imagined Colm, waiting patiently by the door to where he was, waiting and waiting, peering at the slowly approaching figure.

But Sheriff Travis did not die. A concerned citizen, worried because of the storm, had called his house. When he didn't answer, people went looking for him. They found him where we left him, alive. At the hospital my father operated to repair his lacerated kidney and fretted over his hemisected spinal cord.

When Sheriff Travis woke up he said he remembered everything. Despite the darkness of the night, and the falling snow, he gave fairly detailed descriptions of his attackers. Two large black men had done it, he said, one holding him while the other stabbed him and called him "Honky Santa." Police called on the community just outside the Severna Forest gates, and two men were arrested after Sheriff Travis identified them in a lineup. I saw them in the paper.

Molly was furious that Sheriff Travis hadn't died. She stood in my room, kicking my bed so hard that the wall shook and the FIRST MATE sign fell down with a clunk.

"Why?" she said in a loud voice. "Why couldn't he have died?"

I thought about her hungry blue stone while she kicked my bed some more, until my father came to the door and said, "Everything OK in here?"

"Yes, sir," she replied. "We were just kicking the bed."

"Well, please don't."

"Yes, sir," she said, blushing. I looked at the sunlight on the carpet and wanted my father to leave. *Don't make her angry,* I was thinking.

When he was gone she said, "It's just not fair."

I thought it would be many more months before she returned for me at night. I thought we would lie low, but she came back after only two weeks had passed, at the beginning of the second week of January. She had been in Florida with her grandparents over break, while a bitter cold descended over the Atlantic coast from New York to Richmond. The river and even parts of the Chesapeake were frozen over. She came for me the first night she was back.

When we went down the ravine to Beach Road, I thought for sure we were going to Sheriff Travis's house, to finish him off. But upon reaching the road she crossed it and stepped over the riverbank, onto the ice. She turned back to me. "Come on," she said, sliding over the ice in her rubber boots. She went past the pier and the boat slips, out to the wide center of the river. Her voice came drifting back to me: "Don't be such a slowpoke." I hurried after the place where I thought her voice was coming from, but I never caught up with her — perhaps she was hiding from me. It was a clear yet moonless night, and she was wearing a dark coat and a dark hat. I stopped after a while and wrapped my arms around myself. I was cold because my parents were both home and I had not dared go down for my coat. Instead I had worn two sweaters, but they weren't enough to keep me warm. I knelt on the ice and looked down at it, trying to catch Colm's image. I heard Molly's boots sliding over the ice out in the dark, and I thought about a story people told about the ghost of a girl who drowned skating across the river to Westport, to see her boyfriend. On nights like this, people said, you could see her, a gliding white figure. If you saw her face you would die by water one day. I looked downriver, searching for either the ghost or Molly but seeing only the lights of the bridges down past Annapolis. There was a flash, and for a moment I thought it was the winter equivalent of heat lightning, until I heard the Polaroid whirring.

She took my picture again, and again, from different sides. I suppose she was trying to upset me, or make me afraid. Maybe she thought I would run and slip on the ice. I just knelt there, and then I lay down on my back and looked up at the stars. My father had shown me the constellation of Gemini. It was the only one I ever looked for; and though I didn't see it then, I made out my brother's shape in any number of places. Molly came sliding up to me. She stood behind my head; I could not see her, but I could see her panting breath.

I thought she would speak, then. In my mind I had heard her speak this speech; I had played it out many times: "I need you," she would say. "For my parents. They're stuck in here and I must let them out. You don't mind, do you?" Of course I didn't. I would have told her so, if I could have. I had been expecting her to say this ever since she had stabbed the horse, because I didn't know what animal she could turn to after that, besides me. That night Colm had said to me, "So soon!" But it was not so soon, and I had waited.

She didn't say anything, though. She only knelt near me and put a hand on my belly. She wasn't smiling, just breathing hard. The camera hung around her neck and the dagger was in her hand. She raised my sweaters and my pajama top so that I felt the cold on my skin and the goose bumps it raised. She put the tip of the dagger against my belly, and when she looked at me I was so tempted to speak.

"Goodbye," she said, and gently slipped it in. I heard my brother's voice ring in my head: "Now!" For just a moment, as I felt the metal enter me, I wanted it, and I was full of joy; but a tall wave of pain crashed over me and washed all the joy away. A cresting scream rose in me and broke out of my mouth, the loudest sound I had ever heard, louder than Sheriff Travis's scream, louder than my father's scream, louder than any of the dogs or cats or rabbits. It flew over the ice in every direction and assaulted people in their homes. I saw windows lighting up in the hills above the river as I scrambled to my feet, still screaming. Molly had fallen back, her face caught in a perfect expression of astonishment. I turned and ran from her, not looking back to see if she was chasing me, because I knew she was. I ran for my life, sliding on the ice, expecting at any moment to feel her bodkin in my back. I cried out again when I climbed over the sea wall and ran across the road, because of the pain as I lifted myself. I clambered up the ravine, hearing her behind me. On the spruce that led to my bedroom she caught me, stabbing my dangling calf, and I fell. She came at me again, and I kicked at her; she didn't make a sound. I held my hands out before me and she stabbed them. With a bloody fist I smashed her jaw and knocked her down. I got up the tree and into my room, too afraid to turn and close the window. I rushed down the stairs into my parents' bedroom, where I slammed the door behind me and woke them with my hysterical screaming. My mother turned on the light. Despite my long silence the words came smoothly, up from my leaking belly, sliding like mercury through my throat and bursting in the bright air of their room.

"I want to live!" I told them, though my heart broke as I said it; Colm's image appeared in the floor-length mirror on the opposite side of the bed. He was bloody like me, wounded. He looked at me as my parents jumped out of bed with their arms out, their faces white with horror at the sight of me. I cried great heaving, house-shaking sobs, not because of the pain of my wounds, or because my parents were crying, or because I knew Molly was on her way back to the river, where she would turn her knife on herself and at last take a human life for her soul-eating dagger. I didn't cry like that over the animals and people, now that I knew just how much a knife hurt, though I did feel guilty. And I wasn't crying at my pending betrayal of Molly, though I knew I would say I had no part in any of it and there would be no proof that I had. I cried because I saw Colm shake his head, then turn his back on me and walk away, receding into an image that became more and more my own until it was mine completely. I knew it would speak to me only with my own voice, and look at me with my own eyes, and I knew that I would never see my brother again.

2006

BRADFORD MORROW

THE HOARDER

Bradford Morrow (1951–) was born in Baltimore, Maryland, but grew up in Colorado, receiving a BA from the University of Colorado, then undertaking graduate studies at Yale University. He traveled for the next ten years and worked in various jobs, including as a jazz musician, translator, rare-book seller, and medical assistant. He has taught at Princeton, Brown, and Columbia, and has been a professor of literature at Bard College for twenty years, where he has been the editor of *Conjunctions,* the prestigious literary journal, for its more than fifty issues.

After five volumes of poetry, Morrow turned to the novel; his first, *Come Sunday,* was published in 1988. *The Almanac Branch* (1991) was a finalist for the PEN/Faulkner Award. His next novel, *Trinity Fields* (1994), which the author identified as the first volume of his New Mexico Trilogy, was a finalist for the Los Angeles Times Book Award. *Giovanni's Gift* (1997), among readers' favorites of his books, came next, followed by the second volume of the New Mexico Trilogy, *Ariel's Crossing* (2002). He has also written two children's books: *A Bestiary* (1991), illustrated by eighteen contemporary American artists, and *Didn't Didn't Do It* (2007), charmingly illustrated by Gahan Wilson.

Among Morrow's awards are an Academy Award in Literature from the American Academy of Arts and Letters (1998), the O. Henry Prize, for his short story "Lush" (2003), the PEN/Nora Magid Award for Editing (2007), and a Guggenheim Fellowship (2007).

"The Hoarder" was first published in the anthology *Murder in the Rough* (New York: Mysterious Press, 2006).

▪ ▪ ▪

I have always been a hoarder. When I was young, our family lived on the Outer Banks, where I swept up and down the shore filling my windbreaker pockets with seashells of every shape and size. Back in the privacy of my room I loved nothing better than to lay them out on my bed, arranging them by color or form — whelks and cockles here, clams and scallops there — a beautiful mosaic of dead calcium. The complete skeleton of a horseshoe crab was my finest prize, as I remember. After we moved inland from the Atlantic, my obsession didn't change, but the objects of my desire did. Having no money, I was restricted to things I found, so one year developed an extensive collection of Kentucky bird nests, and during the next an array of bright Missouri butterflies preserved in several homemade display cases. Another year, my father's itinerant work having taken us to the desert, I cultivated old pottery shards from the hot *potreros*. Sometimes my younger sister offered to assist with my quests, but I preferred shambling around on my own. Once in a while I did allow her to shadow me, if only because it was one more thing that annoyed our big brother, who never missed an opportunity to cut me down to size. Weird little bastard, Tom liked calling me. I didn't mind him saying so. I was a weird little bastard.

When first learning to read, I hoarded words just as I would shells, nests, butterflies. Like many an introvert, I went through a phase during which every waking hour was spent inside a library book. These I naturally collected, too, never paying my late dues, writing in a ragged notebook words which were used against Tom at opportune moments. He was seldom impressed when I told him he was *a pachyderm anus* or *runny pustule,* but that might have been because he didn't understand some of what came out of my mouth. Many times I hardly knew what I was saying. Still, the desired results were now and then achieved. When I called him some name that sounded nasty enough—*eunuch's tit*—he would run after me with fists flying and pin me down demanding a definition and I'd refuse. Be it black eye or bloody nose, I always came away feeling I got the upper hand.

Father wasn't a migrant laborer, as such, and all our moving had nothing to do with a fieldworker following seasons or harvests. He lived by his wits, so he told us and so we kids believed. But wits or not, every year brought the ritual pulling up of stakes and clearing out. His explanations were always curt, brief, like our residencies. He never failed to apologize, and I think he meant it when he told us that the next stop would be more permanent, that he was having a streak of bad luck bound to change for the better. Tom took these uprootings harder than I or my sister. He expressed his anger about being jerked around like circus animals, and complained that this was the old man's fault and we should band together in revolt. It was never clear just how we were supposed to mutiny, and of course we never did. Molly and I wondered privately, whispering together at night, if our family wouldn't be more settled had our mother still been around. But that road was a dead end even more than the one we seemed to be on already. She'd deserted our father and the rest of us and there was no bringing her back. We used to get cards at Christmas, but even that stopped some years ago. We seldom mentioned her name now. What was the point?

Like the sun, we traveled westward across the country all the way to the coast, though more circuitously and with much dimmer prospects. I'd made a practice of discarding my latest collection whenever we left one place for another, and not merely disposing of it but destroying the stuff. Taking a hammer to my stash of petrified wood and bleached bones plucked off the flats near Mojave, after the word came down to start packing, was my own private way of saying goodbye. Molly always cried until I gave her a keepsake — a sparrow nest or slug of quartz crystal. And my dad took me aside to ask why I was undoing all my hard work, unaware of the sharp irony of his question — who was he to talk? He told me that one day when I was grown up I'd look back and regret not treasuring these souvenirs from my youth. But he never stopped me. He couldn't in fairness do that. These were my things, and just as I'd brought them together, I had every right to junk them and set my sights on the new. Besides, demolishing my collections didn't mean I didn't treasure them in my own way.

We found ourselves in a small, pleasant, nondescript oceanside town just south of the palm-lined promenades of Santa Barbara and the melodramatic Spanish villas of Montecito, where the Kennedys had spent their honeymoon a few years before. By this time I was old enough to find a job. Tom and I had both given up on school. Too many new faces, too many new curricula. Father couldn't object to his eldest son dropping out of high school, since he himself had done the same. As for me, having turned fifteen, I'd more or less educated myself anyway. It was a testament to Molly's resilient nature that she was never fazed entering all those unknown classrooms across this great land of ours. My responsibility was to make sure she got to summer school on time and to pick her up at day's end, and so I did. This commitment I gladly undertook, since I always liked Molly, and she didn't get in the way of my schedule at the miniature golf course where I was newly employed.

Just as California would mark a deviation in my father's gypsy routine, it would be the great divide for me. Whether I knew it at the time is beside the point. I doubt I did. Tom noticed something different had dawned in me, a new confidence, and while he continued to taunt me, my responses became unpredictable. He might smirk, "Miniature golf . . . now, there's a promising career, baby," but rather than object, I would cross my arms, smile, and agree, "Just my speed, baby." When we did fight, our battles were higher-pitched and more physical, and as often as not, he was the one who got the tooth knocked loose, the lip opened, the kidney punched. Molly gave up trying to be peacemaker and lived more and more in her own world. It was as if we moved into individual mental compartments, like different collectibles in different cabinets. I couldn't even say for sure what kind of work my father did anymore, though it involved a commute over the mountains to a place called Ojai, which resulted in us seeing less of him than ever. The sun had turned him brown, so his work must have been outside. Probably a construction job — so much for his touted wits. Tom, on the other hand, remained as white as abalone, working in a convenience store. And Molly with her sweet round face covered in freckles and ringed by wildly wavy red hair, the birthright of her maternal Irish ancestry, marched forward with the patience and hope that would better befit a daughter of the king of Uz than a carpenter of Ojai — which our dear brother had by then, with all the cleverness he could muster, dubbed *Oh Low.*

The change was gradual but irrevocable, and would be difficult if not impossible to describe in abstract terms. To suggest that my compulsion to hoard shifted from objects to essences, from the external world's cast-offs to the stuff of spirits, wouldn't be quite right. It might even be false, since what began to arise within me during those long slow days and evenings at work had a manifest concreteness to it. Whether my discovery of glances, fragrances, gestures, voices, the various flavors of nascent sexuality, the potential for beautiful violence that hovers behind those qualities, came as the result of my new life at Bayside Park, or whether it would have happened no matter where I lived and breathed at that moment, I couldn't say. I do know that Bayside — that perfect world of fantastical architecture and linked greens and strict rules — was where I came awake, felt more alive, as they say, than ever before. I who'd loved lifeless things was now reborn.

The first time I laid eyes on the place was early evening. Fog — which seasonally rolled in at dusk, settling over the coastal flats and canyons until early afternoon the next day — was drifting ashore like willowy, ghostly scarves. I wore my best flannel shirt and a pair of jeans to the interview. My head was all but bald, my old man having given me a fresh trim with his electric clippers, a memento filched from one of his many former employers. Even though it was late June and the day was warm, I wished I'd brought a sweater, since the heavy mist down by the ocean dampened me to the bone. I could hear the surf once I crossed the empty highway, and I started thinking about what questions I might be asked during my interview and what sorts of answers I'd be forced to make up to cover a complete lack of experience. There was a good chance I'd be turned down for the job. After all, I was just a kid who had done nothing with his life beyond collecting debris in forests and fields and reading novels and other worthless books. Weren't I so bent on getting clear of our house, pulling together money toward one day having a place of my own, unaffected by my shiftless father and moron brother, I'd have talked myself out of even trying. Tom called me a loser so often that, despite the contrarian waters running deep in me, I knew he wasn't altogether wrong.

As I approached the miniature golf park, I was mesmerized by a ball of brilliance, a white dome of light in the mist that reminded me of some monumental version of one of those snow shaker toys, what on earth are they called? Those water-filled globes of glass inside which are plastic world's fairs, North Pole dioramas, Eiffel Towers that, when joggled, fall under the spell of a miraculous blizzard. What loomed inside this fluorescent bell jar was a wonderland, a fake dwarf-world populated by real people, reminiscent of snow globe toys in other ways, too. The fantastic impossible scenes housed in each, glass or light, were irresistible. I walked through a gate over which was a sign that read BAYSIDE — FOR ALL AGES. What lay before me, smaller than the so-called real world but larger than life, was a village of whirling windmills and miniature cathedrals with spires, of stucco gargoyles and painted grottoes. A white brick castle with turrets ascended the low sky, its paint peeling in the watery weather. Calypso's Cave, the sixth hole. A fanciful pirate ship coved by a waterfall at the seventh. And everywhere I looked, green synthetic alleys. All interconnected and, if a bit seedy, very alluring.

A result of lying about my age, background, and whatever else, I got the job. When asked at dinner to describe what kind of work was involved, I told my father I was the course steward. In fact, my responsibilities fell somewhere between janitor and errand boy. Absurd as it may sound, I was never happier. Vacuuming the putting lanes; scouring the acre park and adjacent beach for lost balls and abandoned golf clubs; tending the beds of bougainvillea and birds of paradise; spearing trash strewn on the trampled struggling real grass that lay between the perfect alleys; skimming crud out of water traps and ornamental lagoons; retouching paint where paint needed retouching. If Bayside were a museum — and it was, to my eyes — I was its curator. The owner, a lean, sallow, stagnant man named Gallagher, seemed gratified by my attentiveness and pleased that I didn't have any friends to waste my time or his. Looking back, I realize he was quietly delighted that I hadn't the least interest in playing. What did I care about hitting a ball into a hole with a stick?

That said, I did become an aficionado, in an antiseptic sort of way. Just as I had about the classifications of seashells or the markings of dragonflies in times past, I read everything I could about the sport in the office bookcase, surrounded by framed photos autographed by the rich and famous who played here long ago. The history was more interesting than I imagined. In the Depression they used sewer pipes, scavenged tires, rain gutters, whatever junk was lying around, and from all the discards built their Rinkiedinks, as the obstacle courses were called, scale-model worlds in which the rules were fair and the playing field —however bunkered, curved, slanted, stepped—was truly level. Once upon a time, I told Molly, this was the classy midnight pastime of America's royalty. Hollywood moguls drank champagne between holes, putting with stars and starlets under the moon until the sun came up. One of the earliest sports played outdoors under artificial lights, miniature golf was high Americana and even now, though it had a degraded heritage, was something finer than people believed.

My favorite trap in the park was the windmill, which rose seven feet into the soggy air of the twelfth green. Its blades were powered by an old car battery that needed checking once a week, as its cable connections tended to corrode in the damp, bringing the attraction—not to mention the obstacle—to a standstill. One entered this windmill by a hidden door at the back, which wasn't observable to people playing the course, indeed was pretty invisible unless you knew it was there. Gallagher had by August learned to trust me with everything except ticket taking, which was his exclusive province when it came to Bayside, and about which I could not care less. So when, one evening, a couple complained to him that the windmill blades on 12 weren't working, he handed me a flashlight, some pliers, a knife, and explained what to do. The windmill was at the far end of the park and I made my way there as quickly as possible without disturbing any of the players.

Once inside, I discovered a new realm. A world within a world. Fixing the oxidized battery posts was nothing, done in a matter of minutes. But then I found myself wanting to stay. What held me was that I could see, through tiny windows in the wooden structure, people playing, unaware they were being watched. A girl with her mother and father standing behind, encouraging her, humped over the white ball, her face contorted into a mask of concentration, putting right at me, knowing nothing of my presence. One shot and through she went, between my legs, and after her, her mom and dad. They talked among themselves, a nice, dreary, happy family, in perfect certainty their words were exchanged in private. It was something to behold.

I stuck around. Who wouldn't? Others passed through me, the ghost in the windmill, and none of them knew, not even the pair of tough bucks who played the rounds every night, betting on each hole, whose contraband beer bottles I'd collected that very morning. It became my habit, from then on, to grab time in the windmill during work to watch and listen. I found myself particularly interested in young couples, many of them not much older than I was, out on dates. Having avoided school since we came West, and being by nature an outsider, my social skills were limited. The physical urgency I felt, spying on these lovers, I sated freely behind the thin walls of my hiding place. Meanwhile, I learned how lovers speak, what kind of extravagant lies they tell each other, the promises they make, and all I could feel was gratitude that my brand of intimacy didn't involve saying anything to anybody. The things I found myself whispering in the shade of my hermitage none of them would like to hear, either. Of that I was sure.

One evening, to my horror, Tom appeared in my peephole vista. What was he doing here? What gave him the right? And who was the girl standing with him, laughing at one of his maudlin jokes? He had a beer in his pocket, like the toughs. His arm was slung over the girl's shoulder, dangling like a broken pendulum, and his face was rosy for once. They laughed again and looked around and, taking advantage of being (almost) alone, kissed. At first I stood frozen in the windmill whose blades spun slowly, knowing that if Tom caught me watching, he'd beat the hell out of me and back at home deny everything. But soon I realized there was nothing to fear. This was my domain. Tom could not touch me in my hideaway world. Much the same way I used to trespass his superiority with those words lifted out of books, I offered him the longest stare I could manage. Not blinking, not wincing, I made my face into an unreadable blank. Pity he couldn't respond.

Work went well. Some days I showed up early, on others left late. Gallagher one September morning informed me that if I thought I would be earning overtime pay I was mistaken, and he reacted with a smiling shrug when I told him my salary was more than fair. "You're a good kid," he concluded. And so I was, in that what he asked me to do I did, prompt and efficient. Players, it turned out, were more irresponsible and given to vandalism than I'd have assumed. Given the game had so much to do with disciplined timing, thoughtful strategy, a steady hand and eye, what were these broken putters and bashed fiberglass figures about? Perhaps I'd become an idealistic company man, but the extensive property damage Gallagher suffered seemed absurd. I helped him with repairs and thought to ask why he didn't prosecute the offenders; we both knew who they were. Instead, I kept my concerns to myself, sensing subconsciously, as they say, it's best not to call the kettle black. After all, Gallagher surely noticed my long absences within the precincts of the park and by mutual silence consented to them, so long as I got the work done.

In my years of wandering far larger landscapes than Bayside I had learned where the birds and beasts of the earth hide themselves against their enemies and how they go about imposing their will, however brief and measly it may be, on the world around them. All my nest hunts and shell meanderings served me well, though here what I collected thus far were fantasies. I can say I almost preferred the limitations of the park. Finding fresh places to hide was my own personal handicap, as it were. And since this was one of the old courses, ostentatious in the most wonderful way—a glorious exemplar of its kind—the possibilities seemed infinite. They weren't, but I took advantage of what was feasible, and like the birds and crustaceans whose homes I used to collect, having none myself to speak of, I more or less moved into Bayside, establishing makeshift berths, stowing food and pop, wherever I secretly could. Like the hermit crab, I began to inhabit empty shells.

The girlfriend's name was Penny. Penny for my thoughts. Thin, with sand-colored hair that fell straight down her back to her waist, she had a wry pale mouth, turned-up nose, and brown searching eyes, deep and almost tragic, which didn't seem to fit with her pastel halter and white pedal pushers. The haunted look in those eyes of hers quickly began to haunt me and, as I watched, my bewilderment over what she was doing with the likes of Tom only grew. In life many things remain ambiguous, chancy, muddled, unknowing and unknowable, but she seemed to be someone who, given the right circumstances, might come to understand me, maybe even believe in me. I developed a vague sense that there was something special between us, a kind of spiritual kinship, difficult to define. Molly was the one who told me her name. She said they had taken her on a picnic up near Isla Vista, and that Penny had taught her how to pick mussels at low tide. Very considerate of Tom, I thought, very familial.

Meantime, he and I were never more estranged. Our absentee father kept a roof over our heads but was otherwise slowly falling to pieces, a prematurely withering man who spent more time after work in taverns, communing with scotch and fellow zilches. Molly had made friends with whom she walked to school these days, so I wasn't seeing much of her, either. Always the loner, I was never more solitary. Time and patience, twin essentials to any collector, were all I needed to bring my new obsession around. So it was that I took my time getting to know Penny, watching from the hidden confines of the windmill, the little train station with its motionless locomotive, the Hall of the Mountain King with its par 5, the toughest hole on the course. Having wrapped her tightly in my imaginative wings, it was hard to believe I still hadn't actually met Tom's friend.

He, who returned to Bayside again and again with some perverse notion he was irritating me, would never have guessed how much I learned about his Penny over the months. Anonymous and invisible as one of the buccaneer statuettes on the pirate ship, I stalked them whenever they came to play, moving easily from one of my sanctuaries to another, all the while keeping my boss under control, so to say; Gallagher, who had grown dependent on me by this time. She was an only daughter. Her father worked on an offshore oil rig. Chickadee was the name of her pet parrot. She loved a song by the Reflections with the lyric "Our love's gonna be written down in history, just like Romeo and Juliet." Peanut butter was her favorite food. All manner of data. But my knowing her came in dribs and drabs, and the fact that what I found out was strictly the result of Tom's whim to bring her to Bayside began to grate on me. I needed more, needed to meet her, to make my own presence known.

How this came about was not as I might have scripted it, but imperfect means sometimes satisfy rich ends. The first of December was Tom's birthday, his eighteenth. As it happened, it fell on a Monday, the one day of the week Bayside was closed. Molly put the party together, a gesture from the heart, no doubt hoping to bring our broken, scattered, dissipating family into some semblance of a household. When she invited me, my answer was naturally no until, by chance, I heard her mention on the phone that Penny was invited. She even asked Gallagher to come. Thank God he declined. Molly and a couple of her friends baked a chocolate cake, and the old man proved himself up to the role of fatherhood by giving Tom the most extravagant present any of us had ever seen. Even our birthday boy was so overwhelmed by his generosity that he gave Dad a kiss on the forehead. Molly and I glanced at one another, embarrassed. Ours was a family that didn't touch, so this was quite a historic moment. If I hadn't spent most of the evening furtively staring at Penny, I might have thrown up my piece of cake then and there.

It was a camera, a real one. Argus C3. Black box with silver trim. Film and carrying case, too. The birthday card read, *Here's looking at you, kid! With affection and best luck for the future years, Dad and your loving brother and sister.* My head spun from the hypocrisy, the blatant nonsense of this hollow sentiment, but I put on the warm smiling face of a good brother, ignoring Tom while accepting from his girlfriend an incandescent smile of her own, complicated as always by those bittersweet eyes of hers, and said, "Let's get a picture." Tom's resentment at having to let me help him read the instructions for loading gave me more satisfaction than I could possibly express. We got it done, though, and the portrait was taken by a parent who arrived to pick up one of Molly's friends. The party was a great success, we all told Molly. That Argus was a mythical monster with a hundred eyes I kept to myself. Although the idea of stealing his camera came to me that night — Tom would never have used it anyway — I waited a week, three weeks, a full month, before removing it from his possession.

With it I began photographing Penny. At first my portraits were confined to what I could manage from various hiding places at the park. But the artificial light wasn't strong enough to capture colors and details in her face and figure, and of course I couldn't use flashbulbs, so the only decent images I managed to get were on the rare occasions when she played during the day, often weekend afternoons, and not always with Tom. I kept every shot, no matter how poor the exposure, in a cigar box stowed inside a duffel in a corner of the windmill along with the camera. During off-hours I often took the box, under my jacket, down to some remote stretch of beach and pored over the pictures with a magnifying glass I'd acquired for the purpose. Some were real prizes, more treasured, even cherished, than anything I'd collected in the past. One image became the object of infatuation, taken at great risk from an open dormer in the castle. It must have been a warm early January day, because Penny wore a light blouse which had caught a draft of wind off the ocean, ballooning the fabric forward away from her, so that from my perch looking down I shot her naked from forehead to navel, both small round breasts exposed to my lens. The photo was pretty abstract, shot at an odd angle, with her features foreshortened, a hodgepodge of fabric and flesh that would be hard to read, much less appreciate the way I did, unless you knew what you were looking at: her uncovered body laid out on that flat, shiny piece of paper. Thinking back to those heady times, I realize most pornography is very conventional, easily understood by the lusting eye, and certainly more explicit. But my innocent snapshots, taken without her knowledge or consent, seem even now to be more obscene than any professional erotic material I have since encountered.

Things developed. I made the fatal step of finding out where Penny lived. Her house was only a mile, give or take, from ours. It became my habit to go to bed with an alarm clock under my pillow, put there so that only I would hear it at midnight, or one or two in the morning, when I'd quietly get dressed and sneak out. These excursions were as haphazard as what I did at the park, if not more so. I took the camera with me, and often came home with nothing, the window to her bedroom having been dark; or worse—her lights still on, the shade drawn, and a shadow moving tantalizingly back and forth on its scrim. But there were occasional triumphs.

Milling in a hedge of jasmine one moonless night, seeing that the houses along her street were all hushed and dark, I was about to give up my siege and walk back home when I heard a car come up the block. Tom's junker coasted into dim view, parking lights showing the way. The only sound was of rubber tires softly chewing pebbles in the pavement. Retreating into the jasmine, I breathed through my mouth as slowly as I could. Penny emerged from the car many long minutes later and dashed right past me—I could smell her perfume over that of the winter flowers—and let herself into the house with hardly a sound. Good old cunning Tom must have dropped his car into neutral, as it drifted down the slanted grade until, a few doors away, he started the engine and drove away.

The lateness of the hour might have given her the idea that no one would notice if she didn't close her shades. Or maybe she was tired and forgot. Or maybe she was afraid to make any unnecessary noise in the house that would wake her parents. She lit a candle, and I saw more that night than I ever had before. To say it was a revelation, a small personal apocalypse, would be to diminish what happened to me as I watched her thin limbs naked in the anemic yellow, hidden only by the long hair she brushed before climbing into bed. How much I would have given to stretch that moment out forever. Though the camera shutter resounded in the dead calm with crisp brief explosions, I unloaded my roll. After she blew out the candle, I retreated in a panicked ecstasy, dazed as a drunk. When I woke up late the next morning, I didn't know where I was, or who.

The film came out better than I hoped — the blessing that would prove a curse, as they might have written in one of those old novels I used to read. The pimply kid who handed me my finished exposures over the counter at the camera shop, and took my crumple of dollars, asked me to wait for a minute.

"How come?" I asked.

Not looking up, he said, "The manager's in the darkroom. He wanted to have a few words with whoever picked up this roll. You got a minute?"

I smiled. "No problem."

When he disappeared into the back of the shop, I slipped out as nonchalant as possible and walked around the corner before breaking into a run, until I reached the highway and, beyond, the golf park.

Gallagher mentioned I was even earlier than usual, not looking up from his morning paper in the office. I explained I wanted to do some work on Calypso's Cave if he didn't mind. He said nothing one way or the other. Toolbox in hand, I hurried instead to the windmill, wondering what kind of imbecile Gallagher thought I was. Nothing mattered once I spread the images in a fan before me in the half-light of my refuge. Other than having to pay for them to be developed, these new trophies were just as virtuous, as pure and irreproachable, as any bird nest or seashell I'd ever collected — perhaps more innocent yet, I told myself, since nothing had been disturbed or in any way hurt by my recent activities. The camera shop had a fake name and wrong phone number. Everything was fine. To describe the photographs of Penny further would be to sully things, so I won't. She was only beautiful in her unobservance, in her not-quite-absolute aloneness.

Spring came and with it all kinds of migratory birds. This would normally be the season when our family meeting — which the old man called, as we might have expected, one Sunday morning — meant the usual song and dance about moving. Out of habit, if nothing else, we gathered around the kitchen table, Tom thoughtfully drumming his fingers and Molly with downcast eyes, not wanting to leave her new friends. Whatever the big guy had to say, I knew I was staying, no matter what. I was old enough to make ends meet, and meet them I would without the help of some pathetic Ojai roofer. I could live in the windmill or the castle for a while, and Gallagher would never know the difference. Eventually I'd get my own apartment. Besides, where was there left to go?

He came into the room with a grim look on his heavy brown face. "Two things," he said, sitting.

"Want some coffee, Dad?" Molly tried.

"First is that Tom is in trouble."

"What kind of trouble?" my brother asked, genuinely upset.

Our father didn't look at him when he said, "I might have thought you'd make better use of your birthday present, son."

Tom was bewildered. "I don't know what you're talking about." He looked at me and Molly for support. Neither of us had, for different reasons, anything to offer. Surely it must have occurred to my dear brother that his having misplaced his fancy birthday present and kept it a secret would come back to haunt him. On a lark, I'd started using his name when I went to different stores to have the film developed. Seemed they caught up with their culprit.

"Much more important is the second problem."

We were hushed.

"Your mother has passed away."

No words. A deep silence. Tom stared at him. Molly began to cry. I stared at my hands folded numb in my lap and tried without success to remember what she'd looked like. I had come to think of myself as having no mother, and now I truly didn't. What difference did it make? I wanted to say, but kept quiet.

"I'm going back for a couple weeks to take care of everything, make sure she's — taken care of, best as possible."

It was left at that. No further questions, nor any answers. However, when we put him on the flight in Los Angeles, Tom having driven us down, I could tell my brother remained in the dark about that first problem broached at the family meeting. Dull as he was, he did display sufficient presence of mind not to bring it up when such weightier matters were being dealt with. The old man, waving to us as he boarded his flight, looked for all the world the broken devil he was becoming, or already had become.

Things moved unequivocally after this. Mother was put to rest and her estranged husband returned from the East annihilated, poor soul. Molly withdrew from everybody but me. Penny and my brother had broken up by the time summer fog began rolling ashore in this, my year anniversary at Bayside. It fell to me, of all people, to nurture family ties, such as they were. To make, like an oriole, a work of homey art from lost ribbons, streamers, string, twigs, the jetsam of life, in which we vulnerable birds could live. I had no interest, by the way, in mourning our forsaken mother. But for a brief time, I tried to be nice to the old man and avoid Tom.

Which is not to say that my commitment to Penny changed during those transitional months. I continued to photograph her whenever I could, adept now that I had come to know her routines, day by day, week by week. Instead of hiding from her at Bayside, or downtown, or even in her neighborhood where sometimes I happened to be walking along and accidentally, as it were, bumped into her, I stopped and talked about this or that, when she wasn't in a hurry. If she asked me about Tom, I assured her that he was doing great, and changed the subject. Did the Reflections have a new hit song? I would ask. Did she want to come down to the golf course, bring some girlfriends along, do the circuit for free? She appreciated the invitation but had lost interest in games and songs and many other things. Rather than feeling defeated, I became even more devoted. My collection of photographs throughout this period of not-very-random encounters and lukewarm responses to my propositions grew by leaps and bounds. I enrolled pseudonymously in a photo club that gave me access to a darkroom, where I learned without much trouble how to develop film. Hundreds of images of Penny emerged, many of them underexposed and overexposed and visually unreadable to anyone but me. But also some of them remarkable for their poignant crudity, since by that time I'd captured her in most every possible human activity.

The inevitable happened on an otherwise dull, gray day. Late afternoon, just after sunset. The sky was like unpolished pewter, and late summer fog settled along the coast. I was down near my windmill, loitering at Gallagher's not-great expense, with nothing going on and nothing promising that evening, either, except maybe the usual jog over to Penny's to see what there was to see, when, without warning, I was caught by the collar of my shirt and thrown to the ground. I must have blurted some kind of shout or cry, but remember at first a deep exterior silence as I was dragged, my hands grasping at my throat, through a breach in the fence and out onto the sand. The pounding in my ears was deafening and I felt my face bloat. I tried kicking and twisting, but the hands that held me were much stronger than mine. I blanked out, then came to, soaked in salt water and sweat, and saw my brother's face close to mine spitting out words I couldn't hear through the tumultuous noise of crashing waves and throbbing blood. He slapped me. And slapped me backhanded again. Then pulled me up like a rough lover so that we faced each other lips-to-lips. I still couldn't hear him, though I knew what he was cursing about. Bastard must have been following me, spying, and uncovered my hideout and stash.

What bothered me most was that Tom, not I, was destroying my collection. He had no right, no right. None of the photographs that swept helter-skelter into the surf, as we fought on that dismal evening, were his to destroy. Much as I'd like to sketch those minutes in such a way that my seizing the golf ball from my shirt pocket, cramming it into his mouth, and clamping his jaw shut with all the strength I had, was a gesture meant to silence not slay him, it would be a lie.

Lie or not, Tom went down hard, gasping for air, and I went down with him, my hands like a vise on his pop-eyed face. He grabbed at his neck now, just as I had moments before, the ball lodged in the back of his throat. A wave came up over us both in a sizzling splash, knocking us shoreward before pulling us back toward the black water and heavy rollers. Everywhere around us were Penny's images, washing in and out with the tidal surges. Climbing to my feet, I watched the hungry waves carry my brother away. I looked up and down the coast and, seeing no one in the settling dark, walked in the surf a quarter mile northward, maybe farther, before crossing a grass strip which led, beneath some raddled palms, to solitary sidewalks that took me home, where I changed clothes. In no time I was at work again, my mind a stony blank.

Whether by instinct or dumb luck, my having suppressed the urge to salvage as many photos as I could that night, and carry them away with me when I left the scene where Tom and I had quarreled, stood me in good stead. Given that I had the presence of mind to polish the Argus and hide it under Tom's bed, where it would be discovered the next day by the authorities when they rummaged through his room looking for evidence that might explain what happened, I think my abandonment of my cache of portraits was genius. Clever, at least.

Clever, too, if heartfelt, was my brave comforting of Molly, who cried her eyes out, on hearing the disastrous news. And I stuck close to our paralyzed father, who walked from room to room in the bungalow we called home, all but cataleptic, mumbling to himself about the curse that followed him wherever he went. Though they had not ruled out an accidental death — he disgorged the golf ball before drowning — our father was, I understand, their suspect for months. A walk on the beach, man-to-man, a parental confrontation accidentally gone too far. In fact, their instinct, backed by the circumstantial evidence of his having been troubled by his estranged wife's demise, given to drinking too much, and his recent rage toward his eldest kid over having taken weird, even porno snapshots of his girlfriend, led them in the right direction. Just not quite. Molly and I had watertight alibis, so to speak, not that we needed them. She was with several friends watching television, and Gallagher signed an affidavit that I was working with him side by side during the time of the assault. Speculating about the gap in the fence and faint, windblown track marks in the sand, he said, "Always trespassers trying to get in for free," and, not wanting to cast aspersion on the deceased, he nevertheless mentioned that he'd seen somebody sneaking in and out of that particular breach at odd hours, and that the person looked somewhat like Tom.

Our father was eventually cleared. Turned out Sad Sack was a covert Casanova with a lady friend in Ojai. This explained why our annual rousting had not taken place. He need not have been shy about it, as his children would prove to like her; Shannon is the name. Whether Gallagher'd been so used to me going through my paces — efficient, thorough, devoted — that he improved on an assumption by making it a sworn fact; or whether he really thought he saw me at work that night, ubiquitous ghost that I was; or whether he was covering for me, not wanting to lose the one sucker who understood Bayside and could keep it going when he no longer cared to, I will never know. Gallagher himself would perish a year later of a heart attack, in our small office, slumped in his cane chair beneath those pictures of stars who gazed down at him with ruthless benevolence.

The initial conclusions reached in Tom's murder investigation proved much the same as the inconclusive final one. They had been thorough, questioned all of Tom's friends. Certainly Penny might have wanted him dead given how humiliated, how mortified, she was by the photographs that had been recovered along the coast. Asked to look through them, she did the best she could. While she did seem to think Tom had been with her on some occasions when this or that shot was taken — they were all so awful, so invasive, so perverse — she couldn't be sure. Given that he was present in none of the exposures, that the camera used was his, and so forth, there was no reason to look elsewhere for the photographer. Penny had a motive, but also an alibi, like everyone else.

None of it mattered, finally, because good came from the bad. Our family was closer than ever, and Dad seemed, after a few months of dazed mourning, to shake off his long slump. He brought his Ojai bartender girlfriend around sometimes, and Molly made dinner. Penny, too, was transformed by the tragedy. Before my watchful eyes she changed into an even gentler being, more withdrawn than before, yes, but composed and calm — some might say remote, but they'd be wrong, not knowing her like I did. It was as if she changed from a color photograph to black-and-white. I didn't mind the shift. To the contrary.

The morning Penny came down to Bayside to speak with me was lit by the palest pink air and softest breeze of late autumn. I'd been the model of discretion in the several years that followed Tom's passing, keeping tabs on Penny out of respect, really, making sure she was doing all right in the wake of what must have been quite a shock to her. Never overstepping my bounds — at least not in such a way as she could possibly know. Meantime, I had matured. Molly told me I'd become a handsome dog, as she put it. Her girlfriends had crushes on me, she said. I smiled and let them play the golf course gratis. Why not? Then Penny turned up, unexpected, wanting to give me something.

"For your birthday," she said, handing me a small box tied with a white ribbon. There was quite a gale blowing off the ocean that day and her hair buffeted about her head. With her free hand she drew a long garland of it, fine as corn silk, away from her mouth and melancholy eyes. It was a gesture of absolute purity. Penny was a youthful twenty-one, and I an aged nineteen.

I must have looked surprised, because she said, "You look like you forgot."

She followed me into the office, where we could get out of the wind. All the smugly privileged faces in Gallagher's nostalgic gallery had been long since removed from the walls and sent off to his surviving relatives, who, not wanting much to bother with their inheritance of a slowly deteriorating putt-putt golf park, allowed me to continue in my capacity as Bayside steward and manager. Like their deceased uncle — a childless bachelor whose sole concern had been this fanciful (let me admit) dump — they thought I was far older than nineteen. The lawyer who settled his estate looked into the records, saw on my filed application that I was in my mid-twenties, and further saw that Gallagher wanted me to continue there as long as it was my wish, and thus and so. A modest check went out each month to the estate, the balance going to moderate upkeep and my equally moderate salary. What did I care? My needs were few. I spent warm nights down here in my castle, or the windmill, and was always welcome at home, where the food was free. And now, as if in a dream, here was my Penny, bearing a gift.

I undid the ribbon and tore away the paper. It was a snow globe with a hula dancer whose hips gyrated in the sparkling blizzard after I gave it a good shake.

"How did you know?" I asked, smiling at her smiling face.

"You like it?"

"I love it."

"Molly told me this was your new thing."

"Kind of stupid, I guess. But they're like little worlds you can disappear into if you stare at them long enough."

"I don't think it's stupid."

"Yours goes in the place of honor," I said, taking the gift over to my shelves lined with dozens of others, where I installed the hula girl at the very heart of the collection.

Penny peered up and down the rows, her face as luminous as I've ever seen it, beaming like a child. She plucked one down and held it to the light. "Can I?" she asked. I told her sure and watched as she shook the globe and the white flakes flew round and round in the glassed-in world. She gazed at the scene within while I gazed at her. One of those moments which touch on perfection.

"Very cool," she whispered, as if in a reverie. "But isn't it a shame that it's always winter?"

"I don't really see them as snowflakes," I said.

"What, then?"

Penny turned to me and must have glimpsed something different in the way I was looking at her, since she glanced away and commented that no one was playing today. The wind, I told her. Sand gets in your eyes and makes the synthetic carpet too rough to play on. In fact, there wasn't much reason to keep the place open, I continued, and asked her if she'd let me drive her up to Santa Barbara for the afternoon, wander State Street together, get something to eat. I was not that astonished when she agreed. Cognizant or not, she'd been witness to the character, the nature, the spirit of my gaze, had the opportunity to reject what it meant. By accepting my invitation she was in a fell stroke accepting me.

"You can have it if you want," I offered, taking her free hand and nodding at the snow globe.

"No, it belongs with the others." She stared out the window while a fresh gale whipped up off the ocean, making the panes shiver and chatter as grains of sand swirled around us. I looked past her silhouette and remarked that the park looked like a great snow globe out there. How perverse it was of me to want to ask her, just then, if she missed Tom sometimes. Instead, I told her we ought to get going, but not before I turned her chin toward me with trembling fingers and gently kissed her.

As we drove north along the highway, the sky cleared, admitting a sudden warm sun into its blue. "Aren't you going to tell me?" she asked, as if out of that blue, and for a brief, ghastly moment I thought I'd been found out and was being asked to confess. Seeing my bewilderment, Penny clarified, "What the snowflakes are, if they're not snowflakes?"

I shifted my focus from the road edged by flowering hedges and eucalyptus over to Penny, and back again, suddenly wanting to tell her everything, pour my heart out to her. I wanted to tell her how I had read somewhere that in some cultures people refuse to have their photographs taken, believing the camera steals their souls. Wanted to tell her that when Tom demolished my collection of adoring images of her, not only did he seal his own fate, but engendered hers. I wished I could tell her how, struggling with him in waves speckled with swirling photographs, I was reminded of a snow globe. And I did want to answer her question, to say that the flakes seemed to me like captive souls floating around hopelessly in their little glass cages, circling some frivolous god, but I would never admit such nonsense. Instead, I told her she must have misunderstood and, glancing at her face bathed in stormy light, knew in my heart that later this afternoon, maybe during the night, I would be compelled to finish the destructive work my foolish brother had begun.

2007

LORENZO CARCATERRA

MISSING THE MORNING BUS

LORENZO CARCATERRA (1954–) was born in the Hell's Kitchen neighborhood of New York City. He began his career as a journalist for the *New York Daily News* in 1976, first as a copy boy, finally as entertainment reporter, before moving to Time, Inc. as a writer for *TV-Cable Week* and *People,* moving on to write for numerous other magazines both as a staff writer and a freelancer, including *Family Circle,* the *New York Times Magazine,* and *Twilight Zone.*

In 1988 he became creative consultant for the TV series *Cop Talk: Behind the Shield,* leading to a managing editor position for the CBS-TV series *Top Cop,* which ran for four years. Among much other television work, he has written several unproduced pilots, and in 2003 and 2004 was a writer and producer on *Law and Order.*

After his first book, *A Safe Place: The True Story of a Father, a Son, a Murder* (1993), which has sold some 200,000 copies, he wrote the highly controversial *Sleepers* (1995), a semiautobiographical work about child abuse in a state juvenile facility. With nearly 1.5 million copies sold, the number one bestseller was filmed in 1996 with Brad Pitt, Robert De Niro, Dustin Hoffman, Kevin Bacon, and Minnie Driver. Carcaterra was the coproducer of the Barry Levinson–directed film, which has seen worldwide earnings of $500 million. His subsequent novels have regularly made the bestseller list, including *Apaches* (1998), *Gangster* (2001), *Street Boys* (2002), *Paradise City* (2004), and *Chasers* (2007).

"Missing the Morning Bus" was first published in the anthology *Dead Man's Hand: Crime Fiction at the Poker Table* (New York: Harcourt, 2007).

▪ ▪ ▪

I LIFTED THE LID on my hold cards and smiled. I leaned back against three shaky slats of an old worn chair, wood legs mangled by the gnawing of a tired collie now asleep in a corner of the stuffy room, and stared over at the six faces huddled around the long dining-room table, thick mahogany wood shining under the glare of an overhead chandelier, each player studying his hand, deciding on his play, mentally considering his odds of success, in what was now the fifth year of a weekly Thursday-night ritual. I stared at the face of each of the men I had known for the better part of a decade and paused to wonder which of these friends would be the one. I was curious as to which of the six I would be forced to confront before this night, unlike any other, would come to its end.

I wanted so desperately to know who it was sitting around that table responsible for the death of the woman I loved. And I would want that answer before the last draw of the evening was called.

I tried to read their faces much the same as they would the cards in their hand. There was Jerry McReynolds, wide smile as always plastered across his face, a forty-year-old straight and single man free of the weight of day-to-day worries, a millionaire many times over due to a $5,000 investment in a small computer start-up outfit working out of a city he had never heard of, let alone visited. Jerry never missed a Thursday-night game, boasting of his streak as if he were a ballplayer about to make a move on Cal Ripken Jr.'s long-standing record of consecutive games played. He came outfitted in the same casual manner in which he approached the cards dealt his way, catalog-ordered shirts and jeans, nothing fancy, nothing wild. I could count on him to come in with two high-end bottles of Italian reds and quickly ease into the steady flow of cards and chatter that filled our weekly five-hour sessions. Jerry was the guardian of the chips and kept a small pad and a pen by his side, starting off the game with a $50 feed and dispensing out whites and blues to any player running low or chasing empty. Jerry kept his cards close, doing a quick fold if he felt his hand weak, playing the table as he did his life, on the up and up and without a hint of bluff. In five years of play, I could never recall a time when Jerry left the room with less in his pockets than he had at the start.

I sat back, rubbed the stiffness from the nape of my neck, and tried to recall how I came to know Jerry in the first place and couldn't quite place it, my cloudy memory confining it to one of the holiday receptions my wife used to host on a semiregular basis back in the days when our marriage still had the scent of salvation. God, how I hated every one of those parties, forced to make small talk in a room packed mostly with her friends since the few I had were seldom invited or welcomed into her cloistered world. I took a long gulp from a glass of scotch and looked back on those long and tedious nights and did a quick flash of Jerry being dragged by the hand in my direction, a glass of white wine in one hand, my wife's in the other. "You two will be good friends in no time at all," she said as she made a quick U-turn back into party traffic, her short and tight black skirt giving strong hints of the curvy body that rested beneath, long red hair hanging just off the edge of her shoulders. She was about forty-two then, give or take, and looked at least ten years younger, the quick smile and easy laugh a sweet antidote to the onslaught of age. I wasn't quite sure how Dottie and Jerry came to know one another and I never did bother to ask, but there was always more to their friendship than they were willing to let on. There was that look between them. You know the kind I mean? As if someone was in front of them telling a joke and they were the only two in on the punch line.

"Five-card draw, jacks or better to open," Steve said, giving the deck one more shuffle before the deal, waiting for us all to ante.

"I need a refill." I tossed my one-dollar chip into the center of the table, pushing my chair back and walking over to a crowded countertop, filled with half-empty bottles of scotch, bourbon, gin, and wine. I spun open the top of a Dewar's bottle and stared over at Steve as he doled out the cards meticulously, eyebrows thick as awnings shading his eyes. I had known Steve since forever started, both of us only children raised in the same Bronx neighborhood and going to the same Catholic schools straight through till college. And even then, while he froze his ass off studying economics and law at Michigan and I was smoking and doping my way through four years of English, a language I already had a leg up on, at Williams, we never drifted very far apart. We saw each other during breaks and vacations, hustling over to the same parties and looking to score with the same girls. I guess if I had to pick one, I'd point to Little Stevie Giraldo as my best friend, the fast-talker with a good line of shit and an innate ability to talk the unwilling to tag along on any outing he thought was worth the time and money. As he got older and life started dealing him a tougher hand of cards, Steve's youthful edge took a sharp nosedive and by the time he hit his forties, he was a man adrift, moving from one mid-tier job to the next, in debt to credit cards and street lenders, a decade into a loser's marriage and with two kids who cost him ten for every five he earned. I was the only one in the room who knew he tried to do a final checkout about eighteen months back, but even there his bad luck stayed that way. He chugged enough pills and booze to knock off Walter Hudson — that guy who was so fat they had to bury his ass inside a piano — and all it got him was a long night at a crowded hospital, his stomach pumping out everything he had managed to shove in. I was the one who waited for him, rushing over from a nearby bar where I was nursing a few, soon as I got the word from Mackey, a mutual pal working the wood that night.

Dottie came by at sunup, driving the old Nissan she would never let me sell, and took us both back to our place, where she made some coffee and let him sleep the rest of the OD off in the back bedroom. She didn't say all that much about it, and I said even less. But I couldn't help but catch the look of concern on her face, odd since she never much cared for Stevie one way or the other. Made me wonder what kind of look I would have earned if it was me instead of him lying in that bed, one pill removed from the long nap.

"Are you in or not, Ike?" Joe asked. "I mean, you going to pony and play or you just looking to mix drinks all night?"

"I'm in for a dollar," I said, dropping two cubes into my tumbler and glaring over at Joe, decked out as he always was in a battered New York Yankees baseball cap, Detroit Red Wings sweatshirt, and San Diego Chargers workout pants. A walking billboard of sports franchises. Joe was a trash-talking ballbuster of a work-from-home bond trader who left his Upper West Side apartment only for poker games or sporting events. Other than on those semiregular occasions, he shopped, ordered food, chatted with friends, and read for both leisure and business on his laptop. His two-bedroom condo, bought with the inheritance he scored off the daily-double death of his mother and a great-aunt three days apart in 1995, was a smooth blend of Ikea, sports and movie memorabilia, furniture, and utensils. Dottie disliked Joe with an intensity that bordered on the fanatical, which, if he knew how she felt, he would ironically appreciate, able to compare it to his rabid feelings toward both the Boston Red Sox and the New York Islanders.

I guess I liked him for the same reasons she didn't. Joe was filled with passion and was never shy to let anyone with ears know how he felt about his teams, his favorite movie or TV show. Hell, he would even get into a beef and a brawl over the athleticism of pro wrestling. Funny though, in all the years I've known Joe, and I've been doing his taxes now going on ten years this next April, he's never once asked me what my favorite sport was or which team I liked. For all he knows, I can't stand the sight of any sport, let alone follow one close enough to dip into my savings for season tickets and wear the team colors to my best friend's wedding or wake. But Joe *did* know that Dottie liked basketball and that she never missed a New York Knicks game on television during the season and, on rare occasions, the playoffs. I know that only because he mentioned it once during a poker game, after the Knicks by some miracle had beaten the Miami Heat the night before, how happy Dottie must have been to see that happen. How the hell could he have any idea that she was a fan or was even at home to watch the game?

I was back at my seat looking down at a pair of tens and a queen high, the fresh drink by my side. I glanced to my left and caught Tony's eye and was given a warm smile as a reward. "Everything good with you?" he asked.

"Good enough," I said, trying to keep the conversation light and not veer it toward the personal, which is the road Tony always seemed to prefer.

It made sense that he would, of course, what with him being a shrink and all. Tony enjoyed doing hit-and-run probes into the lives of the men around the table, treating the entire night as if it were a casual group session with cards, chips, and money added to the mix. He would keep it all very chatty, never giving the impression he was picking and pawing or even the least bit curious about any one of us but always leaving the table owning a lot more information than he had when he first walked in. When he wasn't busy jabbing at our collective scabs as casually as he would a platter of potato salad, Tony regaled us with tales of his sexual conquests, most of them arriving courtesy of his practically all-female practice. It was difficult not to envy any man who in a given week would bed as many as five different women, so you can imagine how well his tales traveled around a poker table filled with either those who had gone without for longer than they would dare to remember or the few who felt strangled by double-decades' worth of marital gloom.

"This is one you won't believe," he said, dropping his cards on the table in a fold and sitting back, wide grin flashed across a face that looked far too young for a man one month shy of his fifty-second birthday. "I have this new patient, right? Drop-dead blonde with stallion legs and a killer smile. Only on her second visit, asks if it's OK for her to call me at home. You know, just to shoot it whenever the urge hits."

"You ever see any ugly patients?" I asked. I really didn't want to believe that every woman who paid to tell Tony sad tales of an unfulfilled life was poster-girl material even though, deep in my heart, it figured probably to be indeed true.

"Only on referrals," Tony said. "Anyway, I'm supposed to say no to such a request, I suppose. I mean if I'm going to do a line-by-line with the rulebook."

"But you never have before," I said. "No sense finding religion now, especially when it's a different promised land you're looking to find."

"So, I give her my home number and go about the rest of my day," Tony said. "I had no doubt she would make use of it down the road a bit, maybe get a few more sessions under her garters before she made the move."

"Let me take a stab at a guess here," Joe said. "She dialed your private line right about the start of the second period of the Rangers game. Right or not?"

"If that's about eight or so, then yes, you win the stuffed bear," Tony said. "She was very upset, needed to talk, and couldn't make it wait. I offered to do a free phone consult, but she wanted a face-to-face. An hour later we were down a half bottle of red and doing a wild roll on the water bed."

"I didn't think anybody still had a water bed," Steve said. "Or that they even made them. You don't have a lava lamp, too, do you?"

I brushed Steve's question aside with one of my own: "This woman, was she married or single?"

Tony stared at me for several seconds before he answered. "Would it make a difference either way?" he asked.

"It might," I said, "to her husband."

"She is married," Tony said with more a sneer than a smile. "Truth be told, most of the women who come to me for help are bound to the ring. If they weren't, then maybe they wouldn't be so damn unhappy and I wouldn't be pulling down seven figures to dole out my pearls of acquired wisdom."

"Does any of that cause you concern?" I asked. "I mean, forget about the doctor-patient mumbo-jumbo crap. I'm talking here as a man. Does it bother you one inch to be taking another man's wife into your bed?"

"It never has." Tony stared right at me as if his measured words were meant for my ears alone. "And it never will."

"Is there any more pie?" Jeffrey asked. "I don't know what it is lately, but I can't seem ever to get enough to eat."

"That may well be because you're celibate," Tony said. "You need something to replace what the body most needs. If you took my advice, which I rarely offer for free, you would switch gears and reach for a warm body instead of a warm plate."

Jeffrey hated to talk about sex or at least that's the impression he wanted to convey. He was a Jesuit priest when I first met him, waiting in line to see Nathan Lane go for laughs in a Neil Simon play — an original, not a revival. It was a cold and rainy Wednesday and the matinee crowd was crammed as it usually was with the bused in and the walk-ins. We both should have been somewhere else, doing what I was paid to do and, in Jeffrey's case, what he was called to do. We made a valiant attempt at small talk as we snaked our way up toward a half-price ticket window and were surprised when we scored adjoining orchestra seats.

"Now if the show is only half as funny as the critics claim," Jeffrey said, "we will have gotten our money's worth."

We stopped by Joe Allen's for drinks after the show and I had just ordered my second shaken-not-stirred martini of the afternoon when I invited Father Jeffrey to join the poker game, eager to fill the void left by Sal Gregorio's spur-of-the-moment move to Chicago to tend to his father's meatpacking plant. Even back then, Jeffrey seemed to me a troubled man, grappling with the type of demons I would never be able to visualize in the worst of my black-dog moments. I came away with the sense that he had reached the top of the well when it came to his chosen vocation, not sure whether it was the pedophile scandal rocking the church that did it or just the very fact that he was a modern man forced to live a sixteenth-century life. "Do you miss it?" I had asked him that day.

"What, the women?"

"We can start with that," I said, trying my best to make light of what would have to be considered a serious deal-breaker in *any* contract talks that brought into play a lifetime commitment.

"There are moments," Jeffrey said, "when I *don't* think about it. It is, by a wide margin, the biggest obstacle a priest must overcome. At least it has been for me. But hidden beneath the cover of misery, a silver cloud often lies."

"What's yours?" I asked, maybe crossing deeper into the holy water than I should.

"That it's young women who draw my eye and not innocent boys," Jeffrey said, the words tinged with anger and not regret.

"Are you one of those rebels in a collar who think Christ and Mary Magdalene were more than just pen pals?" I asked, doing what I could to steer the conversation away from the uncomfortable.

"I am one of those rebels in a collar who think Christ was too much of a man *not* to be in love with a woman as beautiful and as loyal as Mary was to him," Jeffrey said.

One year later, just about to the day, Father Jeffrey turned his back on his vows, handed in his collar, and walked out of the church life for good. Yet, in the time from that eventful day to this, he stayed celibate or, at least, so he claimed, though not from a lack of effort but more from a lack of experience. Now, of all the guys in the poker group, he was the only one Dottie liked, the one she didn't roll her eyes or mumble beneath her breath if we ran into on the street or in a local restaurant. She even mentioned once that she had gone to church to see him celebrate mass and listen to one of his sermons.

"How was he?" I asked her that day.

"He looked like he belonged up there," Dottie said about Jeffrey in the same awed tone I would have reserved for Frank Sinatra or Johnny Cash. "But then again, it's not like it was his first time."

"Full house, kings high," Jerry said, resting his hand flat on the table and reaching over to drag a small mountain of different-colored chips his way.

"Was that deck even shuffled?" Adam asked, shaking his head, thick hair covering one side of his thin face. "I mean, really, just look at all the face cards that are out. I don't think it was shuffled."

"You only ask that when I win a hand," Jerry said. "There a reason for that?"

"That's because the only hands you ever win usually come off a deck that hasn't been shuffled," Adam said.

Adam and Jerry hated one another and I never understood why one, if not both, didn't just walk from the game. It wasn't as if the city was lacking weekly poker gatherings, and God knows most of them served better food and had a nicer selection of wines to choose from than what I offered and set out. Adam was a doctor and a noted one, often cited in medical journals and in the Science section of the *New York Times* as the gold standard in regard to matters pertaining to women and their bodies. He was handsome, with an easy smile and a scalpel-sharp sense of humor, except of course when he found himself sitting across a table from Jerry, cards in hand and a stack of poker chips resting between them. And while I could never quite put a finger to the pulse that got the feud started in the first place, in many ways I felt myself to be the one responsible. After all, as with the rest of the group, I was the one who brought Adam into the game. And I would just as soon bring the weekly session to an end than to see it go on without Adam holding his usual place at the far end of my table.

Dr. Adam Rothberg had saved Dottie's life.

Three years ago, after a long bout with a flu that wouldn't quite surrender the fight, Dottie, fresh off a five-day siege of heavy-duty antibiotics mixed with cough syrup and aspirin, collapsed on the floor of our tiny barely walk-into-it-and-move-around kitchen. She was doubled up and clutching her stomach, foam thick as ocean spray flowed out of her mouth, and her body shook as if it were resting on top of a high-speed motorboat. I was about to jump for the phone and dial 911 when I remembered that the new face that had moved in down the hall during the last week belonged to a doctor. I rushed out of the apartment and ran out into the narrow hall, banging at a door two down from mine. I felt like a boy sitting under a tree crammed with packages on Christmas morning when I saw Adam's face as he swung open his apartment door.

He saved Dottie's life that day, and we have been friends ever since.

In that span of time, Adam's practice flourished and his stature rose, while mine pretty much hovered at the same level it had been for years. I don't hate the work I do really, it's just that I don't love it, either. I look around this table and don't see anyone happier at their chosen work than I am, except maybe for Adam, who truly loves putting on the white coat and playing God twelve hours a day. I am good at what I do, bringing a financial balance to the lives of my clients, despite the fact I can't seem to accomplish those same goals for myself. I could never get it to where I was a step ahead, with all the bills paid and some money set aside. And I could never figure out where the hell it all went, especially since we didn't have the financial burden of kids and had lived in the same apartment for more or less the same rent since we were first married and, except for a two-week splurge in Italy during our first year together, seldom took long or expensive vacations.

It bothered Dottie — I knew that. Not that I was an accountant, but that I was one without money and minus the drive or the talent to earn it. Women like Dottie go into a marriage and expect more out of it than they first let on, not wanting to be the kind of woman who lives her middle age in a financial and emotional rut. And the truth of that, the belief that I had let her down in some way, ate at me more than I would let on. I had failed her, and over time it chipped away at the love she felt for me. I could see it, sense it, her eyes vacant and drawn when she looked my way, her manner indifferent at best, her kisses directed more to the cheek than the lips, as if she were greeting a distant relative with whom she would prefer to have very little contact. It was so different from when we first met. Back then, I was sure we would love each other forever.

I first saw Dorothy Blakemore at a counter on the second floor of a department store on the Upper East Side. It was a week before Christmas and the place was mad crazy with shoppers with a hunger for gifts, credit cards clutched in their hands. She was staring down at a counter filled with men's gloves and kept shaking her head each time a tall, thin, and harried salesclerk made the slightest attempt at a suggestion. "I don't even know his size" were the first words I heard her say, her voice a sultry mix of Southern warmth mixed with a Northeast education.

"If I had an idea as to his height and weight, then perhaps I can narrow down your choices," he said to her, his tone more condescending than consoling.

Dottie paused for a brief second and then glanced in my direction. When she turned and our eyes met, I knew that I was in the middle of a movie moment, standing a mere distance from a woman as beautiful and striking as any I would ever be lucky enough to see in my lifetime. "He's about the size of this man," she said to the salesclerk as she walked toward me.

I helped her pick out a pair of black leather gloves for her brother, who lived in some town in Maine whose name I could never remember. I wasn't the type to move fast when it came to women, but I knew in my heart if I didn't connect with Dottie on that day, then I would for sure never see her again. There have been few moments in my life when I've been able to manage to put the pieces together and not muck up the works, and that early afternoon was top-of-the-list one of them. I offered to buy her a cup of coffee at a nearby luncheonette that if it were anywhere else other than on the Upper East Side of Manhattan would be called a diner, and she smiled and nodded. I fell in love that day and have been ever since.

"Cards don't look to be falling your way tonight, Ike," Steve said, dropping a three of hearts next to my six of spades. "But then, why should tonight be different from any other game?"

"I used up my run of luck looking for love; there wasn't any left over for cards," I said with a slight shrug, my words sounding much meeker than I intended.

"So things between you and Dottie are good now?" Tony asked.

"Did I ever give you a hint that they weren't?" I didn't bother to disguise my annoyance at the question.

"How about we just play the hand?" Joe advised. "You want to talk about unhappy marriages, let's talk about Isiah Thomas and Stephon Marbury. Not only are they mucking it up with each other, they're destroying any remote chance the Knicks have at ever sneaking into the playoffs."

"Dottie and I are not unhappy," I said with as much vigor as I could muster. "And if I did or said anything to give you that impression, it was wrong and unintentional."

"And there it shall end," Jeffrey said with a nod and a smile. "To be quite honest, I never realized how much men loved to gossip until I started playing poker. Unless it's just this particular group that happens to be so chatty."

"I can only imagine what you and your crew talked about back in your rectory days," Steve said. "I would bet a full load it covered nastier terrain than who was swigging too much of the communion wine."

I sat back, smiled, and listened as the kidding and ribbing continued around me, holding my anger in check, knowing that the moment was at hand, the killer soon to be revealed. It was all very easy in some way to piece it together, deciding who in the group sitting around my table would bear the responsibility that had led to my Dottie's sudden and unexpected death.

It was his fingers that were wrapped around the thick black handle of the carving knife as much as mine. It was his hand along with mine that plunged that blade into Dottie's frail and tender body again and again and again until she fell to the floor of the back bedroom, her head slumped to one side, blood oozing out of the deep, severe wounds and staining the thick Persian rug she had bought with the proceeds from my first-and-only Christmas bonus back during that first year of wedded bliss.

I was a forty-four-year-old man, alone and in debt, out of shape and mentally drained, my hair thinner than it had any right to be and my stomach rounder than anyone my age would prefer. I had a past that was filled mostly with dark and gloomy days and empty nights, touched only on rare occasions by the light and tender glare of happiness. I had a future that promised to be even bleaker, doomed to live out what was left of my time alone and in a constant struggle to survive.

So I needed to keep my focus on the present.

In one room, staring up at a chipped and stained white ceiling, an overhead fan on low, circulating warm air in gusts, was the body of a woman who had shared twenty-two years of my life.

And in this room, surrounded by poker chips, two decks of playing cards, near-empty bowls of nuts and salsa, drinks waiting to be finished, sat the man who had forced my hand and directed it toward murder.

"Looks like it's your deal, Ike," Adam said. "And your call. What's it going to be?"

"Let's make this the final hand," I said.

"It's not even ten," Joe protested. "We usually go to eleven, sometimes an hour or two later. Why make it such an early call?"

"If it's the last one, can we at least make it interesting?" Steve asked.

"I intend to," I said. "Midnight baseball, no peak, threes and nines are wild. You draw a four and you can buy yourself an extra card."

"How about we double the ante, then?" Joe asked. "And let's put no limits on the raises. That square with everybody?"

"You go that route and the pot can start to get a little steep," Jerry said. "It's always been a friendly game. This will take it out of that ballpark, no doubt."

"What, you afraid of losing something off the heavy pile of dough you got stashed?" Joe asked.

"I'm afraid of sitting here and watching you lose money I *know* you don't have," Jerry said. "Nothing more."

"You should all be afraid," I said. "This is the one hand none of you can hide from and not one of you can afford to lose."

"What the hell are you talking about?" Adam asked. "Just deal the cards, and let's get this over with. These weekly games are starting to wear a bit thin. It might just be time for me to move on."

I shuffled the deck one final time and pushed it over to my left, waiting for Tony to cut the cards, and turned to Adam. "And if luck singles you out, then you may well get your wish, Doctor," I said.

I had their attention now, each staring at me not sure whether I was drunk or tired or had totally spun my wheels off the rails. Slowly and with great care, I doled out seven cards to each player, myself included. "This isn't at all like you, Ike," Jeffrey said, more than slightly annoyed. "Maybe Adam is on the right track. We may all need to call it for tonight. You look like you could do with a good night's rest."

"You might be right on that score, Padre," I said. "I might just need a few solid hours of shuteye. But before I push back and trot off to bed, I need to bring our little game to a fitting end. I think that's something we all would want. So how about you sit back and sit tight? This won't take very long."

I caught the glances racing across the table from one set of eyes to another, the looks a mixture of confusion, anger, concern, and indifference, and it made me smile. I had them now, these six friends of mine, men I had trusted and confided in, to some had even bared secrets I would never want spoken outside this room. For a long stretch of time in my troubled life, they were the raft that I could wrap my arms around and ward off, however briefly, the arching waves, dark clouds, and approaching storm of an existence that seemed destined to end with my drowning death. But they all carried with them the Judas coin, and the blood of a good woman was now smeared across it.

We all turned our first card over. Steve was high with a jack and casually tossed a one-dollar chip onto the center of the table. I stared at him and waited for him to return my look. "She cared about you," I told him, "and took good care of you after your minor mishap a while back. It was her idea to put you in bed—*our* bed—and leave you there until you were well enough to walk out on your own. But even after all that, you seemed to act as if you didn't even notice when she was around. Or was that a charade meant only for my eyes?"

Embarrassed that his suicidal secret was now open for discussion, Steve looked around at the others before he turned to me. "I don't know what you're getting at, Ike," he said. "You're a bit out of control and not just tonight, but for a while. We've all picked up on it and let it slide figuring you needed to work a few things out, is all. But now it's reached a tipping point, and maybe we should bring it all to a stop right here and right now."

"It's only a game, Ike," Jeffrey said. "It would be madness to let friendships be cast aside over some silly game."

"What's only a game, Padre?" I asked, turning my attention to Jeffrey. "The hand you've just been dealt, or the deal between you and Dottie?"

"What are you implying?" Jeffrey asked. "I have never had an improper moment with Dottie. Not one, not ever. And for you to even *think* something like that borders on madness."

"If it wasn't you, Padre," I asked, "then who *did* have their moments with Dottie, improper or otherwise? Maybe it was you, Jerry. Dottie always *did* do a fast spin toward a man with money, and you have more than most. Or maybe you, Joe, Mr. Reebok himself. After all, how many games can one man go to without wanting to play in one of his very own? Of course, there's always Adam, the good doctor and the one who once rushed in to rescue her in a time of need. What woman wouldn't want to show how grateful she was for a second chance at an unfinished life? Or maybe it was the one obvious choice in the room. That would be you, Tony, the shrink with the black-book Rolodex. Dottie's main complaint about me was that she talked but I never listened. And who better to listen and be receptive to her problems than someone like you? A man who has devoted his life to soothing and comforting women in need."

"Is that what all this is about?" Joe asked. "You think one of us is having an affair with your wife?"

"You're a fool, Ike!" Tony's voice was crammed with pure hatred. "And you may live under the same ceilings as Dottie, but you don't know the first thing about her, or you would know she is willing to do anything to help salvage the shambles you've made of your marriage."

"You're right about one thing, though," Steve said. "We haven't been square with you about our relationship with Dottie. We've all been seeing her, everyone sitting at this table. She insisted on it."

"All of you?" I didn't bother to mask either the shock or the surprise. "You've *all* been with her?"

"Yes," Jeffrey said, "but not for the reason that's currently racing through your mind. Her visits with us were not of a sexual nature."

"Then what the hell were you seeing her for?" I shouted, pounding a closed right fist onto the table, knocking over Steve's wineglass, the red liquid flowing over a stack of chips. "Why was she spending time with any of you? And if it all was on the up and up like you're trying to sell me, then why didn't she tell me about it?"

"She couldn't — at least, not yet." Adam's words were weighed down with a certain edge of sadness. "There were a few more items she needed to clear up first."

"Dottie was sick," Jeffrey said. "Very sick. That bout with the stomach that Adam helped clear her of was merely the first indication of how deep her illness ran and how serious a final outcome it would lead to. That was what brought her to us, individually at first, and then later in small groups."

"What did she want from you?" I asked, the words forcing their way from my mouth. My throat burned and I felt my heart doing a Keith Moon pounding against my chest. I held on to the edges of the table as if it were a life vest, doing all I could not to scream out in agony.

"She asked us to take care of you, look after you after she was gone," Steve said. "Each in a way she knew we could. Adam would make sure you took care of your health. Jerry would pull you out of debt with whatever was left of the insurance money coming your way, working to set your finances in order. Me? I had been your closest friend, and she asked that I stay that way, no matter how much of an ass you turned into."

"I would take you to as many games as you could stand," Joe said. "Dottie told me how often you wished you had a chance to see one team or the other play, and she felt going with a friend would help take your mind off your loss. Tony could show how good a therapist he really is and would see you free of charge. Only you wouldn't know it, since all your bills would be going to Jerry, anyway."

"And Adam and I were asked to simply look after anything else that fell through the cracks," Jeffrey said, "either spiritually or physically. Dottie covered every base by simply turning to the only friends she knew you had. The men at this table."

"It was also important to her that the game keep going," Jerry said. "She felt the weekly poker nights served as an anchor against all the other crap that was going on in your life. She thought you needed it. But after tonight, I'm not all that sure she was right on that count."

"Your suspicions were right," Steve said, "only they were headed in the wrong direction. We were all involved with Dottie. And Dottie was involved with all of us. We each had a mutual interest, and that was you."

"Feel better now?" Adam asked.

I looked at them, scanning their tired and worn faces, and nodded. "I'm sorry." My mouth was as hot and as dry as an August afternoon. "I wasn't thinking straight. I most likely said a lot of the wrong things. And I did something horrible which I know can never be undone."

"We might be pissed at you, Ike," Joe said. "But trust me, we'll get over it. Dottie is right. We're friends here. Even Adam and Jerry, whether they want to admit it or not. And that gives us all quite a bit of leeway. By the time the next game rolls around, what happened tonight will be only a memory."

"I hope that's true," I said. "You don't know how much I want that to be true."

"It will be," Jeffrey said softly. "There's no reason for it not to be."

"How much time did — excuse me — *does* Dottie have left?" I directed my question mainly to Adam.

"It's a fast-moving disease," Adam said, "and it was caught very late. Based on her most recent tests, I would say a month at best, two if she's at all lucky."

"And is there any chance she might beat it?" I asked.

"No," Adam said. "I can't lie to you about that. There's no chance at all. What Dottie has is terminal."

"And did you all agree to help me?" I asked. "To do all the things she asked you to do for me?"

"What kind of friend would say no to something like that?" Jerry said. "We would do anything Dottie asked. And to be honest, we would have done it even if she hadn't asked us."

"We're all you have," Joe said. "We're all what each of us has. The poker game is just a good excuse to get together. We're family. This is it, all of it, right here in this very room. No matter how crazy or stupid some of us get at times, we are all here and will always be here for each other."

"Dottie was right," I said. "You are my friends and my family. She always could see that in a much clearer light."

"She told me if we could keep it all together, then none of us would ever be alone," Tony said. "And there's no reason why we should ever not let it be so."

"Would you help me then with Dottie?" I asked. "See that she gets buried properly, with respect and with care."

"You know we will," Jeffrey said. "You don't even need to ask."

"Dottie's in the bedroom," I told them. "I'm going to take a few minutes alone with her. Once we're ready, I'll call for you. I will need your help then."

"We'll be here for you," Steve said. "Count on it."

"I will," I told them. I eased out of my chair and began to make my way toward the back bedroom and the bleeding and ruined body of my wife, Dottie.

"Believe me, I will."